J. Arthur Phillips

The Mining and Metallurgy of Gold and Silver

SALZWASSER
VERLAG

J. Arthur Phillips

The Mining and Metallurgy of Gold and Silver

1st Edition | ISBN: 978-3-75253-395-8

Place of Publication: Frankfurt am Main, Germany

Year of Publication: 2021

Salzwasser Verlag GmbH, Germany.

Reprint of the original, first published in 1867.

THE

MINING AND METALLURGY

OF

GOLD AND SILVER.

BY

J. ARTHUR PHILLIPS,

MINING ENGINEER.

London:

E. AND F. N. SPON, 48, CHARING CROSS.

MDCCCLXVII.

Dedication.

TO

HENRY HUSSEY VIVIAN, Esq., M.P.,

THIS WORK,

TREATING OF SOME OF THE BRANCHES OF AN ART

WHICH HIS FAMILY HAS FOR A LONG PERIOD SUCCESSFULLY PRACTISED,

AND WHICH

HE HAS HIMSELF SO GREATLY CONTRIBUTED TO ADVANCE,

IS RESPECTFULLY DEDICATED

BY

THE AUTHOR.

b

PREFACE.

THIS treatise has been undertaken with the hope that it may, to some extent, supply a want in our technical literature, which is very deficient in books treating of the mining and metallurgy of the precious metals.

In preparing this work for publication, care has been taken to obtain data directly from the best and most authentic sources. The connexion of the author, as a Mining Engineer, with various large metallurgical establishments, together with his repeated visits to, and residence in, some of the principal mining districts of both Europe and America, have afforded him many opportunities for observation and investigation.

His object has rather been to render this volume practically useful as a record of well-authenticated facts, and of the results of actual experience, than to advance new theories, or to accumulate additional evidence in support of old ones. He has, therefore, contented himself with merely stating the results both of his own observations, and those of others; or at most with suggesting the nature of the forces producing the effects described. He believes that our knowledge of chemical geology is not, as yet, sufficiently advanced to warrant an attempt to form a general theory of the formation of mineral veins.

Recent observations and experience appear, however, to lead to three important conclusions. First, that the most productive gold-bearing rocks are by no means exclusively confined to the Silurian period; secondly, that aqueous agencies have been, and still are, actively at work in the formation of mineral deposits; and, thirdly, that gold ledges are not more liable than ordinary metalliferous veins to become impoverished in depth.

The general order adopted has been, first to describe, in each instance, the principal gold and silver producing districts, and to give such statistical information as could be obtained respecting their yield and importance. Then follows an account of the methods employed for extracting the ores; and, lastly, a description of the apparatus made use of for their mechanical and metallurgical treatment.

With regard to the yield of silver from the various districts producing ores of that metal, it may be remarked that, in a few instances, it has been found necessary to depart from the official estimates; since ores raised in one country have been metallurgically treated in another, and the resulting metal has consequently figured in the returns of both.

The information derived either from other books or from private sources, has, in most instances, been duly acknowledged; but the Author takes this opportunity of returning thanks to his friends for many valuable suggestions of too general a character to admit of specific mention in the body of the work. He is under especial obligations to the Messrs. Taylor, of London; Mr. T. F. Cronise and Mr. P. N. McKay, of San Francisco; Mr. W. Watt, of Grass Valley; and to the gentlemen of the State Geological Survey of California. He also takes this opportunity of expressing his thanks to the principal mill owners and mining engineers of California and Nevada; without the facilities which these gentlemen have so kindly afforded, the Author would have been unable to give the very large amount of facts relating to the mines of the Pacific Coast which their liberality has enabled him to collect.

The table and formulæ on page 236 have been contributed by Mr. C. W. Merrifield, F.R.S., to whom, and to Mr. F. W. Rudler, the author begs to return his thanks for assistance rendered whilst the book was passing through the press.

KENSINGTON,
July, 1867.

CONTENTS.

GOLD.

CHAPTER I.

MODE OF OCCURRENCE, AND GEOLOGICAL POSITION.

CHAPTER II.

GOLD REGIONS OF THE OLD WORLD.

CHAPTER III.

UNITED STATES OF AMERICA—ATLANTIC OR APPALACHIAN GOLD FIELDS.

CHAPTER IV.

UNITED STATES OF AMERICA—GOLD FIELDS OF THE PACIFIC COAST.

CHAPTER V.

MEXICO, CENTRAL AMERICA, AND SOUTH AMERICA.

CHAPTER VI.

BRITISH POSSESSIONS—NORTH AMERICAN COLONIES.

CHAPTER VII.

BRITISH POSSESSIONS—AUSTRALIA AND NEW ZEALAND.

CHAPTER VIII.

GOLD WASHING IN CALIFORNIA AND AUSTRALIA.

CHAPTER IX.

VEIN MINING IN CALIFORNIA AND AUSTRALIA.

CHAPTER X.

VEIN MINING IN HUNGARY AND BRAZIL—SODIUM AMALGAM.

CHAPTER XI.

ASSAY OF AURIFEROUS ORES—ESTIMATION OF GOLD CONTAINED IN QUARTZ—REFINING—ASSAY OF GOLD BULLION.

SILVER.

CHAPTER XII.

MODE OF OCCURRENCE AND GEOLOGICAL POSITION.

CHAPTER XIII.

PRINCIPAL SILVER MINES OF THE OLD WORLD.

CHAPTER XIV.

SILVER MINES OF NORTH AMERICA.

CHAPTER XV.

CENTRAL AMERICA AND SOUTH AMERICA.

CHAPTER XVI.

TREATMENT OF SILVER ORES BY AMALGAMATION—PATIO PROCESS, &c.

CHAPTER XVII.

TREATMENT OF SILVER ORES BY AMALGAMATION—BARREL PROCESS.

CHAPTER XVIII.

TREATMENT OF SILVER ORES BY AMALGAMATION—PAN PROCESS.

CHAPTER XIX.

TREATMENT OF ARGENTIFEROUS ORES AND PRODUCTS BY SOLUTION AND PRECIPITATION.

CHAPTER XX.

CONCENTRATION OF THE PRECIOUS METALS IN METALLIC LEAD—SMELTING.

CHAPTER XXI.

EXTRACTION OF THE PRECIOUS METALS FROM ARGENTIFEROUS AND AURIFEROUS LEAD OBTAINED BY SMELTING.

CHAPTER XXII.

TREATMENT OF ARGENTIFEROUS GALENA AT PONTGIBAUD.

CHAPTER XXIII.

SMELTING SILVER ORES IN MEXICO.

CHAPTER XXIV.

ASSAY OF SILVER ORES AND BULLION.

LIST OF WOODCUTS.

GOLD.

CHAPTER I.

MODE OF OCCURRENCE AND GEOLOGICAL POSITION.

ANALYSES OF NATIVE GOLD—AGE OF AURIFEROUS ROCKS—GOLD OF THE JURASSIC PERIOD—QUARTZ VEINS OF RECENT FORMATION—GOLD VEINS NOT IMPOVERISHED IN DEPTH—ALLUVIAL DEPOSITS.

MODE OF OCCURRENCE.—This metal occurs in the following forms :—

ALLOYS.

Native Gold.—An Alloy of Gold and Silver, associated with small quantities of copper, iron, and other metals.
Palladium Gold.—Gold and Palladium—Porpezite.
Rhodium Gold.—Gold and Rhodium.

AMALGAM.

Gold Amalgam.—A native Amalgam of Gold and Mercury.

ORES.

Sylvanite, or Graphic Tellurium.—Telluride of Gold and Silver.
Nagyagite.—Telluride of Lead containing Gold, Silver, and Copper.

Of the foregoing combinations, Native Gold is the only one of great commercial importance, as furnishing nearly the whole of this metal annually obtained from the different gold-producing districts of the world. Palladium gold occurs to some extent in the mines of Gongo Soco in Brazil, and a small quantity of graphic tellurium is found in those of Transylvania. The other native alloys of gold can only be regarded in the light of mineralogical curiosities.

Gold is usually found, in alluvial washings, in the shape of fine particles and water-worn plates and scales, but crystallised specimens are occasionally met with. These crystals, which are usually small, are generally in the form of octahedrons, although Shepard describes a pentagonal dodecahedron, from California, two-fifths of an inch in diameter: an octahedral crystal from the same country, described by F. Alger, had a diameter of eight-tenths of an inch.

Native gold, occurring in veins, is most frequently found in a quartzose gangue, in which it is often associated with iron and copper pyrites, arsenical pyrites, blende and galena. Gold and iron pyrites are very intimately associated, although the gold appears always to exist in the metallic state, since in almost every gold-producing district, when sulphide of iron has become decomposed, by weathering, into hydrated oxide of iron, gold becomes apparent, and is readily separated by washing. When this metal is encased in undecomposed copper pyrites, iron pyrites, or any other sulphide, or arsenide, its separation, either by washing or amalgamation, is attended with considerable difficulty, although the whole of the gold may be readily extracted by smelting the concentrated pyrites, either with lead ore, or with litharge.

The gold found in ordinary gold quartz, in addition to being disseminated in a more or less finely divided state in the associated sulphides, presents itself in threads, thin plates, and grains of varying dimensions. These are not unfrequently apparent to the naked eye, but rock showing no traces of visible gold is often sufficiently rich to yield a large profit after deducting working expenses.

Native gold invariably contains a certain amount of silver, and almost always traces of copper and iron. The silver associated with native gold is not combined with it according to the laws of atomic proportion, but forms with it an alloy in which silver represents from one-hundredth to more than one-half the total weight of the mixture.

The gold of Australia averages from 960 to 966 thousandths fine, whilst that of California contains from 875 to 885 thousandths of pure gold.

The composition of native gold from various localities is given in the following table :—

TABLE

Showing the Composition of various Samples of Native Gold.

Locality.	Analyst.	Gold.	Silver.	Copper.	Iron.
RUSSIAN EMPIRE—					
Petropawlowsk washings . .	G. Rose	86·81	13·19	Trace	Trace.
Boruschkoi „ . . .	„	83·85	16·15	„	„
Zarewo-Nicolajewsk, near Miask, washings	„	89·35	10·65	„	„
Berezovsk Mine, in brown Hematite	„	93·78	5·94	0·08	0·04
Berezovsk, in quartz	„	91·88	8·03	0·09	Trace.
TRANSYLVANIA—					
Sta. Barbara Mine, at Füses, scales in porphyry with quartz	„	84·89	14·68	0·04	0·13
Vöröspatak, in porphyry with quartz	„	60·49	38·74	0·77	...
AUSTRALIA—					
South Australia	A. S. Thomas	87·78	6·07	...	6·15
Bathurst	J. H. Henry	95·69	3·92	...	0·16
Ballarat	F. Claudet	99·25	0·65	...	...
NEW ZEALAND—					
Locality not known	„	96·25	3·55	...	...
WALES—					
Vigra and Clogau	„	88·50	5·00	...	
Welsh Gold Mining Co. . . .	„	76·40	22·70	...	...
BRITISH COLUMBIA—					
Locality not given	„	86·10	13·50	...	...
Stephens Creek	„	79·50	19·70	...	...
Cariboo	„	84·25	14·90	...	...
SOUTH AMERICA—					
Marmato	Boussingault	73·45	26·48	...	...
Antioquia, New Granada, washings	„	64·93	35·07	...	...
Brazil	D'Arcet	94·00	5·85	...	...
UNITED STATES AND CANADA—					
Feather River, California, scales	Rivot	89·10	10·50	...	0·20
American Fork, California, scales	„	90·90	8·70	...	0·20
Mariposa Estate, Quartz Gold.	F. Claudet	81·00	18·70	...	...
Georgia	W. W. Mather	95·579	4·421	Trace	Trace.
Rivière du Loup, Canada . .	T. S. Hunt	86·40	13·60	„	„

The larger pieces of water-worn gold are called by the miners *nuggets;* but these seldom exceed a few pounds in weight, and are generally accompanied by more or less of the quartzose gangue forming the original veinstone.

One of the finest lumps of native gold now in existence, is that preserved in the collection of the Russian School of Mines, which weighs about 97 lbs.

The largest piece of gold ever found, was probably the great Australian nugget known as the "Sarah Sands," which weighed 233 lbs. 4 oz. troy.

Geological Position of Gold.—The general characteristics of the gold-bearing rocks throughout the world are exceedingly alike, since, whatever their original structure or composition may have been, they have become so assimilated by metamorphic action as to exhibit a very striking resemblance to each other.

They generally consist of slaty deposits, frequently talcose, although sometimes chloritic or argillaceous, and in these the gold-bearing quartz, which is the almost universal matrix of this metal, is generally found most productive. Valuable gold veins are also occasionally found in granite, gneiss and syenite, but these do not so often form the enclosing rock as the metamorphosed shales and slates above referred to.

Veins of auriferous quartz have most frequently the same strike and dip as the shales in which they are enclosed, but in some instances they not only intersect the shales at varying angles, but have also a separate and independent dip. When rocks remain stratified, in nearly the same position in which they were originally deposited, they are rarely found to be highly auriferous; but when, on the contrary, they have been invaded by eruptive masses, are broken up, or raised on edge, and have assumed a crystalline texture, there is good reason to anticipate the presence of the precious metal.

Generally speaking, it may be said that a considerable proportion of the gold-bearing rocks of the world belong to the two lowest geological groups, the azoic and palæozoic, or rather to the latter. For although we are not aware that rocks proved to be azoic have been found to be auriferous, yet it is often impossible to distinguish between these two groups, since in localities where the formation is metalliferous, the strata have generally so changed their original character, as to render it exceedingly difficult to recognise their exact position in the geological series.*

The metamorphosed auriferous strata of the Ural Mountains have been shown by Sir Roderick Murchison to be palæozoic, and the Australian rocks, associated with veins of auriferous quartz, have also afforded abundant evidence of Silurian origin. Mr. Selwyn, the director of the Colonial Geological Survey, has fully satisfied himself that the gold-bearing veins of Victoria are confined to rocks of the palæozoic age, chiefly to those belonging to the Lower Silurian division, ascending from the Llandeilo to the Upper Caradoc formation inclusive. Arguing from his own experience in the Ural Mountains and elsewhere, as well as from facts collected by other observers in the various gold-producing countries of the world, Sir R. Murchison became impressed with the conviction that all the more productive auriferous rocks belong to the palæozoic period, and he considers this question so fully settled, that he remarks, "My chief article of belief has now proved to be true, namely, that the rocks which are most auriferous are of Silurian age."† It would appear, however, that the gold-producing rocks of California and Nevada present a remarkable exception to this general rule, since Professor Whitney, the State Geologist of California, has collected numerous fossils of undoubted Jurassic origin, found *in situ*, in the immediate proximity of one of the largest and best defined quartz veins of the Pacific coast. When describing the geology of the district in the vicinity of the Pine Tree vein, which is one of the largest comprehended within the limits of the Mariposa Estate, he remarks:‡ "Within the slate formation are interstratified sandstones, which are, in some cases, very distinctly bedded, as for instance on the west slope of Hell Hollow. The beds are often several feet in thickness, and like the slates themselves, in all stages of alteration, as is made evident by the differences of hardness, colour and texture which they exhibit. The region of least metamorphism seems to have been from the Pine Tree mine, west, to the slope of Juniper Ridge, and southward, to near the village of Bear Valley. It was in this region that Mr. King

* The Discovery by Sir William Logan of fossil remains in the Lower Laurentian rocks of Canada, renders it extremely doubtful whether the term *azoic* can be correctly applied, even to the oldest formations known to geologists.

† Siluria, p. 474.

‡ Geological Survey of California, p. 226.

found *in situ* fossils, by which the age of this formation was clearly made out to be Jurassic."*

The period of the formation of auriferous veins is less readily determined than the age of the enclosing rocks, although they may be presumed to have often originated at the time of the metamorphic action, by which the change in the strata themselves was effected. It is, however, tolerably evident that this action has not been confined to any particular geological epoch, and it would appear that these

* The following description of fossils from the auriferous slates of California, is by F. B. Meek; see Appendix, Vol. I. Geological Survey of California, p. 477. "The fossils from the auriferous slates, collected on the Mariposa Estate, having been by mistake sent for investigation in part to Mr. Gabb, and in part to the writer, were regarded by both of us, independently, as most probably of Jurassic age. This opinion was expressed by Mr. Gabb in a communication to the California Academy of Sciences, in November 1864 (see Proceed. Vol. III. p. 172), and by myself at about the same time in a communication to the State Geologist. In his paper alluded to above, Mr. Gabb described the following species, viz., *Lima Erringtoni*, *Pholadomya orbiculata*, and *Belemnites Pacificus*. He likewise mentioned a *Pecten*, and a *Nucula* or *Leda*. Two of these species were also described by the writer, under other names, in a communication prepared for publication, but fortunately not published.

"As it was considered by the State Geologist desirable that I should examine all of the few fossils yet found in these slates, they were placed in my hands for investigation; and drawings and descriptions have been prepared for publication.

"In examining the specimens formerly sent, much difficulty was experienced in determining the generic relations of two or three bivalves resembling an oblique *Inoceramus*, and varying considerably from each other in form and convexity, but agreeing exactly in surface markings. Being all casts, more or less compressed and otherwise distorted, it was difficult to understand how they could belong to one species, as their surface markings and some other points of resemblance seemed to indicate, though this was suspected to be the case. Amongst the collections subsequently sent on, and now under examination, these same forms are observed. One is an obliquely oval rather convex shell, with a very prominent terminal strongly incurved beak, while the other is much more compressed, with a straighter, dorsal outline, and a beak scarcely distinct from the cardinal margin. On examining the collections more recently received it was soon observed that the compressed specimens with an inconspicuous beak, are all right valves, while all of those with a prominent strongly incurved beak are left valves.

"This fact, together with their other characters, leave little room for doubting that these are the opposite valves of one or two species of the genus *Aucella*. As this genus is, so far as known, entirely confined to the Jurassic rocks, while an *Amussium*-like shell from the same slates is closely allied to a Jurassic species, and the genus *Belemnites* is not generally regarded as dating back beyond the commencement of the Jurassic period, I can scarcely entertain a doubt that these gold-bearing slates really belong to that epoch, and probably to some of its lower members, at which horizon most of the known European species of *Aucella* are said to occur."

changes, which are probably exceedingly slow in their progress, may have been repeated at periods of time very far removed from one another.

The impregnation with gold of the rocks of the Ural has been shown by Murchison to have taken place at a comparatively recent date, but in many of the other important gold regions we have not sufficient data to enable us to fix, with any degree of exactitude, the epoch at which the concentration of this metal into veins took place. In California, however, this could not have been effected prior to the deposition of the Jurassic strata in which they occur. A further evidence of the occasional recent formation of quartz veins is derived from the fact, that in one of the detrital beds near Volcano, in Amador County, a distinctly marked quartz vein is observed to cut through the beds of sand and gravel, and presents unmistakeable evidence of having been formed subsequently to their deposition, by the action of water holding silica in solution. This vein is chiefly composed of calcedony and agate, but portions of it are more or less stained by a ferruginous deposit. This is by no means a solitary case, many other localities having been noticed, where quartz veins, almost identical in their general features with those met with in the auriferous slates, must have been formed during the most recent geological epochs.*

Auriferous veins, like all others, vary exceedingly, in not only their dimensions, but also in their productiveness. It is, however, generally observed that the widest veins are not usually the richest, and that some of the laminæ running parallel with the enclosing walls are uniformly more productive than others. It therefore not unfrequently happens that a portion of a vein, sufficiently rich to enable it to be treated with advantage, is separated from another band, comparatively barren, by a distinct heading, or false wall. As a general rule those veins are most productive which afford considerable quantities of disseminated sulphides; although, near the surface, these have, in almost every instance, become decomposed, thereby liberating the enclosed granular gold, and staining the quartz of a brown or reddish colour. When gold occurs in a vein of hard white quartz without sulphides, it is in most instances found in flakes and granules of considerable size, and is consequently visible to the naked eye; but such veins, although sometimes affording fine cabinet specimens, are not often regularly and remuneratively productive. Some of the most

* Geological Survey of California, p. 276.

steadily remunerative veins, on the other hand, are only of moderate size, and seldom exhibit visible gold, and this is particularly noticeable in those which, like the Norambagua lead in Grass Valley, California, are divided by numerous thin seams of slate into bands of various thickness. In such veins the gold is commonly in a finely divided state, and principally occurs in the parallel headings, marking the lines of deposition of the quartz. It was formerly believed that veins of auriferous quartz become gradually less productive as greater depths from the surface are attained, but more extensive experience would tend to show that this is in reality not the case. Gold mines which have for many years been continuously worked in various part of the world, have fluctuated considerably in their richness at different depths, but it has not been found that these variations in any way correspond with a gradual impoverishment in the deeper levels. In a communication addressed to Sir R. Murchison, who inclines to the opinion that gold-bearing veins generally diminish in value as they descend in depth, Mr. Selwyn remarks as follows: "There is undoubtedly good evidence that those upper portions of the quartz veins, which have been naturally removed by denudation, and now form the gold drifts, were often far richer than any we now find at the surface; but in drawing conclusions from this evidence, we should not forget that in all probability many hundreds of vertical feet of quartz veins have been thus naturally broken up, crushed and washed, and the fact of the veins, so abraded, being still frequently very rich on their present surface, goes far, I think, to prove that the diminution of yield in depth, even though admitted to be true, on a large scale, is still so slow as not to be appreciable within any depth to which ordinary mining operations are carried."* Mr. Selwyn concludes by expressing an opinion, "that the extraction of gold from quartz reefs, if properly conducted, may be regarded as an occupation, which will prove as permanently profitable in Victoria, as tin and copper mining have been in Great Britain."

In California, the early quartz miners were also fully impressed with the idea that the outcrops of the leads were more productive of gold than the deeper portions of the same veins, and as soon as the quartz extracted ceased to afford remunerative returns, they usually suspended operations, without extending their explorations to any considerable depth. Within the last few years, however, their opinions in this respect have become materially changed, since the

* Siluria, p. 496.

workings of the deeper mines would lead to the conclusion, that, although leads of gold-bearing quartz, like all other metalliferous veins, vary materially in their yield in different portions of their extent, both in length and depth, there is no evidence to indicate a progressive falling off in their yield in the deeper workings. The North Star, Allison Ranch, and Eureka veins, in Grass Valley, will, among many others that might be selected, serve to illustrate the fact, that the Californian mines do not become sensibly impoverished in depth, as, in common with all the mines of this district, they are at the present time quite as productive as they have ever been at any period since the commencement of operations.

The North Star vein is now worked on its inclination to a depth of 750 feet, and affords quartz yielding, on an average, gold of the value of 7*l.* per ton of 2,000 lbs., whereas in the upper levels the gross value of the gold extracted did not exceed 4*l.* per ton.* The Allison Ranch Mine has now reached the depth of 500 feet from the surface, and, during the first three months of 1866, yielded a net profit of above 20,000*l.*

The Eureka Mine is being sunk to the 400 ft. level, and produces quartz at this depth fully equal to the average of that raised during any former period, having during the last year yielded 12,200 tons of vein-stuff, affording an average of above 9*l.* 12*s.* per ton. Hayward's Mine, in Amador County, is another still more striking instance of the produce of a vein of quartz not decreasing as it goes down. This ledge is worked on its inclination to a depth of above 1,250 feet, and yields quartz of much greater value than that obtained from the same vein at shallower levels. On taking into consideration the whole of the circumstances of the case, it is by no means remarkable that at first the opinion should have become prevalent that quartz veins in most instances become impoverished in depth.

It will be readily admitted that metalliferous veins are exceedingly variable in their yield at different depths, and it may be supposed that those only which showed evidences at the surface of being more or less auriferous would be at first operated on. These, after having been worked to a greater or less depth, will, in accordance with the general law, begin to show signs of having become less auriferous; and although a further prosecution of the operations would probably

* The ton of 2,000 lbs. is the standard of weight almost universally adopted in the United States of America.

have led to fresh discoveries, the miners, in a country where capital is not readily obtained, and where wages are high, become discouraged, and finally transfer their operations to other outcrops, presenting a sufficient amount of gold to render its extraction profitable. Another reason for the former prevalence of this impression may be traced to the fact, that gold is almost universally associated with a greater or less amount of iron pyrites and other sulphides, and these, becoming oxidised at shallow depths, liberate the enclosed gold, which is thus readily collected by amalgamation, although the deeper, and consequently less decomposed portions of the vein, which may in reality have been equally auriferous, afforded to the early miners less satisfactory results. With the improved methods of treatment, however, which have now come into general operation, this difficulty has to a great extent disappeared, and as all the auriferous sulphides are being at the present time carefully collected for subsequent elaboration, the average production of a vein has generally been found to be sustained at all depths to which the miner has hitherto penetrated.*

* The moulds of cubical crystals of iron pyrites are frequently found in the quartz of auriferous veins, and more particularly so near the surface, thus showing that the formation of the pyrites must have been as old as that of the vein itself. In such cases, although the iron has often been entirely removed by chemical action, the cavities left sometimes contain finely divided gold, obviously liberated by the decomposition of pyrites. The gold contained in crystallised pyrites enclosed in quartz, is readily rendered apparent by placing the specimen, for a few hours, in a warm place, in nitric acid, by which the pyrites is dissolved, and finely powdered, or filiform, gold will partially occupy the resulting cavities. With regard to the age of auriferous quartz veins, it has been already shown that many of them must evidently be of comparatively recent date, but in some cases the deposition of gold-bearing quartz would appear to be taking place even at the present time. At Steamboat Springs, near Virginia, in the State of Nevada, and in other localities on the Pacific coast, numerous parallel deposits of quartz, assuming the form of veins, are taking place along a line of boiling springs now in a state of great activity. The quartz from this locality exactly resembles that of the ordinary auriferous quartz veins of California, and besides small quantities of iron and copper pyrites, contains oxide of iron and traces of manganese. On making an examination of this quartz for gold and silver, we were unable to find an appreciable quantity of either of these metals; but Mr. Laur, who made a similar investigation of this quartz, succeeded in finding specimens containing small quantities of gold. (Annales des Mines, Sixième Série, p. 421.) These facts would, therefore, not only tend to lead to the conclusion that auriferous veins are under certain conditions deposited from silicious solutions, but also to explain the action by which many of the slates of the auriferous period may have become metamorphosed and silicified.

We are indebted to Dr. Oxland, formerly manager of the Works belonging to the

In addition to the gold occurring in veins, considerable quantities are sometimes found forming an integral component of the rocks themselves, as in the syenites of Bogoslofsk in the Ural, and some of the schists in Siberia, &c.* M. Laur† has also discovered the

Borax Lake Company, Lake County, California, for the following note on the occurrence of gold and silver in that locality :—

"In the Sulphur Bank at Borax Lake, sulphur is constantly in course of formation, with the evolution of aqueous vapour, carbonic acid, and boracic acid, but without any sulphuretted hydrogen, which might have been expected to be present. The smell of carbonic acid is remarkably pungent. The gaseous matters issuing from the *Soffioni* in gentle blowers are usually at the temperature of about 95° Fahr. They appear to be the agency by which gold, silver, mercury, and iron are brought up from below and deposited in cavities near the surface. Sulphur is deposited on the sides of the cavities, either in groups of crystals, or in highly translucent amorphous masses of a beautiful light lemon-yellow colour. Sometimes the sulphur is intermixed with cinnabar, but more frequently with very fine crystals of iron pyrites, and with pulverulent silica in masses blackened by some hydro-carbon which is difficult to isolate. The iron pyrites may be separated by dissolving off the sulphur with bisulphide of carbon, and washing off the silica with water. It is found associated with silver and a trace of gold.

"On the sides of the cavities of the blowers, gelatinous silica is sometimes found coating opalised silica in varying degrees of induration, according to its depth from the surface, presenting examples of opal or hydrated silica in its various stages of formation, from gelatinous silica up to the hardest opal. The indurated silica is sometimes colourless, but is more frequently permeated with cinnabar or iron pyrites, and blackened by the tarry matter before alluded to. Sometimes from a diffusion of cinnabar throughout the mass, in minute quantity, it is delicately tinted of a pinkish colour. The cinnabar is also found in striæ, and occasionally even in veins and concretionary masses of some thickness. Where the bituminous matter occurs in the largest quantity, and the mass is quite black and friable, cinnabar is replaced by metallic mercury.

"In another locality of similar character, about ten miles distant, gold has been found with cinnabar in crystalline masses of some size. In the same place, a vein of apparently compact quartz, about ten inches in thickness, was found to be so friable that it could be easily taken out with the hand in small conchoidal fragments, most of which rapidly fell into fine powder. From its great resemblance to a vein occurring in the Mexican Mine, Virginia City, which is many feet in thickness, and contains $20 to $30 of gold and silver to the ton, attention was drawn to it, and it proved, on being assayed, to contain silver, with a trace of gold, to the value of $15 per ton.

"These phenomena present indubitable evidences of the volatility of gold, silver, mercury, and iron, in presence of aqueous vapour associated with sulphuretted hydrogen, carbonic acid, and boracic acid. Whether the contemporaneous association of these substances may produce a definite compound possessing peculiar powers of solution and volatilization under the influence of elevated temperature, although probable, yet remains to be proved."

* Siluria, p. 481.

† Annales des Mines, Sixième Série, p. 434.

presence of gold in the metamorphic shales of Mariposa County, California; and similar deposits, containing a considerable amount of the precious metal, are known to occur near Lincoln in that State.

It is not, however, from the treatment of auriferous quartz that the principal portion of the gold of commerce is procured, a very large proportion of it, probably more than two-thirds, being obtained from alluvial diggings, in which the gold is separated from the more or less superficial detritus by washing. In some of these deposits nature has been for ages performing the operations of crushing and concentrating on a vast scale, and has deposited the precious metal in positions from which it can be obtained without a large expenditure of either labour or capital. To this circumstance are attributable the great variations which are observable in the production of gold throughout the world; since, on the discovery of new and extensive alluvial diggings, an almost unlimited supply of unskilled labour can at once be applied to its extraction, whilst the same weight of metal, if retaining its original position, could only be collected by the application of a large amount of capital and skilled labour. Indeed, experience clearly shows, that had not this natural concentration taken place, the larger proportion of the gold annually brought into the market could not have been profitably collected, since, in the majority of cases, the veins, from which it must have been originally derived, are not sufficiently rich to defray the expenses of raising and crushing.

It does not seem to admit of a doubt that these deposits have been principally derived from the degradation or breaking up of auriferous veins, and the distribution of the detritus thus formed, chiefly by the agency of running water. It further appears to be conclusively proved, that this gold-bearing drift is, at least, of two distinct geological epochs, both comparatively modern, although the latter period is distinctly separated from the earlier, and its materials chiefly derived from the disintegration and redistribution of the older placers. In California these appear to be distinctly referable to a river-system different from that which now exists, flowing at a higher level, or over a less elevated continental mass, but sometimes in the direction of the main valleys of the present period.

The sources to which the chief annual supply of gold is referable are, therefore, the following :—

1st. Auriferous veins, most frequently enclosed in metamorphic slates.

2nd. The distribution of placer gold by ancient river-systems, known as *Deep diggings.*

3rd. The distribution of placer gold by the present river-system, giving rise to the *Shallow diggings.*

The separation of gold from its original matrix, and its concentration and deposition among and beneath strata of gravel, sand and clay, are the result of causes acting through immense periods of time, and which, although they have not yet ceased, are probably much less energetic than they were at a former but not very remote, geological epoch. The strata constituting the earth's crust are constantly undergoing abrasion and decomposition from various meteorological causes, of which one of the most active and powerful is the alternate freezing and thawing of water retained in the fissures and crevices of stratified rocks, which tend to disintegrate and wear away the more elevated and exposed portions, and to carry down the abraded and loosened fragments and spread them out over the surface of the country at lower levels. On the declivities of lofty and rugged mountain chains, where torrents, either from the fall of rain or the rapid melting of the snows, are of frequent occurrence, the streams, become suddenly swollen, rush with violence down their flanks into the valleys beneath, and thus develop a force capable of rapidly eroding the rocks over which they pass. In addition to this mechanical force, chemical action frequently lends its aid to effect the disintegration of auriferous rocks. In proportion as the gold-bearing strata are worn away, the sulphides with which they are constantly associated become oxidised, and, being thus disintegrated, the rocks are themselves reduced to fragments, which being carried by the action of water into the valleys, the metallic particles, as the heaviest, are first deposited, and sink to the bottom, whilst the lighter earthy and silicious portions are removed by the current to a greater distance.

Geologists are not yet agreed with regard to the identity in origin of the older auriferous sands and gravels, and the modern alluvial formations affording gold: Sir R. Murchison, in particular, strongly insisting that the more or less superficial deposits, constituting the deep diggings, are in no way to be confounded with the modern drifts resulting from present atmospheric causes, but rather that they are the result of diluvial currents closely connected with great physical changes in the earth's surface, such as the elevation of some of the principal mountain chains, &c. The vast accumulation of this *débris*, in some of the mining districts of California and Siberia, would indeed lead to the conclusion that the forces at present in operation were totally inadequate to produce such stupendous results; but until a much more thorough examination shall have been made of some of the great gold-producing districts, it would be injudicious to attempt to arrive at any definite conclusion on this subject.

Baron Richthofen is, however, at the present time engaged in an examination of the deep placers and ancient river-courses of California, and there can be no doubt but that a large amount of additional information on this subject will be derived from the investigations of this indefatigable explorer and able geologist.

CHAPTER II.

GOLD REGIONS OF THE OLD WORLD.

GREAT BRITAIN AND IRELAND—FRANCE—SPAIN AND PORTUGAL—ITALY—SWITZERLAND—HOLLAND—RUSSIAN POSSESSIONS—GERMANY—AUSTRIAN EMPIRE—CENTRAL AND SOUTHERN ASIA—CHINA AND JAPAN—AFRICA.

HAVING made certain general observations on the occurrence of gold, we will now proceed to a consideration of some of the principal auriferous districts of the world.

GREAT BRITAIN AND IRELAND.—*Cornwall and Devon.*—The tin streams of Cornwall have been long known to afford occasional specimens of gold, but not in sufficient quantities to make its collection a matter of any commercial importance. Carew says—"Tynners doe also find little hoppes of gold amongst their Owre, which they keepe in quils and sell to the Goldsmithes, oftentimes with little better gaine than *Glaucus* exchange." * Pryce mentions a piece of gold, found in Cornwall, weighing 15 dwt. 16 gr.† Many of the copper gossans are also known to contain minute quantities of gold, but we are not aware that it has, in any instance, been extracted with advantage. At the Britannia and Poltimore mines, near North Molton, in Devonshire, gold has also been found in small quantities, but it never paid the cost of extraction.

Wales.—In North Wales, especially in Merionethshire, the older slaty rocks have long been known to be more or less auriferous. The gold-bearing district of this country would appear to be chiefly confined to an area of about twenty-five square miles, principally lying on the north of the turnpike road leading from Dolgelly to Barmouth. In this region the Cambrian rocks are overlaid by the Silurian, and the general geological features of the country strongly resemble those of some other auriferous localities. Among the veins which have attracted the most attention are those of the Dol-y-

* Carew's Survey of Cornwall, 1602, book i.

† Pryce's Mineralogia Cornubiensis, p. 52.

frwynog, Prince of Wales, and Vigra and Clogau mines, of which the latter only is understood to have been ever worked with remunerative results. So long ago as 1844, a paper was read before the British Association by Mr. Arthur Dean, who stated that a complete system of auriferous veins existed throughout the whole of the Snowdonian or Lower Silurian formation of North Wales. In consequence of this statement operations were commenced at Cwn Eisen, but the results obtained not having been found satisfactory, they were finally abandoned. Machinery for crushing and amalgamation was, about two years afterwards, erected at Dol-y-frwynog, but after operating on several hundred tons of quartz, the result was in this instance also a failure. Of all the auriferous veins that have been worked in the neighbourhood of Dolgelly, that of the Vigra and Clogau has certainly been the most productive. This mine is situated at a height of about a thousand feet above the level of the sea, the workings being prosecuted on what is called the St. David's or Gold Lode. This lode, which is almost vertical, runs nearly east and west, and is composed of quartz, more or less impregnated with sulphides of iron, lead, and copper. The veinstone also, at one period, particularly during the year 1862, exhibited for a short distance a considerable amount of disseminated gold. This rich deposit is at present reported to have been entirely worked out; but for a considerable time rather large amounts of gold were returned from the property.

The following table, for which we are indebted to Mr. R. Hunt, keeper of Mining Records, shows the returns made by the various Welsh gold mines from 1860 to 1864, or during the time of their largest yield:—

GOLD PRODUCED IN MERIONETHSHIRE.

	1861.		1862.		1863.		1864.	
	Gold. oz.	Value. £	Gold. oz.	Value £	Gold. oz.	Value. £	Gold. oz.	Value. £
Vigra and Clogau .	2,886	10,816	5,299	20,390	526	1,674	2,331	3,434
Cefn Coch . . .	—	—	—	—	25	73	346	970
Castell Carn Dochan	—	—	—	—	—	—	141	394
Prince of Wales .	—	—	—	—	—	—	63	166
Gwyn-fynydd . .	—	—	—	—	—	—	6	17

The number of tons of quartz crushed in Wales during the year 1865 is returned as having been 4,270, yielding 1,664 oz. of gold, or about 0.39 oz. per ton.

The total quantities of gold raised from the commencement of operations in the North Wales Gold District, up to April 1st, 1866, are estimated as follows :—

	Gold obtained. Oz.
Old Dol-y-frwynog	117
Prince of Wales	63
Cwn Eisen	176
Gwyn-fynydd	6
Cefn Coch	478
Castell Carn Dochan	182
Vigra and Clogau	11,778
Total	12,800

As above stated, the productive portion of the Vigra and Clogau lode appears to have become exhausted, and although expensive and efficient machinery has been erected on a large scale, with a view to the treatment of the average quality of quartz produced from the vein, the results hitherto obtained have been far from satisfactory; and, unless some marked improvement should ere long take place, it is to be feared that the Vigra and Clogau may ultimately add another to the list of Welsh gold mines that have absorbed a much larger amount of this metal than they have ever produced.* The old Dol-y-frwynog was reworked for gold in 1864, but without any commercial success, since the average yield of the quartz obtained was only about 20 grains per ton.

Scotland.—Gold has also been found at Lead Hills in Scotland, several hundred men having been employed there in washing gold sands during the reign of James V. Pennant says—"In the reign of *James IV.* the *Scots* did separate gold from the sand by washing. In the following the *Germans* found gold there which afforded the king great sums; three hundred men were employed for several summers and about 100,000*l.* sterling procured." †

Ireland.—In the county of Wicklow, a considerable amount of excitement was caused, in 1796, by the discovery of gold in the *débris* of the valley, at the base of Croghan-Kinshela. These diggings were carried on for about two years, when the works were destroyed by the Irish rebels; but although a considerable quantity of gold was extracted, one specimen in particular weighing no less than twenty-two ounces, the general results obtained do not appear to have been very satisfactory. In 1801 the operations were resumed

* Some further discoveries of gold at Vigra and Clogau have been recently announced.

† Pennant's Scotland, vol. ii. p. 130.

with a view of discovering the gold-bearing veins; but after the expenditure of large sums, without success, in various mining operations, the locality was again abandoned.

FRANCE possesses no known valuable gold mines, but the sands of some of her rivers are, to a certain extent, auriferous. The only quartz vein which has been found to contain gold, is that of La Gardette in the Department of the Isère, which is from two to three feet in width, and enclosed in gneiss. Gold was discovered in this locality in 1700, and workings were intermittently carried on, up to 1841, but the quantity obtained was exceedingly small. The Rhine has, for centuries, produced small quantities of gold, and, according to the report of Réaumur, presented to the Academy of Sciences in 1718, its sands have been chiefly worked between Strasburg and Philipsburg. Near Strasburg it was formerly the perquisite of the magistrates of that city, who farmed out the right of gold washing, but in the year above referred to they only received some four or five ounces as their proportion of the annual produce. In 1846, M. Daubrée, a French engineer, made a report to the Academy of Sciences, in which he states that the gravel most usually worked is that deposited below a sandbank or gravel island, which has become eroded by the river, and that gold is only found in any degree concentrated in the coarser gravels, which have been freed from the finer sands by the action of currents.* The gold occurs in the form of small scales or dust, and is constantly accompanied by titaniferous iron, the amount of which is proportionate to the richness of the sand for the precious metal. The workable beds are invariably thin, seldom exceeding from four to six inches in thickness, and the particles of gold remarkably small, since the number required to weigh one milligramme varies from seventeen to twenty-two, and one cubic metre of gravel contains from 4,500 to 36,000 of these scales. Besides the auriferous deposits in the bed of the stream, M. Daubrée states that the ancient detritus on its banks, extending from three to four miles in width, also affords an appreciable amount of gold, but that the fine silt, free from gravel, which is daily accumulating, is totally barren.

The sands of the Rhine are still washed on a small scale, but there is reason to believe that the production was formerly much more considerable than at present. The yield of the year 1846 is estimated by M. Daubrée at 1,800*l.* and the washers usually made from one and

* Comptes Rendus, xxii. p. 639, 1846.

a half to two francs per diem, although they occasionally gained from ten to fifteen francs. The same authority estimates the average yield of the sands of the Rhine, Siberia, and Chili to be in the proportion of 1 : 20 : 74; or, if the sand of the Rhine, separated from pebbles of two-thirds of an inch in diameter, be taken as the standard of comparison, the ratio becomes 1 : 10 : 37. In Siberia, sands containing 0·000001 of gold were then not considered worth working; but even this yield is seven and a half times greater than that of the ordinary sands of the Rhine. M. Daubrée, after a careful examination of the subject, came to the conclusion that by the aid of proper appliances these sands might probably be treated advantageously, and goes on to say, that, "by the processes now employed, each washer gains from one and half to two francs a day, and exceptionally even ten or fifteen francs; some of the operations would, however, appear to be susceptible of improvement, since the washing is now entirely effected by manual labour, although there is to be obtained, at the distance of a few steps only, the motive power of the river itself, which, if applied to a dredging machine, could be made to remove the superficial stratum of rich gravel, and deposit it on the head of a washing table."

Although, however, the application of machinery might be made to materially lessen the expense of working the deposits of the Rhine, the yield of gold is so exceedingly small, that it is questionable whether, by any known mode of treatment, such results could be obtained, as would afford satisfactory returns for the capital and labour which would be required. There are several other localities in France which have afforded small quantities of gold, and the River Ariège (*Aurigera*) is stated to have derived its name from the amount of auriferous sands it deposited. The washing of these is said to have afforded, up to the close of the fifteenth century, an annual produce of about a hundred pounds of the precious metal.

Small quantities of gold have also been collected by washing the *débris* produced by the erosion of some of the lower carboniferous strata in the Department of the Gard, and we have ourselves found traces of gold in the quartzose pebbles, forming one of the constituents of a coarse conglomerate, a little above the village of Bessage.

SPAIN AND PORTUGAL.—Gold mines were successively worked in Spain by the Phœnicians, Romans, and Moors; and although the amount at present obtained from that country is exceedingly insignificant, it at one period produced large quantities of the precious metal. Both Strabo and Pliny speak of Spain as being rich in gold, and mention various localities from which it was obtained. Adrien Paillette, who has investigated the subject of ancient mining in the Peninsula, has arrived at the conclusion, that in former times, both Spain and Portugal yielded large quantities of gold, which was not only obtained from washing the sands of the Duero, Tagus, and some other rivers, but also from workings in the solid rock. It would appear, however, from the investigations of Paillette, that however rich the auriferous regions might have originally been, they had become almost totally exhausted previous to their abandonment; since during the whole of his investigations of the old workings, which are very extensive, he only obtained a few slight traces of gold. Among the gold mines of the Peninsula which have been in operation within more modern times, may be mentioned one near Talavera, worked by Donna Isabella:* another at Adissa, near S. Ubes in Portugal, was worked during the present century, and which produced as much as forty-one pounds weight of gold in 1815.† A mine at Domingo Flores in Leon was worked intermittently from 1639 to 1749.

The present production of the precious metal in Spain is exceedingly small, and is chiefly derived from washing the sands of the rivers Sil and Salor, from which the total annual yield may be estimated at about 1,600*l.*

ITALY.—A great number of localities in this country were known to the ancients as producing gold. The whole district of the Noric Alps (Illyria) was considered highly auriferous, and at one period gold was worked so extensively, that the large quantity produced is said to have caused a reduction of one-third in its price throughout Italy.‡ Gold was also found in Dalmatia,§ the River Po,‖ and at Pithecusa, opposite Cuma.¶

The only gold mines at present of any consequence are situated in Savoy and Piedmont. The chief amalgamation works are built on the small streams near Macugnaga, at the foot of Monte Rosa, where a considerable amount of gold is found in the valleys of Anzasca, Toppa, and Antrona, and to a less extent in those of Alagna,

* Jacob's History of the Precious Metals, vol. i. p. 272.
† Ibid. p. 283.
‡ Strabo, lib. iv. cap. 6.
§ Plin. Hist. Nat. xxxiii. 21.
‖ Ibid.
¶ Strabo.

Sesia, and Novara. The chief mines in Anzasca are at Peschiera and Minera di Sotto.

The ore is an auriferous pyrites, containing on an average about 12 dwt. of gold per ton. The whole amount produced in the province of Ossola, to which these works belong, was in 1829 about 250 lbs. troy, with a profit of a little over 3,000*l.** In 1844 the yield was as follows :†—

	Kilos.	Value.
Valley of Anzasca	153	£16,092
„ Toppa	19	2,032
„ Antrona	20	2,150
	Total	£20,274

The yield of Alagna, Sesia, and Novara during the same year only amounted to 280*l.* Pliny states that these mines were extensively worked in his time, and that the number of slaves who were allowed to work in them was fixed by the Senate at 5,000, in order to prevent a serious reduction in the price of the precious metal.

Several of the mines in this district have recently been undertaken by English companies; but these have not as yet been sufficiently long in operation, to allow of a satisfactory estimate being made relative to the probable returns of gold, although the results hitherto obtained have been of a very encouraging character.

SWITZERLAND produces no amount of gold of any commercial importance; but the sands of the rivers Reuss and Aar, two of the affluents of the Rhine, are known to contain small quantities of this metal.‡ The Rhine in the Pays de Gex is slightly auriferous, and the Tessin, or Ticino, in the Canton of the same name, deposits sands sometimes affording small particles of gold.

HOLLAND.—Some operations were carried on in this country in the eighteenth century by a Mr. Beecher, with a view to the extraction of gold from the sea sands, but he did not succeed in his enterprise, and a previous adventurer is said to have been equally unsuccessful.

RUSSIAN POSSESSIONS.—The principal portion of the gold from the

* Whitney's Metallic Wealth, p. 96.

† *Mining Journal*, 1845, p. 610.

‡ Dictionnaire des Sciences Naturelles—Or.

Russian Empire is obtained from the western slope of the Ural Mountains, Siberia, and the Caucasus. The government of Archangel also formerly furnished a small quantity of this metal, but the works in that district have been abandoned since the commencement of the present century. In Asiatic Russia, the most productive auriferous districts are comprised within the governments of Perm, Tomsk, Oremburg, Irkoutsk, Yenisseisk, and the district of the Kirghese. The first discovery of gold was made in the year 1743, near Ekatherinburg, and in 1752 the first mining operations were commenced at Berezovsk. These mines, which are sunk in the solid rock, still continue to be productive, although their yield is at present much smaller than it was formerly. In the year 1823 there were no less than sixty-six localities in the Ural from which gold had been obtained by deep mining, but the whole of these undertakings, with the exception of eight, had at that time been abandoned.

The auriferous veins of the Berezovsk mine are numerous, but generally small, and occur in a sort of decomposed granite, which itself forms veins and dykes in talcose, chloritic, and micaceous shales. The most productive veins are of quartz, cutting the granite nearly at right angles, and having an almost perpendicular dip. These veins seldom extend beyond the granite, and appear to become less productive in depth. Towards the close of the last century, the Berezovsk Mine yielded from 600 to 800 lbs. of gold annually, but the production has of late years much decreased, and in 1850 the total yield had been reduced to 100 lbs. troy. During the most prosperous period of their exploitation, the stamped work from these mines afforded from 6 to 11 dwt. of gold per ton.

The gold washings proper of the Ural, which have produced such a large amount of the precious metal, and which, before the discovery of the deposits of California and Australia, had acquired so much celebrity for their richness, were commenced by the Russian Government in 1814, whilst those of Western Siberia were not opened until 1829, and those of Eastern Siberia remained unworked until 1838. The method of occurrence of gold in some of the more important of the Russian alluvial diggings will be understood from a description of the Soimanofsk Mines, north of Miask. Here, great masses of ancient drift or gravel having been removed for the extraction of gold, the eroded edges of highly inclined crystalline limestone have been exposed, which, from being near the centre of the chain, are believed to be of Silurian age. It is from the adjacent eruptive serpentinous masses and slaty rocks, *b*, Fig. 1, that the auriferous shingle *c*, usually more productive near the surface of the abraded rock *a*, has been derived.

FIG. 1.

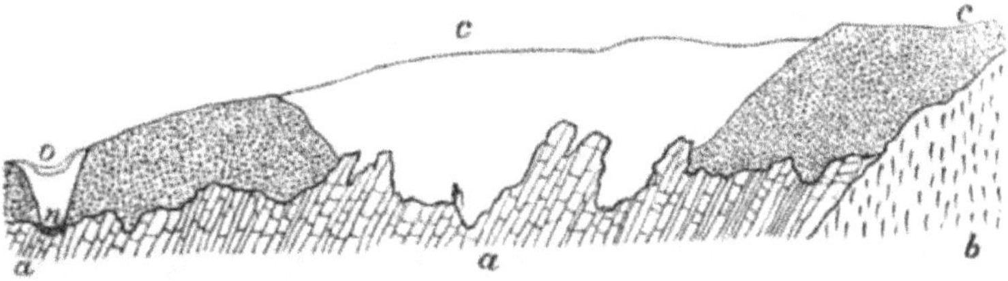

DIGGINGS AT THE SOIMANOFSK MINES.
(*From "Russia and the Ural Mountains,"* vol. i. p. 487.)

The tops of the highly inclined beds *a* are rounded off, and the interstices between them worn into holes and cavities manifestly by very powerful aqueous action. Here, as at Berezovsk, mammoth remains are found lodged in the lowest part of the excavation, at the spot towards which the small figure of a man is pointing, and at a depth of about 50 feet below the original surface of the overlying coarse gravel *c*, before its removal during the progress of the operations. The feeble influence of the existing stream *n* in excavating even the loose shingle, is seen at *o*, the bed of the rivulet having been lowered by artificial means from its natural level *o*, to that marked *n*, for the convenience of working the deposit. In some spots the gold-bearing alluvium is a heavy clay, whilst in others it is made up of fragments of quartz veins, chloritic and talcose shales, and greenstone, which lie on the side of the hillocks of eruptive rock.

It was from one of these gravelly depressions, south of Miask, that the large lump of solid gold was found, which is now preserved in the Imperial School of Mines at St. Petersburg, and which weighs ninety-seven pounds troy.*

The auriferous detritus of the Ural Mountains is, however, poor in comparison with the deposits which have since been found in California and Australia; for although very large nuggets have occasionally been met with, much of the auriferous ground, which in the

* Siluria, p. 484.

Russian Empire, where labour is cheap and water-power abundant, can be worked at a profit, would, if in California or Australia, be neglected as being of no practical value.

The following table shows the production of the Russian washings from their commencement to the year 1860: *—

		Lbs. Troy.
1814 to 1820	Produce of the Crown washings	11,085
1820 to 1830	Crown and private	73,200
1830 to 1840	„ „ „	175,460
1840 to 1850	„ „ „	553,955
1850 to 1860	„ „ „	687,025
	Total	1,500,725

The amount of gold obtained from vein mines in the Russian possessions is very small.

The produce of the Russian mines appears to have nearly reached its maximum in 1847, since which there has been but little increase in their returns. Few new localities producing gold have been discovered, and in the Siberian diggings both the yield of the sand and the amount of gold extracted have somewhat diminished. In the Ural, on the other hand, owing to the skill with which the mines are conducted, and the perfection of the machinery employed, the annual produce of gold is increasing, although the yield of the auriferous drift has decreased to 0·00006 per cent. The washing machinery of the Ural is exceedingly efficacious, being capable of treating large quantities of drift at a very small cost; and were this not the case, it would be impossible to work at a profit, since the proportion of gold, in the material operated on, does not exceed from four to six parts in a million.

Germany.—Austrian Empire.—The amount of gold annually produced in Germany is exceedingly small, although in some localities washing and mining operations in pursuit of this metal have been almost uninterruptedly carried on from remote antiquity. Among the rivers of this country which have afforded auriferous sands, may be mentioned the Rhine, the Reuss, the Aar, the Danube, the Elbe, the Moldau, the Oder, and the Weser.

* Tschewkin Jour. des Mines, quoted in Ann. des Mines (5), iii. p. 805. Archiv für wissenschaftliche Kunde von Russland, 1865, p. 397.

Hungary and Transylvania.—The mines of Hungary have been worked almost without interruption since the eighth century, and are, with but few exceptions, conducted with much skill and economy. In those of Königsberg the gold is disseminated in ores of sulphide of silver, which occur in a partially decomposed feldspathic rock. At Schemnitz, Kremnitz, Neusohl, and Libethen, the treatment of argentiferous and auriferous ores has been carried on for centuries. At Felsöbánya, Kapnick, and Nagybánya, on the western border of Transylvania, there are mines of gold, silver, and copper, which were formerly worked on a very extensive scale. In the mines of Schemnitz, Kremnitz, and Neusohl, the ores afford both silver and gold, together with a sufficient amount of galena to furnish the necessary lead for their metallurgical extraction. The Transylvanian mines afford the rare combination of gold and tellurium, before referred to, but generally yield ores of such low produce as only to admit of being advantageously worked under the united conditions of cheap labour and the application of great mining and metallurgical skill. In Transylvania the gold frequently occurs in veins of considerable magnitude, which have seldom well-defined walls, but abut, without any intervening division, against the enclosing rock. The mine of Kapnik is deserving of notice, from the fact of the gold being frequently associated with orpiment. The produce of gold from the mines of Hungary and Transylvania was, in 1865, 5,395 lbs. troy.

Tyrol and Salzburg.—Small quantities of gold have long been obtained from these districts by the treatment of exceedingly poor ores. At Zell the average yield of the vein-stuff treated was, in 1847, only 4 parts in 1,000,000, equal to about 2¾ dwt. per ton. This is probably the smallest tenure in gold of any auriferous rock mined in any portion of the globe. The annual produce of the mines of Tyrol and Salzburg amounts only to some 65 lbs. troy.

Bohemia.—The mines of Bohemia were worked at a very early period, and it is stated that those of Eula yielded so largely, that, in 734, golden images were manufactured from their produce. There were also gold washings on the Iser, a tributary of the Elbe, within the circles of Bedschow and Turnau, in the Moldau, and at Neuknin, and Bergreichenstein. The produce of the Bohemian mines was from the eleventh to the fifteenth century of some importance to the gold-supply of Europe; but the present total yield does not probably much exceed an annual value of 100*l*.

The different provinces of the Austrian Empire furnished, from the year 1840 to 1847, the following proportional amounts of gold:—

Transylvania	53·30	per cent.
Hungary	45·60	„
Tyrol and Salzburg	0·85	„
Styria, Bohemia, &c.	0·25	„
	100·00	

The total production of the Empire was in 1865 nearly 5,500 lbs. troy.

CENTRAL AND SOUTHERN ASIA.—Thibet has often been referred to as being rich in gold, and more particularly the rivers flowing through the western portion of that country are believed to be highly auriferous. Jacob estimates the annual produce of Thibet at 833 lbs. troy.

That portion of the continent of Asia lying south of the Great Himalayan chain is believed to have formerly yielded large quantities of gold; but although a small amount of this metal is still obtained in many localities in India, the country is far less productive than it would appear to have formerly been.

The washings of the Burrampooter are estimated by Jacob to produce annually from 2,500 to 3,300 lbs. troy.* These workings, however, afford little or no revenue to the British Government, since those employed in this occupation are but barely enabled to subsist on their earnings, and are consequently too poor to pay any kind of royalty. The sands of some of the streams in the Burmese Empire are irregularly worked by the natives; but, according to Jacob, no reliable data relative to their annual yield can be obtained. Mr. Birkmyre estimates the yearly produce of Ava at about 2,000 lbs.

The Malayan peninsula is known to yield gold, but the amount produced is very small, and the character of the inhabitants such as to prevent the introduction of foreign labour and capital.

CHINA AND JAPAN.—The gold-bearing formations of Siberia extend into China, and were formerly worked to some extent, but, according to Sir R. Murchison, operations have been suspended by the Chinese authorities, in accordance with certain theories relative to the maintenance of the balance of the circulating medium. Japan is also

* Jacob's Historical Enquiry into the Production and Consumption of the Precious Metals, ii. p. 330.

known to produce gold, but, from the difficulty of penetrating into the interior, and the entire absence of statistics, little is known, either respecting the method of occurrence, or the amount annually obtained. Some of the East India Islands also yield gold, and many of them in considerable quantities, but we are entirely without information relative to the amount yearly obtained. Gold washing is extensively carried on in Borneo, particularly on the western coast, where, according to Sir James Brooke, the auriferous beds consist of coarse sand and gravel, varying in thickness from one to four feet, and reposing on a bed of clay ten feet in thickness. The same authority states that there are about 5,000 persons, chiefly Chinese, employed in gold washing on the western coast, and that the value of the gold annually collected exceeds 1,000,000*l.**

Timor, Sumatra, Celebes, and the Philippines are also stated by different authorities to afford gold, but in what amount is difficult to ascertain. Whitney estimates the total production of Southern Asia, including the East India Islands, after making allowance for the small quantity exported from China, at 25,000 lbs.

AFRICA was probably the source of a large proportion of the gold possessed by the ancients, and nearly all modern travellers who have penetrated into the interior of that continent agree in their accounts of its wealth in gold.

The whole of the unmanufactured gold which Africa sends into the market is in the form of dust, evidently obtained from alluvial washings. The mines of Bambouk, south of the Senegal, are the most important, and supply the greater portion of the gold which finds its way to the coast; they are open to all, and are worked by the natives of the surrounding villages. The gold occurs in grains and spangles, in the detritus of ancient streams, and the beds of modern rivers, and is generally mixed with ferruginous sands. In these deposits the negroes frequently dig pits to the depth of from thirty to forty feet, out of which they extract the earth from which they subsequently obtain gold by washing. From Mungo Park's description, it would appear that the gold is principally found in a coarse ferruginous gravel, covered by a stratum of rolled pebbles. Another gold-producing district is that of Kordofan on the Upper Nile, between Darfour and Abyssinia. These mines appear to have been known to the ancients, who believed Ethiopia to abound in gold.

* "Narrative of Events in Borneo and Celebes," 1848. London.

The auriferous earths are treated by the natives for the metal they contain by washing in wooden bowls, and the gold obtained is usually stored in quills of the vulture, or some other large bird. Russegger, who travelled through Nubia in 1838, arrived at the following conclusions relative to the occurrence of gold in Central Africa.*

The so-called primitive chain, which, in the interior of Africa, stretches from E.N.E. to W.S.W., as well as the alluvium of the rivers flowing from it, is auriferous, but not to the extent popularly believed. The gold of Sennaar and Southern Abyssinia occurs in the form of scales and grains, in quartz enclosed in granite, gneiss, and chloritic slates. In the granite it is found in quartz veins, associated with hematite and iron pyrites, whilst in the stratified rocks it is disseminated, together with various descriptions of iron ore, in immense beds of quartz. In the gold-bearing alluviums, those beds are most productive which are of an ochreous character and intermixed with coarse pebbles; a fine clay, with roots of plants scattered through it, is also frequently auriferous. The more rapid a stream, and the more rocky its bed, the larger is usually the amount of gold found. The gold of Nubia is of a deep yellow colour, and remarkably pure.

Besides the foregoing localities, gold is also collected in small quantities from that portion of the African continent opposite Madagascar, and lying between the twenty-second and twenty-fifth degrees of south latitude.

The total annual amount of gold furnished by Africa is estimated by Dusgate at 3,744, and by Birkmyre at 4,000 lbs.

* Karsten and Dechen's Archiv. xii. 153, quoted by Whitney.

CHAPTER III.

UNITED STATES OF AMERICA—ATLANTIC OR APPALACHIAN GOLD FIELDS.

DISCOVERY OF GOLD IN THE SOUTHERN STATES—VIRGINIA—NORTH CAROLINA—SOUTH CAROLINA—GEORGIA—TENNESSEE AND ALABAMA—DESCRIPTION OF APPALACHIAN GOLD FIELDS—PRINCIPAL GOLD MINES OF THE SOUTHERN STATES.

THE gold fields of the United States may be divided into two grand geographical sections, viz. those of the Atlantic slope, or the Appalachian gold fields, which have been worked to some extent for the last forty years, and the Californian or Pacific coast gold fields, which, within six years after their discovery, in 1848, had produced more than twelve times the total amount of gold which had, up to that period, been obtained from the regions on the Atlantic shores.

The Appalachian gold fields may be considered to be included within the boundaries of Virginia, North Carolina, South Carolina, Georgia, Tennessee, and Alabama, although some other States have occasionally afforded specimens of the precious metal. The first notice of the discovery of gold in the Southern States which could be found by Professor Whitney, who has carefully examined this subject, occurs in Jefferson's "Notes on Virginia," in which it is stated, that a lump of this metal weighing 17 dwt. had been found near the Rappahannock. Drayton, in his "View of South Carolina," published in 1802, also mentions the finding of a small piece of gold on Paris's Mountain. In 1799 the son of a Mr. Reed is said to have found in Cabarrus County, North Carolina, a piece of gold of the size of a small smoothing-iron, which, after having kept for several years without suspecting its value, he finally sold for about fourteen shillings. Shortly after this, gold was discovered in Montgomery County, and washings were, on a small scale, carried on in these two counties for several years. These operations were entirely confined to the washing of sand and gravel on the banks of various small streams, but several nuggets of considerable size were obtained; and one, found in Cabarrus, weighed 28 lbs. avoirdupois, besides several weighing from 4 to 16 lbs. From this locality it is estimated that over a hundred pounds were collected, previous to 1830, in pieces each over a pound in weight, and in Anson, in 1829, a nugget was found weighing 10 lbs., besides several smaller ones. The first United States gold was coined at the Mint in 1825, and from that time up to 1830, four-fifths of the United States gold coinage was of native gold. From 1804 to 1827, North Carolina furnished the whole of the gold produced in the United States of North America, amounting to $110,000; but in 1829 Virginia contributed $2,500, and in the same year South Carolina yielded $3,500. In 1830 Georgia made its first deposit at the Mint, amounting to no less than $212,000. Previous to 1825 all the gold of North Carolina had been procured from washings, but in that year the auriferous veinstone was discovered *in situ* by Mathias Barringer, who obtained, from an opening about forty feet in length and eighteen in depth, above 625 ounces of gold.

This result turned the attention of miners from the "deposit mines" to "vein mines," and led to the discovery of other leads in Mecklenburg, Guilford, Cabarrus, and Davidson counties. A geological reconnaissance of North Carolina was made by Professor Olmsted about the year 1824, and his observations on the gold fields of that State were published in *Silliman's Journal* in 1825.* At that time the deposit diggings had alone been discovered, and were considered by him to cover an area of 1,000 square miles. Of this region he says that gold, in greater or less abundance, may be found in almost any part of it, and he considers its true bed to be a thin stratum of gravel, which, in low ground, was generally covered by a stratum eight feet in depth of alluvium; when, however, no cause had tended to alter its original depth, it was usually about three feet from the surface. He further remarks that these deposits are not confined to the beds of rivers, but also occur at elevations of 200 feet above the nearest valley. A map of the gold regions was published by Professor Mitchell in 1825, in which nine principal mining localities are laid down, three of which are included by him in the "primary," and six in the "transition" slate.

In Georgia, the first locality known was in Habersham County; but researches were carried on until it was ascertained that the whole of the State lying at the foot of the Blue Ridge was more or less auriferous.

In South Carolina, Brewer's Mine, in Chesterfield, was one of the richest and most extensively worked localities, since in 1830 and 1831

* Vol. ix. p. 5.

between one and two hundred persons were employed there, and were supposed to average from $1.50 to $3 per day each.

In Georgia the gold excitement was not very lasting; but here, as in the other Southern States producing gold, washing has continued to be carried on by the inhabitants as an occasional occupation.

Tennessee and Alabama have each, during the last thirty years, produced a small annual amount of gold, which has been chiefly obtained from alluvial washings.

Professor Silliman, who visited the gold region of Virginia in 1836, states that the principal mines, then working, were Moss and Busby's, in Goochland County, about fifty miles from Richmond—the Moss vein three-quarters of a mile from Busby's, and the Culpeper Mine on the river Rapidan. This gentleman, after describing the several mining properties of this district, remarks: "In my judgment, nothing could be more inauspicious to the mining interest and the welfare of the country, than a spirit of speculation in these concerns. In an excited state of the public mind, it is rare that facts are correctly reported, or correctly viewed. The speculator, who buys merely that he may sell again, is, too frequently, ignorant of the facts, and reckless of the consequences, in regard to those who may succeed him in his obligations; flattering gains from sales of stock are reported from day to day; the property rapidly changes hands; the public mind, being morbidly excited, is of course blinded, and at no distant period accumulated ruin falls heavily on the last in the train."

Professor Tuomey, in his State Geological Report of South Carolina, in the year 1848, mentions the mines then in course of working; and although a great number of localities were being wrought, the operations must either have been conducted on a very small scale, or at a considerable loss, since the annual produce could not have exceeded about $50,000.

In 1852-53 the discoveries which had recently been made in California produced considerable excitement in the public mind with regard to gold mining generally, and, as a natural consequence, attention was directed to the auriferous districts of the Southern States: many English and American companies were formed for the purpose of working the mines of the Atlantic coast, and for a time great activity prevailed in this region.

But before referring to the individual mines which were in operation at this period, we will very briefly describe the principal characteristics of the Appalachian gold fields.

The Appalachian chain takes its origin in Canada, south-east of the St. Lawrence, and forms a series of mountain ridges extending in a south-westerly direction into Alabama. Its width is variable, being greatest near its centre, and diminishing towards its extremities. Its total length is 1,300 miles, and the most remarkable feature of the system is the number of parallel ridges of which it is composed. Along the south-eastern edge of this series of parallel mountain chains, lies a comparatively narrow undulating range of elevations, known by different names in the various States through which they pass. In Vermont they are known as the Green Mountains, in New York they are called the Highlands, in Pennsylvania the South Mountains, in Virginia the Blue Ridge, and in North Carolina the Smoky Mountains. This belt, which is composed of metamorphosed rocks of the lower palæozoic age, varies from ten to fifteen miles in width, and affords but few organic remains. Immediately to the south of this lies the great auriferous belt, running nearly parallel with the Blue Ridge, and apparently of the same geological age. The central axis of this band has, in Virginia, a direction of about north 32° east; but still further north, follows a line more nearly approaching north and south, and towards the south taking a nearly east and west course. Its width, where most developed, on the borders of North and South Carolina, does not exceed seventy miles. Beyond Maryland, on the north, this auriferous belt is not continuous, a few occasional scales, or small lumps, only, being from time to time met with, until we reach Canada, where a considerable area has been proved to afford a notable amount of gold.

The rocks throughout the whole extent of the auriferous belt present very similar characteristics, and consist of slate of almost every variety, alternating with bands of granite and syenite. The predominating rock is a talcose slate occasionally passing into the chloritic and argillaceous varieties, with a prevailing dip to the east at a very high angle.

VIRGINIA.—The amount of gold produced from this State, although small, had been tolerably constant from 1830 up to the commencement of the late Civil War, when, this part of the country becoming the seat of military operations, regular mining was rendered impossible. The talcose slates which predominate in the gold districts of Virginia have generally a reddish colour, and are closely laminated, their general strike being about 30° east of north. The laminæ for the most part stand almost vertically, and enclose masses of granite, syenite, and protogine. For some depth the auriferous rocks are so much decomposed as to admit of being readily worked by the pick and shovel. The gold is almost invariably found in quartz, which, near the surface, is often cellular, from the decomposition and removal of the iron pyrites with which this metal is so frequently associated. The breadth of the gold-bearing belt in Virginia is about fifteen miles.

Professor Whitney, who describes the gold-mining operations carried on in this State during the great excitement of 1853, enumerates the following as being then among the most important:—

Culpeper Mine, on the river Rapidan, seventeen miles from Fredericksburg: in 1850 this mine was working twelve stamp heads, and two Chilian mills.

Freehold Gold Mining Company, established in England in 1853, after an examination by Mr. W. J. Henwood. Vein twenty feet wide, said to have been traced for a mile and a half.

Liberty Mining Company.—Mine situated in Orange County, seventeen miles from Fredericksburg. The vein worked consists of five parallel bands. Gold contained in quartz, and in the enclosing slates, which are much mixed with decomposing iron pyrites. The auriferous belt sometimes widens out to forty feet. This was an English Company, employing eighteen stamp heads, and six Chilian mills. Average yield of the rock estimated at $8 per ton.

Gardiner Gold Mining Company.—Spottsylvania County. But little work done here (1854); machinery in course of erection, calculated to reduce 100 tons daily. Estimated yield of quartz, $12.50 per ton.

Marshall Mine, said to be paying well; depth 100 feet; also in Spottsylvania County.

Whitehall Mine, same county. According to Mr. Henwood, this mine is in deep blue clay slate, the vein running about south-east and north-west. The veinstone is a hard quartz, sometimes marked by ferruginous stains. In this the gold is scantily disseminated, occasionally associated with ores of tellurium. This district is said by Mr. Henwood to resemble closely that of the Morro de San Vicente of Minas Geraes, Brazil.

Waller Gold Mining Company.—This mine is in Goochland County, and was taken up by an English Company in 1853, under the advice of Professor Ansted, who reported the property to be traversed by the great auriferous belt of Virginia. The veins had been proved to a depth of from five to thirty feet, and the average yield was estimated at 1 oz. per ton.

Garnett and Mosely Mines.—Buckingham County. Worked by an English Company; five or six veins on the property, of which two only were in course of exploration. Forty miners employed, and sixty surface hands; crushing power of seventy-two stamp heads.

London and Virginia Gold and Copper Mining Company.—This Company was formed in London, and incorporated in Virginia in 1853, for the purpose of working the Eldridge Mine in Buckingham County.

Buckingham Gold Company.—Organised in 1853, for the purpose of working a continuation of the vein wrought by the foregoing Company. In describing these mines, Mr. W. J. Henwood remarks:—"In this neighbourhood the lowest visible member of the series is a homogeneous lead-coloured clay slate, rather fissile and somewhat contorted, which is succeeded by white quartzose mica slate closely resembling the itacolumite of Brazil, but of no great thickness. The gold formation follows, and is overlaid by a thin-bedded pale greenish-white talcose slate, which is the upper part of the deposit. The strike of all these beds is about north-east and south-west, and their dip 40° or 50° towards south-east. The auriferous deposit had been wrought to a depth of about twenty-six fathoms in the north-eastern part of the mine; it varies in width from three to twenty feet, and the shallower portions consist, for the most part, of quartz, sometimes vesicular, at others, granular, always very slightly coherent; generally much mixed with earthy brown iron ore: irregularly dispersed throughout the silicious ingredients, are masses of iron and copper pyrites, frequently invested with earthy black copper ore, and vitreous copper. Galena and phosphate of lead occur in like manner, although in much smaller quantities, and in the cellular cavities of the quartz there are numerous grains of fine gold which sometimes present crystalline forms." Tellurium is associated with gold in many of the Virginian mines, and there, as well as in Brazil, the gold is of a high percentage produce.

North Carolina.—After a personal inspection of a portion of the gold districts, Whitney was disposed to believe the chances of successful mining to be greater here than in any of the Atlantic States, provided that companies were established with a view to honestly and systematically testing the value of some of the best-known veins. He, however, evidently doubted the *boná fides* of many of the associations then in existence, and appears to have regarded many of them in the light of merely speculative operations.

Gold Hill Mines, in Rowan County, fourteen miles from Salisbury, were the most extensive then worked in the Atlantic States, and are stated to have yielded about $1,500,000 within ten years. The greatest depth to which these mines had been worked was 340 feet.

McCulloch Copper and Gold Mining Company.—The mine formerly worked by this Company was situated in Guildford County, twelve miles from Greensborough. The vein has a known length of about half a mile, and at the time of its purchase by the above Company, in 1853, had been explored over a distance of 1,600 feet. Its average width is about six feet, the enclosing rocks being talcose and micaceous slates. The principal portion of the vein is quartz, and its metalliferous contents, gold, iron, and copper pyrites, and carbonate and oxide of iron. The workings were chiefly above the sixty-feet level, which had been extended 1,200 feet. In 1852, about $31,000 of gold is said to have been taken out at an expense of $60,000. Twenty-five heads of stamps and seven Chilian mills are reported to have been in operation in 1854.

Conrad Hill Mining Company—Davidson County, six miles from Lexington, formerly belonging to Governor Morehead. According to Dr. Genth, there are six known veins on this estate, which are, as usual, composed of quartz, containing a large quantity of disseminated hydrated oxide of iron, together with specular and spathic iron ; near the water level, large quantities of copper pyrites occur. There are no statements of the returns obtained from the property.

Vanderburg Mining Company.—Mines situated in Cabarrus County ; Company organised in 1853. According to the statements of J. T. Hodge, there are several veins with a course north 50° to 55° east, and which occur in greenstone. One of these had been worked to a depth of 100 feet, and varied in thickness from a few inches to 3½ feet. Large quantities of the rock said to yield $40 per ton.

Phœnix Gold Mining Company.—Mines situated in Cabarrus County. Several estates were owned by this Company, of which the principal is the "Conner tract," on which are three veins, on one of which, the "Sulphur Vein," workings have been carried to a depth of 170 feet. This ledge has been traced for a distance of from 3,000 to 4,000 feet, and has a width of from one to three feet. The "Orchard Vein" has a width ranging from one to six feet, and contains sulphate of baryta and copper pyrites. The average yield of this vein, as far as worked, is stated to have been $20 per ton.

Another vein, occurring in granite, in the same county, in addition to gold, affords specimens of wolfram, scheelite, tungstate of copper, and tungstic acid.

Long and Muse's Mine—Cabarrus County. According to Dr. Genth, there are six or eight veins in this property occurring in dioritic slate, passing into chloritic and talcose slates. Four of these veins he considers to be worth working. The veinstone contains much iron pyrites and galena, which render the amalgamation of the gold by the usual methods somewhat difficult.

Lemmond Mine is situated in Union County, eighteen miles from Concord. Fifteen different veins occur in this property, contained in a very ferruginous talcose and clay slate. Of these, thirteen are quartz veins, and the remaining two belong to the class of fahlband deposits, consisting of beds of slate impregnated with sulphide of iron, frequently decomposed into hydrated oxide, and containing disseminated gold.

Mecklenburg Gold and Copper Company—Mecklenburg County, near Charlotte. This association was formed for the purpose of opening the Rhea and Cathay Mines, which were formerly superficially worked on a cluster of veins which pass through the property, and are said to be highly auriferous. We are without information as to the results obtained from the deeper working of these mines.

South Carolina.—The various gold mines of this State had been almost without exception abandoned, previous to the year 1852, when the excitement caused by the discovery of the Dorn Mine again attracted public attention towards them.

The Dorn Mine is situated at the lower end of the Abbeville district, and was for many years perseveringly, but unsuccessfully, worked by a Mr. Dorn, who, in February, 1852, at length struck a very rich pocket of ore. Up to July, 1853, an amount of gold, equal in value to $300,000, is stated to have been obtained by the aid of a Chilian mill from an opening three hundred feet long, twelve feet deep, and fifteen feet wide. Such rich deposits cannot be expected to be continuous, and it is not surprising that, in 1854, the yield of this property began to decrease. From that period up to the commencement of the late Civil War we are without information relative to the progress of the Dorn Mine. An association was also started in New York, under the name of the Dorn Mining Company, for the purpose of working a property adjoining the original Dorn Mine, but the results obtained do not appear to have been satisfactory.

GEORGIA.—The yield of the gold mines of this State has been for many years gradually falling off; and since the commencement of 1860 but little attention has been bestowed on this branch of industry.*

TENNESSEE AND ALABAMA.—Each of these States has annually produced a little gold, but the amount obtained has been very small.

With regard to the various English Companies formed about the year 1853, for the purpose of working gold mines in the Atlantic States, it is generally known, that they were, without exception, complete failures; and it is believed that the success of the different American Companies, started at the same period, can scarcely be said to have been greater. This result cannot, however, be wondered at when the real object of but too many of these associations is taken into consideration, since it is notorious, that in most instances, the working of the share-market received more attention than that of the mines.

Since the cessation of the recent Civil War, however, considerable attention has been paid to the development of the auriferous quartz veins of the South; and it is believed by many, well qualified to form an opinion on the subject, that some of them would be capable of affording continuous and highly satisfactory returns, if judiciously and honestly worked.

* For details relative to the gold mines of the Southern States in 1854, consult "Metallic Wealth of the United States."

CHAPTER IV.

UNITED STATES OF AMERICA — GOLD FIELDS OF THE PACIFIC COAST.

DISCOVERY OF GOLD IN CALIFORNIA—SITUATION AND EXTENT OF AURIFEROUS DISTRICTS—SHALLOW AND DEEP PLACERS—QUARTZ VEINS—MARIPOSA—TUOLUMNE—CALAVERAS—AMADOR—EL DORADO—PLACER—NEVADA AND SIERRA COUNTIES, ETC.—STATISTICS OF GOLD PRODUCED IN THE UNITED STATES.

THERE are now within the American possessions west of the Rocky Mountains, three States, and various Territories, embracing a united area of more than a million of square miles, the whole of which may be considered as a gold-mining country; not that the whole of this region is, strictly speaking, auriferous, as there are large tracts lying within it in which the precious metal has never been discovered in any considerable quantity; but still, everywhere scattered over its surface, are found districts, not only rich in gold, but also affording various other important metals. The gold-bearing States west of the Rocky Mountains, are California, Nevada, and Oregon; besides which the territories of Washington, Utah, Montana, Idaho, Arizona, Colorado, &c. annually contribute to the supply of the precious metal obtained from this portion of the globe.

CALIFORNIA.—It had been long stated that gold existed in California, but until this region had been acquired by the United States, comparatively little was known either of the country or of its productions.

The Jesuit Fathers, who virtually governed California during the Mexican occupation, were, doubtless, aware of the auriferous nature of the country, but refrained from encouraging gold washing, as likely to distract the attention of their neophytes, and ultimately defeat the object which brought them into the country. It is a well-authenticated fact, that gold-bearing quartz was worked by a M. Baric, a Frenchman, at a point near the mission of San Fernando, as early as 1843; placer diggings on a small scale, and with moderate results having been engaged in at a much earlier period. An English naval officer is also stated to have brought with him to Europe from that region, more than forty years since, a magnificent specimen of auriferous quartz; and other travellers had, at different periods, reported this portion of the Pacific coast as affording gold.

The first practical discovery of gold in this State was, however, made, either late in February or early in March, 1858: one of the earliest communications published on the subject being a letter from the Rev. C. S. Lyman, who happened to be in California at the time, and who addressed a letter to *Silliman's Journal*, dated San José, March 24, 1848, in which he says: "Gold has been recently found in the Sacramento, near Sutter's Fort. It occurs in small masses in the sands of a new mill-race, and is said to promise well." This discovery was entirely the result of accident. Colonel Sutter, a retired officer of the guard of Charles X., had contracted with a Mr. Marshall for the supply of a certain amount of lumber; and in order to be able to execute this contract, a saw mill was erected on the south fork of the American River, in El Dorado County, at a place now called Coloma. This mill was completed in the spring of 1848, and on setting it to work, the water, rushing rapidly through the tail-race, exposed certain bright metallic particles, which Mr. Marshall recognised as gold. It was at first sought to keep this discovery a secret, but this was soon found impossible; and the news shortly after reaching San Francisco, caused an excitement which quickly emptied it of its inhabitants, then only amounting to a few hundred in number. Colonel Mason, who was at that time Governor of California, was led by the rumours of the discoveries to visit the locality early in the following July, and found that four thousand people were already employed in washing on the American River and its branches, and were extracting gold of the value of from 30,000 to 40,000 dollars daily.

The fame of these extraordinary discoveries was widely spread during the latter months of 1848 and the spring of 1849, and as soon as the dry season had fairly set in, a large influx of immigration commenced. The first to arrive were those who came from the mining districts of Mexico, Chili, Peru, and other States on the Pacific coast, but these were shortly afterwards followed by immigrants from China and the Sandwich Islands, &c. The arrivals from the United States began to be numerous in July and August, and the overwhelming tide of immigration which from that time rapidly flowed into the country, quickly swept away the Mexicans and Chilians, who, to the number of about fifteen thousand, had first occupied the ground.

Shortly after the receipt of Colonel Mason's communication, the United States Government selected Mr. T. B. King to proceed to California as bearer of despatches, and to report on the population, productions, and resources of the country. This gentleman reached San Francisco, June 4th, 1849, and his first official Report is dated March 22, 1850. In the meantime he had made a rapid journey through the then known gold region, and had collected some valuable information; but not being a scientific observer, his opinions relative to the geology of the country were frequently incorrect. The estimates made by him, however, respecting the probable future supply of gold, although considered at the time as highly exaggerated, have in reality been more than justified by the results obtained. Mr. King estimates, that, during the years 1848 and 1849, about 40,000,000 dollars were obtained from the gold washings, and that, at the close of the last-named year, there were nearly 50,000 Americans and 5,000 foreigners engaged in the occupation. This gold was chiefly obtained from the tributaries of the Sacramento, the branches of the San Joaquin not having at that time attracted much attention. The probable yield of gold for 1850 was set down by Mr. King at 50,000,000 dollars, the actual produce, probably, rather exceeding than falling short of that amount.

The great valley of California is drained by two principal rivers and their tributaries, viz. the Sacramento and San Joaquin, the one flowing north and the other south, but uniting about midway, and finally flowing into the ocean through a lateral opening in the mountain range. The extreme length of this great basin is about 450 miles, and its width from 50 to 90.

The Sierra Nevada rises on the eastern limit of this large area, losing its summits in the region of perpetual snows, and having a central axis of granite, through which volcanic matters have occasionally forced their way to the surface. This great granitic mass is flanked on the west by thick bands of slates and shales, alternating with masses of serpentinous and trappean rocks, and extending into the valleys, where they are overlaid by recent deposits of a sedimentary nature.

Towards the west, this great valley is bounded by the "Coast Range," a series of mountains running parallel with the coast, and situated at no great distance from the Pacific shore. The metamorphic slates of the Sierra Nevada form a belt, having a length of above 300 miles, and an average width of 50 or 55 miles, and are the true gold-bearing rocks of this region. The most prolific source from which the gold of California has been derived, is, doubtless, the veins of auriferous quartz enclosed within the slates and other metamorphic rocks, chiefly occurring on the western slope of the Sierra, and which are believed to be not generally older than the Jurassic period. This great original source of the precious metal is, however, in an historical point of view, secondary to the shallow diggings in which the gold was first discovered, as well as to the deeper diggings, often lying beneath volcanic formations, and from which large amounts have been subsequently extracted.

That the placers owe their origin to the degradation and erosion of veins and bands of auriferous rock, and the distribution, by aqueous agency, of the detritus produced, does not appear to admit of controversy. It is also evident that these gold-bearing gravels, although both comparatively modern, are of two very distinct epochs; the latter clearly separated, in point of time, from the former, and its constituents mainly derived from the breaking up and redistribution of the older deposits.

Placer Diggings.—The attention of the first adventurers in California was exclusively directed to the shallow placers in which the gold lay near the surface, and within the reach of miners whose capital consisted of ordinary working tools. Here their labour was often abundantly remunerated, whilst the capital and skill necessary was extremely limited. In proportion, however, as the surface deposits became gradually impoverished and exhausted, appliances were, by degrees, introduced for sluicing and collecting gold, which involved a greater degree of skill, and the employment of a larger amount of capital. Finally, it was discovered that extensive and valuable auriferous deposits were to be found at levels far above the course of the present streams; and in order to treat these effectually, the application of an entirely new system of washing became necessary. To meet these circumstances, the system known as the *hydraulic process* was introduced; but although it has been already in operation for the last ten years, it has, as yet, barely effected any appreciable diminution of the great masses of auriferous shingle, which remain available for treatment by this method of washing.

At length came the era of deep quartz mining, the successful prosecution of which demanded a greater amount of knowledge, and larger capital, than the early resources of California could afford. In carrying out this operation, man undertakes, through his own skill and industry, by breaking up the original matrix, and extracting the precious metal which it encloses, to effect that which, at an earlier period of the world's history, has been done for him by nature on a gigantic scale.

In many localities, and particularly on the ground between the south and middle forks of the Yuba river, these auriferous gravels have frequently, where they have been exposed to denudation, a thickness of 120 feet, and of more than 250 feet where they have been protected by a volcanic capping.*

These vast beds of gravel are composed of rounded masses of greenstone, quartz, and all the metamorphic rocks found above them in the Sierra. They are often locally stratified, but there appears to be no evidence of there being any continuity in the beddings. As a general rule, the lower portions consist of larger boulders than the upper, but this does not exclude the occasional appearance of large rounded masses of rock among the middle and upper members of the series.

When a fresh fracture of the whole thickness of the deposit takes place, such as may be seen in claims which are in active operation, a striking contrast will be often remarked between the colour of the upper and lower portions of this mass of gravel. This is chiefly caused by the oxidation of iron pyrites, enclosed in the upper layers, by the action of the surface water percolating through them, and thus staining the gravels of a red or yellow colour, in undulating bands and seams, which contrast strongly with the blue colour of the unoxidised detritus. On closely examining the blue-coloured portions of these deposits, they will be found to be highly impregnated with finely-divided iron pyrites, forming one of the chief cementing materials, holding together the sand and pebbles in the form of a compact conglomerate, often requiring the use of gunpowder for its removal.

Isolated patches of fine sand, clearly showing water lines, but never regular for any considerable distance, are frequently observed in the upper portions of the beds, and in these are often found large quantities of fossil wood, still retaining its original structure, but flattened by pressure, and blackened to the colour of coal. Sometimes the masses of this ancient drift-wood have so accumulated in the eddies of the former currents, as to present the appearance of an almost continuous bed of lignite. In Calaveras and Tuolumne

* For information relative to the placers of this district, see Silliman's Report on the Deep Placers of the Yuba River.

counties, the volcanic matters, capping the auriferous deposits, occur in the form of basaltic columns, beneath which are found the layers of sand, gravel, and boulders before described. Here the wood contained in the gravel-beds is beautifully silicified and converted into semi-opal, as is also the case at Nevada, Placerville, and elsewhere. It not unfrequently happens, in these localities, that a piece of wood will be observed, which must have been originally converted into lignite at one end, whilst the other remained unaltered; but the whole having subsequently become silicified, it now presents the appearance of a combination of alabaster and black marble, each portion still retaining the structure of the original wood.

The gravel is also occasionally replaced by bands, and lenticular masses, of a tough yellowish or whitish clay, which, by their coherence and plasticity, frequently present a great impediment to the operations of mining. After a few weeks' exposure to the action of atmospheric influences, the agglutinated gravel is often found to disintegrate, and fall to pieces, from the oxidation of the pyritous cement; but in localities in which silica has formed one of the chief constituents of the cementing material, this alteration by weathering is far less rapid in its action. The cementation of gravel is also frequently effected by the agency of calcareous waters.

Gold is, to a greater or less extent, disseminated throughout the whole mass of these great gravel deposits, not, however, with uniformity, but always in greatest abundance near the bottom, and generally in direct contact with the *bed rock*. The upper portions of the gravels are not unfrequently so poor that of themselves they could not possibly be worked with advantage; but as there is no practicable method of washing the lower strata without removing the upper, it is usually the custom to work the whole thickness of the deposit. Large masses of gold are but rarely met with in these ancient gravels, but on reaching the bed rock, the surface of which is often grooved and polished by glacial or aqueous action, and, separating from it, the superincumbent masses of cemented gravel, the gold becomes visible in the form of numerous scales and water-worn grains. These are frequently so inlaid in, and firmly attached to, the bed rock, as to form a sort of mosaic, the whole surface of the bedding requiring to be carefully worked over by the pick, in order to secure the gold attached to, and embedded in, its surface.

In cases where the bed rock consists of a soft material, such as micaceous and chloritic slates, it is in most cases found advantageous to break it up to a depth of from eight to ten inches. The extent of this auriferous alluvium is exceedingly great in California, and in some instances its richness has been remarkable. M. Laur states that "at Mokelumne Hill the last layer was so rich that the laws limited the extent, that each miner could possess, to fifteen square feet. This was exactly the space for a shaft: the working consisted in sinking this shaft down to the unstratified rock; the upper earths, excellent though they were, being thrown away, the workmen confining themselves to a bed of some centimetres in thickness, consisting of a mixture of pyrites and gold, lying immediately on the bed rock. There are shafts in this region which have thus produced 250 pounds weight of gold, extracted from the fifteen square feet constituting their area." *

It must not, however, be supposed that the yield of gold obtained by working equal areas of these deposits, even in the same district, is by any means constant, since certain localities are invariably found to be far more productive than others.

The poverty or richness of a given mass of alluvium, all other conditions being equal, very much depends on the conformation of the bed rock on which it reposes. If the alluvium rests upon rounded convex rocks, the lower beds are generally but slightly auriferous, and the conditions for working are unfavourable. When, on the contrary, these deposits have been formed over depressions in the bed rock, or still better, a gulley or deep hollow is found in the bottom, an abundance of gold may be anticipated. It has also been observed that, other things being equal, the proportionate yield of gold is larger in the southern portion of the Sierra Nevada than in the northern. One of the most remarkable deposits of auriferous gravel is extensively worked in Tuolumne County, under Table Mountain. The summit of this elevation is occupied by a thick bed of basalt of a very dark colour, and great density of texture, which is occasionally distinctly columnar, and appears to have been poured out in one continuous flow. This, in the neighbourhood of Sonora, is from 140 to 150 feet in thickness, and its width, near the entrance of the Buckeye Tunnel, is about 1,700 feet.

Beneath this capping of basaltic lava is a heavy deposit of detrital matter, distinctly stratified in almost horizontal beds, but with a slight inclination from either side towards the centre of the mass. These

* Du Gisement et de l'Exploitation de l'Or en Californie; par P. Laur, Ingénieur des Mines. Ann. des Mines (vi.), vol. iii. p. 412.

sedimentary beds chiefly consist of a rather fine-grained sandstone, which rapidly disintegrates on exposure to the atmosphere. Interstratified with this sandstone, and more particularly in the proximate vicinity of the bed rock, are clays and fine argillaceous shales, frequently nearly white, and often beautifully laminated. With these are associated beds made up of coarse grains, strongly cohering together, forming the *cement* of the miners; and at bottom is found the *pay gravel*, exactly like that seen in the bed of an ordinary river. The entire thickness of this detrital mass, at its greatest depth, is at least two hundred feet. This thickness, however, diminishes towards the extremities of the deposit, where the edges of the basin formed by the rim rock gradually rise. A good opportunity for measuring the thickness of the various exposed rocks, and for ascertaining the general conformation of the basin, occurs at the Maine Boys' Tunnel near Jeffersonville, the position and relations of which will be understood from the section Fig. 2.

FIG. 2.

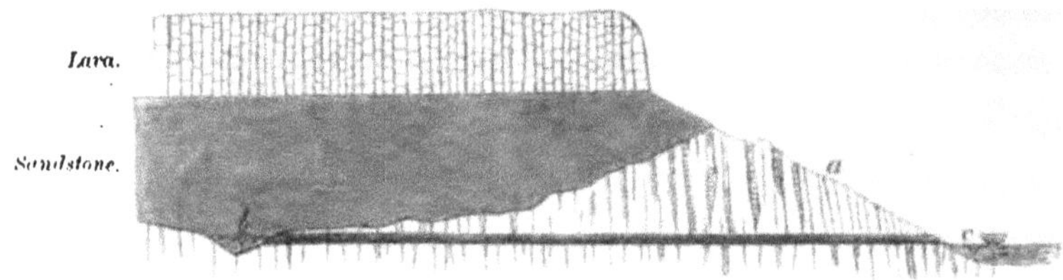

SECTION AT MAINE BOYS' TUNNEL.
(*From "Geological Survey of California,"* p. 247.)

The lava is in this place 140 feet in thickness, and the rim rock *a* rises fully 150 feet above the bottom of the channel *b*, which is drained by a tunnel *c*, driven a thousand feet, with only just the amount of declivity necessary to carry off the water. The channel is about a hundred feet wide, and has a band of slate in the middle, standing about three feet above the ordinary level of the bottom. The depth of the auriferous gravel in this channel varies from four to five feet. Some idea will be formed of the great labour and expense of opening up a deposit of this kind, when it is stated that this tunnel was commenced in October, 1855, and that the pay gravel was not reached until March, 1860; the cost of working during that period having been about 9,500*l*.

The general appearance of Table Mountain, with the shelving sides of the auriferous deposit, beneath the cap of basaltic lava, together with the position of the tunnels, will be understood from the annexed woodcut, Fig. 3.

FIG. 3.

TUNNELS UNDER TABLE MOUNTAIN.
(*From "Geological Survey of California,"* p. 249.)

In most instances the tunnels in Table Mountain are driven through the rim rock, with just sufficient fall to admit of the drainage of the workings; but in some cases they are put down on one of the inclined sides of the basin, or through the detrital matter itself, and in such cases the water can only be extracted by pumping. As soon as the channel is reached, galleries are extended, following the streak of auriferous gravel, or pay dirt, lying in the bed of the ancient watercourse. The dirt excavated from these workings is brought in waggons to the mouth of the tunnel, and there tipped into long wooden spouts, from whence it is washed into sluices, by being played on by nozzles attached to a hose, as in the case of hydraulic mining, to be hereafter described.

The stratified deposits, under the lava, frequently contain masses of wood, and even entire trunks of trees, which are almost invariably silicified and converted into semi-opal. In this the vascular structure is often fully preserved, and specimens which have been partially carbonised, before becoming fossilised, are, when polished, exceedingly beautiful. In the more clayey strata of this sedimentary deposit, impressions of leaves are occasionally found; and an examination of these, made by Dr. Newberry, authorises the conclusion that the auriferous strata lying beneath the lava of Table Mountain are of Tertiary age, and that in all probability they belong to the later Pliocene epoch.

Among the animals of the Pliocene of California, or the group which immediately preceded the period of volcanic activity which covered the great auriferous deposit with lava, have been recognised the rhinoceros, an animal allied to the hippopotamus, an extinct species of horse, and an animal resembling the *Megalomeryx* of Leidy, and allied to the camel.

After the close of the volcanic period, a new fauna, belonging to the Post-Pliocene epoch, makes its appearance, and gradually, though slowly, passes into that of the present day. Among the animals of that time were the mastodon and elephant, whose remains are abundantly found in the superficial deposits of the gold region of California, but have never yet been met with in the deposits under the lava. Associated with these were the tapir, buffalo, and two species of the horse—one of which is not to be distinguished from the mustang, or Indian horse, of the present day. It may be here remarked, that the works of man have been so frequently found among the recent deposits of auriferous gravel, and in such close proximity to bones of the mastodon and elephant, as to lead directly to the inference that man existed in this region before the disappearance of these animals from this portion of the earth's surface.*

During the course of the past year, a human skull, in a state of tolerable preservation, is said to have been found embedded in the deep auriferous gravels of California. The circumstances of the discovery of this skull have been partially investigated by Professor Whitney, who is inclined to the opinion that it was really found, as stated, at a depth of 153 feet, beneath five distinct beds of consolidated volcanic tufa, separated from each other by layers of gravel and sand; but as its geological position is lower than that in which the mastodon

* Geological Survey of California, p. 252.

has yet been discovered in the country, the question of its authenticity becomes one of very great importance, and consequently the results of further investigation will be awaited with considerable impatience.

Quartz Veins.—The auriferous quartz veins of California are not equally distributed throughout the entire region of metamorphic slates, but occur chiefly in the vicinity of crystalline and eruptive rocks, forming a sort of fasciculated aggregation, having a width of from ten to fifteen miles, from east to west, and a length, from north to south, corresponding with that of the metamorphic band. These veins, for the most part, follow the general direction of the strata in which they are enclosed. This parallelism is, in many instances, however, rather apparent than real, since not only is the direction of the vein rarely absolutely identical with that of the stratification of the enclosing rock, but quartz veins are invariably associated with branches and offsets, often cutting through the beds of slate at considerable angles. There can, however, be no doubt but that the dip of many of the most important quartz veins in the country is towards the east, and, further, that the veins of the northern counties, Nevada and El Dorado, run nearly north and south, whilst those of Tuolumne and Mariposa have a course almost south-east and north-west. In some instances, the slaty structure is so indistinct, or so entirely wanting, in rocks of the auriferous formation, as to give to them the character of metamorphosed schists or indurated shales.

If we commence the study of the system of quartz veins of the western slope of the Sierra, by beginning towards the southern extremity of the metamorphic rocks, we find, in the county of Mariposa, an enormous central quartz lead, extending from Mount Ophir to beyond Mokelumne Hill, a distance of at least seventy-five miles. This vein, which varies in thickness from six to sixty feet, frequently crops boldly out above the surface of the ground, and can often be seen from the top of an eminence, traversing the country, for miles, like an immense white wall. This lead may be considered as a kind of axis with regard to the other veins of the district, which are chiefly found within a comparatively short distance of it, and have generally an almost similar direction. The great quartz dyke, commencing at Mount Ophir, in Mariposa, can be traced, almost uninterruptedly, to Jackson, in Amador County; but if we now follow on the same line, we reach Folsom and Marysville, where there are no quartz mines in operation; and, in order to again meet with deep mining, we have to turn eastward to the neighbourhood of Placerville.

This northern assemblage of veins is less regular than that of the south, and we do not here find a large representative quartz dyke, readily distinguishable from all the other veins of the district. The veins in this part of the country are more numerous, and smaller in size, than those of the southern mines, and the belt of metamorphic slates is thinner, and more broken up by the protrusion of eruptive rocks. It is consequently more difficult to trace the direction of the axis of this assemblage of veins, than in the case of those of the southern mines; but if we follow the general line of quartz mills near Log Town, Placerville, Volcanoville, Grass Valley, Nevada, and Downieville, these various localities follow each other, from south to north, according to a line bearing about N. 4° west, which may be taken as the mean bearing of the auriferous belt of the northern district.

Having briefly described the general features of the great gold district of California, we will proceed to notice some of the more important operations, carried on in the different mining counties of the Western Slope.

Mariposa County.—One of the most important features of this county is the "Mariposa estate," which contains some of the most celebrated mines of the southern portion of the gold field, and on which large amounts of money have been expended during the last fourteen years. This estate comprehends an area of seventy square miles, and extends from the Merced river south-eastward about sixteen miles, keeping very nearly on the line of the great quartz vein of this district before described. Placer mining has been here carried on since the earliest days of gold digging in the State, and here also, so long ago as 1852, were made the first attempts at quartz mining. The number and magnitude of the outcrops in this district, together with the amount of gold visible in some of them, were, indeed, well calculated to raise extravagant hopes of the boundless wealth to be derived from working them, but these anticipations have, unfortunately, up to the present time, not been realised.

The Pine Tree and Josephine mines are situated near the north-western extremity of the estate, about a mile and a half from the Merced river. The average thickness of the vein is about twelve feet, but it sometimes expands to a width of at least forty feet. This has been worked, chiefly at a height of 1,300 feet above the river, by levels run in on its direction at three different elevations. A portion only of the veinstone is sufficiently productive to pay the expenses of working, but even this is by no means rich. The average yield of the rock from the Pine Tree, was, in 1860, considered to be 12 dwt. per ton, but since that time, the yield has considerably diminished. The Josephine Mine is situated about half a mile south-west of the Pine Tree, probably on the continuation of the same vein, where there is an outcrop of quartz at least twenty feet in thickness, and from which a large quantity of quartz, containing a small amount of gold, has been extracted. That from the Pine Tree and Josephine mines was crushed at the Benton mill, worked by water power, and provided with sixty-four stamp heads, situated on the bank of the Merced river, and yielded, on an average, about 8 dwt. 23 gr. = $8.98 of gold per ton.*

This mill has been in every respect unfortunate, both with regard to its construction and situation; and not long since, the dam, which had been erected, at a great expense, in order to raise the level of the river for the purposes of the establishment, was carried away by a heavy flood. Relative to this establishment, the State Geologist remarks in his recent Report:—"It yet remains to be shown whether, by a system of judicious changes at the mill, combined with careful selection of the quartz, and skill in following the richer shoots, the Josephine and Pine Tree mines can be worked with profit, which at present is not the case, as there has been a considerable falling off in the yield of the quartz extracted since 1860."†

About six miles south-east of the Josephine is another group of veins, occupying a space of about three miles in length, and which, if not continuous, are very closely connected with each other. Of these, the Princeton vein is the most important, having been, a few years since, one of the most productive in California. It was opened to a depth of above 500 feet, and for a length of 1,400 feet. Its direction is nearly that of the enclosing strata, but is subject to many irregularities; its dip, which is invariably towards the east, also changes considerably in amount. The thickness of the vein varies from a few inches to eight feet, and the rock in which it is enclosed consists of a dark-coloured, fine-grained argillaceous shale, which also forms layers in the veinstone itself. The quartz from this locality differs very materially from that of the Pine Tree and Josephine mines, containing more pyrites, galena, and blende, and often showing beautiful specimens of foliated gold. The average yield from this

* Geological Survey of California, p. 228.

† It was in this region that Mr. King first discovered Jurassic Fossils.

vein was, in 1860, from $25 to $30 per ton, and it is said that gold, to the value of nearly $2,000,000, has been taken from this mine.

It is, however, understood that the yield of the vein has recently very materially fallen off, and that this is one of the prominent causes of the failure of the Company, recently working the mines on this estate, to render their operations remunerative.

At the north-western extremity of the group of veins, of which the Princeton is a member, is a large outcrop of white quartz, known as the Mount Ophir vein. The workings at this place are not of a very extensive character, but the results obtained have not been sufficiently encouraging to warrant further outlay.*

There is another considerable group of veins near the village of Mariposa, on which the first quartz mining in California is said to have been undertaken. The Mariposa vein, which is probably the most important, has been traced for a distance of about two miles, and has afforded some very rich pockets of gold-bearing quartz. The Mariposa estate contains many other outcrops of auriferous quartz on which a large amount of exploratory work has been done; up to the

* The Pine Tree, Josephine, and Mount Ophir veins were worked in 1853-4, by the Nouveau Monde Gold Mining Company, and were reported to be exceedingly rich. No returns of Gold of any considerable amount were, however, forwarded to London, and in 1854 we visited and examined the property. After carefully testing, on a large scale, the quartz from the different locations, we stated their several average yields of gold to be as follows, viz.:

	oz.	dwt.	gr.	
Pine Tree .	0	12	15	per ton of 2,240 lbs.
Josephine .	0	9	17	,, ,,
Mount Ophir	0	6	0	,, ,,

Shortly after this, the mines were abandoned by the Anglo-French Company, whose funds had become all but exhausted, and were taken up by the Merced Mining Company, which worked them for a considerable time, and, in the aggregate, obtained a large amount of gold. Subsequently, however, the Fremont claim to the whole district was enforced, and, after considerable litigation, the Merced Mining Company was deprived of its mines.

Some time after Colonel Fremont came into possession of the grant, a Joint Stock Company, on a colossal scale, was organised in New York, for working all the veins in this district, including the Princeton and some others of known value. Owing, however, to unexplained causes, this Company quickly fell into difficulties, and suspended its operations, although there is reason to believe, that, with the present greatly reduced price of labour and materials, this group of veins, if worked on a large scale and judiciously managed, would yield satisfactory returns.

present time, however, the results obtained have been by no means commensurate with the high expectations, at one time, generally entertained with regard to this property.

Coulterville.—There are several large outcrops of quartz near Coulterville, which are, probably, a continuation of the great quartz vein of which the Pine Tree and Josephine form part. As before stated, this vein appears to run in nearly a straight line from Mount Ophir, on the Mariposa estate, to Jackson, in Amador County, and in the vicinity of the line of these outcrops are found, not only the principal quartz mines, but also the richest surface diggings. There are several localities in the neighbourhood of Coulterville where quartz has been extracted on a small scale, but none of them appear to have afforded results leading to the establishment of permanent works, although some of the outcrops examined are of a very promising nature.

On the banks of the Merced River, near Horseshoe Bend, there is an auriferous quartz vein, possessing considerable interest from the fact of its containing cinnabar in nodules and crystalline plates. The width of this vein, which is enclosed in a highly metamorphosed greenish slate, is about six inches. Its direction is north and south, and its dip towards the west.

McAlpine's.—A few miles north-west of Coulterville a large outcrop of white quartz makes its appearance on the summit of a high hill, known as Peñon Blanco, and forming a conspicuous object for many miles around. On the north side of this great outcrop a quartz mine has been extensively worked on the great quartz lode of the district, and the results obtained are generally understood to be satisfactory. Beneath the productive band there is a thickness of forty feet of totally unproductive white quartz. The quartz above the productive streak differs materially from that beneath it, and contains oxide of iron and laminæ of metamorphic shale. The productive portion of this vein, which varies considerably in width, has been opened for a length of 1,500 feet, and a depth of about 300 feet, at which point it becomes almost vertical, but quite regular. The County of Mariposa, unlike most of the mining regions of California, is without hydraulic diggings, and the shallow placers having become nearly exhausted, the future prosperity of the district must very much depend on the development of its veins of auriferous quartz.

Tuolumne County.—Quartz mining has been carried on at many points in this county, although some of the most productive veins are worked in granite in the vicinity of the metamorphic slates, and not in the slates themselves.

Big Oak Flat.—A large quartz vein passes a little south of this locality, cutting the strata of enclosing slate at an angle; the lines of bedding of the wall rock appearing to run north-west and south-east, whilst the vein itself has a strike of N. 20° W. A considerable amount of mining was done at this point previous to 1863, but in that year the operations were stopped by the burning down of the mill, and we are not aware if they have been since resumed.

Soulsby's.—The Soulsby vein is in granite, is nearly vertical, and runs north and south. The granite in which this vein is enclosed is exceedingly hard, but its walls are well defined; and the lode itself contains a large proportion of the sulphides of iron, lead, copper, and zinc. Near the surface, where the sulphides had become decomposed, the vein, in 1861, gave an average yield of $50 per ton.* In addition to Soulsby's workings, another mine, known as Platt's, is worked on the same vein. Each of these mines has a separate mill; that of the first having twenty stamps, and that of the other, ten. At Lomberdo's Mill, two miles east of Soulsby's, there are several veins occurring in granite, nearly parallel to each other, and running north and south. The only workings on them were, in 1861, on the Louisiana claim, which afforded quartz yielding $20 per ton.

Another group of mills, of considerable local importance, is met with at a distance of about three and a half miles from Soulsby's. The Eureka Mine was here worked in 1861, on a vein in the slates, close to their junction with the granite, bearing N. 25° W. and dipping east at an angle of 40°; the quartz, which was estimated to afford $12 per ton, was crushed in a twenty-stamp mill, driven by water power. The Confidence Mill runs on quartz from a vein in the granite. The width of this vein varies from three to twelve feet, and the average yield is about $15 per ton.

Telegraph Mill.—On the south fork of the Stanislaus, thirteen miles from Sonora, there is a belt of shale, isolated from the main body of the auriferous slate formation, and enclosing a vein of quartz worked at the Telegraph Mill. The thickness of this vein varies from a few inches to twelve feet, and its yield from $15 to $47 per ton; the average yield of one thousand tons of quartz crushed in this mill was $38.80 per ton.

* This vein for some time yielded $50,000 per month, and although it has not recently kept up to that produce, it has still continued to realise large sums.

Jamestown.—The great main vein, or backbone, of the southern portion of the gold field appears to crop out in Tuolumne county, about a mile below Jamestown, where it forms several eminences, known as Whisky Hill, Poverty Hill, Quartz Hill, &c. &c. The main vein is very large, but irregular ; and although it has been repeatedly worked for gold, it has never been found sufficiently rich to pay working expenses. Not far from, and nearly parallel with, the large vein, are several smaller ones, many of which have been profitably worked. One of the most important veins of this district is that of Knox and Company, lying about two hundred feet east of the great main dyke, and running nearly parallel with it. The average thickness of this vein is about twelve inches, and its dip, after the first thirty feet, about 70° towards the east. Beneath the foot wall there is a casing of soft slate, which contains gold, and is often very rich. The average yield of gold from this vein is stated to be $20 per ton. There are several other small mills running in this neighbourhood, but with what results it is difficult to ascertain.

In 1861, a new district was opened up in Sugar-Pine Creek, about twelve miles north-east of Sonora: this when visited by the officers of the State Geological Survey, in 1863, was found to contain some very promising mines. Among them, that which had obtained the largest amount of local celebrity was the Excelsior, on which operations were commenced in 1861. This vein is enclosed in granite, and in 1863 had been explored, by means of an inclined shaft, to the depth of 200 feet. The vein runs N. 40° E., and averages about two feet in thickness. The walls, or casings, of this vein, are rich in gold, and the quartz is said to average from $50 to $75 per ton. It was worked in a ten-stamp mill, on the Tuolumne river; the rock being hauled over the ridge, between the mine and the stream, by steam power.

The quartz-mining interest of this county has, like that of all others in California, been subject to fluctuations; but the operations carried on here do not appear, in the aggregate, to have been attended with that great degree of success attained in some other localities; since, according to Mr. Ashburner's notes, quoted in Geological Report of California, there were in 1859 thirty quartz mills in Tuolumne county, of which about one-half had disappeared previous to 1861; but several new ones have been erected since that time.

The placer diggings of the county of Tuolumne are important, particularly those in, and in the neighbourhood of, Table Mountain, previously described.

Calaveras County.—In the vicinity of Murphy's there is a limestone belt, remarkable for containing quartz veins of sufficient size and richness to admit of their having been extensively worked for gold. At the Blue Wing Mill, there is a vein two feet in width, which runs obliquely across the limestone, the quartz from which has paid as much as $80 per ton. Its run is N. 80° E., and its dip towards the south-east. The great quartz vein of California enters the county of Calaveras at Robinson's Ferry, making itself very conspicuous at Carson Hill, again appearing at Albany Hill, and then at Angel's. It is again seen between that place and San Andreas, and subsequently a little to the north-west of that locality. It has been extensively worked at several points, especially at Carson Hill, and near Angel's.

Angel's Camp was formerly a very active quartz mining centre, there having been at one time thirteen quartz mills at work in the vicinity; but in 1862 only two of them were in operation. The mills at Angel's were all built for the purpose of treating the rock obtained from a lode running parallel with the great quartz vein, and about two hundred feet to the north-east of it. The masses of quartz are parallel with each other, and form somewhat irregular belts enclosed in the talcose slates. A large amount of quartz can be obtained from this place, but its yield in gold is low. The rock crushed at Foster and Company's mill, in 1863, is said to have produced, on an average, $6 per ton. At Carson Hill, a great many exploratory workings have been made; but the gold was found to be very irregularly disseminated. At a place now called the Hope Mine, gold to the value of nearly two million of dollars is reported to have been taken out from a very small space several years since. A band of talcose slates, lying near the back of the great vein, has, in some places, been found exceedingly rich, sometimes paying as much as $80 per ton. Explorations and various attempts at mining have been made on Albany Hill, but hitherto without much apparent success.

West Point.—About sixteen miles east of Mokelumne Hill, near West Point, a great many quartz veins occur in granite. Many of these, which have a course of about N. 50° W. and a westerly dip, have been worked by Mexicans, who grind the quartz in arrastres, and frequently make good wages. These veins are, near the surface, soft, and contain a good deal of oxide of iron, resulting from the decomposition of pyrites; but, as the depth increases, they become harder, and, on reaching the water level, are generally abandoned by the Mexican miners, who transfer their labours to some other outcrop from which quartz can be obtained at a cheaper rate. The Mill vein, which varies from three inches to a foot in width, has afforded quartz, paying as high as $133 per ton. The Myers and Euston lode is very similar to the Mill vein, but is from fourteen inches to two feet in width, and affords quartz yielding satisfactory results. There are also three mills at work on the quartz from the Rathgeber Vein, which is situated three miles east of West Point, and which has afforded some very rich quartz.

The county of Calaveras has been celebrated for the richness of its shallow placers and hydraulic mines. The ordinary river and gulch diggings are now, however, to a very great extent, exhausted, although the surface of the limestone at Murphy's is still being worked, on a rather extensive scale, by means of a long and costly tunnel, which has been brought up at a sufficient depth to command the deepest cavities worn in the rock. Most of the hydraulic diggings, now in operation, are in connexion with the auriferous gravels covered by volcanic deposits, and these are very widely spread over the district.

The deposits beneath the volcanic beds in the vicinity of Mokelumne Hill have been celebrated for their extreme richness, but those in the immediate neighbourhood of the town are now, to a great extent, exhausted. There are others, however, about four miles south, at a place called Chili Gulch, which are still productive, and actively worked. The pay dirt in this place is, as usual, at the bottom of the deposit, and about eight feet in thickness.

Amador County lies between the Cosumnes and Mokelumne rivers, and is considerably smaller than many of the other mining counties. The belt of auriferous rocks, which here occupies a width of about twelve miles, passes directly through its centre, the principal mining towns being Jackson, Sutter, Amador, and Drytown. Ordinary gulch and river mining, although formerly extensively carried on here, is now almost entirely discontinued, whilst quartz mining, on the contrary, has become of great, and rapidly increasing, importance.

Some of the most important quartz mines in the State are situated between Jackson and Drytown, on a belt of quartz which runs nearly north-west from the first-named locality, and which has long been worked with great activity and success. The outcrops, which are by no means those of a continuous vein of quartz, but rather of a series of lenticular masses, occurring in parallel belts, are situated in a line with the great quartz outcrop, commencing in Mariposa County, and which can be traced northward to this place.

The Oneida Mine lies two miles north of Jackson, and is worked on a vein eight feet in width, having the usual strike and dip of the ledges of the district. This mine has been extensively wrought, and affords quartz yielding from $10 to $11 per ton.

Hayward's Mine.—The mines, formerly called the Eureka and Badger, are now generally known as Hayward's, and have been at work for the last twelve years. The vein has a direction of N. 22° W., with a dip of 70° towards the east, and is enclosed in a dark-coloured, rather soft argillaceous slate. Its foot wall is soft and friable, whilst the hanging wall is decidedly harder and more metamorphic. The Eureka and Badger were formerly two distinct concerns, but are now united and worked as one mine. The width of the vein in the Eureka varies from eight to twenty feet, but in the adjoining claim, it suddenly swells out to forty feet. In the two mines, the total length of ground worked is about 500 feet, and to the south of the Badger shaft, which is at the extremity of the claim, nearly all traces of a vein seem to have disappeared, whilst the lode, which is eight feet wide on the north side of the Eureka, pinches out very rapidly in that direction. These mines may therefore be said to be worked rather on a large chimney, or pipe-vein, than on a regular quartz lode. This mine has now reached a depth of more than 1,250 feet, on the underlie of the vein, and still continues to be exceedingly profitable to its proprietors. The quartz is of a greyish-white colour, and is mixed with seams of the enclosing slate, which have a direction parallel to the walls of the vein. The gold is very regularly diffused throughout the veinstone, but is rarely visible to the naked eye. In addition to the free gold, which generally amounts to about $15 per ton, this rock contains nearly three per cent. of auriferous pyrites.

The Eureka Mill has forty stamps, and is worked by water power during the wet season, and by steam when water is not available. The cost of raising the quartz is estimated at $2.50, and the expenses of crushing and amalgamation at $1.32 per ton, thus leaving a large profit on the 90,000 tons annually crushed from the Eureka and Badger mines. The rock from the Badger claim is crushed at the Upper and Lower Badger Mills. The Upper Mill has sixteen stamps, and is run by water; the Lower Mill has but twelve stamps. The stuff from the Badger Mine is very soft, containing a good deal of intestratified talcose slate; it contains about the same amount of gold as the quartz from the Eureka, but, being softer, can be crushed and amalgamated at a cheaper rate. Mr. Ashburner estimates the total cost of these operations at $0.67, which is a lower figure for the treatment of auriferous quartz than can be shown by the books of any other establishment in the State.

The Amador Quartz Mining Company had, in 1862, a twenty-stamp mill driven by steam, and was treating rock from a vein running N. 40° W., with a dip of 57° towards the east. This vein, which has an average thickness of twelve feet, has a hanging wall of soft, black slate, and a foot wall of hard metamorphic rock. At the date above mentioned, it had been worked to a depth of 450 feet on the incline, equal to 377 feet perpendicular; but the workings have been much extended since that time. The yield of the quartz was $10 per ton, and the mill crushed thirty tons daily at an average expense of $1.79 per ton.

The Spring Hill Mills.—There are two mills of this name, situated in Amador

Creek, employed in crushing the quartz of a vein so situated as to allow of the stuff broken, being tipped directly on to the spalling floors behind them.

The average width of the vein is about eighteen inches, although it has in one place suddenly spread out to twenty feet. Its direction is N. 22° W. and its dip towards the east. The average yield of the quartz from this vein is about $10, and the cost of extraction is estimated at $2, whilst the cost of crushing and amalgamation is $1.63 per ton. In some places, this vein is entirely pinched out and replaced by a thin layer of soft black shale, containing finely divided quartz.

Volcano.—Several quartz mines are in operation at this place, and some of them afford rock yielding a good percentage of gold. The Whitman Vein occurs in a band of slate lying between two masses of granite, and is situated about a mile east of Volcano. It can be traced for a distance of above two miles, and has a general direction of N. 22° E. with a dip of 65° towards the west. Its width varies considerably, but may, as an average, be taken at six feet. The Italian's vein occurs in the same band of slate, but its dip is in a contrary direction. The width of this lode is about five feet, and its course N. 40° E. with a dip of 45° towards the east. The Leviathan vein is in the same belt, and has a width ranging from nine to twenty-five feet; its yield is good, although somewhat variable, but seldom declines below $10, or reaches more than $70 per ton. The detrital formation overlying the auriferous slates has a considerable depth in the neighbourhood of Volcano, and is extensively worked for gold. One of the detrital beds in this vicinity is traversed by a distinctly marked quartz vein, passing through the gravel, and evidently formed, since its deposition, by the action of water containing silica in solution. The veinstone is chiefly composed of agate and calcedony, but in some places exhibits ferruginous stains. This is by no means an isolated case, since various other localities have been met with, in which veins of quartz, similar in all their characteristics to those of the auriferous slates, appear to have been formed during the most recent geological period.

El Dorado County lies between Amador on the south, and Placer on the north, comprising that portion of the Sierra extending between the Cosumnes and the middle fork of the American River. The average width of the auriferous belt in this county is considerable, and, at right angles to its direction, must be nearly thirty miles. It would appear from the palæontological evidence, collected by the State Geological Survey, that a portion, at least, of these slates must belong to the Triassic epoch, but this point cannot, as yet, be regarded as being definitely settled with regard to this locality, although it would be impossible not to come to the conclusion that some of the auriferous shales of California belong to that age. A number of fossils have been found in the auriferous slates further north, in Plumas County, which conclusively prove that the slate in that district belongs to the Upper Trias.

This county does not, at present, occupy a very prominent position as a gold-mining region, although it was here that the first discovery of the precious metal was made in 1848. At Logtown, seven miles south of Placerville, there are several veins occurring in the granite, and of which the direction is north-west and south-east, with a dip to the east. There is also a vein at Grizzly Flat, containing gold, associated with large quantities of the sulphides of iron, lead, and zinc. Other quartz veins are known to exist in various parts of the county; but, generally speaking, quartz mining is not extensively carried on. The auriferous detritus covered by volcanic formations does not occupy a large area in El Dorado, but small detached patches are being worked by the hydraulic process.

Placer County lies between Bear River on the north, and the middle fork of the American on the south, and extends from the State line on the east, to the Sacramento River on the west.

Volcanic deposits occupy a large area throughout this county, and consequently its leading interests are connected with hydraulic mining. The known quartz veins are far from numerous, and this branch of industry has not received a large amount of attention.

This county is traversed, from north to south, by an important chain of hydraulic diggings, which are worked on a large scale, the principal mining towns being Iowa Hill, Wisconsin Hill, Yankee Jim's, and Todd's Valley. In many places on this line, the depth of the volcanic and detrital formations is at least five hundred feet, and some of the washings exhibit a vertical section of cement, of more than a hundred feet in thickness. This cement consists of a conglomerate, formed of boulders and coarse gravel, often firmly consolidated by the infiltration of a calcareous or silicious bond, over which lie the usual sedimentary materials, covered by the ordinary capping of hard basaltic lava. At Yankee Jim's, no less than three acres have been stripped of these deposits, and the cemented gravel, which varies in thickness from twenty-five to a hundred feet, has been crushed for its gold. The pebbles and boulders are all thoroughly water-worn, and, to a large extent, consist of quartz; the bed rock is a light-coloured talcose slate, which becomes rapidly decomposed on exposure, and can in many places be readily excavated by the pick and shovel alone.

Much attention has recently been directed to bands of auriferous talcose slates. These deposits are found in the copper-bearing belt, west of the main gold belt of the State, and in the foot-hills of the Sierra. Several of these deposits, now known to contain gold, were first opened as copper mines, the rusty, ochreous outcrops, called among Californian prospecters gossans, or *calico rocks*, from their variegated colours, being supposed to indicate the presence of copper ores in depth. In excavating for copper, these soft ochreous slates were found to contain gold. The Harpending claim, at Whisky Hill, near Lincoln, in this county, is on a vein of this character, and has been worked during the past year on a moderate scale, with a five-stamp mill. The hill rises a hundred feet above the plain, and the metalliferous outcrop is from two to three hundred feet in breadth, and about five hundred in length. Over the whole of this surface the slate outcrops are charged with oxide of iron, and appear in some places almost like blocks of iron ore. On digging down, the rock becomes softer, is more talcose, and, when washed, almost everywhere shows free gold. The material is excavated from an open cut, or quarry, loaded into cars, and conveyed to the mill on a tramway. The softness and abundance of this material allows it to be raised and worked at a very small cost; from thirty-five to forty tons are passed through the mill in twenty-four hours, or at the rate of from seven to eight tons per head. An abundance of water and very coarse grates are used, and the material which passes the batteries is ground in large flat-bottomed pans, known as Moore's grinders. Even with this rude and imperfect way of washing, the material is said to yield from five to six dollars per ton, an amount which it is thought might be much increased by a more effectual system of treatment.

Nevada County comprehends the region lying between Bear River and the Middle Yuba. It is bounded on the east by the State line, and its western boundary is a north and south line, about twenty miles east of, and running parallel with, the course of the Feather River. This county is rich both in quartz mines and hydraulic washings, and mining operations of every description are here carried on, as extensively and successfully as in any portion of California. The width of the auriferous belt in Nevada County is very considerable, but it includes larger areas of granite than any of the counties situated further to the south. Between these masses of granite, the slates are highly metamorphosed, and the sandstones pass into rocks, which can often with difficulty be distinguished from true granite.

The head quarters of quartz mining, is Grass Valley, one of the most prosperous and pleasantly situated towns in the State. The quartz mills in this vicinity are now said to produce about $3,500,000 annually, forming a considerable proportion of the entire produce of the quartz mines in the State. The veins are by no means large, but they more than make up for their want of size by the richness of the quartz which they afford.

Allison Ranch.—The direction of the lode worked on this property is from 5° to 15° west of north, with a dip of from 40° to 45° towards the west. This vein is regular and well defined, its average width being about two and a half feet, with a distinct selvage or flucan on its hanging wall, whilst the foot wall, although distinctly separated from the enclosing rock, is without any clayey division from it. In 1863, the main shaft had been sunk to the depth of 360 feet, on the inclination of the lode; and at the time of our last visit, November 1866, had reached a depth of 500 feet.

The total length of the claim is 1,600 feet, and the ground has been opened, in the direction of the lode, 600 feet north, and 400 feet south, of the central shaft; the average yield of the quartz from the bottom levels being quite equal to that from the upper workings. Mr. Ashburner states, with regard to the produce of the quartz raised from this lode, that 14,858 tons stamped between March 1857 and December 1861, averaged about $50 per ton: some of the rock near the surface, however, which was crushed at the custom mills, in the neighbourhood, is known to have paid as high as $375 per ton. In the early part of 1863, this mine had become, to a considerable extent, impoverished; but in that year a portion of the vein was reached yielding $150 per ton, and since that time, the results obtained continued to be satisfactory up to the commencement of last year, when the yield of the vein again decreased.

The mill has twelve stamps, each weighing 10 cwt. and is driven by steam power, the arrangements for saving gold being similar to those now generally employed in Grass Valley, and which will be described in a future chapter. The Allison Ranch vein contains large quantities of auriferous pyrites, which is carefully collected, and subsequently ground with mercury in a series of cast iron pans. The gross yield of this mine during the last ten years, has been about $2,300,000; the produce for the three years ending December 30th, 1865, having been $1,000,000, but for the past year it has been less than $200,000.

The position of some of the more important quartz mines in the Grass Valley District, together with the direction and dip of the different veins, will be best understood by reference to the Map (Plate I.) kindly prepared by Mr. M. Attwood, Mining Engineer of San Francisco.

The Norambagua Mine has a claim of 3,000 feet, on the course of the vein, which is nine inches in thickness, generally enclosed in syenitic rock, and runs nearly north and south, with a dip of about 15° towards the east. A section of this mine will be found Plate I. fig. 1. Workings have been here extended to a depth of 500 feet, on the inclination of the lode, which is exceedingly flat; and the veinstone, which is a bluish quartz, with interfoliations of a soft blue slate, has been, on an average, found to yield from $65 to $70 per ton. The crushed quartz, on issuing from the mill, is first conducted over riffles, and subsequently passed to the tables of a number of Bradford's separators, by which 1·33 per cent. of auriferous arsenical pyrites is separated and collected. The gold found in this vein is in a very finely divided state, and seldom visible, but the mine has afforded large and regular profits, and has yielded a total produce of more than $1,000,000. The cost of raising the rock is estimated at $30, and the expenses of milling at $5 per ton.

Massachusetts Hill.—The vein here is very flat, and seems to form a kind of basin, being very different, in this respect, to the gold veins usually met with in California. Its greatest thickness is about two and a half feet, and, where best developed, appears to be divided into three distinct bands, with several inches of country rock between each. The proportion of pyrites in this quartz is considerable, amounting to 5 per cent., whilst the average yield of the vein is about $70 per ton. The group of claims on the Massachusetts Hill is stated to have afforded gold to the amount of $3,500,000.

The North Star Mining Company is working on a vein about two miles south-west of Grass Valley, their claim being 3,400 feet in length. This vein, like others in the same district, varies considerably in thickness, but may be taken as having an average width of twenty-five inches. The direction of the lode is nearly east and west, and its dip 27° towards the north. A shaft has been sunk to a depth of 750 feet on the inclination of the vein, and the quartz obtained, by stoping, from that depth, over an extent of 650 feet, is quite equal to any raised from the upper portions of the vein. This mine is worked in a more than usually economical and systematic way, and has reserves of rock amounting to 20,000 tons, yielding on an average, $30 per ton. It has at present in operation, a new mill, consisting of sixteen heavy heads. From 1st January to 1st March of last year (1866), this Company had crushed, in their old mill, 1,400 tons of quartz, which produced gold to the value of nearly $50,000. It is calculated that the reserves in this mine would, of themselves, keep the new stamping mill employed for the next two years.

Eureka Mine.—This mine is situated about one and a half miles north-east of Grass Valley, on a vein more than three feet in thickness, whose direction is nearly east and west, and its dip, south. The ledge has been driven on at the 300 feet level, a distance of 700 feet. This is one of the most valuable mines in California; the gross yield of bullion for the past year amounting to $596,053, and the dividends declared, to $360,000, or an average of $30,000 per month. The company have now on hand about 75 tons of sulphides, worth at least $30,000, and a large amount of wood, timber, and other supplies, valued at $15,000. In addition, $27,000 were expended a short time since for new machinery, and other improvements. It will thus be seen that the earnings of the mine, including actual dividends paid, have for the year 1866 amounted to $432,000. During that period, 12,200 tons of ore were reduced, giving an average yield of more than $48 per ton. A transverse section of this mine will be found Plate I. fig. 2.

The Eureka Mill is probably one of the best in the district, and consists of twenty heads, working in four battery boxes of five heads, each weighing 840 lbs. This machinery usually crushes and amalgamates 43 tons of quartz daily, affording gold to the value of $37 per ton. During the last twelve months, the total cost of raising and crushing the quartz is stated to have amounted to $13.80 per ton.

The Ione Mine is on a vein running north and south, with a dip of 25° to the east. It is enclosed in porphyry, and about two and a half feet in width. The crushing apparatus consists of an eight-head stamping mill, worked by steam, each head weighing 8½ cwt., and crushing 1¾ tons in twenty-four hours. The present perpendicular depth of this mine is 165 feet, the cost per ton of raising the ore $4.50. The total cost of crushing and amalgamation is $1.50, and the average yield of the quartz, hitherto treated, $40 per ton.

Among the more important mines of the neighbourhood of Grass Valley might be mentioned, the Lone Jack, Ophir Hill, and some others, but we have no detailed information respecting these properties. In the neighbourhood of Nevada City there are also some mines and mills of considerable importance.

The Nevada Quartz Mining Company has its mill on the right bank of Deer Creek, about a mile below the town of Nevada, and obtains its quartz from a vein, enclosed in granite, which runs north-west and south-east, and dips at an angle of 45° towards the north-east. The average width of this lode, which contains a considerable amount of sulphides, is about twelve feet. The mill has twelve stamps, driven by water ; the average yield of the quartz is said to be $15 per ton, and the net profit for the year 1863, was a little over $67,000.

Sneath, Clay, and Company's Mill is three-fourths of a mile south-west of Nevada, and has twelve stamps run by steam-power. The vein is in close proximity to the mill, and has an average width of two feet. This mill, at the date of its erection, in 1863, was locally regarded as one of the best in the district, and the returns were very satisfactory ; but we are without data relative to the recent operations either of this or the Nevada Company.

There are various other mines in this neighbourhood, such as the Star-spangled Banner, and Whigham, affording remunerative returns, but presenting no features of special interest, and relative to which we possess no statistical information. The total value of the gold extracted from quartz mines in the Grass Valley district, since their commencement in 1852, is estimated at above $25,000,000.

This county is not only celebrated for its rich quartz veins, but also for its extensive and productive hydraulic washings, second only to those of Sierra County. It is a question still to be decided, whether the great river bed of the Pliocene Tertiary period of Sierra County, known as the *Blue Lead*, passes through Nevada ; but it is known to enter the county at Snow Point : whether, however, it continues its course across it in a northerly direction, to near Red Dog, has not been ascertained. The hydraulic washings near this place are remarkable for the large number of trunks of trees buried in the detritus. These are silicified, and bear evidence of having been subjected to the action of powerful currents, before being deposited in the position in which they are now found. The most important hydraulic washings in this county, at the present time, are those extending along its north-western border, parallel to, and in the vicinity of, the bed of the Middle Yuba.

Sierra County is bounded on the south by the Middle Yuba, whilst its northern boundary is formed by the irregularly curved water-shed between the Feather River and North Yuba; east and west it extends from the State line to Yuba County. The western, or principal mining portion of this county covers an area of about twenty-five square miles. Some of the principal quartz mines are situated fourteen miles above Downieville, within 1,500 feet of the summit of the Buttes, and probably about 7,000 feet above the level of the sea.

The Sierra Buttes Mining Company.—The mine and mills belonging to this Company are situated at an elevation of 2,000 feet above the bed of the river, near the outcrop of an immense vein called the Cliff Ledge, which can be traced for a great distance across the ravines by which the country is intersected. The bearing of this ledge is nearly east and west, with a dip of 42° towards the north. It varies from six to thirty feet in width, and is enclosed in a hard metamorphic rock. That portion only of the lode which is found near the foot wall, and which varies from two to seventeen feet in thickness, is passed through the mill, the remainder of the ledge not being considered sufficiently auriferous to pay the expenses of treatment.

This Company has two mills of twelve stamps each, worked by water power, one of them having been built in 1853, and the other in 1856. These mills are capable of working monthly, 900 tons of quartz, of which the yield in 1860-1, averaged $14.82 per ton. The cost of raising the quartz, and delivering it at the mill, is stated to be $5.87, and the expense of crushing and amalgamating $1.35 per ton.

This mine was first taken up in 1851, and worked by arrastres until 1856, when it was purchased by the present owners, who commenced working it in the spring of 1857, with one Chilian mill, and five arrastres, and have obtained the following annual results:—

	Taken from Mine.	Expenses.	Dividends.
1857	$51,000	$15,000	$36,000
1858	55,000	15,000	40,000
1859	88,000	20,000	68,000
1860	120,000	37,000	83,000
1861	198,000	48,000	150,000
1862	166,000	54,000	112,000
1863	156,000	57,000	99,000
1864	90,000	75,000	15,000
1865	196,000	64,000	132,000
	$1,120,000	$385,000	$735,000

The foregoing item of "expenses" includes all improvements, from taking possession of the mine, up to the present time. No calls were ever made, and therefore the whole outlay for machinery has come out of profits realised. In the fall of 1858, the first stamping mill was erected, to which a second was subsequently added. The smallness of the return for 1864, was the result of a deficiency of water, caused by the great drought of that year, and consequently, in order to avoid the recurrence of similar interruptions, an aqueduct was, in 1864, brought in at an expense of $40,000.

In addition to the vein, from which the principal part of the gold produced has been derived, there is on the property, another parallel ledge, called the Aërial, from which some good quartz has been crushed.

The Independence Mine is also on the same veins, and produces quartz having nearly a similar tenure in gold.

A great many other important quartz mines have been opened, and are in full operation in this neighbourhood, but we are without particulars relative to their yield or situation.

The most important feature of this county is the Blue Lead, one of the many ancient river channels found in various localities in the mining regions. The characteristics of this old river bed do not materially differ from those of the auriferous deposits found under Table Mountain, in Tuolumne County, except that in Tuolumne the course of the ancient currents by which the detritus was deposited, was nearly coincident with that of the streams flowing through the district at the present day, whereas in Sierra County the direction of the Blue Lead is nearly at right angles to that of the modern rivers. As a consequence of this difference of direction, its continuity has been frequently interrupted by the erosion caused by the passage through it of the more recent streams. It is also to be observed that the valley of the river under Table Mountain was evidently filled up by one great continuous flow of lava, whilst, in the present instance, the volcanic phenomena are so numerous and complicated, that it is not easy to determine, whether the changes which first turned the course of the ancient river, and subsequently covered, to a great depth, its former bed, were the results of one, or several successive eruptions. Mr. C. S. Capp observes, relative to the Blue Lead: "Hundreds of tunnels have been run in search of it. Where the line it follows has been adhered to, they have always found it, and have been well rewarded for their labour. Millions of dollars have been taken from this lead, and its richness, even in portions longest worked, is yet undiminished. These tunnels have cost from $20,000 to $100,000 each, and interests in the claims they enter, sell readily at from $1,000 to $20,000; in proportion to the amount of ground within them remaining untouched, and the facilities which exist for working it, many of these claims will yet afford from five to ten or more years' profitable labour to their owners, before the lead itself within them is exhausted." *

Yuba County lies west of Sierra County, and extends to the Sacramento River, one-half lying in the mountains, and the other in the plains, the mining district being principally in the former. The chief mining towns are Camptonville, Timbuctoo, Foster's Bar, Texas Bar, and Long's Bar. The Assessor's report for 1860 mentions only two quartz mills as being at work in this county. Hittell states there are twenty-two ditches in Yuba County, having an aggregate length of 942 miles, giving an average of 43 miles each. The most important of these is the Bovyer Ditch, which supplies Timbuctoo, in winter, with 5,000 inches of water; but this amount somewhat diminishes during the summer months.

Butte County lies west of Yuba and Plumas counties, and is drained by the Feather River. Its principal mining towns are Oroville, Bidwell's Bar, Forbestown, Natches, and Whiterock. In 1860 there were twenty-nine quartz mills in this county. It contains sixty-four mining ditches, having an aggregate length of 583 miles. The most important of these is that belonging to the Cape Claim Company, near Oroville, which has an aqueduct, built in 1857, three-quarters of a mile in length, and twenty feet wide, which furnished employment for 250 men during six months, and cost $176,985. The receipts during the first season amounted to $251,426, showing a profit of $74,441. An extension of this flume was undertaken during the succeeding dry season, but the next year's receipts were considerably less than the outlay.

Plumas County.—This is a large, but not very important mining county, and comprises the whole of the region drained by the Upper Feather River and its affluents. About one-third of its surface is more or less auriferous; but, during the winter months, mining operations are much impeded by ice and snow. The principal mining towns are Quincy, Jamison City, Indian Bar, Nelson's Point, and Poorman's Creek. There are five quartz mills in this county, and a considerable amount of gold is obtained by tunnel and hydraulic mining.

* Quoted in Hittell's "Resources of California," p. 293.

In addition to the gold annually yielded by the great auriferous region which we have thus endeavoured to describe, a certain amount of the precious metal is also procured from various less important localities, in different parts of the State, but which space will not allow us to particularise. We cannot, however, conclude this portion of the subject without noticing the quartz mines of Kernville and Clear Creek, south of Mariposa, whence some patches of the auriferous zone would appear to extend, southward, to those localities. There are several mills at Kernville making satisfactory returns, whilst there is every probability that Clear Creek, at which there are some six or eight already in profitable operation, will eventually become an active and prosperous mining centre.

The gold yield of California reached its culminating point in 1853, and the exportation of treasure, which rose in that year to $57,330,034, gradually fell until 1861, when it was $40,639,080. The silver of Nevada, and the gold of Idaho, then began to flow in, and the amount of the shipments again rose. The following table shows the estimated annual yield of gold, and the annual amount of treasure manifested for exportation, from the commencement of operations in 1848, to 1866, both inclusive :—

Years.	Estimated Amount of Gold produced.	Amount of Treasure exported.	Years.	Estimated Amount of Gold produced.	Amount of Treasure exported.
1848	$10,000,000	(no record.)	Brot. forwd.	$505,000,000	$373,467,283
1849	40,000,000	$4,921,250	1858	50,000,000	47,548,025
1850	50,000,000	27,676,346	1859	50,000,000	47,649,462
1851	55,000,000	42,582,695	1860	45,000,000	42,203,345
1852	60,000 000	46,588,434	1861	40,000,000	40,639,080
1853	65,000,000	57,330,034	1862	34,700,000	42,561,761
1854	60,000,000	51,328,653	1863	30,000,000	46,071,920
1855	55,000,000	45,182,631	1864	26,600,000	55,707,201
1856	55,000,000	48,880,543	1865	28,500,000	44,984,546
1857	55,000,000	48,976,697	1866	26,500,000	44,364,393
Carried on	$505,000,000	$373,467,283	Total	$836,300,000	$785,197,016*

About one-third of the gold annually obtained from California is the produce of quartz mining, whilst the remaining two-thirds are procured from the shallow placers and hydraulic mines.

Other States and Territories affording Gold.—The gold obtained from the State of Nevada is now chiefly derived from the treatment of the auriferous silver ores of the Great Comstock

* This includes about $65,000,000, the produce of Nevada, &c.

Vein, in which the gold usually presents about one-third of the total value of the precious metals contained in the rock. The production of gold from this source, since 1861, has been, according to Richthofen, as follows:—

1862 about		$1,500,000
1863 „		4,000,000
1864 „		5,000,000
1865 „		4,750,000
	Total produce 1862—1865	$15,250,000

In Eastern Oregon, Washington Territory, Idaho, and Montana, large auriferous districts have been recently discovered, every year adding to their extent, in proportion as these hitherto little known regions become more widely explored. Shallow diggings have been worked for nearly ten years near Fort Colville, on the Upper Columbia river, and results have been obtained which would have been highly satisfactory, had it not been for the difficulty and expense of obtaining supplies, and the frequent troubles with the Indians. The production of gold from these northern countries has been for several years considerable, and is steadily and rapidly increasing; but the whole amount of the precious metal hitherto received from these regions, has been exclusively obtained from river diggings, and other very shallow sources.

It is not, however, probable that, for a very long period at least, these countries will at all approximate in their yield to the annual produce of California, since there are many things calculated to deter any but the most resolute and hardy, from seeking their fortunes in these wilds. The winters are long and severe, and for six months of the year travelling and the transport of materials and provisions are impossible. To this must be added the frequent hostility of Indians, and the notoriously bad social condition of the white inhabitants; life being insecure, and property almost without protection.

A certain amount of gold is annually produced by the territory of Utah, but the quantity is believed to be small. The same may be said of Arizona, although, judging from the reports of miners and others who have visited these regions, it would appear that the limited nature of the returns is rather a result of the small number of miners, chiefly caused by the hostility of the Apaches, than from any deficiency in the richness of the auriferous deposits which have been discovered.

The mining districts on the banks of the Lower Colorado continue to possess attractions for a considerable number of miners, who have been at work on them for several years. Hitherto, however, they have produced but a small amount of bullion, but promise to increase in importance, and will, it is generally believed, ultimately supply the market with large quantities of the precious metals.

The following tables contain valuable data, obtained from official sources, relative to the production of gold in the United States:—

STATEMENT OF GOLD OF DOMESTIC PRODUCTION, DEPOSITED AT THE MINT OF THE UNITED STATES AND BRANCHES, TO THE CLOSE OF THE YEAR ENDING JUNE 30, 1866.

1.—MINT OF THE UNITED STATES, PHILADELPHIA.

PERIOD.	Parted from Silver.	Virginia.	North Carolina.	South Carolina.	Georgia.	Tennessee.	Alabama.	New Mexico.	California.	Nebraska.
1804 to 1827	...	...	$110,000·00	...	...	...	...	...	...	...
1828 to 1837	...	$427,000·00	2,519,500·00	$327,500·00	$1,763,900·00	$12,400·00	...	...	...	...
1838 to 1847	...	518,294·00	1,303,636·00	152,366·00	566,316·00	16,499·00	$45,493·00	...	...	...
1848 to 1857	...	534,491·50	467,237·00	55,626·00	44 577·50	6,669·00	9,451·00	$48,397·00	$226,830,521·62	...
1858	...	18,377·00	15,175·00	300·00	18,365·00	...	...	...	1,372,506·07	...
1859	...	15,720·00	9,305·00	4,675·00	20,190·00	240·00	...	275·00	959,191·79	...
1860	...	17,402·62	8,450·11	...	7,556·41	595·88	92 76	...	663,389·02	...
1861	...	7,200·29	7,523·80	...	15,049·41	...	...	...	426,807·81	...
1862	$68,864·66	...	81·38	...	135·40	...	...	...	244,259·81	...
1863	3,468·69	69·00	1,178·84	...	246·66	...	...	514·53	109,778·58	...
1864	7,896·79	...	6,093·85	...	...	...	...	...	91,663·75	...
1865	7,519·76	910·77	16,293·25	...	10,450·12	...	...	...	64,308·07	...
1866	5,916·98	8,704·64	111,401·39	694·54	37,273·11	...	...	3,155·65	107,024·46	$3,645·08
Total	$93,666·88	$1,548,169·82	$4,575,875·62	$541,161·54	$2,484,059·61	$36,403·88	$55,036·76	$52,341·58	$230,878,450·98	$3,645·08

PERIOD.	Montana.	Oregon.	Colorado.	Arizona.	Washington Territory.	Idaho Territory.	Dacotah Territory.	Nevada.	Other Sources.	TOTAL.
1804 to 1827	...	...	...	...	...	...	...	...	...	$ 110,000·00
1828 to 1837	...	...	...	...	...	...	...	...	$13,200·00	5,063,500·00
1838 to 1847	...	...	...	...	...	...	...	...	21,037·00	2,623,641·00
1848 to 1857	...	$54,285·00	...	...	...	...	...	...	7,218·00	228,067,473·62
1858	...	3,600·00	...	...	...	...	...	...	...	1,428,323·07
1859	...	2,690·00	$ 145·00	...	...	...	...	...	...	1,012,701·79
1860	...	2,780·16	346,604·05	...	...	...	...	...	1,402·01	1,048,180·26
1861	...	...	607,502·08	$3,048·37	...	...	...	...	1,507·96	1,068,822·48
1862	...	...	1,122,333·50	...	$ 215·70	...	...	...	...	1,435,890·45
1863	...	7,910·78	1,896,329·87	3,869·75	18,563·88	$ 1,816·97	$2,198·88	$103·68	...	2,046,050·11
1864	...	14,102·90	935,146·72	114·72	7,347·97	847,782·60	...	944·74	...	1,911,184·04
1865	$ 453,250·71	11,491·05	308,590·55	276·80	...	1,400,863·12	...	576·37	...	2,274,530·57
1866	1,778,836·84	46,521·12	425,145·14	...	...	286,400·11	...	897·88	...	2,815,616·34
Total	2,232,087·55	$143,381·01	$5,381,886·91	$7,309·64	$26,127·55	$2,536,862·80	$2,198·88	$2,522·67	$44,364·97	$250,905,913·73

STATEMENT OF GOLD OF DOMESTIC PRODUCTION.—*Continued.*

2.—BRANCH MINT, SAN FRANCISCO.

PERIOD.	Parted from Silver.	California.	Colorado.	Nevada.	Oregon.	Dacotah Territory.	Washington Territory.	Idaho Territory.	Arizona.	Montana.	Refined Gold.	TOTAL.
1854	...	$10,842,281·23	...	...	...	...	...	...	...	...	...	$10,842,281·23
1855	...	20,860,437·20	...	...	...	...	...	...	...	...	...	20,860,437·20
1856	...	29,209,218·24	...	...	...	...	...	...	...	...	...	29,209,218·24
1857	...	12,526,826·93	...	...	...	...	...	...	...	...	...	12,526,826·93
1858	...	19,104,369·99	...	...	...	...	...	...	...	...	...	19,104,369·99
1859	...	14,098,564·14	...	...	...	...	...	...	...	...	...	14,098,564·14
1860	...	11,319,913·83	...	...	...	...	...	...	...	...	...	11,319,913·83
1861	...	12,206,382·64	...	...	...	...	...	...	...	...	...	12,206,382·64
1862	$822,823·01	14,029,759·95	$680·00	$13,000·00	$888,000·00	...	...	...	...	...	...	15 754,262·96
1863	1,108,466·57	13,045,711·69	59,472·00	11,250·00	3,001,104·00	$5,760·00	$12,672·00	...	...	...	...	17,244,436·26
1864	220,890·18	14,863,657·52	...	...	2,139,305·00	...	...	$1,257,497·50	...	...	...	18,481,350·20
1865	217,935·98	11,089,974·52	...	5,400·00	1,108,076·54	...	22,460·94	3,490,281·14	$20,369·48	$3,000·00	$2,598,601·49	18 560,100·09
1866	374,393·28	10,034,775·03	...	43,497·28	858,433·11	...	...	2,880,203·48	30,430·68	549,733·32	2,665,033·00	17,436,499·18
Total	$2,744,509·02	$193,231,872·91	$60,152·00	$73,147·28	$7,989,918·65	$5,760·00	$35,132·94	$7,636,982·12	$50,800·16	$552,733·32	$5,263,634·49	$217,644,642·89

STATEMENT OF GOLD OF DOMESTIC PRODUCTION.—*Continued.*

3.—BRANCH MINT OF NEW ORLEANS.

PERIOD.	North Carolina.	South Carolina.	Georgia.	Tennessee.	Alabama.	California.	Colorado.	Other Sources.	TOTAL.
1838 to 1847 . .	$741·00	$14,306·00	$37,364·00	$1,772·00	$61,903·00	...	...	$3,613·00	$119,699·00
1848 to 1857 . .	...	1,911·00	2,317·00	947·00	15,379·00	$21,606,461·54	...	3,677·00	21,630,692·54
1858	...	...	1,560·00	164·12	...	448,439·84	...	...	450,163·96
1859	...	...	...	...	...	93,272·41	...	...	93,272·41
1860	...	...	...	...	661·53	97,135·00	$1,770·39	...	99,566·92
1861 (to Jan. 31st)	...	...	...	...	...	19,932·10	1,666·81	...	21,598·91
Total . . .	$741·00	$16,217·00	$41,241·00	$2,883·12	$77,943·53	$22,265,240·89	$3,437·20	$7,290·00	$22,414,993·74

STATEMENT OF GOLD OF DOMESTIC PRODUCTION.—*Continued.*

4.—BRANCH MINT, CHARLOTTE, NORTH CAROLINA.

PERIOD.	NORTH CAROLINA.	SOUTH CAROLINA.	CALIFORNIA.	TOTAL.
1838 to 1847	$1,529,777·00	$143,941·00	...	$1,673,718·00
1848 to 1857	2,503,412·68	222,754·17	$87,321·01	2,813,487·86
1858	170,560·33	5,507·16	...	176,067·49
1859	182,489·61	22,762·71	...	205,252·32
1860	134,491·17	...	...	134,491·17
1861 (to March 31st)	...	65,558·30	...	65,558·30
Total	$4,520,730·79	$460,523·34	$87,321·01	$5,068,575·14

STATEMENT OF GOLD OF DOMESTIC PRODUCTION.—*Continued.*

5.—BRANCH MINT, DAHLONEGA.

PERIOD.	UTAH.	N. CAROLINA.	S. CAROLINA.	GEORGIA.	TENNESSEE.	ALABAMA.	CALIFORNIA.	COLORADO.	OTHER SOURCES.	TOTAL.
1838 to 1847	...	$64,351·00	$95,427·00	$2,978,353·00	$32,175·00	$47,711·00	...	...	...	$3,218,017·00
1848 to 1857	...	28,278·82	174,811·91	1,159,420·98	9,837·42	11,918·92	$1,124,712·82	...	$951·00	2,509,931·87
1858	...	...	32,322·28	57,891·45	107·33	...	5,293·52	...	...	95,614·58
1859	...	2,656·88	4,610·35	57,023·12	...	...	699·19	$82·70	...	65,072·24
1860	...	3,485·70	2,004·36	35,588·92	...	...	1,097·37	2,490·86	...	44,667·21
1861 (to February 28)	$145·14	812·79	2,066·91	22,182·14	...	...	4,213·79	32,772·28	...	62,193·05
Total	$145·14	$99,585·19	$311,242·81	$4,310,459·61	$42,119·75	$59,629·92	$1,136,016·69	$35,345·84	$951·00	$5,996,496·95

STATEMENT OF GOLD OF DOMESTIC PRODUCTION.—*Continued.*

6.—ASSAY OFFICE, NEW YORK.

PERIOD.	Parted from Silver.	Virginia.	North Carolina.	South Carolina.	Georgia.	Alabama.	New Mexico.	California.	Montana.
1854	...	$167·00	$8,916·00	$396·00	$1,242,00	...	...	$9,221,457·00	...
1855	...	2,370·00	3,750·00	7,620·00	13,100·00	$350·00	...	25,026,896·11	...
1856	...	6,928·00	805·07	4,052·29	41,161·28	233·62	...	16,529,808·90	...
1857	...	1,531·00	1,689·00	2,663·00	10,451·00	1,545·00	...	9,899,957·00	...
1858	...	501·00	7,007·00	6,354·00	12,951·00	2,181·00	...	19,660,531·46	...
1859	...	436·00	20,122·00	700·00	14,756·00	593·00	...	11,694,872·25	...
1860	...	4,202·00	9,735·00	...	19,368·00	...	...	16,023,628·36	...
1861	...	3,869·00	2,758·00	679·30	6,900·00	818·00	$6,714·00	19,227,658·14	...
1862	$241,029·00	316·00	2,232·00	2,065·00	1,469·00	...	1,543·00	12,580,647·83	...
1863	34,328·00	...	130·00	...	...	...	5,580·00	346,244·60	...
1864	7,618·00	...	...	...	...	...	...	116,101·06	...
1865	14,003·00	...	...	...	3,422·00	2,269·00	3,924·00	2,177,954·04	$1,217,518·00
1866	79,304·00	1,693·00	29,536·00	...	11,161·00	1,135·00	...	4,456,392·00	3,132,370·00
Total	$376,282·00	$22,013·00	$81,695·07	$24,519·59	$135,921·28	$9,124·62	$17,761·00	$146,961,348·75	$4,349,888·00

PERIOD.	Idaho.	Colorado.	Utah.	Arizona.	Oregon.	Nevada.	Vermont.	Other Sources.	TOTAL.
1854	...	...	...	...	...	...	...	...	$9,227,177·00
1855	...	...	...	...	...	...	...	$1,600·00	25,054,086·11
1856	...	...	...	...	...	...	...	...	16,582,129·16
1857	...	...	...	...	...	...	...	...	9,917,836·00
1858	...	...	...	...	$5,581·00	...	...	27,523·00	19,722,629·46
1859	...	$3,944·00	...	...	2,866·00	...	...	405·00	11,738,694·25
1860	...	248,981·00	$4,680·00	$1,190·00	...	...	...	...	6,311,804·36
1861	...	1,449,166·00	73,734·00	16,871·00	3,181·00	...	...	...	20,759,384·14
1862	...	912,403·00	...	391·00	295·00	$40,846·00	...	3,293·00	13,786,439·83
1863	...	937,535·00	...	391·00	7,813·00	...	$298·00	...	1,332,319·60
1864	$201,288·00	715,208·00	...	3,775·00	8,650·00	74·00	...	117,347·00	1,170,061·06
1865	...	938,593·00	...	707·00	9,876·00	949·00	316·00	364,857·00	4,734,388·04
1866	205,844·00	496,805·00	...	...	8,705·00	5,710·00	...	129,100·00	8,557,664·00
Total	$407,132·00	$5,702,635·00	$78,414·00	$23,325·00	$46,877·00	$47,579·00	$614·00	$644,125·00	$148,894,563·01

STATEMENT OF GOLD OF DOMESTIC PRODUCTION.—*Continued.*

7.—BRANCH MINT, DENVER.

PERIOD.	COLORADO.	MONTANA.	IDAHO.	OREGON.	ARIZONA.	TOTAL.
1864	$486,329·97	...	...	...	...	$486,329·97
1865	375,065·90	$93,613·01	$71,310·49	$1,230·16	$339·48	541,559·04
1866	96,521·38	44,134·13	19,549·89	777·54	...	160,982·94
Total . . .	$957,917·25	$137,747·14	$90,860·38	$2,007·70	$339·48	$1,188,871·95

STATEMENT OF GOLD OF DOMESTIC PRODUCTION.—*Continued.*

8.—SUMMARY EXHIBIT OF THE ENTIRE DEPOSITS OF DOMESTIC GOLD AT THE MINT OF THE UNITED STATES AND BRANCHES, TO JUNE 30TH, 1866.

MINT.	Parted from Silver.	Virginia.	North Carolina.	South Carolina.	Georgia.	Alabama.	Tennessee.	California.	Colorado.	Utah.	Nebraska.
Philadelphia	$93,666·88	$1,548,169·82	$4,575,875·62	$541,161·54	$2,484,059·61	$55,036·76	$36,403·88	$230,878,450·98	$5,641,886·91	...	$3,645·08
San Francisco	2,744,509·02	...	...	...	...	...	...	193,231,872·91	60,152·00	...	...
New Orleans	...	...	741·00	16,217·00	41,241·00	77,943·58	2,883·12	22,265,240·89	3,437·20	...	...
Charlotte	...	...	4,520,730·79	460,523·34	...	...	...	87,321·01	...	...	...
Dahlonega	...	...	99,585·19	311,242·61	4,310,459·61	59,629·92	42,119·75	1,136,016·69	35,345·84	$145·14	...
Assay Office	376,282·00	22,013·00	81,695·07	24,519·29	135,921·28	9,124·62	...	136,960,348·75	5,702,635·00	78,414·00	...
Denver	...	...	...	...	...	...	...	...	957,917·25	...	...
Total	$3,214,457·90	$1,570,182·82	$9,278,627·67	$1,353,663·98	$6,971,681·50	$201,784·83	$81,406·75	$584,559,251·23	$12,401,374·20	$78,559·14	$3,645·08

MINT.	Montana.	Arizona.	New Mexico.	Oregon.	Nevada.	Dacotah.	Idaho.	Washington.	Vermont.	Other Sources.	TOTAL.
Philadelphia	$2,232,087·55	$7,300·64	$52,341·58	$143,741·01	$2,522·67	$2,198·88	$2,536,862·80	$26,127·55	...	$44,364·97	$250,905,913·73
San Francisco	552,783·32	50,809·16	...	7,989,918·65	73,147·28	5,760·00	7,736,982·12	35,132·94	...	5,263,634·49	217,644,642·89
New Orleans	...	...	...	...	...	...	...	...	...	7,290·00	22,414,993·74
Charlotte	...	...	...	...	...	...	...	...	...	...	5,068,575·14
Dahlonega	...	...	...	...	...	...	...	...	...	951·00	5,995,495·95
Assay Office	4,349,888·00	23,325·00	17,761·00	46,877·00	47,579,00	...	407,132·00	...	$614·00	644,125·00	148,928,163·01
Denver	137,747·14	339·48	...	2,007·70	...	...	90,860·38	...	...	...	1,188,871·95
Total	$7,272,456·01	$81,774·28	$70,102·58	$8,182,544·36	$123,248·95	$7,958·88	$10,771,837·30	$61,260·49	$614·00	$5,960,365·46	$652,146,656·41

CHAPTER V.

MEXICO, CENTRAL AMERICA, AND SOUTH AMERICA.

MEXICO PRE-EMINENTLY A SILVER-PRODUCING COUNTRY—NICARAGUA—CHONTALES MINING COMPANY—BRAZIL—ST. JOHN D'EL REY COMPANY—IMPERIAL BRAZILIAN —DON PEDRO NORTH D'EL REY—ROSSA GRANDE GOLD MINING COMPANY—EAST D'EL REY—NEW GRANADA—MARIQUITA AND NEW GRANADA MINING COMPANY— PERU AND BOLIVIA.

MEXICO is pre-eminently a silver-producing country, and almost the whole of the gold which it affords is found in combination with that metal. The amount of silver produced is, however, so large, that the associated gold becomes a matter of considerable importance, and will be more particularly referred to when treating of the ores of silver.

The silver of Guanaxuato and Guadalupe y Calvo is rich in gold, whilst that of Tasco, Catorce, and Zacatecas is poor. In 1840 Duport estimated all the gold produced in Mexico, including that separated from silver, at $\frac{1}{138}$th of the production, by weight, of the latter metal, and its value at $\frac{1}{8}$th of that of the silver.

There are some gold veins in Oaxaca, which have been worked for many years, and which Chevalier was of opinion would at some day become of importance.

CENTRAL AMERICA.

But little is definitely known with regard to the auriferous districts of Central America, except that the gold washings of Costa Rica produce a certain amount of the precious metal, which is mostly smuggled out of the country, and consequently no estimate can be made of its amount. The only European Association professing to carry on gold-mining operations in Central America is, we believe, the following:—

NICARAGUA.—The Chontales Gold and Silver Mining Company.—This Company was formed in 1865 to purchase and work gold and silver mines in the Chontales district of Nicaragua, a gold field hitherto unexplored by Europeans, although worked for several years by the inhabitants. The following description of the properties is condensed from the reports of Captain Paul, the mining agent who was sent out for the purpose of inspecting them, and who has since become the local manager.

The San Domingo Mine comprises an extent of 1,000 varas on the course of the lodes, by 2,000 varas wide. There are two large well-defined auriferous and argentiferous veins running parallel with each other through this sett, about 50 varas apart. One lode has been worked, for about 100 yards in length, to the depth of 20 feet, on its entire width, and is said to have yielded from 1 to 10, and as high as even 100 oz. of gold per ton, while the general average is reported to be about 3 oz. per ton. The hard quartz, yielding nearly 2 oz. per ton, is stated to have been thrown aside, owing to inadequate means for grinding. The mine has, hitherto, been badly worked, and on a small scale, yet 230 oz. of gold were raised in the month of January, 1865.

La Trinidad adjoins San Domingo on a parallel lode. It is 800 varas in length, by 100 in width. The workings are in a deep valley, so that a level can be driven, and 30 to 40 fathoms of backs obtained. This mine has hitherto been owned and worked by natives, who have not had the means of erecting proper machinery, and, in consequence, have been obliged to carry the ore to the mill on men's backs. From 60 tons of ore they obtained 112 oz. of gold.

A shaft has been sunk 27 varas, and levels have been driven at 9, 18, and 27 varas, and in each of them the lode is said to yield an average of 2 oz. per ton. The Cabezales sett, on a continuation of the Javali lode, is 1,200 yards in length, by 200 in width. In one place a shaft is sunk 21 feet deep by 8 feet square, on this lode, and has yielded 30 to 40 oz. of gold, extracted by the most primitive processes. Samples taken from the shaft are stated to average about one ounce per ton, and it is said an abundance of quartz can be obtained when the mine has been properly opened. Javali is situated about one and a half miles from San Domingo. An open cutting has been made in the lode, 60 or 70 yards in length, to the depth of from 5 to 20 feet, and 21 feet wide, still leaving a portion standing. The hard quartz, all of which contains sulphide of silver, and from half to three quarters of an ounce of gold per ton, has hitherto been thrown away, unless it contained visible gold, and there are from 1,500 to 2,000 tons of rock now at surface, which, with proper machinery, would yield a good profit. A new shaft is being sunk in the whole ground to get under the old workings, where the lode yields from 3 to 4, and even up to 40 ounces, per ton. At present only four mills are at work, with which they grind about 160 tons per month, and extract from 200 to 300 oz. of gold; employing 40 to 50 men, most of whom are occupied in carrying the ore to the mill on their backs.

Consuelo is about a mile from the San Domingo, and is 800 yards in length on the course of the lode, by 200 yards wide. A shaft has been sunk about 60 yards deep, and levels driven on the lode, at each eight yards in depth. The lode is not uniformly rich throughout its whole width, but the poorest parts will give at least half an ounce of gold per ton, while the richest, for three feet in width, will average 4 oz. per ton; and taking the rich thread by itself, which is from three to six inches wide, it will yield from 10 to 300 ounces per ton.

San Antonio is on a parallel lode immediately to the north of the San Domingo, and adjoins La Trinidad to the west, being a continuation of the same lode. It is 800 yards in length on the course of the vein, by 200 yards wide. In January, 1865, 50 tons of ore yielded 123 oz. of gold; and from the manner in which the ore was ground and amalgamated, it is believed a large quantity was lost. There are about 500 tons of ore on the surface, which will yield about 1 oz. per ton; but, owing to the distance the present workers have to carry it to the mill, it does not remunerate them.

These mines have not, as yet, made either large or regular returns; but, if the foregoing description of the property be correct, it should, with good management, afford large quantities of bullion at a very early date.

South America.

The quantities of gold produced by the mines of South America have never been very large, although they at one time poured forth a stream of wealth, in the form of silver bullion, almost unparalleled in the history of the world. Humboldt estimated, in 1800, the whole produce of gold of the South American Continent at 33,524 lbs., of which 9,900 lbs. were furnished by Brazil; whilst, according to the same authority, the yield of silver during the same period amounted to 691,625 lbs.; the respective weights of the two metals being thus nearly in the ratio of 1 : 29. In the year 1850, the yield of gold had further diminished to about three-fourths of what it was at the beginning of the century, and, according to Chevalier, the total yield of gold from Peru and Bolivia was, in weight, up to 1846, as compared with silver, in the ratio of 1 : 170.

Brazil.—This country has long been famous for its gold mines, which have been worked from the beginning of the last century, and have, in the aggregate, produced very considerable amounts of the precious metal. The large quantities of gold produced during the eighteenth century were almost exclusively the produce of the alluvial washings of Minas Geraes, but these have, to a great extent, become exhausted, and the gold now yielded by Brazil is almost entirely the result of deep mining in the solid rock, which is, for the most part, carried on by English capitalists. The auriferous deposits of Brazil differ considerably in their character from those of other parts of the world, since the gold is often rather disseminated in metalliferous beds, than enclosed in regular veins. The enclosing rocks are supposed to be of palæozoic age, but they have been so changed by metamorphic action, as to render it impossible to assign them to any precise epoch. The gold-bearing district consists of a series of disconnected elevations, which do not assume the appearance of a regular mountain-chain, and in which the eruptive rocks come to the surface in dome-like masses. The most generally prevailing formations are gneiss, and those varieties of rock, known in the country as *itacolumite*, *jacotinga*, and *itabirite*. These are characteristic of the gold-bearing rocks of Brazil, and are not generally met with in the mines of either California or Australia, although some of the rocks of the Appalachian gold mines very closely resemble them. Itacolumite is a quartzose rock, intimately incorporated with particles of chlorite, and frequently occurring in bands of enormous thickness. When this rock includes specular iron in its composition, it becomes either itabirite or jacotinga, according as it is crystallised or compact in its structure. Throughout these metalliferous beds gold is disseminated, and those veins are generally most productive which contain deposits of quartz and specular iron.

The most important of the Brazilian gold mines is the Morro Velho Mine, belonging to the St. John d'El Rey Company, where the various operations of mining and reduction are conducted on a very extensive scale. Through the kindness of Mr. Hockin, the Managing Director of this Company, we are enabled to give the following particulars relative to the St. John d'El Rey Company's Mines :—

The St. John d'El Rey Mining Company was first formed in 1830, for working, on lease, the mines of St. Joaõ d'El Rey and St. José near the town of the former name, in the southern part of the province of Minas Geraes, in the Empire of Brazil. These mines, having been found wholly unproductive, were abandoned in 1834, and the Company then purchased the Morro Velho mine and estate, situate at Congonhas, near Sabara, a considerable distance (a degree and a half of latitude) north of the locality of their first operations. The Morro Velho Mine had been previously worked by native proprietors for more than a century, chiefly by open cuttings, and with varied results.

At the time of the purchase of the property by the St. John d'El Rey Company, the Morro Velho Mine was stated to be yielding a profit ; but a considerable outlay having been found necessary, in order to extend the operations and increase the resources of the mine, the Company, having had to expend large sums in the purchase of stock and erection of buildings, &c., worked at a loss during the first four years of its possession of the estate. In 1839, the returns, under the management of the late Mr. C. Herring, to whose judgment the Company is indebted for the selection of the property, again exceeded the outlay ; but the original capital having been exhausted by the losses incurred at the St. John d'El Rey mines, and the purchase of the Morro Velho property, it was found necessary to apply the greater portion of the proceeds of the gold extracted, to the extension of plant, and it was not until 1842 that the first dividend was declared.

From that date, with the exception of an interval of eighteen months on one occasion (1857-8), and twelve months on another (1864-5), during which the working of the most productive portion of the lode was interrupted by a breakage of the pumping and other machinery, the Company has regularly paid dividends every six months.

The original subscribed capital of the Company was	£135,000
Out of which there was returned to the proprietors	6,600
Net paid up capital	£128,400
There has been paid in dividends	£756,245
Laid out in machinery and buildings on the property, out of profits	140,000
Stores existing on the property of the value of	39,000
A reserve fund and working capital has been provided, out of profits, to the extent of	72,249
Making total profit	£1,007,494

The total value of the precious metals extracted from the mine has been	£2,902,480
The total amount of mineral raised	1,769,050 tons.
The average yield of the ore	4·333 oitavas per ton.

Or as nearly as possible half an oz. Troy, value about 32*s.* 6*d.**

The ores from which these results have been obtained, as will be seen by the following figures, have been, on the whole, poor; the yield has been tolerably uniform, the variations that have occurred being attributable rather to the proportion of slate ground with the ore, than to any fluctuation in the quality of the lode itself. Improvements have, from time to time, been made in the mode of treatment, and the loss sustained has been, year by year, steadily reduced.

The average yield of gold per ton, in oitavas, on the whole quantity of stone annually brought to the surface since the year 1847, has been as follows:—

Years.	Oitavas.†	Years.	Oitavas.
1848	3·77	1857	3·06
1849	3·89	1858	3·25
1850	4·07	1859	4·13
1851	3·89	1860	4·52
1852	4·25	1861	5·44
1853	4·34	1862	5·92
1854	4·17	1863	5·78
1855	3·98	1864	4·82
1856	3·52	1865	5·47

It should be stated, with reference to these figures, that they do not furnish reliable data whereon to form a judgment as to the increasing or diminishing produce of the auriferous formation in depth, inasmuch as, until recently, no account has been kept of the quantity of clay slate or other unproductive stone raised from the mines. During the last six years, excluding 1864, during which a large portion of the killas or clay slate was stamped with the ore, this unproductive stone

* The gold obtained at Morro Velho is usually alloyed with about 20 per cent. of silver.

† An oitava is 2 dwt. 7·343 gr. Troy, or 8·67425 oitavas = 1 oz. Troy.

has been treated separately, and the proportion it bore to the whole quantity of stuff raised has been as follows, viz. :—

Years.	Per Cent.	Years.	Per Cent.
1860	18	1863	22
1861	24	1864	—
1862	24	1865	32

Whether during previous years, the quantity of this comparatively unproductive stone was in excess, or otherwise, of the foregoing, there is no means of ascertaining. The formation affording the gold is a strong, well-defined lode, though irregular in direction, dip, and dimensions ; its inclination or underlie has also been found to vary at different depths, and in different parts of its extent. The vein-stone is mostly composed of quartz with iron pyrites, disseminated, more or less regularly, throughout its mass, and the lode is not unfrequently traversed by clay slate and barren white quartz. When pyrites is absent in these rocks, gold is seldom present.*

In some places the vein is cavernous, and less close in its texture than in others ; but where drusy cavities are frequent, the yield of gold diminishes : the most productive matrix for gold is a compact mixture of quartz and pyrites, with varying quantities of slate. The great metalliferous deposit called the Cachoeira, Bahu, and Quebra Panella, is one continuous, very irregular vein, varying in width from seven to seventy feet, and at one point reaching 100 feet. The average thickness at the present depth, 176 fathoms perpendicular on the Cachoeira, and 165 fathoms on the Bahu, is 19 feet : the stoping space extends over 807 square fathoms. There is a north branch, separated from the main deposit by the enclosing rock called the Gamba, but its working, having been found unprofitable, has been discontinued. The enclosing rock is a clay slate of tolerably uniform texture. The shafts, so-called, for the whole of the lode has been excavated from the surface, are carried down at an inclination of about 45°, and the mineral is brought to the surface by tram carriages of a peculiar construction, carrying large kibbes, containing a ton each. The mineral brought to the surface is first freed from slate and other unproductive stone on the spalling floors, and the ore, after being broken to a uniform size, is stamped fine. The rejected slate and quartz is removed by tramways to another establishment, half a mile distant, and there employed to assist in the further pulverisation of the refuse sand from the first stamping, which is re-stamped.

The stamping mills, as is also the pumping and other machinery, are moved by water-power. The pulverised ore, issuing from the stamp coffers, through finely perforated copper grates, passes over bullock skins, in the first instance, and lower down the inclined tables, over woollen cloths. The bullock skins are taken up and washed in vats every hour, and the woollen cloths at longer intervals. The concentrated sand resulting from washing the bullock skins, is subsequently amalgamated in barrels.

The subjoined table shows the quantities of rock raised and stamped, the amounts of gold produced, and annual net profits made since 1848.

---

* Arsenical, magnetic, and ordinary iron pyrites predominate at different points, and in varying quantities ; carbonate of lime, dolomite brown spar, and, very rarely, copper pyrites, are also present in the vein.

	1849.	1850.	1851.	1852.	1853.	1854.	1855.	1856.	1857.
Stone raised, tons	67,336	67,106	79,810	82,642	85,698	86,048	87,297	89,877	86,407
Stone and Ore stamped, tons	69,004	64,312	81,629	81,236	86,806	86,433	86,848	87,424	86,335
Gold produced, lbs. Troy	2,583	2,517	3,057	3,323	3,623	3,464	3,325	2,992	2,539
	£	£	£	£	£	£	£	£	£
Net Profit	48,136	35,880	51,586	55,391	49,273	44,740	34,466	23,238	787

	1858.	1859.	1860.	1861.	1862.	1863.	1864.	1865.
Stone raised, tons	88,901	88,968	91,361	96,612	90,596	84,758	65,435	78,883
Stone and Ore stamped, tons	87,270	82,880	74,528	71,902	67,508	65,697	62,147	59,607
Gold produced, lbs. Troy	2,733	3,294	3,974	5,051	5,182	4,718	2,852	4,153
	£	£	£	£	£	£	£	£
Net Profit	8,545	38,058	60,466	96,769	87,531	68,285	...	80,438
Loss	...	...	...	...	...	...	14,629	...

Since 1860 the slate and other unproductive stone has been rejected, and the ore only stamped. The clay slate thus separated is crushed in another department of the works. In the above table the profit for that year has been calculated on accounts made up to the end of February, whilst the other figures given are the result of operations up to the end of December in each year. This company employs upwards of 2,400 hands, from 120 to 130 of whom are Europeans. The number of stamp heads at work is 135, for reducing the ore in the first instance, and 56 for re-stamping the residual sand, with slate and quartz: arrastres are also used for re-pulverising the residual sand, and are found very efficient for that purpose. The work performed by the stamps is given in the following table :—

1865.

TABLE OF STAMPS DUTY.

STAMPS.	Heads.	Blows per Min.	Days working.	Tons of Ore stamped.	Tons per Day.	Pounds per Head per Day.
Lyon . .	30	56	357·46	12,100·6	33·85	2,527
Cotesworth .	12	59	356·00	4,932·1	13·85	2,585
Susanna . .	9	60	361·12	2,897·2	8·02	1,996
Herring . .	24	77	357·29	11,495·0	31·89	2,976
Powles . .	36	64	351·24	17,562·6	50·00	3,111
Addison . .	24	67	353·52	10,619·8	30·04	2,803
Total . .	135	—	—	59,607·3	167·65	—

Imperial Brazilian Mining Association.—This Company was formed in 1825, for the purpose of working the Gongo Soco and other mines in the province of Minas Geraes, and in the course of fifteen years produced nearly a million sterling. The following is a statement of the financial operations of the Imperial Brazilian Mining Association at Gongo Soco, from 1st January, 1826, to 31st December, 1856 : *—

RECEIPTS.

Proceeds of gold dust			£1,467,448

PAYMENTS.

Salaries and wages	£432,942		
Materials	451,995		
		£884,937	
Provincial duties paid Brazilian Government	£310,777		
Export duties, ditto	22,403		
		333,180	
			1,218,117
Actual profits			£249,331

Gold was discovered at the surface 122 fathoms above the bottom of the mines, but, owing to the slope of the ground, the deepest shaft was only 56 fathoms in depth ; and for the last eight or ten fathoms, the vein, which had entirely changed its character, afforded only a few particles of gold.†

Don Pedro North d'El Rey.—This Company was, on the recommendation of Captain Treloar, formed in 1863, for the purpose of purchasing and working the mine of Morro de Santa Anna. This gold mine forms a portion of the celebrated range of mountains called the Sierra de Itacolumi. The mine is about six miles north from Ouro Preto, the capital of the province of Minas Geraes, and two miles, west, from the cathedral city of Marianna. It is distant from the St. John d'El Rey Company's mine, Morro Velho, about forty miles in a southerly and easterly direction. The holding, or partition of the mining concession in this locality, differs from that of similar property generally in Minas Geraes. In 1762, permission was given by the Government to open mines in this mountain, wherever the miners might feel inclined, and on doing so they became the lawful possessors of fifty palmos of ground on each side of their levels and shafts. Owing to this, the mountain is studded with mines, which the owners from time to time went on selling, until, with a few unimportant exceptions, the whole became the property of the present Company. At one period, upwards of 5,000 miners were working on this mountain, and, in order to extract the precious metal, most of them crushed the mineral obtained by hand, and it must therefore have been rich to have repaid them for their trouble.

The mountain of Morro de Santa Anna rises some 2,000 feet above the valley, but behind it there are still higher mountains, and the mine is consequently well provided with water ; water is brought in at different levels, and more could be obtained if required. Near the summit the mountain has been, in most places,

* Communicated by W. J. Henwood, F.R.S.

† This mine was ultimately abandoned, about the year 1858, on account of its poverty.

completely honeycombed; but downwards, the auriferous formations are entire for a considerable elevation above the valley. The Morro de Santa Anna contains three auriferous formations; two of them are of jacotinga, and the third is a rock formation. All three have yielded large quantities of gold, but the rock, with the jacotinga next it, have been most productive. The face of the mountain is covered with *canga*, an iron conglomerate, about four feet thick; this is auriferous, and will probably pay for stamping.

Beneath the canga is the first jacotinga formation, about 60 feet in thickness, containing veins rich in the precious metal; the jacotinga partakes more of the character of mica slate, than of iron sand, and the auriferous veins in it are more like quartz than ironstone. This rests on a stratum of hard ironstone about three feet in thickness, which is the second jacotinga formation, but quartz is the predominating constituent, and rock is, according to Captain Treloar, a more correct name for it than jacotinga. This lode averages about four feet wide; it opens and contracts, and where it expands it is generally found most productive. Subjacent to the latter, is a layer of hard clay and mica slate, of about five feet in thickness, and then comes the rock formation, which has yielded the chief returns of gold. In the present workings, it is about ten feet wide; but in its longitudinal course, it so expands and contracts as to become in some places extinct. Where it expands, the dip is northerly.

Besides these, there is another lode in the hill on the opposite side of the valley, at a place called Maquine. Of this lode but little is known; a very large stream of water is issuing from it, and reports say that large quantities of gold, and some nuggets, have been found at the foot of the hill. The general direction of the lodes at Morro de Santa Anna may be said to be easterly and westerly, and their underlie northerly, but both vary, owing to the lodes hugging the contour of the mountain. The late proprietors worked only on a small scale, and on account of their want of knowledge of mining, chiefly confined their operations, during the last three years, to one *canudo*. The first of these three years was mainly devoted to clearing the workings, shifting stamping mill, and other preliminary operations, but even during this period the chief proprietor is said to have made a profit of £7,600.

The Rossa Grande Gold Mining Company.—This Company was formed in 1864, to work an extensive mineral property, called Rossa Grande, in which are said to be several gold mines. The estate is situated in the province of Minas Geraes, in the vicinity of the mine of Morro Velho. The city of Sabara and several villages are within easy walking distances of the property, and the road from Gongo Soco to Sabara and the St. John d'El Rey Company's mines passes through it. It is of great extent, and is estimated to comprise an area exceeding twenty-one square miles, or over 13,000 acres. The climate is said to be salubrious, and the characteristics of the lodes similar to those of the Morro Velho Mine.

The estate contains three distinct auriferous rock formations, which can be traced for miles, besides a jacotinga formation in the direction of Gongo Soco. Diamonds are said to have been found, and the alluvial deposit in the valley is believed to contain sufficient gold to make it remunerative for working. The first rock formation, or upper lode, is about six feet wide. It consists chiefly of white quartz and iron, and has yielded from four to forty oitavas, or from half an ounce to five ounces of gold per ton.

The second rock formation, or middle lode, varies in size from six to twelve feet. It is composed chiefly of quartz and auriferous arsenical pyrites. Lumps of gold have been found in it, and the ore in the swells has sometimes afforded fifty oitavas or upwards of six ounces of gold per ton. The third, or lower rock formation, is of greater magnitude than the other two, being about thirty-six feet wide. Its composition is mainly quartz and brown oxide of iron. The whole mass of this lode is said to be auriferous, and portions of it have yielded fifty oitavas of gold per ton. This mine has not yet produced any considerable amount of gold : the greater portion of the time which has elapsed since the formation of the Company, has been occupied in clearing out the old workings, and the erection of machinery.

East d'El Rey Company.—The Morro Saõ Vicente Mine, worked by this Company since 1863, is situated about twenty-four miles eastward of the Morro Velho Mine, and about twenty-two miles from Ouro Preto, the capital of the province of Minas. The highway to the latter from the interior passes through the estate, and the distance from the Emily Mines, formerly worked by this Company, is about seventeen miles. The estate contains several lodes, but the Champion Lode is considered to be more important than the others. The mine is on this lode, which runs obliquely to the cleavage planes of the containing rock ; its course being S. 50° E., and underlie north, at an angle of 45°.

This vein belongs to the class of auriferous rock formations. It chiefly consists of quartz, pyrites, galena, tellurium, and gold ; it can be traced for some miles, and its width varies from twelve to thirty feet. The rich shoots dip eastward, at an angle of 40° ; the containing rock is clay slate. The mine is situated in a deep hollow, near the western boundary of the property, and, consequently, does not admit of drainage by an adit ; pumping machinery, therefore, is used for this purpose. The excavation has gone down at a less slope than the dip of the lode, and, consequently, it has passed from one layer of the vein into another above it, and, since the returns of gold have been much higher in some months than during others, it follows that they vary in richness ; yet, on the whole, the mine has been generally found to improve in descending. Its present depth is about 100 fathoms. This property has, until very recently, made regular returns of gold ; but having, in common with other mines in the district, suffered much from want of workmen, who, in consequence of the war in which Brazil is now engaged, have been draughted for military service, it has been obliged temporarily to suspend operations.

The value of the gold remitted to England during the time the Emily Mine was being worked by this Company, amounted to 5,306*l.* 15*s.* 5*d.*

From the Morro Saõ Vicente :

	£	*s.*	*d.*
In 1864	2,852	7	4
1865, to May 1866	8,588	17	6
Total	£11,441	4	10

Brazil afforded its largest yield of gold about the middle of the eighteenth century, and from 1752 to 1761 the amount on which the royal fifth was paid, varied from 17,000 to 21,500 lbs. yearly. The production from that time fell gradually off, until in 1822 it was less than 1,000 lbs. From 1810 to 1817, the mean annual production of Minas Geraes, by far the most productive mining district of the country, is given by Humboldt as having been 4,288 lbs.

The gold at present produced in Brazil is almost exclusively obtained by the various large English companies, and particularly that of the St. John d'El Rey, from deep mining.

NEW GRANADA.—From the year 1819 to 1831, the ancient vice-royalty of New Granada was united with Venezuela, and during a portion of the time with Equador, forming the republic of Columbia, but is now, in common with each of the other States, nominally an independent republic. The mines of New Granada have been well described by Boussingault, Chevalier, and others, but we are without much recent information on this subject. The principal washings are situated in the provinces of Antioquia and Veraguas, in the former of which the detritus of all the rivers is said to be auriferous; and some quartz veins occurring in granite, and containing iron pyrites, are worked on a limited scale. The principal mines of gold quartz worked in 1850 were on the river Porce, the veins resembling in every respect the quartz lodes of other auriferous regions, and containing a considerable amount of iron pyrites, and other sulphides. Quartz veins are also numerous in the provinces of Panama and Veraguas, but the amount of gold contained in them is usually small. Chevalier estimated the yield of the Province of Antioquia for the year 1847–8 at 12,500 lbs. Mr. Danson,* from information based on the returns of the British Consuls, estimates the total amount produced from 1804 to 1848 at 40,817,066*l*. There is abundant evidence, however, that New Granada is rich in gold; and with a healthy climate, more energetic inhabitants, and a better government, there is no doubt that it would have annually produced large quantities of the precious metal. Various English Companies have at different times worked mines in New Granada, and even within the last twelve months discoveries were made of placer diggings, which attracted the general attention of Californian miners, and caused them to immigrate to the country in considerable numbers.

We believe, however, that the results obtained were not generally satisfactory, and that the diggings were very unhealthy.

Mariquita and New Granada Mining Company.—The most important gold mines belonging to British capitalists now worked in New Granada are those of Marmato, which are situated in the province of Antioquia. Previous to 1852, these mines were worked by an independent company, but in that year the above association was

* Journal Stat. Society of London, xiv. 40, quoted by Whitney.

formed, for the double purpose of working the Marmato gold mine and the Santa Ana silver mine, both in New Granada.

At the time of their purchase by the present proprietors, the mines of Marmato were provided with twelve stamping mills, representing, in the aggregate, 110 heads; which, during the year 1851, had crushed 12,488 tons of stuff, yielding on an average 11 dwt. 11 gr. of fine gold per ton, and resulting in a net profit of 8,343*l.* 6*s.* 8*d.* The Marmato mines are worked on deposits of auriferous pyrites, usually yielding a little more than half an ounce of gold per ton. The quantity of ore raised during the year ending March 1853, was 15,056 tons, and the quantity stamped 19,089 * tons, the total produce being, gold, 10,711 oz.; silver, 5,988 oz., leaving a profit of 11,449*l.* 10*s.* 2*d.*

During the financial year ending March 1854, the ores raised amounted to 17,372 tons, and the quantity stamped to 18,225 tons, yielding gold, 10,170 oz.; silver, 5,895 oz., and resulting in a net profit of 9,767*l.* 13*s.* 9*d.* From March 1854 to 1855, the ores raised amounted to 14,154 tons, and the ores stamped to 18,288 tons, which produced 6,608 oz. of fine gold, and 4,193 oz. of silver; the profit for the year being 3,932*l.* 5*s.* 7*d.* In the following year, the ores raised amounted to 15,966 tons, and the quantity stamped to 17,668 tons, yielding 6,408 oz. fine gold, and 4,193 oz. of silver, and leaving a profit of 555*l.* 14*s.* 2*d.* on the operations of the twelve months. During the year ending March 1857, the ore stamped amounted to 19,370 tons, yielding 5,635 oz. of gold and 3,353 oz. of silver, leaving a profit of 2,184*l.* 19*s.* From this period to March 1858, 14,820 tons of ore were crushed, and 4,743 oz. of gold and 2,852 oz. of silver obtained; but resulting in a profit of only 541*l.* 0*s.* 8*d.*, as a large amount of machinery was erected in the course of this year. In 1859 the profits were 1,918*l.* 12*s.* 5*d.*, the stuff crushed, 19,598 tons, the gold obtained, 6,476 oz., and the silver, 3,874 oz. The profits in 1860 amounted to 2,778*l.* 8*s.* 4*d.*, but we have no data relative to the amount of ore treated, &c. For the year ending March 1861, the profit was 1,083*l.* 18*s.* 5*d.*; the number of tons crushed, 19,431 the yield of gold, 5,059 oz., and of silver, 3,150 oz. From the 28th February, 1861, to 24th of January, 1862, the operations of the mines were much interfered with by the Revolutionary War: only 16,859 tons of rock were crushed, and 2,592 oz. of gold, and 1,663 oz. of silver obtained. The loss on the operations of this year amounted to 2,745*l.* 15*s.* 9*d.*, and they were afterwards for some time almost suspended.

After the termination of the revolutionary movement, the works were again resumed, and between 31st March, 1864, and 31st March, 1865, 10,283 tons of stuff were crushed, and about 3,000 oz. of gold and 1,800 oz. of silver obtained, but the returns were not sufficient to meet the outlay. The Marmato property is at the present time being worked at a profit, and the Company has recently acquired the Aguacatal mines, in the immediate neighbourhood, from which satisfactory results are anticipated.

PERU.—Gold is found in many of the mountain passes, and nearly all its rivers wash down auriferous sands. Some of the richest gold diggings of the country are about Huaylas and Tarma. It is difficult to estimate with any degree of exactitude the amount of gold annually

* The number of tons crushed is always in excess of the weight of ore raised, as some of it is stamped more than once.

obtained in this country, the business of gold washing being carried on almost wholly by the Indians; but it is believed that the yearly production is somewhere about 2,400 lbs. Troy. In the valley of the river Chuquiaguillo the alluviums appear to be due to the abrasion of Silurian rocks, and are stated by Forbes to be eminently auriferous.* These have been worked from a very remote period, and the great quantities of gold found in Peru at the time of the Spanish conquest, had been, in great part, if not entirely, derived from detrital accumulations.

The rabbit-like burrows made by the Indian gold miners into the more auriferous beds, are still everywhere visible along the sides of valleys, where a supply of water was not too distant to admit of their transporting the pay dirt for the purpose of being washed; and later explorations have not unfrequently disclosed the mummies or skeletons of Indians who have, in these narrow and tortuous holes, perished from the falling in of the superincumbent earth, and have been buried along with their tools and mining implements. The gold-washings in the valley of the Chuquiaguillo are at present conducted in the following way. The valley is, in the first instance, completely closed up, and the course of the river stopped by a rude wall or dam of stones and earth, provided with sluices, and having a portion of the wall somewhat lower, in order to serve as an overflow for any excess of water which may be collected. A longitudinal excavation is then made, close up to one side of the valley, of such a breadth as can be conveniently carried on by the number of hands employed on the works, and any stones or boulders that may be met with, too heavy to be carried off by the rush of water, are piled on one side, whilst the earth, sand clay, and gravel are removed by the force of the stream. On arriving at the several successive auriferous beds, the positions of which are known beforehand, from the results of previous trials, more care is taken in washing; but the whole of the pay dirt is flushed off, and, being heavier than the other constituents of the bank, deposits itself at a short distance from the workings. Here it is collected, and subjected to repeated washings in wooden troughs, until nothing but the grains of metallic gold remain behind.

The excavation is in this way gradually deepened, until the lowest available auriferous stratum has been reached, when the operations are abandoned, in order to commence similar washings on a line parallel

* Report on the Geology of South America, by David Forbes, F.R.S., communicated to the Geological Society, November 21st, 1860.

with the first opening. Any stones or boulders met with in the new workings are thrown into the old one, and the excavation is thus carried directly across the valley.

BOLIVIA.—Gold is found in many of the streams that flow down the eastern side of the cordillera, and at Choquecameta, near Cochabamba, at the sources of the Rio Grande, as well as at Tipoani, near Sorata; and in some other localities, the washing of auriferous sands is still carried on with profit. The gold-bearing strata occurring in the detrital accumulations of Bolivia, are generally known by the name of *veneros*, being, as it were, floors, or clay bottoms, on which gold had become deposited previous to its being covered by alternating beds of sand, gravel, and boulders. Above the first of these there are sometimes one or more similar deposits, again covered by layers of sand and gravel. The diggings are entirely confined to the sides of valleys and the beds of rivers, which afford the necessary supply of water for washing.

The celebrated washings of Tipoani and those of Yungas appear to belong to diluvial accumulations of the same geological age. There are no means of ascertaining the amount of gold annually obtained from the various mining districts of Bolivia, but the total produce is probably about 1,600 lbs. Troy.

Chili annually affords a considerable amount of gold, but we are without any reliable information of a recent date relative to the gold mines of that country. Humboldt estimated its yearly produce, in 1800, at 7,500 lbs. Troy.

CHAPTER VI.

BRITISH POSSESSIONS.—NORTH AMERICAN COLONIES.

DISCOVERY OF GOLD IN NOVA SCOTIA—GEOLOGY OF GOLD REGION—CORRUGATED QUARTZ AT WAVERLY—IMPRACTICABLE MINING LAWS—STATISTICS OF GOLD OBTAINED—CANADIAN GOLD FIELDS—PRINCIPAL GOLD WASHINGS IN CANADA—REPORT OF PARLIAMENTARY COMMITTEE—DISCOVERY OF GOLD IN BRITISH COLUMBIA—EXTENT OF THE GOLD FIELDS—GOLD CHIEFLY OBTAINED FROM ALLUVIAL DIGGINGS.

NOVA SCOTIA.—The whole of the Atlantic shore of this Province is bordered in an unbroken line by strata of a metamorphic character and probably of considerable geological antiquity, frequently broken through by eruptive rocks. These form a coast, in some places low and rugged, and in others boldly undulating; the soil is generally rocky and sterile, although there are large tracts well covered with timber, and affording prosperous agricultural settlements. Along the Atlantic shore, this district is generally low, gradually rising to a height of some three hundred feet, as it advances northward. Its coast line has, according to Dr. Dawson, a general direction of south 68° west, whilst its inland boundary, although presenting some considerable undulations, has a direction of south 80° west. The extreme breadth of this band, at Cape Canso, its northern extremity, is about eight miles; whilst, in its extension westward, it gradually increases, until at the west branch of St. Mary's River, eighty miles west of Cape Canso, it is known to be thirty miles wide. In the western counties its width has not yet been accurately ascertained, but here its entire breadth cannot be far short of fifty miles. Its total length corresponds with that of the peninsula of Nova Scotia. This band, in which almost the whole of the gold discovered has been found, chiefly consists of thick bands of slate and quartzite, highly inclined, and having a general north-east and south-west strike. In different localities these rocks, which probably belong to the Silurian epoch, have been penetrated by masses of granite, and in their vicinity the quartzites and clay slates usually present a highly metamorphosed appearance.

Since the gold discoveries in California and Australia have been generally known, and public attention has been directed to the conditions under which deposits of the precious metal usually occur, reports of similar discoveries have, from time to time, locally arisen in different parts of Nova Scotia. In every instance, however, either mica or iron pyrites would appear to have been mistaken for gold. Some years since, also, a considerable excitement was caused by an article in *Blackwood's Magazine*, in which it was affirmed that gold would be found in the hills to the south of Annapolis, and comparisons were instituted between that locality and the Valley of the Sacramento. Many persons were induced by this article to leave their ordinary occupations to seek for gold, but their researches having in all cases proved unsuccessful, the fever gradually subsided, and the subject was ultimately forgotten. It is also worthy of remark, that Dr. Dawson, so long ago as 1855, when describing the great metamorphic band, observes, "Quartz veins, however, occur abundantly in some parts of this district, and it would not be wonderful if some of them should be found to be auriferous."*

There is, nevertheless, no authentic evidence of the discovery of the precious metal in the province previous to 1860, when some hundreds of persons, tempted by rumours of gold having been found, commenced exploring near the head waters of the Tangier river. The amount of gold obtained in this locality was, however, so small that the miners ultimately became discouraged, and the excitement gradually subsided. In the month of March, 1861, a man who was stooping to drink at a brook, observed a piece of gold among the pebbles at the bottom, and, having picked it up, searched and found more. This took place about a mile to the east of the Tangier river. From this date attention became directed to the locality, numerous claims were taken up, and considerable quantities of gold were obtained by breaking the quartz with hammers, and washing the resulting dust in tin pans.

In June, the discovery of gold was reported near Lunenburg, at a locality called the Ovens. The veins at this place, although generally small, are frequently highly auriferous, and appear to cross each other in almost all directions in a metamorphic slate belonging to the great southern band. On these discoveries being made known, numerous claims were immediately taken up, and various small Companies

* Acadian Geology, p. 362.

formed for working the veins, presenting themselves numerously in the cliff.

Shortly after the discovery of the auriferous nature of the quartz veins, it was found that the sands on the beach beneath the headland also contained large quantities of gold; here claims were likewise rapidly staked off, and worked by means of cradles, so that the aggregate daily yield from the several shore operations soon reached one hundred ounces. Gold discoveries subsequently followed each other in rapid succession, at Lawrencetown, Dartmouth, Sheet Harbour, Isaac's Harbour, Sherbrooke, Waverly, and Oldham.

The most remarkable deposit of auriferous quartz hitherto found in Nova Scotia is undoubtedly that on Laidlaw's Farm, at Waverly.

FIG. 4.

CORRUGATED QUARTZ, LAIDLAW'S FARM, WAVERLY.
(From a Photograph.)

The principal workings are here situated near the summit of a hill composed of hard metamorphic shales, where openings have been made to the depth of some ten or twelve feet upon a nearly horizontal bed of corrugated quartz, of from eight to ten inches in thickness. This auriferous deposit, which is represented Fig. 4, is entirely different from anything we have seen elsewhere, and when laid open, presented the appearance of trees or logs of wood laid together, side by side, after the manner of an American corduroy road.

From this circumstance, the miners have applied the name of "barrel quartz" to the formation, which in many cases presents an appearance not unlike a series of small casks laid together, side by side, and end to end. The rock covering this remarkable horizontal deposit is exceedingly hard, but beneath it, for some little distance, it is softer, and somewhat less fissile. The quartz is itself foliated parallel to the lines of curvature, and exhibits a tendency to break in accordance with these striæ. The headings, and particularly the upper surfaces of the corrugations, are generally covered by a thin, bark-like coating of brown oxide of iron, which is frequently seen to enclose numerous particles of coarse gold, and the quartz in the vicinity of this oxide of iron is itself highly auriferous. The other gold veins of the Province present, generally speaking, few distinctive peculiarities, and very closely resemble those found in California and Australia. Their general course is north 60° west, and their dip towards the south-west, but there are not unfrequent exceptions to this rule.

In addition to gold, the most auriferous veins of Nova Scotia contain variable quantities of iron pyrites, mispickel, galena, blende, and, less frequently, a small proportion of argentiferous and auriferous sulphide of copper. Here, as elsewhere, the presence of the sulphides is regarded as a favourable indication of the richness of a gold vein; and a lead, containing much disseminated galena, almost invariably yields a certain quantity of gold.

The productive veins hitherto discovered have, as before stated, been found in the older rocks on the Atlantic shore, and commonly occur in parallel groups, near the centre of which, and parallel to the productive veins, a large reef of crystallised and comparatively unproductive quartz, is in many instances found to run. These large courses are locally called "bull veins," and usually contain small quantities only of the precious metal. The attention of the Nova Scotia gold miner has, contrary to the usual practice, been almost entirely directed to the exploration of veins of gold quartz, and alluvial digging has consequently been almost entirely neglected. There is, however, reason to believe that a careful examination of the alluvial deposits might lead to the discovery of gold. The thickness of the auriferous veins of this colony is less than those of California and some other countries, but they often contain visible gold.

In 1861, considerable excitement prevailed in the Colony with regard to the gold discoveries; and portions of the country, particularly those in the vicinity of Lunenburg, Tangier, Waverly, Lawrencetown, Sherbrooke, Sheet Harbour, and Isaac's Harbour, were staked off into claims, and more or less worked at a very shallow depth. Several Companies were also established with a view to quartz mining on a more extensive scale; but although many of the veins were found sufficiently auriferous to have warranted more extensive and systematic exploration, the larger Companies were not generally successful. This result appears to have been, in a great measure, the effect of the injudicious nature of the mining laws framed by the local Government, which limited the size of the claims to an exceedingly small area; and a somewhat heavy tax charged on each, rendered the prosecution of deep mining all but impossible. Nearly every man in the Colony thus became the possessor of one or more claims, which could only be taken up in accordance with certain maps prepared by the County Surveyor, by whom each district was laid out in parallelograms almost irrespective of the nature and position of the leads; and consequently, the larger Companies, if desirous to obtain a mining field of suitable extent, had to buy out, at a large price, numerous small claim-owners, who, although they could not work their several minute holdings, did not scruple to demand for them an exorbitant sum of money. It also not unfrequently happened that some claim-owner, whose fragmentary holding was so situated as to render it a necessity for the efficient working of a large location, took advantage of his position to refuse to sell except for an extortionate amount.

It is evident that such a system was totally incompatible with the rapid development of the mineral resources of the Colony, which, as a natural consequence, were most unfavourably affected thereby; but when these obstacles shall have been gradually removed, and reasonable laws have been enacted, there appears to be no reason for believing that gold mining will not become one of the profitable and lasting industries of Nova Scotia. The beach diggings near Lunenburg, which were at one time the most productive, have long since been, to a great extent, exhausted; but many of the associations organised for the purpose of mining and reducing auriferous quartz, still continue their operations, although, it is believed, with somewhat variable success.

The following are the official returns of gold obtained from Nova Scotia :—

PERIOD.	Average No. of Men employed.	No. of Crushing Mills.	Steam Power.	Water Power.	Quartz, Sand, and Gravel crushed.			Yield per Ton.			Gold from Alluvial Mines.			Total Yield of Gold.		
					Tons.	cwt.	lbs.	oz.	dwt.	gr.	oz.	dwt.	gr.	oz.	dwt.	gr.
Year ending Dec. 31, 1862 . . .	484	30	18	12	6,401	0	0	1	1	1	311	0	0	7,275	0	0
,, ,, ,, 1863 . . .	877	35	25	10	17,001	14	15	0	16	12	28	0	0	14,001	14	17
Nine Months ending Sept. 30, 1864	830	35	23	12	15,316	14	0	0	19	0	38	11	8	14,565	9	8
Year ,, ,, 1865	692	33	23	10	23,835	11	0	1	0	21	141	0	7	24,867	5	22

CANADA.—The existence of gold in Canada first attracted public attention in 1847, although it is stated that M. de Léry, a French Canadian, had found specimens of this metal long previous to that date. In 1850, a considerable amount of local excitement was caused by the discovery of alluvial gold in the detritus of the Chaudière and various neighbouring streams ; and an association, under the title of the "Chaudière Gold Mining Company," was formed for the purpose of washing gold in that district. In 1851, specimens of gold were shown in the Great Exhibition of that year, by Sir W. Logan, the Government Geologist, and the then recently formed Chaudière Company. In addition to the Chaudière, other localities have afforded this metal ; among these may be mentioned St. Francis Beauce, Aubert-Gallion, Sherbrooke, and Melbourne. The auriferous region, according to Sir W. Logan, covers an area of from 3,000 to 4,000 square miles, and appears to occupy a great part of that portion of the province lying on the north-eastern side of the prolongation of the Green Mountains into Canada, extending up to the boundary line separating that colony from the United States. The greater portion of the gold hitherto obtained has been procured from superficial washings, none of the quartz veins which occur in the district having been extensively worked. The auriferous detritus frequently contains shells, and bones of animals of existing species.

The coarser materials of the drift are chiefly fragments and rounded pebbles of the clay slates and grey sandstone on which it lies ; but these are more or less mixed with pebbles and boulders of serpentine and talcose slate. Sands containing specular, magnetic, and chromic iron ores, are also associated with this drift, as well as occasional rolled masses of white quartz, derived from the mountain chain bordering the district towards the north. The principal gold washings have been carried on on the Chaudière, Du Loup, and Touffe des Pins rivers, and the results obtained have been, on the whole, satisfactory. During the season of 1851-2, fifteen men collected about 80 ounces, and one nugget weighing two ounces was picked up. On the Touffe des Pins a lump of four ounces in weight was found.

From a personal inspection, made some years since, of the Canadian gold fields, we are inclined to believe that, in many localities, not only would the detritus, if worked on an extensive scale, pay a fair profit on the expenditure, but also that some of the quartz veins could be worked with considerable advantage.* Often, however, the thickness of the deposits is not sufficiently great, and the area locally occupied by the pay dirt is too limited to offer the requisite inducement for the installation of a regular system of sluicing.

On the 16th March, 1865, an elaborate report was made by a Parliamentary Committee, after a searching investigation of the subject, filling a closely-printed pamphlet of one hundred and twenty-six pages. A large number of witnesses, taken from all classes, were examined. Two or three extracts from this Report will show the character of the evidence elicited:—

"In regard to the extent to which gold has been mined or discovered, your Committee have obtained very valuable and reliable evidence. The Gold Mining Inspector, Major de Bellefeuille, states the whole quantity of gold produced during the past season, in the Chaudière Gold Mining Division, to be $116,000; and this, considering the comparatively small number of hands employed, must be regarded as a very handsome return, the average of the season being no less than $4 per day per man. The Gold Mining Inspector's Report, however, cannot be taken as representing the total quantity, as it comes only to the 30th of November, since

---

* In the report of a meeting of the present Chaudière Gold Mining Association, dated St. François, March 7th, 1866, accounts are given of fourteen different shafts now being sunk on quartz veins in the neighbourhood. One of these is twenty-four feet wide; another twenty; another thirty; and in neither have the walls yet been found. The assays reported run from $75 to $150 per ton; but these are evidently results obtained from picked samples. Thirteen cwt. of ore, taken from one vein, crushed, and worked in New York by mill process, yielded at the rate of $40 to the ton.

The whole expense of raising and working quartz at the mines, need not, it is said, exceed from $4 to $8 per ton.

Machinery is also reported to have arrived at Quebec, and only to await the opening of the season to be erected.

which period mining operations have been constantly carried on, and with highly satisfactory results, on the Gilbert. The greater portion of the gold, so far obtained, has been taken from a small area on the Gilbert river, a few miles from its mouth, in the parish of St. Francis. It appears, however, that considerable quantities of gold were obtained in various parts of the country, of which he was furnished with no returns. Thus, for example, on the Stafford Brook, the evidence shows that $2,000 were obtained, while his return shows only $300.

"In regard to the winter operations carried on, on the Gilbert, the evidence of the miners is highly important, as it was to some extent against their interest to give it. They have found hill tunnelling beneath the snow in winter, as profitable as alluvial washing in summer.

"With regard to the general richness of the Gilbert diggings, the evidence of these witnesses is conclusive. William Abbott took from one claim, of only sixty feet front, $1,750 in gold, during the early part of the summer; and in the month of August, he took from another claim, of only twenty-five feet frontage, $595. He had seen or found nuggets worth from $79 up to $300.

"John McCrea exhibited a nugget weighing 12 oz. 14 dwt., besides a quantity of gold in rough nuggets, amounting to many ounces in weight."

British Columbia.—As early as June 1856, Mr. Douglas, the Governor of Vancouver's Island, reported to the Secretary of State the discovery of gold in British Territory, north of the 49th deg. of latitude, and stated that the earnings of the diggers ranged from 2*l.* to 8*l.* per day. In consequence, however, of the hostile attitude assumed by the natives, the number of diggers was very limited. Altogether, this discovery attracted at first less attention than might have been anticipated; but, in December 1857, Governor Douglas reported that the Indians themselves were extensively engaged in the search for gold, and that the accounts which had reached the neighbouring States of America had caused considerable excitement. It was not, however, until May 1858, that a stream of immigration, sufficient to overpower the opposition of the aborigines, had fairly set in, and the British public learnt for the first time, that the mainland of New Caledonia, as the district extending from the Red river to the Pacific was somewhat vaguely designated, was a rich auriferous country, which gave every promise of becoming a flourishing and important colony.

Beginning with the Fraser river, the main artery of the auriferous region, gold is known to exist, and has been worked, at a great many places on its course, from a point about forty-five miles from its mouth, up to near its source in the Rocky Mountains—in other words, from the 49th up to the 53d parallel of north latitude, a distance, taking in the windings, of some 800 miles. The south branch of the Fraser has its sources near Mount Brown, in the Rocky Mountains, in about 53° north latitude, 118° 40′ west longitude. Thence this branch flows for 290 miles to Fort George, a post of the Hudson's Bay Company. The north branch rises in an opposite direction. It receives its supply from a series of lakes lying between 54° and 55° of north latitude, longitude about 124° 50′ west, and runs a course of 260 miles to its junction with the south branch, some miles below the 54th parallel of north latitude. Here the union of the two branches forms the Fraser river proper. Adding the north branch, which is also a gold-bearing stream, the two will give a continuous stretch of auriferous territory, upwards of 1,000 miles in length, extending for many miles back into the country, but not including the tributary rivers which fall into the Fraser. In short, the river itself is known to be auriferous, and to pass through a gold-bearing country throughout its whole course. Gold is also found in most of the tributaries of the Fraser, of which no less than fifty-nine are known. The great length of the main river, and the number of its tributaries, will give some idea of the resources of the country for placer mining.

These facts do not, however, by any means convey an accurate view of the extent of the area of the gold fields, because these observations are limited to the central portions only of the country, while the whole of the upper portion of British Columbia is said to be auriferous.

Besides the gold found in the beds and on the shores of streams, the Fraser itself and many of its tributaries are skirted by terraces which yield gold. These terraces, or "benches," as the miners call them, run at intervals along both sides of the rivers for miles in length, and recede where the mountains fall back into the valleys, varying in breadth from a few yards to several miles. These are objects of curiosity, and add much to the beauty of the scenery in which they occur. They are generally found on both sides of the river, at the same place, sometimes at the same elevation on both sides, sometimes at different elevations, high on this, and low on the other side of the river, and in some places they are multiplied into several successive level plateaux, rising one above the other as they recede from the bank. These terraces are composed of the ordinary alluvial deposits, loam, gravel, stones, sand, and boulders, and are thick masses, generally rising to a height of from 150 to 200 feet.

There would also appear to be a considerable amount of gold in other localities besides the vicinity of the Fraser. Large yields have been obtained from the diggings between Fort Hope and Fort George, about 100 miles from its mouth. These mines are said to have yielded, during the season of 1861, an average of $17 to the hand, and a party of three men took, from three days' digging, $240. At Okanagan, sixty miles distant, the produce is stated to have been $4 to the hand. The Thompson river and its tributaries are also auriferous, and the North river has given good results.

Cariboo, however, appears to be one of the largest and richest gold districts hitherto discovered in British Columbia, and has produced large quantities of the precious metal. The gold regions of this colony appear to be a continuation, northward, of those of Oregon, and although it is difficult to procure any definite information on this subject, it is probable that they are of the same geological age as the great gold field of California. By far the largest proportion of the gold obtained from British Columbia is the produce of shallow placers, from which it is extracted by processes precisely similar to those employed in California and other auriferous countries. With regard to the quantities of gold annually furnished to commerce by this colony, there is some difficulty in arriving at correct figures. Nearly the whole amount obtained finds its way, by some means, to San Francisco; but, as a large proportion of it reaches that city through private hands, it renders impossible any attempt to obtain exact statistics. The total annual yield of British Columbia has been variously estimated at from 125,000 oz. to 150,000 oz.

CHAPTER VII.

BRITISH POSSESSIONS.—AUSTRALIA AND NEW ZEALAND.

DISCOVERY OF GOLD IN AUSTRALIA—VICTORIA THE MOST PRODUCTIVE DIVISION OF THE AUSTRALIAN CONTINENT—GEOLOGY OF THE GOLD-BEARING ROCKS OF VICTORIA—QUARTZ VEINS—AURIFEROUS PLIOCENE GRAVELS—PRIMITIVE MINING—QUARTZ VEINS PRODUCTIVE AT ALL DEPTHS YET ATTAINED—PORT PHILLIP AND COLONIAL GOLD MINING COMPANY—YIELDS OF SOME OF THE PRINCIPAL MINES—TOTAL AMOUNT OF GOLD EXPORTED FROM VICTORIA—GOLD EXPORTED FROM NEW SOUTH WALES—SOUTH AUSTRALIA AND TASMANIA—QUEENSLAND—DISCOVERY OF GOLD IN NEW ZEALAND—PRINCIPAL GOLD FIELDS OF THAT COUNTRY—YIELD OF GOLD—ANNUAL PRODUCTION OF THE GOLD MINES OF THE WORLD.

AUSTRALIA.

THE Australian Cordillera has a direction nearly parallel with that of the coast line, from which it is usually distant from fifty to one hundred miles. This mountain range is principally composed of micaceous, argillaceous, and silicious shales, interlaminated with which the granite makes its appearance at the surface in numerous localities. The Australian slates often stand nearly vertical, and, like almost all other schistose rocks extending over large regions, have a general strike approximating to north and south. These have been much broken up and disordered by what are usually considered to be igneous rocks, such as porphyry, syenite, basalt and trap; and the general resemblance of the formation to that of the Uralian Cordilleras would appear to be so striking, that Sir R. Murchison, after an examination of the collections and maps of Count Strzelecki, in 1844, and without having visited the country, did not hesitate to express the opinion that this portion of Australia would, in all probability, be found to be auriferous. Specimens of gold had, however, been discovered by the Rev. W. B. Clarke as early as 1841, and in 1843 he first communicated the fact of the existence of gold in Australia to Sir George Gipps, then Governor of New South Wales, who enjoined him to silence, under the impression that a widely-spread knowledge of the discovery would be prejudicial to the general interests of the colony. The practical discovery of the presence of gold, in remunerative quantities, was, however, reserved to Mr. Hargreaves, a returned Californian, who was so much struck by the resemblance of the rocks of Australia to those found in the gold regions of California, that without waiting for the reply of Government to his notification that gold would be found there, commenced prospecting on the Macquarie river, New South Wales, and quickly found evidence of the existence of gold in considerable quantities.*

* It may be well to insert here a certificate extracted from the Report of the Commissioners of the International Congress of Australian Statistics in 1861, which will probably be considered an unbiassed decision of the relative merits of the respective claimants to this discovery.

"95. *History of the Discovery of Gold in Australia.*—The first known discovery of the precious metal was made by Count Strzelecki in 1839, and was mentioned by him to some personal friends, and to Sir George Gipps, the then Governor of the colony of New South Wales. It was again discovered and specially noticed by the Rev. W. B. Clarke, of Sydney, in 1841. The attention of the colonial public, however, was not attracted to the subject until the existence of an extensive gold field throughout Australia was announced by Mr. E. H. Hargreaves in 1851. A long time previous to this announcement, namely, in 1844, and without being aware of the finding of specimens of the precious metal by Count Strzelecki and the Rev. W. B. Clarke, Sir R. Murchison publicly asserted the high probability of the existence of gold in Australia. This bold induction was based upon his knowledge of the geological formation of that country; and the wonderful results of gold mining in Victoria and New South Wales, afford a proof of scientific sagacity almost unparalleled in the history of science.

"JAMES MACARTHUR,
"EDWARD HAMILTON, } *New South Wales.*
"STUART A. DONALDSON,
"M. H. MARSH, *Queensland.*
"WILLIAM WESTGARTH, *Victoria.*
"EDWARD STEPHENS, *South Australia.*
"JAS. A. YOUL, *Tasmania.*
"J. E. FITZGERALD, *New Zealand.*

"OFFICES OF THE CONGRESS,
SOMERSET HOUSE, LONDON.
18*th July*, 1860."

The merit of scientific discovery is here awarded to Count Strzelecki. As to why he did not then make it known, we will allow the Count to speak for himself:—"I was warned," writes the Count, "of the responsibility I should incur if I gave publicity to the discovery, since, as the Governor argued, by proclaiming the colonies to be gold regions, the maintenance of discipline among 45,000 convicts, which New South Wales, Tasmania, and Norfolk Island contained, would become almost impossible; and unless the penal code should be amended at home, transportation would become a premium upon crime, and cease to be a punishment. These reasons of State policy had great weight with me, and I willingly deferred to the represen-

On the 8th of May, 1851, the Commissioner of Crown Lands received from him a notification that several ounces of gold had been collected on a branch of the Macquarie, and, shortly after, that a nugget weighing thirteen ounces had been discovered. It need scarcely be added, that the excitement at once became very great, and that all classes of the community left their usual occupations in order that they might rush to the gold diggings. On this discovery becoming an established fact, the Government laid claim to the lands, and began to grant licences, at the rate of thirty shillings per month, to dig for gold; and instituted, shortly afterwards, a geological survey of portions of the country.

VICTORIA.—This colony has hitherto produced a much larger amount of gold than any of the other divisions of the Australian Continent. Long before the appearance of any public announcement of the discovery of gold in Victoria, small pieces of this metal had been collected by shepherds and others, but no particular importance seems to have been attached to this fact, although well known to many of the older settlers, who appear to have made it the subject of conversation, and from whom rumours of its existence probably reached Europe. Mr. R. B. Smyth would appear to be strongly of this opinion, since, in his Paper on the "Mining and Statistics of Gold," page 101, Catalogue of the Victorian Exhibition of 1861, he remarks—"Indeed there is reason to believe, the statements of settlers who had returned to Europe in the early days of the colony, had left no doubt in the minds of scientific men at home that Victoria was a gold-producing country."* Gold is said to have been first found at Clunes in March 1850; and on the 10th June, 1851, it was discovered on a tributary of the river Loddon; on the 20th July at Mount Alexander; on the 8th August at Buninyong; and on the 8th September of the same year at Ballarat. Licences to dig were first issued on the 1st September, 1851, and such large yields of the precious metal were shortly after reported, that the colonists soon left their ordinary occupations to join in the exciting search for gold. The total male population of the colony was at that time only about 46,000, and the sudden withdrawal from their usual pursuits of nearly half this number at once produced a wonderful revolution

tations of the Governor-General, notwithstanding that they were opposed to my private interests."—Quoted by Terry, "Thirty Years in New South Wales and Victoria." (London, 1863.)

* R. B. Smyth, Secretary of Mines for the Colony of Victoria.

in the social conditions of the country. The price of labour became enormously increased, all kinds of provisions rose rapidly in price, the value of property in Melbourne became seriously depreciated, and it was only after the arrival of a great influx of immigrants from Europe and from the adjacent colonies that society, to a certain extent, began to regain its equilibrium.

It would appear, from the investigations of Mr. A. R. C. Selwyn, the Government Geologist, that the age of the gold-bearing strata of Victoria is, geologically, much greater than that of the auriferous rocks of California, and further, that they belong to the lower palæozoic, or Silurian epoch, thus closely approximating in age and constitution to those of the great Uralian Cordillera.

In reference to this subject, we cannot do better than quote Mr. Selwyn's report on the "Geology of Victoria," which gives a concise and lucid description of the gold-bearing rocks of that colony: *—

"So far as at present known, the rocks of this period are the source whence the whole of the gold now produced in Victoria has originally been derived. They are exposed on the surface, at intervals, from the Grampians, on the west, to the extreme limits of the colony on the east. With a few local exceptions, they have a nearly true meridional strike or direction. Their great longitudinal extent is due to the crumpling and folding to which they have been subjected, causing the same beds to recur again and again at the surface, in a succession of synclinal and anticlinal undulations. Making due allowance for this great repetition of the same beds at the surface, the total vertical thickness of the series is probably not less than 35,000 feet.

"The lower members of the group consist chiefly of schistose and slaty rocks, with numerous beds of hard gritty quartzose and soft micaceous sandstones. Among the latter are beds that afford good freestone for building purposes, and, in the former, flags and roofing slates are occasionally met with.

"Various species of *Polyzoa* are the characteristic and most abundant fossils that have been found in the lower beds.

"In the upper portion of the series, which does not extend more than a few miles westward of the meridian of Melbourne, shaly 'mudstones,' associated with sandstones, very varied in colour and texture, are most prevalent. This portion is seldom affected by the true slaty cleavage, so characteristic of the lower beds, and it contains a rich assemblage of fossil animals, indicative of several of the subdivisions

* Catalogue of the Victorian Exhibition of 1861, p. 177.

of the Upper Silurian period. The almost total absence of limestone bands, the number and extent of the quartz veins, and the constantly recurring protrusions, at short intervals, of granitic, and occasionally of plutonic trappean rocks, in dykes and large masses, are the most remarkable features in the physical structure of the lower palæozoic rocks in Victoria. The granite intrusions do not occur along any main axes of elevation, but are dotted about over every part of the area within which the palæozoic rocks are found. The stratified rocks, amongst which they have been intruded, are invariably hardened, and otherwise metamorphosed for a short distance from their junction. This alteration varies, in a very marked degree, with the mineral character of the altering mass; thus the change produced by diorites and feldspar porphyries is often very distinct from that produced by granite. Their intrusion appears very rarely, if ever, to have exercised any influence in determining the general strike, dip, and contortions of the palæozoic rocks; these invariably retain their general meridional direction, which is certainly remarkable, considering that the main water-shed, or axis of elevation, runs from east to west, and consequently almost at right angles to the strike of all the older rocks. It is difficult, under these circumstances, to understand what influence can have determined this feature in the physical geography of Victoria. That no great alteration, or even modification, of the water-shed has taken place, since the earliest tertiary periods, is well proved by circumstances connected with the physical geology of the formations of that period, as exhibited on either side of the dividing range.

"The quartz veins occur throughout the lower palæozoic rocks, from the size of a thread to many feet in thickness. They have mostly a nearly true meridional direction, and are inclined either east or west, at angles varying from horizontal to vertical: occasionally they occur between the planes of the strata; more frequently in those of cleavage, and they often intersect both. They are true mineral lodes, and perfectly analogous in their mode of occurrence to all other mineral veins, whether of silver, lead, tin, copper, or any other crystalline mineral.

"The thickest and most persistent veins are found in the lower or older portions of the series, but the average yield of gold per ton is, however, greater from the generally thinner veins of the upper beds. These occur at Kilmore, Yea, Reedy Creek, Heathcote and Rushworth gold fields.

"The greatest depth to which any reef has yet (1861) been worked is about 460 feet. At this depth a yield of over five ounces per ton has been obtained.

"The total area occupied in Victoria by lower palæozoic formations with their associated plutonic rocks, inclusive of tracts in which the overlying tertiary deposits do not exceed 300 feet, cannot be estimated at less than 30,000 square miles."

It is, however, to be observed, that although the metamorphic rocks enclosing the auriferous quartz veins of Victoria appear to belong to a more ancient series than those in which gold quartz lodes are found in California, the drifts, constituting the deep diggings, seem, in both countries, to be almost, if not identically, of the same period, and are in each instance often capped by volcanic matter. In the report before referred to, Mr. Selwyn gives the following description of the auriferous tertiary gravels of Victoria:—

"The igneous rocks associated with them are strictly volcanic, and in no instance do they appear to be of older date than the close of the Miocene period. Their greatest development has taken place during the deposition of the Pliocene series, and in some instances it has evidently been continued to a period that could not be chronologically separated from the most recent geological events.

"The exact period in the tertiary epoch when the gold drifts commenced, is at present exceedingly doubtful. No beds are yet known in Victoria associated with, or forming a portion of such drifts, that contain fossil marine animals. Neither has any gold been obtained from beds below the known fossiliferous tertiary strata. The volcanic rocks, consisting chiefly of varieties of Trachytic Dolerites, Basalts, Trachytic Porphyries, &c., are in many districts interstratified, in contemporaneous layers, with the sands, clays, and gravels, of what are at present considered to be the oldest gold drifts, in which the lowest stratum, where the gold occurs, almost invariably consists of a water-worn quartz gravel. That there are gold drifts marking at least three distinct deposits, the results of successive upheavals and depressions, is quite certain; and it is now almost equally certain that the earliest of them was the result of the commencement of the oldest Pliocene period. In accordance with this view, they have been divided into Older Pliocene, Newer Pliocene, and Post-Pliocene deposits. These three stages sometimes occur in the same locality without the intervention of any volcanic rocks, in which case three bottoms or gold-bearing strata are found in one shaft, the last being always on the solid, unmoved palæozoic rock. About four hundred feet is the greatest known thickness of these Older Pliocene deposits including the associated volcanic rocks, and at this depth rich deposits of gold are found in them resting on the slopes, and in the hollows of what was once the old Pliocene sea bed. The exact relations of the gold-bearing drifts of the upper Tertiary periods to the marine Tertiary sands, clays, and limestones of the Miocene and Eocene series, is a very interesting point in Victorian geology not yet elucidated, and one which may have an important bearing on the probable extension of the deep gold leads of Ballarat and other gold fields.

"In following the leads they are invariably found to deepen in the general direction of the existing surface water-shed. Thus, at Ballarat and other gold fields on the south side of the dividing range, they deepen in a southerly direction; whilst at Clunes, Bendigo, &c., they invariably deepen in the opposite or northerly direction, and there seems no reason why they should not extend underneath a very large part of the extensive plains that stretch from the northern gold fields to the Murray, and from the southern flank of the dividing range to the sea-board, wherever the tertiary rocks forming these plains rest directly on the lower palæozoic strata."

It may here be observed that in Victoria there are, in addition to the great auriferous gravel beds generally referred to the Pliocene epoch, others of a comparatively non-auriferous character, which are found below them, and believed by Mr. Selwyn to belong to the Miocene period. In order to account for these older deposits being less auriferous than those occupying a higher position in the series, Mr. Selwyn has, we conceive, justly arrived at the conclusion, that there must be at least two distinct sets of quartz veins, that the older ones were formed prior to the Miocene period, and are comparatively barren, whilst the newer, formed after them, but before the Pliocene epoch, are productive. The former, therefore, will have furnished the materials for the barren Miocene gravels, whilst the disintegration of the latter has afforded the detritus forming the productive Pliocene deposits.* Below the basalt, the depth of auriferous alluvium rarely exceeds from ten to twenty feet, more frequently not so much, and in many places the basaltic rock is known to repose, for a considerable distance, directly on the bare bed rock.

In some parts of the country, not covered by basalt, such as Chinaman's Flat, Maryborough and Bendigo, the thickness of the alluvium is known to be as much as from 130 to 140 feet; and a still more

* Mr. Selwyn's Letter to the Victoria "Mining Record," February 22, 1866.

remarkable instance has been exposed, where a shaft has been sunk to a depth of more than 400 feet, passing, from top to bottom, through a conglomerate formed of water-worn pebbles, and blue clay. At this place, the shaft, although not passing through eruptive matter, is surrounded by a volcanic country, and, up to January 1865, had not yet bottomed on the bed rock.

In Australia, as in California, there are three distinct sources from which the supply of gold is directly obtained,—viz., shallow placers, deep diggings, and veins of auriferous quartz.*

In the early days of gold digging, the miner usually contented himself with excavating shallow pits in the clays and gravels, found in beds and gullies of the creeks, or with washing the soil from slopes of hills intersected by auriferous quartz veins.

The methods of extracting gold were in all cases exceedingly primitive, and conducted with the aid of the smallest possible amount of plant and materials. When a light sandy earth had to be dealt with, it was either washed in the tin pan, or passed through a cradle; whilst if, on the contrary, the soil was mixed with tenacious clay, it became necessary to puddle it before passing it through this simple machine. In order to effect this puddling, the auriferous material was thrown into a large tub, with a sufficient quantity of water, and continually stirred with a shovel until the clay became softened and held in suspension in water, which from time to time was run or drawn off, and a fresh supply added, until the sands and gravels remaining in the bottom had become sufficiently free of clay to admit of being cradled without difficulty. The residues, thrown away by the miners, who worked by this system, were necessarily

* "Gold is now found to occur, not only in quartz veins and the alluvial deposits derived from these and the surrounding rocks, but also in the claystone itself, and, contrary to expectation, flat bands of auriferous quartz have been discovered in dykes of diorite which intersect the Upper Silurian or Lower Devonian rocks. Quartz of extraordinary richness has been obtained from these bands, and the new experience of the miner is leading him to look for gold in places heretofore entirely neglected. It is probable that some time may be lost, and that his labours may not always be well directed or successful, but it is commendable that he should not be deterred from exploration by warnings and remonstrances, founded on surmises often baseless. If he had closely followed the older precepts, we should, at this moment, have been dependent for our yield of gold on the shallower alluviums, and the surface only of the veins of quartz. The miner is, however, prospecting the deeper tertiaries with well-grounded hopes of success, and some of the shafts which have been sunk to penetrate the veins are as deep as 590 feet. From these levels very rich quartz has been obtained."—*R. B. Smyth, Intercolonial Exhibition*, 1866, p. 5.

often very rich, and, after exposure to the disintegrating action of the atmosphere, were frequently reworked for gold with considerable profit.

After a time, the small pits sunk in valleys and the bottoms of creeks, were carried down to the bed rock, where it was discovered that the principal part of the gold had usually accumulated. From the bottom of these, small drifts were extended in all directions, and the wash dirt carefully collected from the face of the bed rock, and brought to the surface for the purpose of being washed. The claims originally granted to the Australian miner were exceedingly limited, the dimensions of each being in most instances 10 feet by 10 feet, or 16 feet by 8 feet, and consequently this method of mining was only sufficiently advanced for operations conducted on such a restricted scale. These workings, however, in many cases crushed together, before the whole, or even the largest portion of the gold-bearing stratum had been removed; and hence one of the principal reasons why, in nearly all the more important gold fields, the alluvium has been repeatedly worked over with profitable results. This method of mining is still extensively practised in Victoria, but the puddling is now, in the majority of cases, effected either by horse or steam power.

From the general scarcity of water in the auriferous districts of Australia, all operations connected with the process of gold washing require to be carried on with a view to the utmost economy of this indispensable agent, and consequently the hydraulic mining of California is almost unknown in the country, and even sluicing on a large scale is comparatively little practised. The deep diggings, on deposits of the Pliocene tertiary epoch, are in Victoria most frequently worked by means of shafts of greater or less depth, from which, when the bed rock has been reached, galleries are extended, and the pay dirt is removed, very much in the same way as coal is extracted from seams of that mineral.

The pay dirt, on reaching the surface, is subjected to the operation of puddling, and the residue remaining in the machine subsequently washed for the gold it contains. This method of carrying on operations is not only expensive, but the working of deep leads, as the beds of these ancient watercourses are called in Australia, is frequently much impeded by the influx of water, and a relatively large proportion of the steam-power employed in the gold fields is utilised in pumping water from deep workings.

The time necessary for sinking a shaft from the surface to the pay dirt may vary from a few months to one or more years, during the whole of which time no possible return can be made for the outlay expended; and it is only after reaching the "gutter," that the harvest of the miner begins to be reaped. From a report, in 1861, of Mr. Davidson, one of the mining surveyors of Ballarat, it appears that the average yield of the celebrated leads, named the Golden Point, Inkermann, Redan, and Nightingale, situated in his district, was from 10 dwt. to 2½ oz. per cubic yard, and that the thickness of the pay dirt varied from one to twelve feet. Another mining surveyor states, that at the Waterloo Company's claim, Ballarat, the total quantity of gold obtained was 6,750 oz., which, at 80*s.* per ounce, would amount to 27,000*l.* This company was occupied two years and one month in working out the claim, and the total expense of carrying out the works was 5,824*l.*, thus leaving a clear profit of 21,176*l.* as the result of the operations.

In some localities, as at Sandhurst, where the pay dirt is composed of water-worn pebbles, strongly bound together by ferruginous and silicious cements, it is crushed in an ordinary quartz mill, and the gold extracted by amalgamation in the usual way. The mining surveyors speak favourably in their reports of this system of treatment. These auriferous deposits of the Pliocene epoch are found at Ballarat, Smythesdale, Creswick, Raglan, Ararat, Sandhurst, Indigo, near Beechworth, Maryborough, and various other localities in the province.

Wherever the level of the ancient deposit is above that of the modern valleys, adit levels, or tunnels, are brought in on the leads, and the work is then conducted precisely as if it had been reached by the sinking of perpendicular shafts. This method of mining has, however, many advantages over deep sinking, both with regard to the drainage of the workings, and transport of the stuff to be washed, and is invariably adopted wherever the conformation of the district admits of its introduction. In order to avoid the expense and loss of time involved in the drainage of long levels from the bottom of the shafts, to reach the deposits of pay dirt, it is now usual to explore the ground by means of bore-holes: and the true position of the auriferous channel having been thus approximately ascertained, the shaft is subsequently sunk in such a position as most conveniently to command the lead, and reach it with the least possible time and expense. As far back as 1855, the attention of the local Government was directed to the necessity of supplying the gold fields with water, and in 1860 a first grant of 50,000*l.* was appropriated for that purpose this was followed, in 1861, by a further sum of 75,000*l.*, for the extension of similar works.

In the early days of the colony, the operations of quartz miners were exclusively confined to such outcrops as showed visible gold, and the rock being either broken by a hammer or pounded in a mortar, the gold was afterwards washed out in the ordinary tin pan. It was, however, soon found that the working of veins in depth could be prosecuted with advantage; and at the present time, from one-fourth to one-third of the gold obtained in Victoria is the result of treating auriferous quartz. Whenever metamorphic slates appear at the surface, quartz veins are generally found, the general direction of the greater number being nearly north and south. These veins vary in thickness, from a mere thread to forty or even fifty feet. The magnetic bearings of the northerly and southerly veins are, with rare exceptions, confined within a variation of some 24°, and the strike of the easterly and westerly lodes, which are much less numerous, is nearly at right angles to them.

The machinery usually employed in Australia for the treatment of auriferous quartz, is the ordinary stamping mill, which will be described in a subsequent chapter, each head, on an average, striking sixty blows per minute, and weighing seven cwt. About one horse power is consumed by each of these heads, a nominal ten-horse engine being most frequently attached to a battery of eight. The crushed quartz flowing from the stamping mill is conducted over blankets, mercurial riffles, amalgamated copper plates, and various arrangements similar to those employed in California and other gold-producing countries; the Australian miners experience the same difficulty, elsewhere complained of, in separating gold from iron pyrites, and other metallic sulphides. The miners generally have, in common with those of other countries, come to the conclusion, that better results, with regard to profit, are to be obtained by crushing large quantities of only moderately rich stuff, with powerful and well-arranged machinery, than from treating a limited amount of very rich rock on a small scale.

When, as at first, the cost of crushing and amalgamating a ton of quartz amounted to some 80*s.*, a very small proportion of the auriferous veins of the colony could be treated with advantage; but now that the total expense of raising and treating a ton of rock by steam-power has, under favourable circumstances, been reduced to about 16*s.* 4*d.*, there are numerous reefs throughout the gold-mining region affording satisfactory results, and many others that would do the same, if extensively and judiciously worked. Many of the reefs have yielded quartz of extraordinary richness, as, for instance, one at Castlemaine, from which 266 oz. per ton were obtained, although this cannot be regarded as the average produce of the vein.

Generally speaking, also, the yield of the quartz veins of Victoria has not been found to decrease in depth, and those which have been wrought below 500 feet from the surface have experienced no diminution in their produce. Quartz mining requires a considerable amount of capital, and is subject to all the usual fluctuations of mining enterprises, excepting, however, such as are influenced by the varying prices of metals; but, in spite of all its disadvantages, it has been found a highly remunerative occupation, and from the productiveness and extent of its reefs, it is certain that Victoria presents an attractive field for the investment of capital in this department of industry.

Two of the most productive gold fields of Victoria have been those of Ballarat and Bendigo. The gold field of Ballarat is the largest within the mining district of that name, and the centre of other outlying gold fields, among which are Clunes, Creswick, Smythe's Egerton, Gordon, Steiglitz, Linton's, Carnham, &c.

The town of Ballarat is, with perhaps the exception of Sandhurst, the chief town of the district in which Bendigo is situated; and Castlemaine, the chief town of the district of that name, the most important and largest within the six mining districts. The mining carried on in this district is, for the most part, of the deep alluvial class, the bed rock being seldom found at a less depth than 200 or 300 feet.

Bendigo, the largest auriferous field of the Sandhurst district, was originally a shallow gold field, some of its famous gullies, yielding many ounces to the tub, having been scarcely a yard in depth. The soil from these has now, however, been all cleared away to the bed rock, and passed through the puddling machines, from whence it has issued in the form of a pasty sludge which may be seen in all directions overflowing the surface of the county. In place of the placer diggings, which are at present, to a considerable extent, exhausted, the chief industry of Bendigo is now concentrated on its quartz mines, which extend over an area of some forty square miles. On the north side of the gold field, however, deep placer mining has been extensively carried on, where the bed rock was found to dip rapidly, and this extension of the Bendigo gold field is now being extensively worked.

It would be difficult to ascertain the average produce of the quartz crushed in the different reduction establishments in the colony since the commencement of quartz mining, but it appears from the Surveyor's reports for 1860, that, in that year, 61,075 tons of rock from the Ballarat district yielded 38,378 oz. 6 dwt. of gold = 12 dwt. 13 gr. per ton.

From the Beechworth mines 3,725 tons 16 cwt. of quartz gave 13,862 oz. 6 dwt. of gold = 3 oz. 14 dwt. 10 gr. per ton.

The Sandhurst district afforded 2,678 tons 15 cwt. of quartz, yielding 6,361 oz. 8 dwt. of gold = 2 oz. 7 dwt. 12 gr. per ton.

From the Maryborough district there were crushed 4,548 tons, producing 6,345 oz. 1 dwt. of gold = 1 oz. 7 dwt. 21 gr. per ton.

The district of Castlemaine produced 13,301 tons 15 cwt., affording 14,955 oz. 11 dwt. of gold = 1 oz. 2 dwt. 11 gr. per ton.

Ararat yielded 1,265 tons 10 cwt. of quartz, which gave 2,002 oz. 10 dwt. of gold = 1 oz. 11 dwt. 15 gr. per ton.

In the same year there were 294 steam-engines, of the aggregate horse-power of 4,137, employed in alluvial mining, and 417 engines of the aggregate power of 6,645 employed in quartz mining. There were, in addition, 138 water-wheels and 3,958 horse puddling machines in operation. The total approximate value of the mining plant in the colony was, at the same period, estimated at 1,299,303*l.*

The total number of steam-engines employed for gold-mining purposes at the end of 1864, was 888, of which 441 were used in alluvial, and 447 in quartz mining. In the following year there were 17,326 miners engaged in quartz mining, more than 2,000 distinct reefs had been discovered and named, and 491 steam-engines, equal to 8,606 horse-power, and 62 engines driven by water or horse power, were employed in quartz mines for crushing, winding, pumping, &c.

On the 31st December, 1865, the number of leases in force in the different districts were as follows :—Ballarat, 88; Sandhurst, 318; Maryborough, 228; Castlemaine, 85; Beechworth, 300; Ararat, 24.

There were 62,131 miners engaged in getting gold from the auriferous alluviums, and 4,131 machines of various kinds, 4,428 sluice boxes, and 648 sluices and toms used exclusively in this kind of mining. The quantities of gold obtained by the alluvial miners during three years were, as nearly as can be ascertained, as follows:— 1863, 1,133,567 oz.; 1864, 1,041,830 oz.; 1865, 1,093,801 oz.*

* R. B. Smyth, International Exhibition, 1866, p. 24.

CLUNES.—*Port Phillip and Colonial Gold Mining Company.*—This is the most important and extensive quartz-mining enterprise in the colony. The extent of the claim is 160 acres, held on a lease for twenty-one years, from 1st January, 1857, at a royalty of 7½ per cent. on the gross value of the gold raised. Operations were commenced by the present Company in 1857, and in the following year, Mr. Selwyn, the Government Geologist, thus writes of its mines and establishments :—" Within the last twelve months, I have visited all the principal quartz reefs and crushing establishments on the northern and western gold fields, and the Port Phillip and Colonial, and Clunes Company, is the only one I have seen, of which it would be possible to say, that it leaves little to be desired, either as regards the system of working the mine, or the general arrangement and management of the machinery."

The reefs worked are five in number, and are enclosed in a soft white and brown slaty sandstone, which, like the veins themselves, runs nearly north and south, and generally dips towards the east. With the exception of the overlying tabular basalt, no igneous rocks occur on the surface within three miles of these veins. The nearest granite is at Mount Beckworth, nine miles west of the Company's property. Nearly three-fourths of the land held by the Company is occupied on the surface by a stratum of tabular basalt, and it is only in the south-western corner, where this rock has been removed by denudation, that the shales and sandstones, with their associated quartz veins, come to the surface.

The following section, at the northern extremity of the Company's property, Fig. 5, will serve to give a general idea of the formation of the county, and the relative positions of the different veins worked.

FIG. 5.

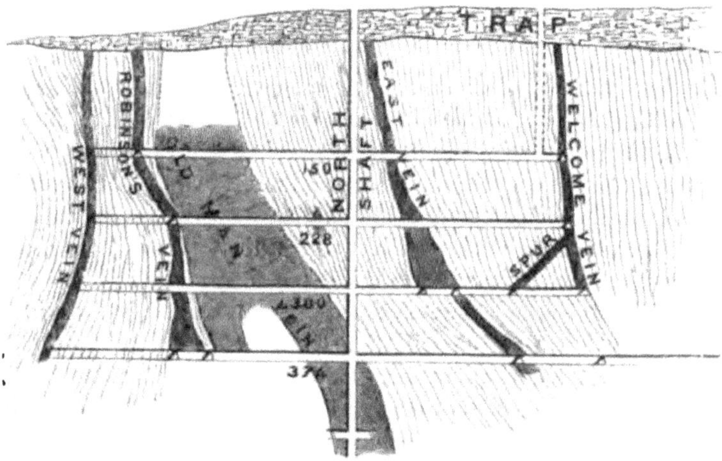

CLUNES.
(*North Cross Section.*)

The extreme irregularity in the width of these veins in different portions of their course, will be at once perceived by comparing the cross section at the southern boundary of the property, Fig. 6, with the foregoing. It will be remarked, that in this portion of the ground, the "Old Man Vein" is very much contracted, whilst the "Welcome Vein" has become entirely obliterated. This alternate swelling and pinching out of quartz veins appears to be peculiarly characteristic of lodes of auriferous quartz in all parts of the world.

FIG. 6.

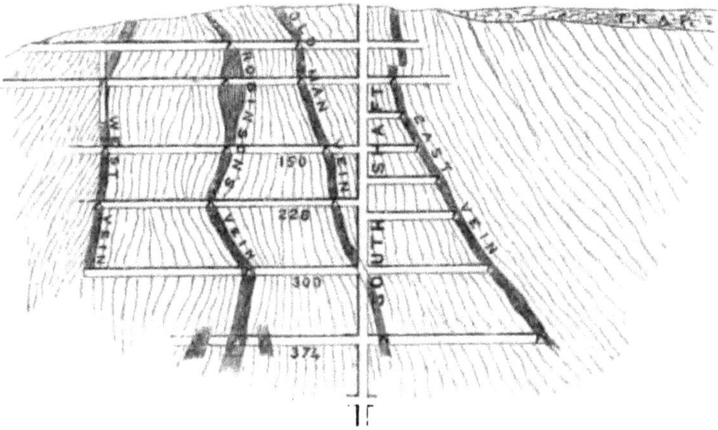

CLUNES.
(*South Cross Section.*)

The greatest depth to which this mine has been worked is 485 feet, and the total amount of quartz treated since the commencement of operations in 1857, to October 1866, has been 319,695 tons, yielding 185,488 oz. 0 dwt. 8 gr. of gold, giving an average produce of 11 dwt. 14½ gr. per ton. We are indebted to Mr. C. H. Fielder, the secretary of the Company, for the information embodied in the following tables:—

TABLE I.

Return of Quartz crushed from June 1857 *to October* 1866.

Period.			Amount crushed.	Net Amount of Gold produced.			Average per Ton.			Royalty.			Total.		
			Tons.	oz.	dwt.	gr.	oz.	dwt.	gr.	£	s.	d.	£	s.	d.
1857	7	Months.	4,146}	6,780	14	8	1	12	17	2,650	11	1	26,764	4	6
1858	9	,,	11,320½	15,764	9	0	1	7	20	6,130	2	2	61,301	3	5
1858-9	12	,,	17,542	18,165	12	12	1	0	17	6,202	15	8	71,497	4	5
1859-60	12	,,	21,694	17,466	16	9	...	16	0	5,135	14	4	68,476	5	8
1860-1	12	,,	32,258	24,326	6	3	...	15	2	7,178	3	2	95,708	13	3
1861-2	12	,,	34,236	22,012	0	17	...	12	20	6,479	18	4	86,398	12	11
1862-3	12	,,	40,360	22,988	1	19	...	11	9	6,850	4	5	91,336	5	8
1863-4	12	,,	44,149	17,611	8	0	...	8	0	5,237	1	9	69,694	7	2
1864-5	12	,,	54,413	20,596	15	12	...	7	13	6,074	3	0	80,692	7	8
1865-6	12	,,	59,576	19,775	16	0	...	6	15	5,893	16	10	78,584	19	1
			319,695	185,488	0	8	...	11	14½	57,822	10	9	730,454	3	9

The subjoined table (II.) gives the monthly results of the operations of the Company in Victoria, from January 1865 to June 1866, both inclusive. The crushing apparatus consists of seven stamping mills or batteries, composed in the aggregate of eighty heads, each weighing, including the stem, from 6 to 8 cwt.

TABLE II.

PORT PHILLIP AND COLONIAL GOLD MINING COMPANY.

Cost and Returns from January 1865 *to June* 1866.

PERIOD.	Quartz Stamped.	Quartz Stamped per Week.	Duty, per Stamp head per Day.	Produce of Gold.	Produce per Ton.	Gold per Ton in Tailings, by Assay.*	Total Mine Cost per Ton.	Total Reduction Cost per Ton.	Pyrites: Treated.	Pyrites: Yield per Ton.	Pyrites: Profit.	Price of Gold per oz.	Proceeds of Gold.
1865.	Tons.	Tons.	cwt. qr.	ounces.	dwt. gr.	dwt. gr.	s. d.	s. d.	Tons.	oz. dwt.	£	£ s. d.	£
January .	3,412	853	49 0	1,039	6 2	1 15	...	...	...	... ...	...	3 16 0	4,147
February .	4,551	910	48 2	1,566	6 22	1 15	...	...	...	... ...	...	3 16 0	6,272
March . .	3,677	919	54 0	1,006	5 11	1 22	15 0	7 9	85	2 7½	460	3 16 0	4,163
April . .	3,826	831	58 0	868	5 5	1 3	16 0	6 6	...	... ...	...	3 16 0	3,434
May . .	6,142	1,024	58 0	1,824	5 22	1 20	15 6	5 2	...	... ...	...	3 16 0	7,213
June . .	4,530	1,132	56 0	1,836	8 2	2 3	14 9	7 0	...	... ...	...	3 16 0	7,322
July . .	4,688	1,172	57 0	1,761	7 12	1 23	13 2	5 6	23	3 1½	208	3 16 0	7,026
August .	4,787	1,197	57 2	2,254	9 10	2 15	12 8	5 6	25	3 1	222	3 16 0	9,019
September	6,817	1,136	54 0	3,465	10 4	1 22	14 11	5 2	30	4 12	413	3 16 0	13,725
October .	4,774	1,193	56 3	1,997	8 8	2 3	11 2	7 3	...	... ...	...	3 15 4	7,876
November	4,676	1,169	57 3	1,661	7 2	2 15	14 7	8 2	...	... ...	...	3 15 1	6,562
December	4,195	1,049	54 3	1,316	6 7	2 6	16 1	11 2	...	... ...	...	3 14 10	5,172
1866.													
January .	4,177	1,044	53 0	1,377	6 14	2 6	15 3	9 4	...	... ...	...	3 14 10	5,438
February .	4,511	1,128	53 2	1,602	7 2	1 22	13 11	8 0	105	3 1	856	3 14 10	6,319
March . .	4,830	1,207	57 0	1,514	6 6	1 23	11 9	6 7	...	... ...	...	3 15 4	5,999
April . .	6,778	1,129	55 0	1,946	5 18	2 6	10 10	6 6	40½	2 10	280	3 15 4	7,728
May . .	4,783	1,196	57 0	1,111	4 15¼	1 16	11 0	6 2	19	2 11	...	3 15 9	4,435
June . .	4,877	1,219	63 3	911	3 17¾	1 17	10 6	7 0	19	3 3	286	3 15 9	3,616

* A portion of this gold is recovered by washing the tailings, and roasting and amalgamating the pyrites obtained.

From estimates very carefully made by the Colonial Secretary of Mines, which, however, are not given as being absolutely correct, it appears that the total quantities of gold obtained in Victoria from quartz veins were, during the three years undermentioned, as follows:—

	oz.	dwt.
1863	493,499	0
1864	503,618	5
1865	450,000	0

The following particulars relative to a few of the principal mining operations in the colony have been collected from the files of *Dicker's Mining Record.*

BALLARAT.—The following workings in this locality are classed as alluvial:—

Cosmopolitan.—Commenced 1857; claim 880 feet on the gutter; basaltic rock 112 feet in thickness; total length of drivages, 2,500 feet; stuff puddled and washed up daily. This undertaking had produced 38,249 oz. 4 dwt. 19 gr. of gold, of the value of 152,442*l.*, and paid dividends to the amount of 125,454*l.* up to November 19th, 1864.

United Extended Band of Hope.—Extent of claim, 36,040 feet; commenced in 1856, and had yielded gold to the value of 259,547*l.*; of which amount 147,200*l.* had been paid in dividends up to 31st December, 1865.

Defiance Company.—Commenced, 1856, and had afforded 20,197 oz. 18 dwt. of gold of the value of 81,102*l.*; out of which 66,483*l.* had been paid in dividends up to December 24th, 1864.

Koh-i-Noor. — Commenced, 1857; produce, 60,332 oz.; value, 241,233*l.*; dividends paid, 176,080*l.*, up to December 6th, 1864.

Prince of Wales.—Commenced, February 1857; gold produced, 22,912 oz. 11 dwt. 19 gr.; value, 90,735*l.*; dividends paid, 51,552*l.*, up to December 10th, 1864.

Alston and Weardale.—Commenced, July 1858; gold produced, 2,585 oz. 15 dwt. 3 gr.; value, 10,451*l.*; dividends paid, 4,884*l.*, up to August 1864.

Great Extended.—Commenced, 1857; amount of gold produced, 82,754 oz. 9 dwt. 14 gr.; value, 325,967*l.*; dividends paid, 274,450*l.*, up to December 4th, 1864.

BUNINYONG.—*Buninyong Mining Company.*—Alluvial. Commenced, November 1857; gold produced, 43,175 oz. 16 dwt. 22 gr.; value, 172,695*l.*; dividends paid, 88,007*l.*, previous to November 26th, 1864.

DAYLESFORD.—*New Wombat Hill.*—Alluvial; commenced April 1861; gold produced, 14,942 oz. 14 dwt. 19 gr.; value, 58,059*l.*; dividends paid, 38,400*l.* up to November 5th, 1864.

BENDIGO.—*Catherine Reef United.*—Quartz; claim, 501 yards, held under a lease from the Government; vein 4 feet wide, with strike 23° west of north, and a dip to the east; commenced, March 1861; gold produced, 24,930 oz. 15 dwt. 12 gr.; value, 95,784*l.*; dividends paid, 29,735*l.* previous to December 17th, 1864.

SCARSDALE.—*Avonclift.*—Alluvial; area of claim, 133 acres; depth of basalt, 84 feet; two gutters running parallel; depth of wash dirt, 4½ feet; gold produced, 4,272 oz. 14 dwt. 12 gr.; value, 17,090*l.*; dividends paid, 4,000*l.* up to September 1864.

HAPPY VALLEY.—*British Gold Mining Company.*—Alluvial; extent of claim,

50 acres; held under a lease from the Government; the gutter is 30 feet in width, and the depth of the wash dirt, about 3 feet; commenced in July 1860; produce of gold, 17,591 oz. 6 dwt. 1 gr.; value, 70,126*l.*; dividends paid, 40,800*l.* up to March 4th, 1866.

Try Again Gold Mining Company.—Alluvial; commenced, September 1859; extent of claim, 49 acres; held under a lease from the Crown; wash dirt from 2 to 3 feet in thickness; gold produced, 6,153 oz. 7 dwt. 8 gr.; value, 24,535*l.*; dividends paid, 9,802*l.* up to December 10th, 1864.

Cleft in the Rock.—Alluvial; commenced, November 1859; extent of concession, 50 acres. held under a lease from the Crown; main lead bearing north and south; thickness of pay dirt, from 2 to 7 feet; produce of gold, 3,848 oz. 14 dwt. 11 gr.; value, 15,287*l.*; dividends paid, 5,960*l.* up to December 12th, 1864.

WOOD'S POINT.—*Alps Great Central Gold Mining Company.*—Quartz; commenced, July 1863; produced 27,500 oz. of gold; value, 92,812*l.* up to July 1865.

Hope Mining Company.—Quartz; commenced, July 1863; produce of gold 8,732 oz. 3 dwt.; value, 27,032*l.* up to July 1865.

By an Act for the better management of the gold fields of Victoria passed by the Colonial Parliament in 1857, the whole of the auriferous region was divided into the six following mining districts, each called after its chief gold field, or rather after the chief town in its most important gold field:—Ballarat, Castlemaine, Sandhurst, Maryborough, Beechworth, and Ararat; but this division is entirely arbitrary, and totally unconnected with any geographical or geological features of the country. The only connecting link between the Colonial Government and the gold fields, is the Warden, whose duty it is to attend to the settlement of small disputes connected with the gold-mining interests; to report on the advisability of granting leases of mineral lands, and to draw up periodical reports relative to the state of the gold fields in his district. Each gold field, and sometimes each division of a gold field, when it is a large one, has its own Warden, whose correspondence with the Government passes through the hands of the Chief Warden. Each district has its own Mining Board, of which the members are chosen by ballot by the gold miners, and which arranges all gold-mining questions within its jurisdiction. Each member receives a small allowance for his attendance at the board, and holds office during three years, at the expiration of which he is eligible for re-election. A Court of Mines is also established within each mining district, before which come all disputes above the adjudication of the Chief Warden. The judges of these courts are independent of the Colonial Government, and hold office *quamdiu se bene gesserint.* From the decisions of the judges of the Court of Mines there is a power of appeal to the Supreme Court of the Colony.

The following amounts of gold have been exported from the Colony of Victoria since 1850:—

Period.	Quantity.			Value.		
	oz.	dwt.	gr.	£	s.	d.
1851 . .	145,137	3	12	580,548	12	0
1852 . .	1,988,526	10	13	7,954,106	0	0
1853 . .	2,497,723	15	16	9,990,895	0	0
1854 . .	2,144,699	9	19	8,578,797	16	0
1855 . .	2,575,745	4	17	10,302,980	16	0
1856 . .	2,985,695	17	0	11,942,783	8	0
1857 . .	2,761,528	8	0	11,046,113	12	0
1858 . .	2,555,263	0	0	10,221,052	0	0
1859 . .	2,280,525	14	0	9,122,102	16	0
1860 . .	2,128,466	11	0	8,513,866	4	0
1861 . .	1,978,864	13	0	7,915,458	12	0
1862 . .	1,662,448	18	0	6,649,795	12	0
1863 . .	1,627,066	0	0	6,508,264	0	0
1864 . .	1,545,449	15	0	6,181,799	0	0
1865 . .	1,545,450	0	0	6,181,800	0	0
	30,422,591	0	5	£121,690,363	8	0

In addition to the above amounts, exported direct from the colony, 1,691,150 oz. of gold, produced in Victoria, are known to have been shipped through the Customs of New South Wales, Tasmania, and South Australia, besides a large amount (estimated at 2,250,000 oz.) that left the country in private hands.

The total exports of the colony, from the commencement of gold-mining operations to the end of 1865, will therefore be nearly as follows:—

	oz.	dwt.	gr.
Returned by Victoria Custom House	30,422,591	0	0
Not returned " " "	1,691,150	0	0
Taken by Private Hands	2,250,000	0	0
Total . .	34,363,741	0	0

The total value of the gold exported from the colony, up to the end of 1865, will consequently be nearly 138,000,000*l.*, exclusive of that absorbed by the currency, &c. of the country.*

* The Colonial Secretary of Mines estimates the quantity of gold produced in the colony, from the first discovery of the gold fields, to the 31st December, 1865, at 30,998,071 oz.; value £123,992,284; but no allowance is made by him for the gold which had been sent off privately, or for the amount used and manufactured in the colony.

New South Wales.—Although the first practical discovery of gold was made in New South Wales, some weeks previous to its being found in Victoria, its total produce of the precious metal has been far less considerable than that of the sister colony. The general description of the gold fields of Victoria is equally applicable to those of New South Wales, but we are without any very definite information relating to the different workings in the latter colony, which are, however, much less numerous and extensive than those of Victoria. Among the principal mining districts of New South Wales may be mentioned Abercrombie, Summerhill, Ophir, Turon, Tamworth, &c. &c. The produce of gold from New South Wales up to the close of 1860, amounted to about 8,000,000*l*., whilst Victoria had exported gold to the value of nearly 90,000,000*l*. during the same period. According to the Government returns, entitled "Statistical Abstract for the several Colonial and other Possessions of the United Kingdom, 1866," the export of coined and uncoined gold from this colony, up to 1864, had been nearly as follows :—

Period.	Quantity.	Value.
	oz.	£
1851	144,120	470,836
1852	818,751	2,660,945
1853	548,152	1,781,272
1854	237,910	773,209
1855	64,384	209,250
1856	46,999	156,151
1857	277,531	1,101,448
1858	443,462	1,773,851
1859	427,558	1,704,774
1860	472,886	1,878,588
1861	507,021	2,010,263
1862	741,055	2,984,269
1863	593,699	2,362,054
1864	740,048	2,952,471
	6,063,576	22,819,381

Although we have not been able to obtain the same amount of statistical information with reference to this colony, as is to be procured with regard to Victoria, it is probable that a very large proportion of the gold exported from New South Wales is the produce of other portions of the Australian Continent. The establishment of a mint at Sydney has naturally caused large quantities of gold to be imported, for the purpose of being converted into coin, but the total produce of the gold fields of New South Wales, since their discovery in 1851, is estimated at only 4,000,000 oz., and the present annual yield at about 320,000 oz.

SOUTH AUSTRALIA AND TASMANIA also annually produce a certain amount of gold, but the quantity is comparatively small, since, from 1851 to the close of 1860, the total weight exported, including the exports from New Zealand, was represented by a money value of 374,000*l.*, of which New Zealand is supposed to have contributed more than one-half. The amounts and value of the gold exported from South Australia and Tasmania, including New Zealand, from the discovery of gold in those countries to the end of 1860, were nearly as follows:—

PERIOD.	QUANTITY.	VALUE.
	oz.	£
1852	5,250	21,000
1853	5,250	21,000
1854	5,250	21,000
1855	5,250	21,000
1856	5,250	21,000
1857	15,639	62,556
1858	18,680	74,720
1859	16,431	65,724
1860	16,500	66,000
	93,500	374,000

QUEENSLAND is likewise, to a certain extent, a gold-producing country, and affords a small yearly yield of the precious metal, but we have been unable to procure any returns of its annual production. According to *Dicker's Mining Record* of 17th April, 1866, there is but one quartz-crushing establishment in that colony, and only one quartz-mining company now at work. This association holds the lease of three quartz reefs from the Crown.

The extent of the ground held is 400 yards in length, on the line of each reef, by a width of 200 yards. The Alexander Reef is twenty-two miles from Gladstone, on the water-shed of the Boyne River. A crushing had been made of 400 tons, which paid satisfactorily. There was only one very indifferent mill of 10 horse-power in the country. The charge for crushing was 25*s.* per ton. On this reef there were five shafts, varying in depth from 80 to 100 feet; the thickness of the vein varies from two to four feet. The reef forming the second lease is on Bell's Run, twelve miles from Gladstone, on the water-shed of the Caliope. There had been six shafts sunk, varying in depth from 50 to 70 feet, and the thickness of the lode is from three to eight feet. The proprietors had sent two tons to Sydney to be crushed, but the result had not been announced at the date of the despatch leaving the colony. The third lease is on a quartz reef, on the range dividing the waters of the Boyne from the Caliope. Not much, however, had been done here up to the spring of 1866, although two shafts were then in course of sinking.

New Zealand.

The first authentic discovery of gold in New Zealand was made at Massacre Bay in 1842, by an exploring party under Captain Wakefield, but did not at the time attract much attention. No further discoveries of this metal were announced until 1852, but in that year gold was almost simultaneously found in the Provinces of Auckland and Otago, and, from the important results which had then been obtained from the Australian gold fields, excited a considerable amount of public attention. The Auckland discovery was made at Coromandel, but only about 1,100 ounces of gold were obtained, and the district was shortly afterwards abandoned. In 1856, attention was called by the Surveyor-General of New Zealand to the existence of gold in the sands and gravels of the Mataura River, and in the same year discoveries were made at Motaeka, in the Province of Nelson; whilst inthe following year, the gold field at Aorore, Massacre Bay, again came into notice. A rush of the population to the gold regions was the result of these discoveries, and about a thousand persons were for some time employed in the diggings with varying success; but the severity of the season, and want of practicable roads, soon led to the discouragement of a large number of the miners. The exports from this district, up to the end of 1858, amounted to 16,473 ounces of gold. The richest diggings on the Aorore gold field were those on the Slate River, which takes its rise in the Anatoki Range, and afterwards falls into the Aorore. This river has high and precipitous banks, composed of granite, slate, and quartz; the gold being found, associated with osmiridium, in a yellow sand met with in the bed of the stream.

In the latter part of 1857, the existence of gold in Otago was made known; and the Sub-Assistant Surveyor, Mr. Gillies, and party, found gold in a creek running between the Waikioi and Makerewa Bush, and emptying itself into the Makerewa. About the same period, Mr. Garvie, another Sub-Assistant Surveyor, found traces of gold in many of the sands and gravels of the south-eastern district of the Province. In March 1858, Mr. Garvie brought into Dunedin the first important specimens, which were obtained by Mr. Buchanan from the river beach of the Dunstan gorge, which four years later proved so highly remunerative to two old Californian miners, named Hartley and Reilly, and which ultimately led to the development of the most extensive gold field in the Province. In the same year, gold was discovered in the surface gravel near the mouth of the Tuapika River, and also in the River Lindis.

Further discoveries continued to be made in the Province of Nelson, and in 1859 some nuggets, weighing from two to nine ounces, were found in the Rocky River.

Gold was found in considerable quantities in the River Lindis in March 1861, in the form of water-worn nuggets of the size of beans as also, in a finer state of division, in the Kakanui, near Moeraki. In June of the same year, a discovery was made from which may be dated the importance of Otago as a gold-producing country. Mr. Gabriel Read was led by curiosity to attempt the verification of the reported presence of gold in that district, and in the course of his expedition examined the ravines and tributaries of the Waitahuna and Tuapika rivers. With a tin dish and a knife for his only tools, he collected seven ounces of gold in about ten hours, and ascertained the existence of the precious metal in many of the creeks and gullies. These discoveries of Mr. Read were shortly afterwards confirmed by the results obtained by other explorers, and caused a great rush to the district, where discoveries followed each other in rapid succession, fully establishing the fact of the existence of a valuable and extensive gold field.

Early in 1862, fresh discoveries were made at Coromandel, where a large number of miners congregated, and several companies were organised for working quartz veins. The gold diggings on the western coast of Nelson also gave promise of being highly productive, and some very large prospects were obtained. In the month of August a discovery was made in the Province of Otago which exceeded in importance those of the previous year. In February, two men, who had been miners in California, started on a prospecting tour up the Molyneux River, and found gold so readily, that, to use their own words, "they had nothing to do but to set the cradle on the edge of the river and keep it going from morning till night, as one man could get rich wash dirt to feed the cradle as fast as the other could wash it." These men, Hartley and Reilly, as the result of three months' work, brought into Dunedin 87 lbs. of gold, and received from the Provincial Government a bonus of 2,000*l*. for making known the locality from which it had been obtained.

In the latter part of 1862 and the beginning of 1863, the area of the gold field of Otago was much extended, and in the latter year large amounts of gold were obtained, and immense areas of auriferous ground opened up, on the Wakatipu Lake and its tributaries. Towards the latter part of 1863, further and important discoveries were made on the western coast of Nelson, and in the early part of the following year the Matakitaki Diggings, in the same province, came into considerable notice.

In April 1864, the first discovery of gold was made in the Province of Marlborough, in the River Wakamarina and its vicinity; but disastrous floods, and the impenetrable nature of the country, have prevented the rapid development of this gold field. During the same year, gold was obtained from the banks of the Teremakau River to the west of Canterbury, and various other localities along the coast.

In the year 1865, another very important discovery of gold was made in the Hokitika River, on the west coast of Canterbury, the yield from which, up to the present time, has been very considerable; and as further discoveries are being made in the district, it is probable that this river, and the district around it, will turn out to be a rich and important gold field. Gold mining is now being successfully carried on at Coromandel in the Province of Auckland, at Massacre

Bay, and on the Buller, Lyell, Wangapeka, and other western streams in the Province of Nelson; in the Grey, Teremakau, and Hokitika rivers, and over a large extent of the western coast of the Province of Canterbury, as well as over a vast area in the Province of Otago.

In New Zealand, as in all other gold-bearing countries, the zones of clay slate and mica slate appear to be the original sources from which the supply of the precious metal has been chiefly derived, but the largest portion of that at present obtained has been procured from workings in the alluviums, some of which, like those of California and Australia, extend under a capping of volcanic rock.

The geological age of the auriferous drifts of New Zealand is probably that of the gold-bearing alluviums of Australia, although this does not appear to have been as yet distinctly proved.

Quartz mining is as yet in its infancy in the colony, but several promising reefs have been opened, and are expected to afford satisfactory returns. The most important quartz mines at present known are at Waipori. A large proportion of the gold produced in New Zealand is obtained by sluicing, and so favourable have been the results of this class of mining, that it may be fairly anticipated, that the Province of Otago will be a large gold-producing country for many years to come. River mining is profitably followed in various parts of the country, particularly in the Wakatipu district, and in the beds of the Molyneux and neighbouring streams. As these deposits gradually become exhausted, the attention of miners will, doubtless, be more exclusively directed to the thicker formations of auriferous drift.

The following statistics relative to the gold production have been compiled from official sources:*—

TABLE I.

AMOUNT OF GOLD EXPORTED.

	oz.	dwt.	gr.
1861-1862, 1st August to 31st July	457,239	10	6
1862-1863 " "	514,385	17	0
1863-1864 " "	497,031	9	0
1864-1865 " 31st March	231,010	11	0
Total quantity exported from Otago . .	1,699,667	7	6

* New Zealand Exhibition, 1865, Reports and Awards of Jurors.

In addition to the above, 63,970 oz. of gold, the produce of the gold fields of Otago, were exported from other ports in the colony, making the grand total exported 1,763,637 oz. 7 dwt. 6 gr., value 7,054,544*l.*

TABLE II.

Showing the quantity and value of gold from the gold fields in each Island, and the whole of New Zealand, exported from the Colony, from 1st April 1857 *to 31st December* 1864.*

Produce of.	During 1864.		From 1st April 1857 to 31st December 1863.		Total exported from New Zealand, to 31st Dec. 1864.	
	oz.	£	oz.	£	oz.	£
North Island	3,448	10,552	6,076	19,323	9,524	29,875
South Island	476,723	1,847,295	1,263,112	4,894,560	1,739,835	6,741,855
Total from New Zealand	480,171	1,857,847	1,269,188	4,913,883	1,749,359	6,771,730

The following table gives the approximate yields, in lbs. troy, of the principal gold-producing countries at the commencement of the present century, and for the years 1850, 1860, and 1865. In cases where the returns for the year indicated could not be obtained, the produce for the nearest years, for which they could be procured, has been substituted. The quoted produce of the mines of the United States and of the British Possessions, may, however, be regarded in each instance as being nearly correct, except that the return for California and the neighbouring States and Territories for 1865, is probably somewhat under the truth, since it is exceedingly difficult to ascertain the precise yields of Idaho, Montana, Colorado, and some other outlying districts. After each absolute sum is given its relative weight, in comparison with the grand total produced throughout the world:—

* The returns state: "The value has been calculated on the uniform estimated rate of 3*l.* 17*s.* 6*d.* per oz., with the exception of the gold from the North Island, for which the ascertained value has been allowed. This table has been compiled from the *Monthly Returns of Gold Exported*, which do not in all cases exactly correspond with the Quarterly Trade Returns of Exports from the Colony, as furnished by the collectors of their respective ports, from which Table I. was constructed."

TABLE SHOWING APPROXIMATE PRODUCTION OF THE PRINCIPAL GOLD FIELDS OF THE WORLD.

	1800.		1850.		1860.		1865.	
	lbs. troy.	ratio per cent.	lbs. troy.	ratio per cent.	lbs. troy.	ratio per cent.	lbs. troy.	ratio per cent.
Russian Empire	1,440	2·7	65,600	19·0	66,000	11·3	69,500	12·4
Austrian Empire			5,600	1·6	5,500	1·0	5,500	1·0
and	3,500	6·5						
Rest of Europe			100	...	350	...	375	
Southern Asia	10,000	18·5	25,000	7·3	25 000	4·3	25,000	4·5
Africa	600	1·2	4,000	1·1	4,000	0·7	4,000	0·7
Chili	7,500	13·8						
Bolivia	1,600	3·0						
Peru	2,400	4·4	34,000*	9·9	34,000	5·9	34,000	6·1
New Granada	12,000	23·4						
Brazil	10,000	18·5						
Mexico	4,300	8·0						
California & neighbouring States & Territories	...	...	208,000	60·2	187,000	31·9	210,000	37·5
Rest of United States	...	...	2,950	0·9	1,020	0·2	140	
Nova Scotia	...	...	...	...	...	...	2,072	0·4
British Columbia	...	...	...	...	20,000	3·4	11,600	2·1
Australia	...	...	...	...	217,500	37·0	156,000	27·9
New Zealand	...	...	...	...	25,000	4·3	41,400	7·4
	53,940	100	345,250	100	585,370	100	559,587	100

* The yields of the different members of this group vary considerably from year to year, but the aggregate produce is believed to remain tolerably constant.

CHAPTER VIII.

GOLD WASHING IN CALIFORNIA AND AUSTRALIA.

PLACER MINING—THE PAN—ROCKER—LONG TOM—PUDDLING BOX—SLUICE—RIVER MINING—BEACH MINING—WATER SUPPLY—EUREKA CANAL—HYDRAULIC MINING —AMOUNT OF WATER REQUIRED—COST OF WATER, AND METHOD OF MEASUREMENT—DRY WASHING.

GOLD mines may be divided into two distinct classes, viz., Placer Mines, in which the metal is found, in a more or less water-worn condition, embedded in earth, clay, sand, or gravel; and Quartz, or Vein Mines, in which gold is met with disseminated in its original gangue, or matrix.

In the former, the gold-producing material is called "pay dirt," which, on being subjected to the action of water, becomes disintegrated, and the lighter portions are mechanically carried off, whilst the gold, from its greater specific gravity, remains behind. In the latter, on the contrary, after first obtaining the rock by the ordinary operations of mining, as practised with regard to other metals, it has to be reduced by mechanical means to the state of a finely-divided powder, before the associated gold can be collected, either by washing or amalgamation.

The amount of skill and capital necessary for the successful prosecution of placer mining, is usually less than is requisite for carrying on quartz mining, on a remunerative scale; and as placer mines are generally those to which attention is first directed in a new country, and from which remunerative returns are most readily obtained, we shall, in the first place, describe the processes employed for extracting gold from the various alluvial deposits, and subsequently pass on to the consideration of quartz mining, and the extraction of the precious metal from the veinstone constituting its original matrix.

Water is the great agent by the aid of which placer mining is carried on: with a large supply, the operations of the miner can be cheaply and rapidly conducted; but without water, or with only a limited amount, a claim that would otherwise have been highly productive, may either become valueless, or only capable of affording very irregular returns.

Placer mines are of two distinct classes, the shallow and the deep; shallow, or surface diggings, are generally found in the beds of ravines or gullies, on the bars and in the beds of modern rivers, and on shallow flats. In the latter, the pay dirt is often found at great depths from the surface, and is not unfrequently covered by thick beds of lava, or volcanic ash, as in the case of the deposits under Table Mountain, Tuolumne County, and near Nevada City, California.

In the deeper placers, the auriferous drifts are reached either by shafts of considerable depth, or by means of levels, or tunnels, driven in from some neighbouring valley. The pay dirt, after being thus extracted, is conveyed to the surface, in order that it may undergo the usual process of washing. In other instances, hydraulic mining is resorted to, in which case jets of water, under great pressure, obtained from a high column, are directed against the deposits of sand and gravel, which are thus not only disintegrated, but finally carried away by the current. This is the most economical and expeditious method of working placer mines, when a sufficient supply and pressure of water can be obtained, and there is also enough declivity below the auriferous beds to allow of the resulting detritus being readily disposed of. The pay dirt is almost invariably covered by various layers of barren clay and sand, which are, in the shallow diggings, removed by the use of the pick and shovel; but, in hydraulic workings, the whole is washed away by the force of a stream of water playing against it, and any particles of gold which it may contain are caught in the sluices through which the lighter materials pass. In many of the deep placers, after reaching the pay dirt by means of shafts or tunnels, it is extracted by a system of levels and headings, not unlike those employed for working a coal seam in this country.

In California, besides classifying the placer mines as shallow and deep, they are again subdivided into hill, bench, flat, bar, gulch, and river diggings, with reference to their topographical position as regards the surrounding country. Hill diggings are in the sides of hills; bench diggings are on narrow benches on the declivities of hills, and above the level of existing rivers; flat diggings are situated on flats or small plains; bar diggings are usually in collections of sand and gravel, on the sides of streams, and, under ordinary circumstances, above the surface of the water; gulch claims are found in ravines and gullies, through which no water passes, except in times of extraordinary floods; river diggings occur in the bottoms of rivers, and can only be worked after diverting the water from its original channel.

Placer claims are likewise spoken of as sluice, hydraulic, and tunnel claims, dry diggings, &c., in accordance with the means employed for reaching the auriferous deposits, and the methods adopted for the separation and collection of gold. In the early days of Californian and Australian gold mining, when paying diggings could generally be found near the surface, and before the large deposits of pay dirt lying at great depths below the ground had been discovered, the greater portion of the gold produced was obtained from shallow workings. These have now, to a great extent, become exhausted, and in Australia shafts are sunk to the older deposits, whilst in California enormous aqueducts have been constructed, and hydraulic mining is extensively introduced. In both countries, therefore, at the present time, the greater portion of the gold obtained is the result of deep mining, the shallow placers being generally abandoned to the Chinamen, who are satisfied to wash over the dirt which has been already passed through the machines, or has escaped the attention of the ordinary miner.

The object of the miner is generally to obtain the largest quantity of gold in the shortest possible time, and with the least amount of labour and expense, rather than to extract the total amount contained in the material on which he operates; and, consequently, without taking into consideration the necessary loss incident to the imperfect nature of the appliances employed, his refuse will naturally retain a certain proportion of the gold originally present. The falling abroad, however, of lumps of clay, by the action of the weather, constantly exposes fresh particles of the precious metal, and from this cause the residues frequently afford an amount of gold that could not have been otherwise obtained from them. Many contrivances have been introduced with a view to obtaining the whole, or a large proportion, of the gold present in the pay dirt, but, in the majority of instances, the result has been a failure; and if an increase of yield has sometimes been obtained, the additional gold extracted has frequently been more than compensated for by the extra expense entailed.

Whilst the supply of shallow auriferous dirt was sufficient to furnish employment for the whole labouring population, the gold produced was almost exclusively obtained either by solitary diggers, or by small private companies of working men, whose capital consisted rather in their united strength, than in an accumulation of money. Things went on in this way until the richer and more easily-worked alluviums had become partially exhausted; when it was found that to carry on successfully the deeper diggings, combinations on a somewhat more extensive scale became necessary, and that capital and intelligence, as well as strength and endurance, were required by the gold miner. While there was no difficulty in finding shallow claims that would pay from 25*s.* to 30*s.* per day to the hand, it was almost impossible to obtain the labour necessary to carry on either deep digging or quartz mining with any chance of success; but when these began to be worked out, this difficulty gradually disappeared, and attention became directed to operations on a more extensive scale, generally conducted either at the expense of a co-operative company, or joint-stock association. In this way, the usages and exigencies of a newly-discovered gold region rapidly change and become more assimilated to those of more commercial and longer established communities. A lucky miner becomes a capitalist, and in the gold regions, as in all other places, money commands labour, and large operations are commenced, often to the doubtful advantage of the speculators, but to the manifest benefit of the general community.

Having thus briefly alluded to the general conditions of recently discovered gold regions, we will proceed to describe the various appliances employed for the separation of gold from the different earthy materials with which it is associated, beginning by the cheaper and more simple, and afterwards treating of the more complicated and efficient arrangements now generally employed.

The Pan.—This is the indispensable companion of the gold miner, and is used by him in all branches of his business, either for washing, or as a receptacle for gold, amalgam, or rich dirt. It is made either of stiff tin plate, or of thin sheet iron, and is at bottom about fourteen inches in diameter. A sheet iron pan is generally to be preferred to one made of tin plate, not only because it is stronger, but also because it is unattacked by mercury, if brought in contact with that metal. The top is from three to four inches wider than the bottom, and consequently the sides, which are about five inches in depth, and strengthened at the edge by a thick wire, have a considerable inclination outwards. In order to wash with the pan, it is first about two-thirds filled with dirt, and then placed in a water-hole, which should not be more than about a foot in depth, in order that the vessel may rest on the bottom, whilst the miner stirs up its contents with his hands. If the water be too deep for this, the pan may be held in one hand, and stirred with the other, but it is more convenient, and less tiresome, to be enabled to let it rest on the bottom. The dirt having been placed in the pan, and the pan itself filled with water, the miner inserts his hands into it, and raises and stirs the dirt, so as to make every part of it thoroughly wet. Having done this, he now takes the pan in his hands, holding it by the two opposite sides, but somewhat behind its greatest diameter; and raising slightly the part which is towards him, and consequently depressing the outer edge, he commences to shake it from side to side in such a way that all the dirt is beneath the surface of the water, and at the same time, by a sort of circular motion, he allows a small portion of it to pass over the edge at each oscillation. The earthy particles, together with the fine sand, soon become suspended in water, and gradually pass over the side in the form of thin mud, whilst the gold, the tough clay, and large stones remain behind.

The stones collect on the top of the sand and clay, and are scraped off with the fingers, while the lumps of clay are rubbed between the hands, and thus prepared for being taken up by water during the next washing. The process is thus continued, the pan being gradually raised in the water, and its outer edge further depressed, until the greater portion of the clay and stones have been removed, and the gold remains, together with a little earthy matter and black sand. At this stage of the operation, the pan is nearly filled with water, and after being removed from the pool in which the washing has been hitherto conducted, is shaken, so as to get the last portions of clayey matter in suspension, and the water carefully poured off, as shown in Fig. 7.

The outer edge of the pan only is now immersed in water, and a further portion of the clayey matter removed by careful washing, leaving the gold, and a small quantity of heavy titaniferous iron sand, in the angle formed between the bottom and side. This black sand, which is mixed with the finer particles of gold, is so heavy that it cannot be separated from the metal by washing, but can, to a great extent, be removed by a simple process of blowing. In order to do this, it is allowed to dry, and a small quantity of it placed in a *blower*, which is a sort of dish, or shallow tin scoop, open at one end. The miner now holds the blower with the open end from him, and with his mouth directs a gentle stream of air along the surface of the mixture of gold and fine sand, taking care so to regulate its force as to remove the latter without causing a loss to the former. To effect this, the blower must be gently shaken, so as to change the position of the particles, and bring them all, in turn, under the influence of

FIG. 7.

WASHING WITH PAN.

the current of air; and although the gold cannot be thoroughly cleansed in this way, any remaining particles are readily removed by a magnet.

The pan is always employed for washing up the rich dirt which collects in the cradle and sluice heads, and is exceedingly convenient for cleaning small quantities of gold-bearing sand collected in the different arrangements made use of in placer mining. Amalgam can be separated from sand by washing, almost as readily as gold, and the pan is therefore frequently used for this purpose. Panning is apparently a very simple process; but in order to use a pan so as to wash quickly, and at the same time without loss of gold, considerable practice is required.

The Cradle.—This apparatus somewhat resembles in size and shape a child's ordinary wooden cradle, and stands on similar rockers. The box is usually about forty inches in length and twenty in width, with one end from fifteen inches to two feet in height, the sides being sloped off at the lower extremity like those of a coal-scuttle. The construction of a cradle and the method of using it will be understood by reference to Figs. 8 and 9.

At the upper end of the cradle is the hopper, or riddle box, *a*, twenty inches square and six inches in depth, of which the bottom is composed of sheet iron, thickly perforated with holes half an inch in diameter. This is not fastened to the cradle, but can be lifted on and off at pleasure, and fits into it so as to be quite steady when in its right position. Beneath the riddle is placed an apron, *b*, made by stretching a piece of canvas on a framework resting on fillets, inclined

FIG. 8.

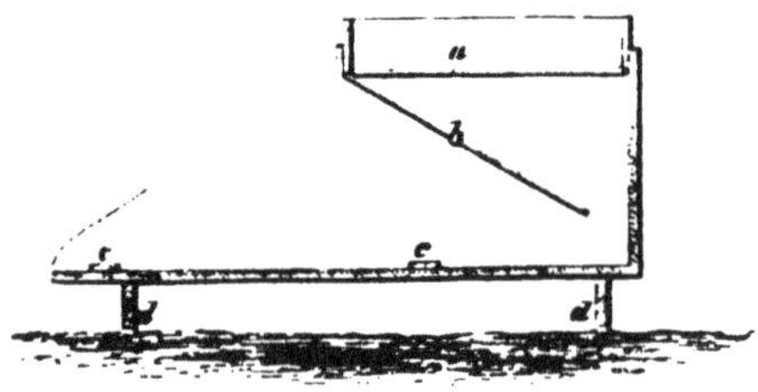

SECTION OF CRADLE.

FIG. 9.

WASHING WITH CRADLE.

from the bottom edge of the riddle towards the head of the cradle, whilst across the bottom are nailed two riffle bars, *c*, about three-quarters of an inch in height, one towards the middle, and the other at the lower end.

In order to work with this apparatus, which stands on rockers, *d*, the dirt is shovelled into the hopper; the cradler sits or kneels by the side of his machine, and whilst, with a ladle or dipper in one hand, he pours water upon the dirt, he with the other gives a rocking motion to the cradle. By the action of the water and motion together, the dirt is rapidly disintegrated, and passing through the riddle falls upon the apron, by which it is carried to the head of the cradle box, and from thence flows along the bottom, and finally escapes at the lower end, leaving the gold, black sand, and heavier particles of gravel, behind the riffle bars nailed across it. The pay dirt usually contains a great many large stones, which remain on the hopper, from whence those which are so large as to give an unpleasant jerk to the cradle in rocking are removed by hand. The smaller ones, however, are allowed to remain until a hopperful of clean stones has accumulated, when the cradler, rising from his seat, first looks them over to see that there is no gold among them, and then takes out the riddle box, and with a jerk throws out its contents. The rocking motion of the cradle not only assists the disintegration of the dirt, but also tends to keep the sandy deposit behind the riffle bars from becoming too solidly packed, which, by preventing the particles of gold from settling at the bottom, would cause a considerable loss.

The operation of washing with the cradle is merely a repetition of the processes above described; but, in order to prevent loss of gold, it is necessary to clean up the cradle box from two to three times a day, according to the richness and nature of the wash dirt which is being worked. To do this, the hopper is first lifted off, and the apron removed, in order to get readily at the bottom of the cradle, which is then carefully scraped with an iron spoon, and the dirt collected in a pan for the purpose of being subsequently panned out. The larger proportion of the gold naturally collects above the riffle bars; and when it is in a very finely divided state, it is sometimes found advantageous to place the hopper over the lower end of the cradle, which will thus take double the length of apron, and oblige the stuff washed to pass over a longer surface before leaving the machine. If, in this case, the apron be made of a thick woollen cloth, a considerable amount of fine gold will be retained on its surface, and on cleaning up the machine, it can be readily washed off into a pan. For the convenient supply of a cradle, water should be conducted, by means of a small ditch or gutter, to a pit sunk near its head, serving as a reservoir, and from which it is dipped out by means of a basin-shaped ladle, provided with a short wooden handle, and capable of containing from three to four quarts.

The difference of level between the upper and lower ends of the machine should, under ordinary circumstances, be about two and a half inches, but this may be slightly varied in accordance with the fineness of the gold, and the nature of the dirt to be washed. The amount of dirt that can be washed by one man in a day, will evidently depend on the quantity of clayey matter it contains, and varies from one to three cubic yards. The dirt is shovelled into a pan or bucket, and from thence thrown into the hopper, the miner estimating the amount of work done by the number of pans or buckets washed.

Although the cradle is frequently worked by one man, washing by this machine can be more expeditiously and cheaply conducted by two persons, since, in order to keep it in constant operation, there is always sufficient work for a cradler and a shoveller. In that case, one of the miners attends the cradle, whilst the other, who is provided with a couple of buckets or pans, fills them alternately with dirt, always keeping a full one near the cradle, so that he can at once pick it up and empty it into the riddle box. When a cradle is worked only by one man, he has continually to stop working in order to discharge the stones from the riddle, and fetch more dirt, and during this time the sand and clay retained by the riffle bars are liable to pack, and have to be loosened with a spoon, or scraped, before again beginning to wash. It has been found in practice that the weight of water required for working a cradle is at least three times that of the dirt washed, and consequently, where there is no means of conducting a supply to the cradle, it is taken to water, and the wash dirt transported to it. It is of great advantage to the miner when he can place his cradle within a few feet of the pit from which he obtains his pay dirt, and it is also essential that he should have an adequate supply of water and a sufficient fall to enable him to get easily rid of his tailings.

The rocker is neither an expeditious nor economical method of washing, as it not only loses fine gold, but also gets through but one-fifth the amount of work that the same number of hands can perform with a tom, and less than one-tenth of that which an ordinary sluice will accomplish, but is nevertheless peculiarly adapted to certain descriptions of diggings. In all gold-producing countries there are numerous little gullies and ravines containing coarse gold, but in which no water can be obtained for washing, except immediately after heavy rains, and then only for a few days at a time; and in such situations the cradle can often be used with advantage. It is in the first place cheap, does not require a large quantity of water, and being exceedingly portable, can, when the supply fails, be readily removed to the bank of some pool, where a supply of pay dirt can be obtained.

The great defect of the cradle is the tendency of the sand to pack behind the riffle bars, which causes the bottom of the box to assume a plain even surface, over which gold is liable to pass off and become lost. It is consequently necessary, after the machine has been allowed to stand, if only for a few minutes, without rocking, to stir up the sand in the bottom before recommencing the operation. Mercury is sometimes employed in the rocker, but this is not general, and its use in this apparatus is not generally to be recommended. In the early days of Californian and Australian gold mining the rocker was very commonly employed; but now that the supply of rich shallow pay dirt has become nearly exhausted, it is but little used by European and American miners, although still a general favourite with Chinese diggers.

The Tom.—The tom or long tom was almost universally employed in the Californian placers up to the year 1852, but is now rarely met with. It consists of a roughly-made wooden trough, or spout, about twelve feet in length, twenty inches in width at its upper end, and gradually widening to thirty inches at the other extremity, with its bottom covered by a plate of iron to prevent wearing. The sides, from eight to ten inches in depth, are cut off obliquely from the bottom upwards, so that the wide end may be closed by an inclined riddle of punched sheet iron, precisely similar to that forming the bottom of the hopper of an ordinary rocker. This trough is supported on trestles or logs, so as to have an inclination from the head downwards of about twelve inches, and beneath the strainer of sheet iron is placed the riffle box, which may be used either with or without quicksilver, and from which the rich dirt is, from time to time, cleaned out and panned up, as in the case of the rocker.

The general arrangement of the tom and its riffle box will be understood by the aid of Figs. 10 and 11, which show the method of fixing this apparatus.

A stream of water is brought by the spout, A, on to the tom, B, and the dirt is thrown in near its head by one man, whilst another keeps it constantly stirred, either by a shovel, or by a fork provided with numerous prongs, with which he from time to time removes the large stones, and throws back against the current such pieces of clay as continue to hang firmly together. The number of men working at a time varies from two to four, according to the tenacity of the dirt, and the quantity of water available. The small stones which gradually accumulate in the angle between the bottom and the perforated iron plate, *b*, are removed when necessary, and a fresh supply of pay dirt is continuously shovelled in at the head of the trough.

Fig. 10.

Section of Tom and Riffle Box.

Fig. 11.

Plan of Tom and Riffle Box.

This arrangement is most applicable to diggings yielding but a limited amount of pay dirt containing coarse gold; but even when quicksilver is used behind the riffles *c*, in the riffle box C, the loss of fine gold is considerable, although the constant falling of the water on it generally prevents packing.

The sluice, which has now generally superseded the tom, is not only capable of washing a much greater quantity of dirt in a given time, but is also attended with a less loss of gold.

Puddling Box.—The puddling box is a rough wooden case, usually about six feet square, and eighteen inches in depth, which is used for disintegrating very tough clay. The dirt is thrown into this box, and a considerable quantity of water added, with which it is stirred up by a rake, having very long and strong teeth, until the whole of the clay is held in suspension, when a plug, a few inches from the bottom, is removed, and the slimy matters run off. More clay and water are now introduced, and the operation is repeated until the box becomes filled with gravel and coarse sand to the level of the plug hole, when it is removed for the purpose of being washed up by the pan, cradle, or some similar appliance. In California, the puddling tub is only employed in diggings carried on on a very limited scale, and never where the sluice or the hydraulic process can be introduced. In Australia, on the contrary, where the supply of water is often scanty, washing by the aid of a puddling machine is generally resorted to. For small operations, half a porter barrel is sometimes used, the clay being stirred with a shovel; but in works conducted on a more extensive scale, an arrangement not unlike a brickmaker's pug-tub, set in motion either by horse or steam power, is generally used. This machine, when worked by steam power, consists of a large shallow tub with an upright shaft standing in its centre, provided with strong rake-like arms, set in motion by a mitre wheel attached to the perpendicular shaft. From these tubs the thin mud is tapped off, in the same way as from the puddling box, and the residues afterwards subjected to some process of washing. These machines are so general in Australia that in 1860 no less than 3,958 of them, worked by horse power, were in use in Victoria alone.

The Sluice.—This arrangement is now almost universally employed by Californian miners, and by it are, probably, collected at least eight-tenths of the gold furnished by the placer mines of that country. The sluice is generally a long wooden trough, having a considerable inclination or declivity, into which the pay dirt is shovelled, and through which a rapid stream of water is continually flowing. The bottom of this trough is provided with a series of riffles, generally containing mercury, by which the gold is retained, whilst the clay, sand, and gravel are carried off by the force of the current. The ordinary sluice is composed of a series of rough wooden boxes, each twelve feet in length, generally varying from sixteen to twenty inches in width, and from ten inches to a foot in depth, made of inch-and-half pine planks. In order to facilitate the making of these sluice boxes, the boards for the bottom are sawn, at the mill, four inches wider at one end than at the other. This enables the narrow end of one box to be fitted into the wide end of another, and in this way a sluice, several hundred feet in length, can be rapidly put together, or, if necessary, taken apart and removed. The descent of a sluice is called its *grade*, and is commonly from ten to eighteen inches on each box of twelve feet in length, and, consequently, a sluice having the latter inclination would be said to have an eighteen-inch grade. The grade to be employed is regulated by the position and length of the apparatus, and the nature of the dirt to be washed. The greater the descent, the more rapid will be the current, and, as a consequence, the greater is the danger of fine particles of gold being carried off by the water and lost. If the angle at which the boxes are set be considerable, the dirt will be rapidly disintegrated, but the danger of losing fine particles will be increased; whilst if the stuff to be washed contains much clay, a small inclination will not easily effect its disintegration. Generally speaking, therefore, a sluice with a rapid current of water requires to be made longer than one set more nearly on a level, and, for this reason, where a long sluice cannot be employed the inclination must be diminished.

Economy and the convenience of working render it necessary that the sluice should not be raised too high above the surface of the ground, and therefore the angle at which it is laid is somewhat influenced by the conformation of the country. There are, obviously, various considerations to be attended to in finding the proper grade; but in most instances a fall of less than ten inches, or more than twenty inches, on the length of a twelve-foot box, is not regarded as suitable for the ordinary sluice. In many claims the pay dirt contains large blocks of stone and boulders, each weighing from fifty to several hundred pounds, which have to be passed through the sluice, either whole or after being broken, and in such cases a large body of water and a rapid current are essential. The upper part of a sluice is sometimes made steep in order to effect the disintegration of the dirt, whilst the lower is placed at a less inclination for the purpose of collecting the gold, and this arrangement is often found advantageous. The ordinary clay met with in pay dirt is entirely taken up in suspension by the water of a sluice with a moderate grade, within the first two hundred feet, and the remainder of the boxes beyond that point are only useful in collecting gold. It is scarcely necessary to observe that when the gold is coarse, the inclination may be safely made greater than when it occurs in a finer state of division. In some claims the clay is so extremely tenacious that it will roll into balls, which are carried the whole length of an ordinary sluice without being much diminished in size. This has to be carefully avoided, by breaking up the lumps at the head of the sluice, since balls of plastic clay passing through the boxes not only do not give up the particles of gold they may contain, but are also liable to pick up others over which they may pass in their course.

Sluice boxes are always provided with some sort of false bottom for the purpose of retaining the gold, which would otherwise not only be taken away by the force of the current, but the bottoms themselves be rapidly worn out by the attrition of the stones and gravel passing over them.

In the majority of cases the false bottoms employed are composed of longitudinal bars *a*, from two to four inches in thickness, from three to seven inches in width, and about five feet six inches in length. These are wedged in the boxes, from an inch to two inches apart, by the cross pieces *b*, so that two lengths of bars are fitted in the bottom of each box, as seen in Figs. 12 and 13.

FIG. 12.

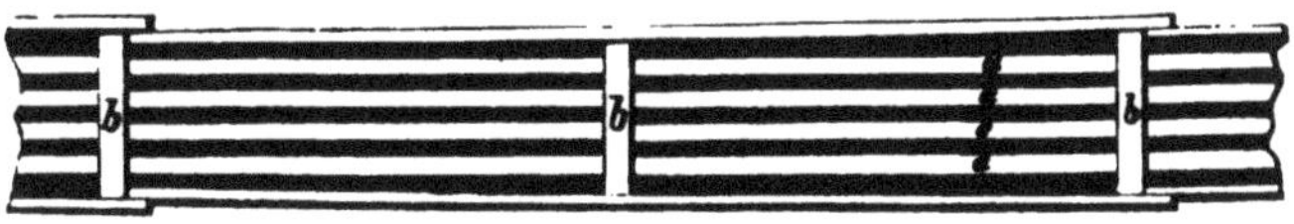

PLAN OF SLUICE BOX.

FIG. 13.

SECTION OF SLUICE BOX.

The whole of the boxes are thus fitted with these bars, and the bottom of the sluice consequently represents a series of rectangular depressions, of the thickness of the bars, and several feet in length, in which the gold, mercury, and amalgam are caught. It is evident that the larger pieces of gold will be readily caught by such an arrangement without the use of quicksilver; but in order to retain the finer particles, the employment of this substance becomes essential.

When the sluice boxes have been all joined together, and the bars wedged into the bottom of each, the apparatus is ready for working; for although the boxes are generally made of planks rough from the saw, the swelling of the wood, on the introduction of water, and the clay which gets into the joints, as soon as the wash dirt is thrown in, quickly closes them, and renders the whole arrangement water-tight. The pay dirt is now shovelled in at the head, the number of men employed being regulated by the size of the sluice, and the nature of the dirt, which the current rapidly disintegrates, carrying off the clay in suspension, and rolling the pebbles and boulders onward by the force of the stream. The first dirt thrown in closes the joints of the troughs, and fills the spaces between the riffles, but nevertheless leaves a sufficient number of pits and inequalities for retaining the particles of gold and amalgam.

The amount of dirt which can be thrown into an ordinary sluice in a day by one man, depends on the compactness and state of aggregation of the deposit, and varies from about two to five cubic yards. About one hour and a half or two hours after the commencement of sluicing, some mercury is poured into the head of the apparatus, from whence it gradually finds its way downwards, in the direction of the current, but is still chiefly retained by the upper boxes of the series. Smaller quantities of quicksilver are also introduced between the bars, along in various places in the boxes; and the greater the amount of fine gold present, the larger must be the quantity of mercury used.

When the gold contained in the dirt is exceedingly fine, an amalgamated copper plate is sometimes resorted to. This plate is generally three feet in width, and six in length; is set nearly level, and, when the sluice is a very large one, the stream is frequently divided into two or three separate portions, each of which is conducted over a distinct amalgamated plate.* A well-amalgamated copper plate is considered as effective for saving fine gold, as an equal surface of pure mercury, and is not only cheaper, but also more easily managed. The copper plate is, in most instances, placed at a considerable distance from the head of the sluice, and the dirt and water falling upon it first passes through a sheet iron screen, having apertures half an inch in length, and a sixteenth of an inch in width. The amalgamation of the copper plate is effected by first washing over its upper face with dilute nitric acid, and then rubbing on, with a rag, quicksilver

* For the purposes of hydraulic mining sluices from four to seven feet in width are frequently employed.

on which a little diluted nitric acid has been first poured, so as to form a certain amount of nitrate of mercury. When a plate has been thus well covered, this operation need never be repeated, it being only necessary to sprinkle its surface occasionally with a little fresh quicksilver, in proportion as the gold caught converts it into a solid amalgam.

In order that these plates should act satisfactorily, it is essential that the current should be slow, and the water shallow, since otherwise a considerable portion of the fine gold might escape without coming in contact with the face of the plate; and it is for this reason that in large sluices it is usual to divide the stream, and to pass each portion over a separate surface of amalgamated copper. Wherever a particle of gold has attached itself to the face of an amalgamated plate, others will be found to arrange themselves around it, evidently becoming more readily attached to those portions of the surface on which gold has been already caught, than on those on which no deposit of this metal has previously taken place. When a newly amalgamated plate is first used, its surface is apt to become tarnished by the formation of subsalts of copper, which forming a green slime, interfere with the adhesion of gold. This should be carefully scraped off, and the place from whence it has been removed rubbed with a little fresh mercury. The larger the amount of gold deposited on the surface of a copper plate, the better it is considered for the purpose of arresting the progress of fine particles of that metal; but as the accumulation of a very large quantity of auriferous amalgam might give rise to losses through theft, it is injudicious to allow too great a thickness to accumulate before being removed. For this purpose, the plate is taken up and heated over a fire, until the hand cannot bear to remain on it beyond about a second, when the amalgam becomes softened and loosened, and can be easily removed by scraping. The plate, after cooling, may now be again rubbed with quicksilver, without the aid of nitric acid, and is again ready for use. A copper plate, to be employed for this purpose, should not be too thin, since it would quickly become permeated by the quicksilver, and break almost as readily as glass; a plate of one-sixteenth of an inch in thickness will, however, with careful management, last several years. It is evident that the coarser gold will be caught near the head of the sluice, and the finer particles be arrested further down, in proportion to their state of division. When dirt contains a large proportion of coarse gold, the mercury is frequently introduced, at a distance of from forty to sixty yards from the head, so as to catch only the fine gold in the form of amalgam.

The collection of the dirt which accumulates in the bottom of the sluice, and the separation from it of the gold, amalgam, and quicksilver, is called the *cleaning up*, and the time between one cleaning up and another is called a *run*. In most cases, an ordinary sluice runs only during the day, but, in some instances, the work is continued throughout the whole twenty-four hours. A run commonly lasts about a week, and the cleaning up is not unfrequently reserved for the Sunday. This usually occupies about half a day, and consequently, on account of the loss of time entailed, must not be too frequently repeated. In some claims it is not done until the riffles are so worn and damaged, as to require to be overhauled and repaired.

When a cleaning up has been decided on, no more dirt is thrown into the sluice, and the water is allowed to run through it until it passes off quite clear at the lower end. Some six or eight sets of bars are now taken up from the head of the sluice, and the dirt is washed down; whilst the gold and amalgam, which had been caught between them, is arrested by the first remaining set of bars, from whence it is taken out with a scoop into a pan or bucket. Another six or eight sets of riffle bars are now taken up, and the operation repeated, until the whole length of the sluice has been cleaned up.

The amalgam and mercury taken from the sluice are first separated from any admixture of sand by panning, and then strained, either through buckskin, or a piece of close canvas, which allows the liquid quicksilver to pass through, but retains the more solid amalgam. In order to obtain the gold in a metallic state, the amalgam must be subjected to a degree of heat capable of volatilising the quicksilver, which is thus expelled, leaving the gold in the form of a porous mass, of a light yellow colour. This operation is most economically performed in a cast iron retort, provided with a refrigerator, by which the mercury is condensed, and can be collected for subsequent use; but in many cases, and particularly in small claims, the miners drive off the quicksilver by heating the amalgam on a shovel, or on an iron plate, by which method of proceeding it is of course volatilised and lost, besides exposing those around to the danger of injury from the metallic vapours evolved. The amalgam obtained, after squeezing the superfluous mercury through cloth or buckskin, is generally calculated to afford from thirty-five to forty per cent. of retorted gold.

As before stated, the riffle bars are often between five and six feet in length, and sawn in the direction of the grain of the wood; but these, in claims where large quantities of pebbles and boulders are enclosed in the dirt, are rapidly worn away, and in some cases the bars are cut across the grain of the timber, and placed end upwards in the sluice. Riffles so constructed are found to last three times as long as those cut in the ordinary way, but it is generally difficult to get them more than about three feet in length, and consequently they require a little more time for fixing than the usual longitudinal bars. These *block riffles*, instead of being placed longitudinally in the boxes, are sometimes fixed transversely across them, and at distances of about two inches apart.

In small sluices, the bars are not always placed either longitudinally or transversely, but sometimes in a series of zigzags, as seen in Fig. 14.

FIG. 14.

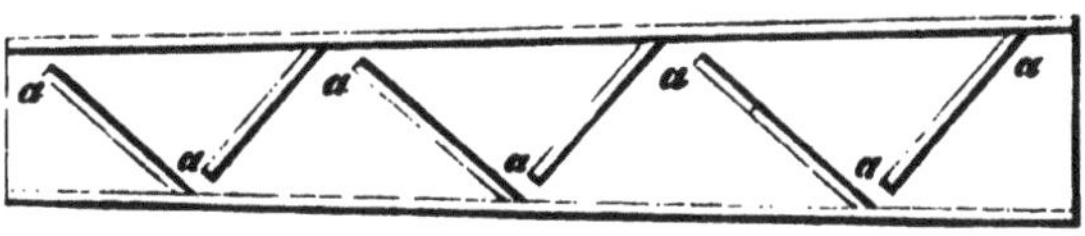

ZIGZAG RIFFLES.

The first bar in the sluice is nailed at an angle of 45° with the course of the box itself, but does not touch the opposite side, between which and its extremity is left a space *a*, of about an inch in width. Immediately below this open space another bar is fixed, at right angles to the first, touching the side of the box beneath the opening, and stopping an inch short of the other side. This is continued until near the lower end of the sluice, where there are either longitudinal riffles, or transverse blocks, as before described. When this arrangement of the bars is employed, it is evident that, although a large proportion of the dirt and water will pass over them directly down the trough, the heavier particles will sink to the bottom of the boxes, and being directed by the oblique riffles, will assume a tortuous course through that portion of the sluice. At a short distance from the head of sluices of this description is placed a vessel containing mercury, in which is a small hole, from whence it is allowed, very slowly, to escape into the sluice. This quicksilver runs down the arrangement, following the course of the riffles; and overtaking, and coming in contact with, the particles of gold, unites with it, and forms an amalgam, which is retained in that portion of the sluice provided with ordinary longitudinal riffles. It is necessary that these, and all other descriptions of sluice, should be carefully watched, in order to prevent any jamming of the larger boulders, or any local accumulations of dirt, which would interfere with their efficient action, and result in loss of gold.

In small sluices, it is sometimes customary not to allow the large pebbles to run throughout their whole extent, and stones of more than a few pounds in weight are therefore thrown out by a man provided with a prong, having numerous blunt parallel teeth, which, without being liable to injure the wood of which the boxes are made, enables him to remove the stones. Another contrivance for collecting fine gold is to impregnate the wood of which the riffles are made, with mercury. This is done by means of an ordinary gas-pipe, which is first ground to a thin edge at one end, and then driven into the wood forming the block riffles. On subsequently filling this pipe with quicksilver, the pressure of the column forces it into the pores of the wood, which afterwards acts somewhat similarly to the amalgamated copper plates before described, except that the resulting amalgam is removed by simply scraping the surface of the blocks. This process is not, however, often adopted, and is not generally to be recommended, since it requires more time to prepare the blocks than to amalgamate an ordinary copper plate, besides which its action is, on the whole, not so satisfactory.

When two companies are working claims side by side, a double sluice is, for the sake of economy, sometimes employed. In this case the boxes are made of double the usual width, and are divided in the middle by a longitudinal partition, so as to form two distinct sluices. This arrangement is also employed in claims where, to prevent loss of time, one side of the trough is made use of, whilst the other is being cleaned up; or in localities in which the supply of water is, during a portion of the year, sufficient for working both sluices, whilst in the dry season the quantity at command is only enough for one.

The *under-current sluice,* another modification which is often found advantageous, is represented Fig. 15.

In this arrangement a grating is placed in the bottom of the lower extremity of the last box in the series, and beneath this is introduced another sluice with a lower grade and fresh supply of water. The impetus acquired by the large boulders, in the first sluice, causes them to roll off over the grating, and, together with a portion of the water, to escape at the lower end; whilst the introduction of clear water, the less inclination, and more moderate current, determine the arrest of many particles of gold that would, under ordinary circumstances, be carried off and lost.

FIG. 15.

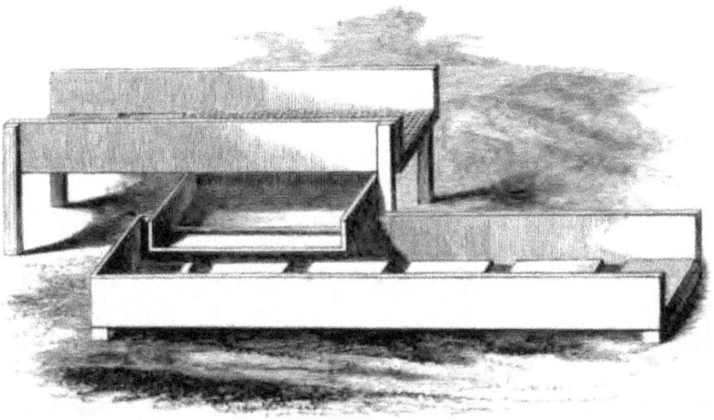

UNDER-CURRENT SLUICE.

The rapid wearing of all kinds of wooden riffles, and the facilities they afford for stealing the auriferous amalgam by night, has led to the introduction of what are known as *rock sluices*, but these are attended with the disadvantage of being more difficult to clean up, and consequently to prepare for working after being cleaned up, than any of those before described. The sluice itself is formed of the ordinary rough wooden boxes, which are coarsely paved with lenticular rolled pebbles, laid on edge, and which, when the wash dirt has passed over them for a short time, become securely embedded by the sand which collects between them. In *tail sluices* the paving stones employed are generally larger than those used for the bottom of an ordinary sluice. These stone bottoms are only employed in wide boxes, and have generally an inclination of about an inch to the foot. When the sluice is cleaned up, the stones have necessarily to be removed, and the bottom of the boxes repaired before again commencing to wash; but this, with experienced hands, is performed with considerable rapidity, since a miner, accustomed to the business, will pave some 200 feet of an ordinary sluice in the course of a day.

Tail sluices are arrangements for collecting gold still retained by the dirt which has passed through the ordinary sluice, and escaped being thoroughly impoverished in its progress. They are usually placed in a ravine through which the tailings from one or more sluices of the ordinary construction flow, and are only cleaned up after the

FIG. 16.

TAIL SLUICES, YUBA RIVER.
(From a Photograph.)

expiration of several weeks, receiving, in the meantime, no further attention than is necessary to prevent their choking. Tail sluices are generally large, long, and paved with blocks of stone, or wood placed on end, and often afford large profits to their proprietors. Both the dirt and water with which they are supplied is furnished by the sluices emptying into them, and they are in some instances made double, so that one side may be in working order whilst the other is being cleaned up. Many of the tail sluices on the Yuba are of extraordinary length, and some of them have been constructed as much as twenty feet in width. Fig. 16 is a view of two of the tail sluices on this river.

All the varieties of the sluice which have been hitherto described require wooden boxes or troughs, through which the water is conducted; but in localities where there is a large supply of water, plenty of pay dirt of low produce, and the necessary declivity, a sluice is sometimes improvised without the use of wood. Such arrangements are called *ground sluices*, and in order to prepare one, a small gutter is first made with a sufficient inclination through the dirt to be washed, and into this is directed a stream of water, by the action of which the channel rapidly becomes deepened and enlarged. As soon as the sides and bottom of this ditch have ceased to become rapidly eroded by the action of the current alone, the miners begin to assist the operation by pinching off scales of ground from the bank, which, falling into the stream, are acted on precisely as in the case of the ordinary board sluice. No mercury or riffles are employed in the ground sluice, but unless the bottom consists of a rough and irregular bed rock, a few large stones should be roughly thrown in for the purpose of arresting the gold, which, if the surface were not more or less uneven, would be liable to pass off and be lost. When a considerable amount of dirt has been passed through a sluice of this description, the water is diverted, and the auriferous matters, thus partially washed, collected, and cleaned up in a tom, cradle, or short box sluice. The ground sluice is seldom employed on claims where mining is continuously carried on, and is most advantageously introduced in localities in which water is abundant for a few days only, after heavy rains, and consequently where it would not be judicious to erect large and expensive sluices. When, as is sometimes the case, either in hydraulic or other mines, a sluice passes through an adit level, or day tunnel, it is called a *tunnel sluice*, but these differ in no respect from other sluices except in their situation.

River Mining.—River mining consists in turning the stream of a river, by means of a dam in connexion with a ditch or large wooden flume, and subsequently washing the dirt, found in its bed, for the gold which it may contain. The streams selected for this purpose are generally mere mountain torrents, of which the banks are steep and irregular; and consequently a ditch being impracticable, recourse is had to a rough wooden trough or flume. River mining can only be successfully carried on during the summer and early fall, when the water is not only low, but the miner will not be subject to have all his work destroyed by a sudden freshet, which might sweep before it his flume, dam, and all his tools together. This branch of mining is, however, subject to many disadvantages, from which the other descriptions are comparatively free. In the first place it cannot be carried on during more than half the year, and as the miner has no means of prospecting under the surface of the water, and thereby ascertaining the value of the dirt, it may, after he has expended a large amount of time and labour, prove almost worthless when the diversion of the stream has been effected. Secondly, he is constantly exposed to the danger of floods, which may, by carrying away his flume and destroying all his work, suddenly deprive him of the advantages to be derived from his outlay of capital and labour.

These disadvantages, coupled with the fact that the principal river washings have been already exhausted, have almost done away with this description of mining in California. In some few instances enterprises of this kind have been attended with highly remunerative results ; but in the majority of cases, the gold extracted has not repaid the labour and capital expended to procure it. A long flume of a sufficient capacity to carry off the whole of the water of a considerable river, is in itself an expensive piece of work ; but when it is taken into consideration that a greater or less amount of leakage from the dam has always to be contended with, and that water is constantly finding its way into the river bed from the various ravines trending in that direction, it becomes evident that the difficulties of river mining are of no ordinary character. It is therefore necessary to provide machinery for pumping out this influx of water ; and as large rocks, often weighing several tons, are frequently met with, they have to be removed, by means of cranes, before the most valuable dirt can be reached. River mining is consequently never attempted by single individuals, but is always carried on by associated companies, either entirely composed of working miners, or by miners assisted by the storekeepers and other substantial inhabitants of the neighbourhood. In the latter case, those who are not directly connected with the business pay their proportion of the expenses in money, the merchants supply the necessary provisions, the saw-mill proprietors the wood, and the carpenters make the flumes, whilst the miners prepare the dam, and perform any other work that may be required.

Beach Mining.—Beach mining is the process of extracting gold from the sands on the sea-shore, and has been extensively carried on between Cape Mendocino in California, and the mouth of the river Umpqua in Oregon. The beach is here narrow, and lies at the foot of a bluff of auriferous sand, which, in stormy weather, is undermined by the waves, and the lighter constituents being washed away, leave sands which are often rich in gold. The gold is here found in a finely divided state, associated with the heavier and darker coloured sands, the position of which is frequently changed by the action of the tides and currents. In this way, a part of the beach which may, on one day, be deeply covered with sand, in which particles of fine gold can be readily seen, will, on the following, be left either bare, or covered with sand containing little or no gold, and it therefore requires constant attention on the part of those directing the operations, in order to select the most auriferous descriptions for treatment.

The Companies engaged in this kind of mining usually consist of about ten men, including the foreman, who every morning rides along the beach for a distance of about two miles, on either side of the camp, for the purpose of ascertaining where, on that day, the richest sands are to be met with. When this has been determined, each man of the company proceeds to the spot with two pack mules provided with raw hide sacks, *alforjas*, in which the sand is collected and carried to the washing place, which is sometimes several miles distant. Sea water is occasionally employed for this purpose, but fresh is generally preferred; and for this reason, the sand is in most cases transported to a running stream at no great distance from the shore. It sometimes happens that rich sand is not met with within twelve miles of the camp, but in such cases it requires to be highly auriferous in order to support the expenses of transport. The richest sands are found far down the beach at low tides, and consequently when such a tide occurs during still weather, every exertion is made to obtain as large a supply as possible; since with high tides and a rough sea, there is little to be done in this class of mining. The sands thus obtained, being entirely free from clay, are very readily treated, and a couple of days' working with a sluice will generally effect the washing of all the sands collected during a month.

Water Supply.—In proportion as the shallow placers in the ravines and river beds of California, from which the first supply of gold was obtained by simple means and at a small cost, became more or less completely exhausted, the necessity of devising some ready method by which the deep placers could be economically worked, naturally forced itself on the attention of the mining community. In order to accomplish this object, it was necessary to convey a copious supply of water to auriferous deposits far above the level of the rivers in the vicinity, and often situated at a great distance from the present streams of the country. This required the expenditure of large sums of money for the construction of the canals and aqueducts, by which it was brought from springs and reservoirs, at elevations such as to command the largest and most important diggings. This demand for the association of labour and capital soon called into existence numerous canal and ditch companies, the shareholders being for the most part miners, whose limited resources generally obliged them to borrow money from the local bankers, at rates of interest varying from three to five per cent. per month. In this way the Middle Yuba Canal Company was organised in 1853, the water being brought from a point on the Middle Yuba a little below Woolsey's Flat, where the river was dammed and the aqueduct commenced. The total expenditure involved in this enterprise, including the various branches, ditches, reservoirs, and extensions, has amounted to $600,000 or about 120,000*l.*; and the works are now capable of supplying thirty-eight cubic feet of water per second, which could at a comparatively small expense be increased to sixty cubic feet.

The first-named quantity is considered equivalent to nearly 1,500 inches, miner's measurement, and the second to 2,280 miner's inches.* The Eureka Canal was commenced in 1856, and has cost, including the various reservoirs and branches, $1,000,000, or 200,000*l.* The Eureka Lake is the largest reservoir now in connexion with this aqueduct, although it has been proposed to connect it with the Truckee Lake, which is a still more considerable body of water. At the outlet of the Eureka Lake a substantial granite dam raises its waters to the height of forty-two feet above their natural level. This is retained by a natural abutment of granite, capable of receiving, if necessary, an additional height of twenty feet. The width of this structure, at the base, is 120 feet, its height is seventy feet, and its length from bank to bank 250 feet. Its water face has a double lining of securely-fastened two and a half inch planking, and the flow of water is regulated by a sluice placed in a tunnel of strongly-arched masonry. The capacity of this reservoir is estimated at 933,000,000 cubic feet, or about five months' full supply of the canal. During from four to five months in

* The miner's inch of water, in California, is the quantity which will flow through an opening one inch square under a mean head of six inches, and the working day is generally calculated at ten hours.

each year, however, it obtains the necessary amount of water from other sources. The snow accumulates in the Sierras, in great quantities during the winter months, and the melting of this not only supplies the flow of the streams, but also fills, to overflowing, the various mountain lakes and artificial reservoirs, in which the waters are stored in reserve against the droughts of late summer and autumn. Besides this main reservoir, there are several others, of which Lake Faucherie is the most important.

The Eureka Canal is constructed partially of earth and partially of a wooden fluming: the dimensions of the main flume are five feet nine inches in width, and three feet in depth, with a fall of sixteen feet per mile* The discharge is ninety-six and a half cubic feet of water per second, or 3,667 miner's inches. We shall therefore be below the truth if we assume that this canal is capable of supplying, after allowing for leakage, 3,000 inches of water in a working day of ten hours, which is equal to 7,200 inches during the twenty-four hours, or, as the discharge per second is ninety-six and a half cubic feet, it will afford 8,337,600 cubic feet of water in twenty-four hours.

Among the most remarkable objects that strike the traveller on first visiting the mining regions of California, are the lofty aqueducts, constructed of trestle-work, for the purpose of conveying water across deep valleys and ravines. The Magenta and National aqueducts are the most considerable constructions of this description on the line of the Eureka Canal. The Magenta aqueduct is 1,400 feet in length, whilst the length of the National is 1,800 feet. The greatest height of the former is 126 feet, and that of the latter 65 feet. The dimensions of the flume are seven feet in width by fifteen inches in depth, and its inclination one foot in a hundred. In order, as much as possible, to avoid the action of the wind, which often blows strongly up the valley, the sides are made low, and considerable width given to the bottom. The legs of the trestles were all cut out of trees which grew in the vicinity, and are without a splice from foundation to top. The sides of the flume are made of whole scantlings, seven and a half inches in width, and thirty feet in length. The trestles are placed thirty feet from centre to centre, and are well and securely braced. This aqueduct was put together in sections of thirty feet, and each, when completed, raised into its place from the spot on which it was constructed, by which means the use of scaffolding

* When a less inclination is given, the water is liable to freeze in winter.

was rendered unnecessary. The aggregate length of all the ditches belonging to the Eureka Company is about 200 miles.

The foregoing description of the works of the Eureka Lake Water Company will afford some idea of the extensive scale on which such enterprises are conducted in California, as nearly all the more important mining districts now receive a plentiful supply of water by similar means. The following woodcut, Fig. 17, will serve to illustrate

FIG. 17.

FLUME NEAR SMARTSVILLE, YUBA COUNTY.
(*From a Photograph.*)

the method adopted for the construction of high aqueducts for mining purposes.

Hydraulic Mining.—In order to treat most successfully the extensive beds of detritus forming the deep placers previously described, the following conditions are involved :—

1st. Whatever may be the depth of the auriferous gravel, the whole must be removed down to the bed rock.

2nd. This must, as far as possible, be effected by the force of a column of water, since manual labour becomes too expensive when from 1,500 to 4,500 cubic yards of dirt have to be disposed of during each working day of ten hours.

3rd. The mechanical disintegration of the more or less indurated gravel must go on contemporaneously with the washing of the resulting debris, and be effected by the same supply of water.

4th. Provision must be made for readily disposing of the large amounts of refuse resulting from the removal of such vast masses of auriferous gravel.

In practice these conditions are fulfilled in the following way :—

After having selected a sufficient extent of suitable ground, the water from a canal is brought, by side flumes or aqueducts, to the head of the mining ground, with an elevation of from 120 to 160 feet above the level of the bed rock, where it is conducted into a wooden tank, into which it constantly flows. This box is provided with a valve, and from it the water is conveyed to the bottom of the claim by means of a strong sheet iron rivetted pipe, from eight to fourteen inches in diameter, communicating at the bottom with a thick rectangular cast iron chamber, in the sides of which are apertures provided with slide valves and union joints, to which can be fitted strong flexible hose terminating in bronze nozzles from two and a half to three inches in diameter. The arrangement of the bulk head or pressure box, into which the water is conducted at the head of the column, will be understood by reference to Fig. 18.

The flexible hose are usually made of closely-sewn heavy duck, and will, without any external support, bear the pressure of a column of about fifty feet in perpendicular height; when however, as is most frequently the case, the pressure employed is greater than this, they require to be strengthened by iron rings. The bands employed are placed over the hose at intervals of three inches from each other, and connected by means of four longitudinal cords, dividing the circumference into equal divisions. These *crinoline hose* are very flexible, and will, if well made, support, without danger of bursting, the pressure of a column of water a hundred and eighty feet in height. Instead of increasing the strength of the canvas hose by the use of iron rings, they are sometimes tightly covered with a netting of cord, half an inch in diameter, forming meshes two inches square. In some claims also the cast-iron chamber at the bottom of the pressure pipe is dispensed with, and a separate iron pipe connected with each nozzle, or two or more hose joined to each by means of T pieces; but the use of one large pressure pipe with the close chamber at the bottom is, in most cases, to be preferred. From each of these

FIG. 18.

PRESSURE BOX, YUBA RIVER.
(From a Photograph.)

nozzles streams of water are directed against the face of the gravel to be washed, with a force which can only be compared with that of ordnance, and the power developed by this means, where the supply of water is large and the height of the column considerable, is perfectly astonishing. The volume of water employed varies in accordance with various local circumstances; but it is not uncommon to see four or five such streams acting simultaneously against the face of the same bank—five hundred miner's inches of water constantly discharged against the face of a bank, under a pressure of from sixty to a hundred pounds to the square inch, aided by its disintegrating and softening action, bring down large sections of the gravelly mass, which fall with violence, and render it necessary for the workmen directing the operation to exercise great caution in order to avoid accidents.

The number of men necessary to carry on the operations of a hydraulic claim is very limited, since, in addition to those engaged in directing the nozzles, only one person is generally employed in attending to the sluice, so as to prevent its being choked by the dirt washed down from above.

The following woodcut, Fig. 19, shows the method of applying the jets of water against the side of a bank of dirt.

FIG. 19.

HYDRAULIC MINING, WASHING DOWN BANK.

(*From a Photograph.*)

The debris thus produced becomes rapidly disintegrated, and, borne along by the resistless force of the water, is carried forward to the sluice, through which it passes with the whole volume of the turbid stream.

Banks of more than eighty feet in height are generally worked in two benches. The upper half is never so rich as the lower, but is usually less compact and more easily removed by the action of water. The lower section, on the contrary, is often very closely cemented together, and most frequently requires the aid of gunpowder in order to loosen it, so as to enable the water to remove it with sufficient rapidity. For this purpose a tunnel is driven into the bank, at the level of the bed rock, for a distance of some fifty or sixty feet, and from its extremity another drift is extended on either side, at right angles, in which a large quantity of gunpowder is placed. The charge usually varies from fifty to two hundred barrels, which after being securely built in, is fired by a slow match, and by its explosion loosens a large mass of the compact conglomerate, which is afterwards readily acted on by the force of the currents of water brought to bear against it.

When the conformation of the country admits of it, a tunnel is sometimes brought in from the nearest and most convenient ravine, at a considerable depth in the bed rock, at a gradient of from one in twelve to one in twenty, and varying in length from a few hundred to several thousand feet. Such tunnels have not unfrequently occupied from three to four years in driving, and have cost very large sums of money. On the extremity of this long tunnel a shaft is sunk, through which the pay dirt is washed, and the level itself becomes a channel in which the sluice boxes are fixed, for the double purpose of directing the stream and collecting the gold. In such cases it is usual to employ a double sluice, in order that one side may be cleaned up whilst the other is in active operation, by which means all loss of time in working the claim is avoided. When this method of proceeding is adopted, the debris produced by the united action of the jets of water directed against the bank is rapidly carried forward by the current to the mouth of the shaft, down which it is precipitated with great violence, and being often accompanied by boulders of a hundred or two pounds in weight, a powerful disintegrating action is the result of the fall.

In some claims a system of tunnels is extended in the bed rock, very much as in a coal mine; and after dividing the ground into separate blocks by proper levels, they are washed away by the hydraulic process, after which the whole mass settles down and is easily disintegrated by the action of water.

The sluices employed in connexion with hydraulic mining are made wider than those used for other purposes, and are sometimes provided with wooden riffles, kept apart by slips of wood; in others their bottoms are paved with stone, as previously described. When wooden riffles are employed, they are composed of blocks of wood cut transversely across the tree, and placed end upwards in the sluice box. In this case the cavities which occur between the different blocks form the spaces in which the gold is collected, and are found very efficient for this purpose. A good general idea of the appearance of the sluice belonging to an ordinary hydraulic claim is afforded by Fig. 20.

FIG. 20.

SLUICE AND TUNNEL, TIMBUCTOO.

(From a Photograph.)

Rude as this method of saving gold appears, experience has shown that a larger proportion of the metal is collected by it than by any other process, and that at the same time the cost of handling a cubic yard of dirt is infinitely less by the hydraulic, than by any other system of mining. In fact, it would be utterly impossible to treat such enormous masses of dirt, as are now daily operated on, by any other known means.

As an illustration of the amount of work which can be performed in a given time by hydraulic mining, we give the results obtained at the Eureka Claim, near San Juan, California, where the bed of pay dirt is about 135 feet in depth.*

The upper portion of this deposit to the depth of seventy feet does not contain a large amount of gold, but is easily washed, whilst the lower portion, having a thickness of sixty-five feet, is much richer, but cemented together, and the work is therefore carried on under conditions of considerable difficulty. The pay dirt is reached by a bed-rock tunnel of a great length, which cost on an average $8 per foot, and of which the total expense was $28,000. The work is carried on by means of four *jets d'eau*, discharging together about 208 gallons per second, or 12,500 gallons per minute, under a pressure of 140 feet. The whole of the operations are conducted by four men, and after the expiration of ten working days, the washing down of fresh earth is suspended and the sluices cleaned up.

During this period of ten days about 36,500 cubic yards of gravel are worked over, the cost of working being nearly as follows:

Cost of Water	$1,000
Labour	173
Sundries	100
Total	$1,273

* The following statistics relate to another hydraulic claim near the same locality:—Capital invested, $7,000. Length of time during which the claim has been worked, 16 months, in two seasons of 8 months each. Water used, 350 miner's inches; pressure, 160 feet: water brought 2,800 feet, through 13-inch pipe; used through two nozzles of 2½ inches, and one nozzle of 2 inches diameter; water all used through the pipes. Running night and day; twenty-four hours estimated as a day's work; water costs 20c. per inch, or $70 per day. Total expenses per day, about $115. During the two seasons this company has paid all its expenses, and repaid $4,000 of its capital. The gravel has averaged, gross returns, about 3c. per ton of 15 cubic feet; the quantity removed daily has been about 4,250 tons. If this gravel had been even slightly cemented, the cost of working would have been materially increased. The above are supposed to be about the poorest gravels worked in California.

The gold taken from the sluice at the end of this period fetches, on an average, $6,000; and when the operations are confined to the lower portions only of the gravel, the value of the gold obtained increases from $16,000 to $20,000.

As an evidence of the enormous advantages possessed by the hydraulic process over every other system of placer mining, it may be stated, that taking a miner's wages at $4 per day, the cost of handling a cubic yard of gravel will be nearly as follows:—

With the pan	$20·00
„ rocker	5·00
„ long tom	1·00
By hydraulic process	·05

With reference to the enormous power of this system, Professor Silliman observes, "Man has in the hydraulic process taken command of Nature's agencies, employing them for his own benefit, and compelling her to surrender the treasure locked up in the auriferous gravel by the use of the same forces which she employed in distributing it." *

The water is usually supplied to the various mining claims by independent associations, who charge for it at rates varying from 10c. to 40c. per miner's inch per working day of ten hours, but the average charge may be estimated at 16c. The consumption of each mining claim in active work may be taken at about three hundred miner's inches; and this quantity flowing for ten hours will be equal to 284,210 cubic feet, or 1,771,219 imperial gallons. †

The amount of water distributed to the various claims is ascertained by conducting a stream from the canal into a measuring box, from twelve to fourteen feet square, in the sides of which openings are made two inches in height, and extending nearly across three of its sides. These openings are closed by slide valves when not required,

* Report on the Deep Placers of the North and Middle Yuba, p. 22. Silliman.

† In order to soften the bank, when the gravels are slightly cemented, it is usual to cut a trench across it, a short distance in advance of the breast. Water is allowed to flow into this, and, by percolating through the gravels, it has a tendency to soften the cementing ingredients of the deposit. When the bank is naturally soft, and consequently removed with great facility, it is customary to admit a certain amount of water into the sluice in addition to that passing through the nozzles. This is done for the purpose of so diluting the clay and fine sand as to allow the gold an opportunity of coming in contact with the mercury between the riffle blocks.

and the sectional area through which the water flows determines the number of inches used. The amount of water discharged by one miner's inch, in ten hours, is equivalent to 947 cubic feet.

In some cases, instead of bringing the water directly into a claim by means of an open aqueduct, it is found more convenient to place the pressure box on some neighbouring elevation, from which the supply is conducted, by an inclined iron pipe, to the hose box at the face of the diggings. Fig. 21 represents this method of arrangement.

FIG. 21.

IRON PIPES.
(From a Photograph.)

The iron pipe, although, in California, generally more expensive than a wooden flume, has the advantage of preventing loss by evaporation and leakage, whilst the full pressure can be obtained at any point along its course by the introduction of a union joint, to which a valve may be attached, for the purpose, when necessary, of cutting off the supply; such a branch and valve are seen in the woodcut to the left of the main pipe. It sometimes happens that the pay dirt in a hydraulic claim contains a thick band of non-auriferous clay, which is not readily taken up by water, and is liable to pick up gold if allowed to pass through the sluices in the form of rolled pellets. In such cases the clay band is undermined by the judicious use of the nozzles, and, after dividing the detached portions into fragments of a manageable size, they are taken up by a crane provided with a long jib. This, by making half a revolution, deposits the mass behind the workings, and at a distance of many yards from the face of the pay dirt; after the removal of the clay, the washing of the dirt proceeds in the usual way. This arrangement is also used for the removal of any very large boulders that may be met with in the dirt.

Cranes used for this purpose are frequently worked by hydraulic pressure supplied by a branch pipe from the main, and are very simply constructed. To the pinion shaft of the winch is attached a S-shaped flyer, through which the water rushes, as in Barker's mill, and a rotary motion is the result. The orifices of the revolving fly are provided with valves so constructed, that, in case of the speed becoming too great, they become partially closed by the centrifugal force acquired, and the action of the machine is consequently as easily controlled as that of the steam-engine by its governor. Companies formed in California for the purpose of supplying the various diggings with water have, as a general rule, been highly remunerative to the shareholders, and the large annual revenue derived from some of them will be understood when it is stated that the receipts of the Eureka Company alone, during three years, amounted to $626,560 (= 125,312*l.*). The expenses during the same period were about $120,000, or 24,000*l.*, leaving a clear profit of $506,560, or 101,312*l.* on the three years' operations.

Dry Washing.—Dry Washing is a process for winnowing gold from dirt, which in the early days of Californian mining was much employed, by Mexicans, in localities where water could not be procured for the purpose of washing. In diggings of this description the richest dirt only is selected and placed on a raw hide, on which, after it has become thoroughly dry, it is pulverised by rubbing between the hands, and the coarser particles of stone and pebbles picked out. The miner now takes a large shallow basin, called a *batea*, and with a circular motion throws the dirt into the air, allowing the wind to carry off the lighter portions, and catching the remainder as it falls in the batea. This operation is repeated until what remains in the basin contains a large proportion of gold, when its further purification is effected by blowing with the mouth. This operation is similar to the old method of separating corn from chaff, and is conducted in very much the same way. Instead of using the wooden dish, two men sometimes take a hide, or blanket, in which they throw up the dirt for the purpose of exposing it to the action of the wind. The dry digger never goes very deep for his dirt, but unless it be rich in gold this method of operating cannot yield him remunerative returns. Instead of removing the surface earth, he frequently digs a pit six or eight feet deep, and then burrows after the pay dirt. This method of mining, which is not entirely confined to dry washings, is called *coyoting*, from the supposed resemblance of openings so made to the burrows of the coyote, or Californian wolf.

CHAPTER IX.

VEIN MINING IN CALIFORNIA AND AUSTRALIA.

QUARTZ MINING—TESTING GOLD QUARTZ—BATEA—HORN SPOON—ARRASTRE—CHILIAN MILL—STAMPING MILL—AMALGAMATING IN BATTERY—IRON BATTERY BOX—SCREENS—SINGLE CAMS—SEPARATION OF GOLD—BLANKETS—AMALGAMATED COPPER PLATES—CLEANING UP—SETTLING PITS—AMALGAMATOR—ATTWOOD'S SYSTEM OF AMALGAMATION—LOSS OF GOLD—CONCENTRATION OF TAILINGS—ROCKER—CONCAVE BUDDLE—BRADFORD'S SEPARATOR—EXTRACTION OF GOLD FROM SULPHIDES—BAUX AND GUIOD'S AMALGAMATOR—CHLORINATION PROCESS—ANALYSES OF CALIFORNIAN PYRITES—RETORTING—MELTING—TABULAR STATEMENT OF THE OPERATIONS OF THE PRINCIPAL CALIFORNIAN QUARTZ MILLS.

THE processes employed for the extraction of gold quartz differ in no respect from ordinary mining operations applied to the working of regular mineral veins, and will consequently require no special description. When the conformation of the country admits of working by means of a day level, it is driven in from some convenient valley in the neighbourhood of the vein, and the rock is obtained by stoping in the usual way. If, on the contrary, there be no facilities for this method of commencing the work, shafts are at once begun from the surface, either perpendicularly, so as to intersect the lode at some convenient depth, or, still more frequently, an inclined shaft is put down on the course of the vein itself. When the mine is worked by means of an adit level, the rock broken in the interior is trammed through it into the open air for subsequent treatment; but if the extraction be conducted by the aid of shafts, the auriferous quartz is drawn to the surface by skips or waggons running on inclined tramways in connexion with a horse whim or steam-engine. In the case of very narrow veins some of the enclosing rock has frequently to be broken with the lode in order to afford room for the miner, whilst, in wide ones, it often happens that a portion only is sufficiently rich to pay the expenses of extraction and treatment, and the remainder is consequently allowed to remain in the mine. Sometimes also the walls of a vein, and particularly the foot wall, contain a sufficient amount of gold to make its extraction a matter of importance, and when this occurs a portion of the enclosing rock is necessarily excavated. In some veins the rock is, generally speaking, barren, containing traces merely of the precious metal, the gold only occurring in paying quantities in pockets, at considerable distances from each other. In others the pay rock forms bands or streaks, running more or less parallel with the walls of the lode, and frequently separated from the non-productive portion by a distinct heading or band of country rock. Other veins are productive throughout their entire width, but seldom contain visible gold. These veins are not unfrequently lamellar in their structure, and contain thin interfoliations of slate parallel with their walls, as in the case of the Norambagua lode in Grass Valley. The most profitable leads are usually those which afford a large supply of rock obtainable at a cheap rate, and uniformly yielding an amount of gold in excess of the cost of extraction and treatment.

In all mines, however, the produce is, to a certain extent, variable, and in the majority of cases the best rock occurs in shoots having a known inclination in the direction of the extension of the vein in length.*

From the general irregularity of the produce, it is impossible to ascertain the average yield of vein-stuff without crushing and experimenting on large quantities; but the most usual method of judging, approximately, of the value of rock, is to pulverise a small quantity and wash the resulting powder in a batea or horn spoon. In selecting the rock for this purpose, it is evidently of the greatest importance that it should represent a fair average of the vein or streak from which it is taken, and consequently several hundred-weights should be broken from the whole area of the exposed surface, taking care that every part be represented by samples of nearly equal weights. The whole must now be broken by a hammer on an iron plate, into pieces of about the size of walnuts. The resulting heap is then carefully mixed, by turning over with a shovel, and subsequently cut through the middle, so as to leave a trench through its centre, extending to the floor on which it has been placed. The two sides are afterwards carefully scraped down, and removed as a representative sample on which the yield of the vein is to be estimated. For the

* These pay shoots have generally the direction of the striæ formed by dynamic action on the walls of the vein.

purpose of a rough approximation this may be at once pulverised in a mortar or otherwise, and its contents judged of in accordance with the results obtained by washing. Where, however, greater accuracy is aimed at, and the original heap contained a large quantity of broken rock, at least a hundred-weight should be scraped down from the sides of the cutting, and this, after being further reduced to the size of peas, must be again cut through, and a sample of about four pounds obtained, by the means employed in the first instance, as the final sample. This is pulverised in a mortar, and the whole of it passed through a sieve of wire gauze, of forty holes to the lineal inch, after which it is ready for treatment, either by washing or assay.

The most accurate results are obtained by carefully washing a four-pound sample in the batea (Fig. 22), which is about twenty inches in diameter, and two and a half in depth.

Fig. 22.

Batea.

After having in this way concentrated the gold in about an ounce of sand and pyrites, this residue may be either subjected to assay, or the sulphides dissolved by nitric acid, and the gold extracted by amalgamation with a little mercury, which is subsequently volatilised, and the gold weighed. In either case, calculations are made on the four-pound sample, and when the residue has been subjected to fusion very accurate results are obtained. When amalgamation of the residue is resorted to, allowance must be made for the increase of weight arising from the impurities usually contained in the gold of the district.

The spoon employed for washing small samples of pulverised quartz is made by cutting a large ox horn as shown at Fig. 23, and is generally about three inches in width and eight or ten in length.

In this spoon about a pound of the powdered quartz is carefully washed, and from the results obtained the miner is enabled, by practice, to judge, with a certain degree of accuracy, as to the probable yield of the rock. The quartz, after being broken from the vein, must be finely pulverised before the extraction of the gold it contains can be effected. Various contrivances are used for this purpose, but one of the simplest forms of apparatus employed is the arrastre.

FIG. 23.

HORN, SHOWING METHOD OF CUTTING SPOON.

Arrastre.—The arrastre consists of a circular pavement of stone, about twelve feet in diameter, on which the quartz is ground by means of two or more large stones, or mullers, dragged continually over its surface, either by horses or mules, but more frequently by the latter. The periphery of the circular pavement is surrounded by a rough kerbing of wood or flat stones, forming a kind of tub about two feet in depth, and in its centre is a stout wooden post, firmly bedded in the ground, and standing nearly level with the exterior kerbing. Working on an iron pivot in this central post is a strong upright wooden shaft, secured at its upper extremity to a horizontal beam by another journal, which is often merely a prolongation of the shaft itself. This upright shaft is crossed at right angles by two strong pieces of wood, forming four arms, of which one is made sufficiently long to admit of attaching two mules for working the machine. The grinding is performed by four large blocks of hard stone, usually porphyry or granite, attached to the arms, either by chains or thongs of raw hide, in such a way that their edges, in the direction of their motion, are raised about an inch from the stone pavement, whilst the other side trails upon it. These stones each weigh from three to four hundred pounds, and in some arrastres two only are employed; in which case, a single mule is sufficient to work the machine. The following woodcut,

Fig. 24, is a sectional view of a Mexican arrastre, as usually constructed; in which A is the upright shaft; B, arms to which mullers C are attached; and D, the central block of wood in which the lower bearing works.

FIG. 24.

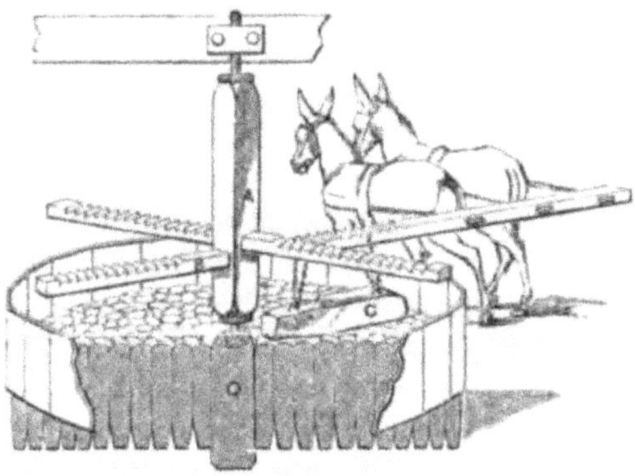

ARRASTRE.

Some of the arrastres used by Mexican gold miners, and for the purpose of testing the value of quartz veins, are very rudely put together, the bottom being made of unhewn flat stones laid down in clay; but in a well-constructed arrastre, intended to be permanently employed, the stones are carefully dressed and closely jointed, and, after being placed in their respective positions, are grouted in with hydraulic cement.

The charge for an ordinary arrastre is four hundred and fifty pounds of quartz, previously broken into pieces of about the size of pigeons' eggs. The machine is now set in motion, a little water being from time to time added, and at the expiration of from four to five hours the quartz has become reduced to a finely-divided state, and more water is added, until the contents of the arrastre assume the consistency of tolerably thick cream. Quicksilver is then sprinkled over its surface to the amount of one ounce and a quarter for every ounce of gold supposed to be contained in the finely-divided rock, which is generally known, with a considerable degree of accuracy, from the results obtained from previous charges. The grinding is after this continued for another two hours, during which time the mercury is divided into minute globules, and becomes disseminated throughout the mass, which should be of such a consistency as not to allow it to sink to the bottom, but be so held in suspension as to meet, and amalgamate with, all the particles of gold. At the expiration of this time the amalgamation is considered complete, and the process of settling the amalgam from the ground silicious matter is commenced. Water is now let into the paste so as to render it very thin, and perfectly mobile, the mules being driven very slowly, in order to allow the particles of gold and amalgam to yield to the influence of their densities, and to sink to the bottom. After having in this way slowly agitated the mixture for about half an hour, the thin mud is allowed to run off, leaving behind it, in the bottom of the arrastre, the gold combined with mercury in the form of amalgam. Another charge of broken quartz is now put in, and the operation is repeated, time after time, until it is thought desirable to stop for the purpose of cleaning up. The length of a run, or the period which is allowed to elapse between one cleaning up and another, varies according to circumstances. In the roughly constructed arrastre, having a bottom of uncut stones laid in clay, the run is seldom less than ten days, and is sometimes extended to three weeks or a month. In this case the amalgam settles in the crevices between the paving stones, which have to be dug up, and all the sand and mud between them carefully washed. If, however, the machine be well constructed, and provided with a closely-paved bottom, the cleaning up is more frequently repeated, since the quicksilver and amalgam do not find their way so readily between the stones, but remain on the surface, from which they are easily collected in an iron vessel, for subsequent treatment by straining and retorting.

The arrastre does its work slowly, and consumes a large amount of power in proportion to the quantity of rock crushed, but is an excellent amalgamator, and is often valuable for the purpose of testing newly-discovered veins, and ascertaining their approximate yield. It is also the arrangement most commonly adopted by a miner, who, having found a rich pocket in his vein, is desirous of converting a portion of it into money, and of ascertaining whether it be likely to continue productive, before incurring the expense of erecting more costly and complicated apparatus. A modification of the arrastre is not unfrequently employed for the treatment of pyrites separated from tailings by washing, and is generally considered to be well adapted for that purpose.

The Chilian Mill.—The Chilian Mill consists of a vertical runner, frequently of granite, revolving on a horizontal arm projecting from a perpendicular shaft, to which motion is given either by water or steam power, or by being attached to horse gearing. The basin in which the runner revolves is usually slightly conical, and may be made either of stone or cast iron. In this arrangement the grinding area is regulated by the difference of the circumference of the circles described on the bed stone, by the inner and outer edges of the runner. In the majority of cases the Chilian mill, instead of having only one runner, has two, one on each side of the vertical shaft; and in such mills they are fastened at different radial distances from it. The method of working rock by the Chilian mill is very much like that employed with the arrastre, but the former is now seldom used, as the latter is generally considered to be a more efficient machine.

In order to show how expensive and inefficient this method of crushing is, we quote the following particulars relative to a Chilian mill, employed at the Silver Works of Constante, in Spain, given by Mr. Darlington, in an article on crushing and grinding machinery, contributed by him to "Ure's Dictionary:"—

Diameter of edge runner	6 feet.
Width " "	centre, 20 in.; edge, 16 in.
Weight " "	3 tons, 15 cwt.
Speed " "	200 feet per minute.
Diameter of interior circle	4 feet.
Size of stuff previous to its being ground .	10 holes to the lineal inch.
" " after its leaving the mill . .	60 " " "
Quantity of stuff reduced per 10 hours . . .	350 lbs.
Horse-power employed	7

Stamping Mill.—In addition to the arrastre and Chilian mill, there are various other contrivances for the reduction of ores, and the extraction of the gold they contain; but although a vast amount of ingenuity has of late years been expended on this subject, none of the numerous modern machines can in any way compare in efficiency with the ordinary stamping mill. This may be said to be the only apparatus extensively employed for the reduction of auriferous rock in all parts of the world, and, in spite of local peculiarities, differs but little in its arrangements from the same machine, as applied to the crushing of tin and lead ores in various parts of Europe. The stamping mill essentially consists of a series of heavy pestles, working in a rectangular mortar, each of which is alternately lifted by means of a cam, and subsequently let fall with its full weight upon the ore to be operated on, and of which, after being previously reduced to fragments of proper dimensions, a constant supply is introduced into the mortar, or battery box.

When quartz mining was first practised in California, the lifters or stems of the pestles employed were made of wood, furnished with cast iron heads, attached by means of a wrought iron shank driven into the lifter, and secured by two strong rectangular bands of flat iron. In most mining districts in which these wooden stems are used, the lifting of the pestle is effected by a large wooden or cast iron drum, around the periphery of which cams are arranged in a spiral form, which, coming in contact with tongues, or tappets, fixed in the lifters, they are raised to a certain height, and, being suddenly released by the continuous motion of the axle, fall with their whole weight on whatever may happen to be beneath them. In California, however, another arrangement is employed for imparting motion to the pestles or stampers of a battery with wooden stems. Instead of a large cylindrical axle, a wrought iron shaft is made use of, and on this are keyed a series of long curved cams, which enter mortise or slot holes, in the several stems, and cause them to be alternately lifted and released, precisely as in the case of the ordinary stamping mill, provided with tappets and a drum axle. When wooden stems are made use of, they are usually about six inches square, and cut out of ash, or some other hard wood, having a straight grain. These wooden stems with square heads have, however, been almost universally superseded by the rotary stamp, with a round stem of iron, to which a circular motion is given by the friction of the cam in lifting, and which, being continued up to the moment of its release, is prolonged during its descent, thus imparting a grinding action to the cylindrical head at the moment of its coming in contact with the rock to be broken.

The rotary stamp is said to be more efficient than the rectangular one, and to grind a larger quantity of rock in a given time; but however this may be, it is certain that the faces of the heads wear more evenly, and that a rotating battery requires less frequent repairs, than one made on the old principle. The battery box is generally composed of one solid casting, and usually receives either four or five stampers; when additional reducing power is required, other similar boxes are placed on the same line. In most instances, such batteries are arranged in sets of five stampers in each mortar, two of which are placed side by side in the same framing, ten stampers being thus set in motion by one shaft. Two five-stamp batteries, of a construction frequently employed, are represented Plate II., fig. 1 being a back elevation, and Fig. 2 a transverse section; the iron rods A are the stamp stems, B the shaft, and C the cams. This shaft is provided at one end with a large pulley D, which is generally constructed of either kiln-dried wood on arms, inserted in a cast iron boss, and then turned off in place, or is built solid of well-seasoned planks on a bored boss, and, as in the other case, turned, after being keyed to the shaft. When several of these batteries are arranged in one house, the motive power is communicated, by means of a broad belt, to the intermediate shaft B′, which is fitted with pulleys corresponding to those on the shafts B, with which they are severally connected by belts. These belts, which are manufactured out of a combination of canvas and india-rubber, are, from the first motion to the intermediate shaft, sometimes as much as two feet in width. The belts from the second motion to the shaft on which the cams are keyed, are made of a thinner material, and are from a foot to fourteen inches wide. The lift of the stampers varies from nine to twelve inches, but ten inches may be considered as about the average, and their weight, including the iron stem, varies from 550 to 900 lbs. The order in which the several stampers, included in one box, strike their blows, in a five-stamp battery, is not always the same in all establishments, but in most instances the first blow is struck by the central stamp. This is followed by the outside one to the right, then by the second to the left, afterwards by the second to the right, and finally by the stamper on the extreme left of the series. The number of blows struck by each stamper is from sixty to eighty per minute. The first portion of the stamper *a* is sometimes cast on to the stem, but more frequently it is fastened by wedges, and has a round aperture, in which is inserted the spill of the shoe *a′* firmly driven in or fastened by dry wooden wedges, which expand on coming in contact with water, and hold it securely in its place. The battery box is either of iron, cast in one piece, or its bottom alone may be of cast iron, and its sides of wood; in which case the lower portion of it, together with the inside of the feed hopper, must be lined with sheet iron, half an inch in thickness, fastened by five-eighth bolts. Immediately under each of the stampers is placed a short cylinder of cast iron *a″*, which is retained in its position, either by fitting into a circular bedding, in which it may be keyed by wooden wedges, or it is provided with a square flange, which, coming in contact with those of the other dies and the sides of the box, act as distance-pieces, by which it is kept in its proper position. These, and the shoes of the stampers, are, when worn out, readily replaced by new, a considerable economy of time and money being the result; the parts worn out are merely coarse castings of chilled iron, without any kind of fitting. The hole *x* is for the purpose of forcing in a drift above the spill of the shoe, and thus removing it when a new one is required, whilst the hole *x'* is employed in the same way for getting off the boss from the stem. In Grass Valley, and some of the other more important mining districts, the boxes E are, almost without exception, composed of single iron castings; but in localities where amalgamation is conducted in the battery itself, the sides and ends are sometimes of wood, the bed alone being made of iron; and when this method of construction is adopted, two plates of amalgamated copper, one-eighth of an inch in thickness, are often bolted at *b* on either side of the row of stampers. The rock to be crushed is introduced by a shovel at *c*, and a plate of perforated sheet iron, fastened either in a wooden frame, or retained in its place between the two rectangular iron bands, tightened by cotters, is introduced before the opening *d*. The battery bed, whether entirely of iron, or consisting only of an iron bottom, with lined wooden sides, is firmly bolted to a block of wood, at least two feet square, and of which the dimensions, when very heavy stampers are employed, are even much greater. This either forms, as in the drawing, a portion of the general framing of the arrangement, or is now more frequently, to prevent jarring, made quite independent of it. It is, however, essential that this portion of the structure should be well bedded on a solid foundation, and, if possible, rest directly on the bed rock. Occasionally quartz is crushed dry, but much more frequently water is admitted, and for this purpose a gas-pipe *e* affords the necessary supply, which enters the boxes through the branch pipes *f*, fitted with cocks for regulating the quantity introduced. The studs *g*, against which the cams come in contact, and by which the stampers are raised, are fitted on the iron stems by means of keys, which admit of their positions being readily shifted, when rendered necessary by the wearing of the shoes.

The props *h* shown in one of the batteries, but omitted in the other to avoid complication, are used for keeping up the stampers, either when the battery box is being cleaned, or when a portion of the machinery is thrown out of action for the purpose of repair; to do this they are successively pushed forward, so as to catch beneath the several bosses *g*, when lifted by the cams to their full height. When not so employed the props are allowed to fall back out of the way of the stems, as shown in the sectional drawing. The size of the apertures in the gratings or sieves at *d*, differ in accordance with the fineness of the gold contained in the rock treated, and is also, to a certain extent, varied in conformity with the particular views of the superintendent of the mill on that subject; but it is evident that with very small apertures the amount of quartz crushed, all other conditions being equal, will be less considerable than when a coarse screen is employed. The size of grating commonly made use of in some of the best mills in the Grass Valley district, is shown Fig. 25, which is known as "No 8."

FIG. 25.

STAMP GRATE, WITH ROUND HOLES.
(Full Size of Apertures.)

In order to combine strength with the largest possible open surface, the apertures are sometimes made of an oblong form, and arranged as in Fig. 26.

FIG. 26.

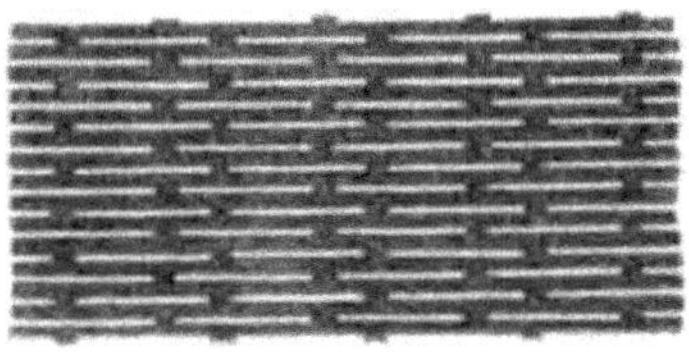

STAMP GRATE, WITH OBLONG HOLES.
(Full Size of Apertures.)

In some establishments these gratings are fixed perpendicularly, as seen in Plate II.; but more generally they are slightly inclined outward, and this arrangement is evidently attended with certain advantages.

When the grating is placed perpendicularly, a particle of quartz or other pulverised matter, splashed against the screen by the fall of the stampers, can only pass through it in case of being projected directly through one of the openings, and should it strike against a portion of the solid plate between the holes, will run down with the water on the inside, and again settle in the battery box. If, on the contrary, the grating be placed at a considerable inclination outward, as shown Plates III. IV. and VIII., a particle of pulverised rock, which has not been projected immediately through the grate, may, on running back with the water over its inner surface, pass through one of the apertures and escape into the trough on the outside of the battery.

In all machines of this description, it is of importance that each particle of the rock operated upon, should escape from the action of the stampers, as soon as it has become sufficiently reduced in size, and with this view the grate surface is in the Californian mills extended as much as possible, being generally made of nearly the full length of

Fig. 27.

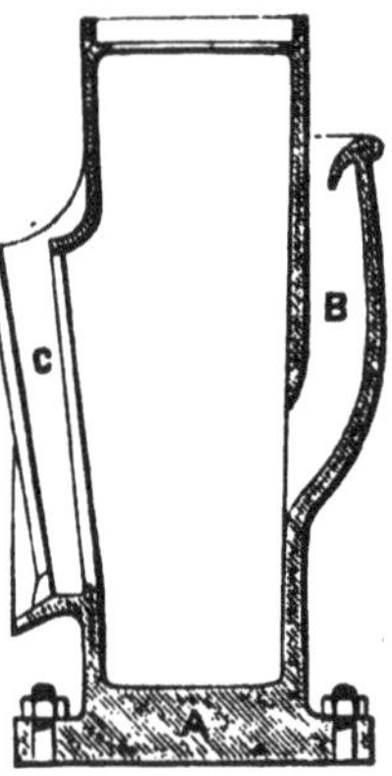

Fig. 28.

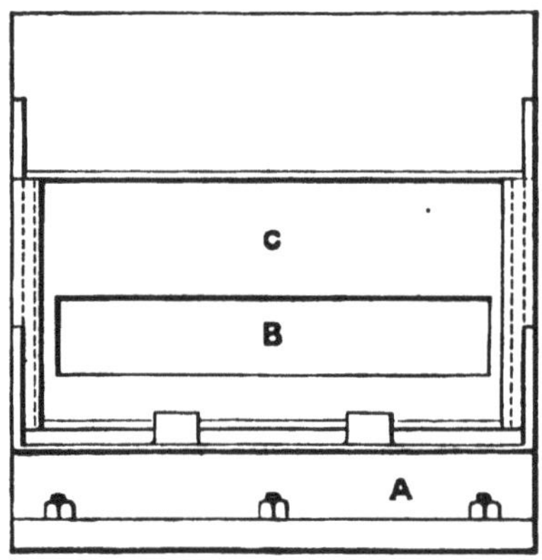

Iron Battery Box.

the battery box. With a view of supporting the grating, and protecting it against injury from the impact of the water dashed against it by the falling stampers, the sheet iron plate is externally strengthened by the application against it of some thin iron bars.

When the high cast iron mortar is made use of, which is now generally the case, it has the form represented Figs. 27 and 28, which the first is a transverse section, and the second a front elevation; the dies are fitted on the bottom A, and the quartz fed through the opening B, whilst the screens are fastened, by nails or screws, to a frame which is firmly secured in grooves provided for its reception at the ends of the mortar, and by two lugs at the bottom of the opening C.

In some cases, instead of employing a double cam, as seen in Plate II. fig. 2, a single one is made use of. This has generally the form shown Fig. 29, and possesses the advantage of allowing the axle to be placed nearer the stamp stem than it can with any other cam, and also that by its use a greater number of blows can be struck per minute, without danger of breakage.

FIG. 29.

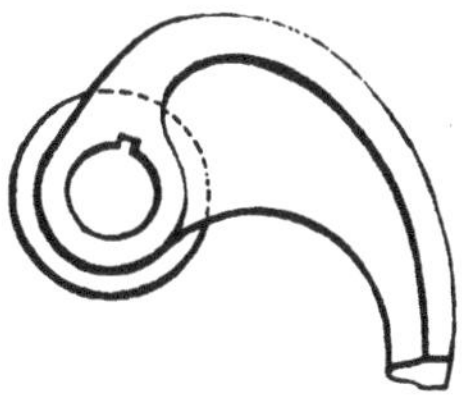

SINGLE CAM.

The auriferous material having been reduced to the state of a finely-divided powder, it becomes necessary to provide means for the concentration and separation of the gold, which is more or less perfectly effected by an almost infinite number of different contrivances, varying slightly in their details in almost every establishment that may be visited. However much the processes employed may differ in this respect, only two decidedly distinct systems are now practically in use in California, viz. amalgamation in the battery; and crushing without the use of mercury, amalgamation being subsequently effected by means of appliances specially designed for that purpose.

Amalgamation in the Battery.—When this method is adopted, the batteries are often provided with amalgamated copper plates *b* (Plate II. fig. 2), about five inches in width, extending the whole length of the box; one on the feed side and the other at the discharge, the latter being protected by the sheet iron lining of the feed hopper, and each having an inclination of from forty to forty-five degrees towards the stampers.

When these are not employed, spaces for the accumulation of amalgam are allowed between the dies and the sides of the box, and vertical iron bars are placed inside the gratings, between which the hard amalgam is found to collect. The copper plates are covered with mercury, by means of a rag dipped in dilute nitric acid, with which quicksilver is rubbed over the surfaces to be coated, in the same way as on those used in ordinary sluices. Quicksilver is also sprinkled into the boxes, by the feeder, at intervals of about an hour, and in quantities varying with the richness of the rock operated on. One ounce of gold requires for its collection about an ounce of mercury; but when the gold is in a finely-divided state, the addition of another quarter of an ounce of this metal is thought advantageous. The proper proportion is, however, readily ascertained by closely watching the discharge. If any particles of amalgam which may pass through be hard and dry, a little more quicksilver must be introduced; but if, on the contrary, they be soft and pasty, or globules of mercury make their appearance, the supply in the battery must be diminished.

When the proportion of mercury has been properly adjusted, the amalgamation of the gold is very completely effected, except in cases in which the ores contain large quantities of lead or antimony, and have been previously burned for the purpose of expelling their more volatile constituents, by which treatment the particles of gold often become coated in such a way as to interfere with their combination with mercury. When the proper proportion of quicksilver has been regularly introduced, and the rock contains coarse gold, from sixty to eighty per cent. of the gold saved is caught in the battery; but when, as in the case of some of the ores of Nevada, the gold is in a very finely-divided state, and is associated with ores of silver and other sulphides, the results obtained are less satisfactory. The alloy resulting from the treatment of such ores contains silver, and in some cases affords from 300 to 400 thousandths only of gold, often producing a spongy amalgam of a dark colour, made up of an aggregation of numerous finely-divided particles. Küstel is of opinion that this effect is partially due to the presence of manganese, but it appears difficult to understand how this substance should influence, to any important extent, the combination of gold and mercury. This amalgam is exceedingly light, and is, therefore, difficult to collect, either by riffles, copper plates, blankets, or any of the other appliances commonly employed for the purpose.

When, therefore, ores contain much lead or antimony, amalgamation in the battery is not to be recommended, since this spongy amalgam is more difficult to retain than the most finely-divided gold, and a large proportion of it floats off over the blankets, riffles, or copper plates, which may be arranged for the purpose of arresting its progress. There is, besides, no evidence that battery amalgamation possesses, under any circumstances, a decided advantage, for gold ores not associated with sulphide of silver, over stamping without the use of mercury, and in some of the most productive gold districts it is seldom resorted to.

In order to collect the particles of gold and amalgam escaping from the battery box, various ingenious contrivances are employed; but as these arrangements differ but little in their details, whether mercury be employed in the battery, or the amalgamation entirely effected after the escape of the pulverised material through the screens, we will proceed to describe the system generally in use in the northern quartz mines, in which the various arrangements are of the most improved description.

Blankets.—At Grass Valley, which, from the richness of its quartz veins and the excellency of the machinery employed for the reduction of the ores, may be considered as the head-quarters of quartz mining in California, the rock is generally crushed without the introduction of quicksilver into the mill. In this district the sand and water issuing from the battery are conducted over blankets spread on the bottoms, and lining the sides of shallow troughs or sluices, inclined at an angle of from three to four degrees with the horizon. Beyond the blankets there are, in most cases, riffles or amalgamated copper plates, which are again followed by some contrivance for collecting the pyrites remaining in the tailings. At the further extremity of this system of appliances there is sometimes a long tail sluice for the purpose of arresting any auriferous material that may have escaped being caught by the other arrangements.

The blanket boards are from fourteen to sixteen inches in width, inside measure, and three inches in depth, being so laid, with a regular longitudinal inclination, that transversely the bottom is perfectly level. It is necessary that this should be carefully attended to, in order that an equal depth of water may, when the mill is in action, flow over every portion of its surface, and thus prevent the occurrence of a rapid current on one side, whilst an accumulation of sand is taking place on the other. The blankets employed are, for the most part, woven expressly for the purpose, of coarse grey wool, and are made of such a width that, when laid in the troughs, and fitting closely over the bottom and sides, they hang down about six or eight inches beyond the top of the woodwork; and in order that they may be readily adjusted, and that no portion of the stream may flow down behind them in the angles, a triangular piece of wood is sometimes fitted into the corners made by the junction of the bottom and sides. The section of one of these troughs (Fig. 30) shows the position of the blanket when fitted in its place.

Fig. 30.

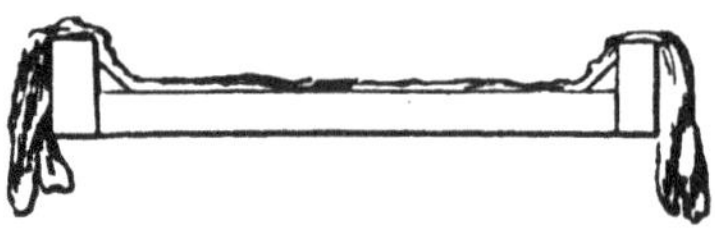

Section of Blanket Board.

In laying these blankets in their troughs, they are so placed as to overlap each other, like tiles on a roof, in order that the water flowing from one may run directly over the other, being prevented by the lap given to them, from finding its way between the blankets and the bottom. The troughs are also themselves made in two or more lengths, and are so arranged that the water in passing through the first, falls into the second, from a height of about three inches.

The general disposition of the batteries and blankets in a well-arranged Californian establishment, will be understood by reference to Plate III., in which fig. 1 is a sectional elevation, and fig. 2, a plan of the apparatus. The battery box A is fitted in front with a water-tight wooden trough B, running its whole length, and provided with an aperture *b*, opening on the blanket board C, and with a second aperture *b'*, at its inner end, which, like the first *b*, can be closed by a small wooden slide, or by placing a bit of plank before it. Immediately before the centre of each battery is placed a blanket board C, and, between each pair a third C', to be used when either of those on each side of it is thrown out of action, for the purpose of removing the blankets. The troughs C and C' are sixteen inches in width, three inches in depth, and have a length of twelve feet; these empty themselves into the troughs D D', having the same width, depth, and inclination, but only nine feet in length. When the batteries are in their normal state of working, the water and crushed ore flow from the apertures *b*, passing through the troughs C, and running over the surface of the blankets with which they are lined; a large portion of the gold and iron pyrites thus becomes entangled in the fibres of the wool, and remains behind, whilst the lighter particles of quartz are carried off by the force of the current, and escape at the lower end of the troughs. If this were allowed to go on without interruption, the fibres of the blanket would soon become so charged with the heavier fragments of crushed ore as at length to cease to act, and the whole of the products of stamping would pass off and be lost. To obviate this, the blankets are frequently washed up, and are then again ready to arrest any particles of gold or pyrites with which they may come in contact. In well-managed mills the blankets at the upper end of the arrangement are now washed every fifteen minutes, and this operation is conducted as follows:—The orifice *b*, opening from the trough B, on one of the blanket boards C, is closed, and the aperture *b*′, communicating with the board C′, standing between the two batteries is opened. This has the effect of leaving the first trough C without water, whilst the stream which before flowed over it is directed through the central trough C′. The blanket over which the current is no longer flowing is now taken up, being at the same time so folded as to prevent the loss of any portion of the adhering matter, and then taken to a rectangular tank prepared for the purpose, where it is carefully washed, and again laid in the trough from whence it was taken. The flow of water and sand from the battery is now cut off from C′, and admitted into its original channel; the same operation being repeated on the trough belonging to the other battery. When the blankets in the intermediate trough require changing, it is done whilst the others are in use. The blankets at the upper end of this system only, are changed so frequently as above mentioned; whilst those on the lower boards D D′, often remain some hours without being washed up. In some mills instead of the intermediate trough C′, there are two blanket boards to each battery, in which case one is being cleaned up whilst the other is in operation.

The cistern, or tank, Fig. 31, in which the blankets are washed, is always situated in the immediate proximity of the troughs containing the blankets requiring most frequent washing, and is generally four feet in height and four feet square at the top, but somewhat smaller at the bottom. On one of its sides is an inclined ledge on which the blankets are rolled after washing, and when again laid down they are rapidly unrolled from the bottom of the trough upwards, so as to fall directly in their places.

FIG. 31.

SECTION OF WASHING TANK.

Sometimes, although rarely, ox hides have been employed instead of blankets, and are placed in the troughs with the grain of the hair against the current, but these are only used in mills of very primitive construction. Sheep skins have also occasionally beeu tried, but these, like ox hides, make bad substitutes for blankets. In some mills, a small stream of clear water is admitted into the troughs at the head of the blankets, for the purpose of rendering the mixture of sand and water issuing from the battery so dilute as to enable the gold and pyrites to settle with greater facility, and this is by some mill-managers considered advantageous; but when the volume of water passing through the troughs is thus increased, their inclination should be made proportionately less considerable. In the majority of cases the gold retained in the battery, together with that collected on the blankets, will represent at least nine-tenths of the total amount obtained from the rock under treatment; but there is, nevertheless, a notable quantity of the precious metal which passes over the blankets, and of which it is desirable to recover the largest possible amount.

Amalgamated Plates.—With this object amalgamated copper plates, often arranged in the form of riffles, are employed, and at the end of these are cisterns or tyes for the collection of the auriferous pyrites, which is subsequently concentrated and treated for the gold it encloses.

At some of the mills in Grass Valley, after running over two blanket boards, respectively twelve and nine feet in length, and having an inclination of three and a half degrees, the water is conducted through troughs E E′ (Plate III. fig. 2) eleven inches wide, of which the bottoms are formed of amalgamated copper riffles, and which have the same inclination as the blankets. From this, the current passes through troughs F F′ set with a less inclination, and of which the bottoms are also formed of amalgamated plates, whilst at the end of these are two reservoirs for the retention of tailings. The plates *e*, forming the bottoms of the riffles in the troughs E E′, are made so as to slide easily in and out of their places for the purpose of being cleaned, or re-amalgamated, and are about eight inches in length.

The riffle plates in the troughs F F′, are also movable, although considerably longer than in those above them; but it is probable that, if instead of contracting these spouts they had been widened, or still better, if two of them had been employed to carry off the current flowing from each of the riffle boxes E E′, and a little fresh water admitted for the purpose of diluting the mixture of water and pulverised ore, the fine particles of gold would have had increased facilities for settling and becoming attached to the surface of the amalgamated plates.

Cleaning up, &c.—The stampers, except when undergoing repair, or stopped for the purpose of cleaning up the gold which accumulates in the battery boxes, are kept constantly at work day and night, the frequency with which the boxes are cleaned of course depending on the richness of the rock operated on. Generally speaking, however, the cleaning up of the battery box takes place at least every week, and often more frequently, particularly when mercury is introduced during the process of crushing. When quicksilver is used in the battery, a very large proportion of the gold obtained is taken from it in the form of amalgam, and even when this metal is not introduced the cleaning up of the battery affords a considerable percentage of the produce, which accumulates in the cavities around the dies, in the form of metallic spangles. The coarser the gold in the rock treated, the larger will necessarily be the percentage of the total produce retained in the battery. Instead of blankets, employed as above described, Brunton's separators, with revolving woollen cloths, have been sometimes used; but these not having been found efficient, have been generally abandoned.

Settling Pits.—When settling pits are used for the purpose of collecting the tailings for subsequent treatment, it is necessary that at least two of them should be provided, so that whilst one is being filled the other may be cleaned up, but in many cases a long pit resembling a Cornish tye is substituted, which, instead of being allowed to fill, and then emptied, is constantly under the superintendence of a lad, who shovels the sand out of it as rapidly as it is brought in by the current, thus causing an amount of agitation, resulting in a further portion of the lighter particles flowing off, and conducing to a greater degree of concentration in the product obtained. It is, moreover, necessary that every mill should be furnished with at least two tanks for washing up blankets, so that one may be ready for use whilst the other is in course of being cleaned up. In some mills, also, the tailings, instead of being allowed to accumulate in a reservoir or tye, prepared for that purpose, and from which they are subsequently removed by manual labour before being submitted to further treatment, are conducted directly into concentrating apparatus, from the end of troughs lined with amalgamated plates.

Amalgamator.—The separation of gold from the matters caught on the blankets, and collected in the washing tanks, is generally effected in California by a very simple piece of apparatus, introduced, many years since, into the northern mines by Mr. M. Attwood, Figs. 32, 33.

This machine consists of two wooden rollers A, eight inches in diameter and two feet in length, furnished on their circumference with numerous small flat knife-bladed pieces of iron arranged around them with their edges at right angles to the axes of the cylinders, and working in cisterns containing mercury; above these rollers, which are set in motion by the pulleys B, over which a belt is stretched so as to cause them both to revolve in the same direction, but contrary to that of the water flowing through the apparatus, is a hopper C, for receiving the sand to be washed. Another pulley D, is connected by a second belt to a rigger keyed on a small shaft fixed in the roof of the mill house, and communicating motion to the whole arrangement. Below the cylinders A, is a riffle board E, having an inclination of seven degrees from the horizontal, and generally covered with plates of amalgamated copper, which can be readily slipped out for the purpose of having the gold amalgam, which may become attached to them, removed. When copper plates are not employed for this purpose, the steps of the riffle are reversed and charged with mercury.

To use this apparatus, some of the sand taken from the cistern in which the blankets have been washed, is placed in the hopper, and a small stream of slightly-warm water allowed to play on it from C′, in such a way as to gradually wash it under the spiked cylinders A, and from thence over the amalgamated riffle board E.* This riffle board is

* The use of warm water is found to facilitate amalgamation, particularly during cold weather.

PLATE

FFLES

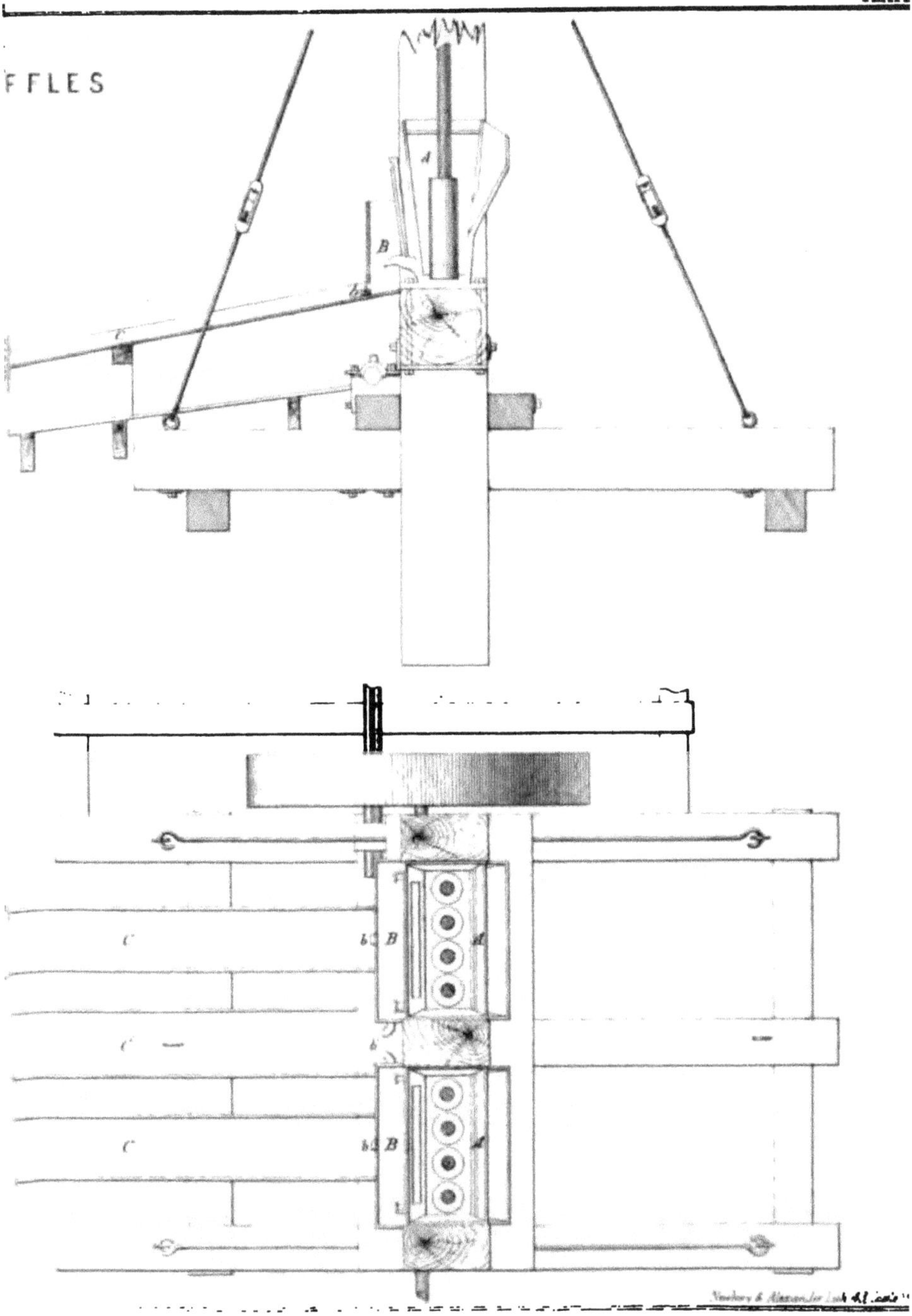

usually nine feet in length, is divided into several channels, and has at its end a cistern for retaining the pyrites and other matters, which, not combining with mercury, escape amalgamation.

As the material operated on in this machine is always highly auriférous, and consequently very valuable, great care is taken to exactly regulate the feed at the upper end, and to keep the surface of

FIG. 32.

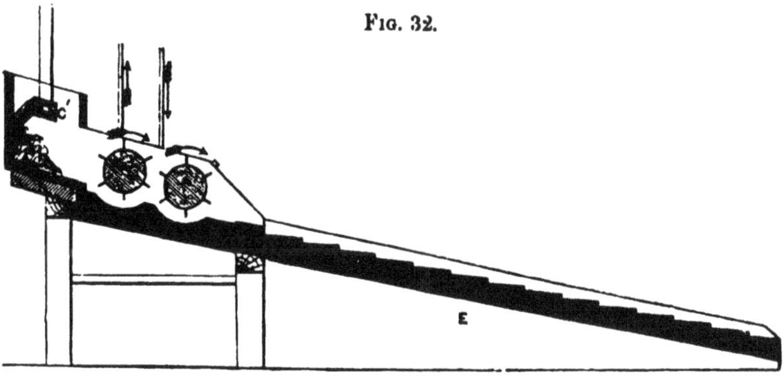

SECTION OF AMALGAMATOR.

FIG. 33.

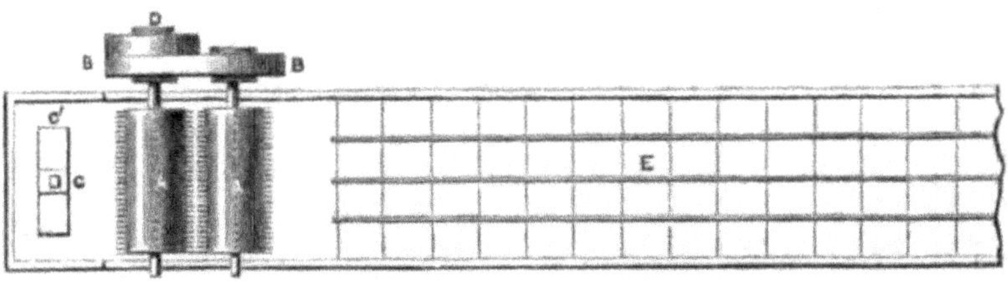

PLAN OF AMALGAMATOR.

the riffles perfectly bright, and clear of any accumulation of pyrites. A boy is therefore stationed at the riffle board, who skims off any scum or impurity which may accumulate on the surface of the plates, and collects it for subsequent treatment in small cast iron arrastres. The sulphides deposited in the tank at the extremity of the riffle board are sometimes ground with mercury, in a Varney or Wheeler pan, and, after thus extracting as much gold as can be so obtained, they may, if they still retain a sufficient amount of gold, be drawn off, and, after settling, are collected and sold for treatment by smelting or chlorination. In many establishments, however, the pyrites from the tanks at the end of the amalgamators, undergoes no further treatment, but is collected and sold as an auriferous sulphide of iron, or it may, previous to being sent to market, be subjected to a simple washing in a rocker, or otherwise, for the purpose of eliminating the sand. The annexed diagram shows the various processes to which gold-bearing quartz is subjected in the neighbourhood of Grass Valley, and explains at a glance the series of operations which the rock undergoes in some of the best mills in that district.

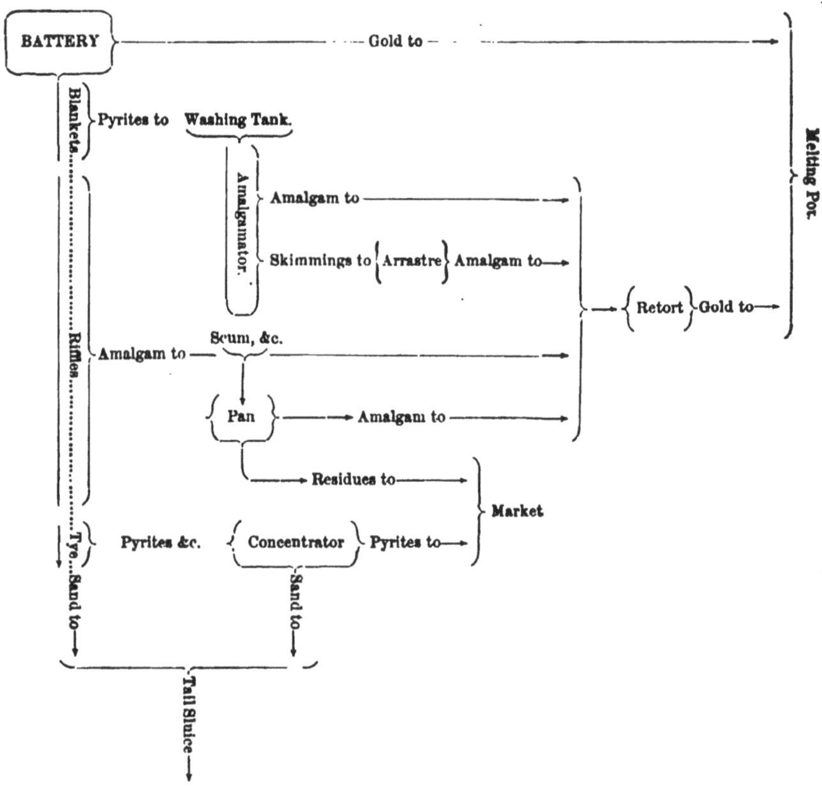

It must, however, be understood, that there are scarcely two mills in which the various manipulations are conducted in precisely the same way, and consequently in the chart of operations mere non-essential differences have been disregarded.

Attwood's System.—Mr. M. Attwood, of San Francisco, has recently designed an arrangement, of which a drawing is given, Plate IV., for saving the gold issuing from a stamping mill. In this Plate, fig. 1 is a sectional elevation; fig. 2, plan; fig. 3, lower end of tyes; and, fig. 4, end of steam chest.

In this arrangement Mr. Attwood does not make use of blankets, but the ground ore issuing from the battery screens, flows directly on to the amalgamator, where it is gently stirred by the action of the cylinders A, turning in the direction indicated by the arrows, and then passes on to a riffle board B, covered by amalgamated copper plates, where a great portion of the amalgam, escaping from the cast iron mercury boxes *a*, will be collected. In order that the mercury in the boxes under the rollers may not become too cold, and its affinity for gold be thus rendered sluggish, they are cast with a double bottom, through which a current of steam can be made to pass, and which is easily regulated by an ordinary tap.

From the riffles B, the ground material passes into the tye C, of which the bottom is inclined at a considerable angle, and which is provided at the lower end with a slot *c*, for regulating the depth of water within it. This is done by means of the stops *c'*. In order to catch any globules of soft amalgam or mercury, which may become detached from the surface of the amalgamated plates, a small cistern D, running the whole width of the riffle board, is provided; in this is an agitator *d*, turning in the direction indicated by the arrow, and which constantly keeps the box, to the depth of its arms, free from accumulations, so as to form a depression in which the mercury and amalgam may become deposited.

To use this apparatus, one of the stops *c'* is placed in the slot *c*, and the mill started in the usual way; the sand which has passed through the amalgamator soon reaches the tye, and the heavier portions begin to accumulate behind the stop, whilst the lighter particles are carried off by the current. The removal of the light sand is facilitated by gently sweeping the surface of the deposit upwards against the stream with a light broom, a boy being stationed there for that purpose; and when the pyrites which is deposited, accumulates to the height of the top of the first stop, another is inserted, and the operation carried on continuously. When one of the tyes has been filled in this way, the tongue E is so turned as to direct the sand and water into the other, which is thus filled whilst the first is being emptied.

It is evident that by this means the pyrites will be collected in the tyes in a very concentrated form, and that the amount of labour required is but small; we have, however, never seen this apparatus in operation, and are without any precise data showing its efficiency, as compared with the blankets and riffles now in general use.

System employed in Australia—Port Phillip Company.—Mr. Bland describes the treatment to which the auriferous quartz is subjected, as follows:*—

"The quartz when brought to the surface is separated into two lots. The small size is tipped into a large hopper, and from thence drawn and delivered, direct, to the stamps, and the larger lumps are sent to the stone-breaking machines to be reduced to a size suitable for the stamps. Two of these machines are in constant use, working on an average about ten hours per day. Each machine will break about eight tons per hour when in good order, at a cost, including wear and tear, of about 10*d*. per ton. They are driven by a shaft from one of the battery engines, and take about twelve horse-power to drive the two. The number of stamps at work is eighty, as follows:—Fifty-six heads of about six cwt. each, including lifter and tongues, driven by one twenty-four-inch engine, giving seventy-five blows per minute, taking about one horse power per head, and crushing an average of about two tons four cwt. per head, for twenty-four hours; twenty-four heads of about eight cwt. each, including lifter, &c., driven by a twenty-four-inch engine, giving seventy-five blows per minute, taking in the aggregate about thirty horse power. These stamps crush about four tons per head per diem, and they have a larger proportion of the small material sent to them. The average quantity of quartz crushed per week, of five days, is about 1,130 tons.

"The following is a return of quartz crushed for the twelve months ending September 1865:—

54,413 tons . . 20,596 oz. 10 dwt. 12 gr. . . 7 dwt. 13 gr.

"The gold above mentioned was collected in the following way:—

In stamp beds	66·08 p. c.
Mercury boxes	22·95 p. c.
Blankets	10·97 p. c.

* The quartz, at the works of the Port Phillip Company, is stamped much coarser than in California. The screens have only ten holes to the lineal inch, and hence the larger amount got through within a given time.

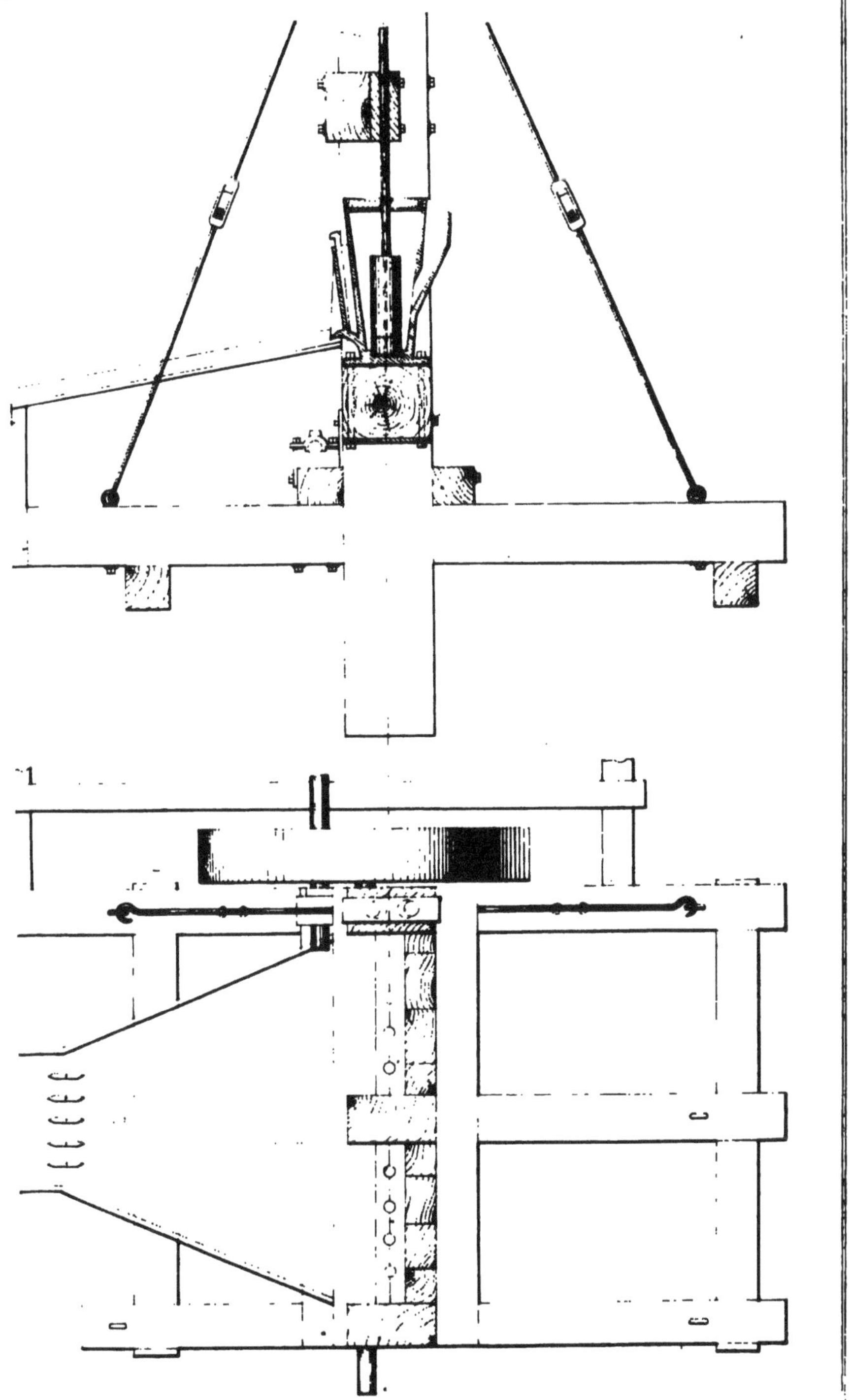

Newbery & Alexander, Lith. 43, Castle St Holborn.

"The quantity of water required to work the stamps efficiently is about eight gallons per head per minute, which is 921,600 gallons per diem. The tailings on leaving the stamps run into settling boxes, where the current is checked, and the heavier material settles. These boxes are cleaned out every few hours, and the material sent to the buddle, where it undergoes a further concentration, and is dressed up to an average of three or four ounces of gold to the ton of material. This is then sent to the roasting furnace, and afterwards ground in Chilian mills with mercury, and an average of about eighty-five per cent. of the assay contents of the gold is thus extracted. The cost of operating on the pyrites, including the buddle, roasting, grinding, loss of mercury, &c., averages about 2*l*. 14*s*. per ton, or about 1*l*. per ounce of gold obtained.

"The expense will diminish as the quantity of pyrites increases, and improves in richness.

"The quantity of quartz crushed, and yield of gold from the commencement of the Company's operations in 1857 to the 31st July, 1866, was as follows:—

Quartz crushed.	Yield of Gold.
308,661 tons.	180,723 oz. 15 dwt. 10 grs.

Equal to six tons of 2,000 lbs. each."

Loss of Gold, &c.—In California the tailings escaping from the last of the appliances employed for the separation of gold, are never carefully and regularly assayed, and consequently it would be impossible to arrive at a correct estimate of the losses resulting from the imperfections incident to the modes of treatment adopted. It would, however, seem that there is comparatively little difficulty in effecting the separation and amalgamation of the free gold, and that the principal losses attending the working of ordinary gold quartz, arise from the escape of small particles of this metal enclosed in pyrites, and which the concentrating apparatus fails to collect. Nevertheless, in some instances the surface of the gold would appear to be coated with a thin glaze of silica, or some other substance which protects it from amalgamation, and in such cases its combination with mercury can only be effected by grinding in a pan, arrastre, or some similar contrivance. The only data relative to this subject which we have been able to procure, have been obtained from the officers of the Port Phillip and Colonial Gold Mining Company, at whose establishments, in Australia, the tailings are regularly sampled and assayed, and found (see table, page 116) to contain on an average about 2 dwt. of gold, of which some portion is again recovered from the washed sulphides, by roasting and grinding in Chilian mills.

The weight of the stampers employed in the Californian mills differs considerably, and, as a natural consequence, the amount of work done by each in a given time varies in nearly the same ratio. In the neighbourhood of Grass Valley, heavy heads are almost universally employed. At the North Star works, the stampers, including the stems or lifters, weigh 9 cwt. and crush weekly 13¾ tons of quartz, or very nearly two tons each in twenty-four hours. The stampers at Allison Ranch are of the same weight, and perform the same amount of work. At the Eureka mill the stampers weigh 840 lbs. and are estimated to crush about two tons each in the course of the twenty-four hours. The table at the end of this chapter, constructed from data collected by Mr. Ashburner in 1861, gives the cost of stamping, weight of stampers, loss of mercury, and many other particulars relating to the various quartz mills then at work in California, since which period the cost of treatment has been somewhat reduced.*

Concentration of Tailings.—In the earlier days of quartz mining, the pyrites and other metallic sulphides were generally allowed to escape with the earthy and silicious portions of the vein-stuff, and a considerable loss was naturally the result, although an attempt to extract the gold which they enclose was sometimes made by roasting the quartz in kilns or heaps, before subjecting it to the action of the stamping mill. This was, however, found to be of little practical advantage, and quartz is therefore now stamped without any kind of preparation beyond that of *spalling*, or breaking it into fragments of a convenient size, but much care is devoted to recovering from the tailings the largest practicable proportion of auriferous material.

The machinery and contrivances employed with this object are of the most varied description, and it would be therefore impossible to attempt a description of the whole of them, and we shall consequently

* An interesting paper has been recently published by the Geological Survey of California, entitled "Mining Statistics, No. 1. Tabular Statement of the Condition of the Auriferous Quartz Mines and Mills in that part of Mariposa and Tuolumne Counties, lying between the Merced and Stanislaus Rivers, by A. Rémond."—Philadelphia, 1866.

From this it would appear that the cost of milling at the present time is lower than when Mr. Ashburner compiled his tables; but the information afforded being of a comparatively local character, we abstain from making extracts.

confine ourselves to noticing such as are most commonly made use of in the best-conducted establishments.

Rocker.—The rocker consists of a trough about twelve feet in length, fourteen inches in width, and ten or twelve inches deep at the sides. In appearance this contrivance is not unlike a school form, of which the top constitutes the bottom of the trough, and of which one leg is shorter than the other, so as to give a slight inclination to the machine. The two legs, which are very short, are rounded at bottom, like rockers, and kept in their positions by articulations which allow of the arrangement working from side to side, this motion being communicated to it by means of a crank, or eccentric and small sweep rod, attached to a pulley, driven by a narrow belt. The trough thus formed is rocked at the rate of forty-five strokes per minute, with a one-inch throw, and is furnished with an end at the higher extremity only, the other remaining open, and forming a spout for the escape of water and sand. Water is admitted at the upper end by means of a flexible tube, and the bottom is lined with sheet iron to prevent wearing. To use this machine, the workman stands at one side of it, near its upper end, and after having turned on the supply of water, he throws in a few shovelfuls of the sand, which has been collected either in the settling pits or tyes. The rocking motion, together with the stream of water, aided by the judicious use of the shovel, causes the lighter silicious particles to be carried off, whilst the heavier pyrites remains in the trough of the rocker. This is removed by the shovel, and another charge of unwashed tailings introduced, the operation being carried on continuously in the same way. This machine washes the pyrites very clean, but appears to allow too large a proportion of it to be carried off in the final tailings.

Concave Buddle.—This apparatus, invented by Mr. Hundt, a Prussian engineer, and patented in this country by a Mr. Borlase, has been successfully introduced at the Port Phillip Company's works in Victoria. This arrangement possesses the advantage of affording a large working area at the head, and at the same time effects a better separation of the waste than can be produced by round buddles of the ordinary construction. Also, when the lighter portions of the tailings have become separated from the heavier near the periphery of the circle, the area over which they are distributed gradually diminishes, which by increasing the rapidity of the flow, enables them to be more readily and effectually carried off. In Australia this apparatus is employed for concentrating tailings from which a large proportion of the gold has been previously extracted by the usual appliances. The woodcuts, Figs. 34, 35, represent a plan and section of one of the best forms of the concave buddle.

FIG. 34.

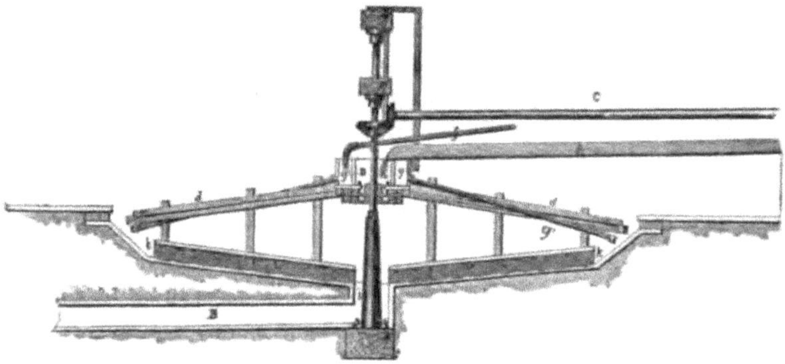

SECTION OF CONCAVE BUDDLE.

The spout bringing in the mixture of water and sand is represented by A; B is the outlet for carrying off the earthy impurities, or final tailings; C, shaft communicating motion to the buddle arms *d*, the distributing launders *e*, and pipes *g′* attached thereto; *f*, pipe for supplying clean water to the annular cistern *g*, from whence it passes by the pipes *g′* with rose apertures at the ends, and serves to dilute the mixture of water and tailings discharged by the launders *e*, on the annular incline at the periphery. The whole of this arrangement revolves on the shaft D; *i* is a circular pit, into which the final tailings fall, previous to being carried off by the channel B.

To the wooden bars *k*, are attached pieces of canvas which sweep over the surface of the stuff deposited in the buddle, and keep it even and free from ruts. The tailings, entering the receiver *h*, are distributed at the periphery of the buddle through the four launders *e*, which at their extremities are turned at right angles to the direction of their motion, when in action; and at the same time clean water is distributed by the apertures pierced in the terminations of the pipes *g′*.

The speed given to this arrangement of arms, launders, and pipes, revolving on the shaft D, varies in proportion to the state of division of the sands to be treated; when these are rather coarse, the machine may make from six to eight revolutions per minute, but when very fine stuff has to be dealt with, the speed is considerably increased. The influx of tailings and water must be regulated in accordance with the speed of the arms and the density of the stuff operated on; and although no very definite instructions can be given with regard to this subject, a short trial of the apparatus will enable any intelligent workman to make the necessary adjustments. The bed may be from twelve to eighteen feet in diameter, and have an inclination of from six to nine inches from the edge to the centre.

FIG. 35.

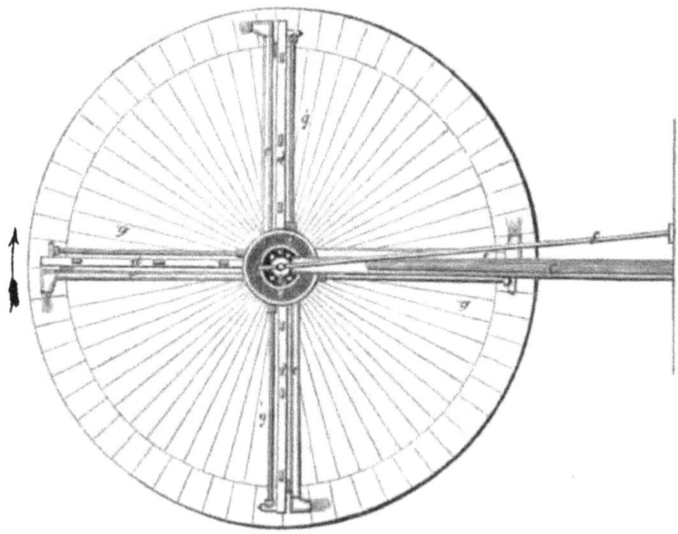

PLAN OF CONCAVE BUDDLE.

At the Port Phillip Works, the tailings cleaned by machines of this description are subsequently roasted, and passed through Chilian mills; but where, as in California, the enriched pyrites has to be transported to considerable distances, it would require to be more than once passed through the machine, or, after being once buddled, the heads might be further enriched, either in the rocker, or by a hand buddle or shaking table. A buddle of this kind can be filled in about four hours, and forms an excellent apparatus for enriching ores with but little waste. If it be intended to dress sulphides directly from the riffles, so as to render them almost entirely free from silicious matter, the first heads will require to be re-washed at least once, and the second heads twice; but when this is done, it is necessary to be provided with other buddles besides those which first receive the tailings direct from the riffles, and which will be constantly in use for that purpose.

When the tailings to be washed are not conducted directly from the blanket boards, but are taken either from tyes or the heads of other buddles, they are charged with a shovel into a hopper connected with a circular sieve, working in water, which discharges into the spout A.

Bradford's Separator.—Various modifications of this machine are employed in the mines of Grass Valley, and particularly at the Norambagua mill, about three miles south of the town. This machine is nothing more than a very compact form of the shaking table, by which the pyrites and other sulphides are discharged over the head of the platform, whilst the lighter silicious matters escape at the lower end. In order that this may be effected without too great an admixture of quartz with the pyrites on the one hand, or without a considerable quantity of pyrites escaping with the quartz on the other, very nice adjustment is required; but, if carefully attended to, this machine appears capable of affording satisfactory results, and the washed pyrites retains but a small amount of impurity. It is, however, evident that when the pyrites is thus rendered free from any admixture of silicious sand, there is some danger of a loss taking place through the escape of a portion of the sulphides from the other extremity of the table. These tables are, in California, sometimes employed for the direct concentration of tailings flowing from the riffles.

The tailings enter by a spout, five inches wide, but which expands at the extremity into a fan-shaped form, so as to be of nearly the same width as the table itself. This has its end closed by a fillet, in which is a line of numerous small holes, fitted with regulating pegs. The table is formed of a perfectly flat sheet of copper, two feet two inches in width, and about three feet in length, suspended by iron rods in such a way that its degree of inclination can be readily varied by means of simple regulating gear. In order to render the motion perfectly regular, the table is held in its position by means of spiral springs, attached near the middle of each side, and connected with a wooden framing. The necessary shaking motion is imparted to the table by rods on either side, moved by eccentrics on a shaft, on which is a small fly wheel, which is driven by a pulley and belt connected with a conical roller, opposite to which is a reversed roller of the same kind, with which it is connected by a belt, by changing the position of which, the speed may be easily regulated. The throw of this table is about two inches, and the speed at which it works very great. When this machine is in operation, the pyrites is discharged over a lip into a small box, whilst the impoverished tailings pass off at the other extremity, and are washed away by a stream of water. This is a very ingenious apparatus, and may be made to do its work remarkably well; but the rocker is, nevertheless, more frequently employed, and possesses the advantages of being cheaper, doing its work more expeditiously, and not requiring such nice adjustment.

In addition to the contrivances which have been described, innumerable appliances have been invented, and in many cases patented, for the reduction and amalgamation of gold quartz, and the concentration of tailings. An immense amount of ingenuity has been expended on various machines for effecting all these operations at a cheap rate, and some of them bear evidence of great mechanical skill: up to the present time, however, it may be certainly said that most of them have been more extensively advertised than employed.

Extraction of Gold from Sulphides.—The Hepburn and Peterson, as well as the Wheeler, Varney, and other pans, extensively employed in Nevada for the treatment of silver ores, are sometimes used for this purpose; but as these machines were originally designed for the extraction of silver from its ores, they will be described under the head of silver.

The arrastre, used in the Grass Valley district for the treatment of scrapings taken from the copper plates of the amalgamator, and other residues rich in gold, consists of a basin of cast iron, four feet in diameter, and of which the mullers are also generally of iron, although they are sometimes, but more rarely, made of stone. These are set in motion by a central shaft connected by a belt with the other machinery of the mill, the cleaning up being effected in the usual way, except that, as the iron pan is free from joints in which an accumulation of mercury and amalgam could take place, it is more easily managed than the same machine with a stone bottom.

In some establishments, as at Allison Ranch, the tailings are passed through a series of iron basins warmed by steam, and provided with mullers, not unlike, in their construction, those of the ordinary Wheeler pan; but they are less efficient than the pans employed for the treatment of silver ores, and are by no means generally adopted.

Baux and Guiod's Amalgamator.—This machine, which is represented Fig. 36, is occasionally used for the extraction of gold from tailings.

FIG. 36.

BAUX AND GUIOD'S AMALGAMATOR.

In this apparatus the water and ores are introduced at the bottom of the pan, through a hopper bolted on its side, and the discharge of tailings is so arranged as to be from the highest point, which is the centre of the lid, whilst the substances being ground are thrown by centrifugal action upon a bed of mercury lying in a groove around the internal circumference. This apparatus is worked continuously, the tailings from the blankets entering at A, and flowing off by the spout B, cast on the cover of the machine.

Chlorination Process.—Several establishments employing this process are carried on, on a small scale, in the neighbourhood of Grass Valley; and when the gold is in a finely-divided state, satisfactory results are obtained.

The concentrated tailings are first roasted in reverberatory furnaces of the ordinary construction, generally heated by wood, until no further smell of sulphur is evolved, a little charcoal or salt being sometimes added, towards the close of the operation, for the purpose of decomposing any sulphates or arsenical salts which may have been formed. This roasting is conducted at a very low temperature, and consequently ordinary bricks are alone employed in the construction of the furnaces, which are of sufficient capacity to work a charge of from a ton and a half to two tons. After the expiration of from six to eight hours the charge is withdrawn and spread evenly on the floor to cool, after which it is repeatedly sprinkled with water, and turned over in order to get it regularly and suitably moistened throughout, since on the degree of humidity of the mass greatly depends the success of the subsequent operations. When properly moistened, the roasted pyrites is introduced into large wooden tubs, about seven feet in diameter, and from twenty-five to thirty inches in depth. These tubs are provided with false bottoms, beneath which chlorine gas is introduced, and allowed to permeate the mass of damp auriferous oxide of iron. At the bottom of each tub are two holes, one for the introduction of chlorine through a lead pipe connected with a leaden gas generator, and the other for running off the solutions. The gas is produced from a mixture of common salt, peroxide of manganese, and sulphuric acid; and after covering the tub, and keeping up the evolution of gas during from twelve to fifteen hours, the cover is removed and clean water introduced. Water is thus added until it reaches the surface of the charge, when the discharge pipe is opened and the liquid, containing chloride of gold in solution, drawn off into glass carboys. Solution of sulphate of iron is now added, which precipitates the gold in the form of a dark brown powder, readily separated by decantation, and filtration, and subsequently melted into bars, which generally contain about 995 thousandths of gold.

This process, when the gold is in a finely-divided state, affords good results; but the larger particles of metal not being dissolved in the time necessary for effecting the solution of the smaller ones, they are often partially attacked only, and unless great caution be exercised, a loss is the result. A sample of the residues from the chlorination vats of one of the establishments at Grass Valley, afforded us, by assay, 18 dwt. of fine gold per ton.

The compositions of three samples of pyrites concentrated from tailings, are given in the following analyses by Mr. F. Claudet, who has kindly communicated his results.

ANALYSES OF AURIFEROUS CALIFORNIAN PYRITES, CONCENTRATED FROM TAILINGS.

	From Grass Valley.	From near Sonora.	North Star, Grass Valley.
Sulphur . . .	46·700	37·250	43·720
Arsenic. . . .	0·310	8·490	1·360
Iron	41·650	36·540	39·250
Copper	trace	trace	0·220
Lead.	"	0·400	trace
Gold	0·037	0·302	0·026
Silver	0·036	not determined	0·012
Cobalt	"	"	0·150
Silica	10·970	17·180	14·230
	99·703	100·162	98·968
Per Ton of 20 cwt.			
	oz. dwt. gr.	oz. dwt. gr.	oz. dwt. gr.
Gold.	12 2 0	98 13 0	8 10 0
Silver	11 16 0	..	3 18 0

Amalgamation in Pans.—Instead of stamping auriferous quartz, either with or without mercury, in the battery, and subjecting the sands flowing from the gratings, to the different operations which have been described, they are sometimes, on issuing from under the stampers, at once collected in settling pits, from whence they are removed by manual labour, in order to be afterwards ground in pans, similar to those employed for working silver ores, and which will be described when treating of that subject. However suitable this method may be for operating on small quantities of very rich quartz, it is evidently not adapted for working large amounts of moderately auriferous rock, and we are not aware of there being, at the present time, any establishment operating extensively and regularly on this principle.

Retorting.—The amalgam of gold and mercury collected during the progress of the various operations connected with the treatment of gold quartz, is first filtered, in order to remove the excess of mercury, and afterwards retorted and melted into bars for the market. In California this expulsion of the redundant mercury is generally effected by well wringing the amalgam in a buckskin, although a piece of closely-woven canvas may, after being wetted, be employed for the same purpose. The amalgam is in this way formed into balls of about the size of large apples, which, after being well squeezed, afford from 35 to 40 per cent. of retorted gold. The retort commonly employed in quartz mills resembles in form and size a large black-lead crucible, furnished with a well-fitting cover, kept in its place either by a screw clamp, or by a clamp and wedge, and into which is screwed an inch iron pipe bent, with a gentle turn, at right angles, and, at a distance of about thirty inches, again so bent downwards as to form another angle.

Before using this retort, it must be slightly covered on the inside, by the use of a rag attached to a stick, with a paste made of water and clay, or sifted wood ashes, to prevent the adhesion of gold in case of too much heat being accidentally applied. The lumps of amalgam are now introduced, and the face of the lid carefully luted with a mixture of clay and wood ashes, after which it is placed on the retort, and securely fastened in its place by means of the clamp.

The crucible and its charge are now introduced into the furnace employed for melting retorted gold into bars, and which for this purpose may be fourteen inches square, and 1 ft. 8 in. deep above the fire bars. The end of the pipe will now be a short distance only from the floor of the furnace room, and beneath it is placed a vessel of water into which a piece of canvas, which is bound round it so as to form a short hose, is allowed to dip; the level of the liquid being constantly maintained by the flowing off of the water in the receiver, in proportion as the condensed mercury accumulates. The condensation of quicksilver is often effected by means of wet cloths bound around the descending limb of the pipe, and which are constantly kept cool by the application of water: the same result is sometimes more neatly and readily produced by the application of a Liebig's condenser.

When it has been thus arranged in the furnace, the fire may be lighted and gradually increased, until the retort has acquired a dull red heat, care being at the same time taken to effect the perfect condensation of the mercury by a constant supply of fresh water to the eduction pipe. The heat is thus kept up for several hours, according to the size of the retort and the amount of amalgam operated on; but the production of a decided light red heat, visible in daylight, should be avoided, since at that temperature the gold might not only be partially melted, but the retort itself seriously injured. When the pipe begins to get cool, and no more drops of quicksilver are observed to fall from its extremity, the operation is completed, and the fire may be withdrawn; but the cover should not be immediately removed, since a hot retort, even after the operation has been slowly and carefully conducted, gives off mercurial vapours, which would be, if inhaled, highly injurious. The water covering the mercury in the receiver, should, during a properly conducted retorting, remain perfectly clear and free from turbidity, since if it becomes milky it may be regarded as a proof that the heat employed has been too great. A forced retorting saves little or no time, and the mercury under such circumstances is imperfectly expelled, whilst the retort itself is rapidly destroyed, and soon rendered unserviceable. In order to obtain satisfactory results, the retort should be heated gradually, kept a long time at a black red heat, and allowed to cool before being opened. The fuel employed in the furnace is either coke or charcoal, and as soon as it has sufficiently cooled, the retort may be opened, and the spongy gold, which is of a light yellow colour, may be removed for the purpose of being melted into bars. When very large quantities of amalgam have to be dealt with, a fixed retort not unlike those employed in the manufacture of coal gas may be made use of, and, particularly when employed for the retorting of silver amalgam, is frequently made of a large size.

Melting Retorted Gold.—The fusion of retorted gold is commonly effected in the furnace employed for the distillation of amalgam in the small crucible-shaped retort. The melting is performed in black-lead crucibles, and the fuel employed, coke or charcoal. The crucible should be annealed by being gradually warmed, before being subjected to the full heat of the furnace, and a small quantity of borax is placed in it with the retorted gold. The gold from the retort being porous, occupies a considerable space, but after melting takes up much less room; so that as soon as the first charge has become fused, the cover may be removed and a further addition of retorted gold made. When the gold has become thoroughly fused, the crucible is withdrawn by the aid of a pair of strong tongs, furnished with jaws for enclosing and supporting its sides, and the metal is poured into moulds of cast iron. In order to render the handling of the pot perfectly safe, and to prevent any chance of the slipping of the tongs, its handles should be provided with a movable link, which, by keeping them tightly together, prevents the jaws from relaxing their hold on the crucible.

TABULAR STATEMENT.

OF THE OPERATIONS OF THE PRINCIPAL QUARTZ MILLS RUNNING IN CALIFORNIA IN THE YEAR 1861.—BY W. ASHBURNER.*

Name and Locality of Mill.	Water, or Steam.	No. of stamps.	Weight of each stamp.	No. of blows per minute.	No. of inches fall.	Horse-power developed by each stamp.	Height of screen above die.	No. of tons stamped per 24 hours.	Amount of wood consumed per ton.	Loss of mercury per ton.	Cost of extracting quartz from the Mine.	Yield per ton.	Cost of stamping per ton.	Total cost of treatment per ton.
			lbs.		in.		in.	tons.	cords.					
MARIPOSA COUNTY.														
Benton	water	64	550	60	12	1·00	5	80	...	0·0027	$3·53	$8·98	$·559	$1·04
Bear Valley . . .	steam	8	1000	65	12	1·97	...	20	0·158	0·007	6·00	25·24	1·618	3·10
Mount Ophir . .	steam	24	500	56	10	0·71	...	26	0·176¼	0·019	6·00	16·94	1·909	2·96
Princeton . . .	steam	12	600	60	14	1·27	5	23	0·118	0·026	5·43	27·42	1·423	3·18
TUOLUMNE COUNTY.														
Union	water	20	500	60	13	0·98	...	20	...	0·031	13·00	50·00	3·145	3·81
Platt	steam	10	500	58	13	0·95	...	8¼	0·130	0·030	5·00	25·36	2·820	2·83
Lomberdo's . . .	water	8	650	58	14	1·33	...	15	...	0·016	8·00	20·00	1·243	1·64
Eureka	water	20	600	65	11	1·08	...	40	...	...	2·33	12·00	...	1·03
Confidence . . .	steam	10	480	54	12	0·78	9	10	0·175	...	1·50	10·00	2·204	2·29
Telegraph . . .	water	10	475	62	...	...	10	8	...	...	3·00	30·00	...	2·00
Knox and Co. . .	water	5	...	...	...	...	...	6	...	...	6·00	20·00	...	1·25
Yaney (Dry) . . .	water	6	800	...	...	...	...	4	...	...	...	...	...	...
CALAVERAS COUNTY.														
Crystal (Dry) . .	steam	12	600	60	10	0·91	6	8	0·500	0·128	1·50	80·00	3·916	8·31
Angels Q. M. Co. .	steam	16	490	50	...	0·62	10	24	0·130	0·125	2·00	5·00	1·827	2·03
Blue Wing (Dry) .	steam	24	...	...	...	...	...	8	...	...	...	...	...	...
AMADOR COUNTY.														
Oneida	steam	16	...	52	10	...	...	16	0·250	0·089	...	10·50	2·351	2·84
Eureka	steam & water	40	500	80	10	1·19	6	60	0·066	0·064	2·50	10·25	0·963	1·32
Badger (Upper) .	water	16	400	80	10	0·81	...	25	...	0·055	2·50	10·25	0·646	0·67
,, (Lower) .	water	12	400	80	10	0·81	...	20	...	0·057	2·50	10·25	0·759	0·78
Herbertville (Dry).	steam	30	500	65	12	0·98	...	14	0·371	0·114	4·50	20·00	3·043	4·59
American Q. M. Co.	steam	20	575	70	10	1·01	...	25	0·160	0·067	2·93	10·00	1·476	1·79
Spring Hill . . .	steam	31	400 & 600	70	10	...	...	36	0·144	0·050	2·00	10·00	1·394	1·63
EL DORADO COUNTY.														
Empire (Logtown).	steam	10	600	60	13	1·18	6	12	0·145	0·054	2·75	10·00	0·990	1·49
Union (AurumCity)	steam	10	450	70	...	...	...	20	0·175	...	...	30·00	2·046	2·05
Tulles (Grizzly Flat)	water	11	1000·500	42	...	...	...	...	...	...	5·00	10·00	...	...
PLUMAS COUNTY.														
Eureka	water	28	...	...	...	...	...	...	...	...	3·73	15·45	...	6·27
Mammoth . . .	water	12	800	40	8	0·65	...	10	...	0·022	...	25·00	...	...
SIERRA COUNTY.														
Sierra Buttes . .	water	24	600	50	10	0·76	9	30	...	0·027	5·87	14·82	0·633	1·36
Independence . .	water	12	550	48	9	0·60	8	10	...	0·033	5·00	15·00	0·858	2·90
NEVADA COUNTY.														
Nevada Q. M. Co. .	water	12	850	60	12	1·54	3	15	...	0·198	4·00	17·14	1·466	2·65
Gold Hill	steam	21	730	52	14	1.34	1½	35	0·171	0·044	...	custom	1·600	2·30
Massachusetts Hill	steam	16	1000	55	12	1·67	4	33	0·183	0·024	26·00	70·00	...	2·91
Empire No. 1 . .	steam		...	...	...	...			0·104	1·120	...	5·00	...	1·37
,, No. 2 . .	steam	6	900	62	14	1·97	5	18	0·141	0·109	10·00	28·00	...	1·66
Orleans	steam	9	600	32	10	0·48	2½	8	0·241	0·046	3·00		...	3·23
Allison Ranch . .	steam	8	950	55	13	1·71	5	17	0·176	0·023	20·00	50·00	1·678	3·60
Lady Franklin .	steam	8	950	60	14	2·02	4	22	0·130	0·011	...		1·279	2·05
Forest Springs . .	water	10	800	60	...	...	4	8·76	...	0·044	15·00	52·35	1·348	2·98

* Geological Survey of California, vol. i. p. 475.

The present average cost of treating gold quartz in California is estimated by Mr. Ashburner as follows:—

	Per ton of 2,000 lbs.
In Water Mills, water free	$1·22
„ „ purchased	1·60
In Steam Mills	2·14

CHAPTER X.

VEIN MINING IN HUNGARY AND BRAZIL—SODIUM AMALGAM.

AURIFEROUS VEINS AT SCHEMNITZ — STAMPING MILLS—HUNGARIAN BOWLS—SHAKING TABLES — CONCENTRATION OF AURIFEROUS SLIMES — GOLDLÜTTE SCHEIDETROG — RESULTS OBTAINED — MODE OF OCCURRENCE OF GOLD AT MORRO VELHO — STAMPING — STRAKES — TREATMENT OF FIRST TAILINGS—TREATMENT OF SECOND TAILINGS—AMALGAMATION OF CONCENTRATED ORES—LOSS OF GOLD AND MERCURY—COST OF WORKING—APPLICATION OF SODIUM AMALGAM—NOT GENERALLY EMPLOYED IN CALIFORNIA—ADVANTAGES STATED TO RESULT FROM ITS USE.

HUNGARY.—The metalliferous deposits of Schemnitz, in Lower Hungary, are generally regarded as being true veins, although they do not always exhibit distinct walls separating them from the enclosing rock, which is, however, in the neighbourhood of the veins, usually more or less decomposed, and often contains a considerable amount of iron pyrites. Some of these lodes are sixty feet in width, and have been worked to a depth exceeding two hundred and fifty fathoms. The veinstone is principally quartz, through which are disseminated, in a finely-divided state, galena, iron pyrites, gold, and sulphide of silver.

Stamping Mill.—These ores are treated in stamping mills, constructed according to the usual continental system.*

Each stem or lifter consists of a wooden beam, usually made of oak or beech, twelve feet in length and six inches square, the lower extremity of which is provided with a head of hard white cast iron. These are cast with a shank, which is inserted into the wood, and securely held in its place by two strong iron bands, driven on over the lifter and tightly wedged. The stamper thus prepared weighs two hundred and fifty pounds, although in some cases they do not exceed

* Our data relative to the treatment in Hungary of gold ores by amalgamation, have been chiefly derived from a paper published in 1846, by M. Pache ; and as we are without any precise information relative to the modifications which may have been since introduced, the descriptions of the various processes must be considered as applying to that date. The title of the paper referred to is as follows :—" Sur la Préparation mécanique des Minerais dans le district de Schemnitz (Basse Hongrie), par M. H. Pache."—*Ann. des Mines*, Tome x. série 4.

one hundred and twenty pounds in weight. The axle is of wood, nineteen inches in diameter, and provided with iron journals, the stampers being lifted by means of wooden cams and tappets. Each pestle has a lift varying from eight inches to a foot, and strikes, on an average, seventy blows per minute. The battery box is composed of thick planks, firmly put together; and the bottom on which the stampers fall is prepared by tightly beating in, with a heavy iron ram, fragments of hard quartz, which are introduced in successive layers.

These mills are generally so constructed as to be self-feeding, although in some cases they receive their supply of ore from a small inclined hopper, into which the stuff to be stamped is thrown by manual labour. They have no gratings, and discharge the pulverised ore over the edge of an aperture running the whole length of the battery box, the height of which, from the face of the stampers, can be regulated by means of a sliding apron. The stamping is conducted wet, about three cubic feet of water per minute being supplied to each battery of five stampers.

The apparatus employed for the extraction of gold at Schemnitz is represented, Plate V. fig. 1, being an elevation, and fig. 2, a plan of the arrangement; B is the last battery of a range of stamping mills, A the axle, *b* the table before *flosh holes*, *c* the canal through which the stamped ore escapes from the battery box; *d*, *e*, *f*, are three canals or spouts at different levels, for the passage of slimes.

Hungarian Bowls, &c.—The eight amalgamating mills, 1, 2, 3, 4, and 1′, 2′, 3′, 4′, are disposed in two rows, of which the first is placed four inches above the other. The divisions *g* are seven inclined planes having the same flooring, but separated from each other by partitions two inches wide, and an inch and a half deep. The distance between these divisions is eighteen inches, and the length of the table six feet ten inches, with an inclination of fifteen inches between its two ends. Each of these inclined planes is completely covered over by two pieces of canvas a little wider than the platform, and slightly exceeding half its length.

The mills are composed of a cast iron basin, *a*, Plate V. fig. 3, half an inch thick in the metal, twenty-two inches in diameter at top, and seventeen and a half inches at bottom, with an internal depth of seven inches. This basin is simply placed, without any special foundation, on the floor, to which it is secured by means of two iron ears. The wooden cylinder *b* is bolted vertically in the centre of the pan, and is bound at top and bottom by iron rings, whilst at its upper extremity is an iron thimble, for the reception of the lower end of a vertical shaft. The runner, figs. 4, 5, 6, destined to revolve in this basin, is of wood, the pivot *c* of the spindle being so placed as to be exactly vertical, both with regard to the bottom of the basin and the face of the wooden block forming the revolving portion of the mill. This adjustment is readily managed by means of the tripod *e*, *f*, *g*, attached to the wood at its extremities, and of which the central boss *h* fits on to the square part of the spindle. The circumference of the wooden block *a′* is bound by two strong iron hoops, its lower face being provided with twelve blades or stirrers of thick sheet iron, driven into the wood, and projecting about half an inch, arranged as the radii of a circle. The space between the runner *a′* and the pan *a* receives 28 lbs. of mercury, the distance between the two surfaces being regulated by means of the nuts, *i*, *i′*. Formerly this was so arranged that the blades penetrated slightly beneath the surface of the quicksilver, but it has been ascertained that the amalgamation progresses more rapidly, and with less loss of mercury, when the lower edges of the iron stirrers are kept slightly above its level. The distance allowed between the circumference of the runner and the inside of the pan within which it revolves, is about one-sixth of an inch, and the upper extremity of each vertical shaft is retained by two bearings, K K′, fig. 1. These shafts have also a coupling in some portion of their length, which enables one or more of the runners to be thrown out of action, without interfering with the remainder.

Motion is communicated to the various mills by means of two mitre wheels, one of which is attached to the axle, whilst the other is keyed on a shaft on which is a pulley, *l*, around which is an endless strap bearing on the riggers of all the mill runners, as shown by the dotted lines. The relative diameters of the mitre wheels are so calculated as to cause the runners to make eighteen revolutions per minute. Higher and lower speeds have occasionally been given to these mills, but the above number of revolutions per minute has been found to afford the most satisfactory results. It has also been ascertained that from eight to nine mills are required for the treatment of the sands and slimes resulting from the action of every ten stampers, which amounts to about seven thousand pounds in the course of twenty-four hours. The working of this apparatus proceeds concurrently with that of the stamping mills, and requires but little supervision. The slimes are discharged into the canal or launder, *c*, from which they pass through a screen of wire gauze, *m*, by which any impurities, such as fragments of wood, are separated; and then flow into the canal *d*, from which they pass through four small spouts into the basin-shaped cavities in the runners of the mills 1, 2, 3, and 4. The slimes now descend so as to come in contact with the mercury contained in the basins, *a*, where they are constantly agitated by the iron blades fixed in the revolving wooden blocks, and finally rising through the annular cavity, between the edge of the runner and the inside of the basin, escape by the lip *n* into the mill immediately below it. Here precisely the same action takes place as in the first; and the slimes flowing off into the canal *e*, are distributed over the inclined tables, *g*, by means of apertures prepared for that purpose in the side of the launder.

Once every month the mills are thrown out of action, and the whole of the mercury removed. The quicksilver is now subjected to two successive filtrations, and an amalgam is obtained, which usually contains from twenty-eight to thirty-three per cent. of gold, and which is treated by distillation. The mercury separated by filtration, and which still retains a little gold, is returned to the pans, and the apparatus again put into operation. The monthly loss of mercury in an arrangement of eight mills, is usually from two and a half to three ounces.

One boy readily manages the supervision of from ten to a dozen of the tables, *g*, and every two hours removes the cloths from each in succession, and, after having washed them in a tank prepared for the purpose, replaces them as before. In the case of ordinary ores, affording from fourteen to fifteen loths per thousand quintals (about three dwt. per ton), eight loths are extracted by the mills, and from five to six by the inclined tables, so that from one to two loths only are obtained from the slimes by smelting. The sands and slimes passing off from the tables are collected in settling pits and labyrinths, from whence they are subsequently removed for concentration, principally on shaking tables.

Shaking Tables.—The shaking table employed at Schemnitz, which is somewhat peculiar in its construction, is represented Plate V. figs. 7, 8, 9, and 10; the first being an end, and the second a side elevation. The part *a* of the table is called its head, *b* is the tail, and *c* (figs. 9 and 10) is known as the tongue. Of the four chains by which the table is suspended, the two at the tail *b* are the longest, and are attached to the wooden rollers *d*, furnished at each end with ratchet wheels by means of which their length may be easily regulated. The wooden axle *e* is furnished with either two or three cams, which successively throw forward the lever *f*, articulated at *g*, carrying with it the rod *h*, which pushes the table in the same direction, as long as the cam continues to act on it, but, as soon as it is released, allows it to fall back with a sudden jerk into its original position, the tongue *c* at the same time striking against a stout bar placed before two of the pillars of the framework for that purpose. The elasticity of this bar causes a series of vibrations in the table, which gradually become less, until it is again forced forward and thrown by the cam as before described. The position of the elastic bar forming the stop is easily regulated by wedges, whilst the length of the rod *h* admits of being adjusted by the use of the screw *i*, and wheel and pinion *k k'*, in such a way as to increase or diminish the throw of the apparatus. Above the axle of each table is a wooden platform, on which are stored the slimes to be treated, and which are from thence transferred to the cistern *l*, of which the bottom has a considerable inclination. Below the semicircular opening *m*, in this box, is a small spout or gutter *n*, leading to the higher end of the inclined plane *o*. This head-board is composed of two distinct planes, placed one above the other, but both inclined at the same angle, and on the upper one are arranged a number of little wooden buttons, *o'*, by the arrangement of which the regularity of the flow of slime over the whole surface is readily secured. In some cases, a strainer of wire gauze is placed across the head of the lower portion of the table head, for the purpose of collecting chips or any other impurities that may have accidentally become mixed with the slimes.

The two launders, *p* and *q*, run the whole length of the establishment, the first being used for the purpose of supplying clean water, and the second for carrying off the impoverished slimes.

These tables are set in motion by water-wheels, one horse power being sufficient to keep in operation ten tables, each of which is capable of washing the slimes produced by four stampers.

The working of these tables is conducted as follows:—Slime is thrown with a shovel into the cistern *l*, and a small stream of water allowed to fall into it, which, mingling with the slimes, escapes by the aperture *m*, and descending in an even flow over the inclined plane *o*, covers the whole width of the head of the table. In order to facilitate the mixture of the slimes and water, it is generally necessary to use a shovel, by which the contents of the box are occasionally stirred; and when the sands mixed with the slimes are somewhat coarse, a small wooden hoe is employed to rake the deposit, on the head of the table, gently against the current.

The tension of the table, or the sine of the angle formed by the suspension chains with the perpendicular, from the point at which they are attached, is made to vary in accordance with the nature of the slimes to be treated, although those of the lower end *b*, generally remain the same for all descriptions of slimes. The tension of these chains is generally about five and a half inches, but for the chains of the head *a*, it is not more than two inches for coarse slimes, whilst for very fine slimes it may be as much as eight inches. The extent of the throw of the table is also made to vary in accordance with the nature of the stuff to be wrought. For coarse slimes it may be as much as five and a half inches, whilst for very fine ones it is sometimes reduced to two inches. The number of oscillations of the table is so managed that it shall be constantly in motion, without any period of repose, the number of throws per minute, for coarse slimes, being about sixteen, and for very fine ones, from thirty-five to forty; but it must be remembered that in each case the elasticity of the bar against which the tongue is made to fall, produces from ten to fifteen secondary oscillations, gradually becoming less decided, until the table is again thrown forward by the cam.

After the apparatus has been in action a certain period, varying according to the nature of the slimes worked, from a few hours to two, or even three days, the deposit of enriched matter, towards the head of the table, accumulates to a depth of some six or seven inches, so that the operation could no longer be continued without danger of its flowing over the sides. The apparatus is then stopped for the purpose of being cleaned up; and as the deposit varies in richness in different parts of the table, it is divided into three distinct portions, each of which is differently disposed of. Even that at the head is, however, rarely sufficiently rich to be sent directly to the smelting works, and is generally again worked over. The deposit in the middle, which is divided into two classes, is invariably re-treated, whilst that at the lower end is usually rejected as useless. The different products thus obtained from the first table are further enriched by being subsequently re-treated on separate tables.

At Schemnitz, in addition to shaking tables, sleeping tables are sometimes employed for the concentration of the finer slimes, but these are of the usual construction, and are rather used for the purpose of washing lead slimes, than for those of which gold forms an important constituent.

Having described the amalgamating mills and shaking tables, it remains for us to follow the treatment of the rich auriferous materials collected on the cloths spread on the inclined tables, and subsequently accumulated in the tanks into which they are washed. The final washing of these rich deposits is a delicate operation, performed first in the gold box (goldlütte), and afterwards in a kind of scoop-shaped batea, called a scheidetrog.

Goldlütte.—This apparatus is represented, in plan and elevation, Plate V., figs. 11 and 12. It consists of an inclined trough, twelve feet in length, and twenty inches in width, with an inclination of about three feet on its entire length. Its end and vertical sides are nailed to the bottom, and are ten inches in depth. The upper portion of the plank forming the bottom of this arrangement has, cut in its surface, numerous small riffles, which form zigzags, running at an angle of 45° with the upright sides. At a distance of seven inches from the upper end of this box, is a dam *a*, rather shallower than the sides, behind which a stream of water is introduced by means of a tap, and which, flowing evenly over its upper edge, distributes itself regularly on the auriferous slimes placed at *b*. The bottom of this arrangement must be so fixed on the woodwork which supports it, that its transverse section is at all points perfectly level. The workman stands on the plank, *c*, and the three rectangular reservoirs, *d*, *e*, *f*, are for the purpose of receiving the products of the operation.

The working of this arrangement is conducted very much like that of an ordinary sleeping table. The ore is added in small quantities with a shovel, water is allowed to play over its surface so as to distribute it in the box, and then clean water alone is made to flow over it; whilst, at the same time, its surface is gently swept upwards, in a contrary direction to the current, with a brush or small heath broom. The products obtained are:—

1st. A coarse argentiferous slime containing gold, galena, and iron pyrites.
2nd. A fine slime containing the same substances.
3rd. A concentrated slime, rich in gold.

The two first products are usually re-washed in the same apparatus before being sent to the smelting works. The third, on the contrary, contains nearly the whole of the gold, and is at once washed in the scoop-shaped batea.

Scheidetrog.—This instrument is represented, in plan and elevation, Plate V., figs. 13 and 14. It is neatly cut out of a single block of wood, elm or sycamore being generally employed for the purpose. The workman holds this below the lower end of the washing box, and when in that position, the auriferous slimes are carefully brushed into it by the aid of a broom, assisted by a gentle current of water. He now holds it in both hands, placing his thumbs in the semicircular depressions *a a'*, and stationing himself before a tank of water, he begins giving to the instrument a motion similar to that of the shaking table, striking at each oscillation the end *b* against his thighs. After working in this way during a few minutes, the greater portion of the sulphides are washed off, and, in order to eliminate the remainder, he holds the batea in a slightly inclined position with the left hand, whilst with the right he directs on it a small stream of water from a horn in which a minute hole has been bored. This operation is commenced at the upper end of the instrument and gradually continued downward, by which means the gold, gradually freed from impurities, begins to make its appearance in the form of a pale yellow crescent-shaped streak. The product of each operation thus conducted is washed into a receiver, the contents of which are again re-washed, in the same way, at the close of the day's work. The final product thus obtained is amalgamated, by agitation with mercury, and after filtration in the usual way, retorted, and melted into bars.

The relative values of the products obtained at Schemnitz from ores operated on in this way, after deducting the cost of metallurgical treatment, were, in 1846, nearly as follows:—

	Per cent.
Gold	50·5
Silver	33·0
Lead	16·5
Total	100·0

BRAZIL.—The rock treated at the Morro Velho mines is principally a mixture of magnetic, arsenical, and common iron pyrites, finely disseminated in, and intimately mixed with, a quartzose gangue. The composition of what is called pure ore may be taken at about forty-three per cent. of silica, and fifty-seven per cent. of pyritous matter. Of these minerals, arsenical pyrites is usually the most auriferous, although it does not occur in large quantities. Pure specimens of this substance afford, by assay, from four to six ounces of gold per ton, and wherever crystals of this mineral make their appearance the yield of the precious metal is large. Cubical pyrites is of more frequent occurrence, but is far less rich in gold; solid specimens of this substance, but slightly mixed with quartz, yield about an ounce and a half of gold per ton by assay.

Magnetic pyrites constitutes the largest proportion of the sulphides found, but this is very slightly auriferous, since pure specimens generally yield rather less than four dwt. per ton. Branches of clay slate are often found in the principal veins, and this rock, under such circumstances, commonly affords, by assay, from five to seven and a half dwt. of gold per ton. Quartz without any admixture of sulphides has never been found to be auriferous, and it is a remarkable fact that the smallest speck of gold is rarely seen, previous to concentration, in any of the ores from this mine.*

Spalling.—The ores on being drawn from underground are delivered on the spalling floors, where they are broken into fragments of a proper size for the stamping mills; and the clay slate, and other comparatively sterile rock, are picked out and thrown into separate heaps. Iron hammers were, until 1857, employed for breaking the ore on the spalling floors, but in that year cast steel was substituted for iron, the result of which has been a saving of at least fifty per cent. on the annual cost of these tools.

Stamping.—The stamping mills employed at Morro Velho are worked by water, and are of the ordinary Cornish form of construction, except that each lifter is provided with four iron guides for keeping it in its proper position. A new stamp head weighs 230 lbs., and when entirely worn out is reduced to 59 lbs. The average weight of a stamp head may thus be taken at about 150 lbs., and the period of its duration at four months. The total weight of a new pestle, *i. e.* head, lifter, tongue, and all the other work attached, is about 640 lbs. The lift of the stamper is from ten to twelve inches, the number of blows struck per minute varying from 60 to 80, in accordance with the greater or less supply of water for the wheels.

The battery box, or coffer, differs slightly in dimensions in the different mills, but is composed of wood lined with sheet iron. The heads are generally worked about three inches from each other,

* We state this on the authority of Mr. Hockin, the Managing Director of the Company.

and the same distance from the sides of the coffer. The height from the bottom of the coffer to the grate openings is a matter of great importance, and one that requires much attention, since on this greatly depends the degree of fineness to which the ore will be crushed, as well as the amount passed through the apparatus in the course of twenty-four hours.

The stamping mills in this establishment are self-supplying, a blow being given to the feeding hopper, by a peg driven in the central lifter of each set, whenever the absence of ore in the coffer admits of its falling sufficiently low to come in contact with it. It therefore follows, as the stamps do not work on iron blocks, but form their own beds of tightly-compressed ore, that as the heads wear, the bottom of the coffer will grow higher, and the space between the grated openings and the faces of the heads become proportionately less.

In order to keep a series of stamping mills in a regular and efficient state of working, considerable attention is required to be bestowed on their adjustment; and when the bottom of the coffer has become too high, the working of the heads is so arranged, that before feeding themselves with fresh ore, they shall so far wear down the stamp bed as to reduce it to its proper level beneath the grate opening.

This adjustment is readily effected by taking out the pin from the middle lifter, and shifting it higher or lower, as the case may require.

It is probable that this operation may have given rise to the term applied to the regulation of stamps, which is called "pitching."

The grates employed at the St. John d'El Rey mines are nineteen inches in length, nine inches in width, and made of sheets of copper one-eighth of an inch in thickness. These are pierced with conical holes one-twelfth of an inch in diameter on the outside, tapering off on the other to one-forty-eighth of an inch, where a projecting burr is raised, which is placed toward the inside of the coffer. Copper plates have been found, on the whole, more durable than iron; besides which they possess the advantage, that when worn out they are readily converted into gun-metal by the addition of a little tin, and can then be employed for axle bearings and other purposes.

Results obtained.—The rock stamped at Morro Velho is reduced to the state of a mixture of fine sand and impalpable slime, the relative proportions of which will be seen from the following tabular statement of experiments:—

TABLE I.*

Size of Mesh.	Mixture from all the Mills.	From Herring's Stamps.	From Lyon's Stamps.
Of 1,000 grains sifted, on sieve of 10,000 holes per square inch—	per cent.	per cent.	per cent.
Passed through	88·25	95·25	93·22
Did not pass through	11·75	4·75	6·78
	100·00	100·00	100·00
Did not pass through 2,500 holes to square inch	0·50	0·25	0·33

This auriferous material issuing from the stamping mills is associated with gold in three different states, viz.—

1st. Free gold capable of concentration by washing.

2nd. Ditto in a lamellar form liable to be carried off in suspension by water.

3rd. Mechanically combined gold, enclosed in particles of pyrites, but capable of being liberated by further grinding.

The following table, from the notes of Mr. Dietzsch, affords much practical information relative to the stamping mills now in operation at this establishment:—

TABLE II.

Name of Stamps.	No. of Heads.	Blows per minute.	Lift of Stamp Heads.	No. of Cams on the axle.	Dimension of Stamps Coffer.						Dimension of Wheels.				Ore stamped.		
					length.		width.		depth.		diameter.		width.		Tons per day.	Tons per head per day.	lbs. per head per day.
			in.		ft.	in.	ft.	in.	ft.	in.	ft.	in.	ft.	in.			
Lyon . . .	30	63	10	...	2	2	1	3	2	0	40	6	3	3	36·73	1·22	2,733
Cotesworth .	12	61	11	4	2	2	1	1	1	6	31	0	3	0	16·92	1·41	3,158
Susannah .	9	65	12	6	2	3	1	3	2	0	19	2	4	4	10·94	1·21	2,710
Herring . .	24	78	12	...	2	6	1	6	2	0	42	6	6	0	34·56	1·44	3,225
Powles . .	36	67	12	4	2	2	1	3	1	10	51	0	5	0	66·10	1·83	4,100
Addison .	24	73	12	4	2	2	1	3	1	10	42	0	6	0	35·54	1·48	3,315
	135																

* From MS. notes of Mr. F. Dietzsch, Superintendent of Reduction Works.

Strakes.—The slimes and water issuing from the gratings in front of the coffers, to which a certain amount of clean water is added, are conducted over inclined platforms about eighteen inches in width, and from twenty-seven to thirty-five feet in length, which have a fall of one inch per foot. The first sixteen feet of these strakes are covered with bullock skins two feet two inches long, and of the width of the strake, tanned with the hair on them ; a series of baize cloths, each two feet ten inches long, are employed below these, which are again followed, at the lower end of the arrangement, by another series of overlapping skins. A certain quantity of finely-divided gold is caught even on the last of these skins, whilst a considerable proportion, estimated at ten per cent. of the total amount present, is carried off in suspension by the water.

The skins and strips of baize are removed and washed at regular intervals during the day and night, the time allowed to intervene between each washing up, depending on the nature and richness of the ores treated. In each of the houses erected over the strakes, are boxes or tanks, in which the skins and pieces of baize are carefully beaten and washed, and of which those destined for the reception of the most concentrated slimes are divided by partitions into three separate divisions. Into one of them the first three skins from the upper end of the strakes are washed, and into the second is removed the ore collected on skins 4 and 5 of the series, whilst the third division contains water in which the final washing of skins 1, 2, 3, 4, and 5, is effected, after having previously removed the coarser particles in one of the other divisions.

The skins and cloths below No. 5 are washed in the same way, but into separate tanks, from which they are subsequently removed and washed over another series of skins and cloths, in order to effect their further concentration. The deposit on the first three skins, known as *head sand,* amounts to about 0·42 of a cubic foot per ton of ore stamped, and contains from twenty-seven to thirty ounces of gold per ton, all of which, with the exception of about one ounce, is in a free state. This sand is sent without further preparation to the amalgamating house.

The *middle sand* consists of the deposit collected on the skins Nos. 4 and 5, and contains about six ounces of gold per ton, of which some sixteen dwt. only are mechanically combined with particles of pyrites. This sand is further enriched by being washed over another system of strakes.

The deposit taken from the third compartment of the tank in which the upper five skins are finally washed, is called *swim sand*, and being exceedingly fine, could not be safely subjected to concentration, and is consequently sent, with the head sand, directly to the amalgamating house.

All the products caught below the fifth skin are known as *tail sands*, and are like the middle sand, concentrated by being washed over a second system of strakes. The apparatus employed for this purpose consists of three strakes, each covered with four skins and seven cloths.

At the Herring, Lyon, Powles, and Addison stamps, the skins and cloths are changed every hour, whilst at the others this is only done every two hours. Previous to 1854 the strakes above described constituted the only arrangement for the collection of the auriferous materials issuing from the batteries, but in that year some extra strakes were added, as it had been long known that a considerable amount of the precious metal passed off in the slimes. These extra strakes are so fixed as to receive the slimes from the lower end of the original ones, after being first diluted by the addition of some clean water, and the sands collected are subjected to amalgamation without further concentration. The saving of gold effected by these additional strakes amounts to about 38 ounces per month.

The valuable nature of the products resulting from the above processes of concentration, renders it necessary that all parts of the establishment in which they are collected should be protected from theft, and for this purpose the strake heads are securely railed off, and the tanks in which the head sands are washed provided with locked covers.

In Californian mills, where the amount of blanket surface employed is proportionately much less than at Morro Velho, that part of the establishment which contains the various contrivances for the separation of gold from the crushed rock, is securely enclosed in a wooden building, under the immediate control of the chief amalgamator. No part of the gold-saving apparatus is, as a rule, kept under lock, with the exception of the tanks, when full, in which the blankets are washed, and the rollers with the mercury boxes of the amalgamators, which are frequently secured by locked covers.

The following table gives some important details relating to the strakes employed at the Morro Velho mines:—

TABLE III.

Name of Stamps.	No. of Heads.	No. of Strakes.	Length of Strakes.	Width of Strakes.	Area of Strakes, square feet.	Square Feet per Ton of Ore stamped.	Tons of Ore passing per 24 hours.	No. of Skins on Strakes.	No. of Baizes on Strakes.	Quantity of Head Sand per day.
			ft. in.	ft. in.						cub. ft.
Lyon . .	30	36	31 10	1 6	1,719	46·83	36·73	288	210	20·00
Cotesworth	12	13	30 6	1 4½	545	32·21	16·92	104	65	5·50
Susannah .	9	8	27 0	1 6	324	29·61	10·94	48	48	2·75
Herring .	24	29	35 0	1 6	1,232	35·64	34·56	228	174	18·00
Powles. .	36	42	33 7	1 3½	1,821	27·55	66·10	336	252	28·47
Addison .	24	30	31 10	1 5	1,352	38·04	35·54	240	170	17·00
	135	158			6,993		200·79	1,244	919	91·72

Mr. Dietzsch remarks that straking may, on the whole, be considered a cheap, simple, and economical process, by which 67 per cent. of the gold originally present in the ore is obtained in a highly concentrated state, whilst the 33 per cent. which escapes is in two distinct forms.

1st. Light free gold.

2nd. Gold enclosed in the coarser particles of pyrites.

The first, which has, to a great extent, been laminated by the action of the stampers, exposes so great an amount of surface, in proportion to its weight, that it cannot be economically saved by any known process, and floats off with the lighter portions of the slimes. It is difficult to determine the exact amount of loss resulting from this cause, but from experiments which have been made on the residual sands, it is believed to be about 10 per cent. of the gold present in the original ore. The second, which is in the form of fine gold enclosed within particles of pyrites, is partially recovered by separating the coarser from the finer sands, and subsequently grinding them in arrastres, and subjecting the resulting secondary slimes to the action of another system of strakes.

Re-treatment of First Tailings.—This is effected by running the whole of the waste from the different systems of strakes above described, through ordinary tyes, similar in construction to those represented Plate IV. c c′, in which small wooden stops are from time to time placed at the end, thus allowing the slimes to run off, whilst the coarser sands remain behind. These tyes are arranged in couples, so that whilst one is being cleaned out, the other may be in operation.

When one of these tyes has been thus filled, the sand from it is taken out into another box, from which it is conveyed by a stream of water into arrastres, which have an opening in the side about a foot from the bottom. Into these arrastres, of which there is a series, driven by water power, the coarse sands are constantly flowing, mixed with a stream of water; and becoming ground under the mullers, are so reduced in size as to float, and then escaping through the apertures in the sides, are concentrated on a system of strakes. It is evident that the action of these machines will be continuous, since the supply of sand to be pulverised is constantly flowing in, and being heavier than the finer particles, it will sink to the bottom, where it remains until it has been ground into an impalpable state, when it escapes in suspension over the strakes.

Each arrastre is supplied with three cubic feet of water per minute, each cubic foot holding in suspension 1·75 lbs. of sand, and discharges over three strakes, 15 feet in length, covered with either five or six skins. The quantity of sand passed through in the course of twenty-four hours, is about three tons. The deposits collected on the first skin are regarded as head sands, and washed off every two hours into tanks, from which they are sent directly to the amalgamating house. These sands usually contain about 16½ dwt. of gold per ton. The deposit on the second skin is removed every four hours, and, like that on the first, subjected to direct amalgamation, whilst the other skins are only washed every twelve hours, and the slimes afterwards subjected to concentration.

Below the first series of strakes, a number of extra strakes are laid down, which are worked precisely like those attached to the first system before the stamping mills.

Re-treatment of Second Tailings.—Up to the year 1855, the tailings from the system of apparatus before described were treated as worthless, and sluiced into the river accordingly, although it had been determined, by numerous experiments, that they still retained a notable amount of gold. At that period, however, a distinct system of works was erected on the banks of the river, and at a low level, for the elaboration of the whole of the refuse escaping from the upper floors.

These are provided with a series of tyes, in which the sands are separated from the slimes, and from which they are subsequently taken to be again ground in stamping mills and arrastres.* The sand from these tyes contains about 11 dwt. of gold per ton.

As these sands could not be advantageously ground in stamping mills, without the admixture of some coarse and hard material, they were for some years stamped with the addition of a portion of a deposit, known as "Cascalho," containing small quantities of gold; but in 1861, the supply of this substance having become to a great extent exhausted, the refuse portions of the lode, picked out at the spalling floors, were substituted for it. The result of this experiment proved highly satisfactory, and consequently the employment of these wastes, which contain a small amount of gold, has been since continued.

The system of enrichment on strakes is conducted precisely as in the case of the upper floors, and about 16 cubic feet of concentrated sand is daily produced. These sands, however, contain large quantities of decomposing sulphides, giving rise to the formation of sulphates of iron, which rapidly flour and sicken any mercury brought in contact with them, and the tailings are consequently not adapted for direct amalgamation. They are therefore again further concentrated, by being passed over another set of strakes, until they have become reduced from 16 to 1½ cubic feet, and are then carefully washed in a batea. This batea is a shallow wooden bowl, used in the same way as the tin dish of the Californian miner, and in which some six or eight pounds of sand are operated on at a time. The product of this last washing chiefly consists of finely-divided gold, associated with small quantities of various mineral impurities, from which it is separated by trituration with mercury in large Wedgewood-ware mortars.

Amalgamation of Concentrated Ores.—The apparatus employed at Morro Velho is represented Plate VI. In this drawing fig. 1 shows the machinery in elevation, and fig. 2 in plan, whilst fig. 3 is a vertical section of the triturator, or "saxe."

The water-wheel A, by means of intermediate gearing, gives motion to a set of barrels H, 4 feet in length, and 2 feet 5 inches in diameter, each having a capacity of 20 cubic feet. The charge of each barrel is 16 cubic feet, or one and a half ton of wet sand, and 60 lbs. of mercury. There is also a sufficient amount of clean water at the

* The stamping mills employed at this part of the establishment have no grates, but, like those of Schemnitz, discharge once over sluices or dams.

same time introduced, to give to the slimes the necessary degree of fluidity to enable the globules of quicksilver formed to become properly incorporated, without allowing them to become sufficiently mobile to admit of the settling of the mercury and amalgam at the bottom.

The barrels, when thus charged, are allowed to revolve in accordance with the nature of the ores treated, and the state of the atmosphere at the time, during from thirty to thirty-six hours; and the bungs L, being then removed in succession, the contents of the barrels are discharged into the hoppers M. The stop-gates *a* are now slightly raised, and a small stream of water is introduced into the hoppers, which gradually washes their contents into the spouts N, where an additional supply of clean water is added from the launder F, and the united streams, carrying with them in suspension a portion of the slimes from M, fall into the transverse conduit O, from whence they pass through the funnels *b*, into the trough, or saxe W.

The saxe consists of a trough, sixteen feet in length, and two feet in width, divided into six compartments by the partitions *w*, and provided with a movable agitator, or runner V, which can be removed at pleasure by being vertically drawn out of the trough W. This is supplied with rakes, fixed on the faces of solid wooden blocks *w'*, corresponding to the number of divisions in the saxe, and supported on a bar, running on guide wheels, in such a way, that the depth of the rakes can be easily regulated by means of screws; a certain amount of play being at the same time allowed them by the introduction of springs.

Motion is given to the rakes by the eccentric Q, and the rods S, U, and bell-crank T, the rod U being at one end connected with the movable bar of the runner.

The working of this apparatus is conducted as follows:—The contents of the barrels are first discharged into the hoppers M, and from thence slowly washed, by a constant stream of water, into the saxe through the funnels *b*, traversing the two central runner-blocks, and discharging beneath the surface of the mercury, whilst the rakes are slowly drawn backwards and forwards, by the action of the eccentric Q, over the surface of the mercury, which accumulates in the trough of the saxe W.

In this way the globules of quicksilver and amalgam are deposited from the diluted slimes, in the bottom of the various divisions, while the slimes themselves flow regularly through the apertures in the divisions, shown by the dotted lines, fig. 3, and, escaping at each end, pass over strakes Y, covered in the usual way with bullock skins, by which a large portion of the mercury, which might otherwise be lost, is collected. It will be observed, by referring to fig. 3, that the central division of the saxe is not, like the others, provided with an aperture; and consequently the slimes entering by one funnel are discharged to the right, while those arriving by the other escape to the left of the apparatus. Extra strakes are arranged below the first, which are worked with the addition of clean water, as in the system of supplementary strakes employed below the stamping mills, and the supply of clean water admitted on the strakes Y is regulated by means of the stop-cocks X. The usual loss of gold per ton of ore treated is, at the St. John d'El Rey mines, estimated at about 2 oitavas or nearly 5 dwt. per ton. The mercury can be drawn off when required, and the amalgam is cleaned up, strained, and retorted every ten days, the gold being then melted into bars.

The loss of quicksilver, taken on the average of the last three years, has been 2·923 oz. per ton of ore stamped. The average cost of extracting the mineral from the mine, and its reduction, including every expense incurred by the Company for general management, &c. &c., for the last ten years, has been 25*s.* per ton; out of which the cost of stamping alone has been 2*s.* 10*d.* per ton.

SODIUM AMALGAM.

The extraction of gold by amalgamation has, hitherto, been often attended with difficulties occasioned by the presence of compounds of sulphur, arsenic, antimony, bismuth, or tellurium in the ores; which by covering the gold with a thin film of tarnish, prevents its entering into combination with mercury. The use of sodium amalgam, however, is stated not only to facilitate amalgamation under such circumstances, but also to prevent the "sickening" of mercury, which in the presence of certain chemical compounds, and among others sulphate of iron, is apt to take place. It is also claimed for sodium amalgam that by its use the "flouring" of mercury when ground with compounds containing sulphur, arsenic, tellurium, &c. may to a great extent be avoided.

Two claimants dispute the honour of having first discovered these properties of an amalgam of sodium and mercury, but the truth would appear to be that the discovery was made by each, almost at the same time, and without any knowledge of what was being done by the other. Dr. Wurtz of New York applied for an American patent in November 1864, whilst Mr. Crookes made a similar application in England in February 1865, and consequently before anything was known in Europe of the existence of the American patent. It must, however, be conceded that the first application for a patent was undoubtedly made by Dr. Wurtz.

Not having any personal experience of the effects produced by the addition of sodium amalgam to mercury employed for the amalgamation of gold ores on a large scale, the following description of its action is given on the authority of the inventors of the process, and has been chiefly derived from an article by Dr. Wurtz, published in the *American Journal of Science and Arts,* vol. xli. March 1866, and from a pamphlet on the same subject, published for private circulation, by Mr. Crookes. It may be remarked that at the date of our leaving the mining districts of California in December 1866, although its use had been extensively experimented on, it had not become generally adopted, and that the evidence with regard to its efficiency was considered to be of a conflicting nature. It may, nevertheless, be regarded as certain, that no time was lost in practically testing the efficiency of sodium amalgam, and that, had it possessed all the advantages claimed, its use would have long since become general.

A quantity of sodium amalgam dissolved in a hundred times or more its weight of quicksilver, is said to communicate to the whole a greatly enhanced power of adhering to metals, and particularly to those which, like gold and silver, are situated towards the negative extremity of the electro-chemical scale. This power of adhesion in the case of the two metals is so great, that the resistance which their surfaces, when in their native state, often oppose to amalgamation (a resistance much greater, and more general than has been hitherto recognised, and due to causes as yet uninvestigated) is instantly overcome, whether their particles be coarse or impalpable. Even an artificial coating of oil or grease, which is usually such an enemy to the combination of mercury with other metals, forms no obstacle to immediate amalgamation by this prepared quicksilver. The atoms of quicksilver are, as it is described, put into a sort of polaric condition, by a minute addition of one of the metals which range themselves toward the electro-positive end of the scale; so that its affinity for the more electro-negative metals is stated to be so greatly exalted that it seizes upon, and is instantaneously absorbed by their surfaces, just as water is absorbed by a lump of sugar, or other porous substance soluble in it.

Such quicksilver even adheres strongly to surfaces of iron, steel, platinum, aluminium, and antimony; an adhesion which, however, in the case of these metals is not a true amalgamation, there being no penetration into the substance of the metal; so that the superficially adherent quicksilver may be readily wiped off, just as water may be removed from glass: the only metal as yet experimented on, which cannot be enfilmed by the use of sodium amalgam, appears to be magnesium.

Application of Sodium Amalgam to working Ores of the Precious Metals.—This consists in adding from time to time, to the quicksilver used in amalgamation, about one hundredth part of its weight of sodium amalgam. The frequency with which the amalgam is to be added cannot be exactly specified, as it will be found to depend on a multitude of circumstances, such, for instance, as the temperature, the purity and quantity of the water used, the ratio borne by the surface of the quicksilver to its mass, the amount and mode of agitation of the quicksilver, the nature of the process and apparatus used, the character of the ore, strength of the amalgam, &c.; so that this important point can only be determined in each case by experience. Some general indications may, however, be derived from the experiments which have been made. It is said that less sodium is requisite in cases in which much water is employed, and when the water is frequently renewed, as, for instance, in the riffles of a sluice, and in all forms of amalgamators through which a continual current of water is kept running; since mercurial solutions of sodium are but little affected by water free from acid, alkaline, or saline impurities. In cases, however, in which but little water is employed, and especially where the ore and quicksilver are ground together into a slime, the water soon becomes alkaline, and oxidation of the sodium sets in, necessitating its frequent renewal. In such cases the following manipulation is recommended. The whole amount of quicksilver to be used for working up a batch of slimes, say fifty pounds, is prepared by dissolving in it one per cent. of amalgam No. 2; or better, two per cent. of the soft amalgam No. 1, which dissolves more readily:* one-

* No. 1 amalgam contains two per cent., and No. 2, four per cent. of sodium, and is a hard brittle solid, remarkably infusible, requiring a temperature nearly as high as the fusing point of type metal to melt it, and may be cast into ingots, and packed either under petroleum, or in air-tight iron cans filled with dry lime.

half, or twenty-five pounds, is then thrown into the mill with the ore, and as the incorporation proceeds; certain fractional parts of the other half are added at intervals, varying according to circumstances, until the whole has been introduced. If, as is usual, the quicksilver has been separated from the slimes of a previous operation, it will retain a certain amount of sodium, and therefore require fresh amalgam in proportionately smaller quantities.

In sluicing operations, the soft amalgam No. 1 is, on account of its ready solubility in mercury, most recommended; and in these cases it is practicable to test the quicksilver in the riffles, and ascertain when the magnetic quality requires restoration, by throwing in a few grains of gold dust.* Similar tests are easily applied to slimes, and in amalgamating generally, a slip of tarnished sheet copper is a suitable agent for such testings.

It may be remarked that the amalgam No. 1 is at any time easily prepared from No. 2, by melting it in an iron ladle with its own weight of quicksilver. In copper-plate amalgamation,—that is, in cases in which auriferous materials are brought into contact with amalgamated metallic surfaces,—it is recommended to substitute for quicksilver itself the pasty amalgam No. 2. In these modes of amalgamation great economy in wear and tear of apparatus, as well as in first cost, is said to be effected by using plates or surfaces of iron instead of copper. The power of coating or enfilming iron is stated to render these amalgams peculiarly valuable in every form of apparatus for amalgamation, which has internal surfaces of iron; for these becoming coated with quicksilver immensely extend its chances of contact with particles of gold, so fine as to remain suspended in the water.

Other important services are expected by the inventors to arise out of this power of enfilming iron, such as keeping the surfaces of stamps and of other apparatus used in crushing ores continually coated. In like manner, as the power of adhesion of quicksilver to other metals is exalted by the presence of the alkali-metals, so also is its own cohesion stated to be greatly increased. It is rendered more difficult to mechanically divide, and when thus divided again runs instantly together upon contact. Hence new results of great value are said to have been obtained. For instance, the so-called flouring or granulation of quicksilver, which in the amalgamation of ores always occa-

* From the attraction which it appears to possess for other metals, Dr. Wurtz calls the compound of sodium and quicksilver, "Magnetic Amalgam."

sions losses both of the quicksilver itself, and of its amalgams with the precious metals, is stated to be reduced to a minimum, or altogether prevented.

The recovery of floured quicksilver and amalgams from slimes and similar mixtures, is also said to be greatly facilitated and accelerated thereby. For this purpose some sodium amalgam is thrown into the separator, and collects and incorporates all the scattered globules of auriferous amalgam.

It is here necessary to call attention to a method of manipulation generally applicable when sodium amalgams are used, and particularly so in all cases in which the ore is ground or agitated with quicksilver in contact with metallic iron. This arises from the liability of abraded particles of iron to adhere to the amalgam.

The following plan is therefore in such cases recommended. The amalgam, after separation from excess of quicksilver, and before retorting, is fused in an earthen dish or iron ladle, with, if necessary, addition of a little quicksilver to make it more liquid; and the iron, which forms a scum on the surface, is skimmed off. The excess of quicksilver may, after cooling, be again separated from the amalgam in the usual way. Any amalgam which adheres to the iron scum is readily detached by boiling in water to remove the sodium. This process depends on the fact that adhesion to the iron totally disappears with the extraction of the last traces of sodium from the quicksilver. It is in fact possible to remove all iron from the amalgam by boiling in water without any previous fusion, particularly if the water be made somewhat acid or alkaline. The presence of iron can be readily detected by the magnet, which may also be sometimes used with advantage in separating iron from amalgam after all the sodium has been extracted. There are still other substances which may be found adherent to the amalgam when sodium has been used, such as platinum and osmiridium. These, like iron, immediately detach themselves on the removal of the sodium by boiling the amalgam in water. A mixture of platinum, or osmiridium, or both, with iron, may be freed from the latter by the magnet.

The sodium amalgams prepared in this country in accordance with the recipes of Mr. Crookes, and sold by his agents, are known respectively as A, B, and C amalgams.

Each of these contains three per cent. of sodium, in addition to which B has a small quantity of zinc in its composition, and C a little tin. An amalgam (A), of seven times the strength of the above, is prepared in solid bars for shipment when the expense of freight or land carriage is great. Amalgams B and C cannot be prepared in the concentrated form. It is recommended that one part by weight of amalgam B or C be dissolved in thirty parts of the mercury which is to be used in the amalgamating, triturating, or grinding machines, and the effect which it produces on the mercury noted from time to time during the operation. If it retain its fluidity and brightness to the end of the operation, it is a sign either that a sufficient amount, or too much has been added, and a second experiment should be tried with a less quantity of amalgam. But if it be floured, or sickened, or any loss occur, more amalgam may be added until the best proportion is arrived at.

Mr. Crookes states that amalgam B will generally be found effective, but if the ore contain an excess of any mineral which has a deleterious action on mercury, more especially if it contain bismuth, it will be advantageous to employ amalgam C instead of B.

When the best proportion of amalgam B or C is determined, small quantities of amalgam A should be introduced into the mercury, already containing amalgam B or C, in the proportion of one part of amalgam A to one thousand of mercury. This quantity of amalgam A can be added every few hours, according to circumstances, but one charge of amalgam B or C will, it is stated, usually be sufficient for several days. Under some circumstances it will be found advisable to add amalgam B or C every few days, but a little experience, and comparison with the results obtained by the old plan, will soon show how these several agents are best utilised.

CHAPTER XI.

ASSAY OF AURIFEROUS ORES—ESTIMATION OF GOLD CONTAINED IN QUARTZ—REFINING—ASSAY OF GOLD BULLION.

ASSAY OF GOLD QUARTZ—FUSION WITH LITHARGE OR RED LEAD—AURIFEROUS PYRITES—CUPELLATION—INQUARTATION—PARTING—ASSAY TABLE—TABLE SHOWING PROPORTION OF GOLD IN AURIFEROUS QUARTZ—REFINING—PLATINUM VESSELS—CAST IRON PANS—ASSAY OF BULLION—QUANTITY OF LEAD NECESSARY FOR CUPELLATION OF ALLOYS OF GOLD AND COPPER—ASSAY LABORATORY—THE TOUCHSTONE.

ASSAY OF AURIFEROUS ORES.—Although the exact amount of gold contained in a given specimen of rock is readily ascertained, it is often much more difficult to obtain a fair average sample of the whole produce of a vein. When the gold is in a finely-divided state, and equally disseminated throughout the rock, this presents comparatively little difficulty; but when, on the contrary, it is granular, and occurs in pockets and irregular deposits, great care and labour are sometimes necessary in order to obtain representative samples of the mass.

It is, therefore, of the highest importance that whenever rock is to be assayed for gold, the greatest care should be observed in preparing the samples on which the operation is to be subsequently conducted. With this view, the rock, of which it is desired to ascertain the yield, should be broken, and the heap cut through in the usual way, at least a ton being taken from each pile of importance, and reduced to fragments of the size of beans. This may be done, where machinery for dry crushing is not at hand, by means of a flat-faced hammer on an iron plate. After well mixing, this pounded ore is again cut through, and about ten pounds of it taken for the purpose of being still further reduced in size, and passed through a sieve of fine wire gauze; on this last from three to six different assays are made, and their mean result taken as the produce of the rock examined. By operating in this way a great degree of accuracy may be ensured; but where a less amount of exactitude is required, the quantities of rock crushed may be somewhat reduced, and the number of assays made, fewer.

Instead of operating as above described, a given weight of

finely-powdered rock, from the last cutting, may be reduced in volume by careful washing in a batea, and the residue dried, and assayed in the usual way. From the results obtained, the amount of gold present in a ton of original rock can be readily calculated.

In establishments for the crushing and amalgamation of auriferous rock, it is, however, generally of more importance to determine the amount of gold retained by the tailings, than to ascertain by assay the actual produce of the original ore; since the quantity yielded by amalgamation on the large scale, added to that present in the resulting sands and slimes, will, for many practical purposes, sufficiently represent the total contents of the rock. It is also desirable to know exactly the amount of gold carried off in the final tailings, in order, not only to be enabled to judge of the effect of any modifications which may have been introduced in the machinery or methods of working, but also for the purpose of ascertaining if due attention has been exercised during the various stages of the different processes to which the ore has been subjected. When required for this purpose, the tailings should be caught at regular intervals throughout the day, by placing a bucket, or some other convenient vessel, under the spout from which they finally make their escape; and when full of water and sand, it must be placed aside, in order to give the matters in suspension time to settle. As soon as the water in the bucket has deposited the whole of the solid matter which it held in suspension, it is carefully decanted off, and the deposit, accumulated at the bottom, removed into a box prepared for that purpose.

This is repeated at intervals of about two hours, and at the termination of the experiment the contents of the box are dried, thoroughly mixed and submitted to assay. In the case of samples of tailings thus obtained, the discrepancies between the several assays will, in general, not be very considerable, since the coarse particles of gold will, as a rule, have been retained by the blankets and other appliances over which the stamped rock has passed, and the remaining fine gold is disseminated with a considerable degree of regularity throughout the mass.

Fusion with Litharge or Red Lead.—When the rock to be operated on does not contain an appreciable quantity of iron pyrites, or any other metallic sulphide, weigh 600 gr. in a finely-pulverised state, and intimately mix it with 4,000 gr. of litharge or red lead, and from 15 to 20 gr. of flour, starch, or finely-powdered charcoal.* Introduce this into a

* The weight of pounded ore is fixed at 600 grains, because this quantity can be easily fused in an ordinary No. 10 French crucible.

crucible, of which it should occupy about one-half the capacity, and heat it in an ordinary assay furnace, until the whole has entered into a state of perfect fusion, when the crucible is withdrawn and allowed to cool. When sufficiently cold, it is broken, and the button of lead extracted, cleaned, and cupelled. In the case of ores containing a large amount of gold, it is far better to break the crucible than to pour its contents into an iron mould; but in works in which tailings are being daily examined, the practice of pouring assays may be adopted with advantage, as from the smallness of the quantity of gold contained in the material operated on, no appreciable error will be the result, whilst, on the other hand, the saving in crucibles will be considerable.

In quartz-crushing establishments generally, the assays of ores and tailings may be conveniently conducted in the furnace employed for retorting and melting, which is generally of sufficient size to admit of three or four fusions being carried on at the same time. In regular metallurgical laboratories, for the sake of durability, and to prevent the cracking of the brickwork, the outside of the melting furnace is usually secured by iron plates as shown Fig. 37, which represents that employed by Mr. F. Claudet, and in which A A′ are the fire-places, B B′ the fire-bars, and *b b′* the ash-pits. The dampers C C′ permit of regulating the draught, and the mouths of the furnaces are closed by the hinged doors D D′, lined with baffle-plates. Instead of hinged doors, sliding plates are sometimes employed, and are, for general purposes, probably preferable. The dimensions of this furnace are, 10 inches square and 16 inches in depth above the fire bars, which can, when necessary, be drawn out from the front for the purpose of allowing the coke to fall into the ash-pits *b b′*, or for unclinkering the grate. When used with charcoal, the crucibles must be supported on the bars on pieces of firebrick; but when coke is employed, it has in itself sufficient resistance to allow of their being embedded in the fuel without any other support.

The best crucibles for this purpose are ordinary French pots, which, before being introduced into the fireplace, should be annealed by being gradually heated on the top of the furnace, in order to expel any moisture they may have imbibed, and which, if they were too suddenly heated, might cause them to crack.

When, in addition to gold, the rock contains iron pyrites or any other sulphurised mineral, it frequently happens that the admixture of charcoal becomes unnecessary, and the fusion may be made with litharge alone, since one part of iron pyrites reduces eight and a half parts, blende seven parts, and sulphide of antimony, or grey copper ore, about six parts of lead, to the metallic state.

FIG. 37.

MELTING AND ASSAY FURNACE.

Auriferous Pyrites.—To determine the amount of gold contained in quartz much mixed with iron pyrites or other metallic sulphides, or to assay auriferous pyrites resulting from the concentration of tailings, the following process is generally resorted to. The amount of the substance on which it has been determined to operate, is weighed into a shallow scorifier, and then introduced into the mouth of the muffle of the cupelling furnace, care being taken not to heat it at first too strongly. The powdered ore is from time to time stirred with a bent iron wire fitted into a wooden handle, and in proportion as the sulphur is evolved, and the substance becomes less fusible, the scorifier is pushed further into the muffle, and consequently subjected to a higher temperature; the stirring, by means of the iron rod, being at the same time continued. The roasting must thus be carried on until all odour of sulphur has ceased to be evolved, and the scorifier with its contents is then withdrawn, and allowed to cool.

When sufficiently cold, the roasted ore is united with six times its weight of litharge, its own weight of dry borax, and from fifteen to twenty grains of charcoal, and the whole fused in the furnace as above described. In making the addition of the reducing agent it is necessary to add such a quantity as will afford a button of lead sufficiently large for the collection of the whole of the gold present, and at the same time of a size convenient for cupellation, since, if the amount of lead were too small, a loss of gold would be the result, whilst a very heavy button would require a large cupel, and occupy a long time in working off.*

Cupellation.—This process is founded on the circumstance that when an alloy of lead and silver, lead and gold, or of lead, silver, and gold, is exposed in a state of fusion to the action of a current of air, the precious metals are neither perceptibly volatilised, nor become oxidised, whilst the lead rapidly absorbs oxygen with the formation of a readily-fusible oxide. In order, therefore, to obtain the gold and silver contained in the assay buttons, it is merely necessary to expose them, on a porous fire-proof support, to such a temperature as will cause the oxidation of the lead, whilst the precious metals are not so affected. The litharge thus produced is absorbed by the porous body on which the assay is supported, and nothing but a button of gold or silver, or of an alloy of the two, in case of their being both present, ultimately remains on the test. These supports, which are called *cupels*, are made of bone-ash slightly moistened with water, and consolidated, by pressure in an iron mould, into the required form.

* Instead of operating as above, the assay may be made by scorification.—See Assay of Silver Ores.

Cupels should be perfectly dry before being used, and ought to be kept for at least a fortnight in a warm place in the laboratory, previous to being employed for making cupellations. The muffle, which is made of baked fireclay, has the form of a small D-shaped retort, closed at one end, and is generally provided with openings in the sides and ends, in order to allow of the circulation of air through it.

The furnaces used for cupellation differ considerably in shape and method of construction, but the muffle, when fixed, is so arranged that whilst its closed extremity is supported by a proper shelf, the other corresponds with an opening in the front of the furnace, to the sides of which it is luted with a little clay, and has before it a small platform, on which the hot cupels can be allowed to stand when withdrawn from the muffle.* The muffle thus placed can be equally heated in every part, whilst the apertures, in the sides and end, admit of the passage through it of a current of air from the mouth, through the interior of the muffle, into the furnace itself. To light this apparatus, a little ignited charcoal or coke is thrown into the furnace, which is afterwards filled with fuel; and as soon as the muffle has become heated to bright redness, six or eight cupels, that have been annealing at the mouth of the opening, are introduced by means of proper tongs; the bottom of the muffle having been previously covered with a little loose bone-ash to prevent its being attacked in case of any litharge passing through the cupels in the course of subsequent operations. The open end of the muffle is now closed by a tile or door provided for that purpose, to prevent the introduction of cold air, and the cupels are raised to the temperature of the muffle itself. When this takes place, the door is removed, and a button, obtained from the fusion with litharge, introduced into each of the cupels by a pair of slender tongs. The mouth of the muffle may now be again closed for about a minute, in order to facilitate the fusion of the alloy; and on its removal, each of the cupels will be found to contain a bright metallic bath, in which state the assay is said to be *uncovered.* Under these circumstances, the lead is rapidly converted into litharge, which is absorbed by the cupel as quickly as it is formed, whilst at the same time a little white vapour rises from the cupels, and is gradually carried off through the end, and through the openings in the sides. A circular stain is at the same time formed around the metal in the cupels,

* The best fuel for the cupelling furnace is hard coke broken into small pieces.

which gradually extends and penetrates into their substance. When nearly the whole of the lead has been thus removed, the remaining bead of rich alloy appears to become agitated by a rapid circular motion, which seems to make it revolve with great rapidity. At this stage, the rotation of the bead will be observed to cease, and the button, having for an instant emitted a bright flash of light, becomes suddenly immovable. This is called the *brightening*, and a button remains on the cupel, composed of an alloy of gold, with the silver derived from the litharge, added to that which may have originally existed in the ore operated on.

When the proportion of silver is, in comparison with that of gold, very considerable, and the button of alloy is itself a large one, the abrupt removal of the cupel from the muffle might cause the metallic bead to spirt or *vegetate*, by which a portion of the metal might be thrown off, and a certain amount of loss thereby entailed. To prevent this taking place when a large button has been obtained, the cupel must be gradually withdrawn towards the mouth of the muffle; or the cupel in which the assay has brightened, may be covered by another, kept hot for the purpose, and then removed to the small platform in front of the muffle.

From the fact that silver becomes sensibly volatile at very elevated temperatures, it becomes necessary, when this metal is present, to make the cupellations at the lowest possible heat at which they can be effected. The temperature best fitted for this operation is obtained when the muffle is at a full red heat and the vapours which arise from the assays curl gradually away, and are finally removed by the draught. When the muffle is heated to whiteness, and vapours rise to the top of the arch, the heat is too great; and when, on the contrary, the fumes lie over the bottom, and the sides of the openings in the muffle begin to darken, a little more fuel must be added, or the draught increased. Should the temperature fall below this point, and the lead *set* in the cupels, they may generally be again started by closing the mouth of the muffle with a few large pieces of charcoal. These should be removed when the complete fusion of the alloy in the cupels has been again effected. If an assay has been properly conducted, the button obtained is round, bright, and smooth on its upper surface, and is readily removed from the cupel.

Inquartation.—In order to be enabled to completely remove silver from an alloy of that metal with gold, by the use of nitric acid, it is essential that the weight of the silver present should be about three times that of the gold. It is consequently necessary that when the amount of gold in the button of lead is approximately known, a piece of pure silver should be added to it before cupellation, of such a weight, that with the quantity of that metal derived from the litharge (ascertained by a separate assay) it will, as nearly as possible, fulfil these conditions. The only inconvenience, however, attending the addition of too large a proportion of silver is, that the gold obtained by the subsequent action of acid is thereby rendered flocculent, and somewhat more difficult to collect. When the object of the assay is to ascertain only the amount of gold present, without estimating the associated silver, the necessary addition of this metal is best made by placing a piece of the required weight on the leaden button obtained from the fusion with litharge, and driving it into the lead by a blow with a bright-faced hammer. In the case of poor ores, containing less than 10 dwt. of gold per ton, the silver derived from the litharge will of itself frequently be sufficient for the purpose of inquartation, whilst, as before stated, for the estimation of gold in richer ores, the addition of a little pure silver before placing the leaden button in the cupel becomes necessary.

When the ore treated contains silver in addition to gold, and it is desirable to ascertain its amount, it becomes necessary to first cupel the button of lead without the addition of silver: the metallic globule thus obtained is weighed, and its weight noted, as is also that of the amount of silver derived from the reduced litharge. If necessary for the operation of parting, more silver is now added by folding the globule obtained from the cupel, together with a bit of silver, in lead foil, and again passing it to the cupel. Lastly, the button of alloy resulting from the second cupellation, is dissolved in nitric acid, and the gold weighed. The amount of silver present in the ore will consequently be represented by the weight of the button of alloy obtained from the first cupellation, less the united weights of the gold, and of the silver yielded by the reduced litharge.

Parting.—The button obtained by cupellation is first allowed to cool, squeezed laterally between the jaws of a pair of strong pliers, and brushed with a hard brush to remove any adhering litharge, and then flattened by a bright-faced hammer on a steel anvil. After being carefully examined, in order to ascertain that it is perfectly free from extraneous matter, the flattened button is taken between the points of a pair of steel forceps, and dropped either into a long-necked flask of about two ounces' capacity, or into a large test-tube, and about half an ounce of nitric acid of 22° Baumé = 1·18 sp. gr. perfectly free from any trace of hydrochloric acid, added. The acid must now be boiled over a spirit lamp or gas jet, until all action on the alloy has ceased, and the liquid carefully decanted off. About a quarter of an ounce of pure nitric acid of 32° B. = 1·28 sp. gr. is then introduced, and boiled for about ten minutes, when it is, in its turn, poured off, and the flask or tube filled with distilled water. Its mouth is now covered by a small crucible, and its position reversed in such a way, that the gold which it contains may fall through the water into the crucible beneath it; and when this has taken place, its mouth is raised to the surface of the water in the crucible, and by a sidelong movement withdrawn altogether from it. The water is now carefully decanted off, and the crucible laid in a hot place to dry, after which it is heated to redness in the muffle, and when cold the gold is removed and weighed. Instead of using a flask, a thin crucible of porcelain may be employed for the operation.

Weighing.—The balance employed for assays of gold and silver should weigh to one-thousandth of a grain, and be provided with a set of decimal grain weights. A good balance should be fitted with an apparatus for steadying the pans, connected with the axis which moves the beam, in such a way that one movement of the handle first releases the beam, and subsequently the pans. The knife-edges should be made of agate, so that all the working parts may be enabled to resist injury from the fumes of the laboratory, or the effects of a damp climate.

The beam of such a balance ought not to be less than eight inches in length, and must be divided for the use of a sliding weight moved by an apparatus provided for the purpose. The whole is enclosed in a glass case supported by adjusting screws for placing the instrument level. To prevent wearing, the weights should be handled by the aid of a pair of forceps provided with ivory points.

From the result obtained by weighing the gold yielded by assay, the amount contained in a ton of ore of 20 cwt. may be readily calculated, either directly or by the aid of the following table :—

TABLE

*Showing, from the weight of Metal obtained from an Assay on 600 grains, the amount of Gold in oz. dwt. and gr. contained in a ton of Ore.**

If 600 grains of Ore give Fine Metal,	One ton of Ore will yield Fine Metal,	If 600 grains of Ore give Fine Metal,	One ton of Ore will yield Fine Metal.
gr.	oz. dwt. gr.	gr.	oz. dwt. gr.
0·001	0 1 2	0·100	5 8 21
0·002	0 2 4	0·200	10 17 18
0·003	0 3 6	0·300	16 6 16
0·004	0 4 8	0·400	21 15 13
0·005	0 5 10	0·500	27 4 10
0·006	0 6 12	0·600	32 13 8
0·007	0 7 14	0·700	38 2 5
0·008	0 8 17	0·800	43 11 2
0·009	0 9 19	0·900	49 0 0
0·010	0 10 18	1·000	54 8 21
0·020	1 1 18	2·000	108 17 18
0·030	1 12 16	3·000	163 6 16
0·040	2 3 13	4·000	217 15 13
0·050	2 14 10	5·000	272 4 11
0·060	3 5 8	6·000	326 13 8
0·070	3 16 5	7·000	381 2 5
0·080	4 7 2	8·000	435 11 2
0·090	4 18 0	9·000	490 0 0

TO FIND THE WEIGHT OF GOLD IN A MIXTURE OF THAT METAL AND QUARTZ.—In purchasing fragments of rich gold quartz, it is sometimes desirable to be enabled to ascertain their intrinsic value, without separating the gold, and thereby destroying the specimen. From the

* To use this table, write beneath each other, on a slip of paper, the number of oz. dwt. and gr. corresponding to the several decimal figures obtained by weighing, and add them together for the yield per ton of ore. As an example, let it be supposed that the gold resulting from an assay, on 600 gr. of ore, weighs 0·235 gr. On consulting the table we find—

gr.	oz.	dwt.	gr.
0·200	10	17	18
0·030	1	12	16
0·005	0	5	10
	12	15	20

as the yield of gold per ton of ore.

known specific gravities of gold and quartz, it becomes easy, after determining the density of the mass, to ascertain approximately the amount of each present in any particular specimen.

The following Table exhibits the proportion, by weight, of gold in auriferous quartz of a given specific gravity; the formula from which it was calculated being found as follows:—

Let g be the specific gravity of gold (taken as 19).
q „ „ of quartz (taken as 2·6).
m „ „ of the unknown mixture.
x the unknown proportionate *bulk* of gold, to a unit of bulk of the mixture.

Then xg is the proportionate weight of gold, and $(1-x)q$ is the proportionate weight of quartz, and of course the sum of these must give the weight of the unit of mixture. That is to say, $xg+(1-x)q=m$. This is a simple equation, from which we find $x=\frac{m-q}{g-q}$, for the proportionate *bulk* of the gold. The proportionate *weight* is $\frac{gx}{m}$, or $\frac{g}{g-q}\times\frac{m-q}{m}$.

The formula may be verified as follows. Let y be the proportionate weight of the gold. Then $\frac{y}{g}$ is its bulk, and $\frac{1-y}{q}$ the bulk of the quartz. Hence the bulk of the mixture $\frac{1}{m}=\frac{y}{g}+\frac{1-y}{q}$, which gives $y=\frac{g(m-q)}{m(g-q)}$ as before.

With the values given above, $\frac{g}{g-q}=\frac{19{\cdot}0}{16{\cdot}4}=1{\cdot}1585366$; and the logarithm of the fraction is 0·06391.

The table is read thus: Auriferous quartz, whose specific gravity is 5·2, contains 0·5793 of its weight of gold; or, which is the same thing, 10,000 ounces of the quartz contain 5·793 ounces of gold.

TABLE

Showing the proportionate weight of Gold in a mass of auriferous Quartz, when the specific gravity of the mass is known.

Specific Gravity.	Proportion of Gold.	Specific Gravity.	Proportion of Gold.	Specific Gravity.	Proportion of Gold.	Specific Gravity.	Proportion of Gold.
2·6	0·0000	3·7	0·3444	5·2	0·5793	8·5	0·8042
2·65	0·0219	3·8	0·3659	5·4	0·6007	9·0	0·8239
2·7	0·0429	3·9	0·3862	5·6	0·6206	9·5	0·8415
2·75	0·0632	4·0	0·4055	5·8	0·6392	10·0	0·8573
2·8	0·0828	4·1	0·4239	6·0	0·6565	10·5	0·8717
2·85	0·1016	4·2	0·4413	6·2	0·6727	11·0	0·8847
2·9	0·1198	4·3	0·4580	6·4	0·6879	11·5	0·8966
2·95	0·1375	4·4	0·4739	6·6	0·7021	12·0	0·9075
3·0	0·1545	4·5	0·4892	6·8	0·7156	13·0	0·9268
3·1	0·1869	4·6	0·5037	7·0	0·7282	14·0	0·9434
3·2	0·2172	4·7	0·5176	7·2	0·7402	15·0	0·9577
3·3	0·2458	4·8	0·5310	7·4	0·7515	16·0	0·9703
3·4	0·2726	4·9	0·5438	7·6	0·7622	17·0	0·9813
3·5	0·2979	5·0	0·5561	7·8	0·7724	18·0	0·9912
3·6	0·3218	5·1	0·5679	8·0	0·7820	19·0	1·0000

REFINING.—SEPARATION OF GOLD AND SILVER.—The silver produced from some of the mines of the American continent, ancient European money, old Mexican and Peruvian dollars, and bars obtained from goldsmiths' sweep, are composed of silver which usually contains a certain proportion of both copper and gold. The processes for the separation of these metals from each other have been rendered so inexpensive and simple, that bars containing but half a thousandth of gold can now be refined at a profit.*

The auriferous silver is first melted, and granulated by being poured into water, and then attacked by boiling in a platinum vessel with from two to two and a half times its weight of sulphuric acid of 66° Baumé. Each attack is made on about 80 lbs. of the granulated alloy, and occupies from three to four hours; the operation being considered finished when effervescence has ceased, and sulphuric acid begins to be evolved.

The attack of the granulated alloy by sulphuric acid is necessarily attended with a copious evolution of sulphurous acid gas, which is generally allowed to escape into the atmosphere, but may be conducted into a sulphuric acid chamber, and thus utilised.

Before passing into the air, or into a sulphuric acid chamber, the gases and vapours are conducted for a distance of some 20 or 30 feet through a leaden tube into a receiver of the same metal, for the purpose of condensing the sulphuric acid distilled off, together with a certain amount of sulphate of silver mechanically drawn over with it. This liquid, which contains large quantities of sulphuric acid in solution, marks from 40° to 45° on Baumé's scale.

When the attack on the granulated metal is terminated, from 4 lbs. to 5 lbs. of sulphuric acid of 58°, derived from the concentration of acid liquors obtained during the preparation of sulphate of copper, are introduced into the boiler, and, after being boiled for a few minutes, the vessel is withdrawn from the fire, and its contents allowed to settle. In this way the gold falls to the bottom; the supernatant liquor is decanted off into another receiver, and diluted with water until it marks from 25° to 30° on the hydrometer.

This solution is now introduced into a large leaden cistern, heated by steam, in which are hung copper plates, by which the silver is precipitated in the form of minute granular crystals. In order to

* When gold bullion is refined, it must be alloyed with sufficient silver to make the proportion of gold as 1 : 2½. It is then granulated and treated in the same way as silver bars containing gold.

ascertain when the whole of the silver has been precipitated, a little of the liquor is filtered, and tested with a solution of common salt; when no further turbidity is caused by its introduction, it is evident that no traces of silver remain in the liquid. In some establishments the liquor is drawn off into leaden reservoirs, where it is allowed to remain in contact with copper plates during several days, in order that the last traces of silver may become precipitated.

When the argentiferous and auriferous alloy is very impure, the solution in sulphuric acid is often turbid, and gives rise to deposits in the bottoms of the vessels in which it is allowed to stand. These sediments are transferred to a separate boiler, diluted with water, and precipitated by sheets of copper. The precipitate thus obtained is then washed and dried, and, after being melted and granulated, is again treated by sulphuric acid. The clear solutions obtained in this way are subsequently transferred to the vessels in which the precipitation of silver is effected.

In some cases, instead of proceeding as above described, the muddy deposits are first washed with warm water, and then allowed to settle. The residue, which principally consists of a mixture of gold and metallic sulphates, is filtered, and then boiled in a platinum vessel with sulphuric acid; by which means a clear solution of silver is obtained, and the gold is deposited at the bottom of the vessel. This is again treated with sulphuric acid, after which it is sufficiently pure to be run into ingots, whilst the solution of silver is transferred to the precipitating tank.

When, instead of using platinum vessels, cast iron boilers are employed, the alloy to be attacked may be either in a granulated form or in the state of ingots, and the operation can be conducted on from five to ten cwt. of metal at a time. If this method be adopted, acid of a less degree of purity may be employed; and it is also found that solution is effected in cast iron vessels with a less expenditure of acid than when platinum is the material used.

The solutions are transferred in an almost boiling state from the iron vessels in which they have been prepared, to a leaden tank, which is afterwards filled up to about two-thirds its capacity with mother liquors from the crystallisation of sulphate of copper. A jet of loose steam is introduced into the tank, and the liquor boiled until it has become saturated with sulphate of silver. When this takes place, the steam is turned off, and the liquid, after standing an hour to settle, is drawn, either by a syphon or tap, placed about ten inches from the bottom, into the precipitating vat. After several successive washings, the gold is removed, again boiled with sulphuric acid in a platinum vessel, and then melted into bars.

The silver precipitated by copper plates is carefully washed and dried in an iron pan over a coke fire, or is formed into blocks by means of an hydraulic press. These must be gradually heated before being fused, as they invariably retain a considerable amount of moisture, and might cause the crucibles to crack if at once introduced into them. When sufficiently dry, the compressed silver is fused into ingots. The silver thus refined contains an inappreciable amount only of gold, but is still alloyed with about two thousandths of copper.

In most instances the gold obtained by treatment with sulphuric acid is again boiled, in the same way, in a platinum vessel with fresh acid, and then melted into bars. In some cases the alloy is fused with three times its weight of silver, treated with nitric acid, and the residue, after being carefully washed, melted into bars. The ingots obtained at refineries working as above described generally contain about 998 thousandths of gold.

The acid solution of sulphate of copper obtained by decantation from the crystals of precipitated silver, contains, in addition to the copper originally present in the alloy, that which corresponds to the amount of sulphate of silver decomposed by the copper plates. This is evaporated in leaden vessels, until it marks 40° Baumé; when, on cooling, it deposits pale blue crystals, which contain a less amount of water of crystallisation than ordinary sulphate of copper. By means of successive evaporations, the mother liquor furnishes other crops of crystals of sulphate of copper; and, finally, a dark-coloured liquid, of from 52° to 58° Baumé, is obtained, which chiefly consists of dilute sulphuric acid, and is employed in the course of succeeding operations. Sulphate of copper, which has crystallised from solutions containing a large excess of sulphuric acid, is not of a marketable quality, but requires to be dissolved in water, and re-crystallised, when it affords the usual crystals of a deep blue colour, containing five equivalents of water of crystallisation. The crystallisers are of wood, lined with lead, three feet wide, three feet deep, and four feet six inches in length. The floor of the crystallising house is of lead, and provided with gutters for carrying off, into suitable reservoirs, any liquors that may be accidentally spilt.

Some experiments made in the Lille Mint, with the view of substituting iron for copper plates in the process of refining, did not, on the whole, afford satisfactory results.

When the proportion of silver in the alloy does not amount to from 20 to 30 per cent. of the whole, instead of treating it directly by sulphuric acid, it is first granulated, and roasted in a furnace at a low red heat. The oxidised mixture is afterwards boiled in the weak acid liquors from the crystallisation of sulphate of copper, by which a portion of the copper is removed, and the residue subsequently refined in the usual way.

ASSAY OF GOLD BULLION.—The process employed for assaying gold bullion by the assayers of the Mint and the Bank of England is similar to that employed at the Paris Mint, and the weight operated on is often the same. One-half gramme is accurately weighed, and subjected to cupellation with a proper quantity of lead, and a portion of pure silver, about three times the weight of the gold supposed to be present in the alloy.

The resulting button is then flattened into a disc, about the size of a sixpence, and, after being annealed, is passed through a flatting-mill until it has been drawn into a riband from 2½ to 3 inches long, which is again annealed, and coiled into a spiral by rolling between the finger and thumb. The *cornet* is now introduced into a long-necked flask, containing about an ounce of pure nitric acid, of 22° Baumé = 1·18 sp. gr., and boiled until red fumes have ceased to be evolved. This acid is carefully poured off, and the cornet again twice boiled, for about ten minutes each time, with acid of 32° Baumé = 1·28 sp. gr. In the two last boilings, a piece of charcoal, consisting of half a charred lentil, is introduced into the flask for the purpose of preventing the ebullition from taking place irregularly and with sudden bursts, which would be liable to break the cornet and project a portion of the liquid out of the flask.

After this second attack, the cornet is washed twice with distilled water. The flask is then filled with water, and reversed, with care, into a small crucible of fine clay, into which the cornet is allowed to fall, gently and without breaking. The water which covers the cornet is now poured off, and the crucible and its contents are heated to redness in the muffle; taking care, however, not to raise the temperature sufficiently to cause the fusion of the gold. From the weight of the cornet obtained, the fineness of the alloy is calculated.

The cornet, after boiling in nitric acid, is of a spongy texture, of a brownish-yellow colour, and exceedingly fragile, so that it would be impossible, in this state, to touch it with the fingers without breaking it; and it is consequently necessary to transfer it carefully with the water contained in the flask. By heating it to redness, in the way described, its volume is reduced to about one-third its original size; it at the same time assumes a metallic lustre, and acquires a degree of cohesion which admits of its being readily handled without fear of loss.

The return is made to the Mint in decimals, the assayer's weights being so subdivided as to give him the value in thousandths of the original half gramme. The Bank return is made to the one-eighth of a carat grain "better" or "worse" than standard, and tables are employed for the conversion of assays expressed in decimals, and conversely.

The quantity of lead necessary for passing an alloy of gold on the cupel depends on the amount of copper present. The following proportions have, after numerous experiments, been adopted at the Paris Mint:—

Amount of Gold in Copper Alloy.	Amount of Lead necessary to remove the Copper by Cupellation.
1000	1 part
900	10 parts
800	16 „
700	22 „
600	24 „
500	26 „
400	34 „
300	34 „
200	34 „
100	34 „

For the assay of ordinary bar gold from California, Australia, or New Zealand, &c., in which the proportion of copper is always exceedingly small, the gold is passed to the cupel, with the necessary amount of silver and two grammes only of lead. But even when the operation of parting has been skilfully conducted, the weight of the cornet of gold will often be increased by a very slight *surcharge* occasioned by its retaining minute traces of silver.

This surcharge is most observable in cornets obtained from alloys containing a very small proportion of copper; since, in cases in which large quantities of this metal are present, and a considerable amount of lead has consequently been employed for cupellation, it is more than compensated for, by the loss of gold absorbed by the cupel. In the assay of alloys having an intermediate composition, the loss of gold is not unfrequently counterbalanced by the surcharge of silver, and the true fineness of the alloy thus directly obtained.

The following results of numerous synthetical experiments made in the Paris Mint, furnish the necessary data for the calculation of a table of corrections :—

Fineness of Gold.	Result obtained.	Differences.
900	900·25	0·25
800	800·50	0·50
700	700·00	0·00
600	600·00	0·00
500	499·50	0·50
400	399·50	0·50
300	299·50	0·50
200	199·50	0·50
100	99·50	0·50

The above experiments were made on mixtures of fine gold and pure copper, in the proportions indicated in the table.

The last traces of silver may be removed from the cornet by treating it, before annealing, with fused bisulphate of potash in a porcelain crucible. When sufficiently cool, the whole is heated with water containing a little sulphuric acid, and the cornet dried and ignited. By this means gold of almost absolute purity may be obtained.

The arrangement of Mr. Claudet's laboratory, Coleman Street, London, which is probably one of the most complete for the assay of gold and silver bullion, is represented Fig. 38.

The cupellations are performed in two French cupel furnaces, made of fireclay, bound with flat iron bands, and standing in an arched recess in the wall of the laboratory, before which is an iron screen (divided in the drawing for the purpose of showing furnace) in order to prevent radiation.

Slides in this screen can be raised or lowered at pleasure, and are provided with counterpoises similar to the sash weights of a window. The tongs for handling the cupels, with its pasteboard guard to protect the hands of the operator from the heat, are seen between the furnaces, whilst a side view is obtained of another similar pair lying on the bench beneath. Under this is kept the coke to be employed as fuel, and to the left of the furnace, lying against the wall, is the pasteboard shield, with a piece of green or blue glass in it, used by the assayer to protect his eyes from injury whilst looking into the

Fig. 38.

Assay Laboratory.

muffle. The racks in the upper left-hand corner are for the storage of cupels, which, after being made in a screw press, are laid aside in shallow iron trays until nearly dry, when they are removed, together with the trays, to the racks seen, behind the tongs, on the shelf below the furnaces, where the last traces of moisture become expelled.

On either side of the furnaces are ranges of flasks for the attack of the inquartated gold, each of which rests on the top of a small button-shaped piece of metal, which has around its edge, apertures for the issue of gas jets. Each of these burners is provided with a separate tap; and a large stopcock, seen at the end of each series, is used to turn on, or cut off, the supply. A guard with holes in it, corresponding to the different burners, keeps the flasks in their respective places, whilst their open ends are inserted into holes in the tile work at the back, which communicate with the chimney and carry off the gases generated.

The vessels resembling teapots are employed for pouring acid into the parting flasks.

This gas apparatus, which was first employed by Mr. F. Claudet, is now adopted by most of the principal assayers, both in this country and on the continent of Europe, and has, among other similar establishments, been introduced into the French Mint.

In estimating the fineness of gold, it is sometimes usual to regard the whole mass as weighing 24 carats; and thus when gold is said to be 18 carats fine, it means that if the whole weight be represented by 24, the proportion of gold will be 18, or that the weight of gold is $\frac{18}{24}$ths of the whole.

Touchstone.—In order to ascertain the fineness of articles of jewellery, and of other small objects from which a sufficient amount cannot be scraped off for the purpose of an ordinary assay, trial by touchstone is sometimes employed. This is a method of ascertaining the approximate value of an alloy of gold with other metals by comparing the colour, &c. of a minute portion of the object to be examined with small bars of similar alloys, of which the proportional composition has been previously determined. These bars are called *touch needles*, and are rubbed on a smooth piece of black basalt or slate, called a touchstone. Sets of touch needles may consist of pure gold; of gold of 23½ carats; of 23 carat gold; and thus down to 20 carats, after which the difference between each needle may be a whole carat.

The marks made respectively by the several needles and the object to be tested, are afterwards wetted with a little aquafortis, and, from the effects produced, the composition of the alloy is inferred; since its fineness is supposed to correspond with that of the bar, which affords a trace on the stone similarly affected by the action of acids. In some countries where trinkets are required to be assayed in this way, a great variety of needles is necessary; but in England the touchstone is very little employed, although it can sometimes be used with advantage to indicate the quantity of silver necessary for inquartation. The British standard for gold coin is 22 carats, and the alloy employed consequently contains 916·66 parts of gold in a thousand. The standard employed in France and America for the gold currency is 900 thousandths.

SILVER.

CHAPTER XII.

MODE OF OCCURRENCE AND GEOLOGICAL POSITION.

NATIVE SILVER—ANTIMONIAL SILVER—NATIVE AMALGAM—PRINCIPAL SILVER ORES—SULPHIDES—ARSENIDES—SELENIDES—TELLURIDES—CHLORIDE—IODIDE—BROMIDE—CARBONATE—SILICATE—CHIEF SOURCES OF SILVER—GEOLOGICAL POSITION.

MODE OF OCCURRENCE.—This metal occurs in the following forms of combination :—

NATIVE METAL AND ALLOYS.

Native Silver.—This metal sometimes occurs in a state of almost chemical purity, but it is more frequently associated with copper, gold, bismuth, antimony, or some other metal or metals. Native silver is often found in connexion with various argentiferous ores, and has sometimes been met with in masses of considerable size. The most remarkable of these have been obtained from the mines of Freiberg in Saxony, Kongsberg in Norway, and those of Huantaya in Southern Peru, from which a specimen weighing over eight cwt. was once procured. A mass of native silver from Kongsberg, in the Royal collection at Copenhagen, weighs about five cwt. It is found both crystallised and in arborescent and filiform shapes. The filiform varieties are often composed of one or more series of octahedrons, closely united, or arranged in parallel rows ; this structure is apparent in many of the specimens from Norway and Mexico.

The alloys of silver and gold are exceedingly numerous, and although native gold has never been found free from silver, it is in some cases alloyed with that metal to such an extent, that the resulting compound can only be regarded as native silver containing traces of gold. Silver obtained from the treatment of ordinary argentiferous ores frequently contains gold, but generally speaking in small quantities only. In some districts, however, as at Virginia City in the State of Nevada, one-third of the value of the bullion produced, arises from the amount of gold which it contains.

Antimonial Silver.—Discrasite occurs in veins at Altwolfach in Baden, Wittichen in Suabia, Andreasberg in the Hartz, near Coquimbo, Chili, and elsewhere. Colour, silver white; composition, antimony 23, silver 77 per cent.; formula, Ag^2 Sb. Heated before the blowpipe, gives off fumes of antimony.

This substance does not occur in sufficient quantities to possess any great commercial value.

Bismuth Silver.—A rare alloy of silver and bismuth, with a little copper and arsenic; occurs in the mine of San Antonio, near Copiapo, Chili. It contains 60 per cent. of silver.

AMALGAM.

Native Amalgam.—Is found in the Palatinate, at Sala in Sweden, Almaden in Spain, and in various mines in Chili, &c. It is frequently crystallised, of a silver white colour, is brittle, and emits a grating sound when cut. There are two known varieties: the one is represented by the formula Ag Hg^2, and the other by Ag Hg^3. The first is composed of silver 34·8, mercury 65·2, and the second of silver 26·25, mercury 73·75 per cent.

A silver amalgam of some commercial importance is found in the mines of Arqueros in Chili, and has been hence named *Arquerite.* According to Domeyko, its composition is represented by the formula Ag^6 Hg; it consists of silver 86·49, mercury 13·51 per cent.

ORES.

The ores of silver which occur in greatest abundance, and which are consequently the most important, are the following:—

Silver Glance.—Vitreous Sulphide of Silver.—This is the most important ore of silver, and contains, when pure, silver 87·04, sulphur 12·96 per cent. Its formula is Ag S. It is found in Europe in the mines of Annaberg and Joachimstahl, and other mines of the Erzgebirge; at Schemnitz and Kremnitz in Hungary, and at Freiberg. It is abundant in the mines of Peru and Mexico, and also in those of the State of Nevada.

Stephanite.—Brittle sulphide of silver is the ore of next greatest importance. This is a double sulphide of silver and antimony, containing, when pure, silver 70·4, antimony 14·0, and sulphur 15·6 per cent. Its formula is $Ag\,S + \frac{1}{6}\,Sb^2\,S^3$. It is found in nearly all the silver mines of Europe, and occurs abundantly in Mexico, Peru, and in the Comstock lode, State of Nevada; beautifully crystallised specimens have been frequently obtained from the California mine worked on that vein.

Pyrargyrite.—Ruby Silver.—An important ore in the Mexican mines, as well as of those in the Reese River district in Nevada. It is composed of the same substances as Stephanite, but in different proportions. When pure, its composition is, silver 58·98, antimony 23·46, and sulphur 17·56 per cent. Its formula is $Ag\,S + \frac{1}{3}\,Sb^2\,S^3$.

Chloride of Silver.—Horn Silver.—This ore is composed of silver 75·33, chlorine 24·67 per cent., and is represented by the formula Ag Cl. This substance is found in most of the silver mines both of Europe and America, and occurs in greatest abundance near the outcrops of the veins. It fuses in the flame of a candle, giving off acrid fumes; and if moistened and rubbed with a piece of iron or zinc, becomes externally coated with a thin film of metallic silver. With a little carbonate of soda it is readily reduced before the blowpipe, and affords a button of silver.

In addition to the foregoing, which yield the larger proportion of the total amount of silver annually produced, there are numerous other minerals containing this metal, but which, from their rarity, may be regarded rather in the light of mineralogical curiosities than as ores of silver. A large amount of silver is likewise extracted from galena, with which it is associated in the form of sulphide.

The following is nearly a complete list of the minerals formed by the combination of silver with other bodies:—

SULPHIDES, ARSENIDES, SELENIDES, AND TELLURIDES.

1. *Silver Glance.*—Sulphide of silver.
2. *Discrasite.*—Antimonial silver.
3. *Naumannite.*—Selenide of silver; occurs in the Hartz.
4. *Stromeyerite.*—Sulphide of copper and silver.
5. *Eucairite.*—Selenide of copper and silver; found in Sweden.
6. *Sternbergite.*—Sulphide of silver and iron, flexible, and marks like plumbago; found in Bohemia and Saxony.

7. *Hessite.*—Telluride of silver; found in Siberia.
8. *Miargyrite.*—A rare sulphide of silver and antimony.
9. *Pyrargyrite.*—Ruby silver.
10. *Proustite.*—Light red silver ore, composed of sulphur, arsenic, and silver; found in Bohemia, Saxony, &c.
11. *Polybasite.*—A variable combination of silver, copper, antimony, arsenic sulphur, and iron; chiefly found in the Mexican Mines.
12. *Freislebenite.*—Antimonial sulphide of lead and silver; containing twenty-two per cent. of the latter metal.
13. *Stephanite.*—Sulphide of silver and antimony.
14. *Xanthocone.*—Sulphide and arsenide of silver; occurs at the Himmelsfürst Mine in Saxony, and various other localities.

CHLORIDE, IODIDE, AND BROMIDE.

15. *Horn Silver.*—Chloride of silver.
16. *Iodyrite.*—Iodide of silver; found in Mexico, Chili, and at the Mines of Hiendelaencina, in the province of Guadalajara, Spain.
17. *Bromyrite.*—Bromide of silver; occurs in Chili, Mexico, and at Huelgoët in Brittany.
18. *Embolite.*—Chlorobromide of silver; found in Chili, Mexico, and in the State of Honduras.

CARBONATE.

19. *Selbite.*—Regarded as a carbonate of silver, but probably only a mechanical mixture.

SILICATE.

20. . . . . This combination is stated by Mr. J. Napier, Jun. to exist in the ores of the district of Reyes, Mexico.*

Few metals enter into a greater variety of natural combinations, or are found over a wider geological range than silver. It is said to exist in minute traces in some organic bodies, and in the waters of the ocean. A certain amount of this metal invariably accompanies native gold, and it would be almost as difficult to find a specimen of galena from which traces of silver could not be extracted, as to meet with native gold entirely free from it.

The whole of the silver of commerce is derived from the three following sources:—

1st. From silver ores proper, in which this metal predominates in value over those with which it is associated.

2nd. From refining the native alloys of gold and silver.

3rd. From the desilverising of lead, and the treatment of certain argentiferous copper ores.

* *Mining and Smelting Magazine*, vol. i. p. 105.

We shall at present chiefly confine our attention to a description of the principal localities producing ores belonging to the first class, since the second source of silver has been already treated of in the portion of this volume devoted to gold, and the third will receive some attention in subsequent chapters.

The principal mining districts in Europe which have been extensively worked for ores of this description, are those of Saxony and Bohemia, some localities in Hungary and Transylvania, the neighbourhood of Kongsberg in Norway, and that of Hiendelaencina in Spain. On the continent of America, Mexico, and the Cordilleras of Southern America, furnish examples of the occurrence of vast deposits of these ores; whilst more recently the discovery of the Great Comstock and some other veins in the new State of Nevada, has been followed by the production of an amount of silver almost without parallel in modern history.

GEOLOGICAL POSITION OF SILVER.—As before remarked, the rocks enclosing deposits of ores of this class differ widely with regard to their geological age. They occur in true veins in the older crystalline and metamorphic rocks, and when so situated have often been worked to great depths without any apparent change of character or diminution of produce. The mines of Kongsberg in Norway and Freiberg in Saxony, are remarkable examples of this mode of occurrence. In South America, on the contrary, a great portion of the silver ores are found forming veins in calcareous rocks, and often running parallel to their stratification. The age of the silver-bearing rocks of Bolivia and Peru is apparently carboniferous, whilst in Chili the strata in which the ores of silver are most abundant are believed to belong to the cretaceous period.*

* Mr. Rémond has obtained fossils in sufficient numbers from the rocks in which are situated the famous silver mines of Chañarcillo and Tres Puntas, to fix their age as belonging to the Lower Cretaceous.—*Proceedings of the California Academy of Natural Sciences, December 3rd,* 1866.

CHAPTER XIII.

PRINCIPAL SILVER MINES OF THE OLD WORLD.

SILVER MINES OF THE UNITED KINGDOM—NORWAY—SWEDEN—TRANSYLVANIA AND THE BANAT—SAXONY AND BOHEMIA—MINES OF THE HARTZ—SILVER MINES OF THE ALPS—FRANCE—SPAIN—ALTAI MOUNTAINS—DAOURIA.

SILVER mines were extensively worked in Europe long before the discovery of the richer veins of America, and some of them still continue in operation, affording considerable annual returns of this metal.

GREAT BRITAIN AND IRELAND.—The whole of the silver produced in the United Kingdom is extracted from argentiferous lead, and consequently an account of the different districts from which it is obtained, would involve a description of the principal lead mines of the country.

It may, however, be remarked that the ores obtained from the North of England, generally speaking, contain but a small proportion of silver, usually not above 1½ oz. per ton. The ores of the Isle of Man are highly argentiferous, yielding from 50 to 60 oz. of silver per ton of lead, whilst the ores of Cardiganshire and Montgomeryshire are moderately so, containing, on an average, from 15 to 25 oz. of that metal per ton of lead. The lead ores of Denbighshire usually contain a very small amount of silver. Those of Cornwall and Devon are generally richer in silver than any others in the United Kingdom, with the exception of those from the Isle of Man. The Cornish ores contain on an average about 30 oz. of silver per ton.

The produce of silver, separated from lead ore, raised from mines in the United Kingdom, from the year 1856 to 1865, both inclusive, has been, according to Mr. R. Hunt, F.R.S., as follows :—

	Ounces.		Ounces.
1856	614,188	1861	569,530
1857	532,866	1862	686,123
1858	569,345	1863	634,004
1859	576,027	1864	641,088
1860	554,002	1865	724,856

NORWAY.—The celebrated mines of Kongsberg were discovered in 1623, and have been worked, with but comparatively little interruption, from that time up to the present. On the separation of Norway from Denmark in 1814, the present Government took the mines of the territory of Kongsberg into its own hands, and appointed a Commission for the purpose of deciding which of them should be re-opened. In addition to the Gottes Hülfe their choice fell on the Kongens and Armens mines, but, at a depth of forty fathoms from the surface, the former became so impoverished that it was abandoned, and the working of the Armens alone for some time proceeded with.

At the depth of sixty fathoms the condition of the Armens mine was considered so satisfactory that it was thought advisable to extend a level from it into the adjoining mine. This operation resulted in making important discoveries, and the two properties have been since worked as one establishment. During the early part of the eighteenth century the mines of Kongsberg were remarkably productive, but from the middle of that century up to 1832 their yield was comparatively insignificant. Since that time they have been regularly worked with uniform and satisfactory results, and have now reached the depth of 280 fathoms from the surface.

These mines are situated in gneiss and crystalline slate, of which the district for a length of a hundred miles and a breadth of fifty, is chiefly composed. The silver occurs in what are called *Fahlbands*, which consist of parallel belts of rock, of considerable length and breadth, impregnated with sulphides of iron, copper, and zinc, and sometimes also with those of lead, cobalt, and silver. The iron pyrites is often more or less decomposed, giving rise to the formation of hydrated oxide of iron, the presence of which is considered in the district an indication of silver.

The direction of the ore-bearing belts is nearly north and south; they are irregular in their dimensions, but constantly preserve a certain degree of parallelism with each other, and may be traced for an extent of several miles. The amount of ore disseminated through them is usually small, but in some places it is sufficiently concentrated to admit of being profitably worked. In the Kongsberg district, there are several of these fahlbands, parallel in strike and inclination with the gneissoid and schistose strata in which they occur, and subject to the same local structure and disturbances of stratification. The fahlbands are themselves traversed by true veins containing silver ores, and experience has shown that these are never argentiferous except where they intersect the fahlbands. From this it would appear that the impregnation of the veins is dependent on the nature of the enclosing rock, which renders it probable that their metalliferous constituents were originally derived from the fahlbands, from which their removal and subsequent concentration have been effected by chemical action.

The total produce of silver from the Kongsberg mines from 1624 to 1864,—240 years,—has been, according to official returns, as follows viz. :—

From 1624 to 1805 . . .	2,360,140 marks,*	equal to	1,332,495 lbs. troy
„ 1805 „ 1815 . . .	38,112 „	„	21,517 „ „
„ 1815 „ 1864 . . .	820,956 „	„	463,498 „ „

The average annual produce has been—

From 1815 to 1833 . . .	4,141, marks,	equal to	2,338 lbs. troy
„ 1834 „ 1838 . . .	27,423 „	„	15,483 „ „
„ 1839 „ 1843 . . .	25,454 „	„	14,361 „ „
„ 1844 „ 1848 . . .	23,464 „	„	13,247 „ „
„ 1849 „ 1853 . . .	20,552 „	„	11,603 „ „
„ 1854 „ 1858 . . .	32,862 „	„	18,553 „ „
„ 1859 „ 1863 . . .	16,091 „	„	9,084 „ „

From 1859 to 1864 the annual yield has been—

1859	20,515 marks,	equal to	11,582 lbs. troy
1860	18,139 „	„	10,241 „ „
1861	14,823 „	„	8,369 „ „
1862	13,088 „	„	7,389 „ „
1863	13,890 „	„	7,842 „ „
1864	13,046 „	„	7,365 „ „

In addition to the mines of Kongsberg, some veins in the district of Skara were formerly of considerable importance, but are now abandoned, although the fahlbands of this locality closely resemble those which have proved so productive in the adjoining district.

The produce, expenses, and net profits of the Kongsberg mines, during the last thirty-one years, have been as follows :—

* The mark of Norway and Sweden is equivalent to 3,252 gr., or 6·775 oz. troy.

STATISTICS OF THE KONGSBERG MINES.

Year.	Produce Sold.	Expenses.	Net Profit.
1834	£87,558	£17,407	£70,151
1835	50,171	16,215	33,956
1836	70,244	13,585	56,659
1837	52,087	21,015	31,072
1838	58,137	21,258	36,879
1839	69,879	20,110	49,769
1840	64,236	20,497	43,739
1841	50,009	22,030	27,979
1842	42,915	19,524	23,391
1843	41,398	19,811	21,587
1844	39,462	18,117	21,345
1845	36,772	16,462	20,310
1846	37,297	12,642	24,655
1847	51,831	19,146	32,685
1848	75,788	16,268	59,520
1849	49,934	18,621	31,313
1850	47,518	16,362	31,156
1851	38,140	15,975	22,165
1852	40,770	16,905	23,865
1853	36,363	16,444	19,919
1854	51,616	17,984	33,632
1855	82,448	20,294	62,154
1856	66,922	19,613	47,309
1857	49,627	17,886	31,741
1858	84,356	20,136	64,220
1859	41,888	20,996	20,892
1860	37,157	23,420	13,737
1861	30,141	24,037	6,104
1862	26,708	20,551	6,157
1863	28,836	20,982	7,854
1864	28,090	21,171	6,919
Averages.	£50,750	£18,885	£31,704

SWEDEN.—The silver mines of Sweden were formerly of considerable value, but are at present less productive. Three mines of this metal were working in 1767, viz.: that of Hellefors in the Province of Wermland, that of Segersfors in Nericia, and that of Sala in Westmannia, the last being the only one of any importance. It is very ancient, and is said at one time to have yielded large quantities of silver, but its present annual produce is only from 2,258 to 2,823 lbs. troy. The ore is a highly argentiferous galena.

HUNGARY, TRANSYLVANIA, AND THE BANAT.—The mines of this region may be divided into four principal groups. The Schemnitz district comprehends the mines of Schemnitz, Kremnitz, Neusohl, and Schmölnitz.

Schemnitz.—Schemnitz, a royal free city of mines, is situated twenty-five leagues to the north of Buda, at a height of 1680 feet above the level of the sea, in the midst of a group of mountains covered with forest. These mountains are for the most part composed of trachytes, enclosing a formation consisting of porphyry associated with syenite, passing into granite and gneiss, with subordinate beds of slate and limestone. All the mines occur in this formation. Beudant, who compared these rocks with specimens of the metalliferous porphyry, &c., brought from South America by Humboldt, long since recognised their exact identity, not only in the most minute details of colour, structure, and composition, but also in the respective positions of the different varieties, and the same similarity of the enclosing rocks would seem to exist with regard to the recently-discovered silver districts in North America.

The metalliferous rocks of Schemnitz occupy a tract of some miles in extent, and are traversed by a group consisting of five principal veins running north-east and south-west, in addition to which there are numerous others of less importance on the north side of the Paradise mountain. The largest of these, the "Spitaler gangue," has occasionally a width of sixty feet, and may be traced for upwards of four miles in length. These lodes have seldom any distinct walls, but the enclosing porphyry is frequently more or less decomposed and impregnated with iron pyrites in the vicinity of the planes of contact. The veins are rarely subject to interruption or dislocation by slides or cross-courses. The veinstone consists of fragments of the enclosing rocks (which are often decomposed to the consistency of clay), cavernous quartz, ferruginous limestone, and sulphate of baryta, with which are associated blende, iron and copper pyrites, argentiferous galena, sulphide of silver, ruby silver, and metallic silver, in addition to a small quantity of gold which is rarely visible. Sulphide of silver and argentiferous galena are the two most important minerals, and sometimes occur in distinct patches, whilst at others they are intimately mixed and disseminated throughout the gangue. The gold and silver are usually found to accompany each other, but they do not now occur in such large quantities as formerly, since the proportion of galena present in the veins evidently increases in depth.

The argentiferous ores from Schemnitz are smelted near the mines, the resulting work lead being sent to refining establishments at Kremnitz, Neusohl, and Scharnowitz, where the silver ores obtained from the other mines in the neighbourhood are also treated. The mines of Schemnitz were first opened more than eight hundred years ago, and have been worked to a depth of over two hundred fathoms; the works have been generally conducted with great care and skill, but from the falling off of the produce of the ores, they are not now in so prosperous a condition as they were a century or more since.

The Empress Maria Theresa founded a School of Mines at Schemnitz in 1760, which was for many years celebrated throughout Europe, but since the year 1848 the number of students has considerably declined, and the rival schools of Przibram and Gratz have proportionately increased in importance.

Kremnitz is situated about five leagues north-west of Schemnitz, in a valley bounded on the right by a range of hills composed of rocks similar in their character to those constituting the metalliferous formation in the vicinity of the latter town. Enclosed in these rocks are veins closely analogous to those of Schemnitz, except that the gangue contains a larger proportion of quartz, and that the ores are generally more uniformly auriferous. The metalliferous area is here of very moderate extent, and is surrounded by a trachytic formation, which geologically belongs to a more recent epoch.

Kremnitz is one of the most ancient royal free cities of mines in Hungary, and has a mint where all the bullion obtained is sent to be parted and refined.

Neusohl lies about six leagues north-east from Schemnitz, on the banks of the river Gran, and was originally founded by a colony of Saxon miners. The mines are here situated in grauwacke, covered by limestone, and afford argentiferous copper ores. They have been worked since the thirteenth century, and annually produce about 105 tons of copper and 1,053 lbs. troy of silver.

The mines of Lower Hungary afford employment to 15,000 workmen, and yield metals of the total annual value of 360,000*l.*

In the neighbourhood of Schmölnitz are copper and other mines belonging to private individuals, which produce, in addition, a certain amount of silver and mercury. They are chiefly worked by a Company called the Waldbürgerschaft, which produces annually 850 tons of copper, 3,535 lbs. troy of silver, and about a hundred flasks of mercury.

Nagybanya.—The veins of this group lie in a chain of mountains which, proceeding from the frontiers of Buckowina, where it unites with the Carpathians, finally disappears among the sandstones on the northern frontier of Transylvania. This district produces some gold, but its annual yield of silver is small.

Abrudbanya.—Nearly all the mines of this district occur in the mountains which rise in the western part of Transylvania, between the Lapos and Maros, in the vicinity of Abrudbanya. The most productive veins are principally found in porphyries analogous to those of Schemnitz, although some of them are enclosed in mica slate grauwacke, and limestone. The principal veins are those of Nagyag, Körösbanya, Offenbanya, Vöröspatak, Boitza, Csertesch, Fatzbay, Füzes, Vulkoj, Porkura, Butschum, and Toplitza. The mines of all these localities produce gold, together with a certain amount of silver, which is smelted at the works at Zalathna. They are celebrated for producing ores of tellurium.

Banat of Temeswar.—The mines of the Banat chiefly occur in the mountains that enclose the valley of the Danube at Orsova, through a narrow gorge in which the river finds a passage. The most important mines of this district are those of Oravitza, Moldawa, Szaszka, and Dognaczka. They principally afford argentiferous copper ores, yielding about 120 oz. of silver to the ton, together with a little gold.

These ores are obtained from veins and deposits chiefly occurring between the mica slate and limestone, or between syenite and limestone. Well defined veins are also found enclosed in syenite and mica slate.

The mines of Hungary, Transylvania, and the Banat, produce about 92,000 lbs. troy of silver annually.

SAXONY AND BOHEMIA.—The chain of the Erzgebirge, which, on the western bank of the Elbe, separates Saxony from Bohemia, has for many centuries produced a certain annual amount of silver. The silver mines of this district have been opened on veins which are, for the most part, enclosed in gneissoid rocks; their thickness rarely exceeds a few feet, and they are associated in groups, whose relative importance has varied considerably at different periods. Mining operations are said to have been first commenced in this district as far back as the beginning of the tenth century, but there are no authentic records on this subject dating prior to about the close of the twelfth, when the still productive mines of Freiberg began to be worked. The mines of Saxony suffered severely from the effects of the Thirty Years' War, during which, many considerable mining towns were entirely destroyed, and some of them have never recovered their former importance and prosperity. Freiberg, Marienberg, Annaberg, Schneeberg, Johann-Georgenstadt, and Schwarzenberg in Saxony, and Joachimsthal in Bohemia, have at various periods been the chief local centres of this mining region. More than nine hundred different veins are said to exist in the Erzgebirge district, which, in accordance with the nature of their gangues, have been divided by Von Weissenbach into the four following classes: *—

1. Quartz veins, containing iron pyrites, mispickel, blende, and galena; and affording silver ores of a moderate percentage.

2. Brown spar veins, yielding the same ores as the preceding, but richer in silver.

3. Veins of which the gangues are composed of carbonate and oxide of iron, fluor spar, and sulphate of baryta; but not so metalliferous as the two preceding. These sometimes extend into the Zechstein formation.

4. Veins with calcareous gangues, occasionally affording rich ores.

The characteristics of the different classes of veins do not, however, appear to be so marked as to admit of their being divided into any definite number of well-defined systems.

Freiberg.—The Freiberg mines afford an interesting example of silver veins retaining their character and richness at considerable depths. Many of the mines now exceed 230 fathoms in depth, and notwithstanding the increasing expenditure incident to this circumstance, their prosperity has continued to be constantly progressive. The most celebrated and productive of the Freiberg mines during the present century, have been those of Himmelsfürst, Himmelfahrt, and Beschertglück; and with a view to facilitate their drainage, it has been

* Annales des Mines, S. 4, t. xi. p. 27.

proposed to bring up a deep adit from the valley of the Elbe, a distance of about eighteen miles.

The ores of the Freiberg mines consist of the various sulphides, particularly vitreous silver, pyrargyrite, light red silver ore, stephanite, freislebenite, and native silver. The latter sometimes occurs in large masses, and the veins occasionally yield considerable amounts of argentiferous galena. The total yield of silver from the mines of Freiberg from 1524 to the end of 1850, was 5,613,228 lbs. troy. As a general rule, the productiveness of these mines has, subject to temporary fluctuations, increased with their progressive depths. At the time of the publication of the work of Heron de Villefosse, "*Sur la Richesse Minérale*" (1819), the Himmelsfürst was the most productive mine, but since 1830 its yield has declined, and the Himmelfahrt has occupied the first position, having afforded, from that time up to 1850, 146,869 lbs. troy of silver.

Marienberg.—Formerly the mines of Marienberg, a small town twenty-five miles south-west of Freiberg, were exceedingly flourishing, and in the sixteenth century ores were frequently found there producing 85 per cent. of silver. The troubles attending the Thirty Years' War put an end, however, to their prosperity: since that period they have never exhibited any degree of activity, and their annual returns are now very inconsiderable.

Annaberg.—The production of the Annaberg district during one hundred and ninety-one years, from 1654 to 1845, amounted in value to about 850,000*l.* but the yield of the veins has decreased in depth, and their annual returns are now exceedingly small.

Schneeberg.—The Saint-George mines, near Schneeberg, were opened in the fifteenth century, in search of ironstone, but soon became celebrated for their large production of silver. Towards the close of that century a mass of ore was discovered in them which afforded nearly twenty tons of that metal; but after this period they became rapidly impoverished as silver mines, but have been worked during the last two hundred years for ores of cobalt, for which they are celebrated, and which are found in the veins formerly yielding such large quantities of silver. Mining operations at Schneeberg are now carried on only on an exceedingly limited scale.

Johann-Georgenstadt.—There are several small mines in the neighbourhood of this town, producing a little silver, but the aggregate amount is exceedingly small. The veins in this district yield a certain amount of bismuth and uranium, and some of them are worked for the ores of these metals. The mines of Schwarzenberg are no longer of any importance.

The average richness of the silver ores throughout Saxony is from sixty to seventy ounces per ton, and the annual production of the country about 80,000 lbs. troy, of which the mines of Freiberg alone yield about ninety-seven per cent.

Joachimsthal.—These mines, which are of great antiquity, and were formerly of much importance, have been worked to a depth of 325 fathoms, but their produce has for many years been gradually declining in amount, and their annual yield is at present insignificant.

MINES OF THE HARTZ.—The most productive silver mines of the Hartz are those in the neighbourhood of Andreasberg, of which the most extensive are the Samson and Neufang mines, which are worked to a depth of 430 English fathoms. They were discovered in 1520, and produce argentiferous galena, in addition to silver ores properly so called. The district yielding the largest amount of argentiferous galena is that of Clausthal, which comprehends several mines worked at a depth of above 300 fathoms. The most extensive of these are the Dorothea and Carolina, the latter of which furnishes a large proportion of the annual produce of the district. The grant of the Dorothea mine extends over a length of 257 yards on the run of the vein, with a moderate width at right angles to its direction. Within this small area there were extracted, from 1700 to 1807 inclusively, 553,200 lbs. troy of silver, besides 38,441 tons of lead, and 1,192 tons of copper. The profits realised from this mine, together with that of Carolina, during the same period, amounted to 1,120,000*l.*, besides which the shareholders contributed largely, by means of loans without interest, to carry on the exploration of various less productive mines in the district.

The annual production of silver from the Hartz mines is about 27,540 lbs. troy.

MINES OF THE ALPS.—The mine of La Gardette in the Oisans, Department of the Isère, was worked during the latter portion of the eighteenth century, on a quartz vein containing small quantities of gold and silver, but it never paid the expenses of extraction, and has long since been abandoned. The mine of Chalanches or Allemont, in the same Department, was regularly worked from 1768 to 1815, but is now also abandoned. The ore consists of various minerals, containing silver, disseminated in a clay which fills the fissures and irregular cavities in talcose and hornblendic rocks. This mine yielded annually, towards the close of the last century, 1,252 lbs. troy.

The mines of Kitzbühel and Röhrerbüchel in the Tyrol were formerly worked on a considerable scale, and in the middle of the eighteenth century were considered among the deepest in Europe, but were shortly afterwards abandoned. They produced copper pyrites, and argentiferous fahlerz, occurring in a clay slate. The ores from these mines, together with the products from some smaller workings in the neighbourhood, were smelted at the works of Brixlegg, near Schwatz. The produce of the mines of the Tyrol, towards the middle of the last century, amounted annually to 6,296 lbs. troy, and was before that time considerably greater, but has since declined in importance. There are mines of argentiferous copper ore at Schladming, Feistritz, Walchern, and Kallwang, but their annual product of silver is unimportant. The mines of l'Argentière, Hautes Alpes, were probably worked by the Romans, but are known to have been in active operation in the twelfth century. The ores contain about 50 per cent. lead, and 0·0024 of silver. These mines are worked on three veins, of which the largest is 16 feet in width. Although not belonging to the above category, it may be mentioned that the mines of Wittichen in the Black Forest produced, some years since, 880 lbs. troy of silver per annum.

NORTHERN AND CENTRAL FRANCE, &c.—Huelgoët in Brittany, although strictly speaking a mine of argentiferous galena, produces an ochreous substance containing about 30 oz. of silver per ton, in the form of *chloride*, which was until recently extracted by a process of amalgamation somewhat similar to that formerly employed at Freiberg.

The mines of Pontgibaud produce large quantities of argentiferous galena, rich in silver; these are treated by a process of smelting which will be described with considerable detail in a subsequent chapter. In addition to the mines of Pontgibaud, Puy-de-Dôme; of Poullaouen, and Huelgoët in the Department of Finistère; of Vialas in the Lozère; and of Pontpéan, Department of Ille-et-Vilaine, there are in France various other localities affording argentiferous lead ores; but as these cannot be strictly regarded as ores of silver, a detailed description of them does not come within the limits which we have assigned ourselves.

SPAIN.—The silver mines of Gaudalcanal and Cazalla, to the north of Seville, occur in mica slate, and were formerly highly productive, but are now of little importance; there were also mines at Villa-Guttier, not far from that city, which are said to have furnished 170 marks of silver daily during some portion of the seventeenth century. A silver vein was also formerly worked in the Sierra Almagrera, and was followed to a depth of above a hundred fathoms. The most important silver mines of Spain are, however, those of Hiendelaencina.

The mines of this district are situated about 70 miles north of Madrid, in the province of Guadalajara. They were discovered in 1843 by a peasant who had been in Mexico, and who on his return to his native country, remarked the resemblance which a large stone situated by the side of the road, near the village of Hiendelaencina, had to the ores he had assisted to work in the Mexican mines. On examination, by the celebrated chemist Orfila, this stone was found to be an exceedingly rich ore of silver, and proved to be part of a lode which outcropped at that point.

Shortly after this discovery a concession was obtained, and the first of the numerous mines of this now widely-known district was commenced under the name of The Santa Cecilia, in honour of the patron saint of the village. Of the other mines which were subsequently opened, the most remarkable are the Suerte, Fortuna, Verdad de los Artistas, Relampago, San Carlos, and Vascongada, all of which have yielded immense wealth. There are numerous other lodes in the district, but, up to the present time, that on which these mines are situated has alone been worked with advantage. Its direction is east and west, with an underlie south, and its average thickness scarcely two feet; the enclosing rock is gneiss, accompanied by a coarse talcose slate. The vein is chiefly composed of sulphate of baryta, together with a little quartz; carbonate of iron is, however, often found associated with them, especially in the richer parts of the lode.

Many varieties of silver ores have been found in this district, but by far the most abundant is silver glance; beautiful specimens of ruby silver are also frequently met with. The average yield of the ores produced is about 4½ oz. of silver per quintal, or 90 oz. per ton.

The greater portion of these ores has been purchased by the Bella Raquel Company, and reduced at their establishments at Constante, about three miles from the mines, to which there is an excellent cart road. A portion of the richest ore was, however, at one time sent to England for treatment, but the whole produce of the mines is now again purchased by the Bella Raquel Company. These mines have declined in their yield since 1858, many of them being at the present time far less productive than formerly. The mines of Hiendelaencina have been worked to a depth of about 200 fathoms, and the concessions are generally 200 yards in length by 100 yards wide.

The production of these mines since 1846, when they were first extensively opened, has been as follows :*—

Year.	Fine Silver.				
	marks	oz.	ochs.	Spanish ounces.	
1847	4,958	1	6	39,665·7	7,578,536·20 English ounces.
1848	17,345	6	4	138,766·5	
1849	21,633	6	4	173,070·5	
1850	48,516	6	6	388,134·8	
1851	68,029	7	2	544,239·3	
1852	64,616	4	2	516,932·3	
1853	69,178	1	5	553,425·6	
1854	89,784	3	4	718,275·5	
1855	80,359	3	4	642,875·5	
1856	67,730	2	4	541,842·5	
1857	65,072	0	0	520,576·0	
1858	86,052	1	5	688,417·7	
1859	67,412	2	4	539,298·5	
1860	50,639	6	3	405,118·3	
1861	40,780	3	5	326,243·6	
1862	31,745	2	3	253,962·4	
1863	24,598	2	3	196,786·4	
1864	19,019	0	3	152,152·4	
1865	9,362	5	4	74,901·5	
1866 June 30, 6 months	5,226	1	1	41,809·1	
Silver in Ore sent to England, as per Assay . .				740,210·2	
Total Produce, 19½ years .				8,196,704·3	

Altai Mountains.—The most important silver mine of this district is that of Zméof, situated to the north-west of the high mountains in 51° 9′ N. lat., and 79° 49′ long., east of Paris. It is worked on a vein containing chloride and sulphide of silver, native silver and

* Communicated by Messrs. Taylor and Sons.

native gold, together with various ores of copper, generally more or less argentiferous. The gangue consists of sulphate of baryta, carbonate of lime, quartz, and occasionally, fluor spar. The principal vein, which is very large, has been traced for a distance of several hundred fathoms, and is worked to a depth of 95 fathoms. This vein has near the surface a considerable inclination, but becomes nearly vertical in depth. Its roof is of clay slate, but on the foot wall the slate is much mixed with hornstone. It throws out numerous branches, is not unfrequently intersected by cross-courses, and was more productive near the surface than at the present time.

The other silver mines of this region are those of Tcherepanofsk, three leagues south-east of Zméof; those of Semenofsk, ten leagues south-east; those of Nicolaiefsk, twenty leagues to the south-west; and of Philipofsk, ninety leagues north-east of the same locality. The last mine lies on the extreme frontier of Chinese Tartary.

DAOURIA.—The name of Daouria is given to the great mountainous tract extending from Lake Baikal to the Eastern Ocean. The metalliferous portions of this district consist of granite, hornblendic shales, and slates, overlaid by a grey limestone, sometimes silicious and argillaceous, in which are veins of argentiferous lead ores. The silver from this district appears to be chiefly, though not entirely, derived from galena, and is estimated to amount to about 21,000 lbs. troy annually. This silver contains a small proportion of gold. Many of the mines of Daouria are reported to be, at the present time, nearly exhausted.

CHAPTER XIV.

SILVER MINES OF NORTH AMERICA.

PRINCIPAL MINING DISTRICTS OF MEXICO—PRODUCTION OF SILVER IN MEXICO UP TO 1845—PRODUCE OF ORES TREATED—GUANAXUATO—ZACATECAS—FRESNILLO—REAL DEL MONTE—HISTORY AND OPERATIONS OF THE REAL DEL MONTE MINING COMPANY—PRINCIPAL MINING DISTRICTS OF NEVADA—COMSTOCK VEIN—DISCOVERY OF SILVER AT VIRGINIA—YIELD DURING FOUR YEARS—SUTRO TUNNEL—REESE RIVER DISTRICT—SYSTEMS OF VEINS—AMADOR DISTRICT—RAVENSWOOD—CORTEZ—WASHINGTON—UNION—SMOKY VALLEY—TWIN RIVER—SAN ANTONIO—OTHER MINING DISTRICTS—TABLE SHOWING NUMBER OF REDUCTION WORKS, &c.

THE principal silver mines of North America are those of Mexico, although large quantities of this metal have of late years been afforded by the State of Nevada. In addition to Nevada, other portions of the possessions of the United States, and particularly Idaho and Colorado, are known to contain valuable mines of this metal; but they have been, as yet, for the most part, imperfectly explored, and it is extremely difficult to obtain reliable data from these comparatively new and outlying countries.

MEXICO.—Our information relative to the mines of Mexico is chiefly derived from the works of European authors, who have either visited the country for scientific purposes, or who, for a time, lived there in connexion with some of the different mining and metallurgical enterprises, which have at various periods been established on that portion of the American Continent by the capitalists of the Old World. By this means, although a large amount of information has been accumulated with regard to the quantities of silver obtained from the different districts, and connected with the various processes employed, both for the extraction and reduction of the ores, we are, nevertheless, without such exact geological data as would enable us to become thoroughly acquainted with the characteristics of the mining regions, and the precise nature of the relations and differences existing between the principal metalliferous centres.

The workings have, for the most part, been excavated on true veins; and deposits in the form of beds or interfoliated masses, running parallel with the stratification of the enclosing rocks, are by no means of frequent occurrence. The veins are chiefly enclosed in what have been designated, by those describing them, as primitive and transition rocks, but of which, a careful and minute examination would doubtless enable the geologist of the present day, not only to determine the relative ages, but also to assign their true position in the geological series. Humboldt calls the limestones of the district of Tasco and Catorce "Alpine" and "Jurassic limestone," whilst Burkart speaks of them as "mountain limestone;" from which it may be inferred that at least a portion of them belongs to the carboniferous period.

The summits of the highest mountains generally consist of granite, gneiss, and mica slate, but their flanks are in most cases covered by deposits of porphyritic and trappean rocks, through which the granite seldom makes its appearance. The most metalliferous rocks of Mexico are varieties of syenite and porphyry, but Humboldt considers that the determination of their relative geological ages would be an exceedingly difficult problem. They are, however, generally characterised by the presence of hornblende, and the absence of quartz. The veins of this country have generally a direction north of west and south of east, with a considerable dip, which is more frequently towards the south than towards the north, and they generally intersect the enclosing rocks at a very decided angle. The largest vein which has been worked in Mexico is the Veta Madre of Guanaxuato, which is sometimes two hundred feet in width, and which has been opened on at various points over a distance of more than three leagues. In 1845 the workings on this lode had already attained a depth of above three hundred fathoms. The lode next in magnitude is the Veta Grande of Zacatecas, which is sometimes seventy-five feet in width; although the generality of the argentiferous veins of Mexico do not possess these extraordinary dimensions, but vary in width from a few inches to six or eight feet.

The veinstone is generally quartz, and the outcrops or *crestones* can frequently be traced for long distances on the surface, standing above the level of the enclosing rocks. The ores consist of the various simple and compound sulphides of silver, which have, near the surface, frequently become decomposed, and given rise to the formation of native silver, and various secondary combinations, of which the chloride is the most important. The outcrops and shallow portions of the veins are generally drusy, and much stained by oxide of iron; and from their red colour are called *colorados* by the Mexicans, corresponding to the gossans of the Cornish miner. Below the point at which this decomposition has taken place, and consequently where the sulphides remain in their original state, the ores are called *negros* (black ores), which, according to Duport, afford seven-eighths of the total produce of Mexico.

At the date of the publication of Humboldt's "*Essai Politique,*" the richest mines of Mexico, arranged in accordance with the importance of their several yields, followed each other in the annexed order.*

Guanaxuato . .	Intendancy of	Guanaxuato
Catorce . . .	" "	San Luis Potosi
Zacatecas . . .	" "	Zacatecas
Real del Monte .	" "	Mexico
Bolaños . . .	" "	Guadalajara
Guarisamey . .	" "	Durango
Sombrerete . .	" "	Zacatecas
Tasco	" "	Mexico
Batopilas . . .	" "	Durango
Zimapan . . .	" "	Mexico
Fresnillo . . .	" "	Zacatecas
Ramos	" "	San Luis Potosi
Parral	" "	Durango

The veins of Tasco, Tlalpujahua, Sultepec, Moran, Pachuca, and Real del Monte, as well as those of Sombrerete, Bolaños, and Batopilas, have, from time to time, afforded immense wealth, but their produce has been generally of a less uniform character than that of the mines of Guanaxuato, Zacatecas, and Catorce. The silver extracted from the mines of Mexico, from January 1, 1785, to December 31, 1789, is stated by Humboldt to have been as follows:—

* With regard to the production of the precious metals, McCulloch remarks: "The silver and gold mines of Mexico have always been deemed the main source of its wealth, and unquestionably its mineral riches far exceed those of any part of America, except perhaps Peru. Before the War of Independence there were in the thirty-seven mining districts of New Spain somewhat more than 3,000 mines, producing annually about $21,000,000 in silver, and about $2,000,000 in gold."

Name of Provincial Treasury.	Silver extracted by amalgamation.	Silver extracted by smelting.
	marks.	marks.
Mexico	950,185	104,835
Zacatecas	1,031,360	173,631
Guanaxuato	1,937,895	531,138
San Luis Potosi . . .	1,491,058	24,465
Durango	536,272	386,081
Guadalajara	405,357	103,655
Bolaños	336,355	27,614
Sombrerete	136,395	184,205
Zimapan	1,215	247,002
Pachuca	269,536	185,500
Rosario	477,134	191,368
Totals . . .	7,572,762	2,159,494

The above is equal to a returned production of 9,732,256 marks, or about 6,100,000 lbs. troy. Humboldt, however, estimates that silver to at least one-fifth of the above amount, had not passed through the Government Offices; and consequently the true produce would thus become 11,678,659 marks, or 7,314,344 lbs. troy.

The mines of Zacatecas were first opened in 1548, and those of Guanaxuato ten years later, about which time the patio process of amalgamation was also introduced. The annual total yield of the Mexican mines at this period has been estimated by Humboldt at from $2,000,000 to $3,000,000, and it subsequently increased, during the eighteenth century, until it finally reached $23,000,000. The production appears to have reached its highest point between 1800 and 1810, when the average coinage of gold and silver at the various mints in Mexico was $23,664,622, the ratio of the former metal to the latter being, by weight, 0·0029 : 1; and in value, 0·05 : 1. During the War of Independence a great falling off took place in the production of the precious metals, which between 1810 and 1845 did not average above $12,000,000, for silver, with a little over $100,000 in gold. Since 1850, however, the mines of Mexico have regained their ancient prosperity, and their present annual produce cannot be much less than $26,000,000 in silver, and $3,200,000 in gold. It is, however, to be regretted that our information with regard to the production of the Mexican mines does not come down to a recent date; since no investigations on this subject appear to have been made, by any competent authority, since the appearance, more than twenty years since, of the works of Duport and Chevalier. The latter author estimates the total produce of silver from the Mexican mines from the earliest period up to 1845, at 162,858,700 lbs. troy.

The quantity of silver obtained from the ores by amalgamation was, at the close of the last century, in the proportion of 3·5 : 1 of that produced by smelting. This ratio was ascertained from the general table prepared at the provincial treasuries of the different mining districts. In some of the districts, however, as for instance, those of Sombrerete and Zimapan, the produce from smelting was greater than that from amalgamation. In 1846 it was, however, estimated by Mr. J. Phillips, that one-eighth only of the silver produced in Mexico was at that time obtained by smelting.* The result of investigations made some years since, showed that the average richness of all the ores treated from the Mexican mines was from 2½ to 3 oz. per quintal, or that the 1,878,400 lbs. troy of silver, produced from the country in prosperous years, were extracted from 446,428 tons of mineral, of which a portion was smelted and the remainder amalgamated. This would give a mean average produce of a little more than 50 oz. per ton.

In the district of Pachuca, the ores of the Biscaina vein were, in 1803, divided into three classes. The minerals of the first class contained, on an average, about 110 oz. per ton, those of the second 45 oz. and the poorest only 30 oz. per ton. In the district of Tasco, the ores of Tehuilotepec afforded, on an average, about 40 oz. of silver per ton. In 1791 the Valenciana mine of Guanaxuato, then in its most flourishing condition, yielded ores of different degrees of richness, in nearly the following proportions :—

In 1,000 parts.	Yield of silver per ton.
5	3,630 oz.
8	1,500 „
152	560 „
815	60 „

In the above year the total amount of silver extracted from the mine was 360,000 lbs. troy, of which the ores affording 50 oz. of silver per ton represented 123,508 lbs.

Space will not allow us to give even a brief description of all

* "Descriptive Notice of the Silver Mines and Amalgamation Process of Mexico." By John Phillips. London, 1846.

the productive mining regions of Mexico, and we shall consequently confine ourselves to certain details relative to some of the best known and most important districts of that country, at the same time selecting such as may serve as types of silver mining generally, on this portion of the American continent. About the year 1821, it having become evident to the Mexican Government that the pecuniary resources of the country were not sufficient to admit of the efficient development of its mines, a proposition was made to allow foreigners to participate with the natives in mining undertakings, and thus to allow of the introduction of foreign capital. This proposition was eagerly responded to by European capitalists, and in 1829 seven large English Companies, one German, and two American Companies were in operation. The English Companies were the Real del Monte, the Bolaños, the Tlalpujahua, the Anglo-Mexican, the United Mexican, the Mexican, and the Catorce. Of these the United Mexican and the Real del Monte are now alone in operation.

Guanaxuato.—The Veta Madre traverses at the surface a conglomerate possessing many of the characteristics of a red sandstone, and subsequently enters a foliated rock of greenish colour, sometimes talcose, enclosing beds of serpentine, occasionally including syenite and a bluish clay slate. The inclination of the vein is about 45° southwest, and its width is seldom less than thirty feet, but it sometimes increases to two hundred. It is generally divided into three bands, separated by intervening sterile rock. The central band is the widest and most productive, but the upper division has also been much worked, and has produced large quantities of ore, whilst the lower branch is, generally speaking, less rich than the other two. This lode, although partially explored over a length of more than three leagues, produced the chief portion of its silver within a space of about 1,000 fathoms, and particularly from that part of the vein comprehended within the concessions of Valenciana, La Cata, Mellado, and Rayas. The Veta Madre is not, however, the only silver vein which has been successfully worked in the neighbourhood of Guanaxuato, as there are others situated a few leagues to the north, which have been opened in the concession of the Pavillon and La Luz. The first of these yields ores containing a large proportion of ruby silver, whilst the veinstone of the latter is much stained by blue carbonate of copper.

The vein worked in the mine of the Asuncion, which is about a league to the north of the Veta Madre, and runs parallel with it, is, like the principal vein of the district, divided into three bands, has the same inclination, and affords ores of a very similar character. The gangue of the Veta Madre is composed of a very white quartz, containing numerous reniform cavernous concretions. The ores consist of native silver, black antimonial sulphide of silver, and small quantities of red silver ore, rarely associated with iron pyrites or galena, but occasionally with very small quantities of blende and mispickel. Gold also occurs in a very finely-divided state, and is consequently seldom visible, although grains of considerable size are sometimes met with, disseminated in the quartz. The ores of Guanaxuato generally contain less than three per cent. of metallic ingredients intermixed with the quartzose gangue.

According to Duport the average assay produce for silver, is from 0·0015 = 49 oz. to 0·0020 = 65 oz. per ton, and when the assay was below 0·0009, or 29 oz. per ton, the ores could, in 1843, be no longer extracted with advantage.* Ores containing more than 0·003 = 98 oz. per ton, are rarely met with, in any considerable quantities. The proportion of gold by weight is generally about 0·005 of that of silver, but this is subject to slight variations in different parts of the vein.

Little is known with respect to the produce of Guanaxuato previous to 1760, when the mine of Valenciana was first opened; but even at that time some of the other workings had attained considerable importance, since Gamboa speaks of the large gallery at Rayas as being a remarkable undertaking, and states that it was of such dimensions as to allow of mules entering the interior of the mine for the purpose of receiving their burdens.† In 1803, the workings in the Valenciana had already exceeded 200 fathoms in depth, which, as Duport remarks, is below the point at which the mines of Mexico usually begin to become impoverished. This gradual diminution in the average produce of a vein is called by the Mexican miners the *enborrascado*, and begins to take place in many instances even at less considerable depths. At the Valenciana, however, the great width of the lode, and the expectation of fresh discoveries, encouraged the proprietors to continue their operation to a depth of 350 fathoms, and efforts were made to compensate for the falling off in the produce of the ores, by the increase of the quantities treated. In this way the enterprise struggled forward until 1810, when the breaking

* "De la Production des Métaux Précieux au Mexique," par St. Clair Duport. P. 212. Paris, 1843.

† Gamboa, "Comentarios a las Ordenanzas," cap. 19-20.

out of the War of Independence caused the suspension of all operations at the Valenciana and many other Mexican mines.

In 1822 the re-opening of the Valenciana mine was undertaken by the Anglo-Mexican Company, who agreed with the proprietors to furnish the necessary working capital on condition of receiving one-half the net profits accruing from the operations. This Company erected at a great expense powerful steam-engines for the drainage of the mines, but, on getting out the water, it was found that the ores at the lower levels were not sufficiently rich to repay the expenses of extraction and reduction, and the deeper portions of the vein were consequently abandoned, and operations entirely confined to the extraction of ores which remained standing nearer the surface. The working of the property was for some time continued in this way, but the results obtained were so far from satisfactory that the English proprietary finally resolved to sacrifice their expenditure and abandon the enterprise to the original proprietors. The operations which have been carried on since that period have afforded but very moderate returns for the capital employed, having been sometimes barely sufficient to cover the current expenses of the undertaking. The Valenciana is the deepest mine in Mexico, and the non-success of the Anglo-Mexican Company has consequently tended somewhat to discourage further attempts at deep mining in the country.

The extraction of the water and ore from the Mexican mines is usually effected by means of *malacates*, or horse whims, around which a rope is so wound that whilst one sack of raw hide is descending the shaft another is being raised to the surface. The Valenciana mine has several shafts, but the principal one, or *tiro general*, which is 734 varas,* or 343 fathoms in depth, has a diameter of nearly thirty feet, and is one of the most remarkable engineering works in Mexico.

Next to the Valenciana, the mine of Rayas is the most important. The main shaft is the largest in the country, and was made to rival that of Valenciana. It is in the form of an octagon thirty-one feet in diameter, and secured by masonry for a depth of about thirty varas from the surface. Its total depth is 465 varas, or 215 fathoms; but its diameter is smaller downward than towards the surface. Some of the best constructed malacates in Mexico have been erected at the mine of Rayas, and at the time this neighbourhood was visited by Mr. J. Phillips (1840), each of them was worked by twelve horses driven round at a fast trot, and drew the *bota*, which when full of water

* The Vara equals 33·384 inches.

weighed 1,500 lbs., from a depth of 465 varas to the surface, in eight minutes.

In the district of Zacatecas and Real del Monte the veins are very numerous and cross each other in various places, although generally at the same angle, whilst at Guanaxuato the riches are to a greater extent concentrated in one enormous lode. The large size of this vein, and the impossibility of thoroughly trying the ground without having recourse to numerous cross-cuts, gave rise at Guanaxuato to a method of working very much resembling the tribute system of Cornwall. The miners who work on this system, which has been attended with the best results, and has led to the discovery of some of the richest deposits of ore, are called *buscones.* In this way the men, to a great extent, work the mines at their own risk, and by following up such indications as may appear to them favourable, they often meet with valuable courses of ore; whilst, on the other hand, they sometimes work for many months without gaining more than sufficient to provide themselves with the means of bare subsistence. The *buscon* receives a certain proportion, sometimes one-half the produce of the ore which he breaks, and should he fall in with a rich deposit his gains will necessarily be very large, instances not being wanting of a man making in this way from a thousand to fifteen hundred dollars per month.

In cases of this kind, however, it is optional with the owners of the mine to take the discovery out of the hands of the miners after giving them a certain notice; when this is done, each man is paid a dollar per diem without allowing him any portion of the ore. A very large proportion of the ores at Guanaxuato are, however, raised by buscones, who divide the produce of their labour with the proprietors of the concessions. The ore, after being broken and separated as much as possible from sterile matter, by hand picking, underground, is usually put into botas of bullocks' hide, and drawn to the surface by malacates. In some of the mines, however, the ore is taken to the surface on the backs of labourers, who, with a load of from two to three hundred pounds, make several journeys daily from the bottom of the mine, often a depth of from four to five hundred varas, to the surface. At the mine of Mellado an inclined railway is employed for this purpose. When brought to the surface, the ore is conveyed to the mine yard, where it is placed in separate heaps under the care of the buscon, who picks out a further amount of sterile matter, and prepares the ore for sale. One day in each week is generally fixed for the sale of the ores, and the miners may then be seen laying out their several parcels, so as to make them appear to the best advantage, by turning each stone in such a way as to expose the best side of it, and keeping his lot constantly sprinkled with water, which has the effect of making the mineral look darker and richer.

The various purchasers, or *rescatadores* as they are called, take, as nearly as possible, an average sample from each lot, which is ground into a fine powder, and subjected to a sort of assay on the spot. This is effected by washing a handful of the pulverised ore in a *jicara* or small bowl, formed of half a gourd; and after washing away the lighter earthy particles, the richness of the parcel is estimated in accordance with the amount and appearance of the mineral deposit remaining in the bowl. Long practice enables those who constantly employ this process to arrive at results very closely approximating to the true yield of the ores, but many of the purchasers now prefer to regulate their bids by the result of fire assays, and in this case the samples are taken on the day previous to that on which the sale is to take place.

When the hour of sale arrives, a bell strikes as a signal that it is about to commence, and the person entrusted with its management takes his place successively at the foot of every parcel. Each purchaser, in turn, now approaches, and whispers in the ear of the salesman his bid for the parcel at the foot of which he stands; and when all have given in their prices, the lot is adjudged to be the property of the highest bidder. When two persons offer the same price, the first bidder obtains the parcel. The salesman and purchasers thus move from lot to lot, until the whole of the ore in the yard has been disposed of, after which it is removed by the various buyers at their own expense. The quantity of ore contained in each parcel is not ascertained by weighing, but, like the assay by washing, is determined with great accuracy, by the eye, by those who have had long practice in the business.

Zacatecas.—The district of Zacatecas is situated about fifteen leagues east of the elevated mountains which join the principal chain of the cordillera extending from Durango to Guanaxuato. Burkart, who lived many years in this vicinity, and who had consequently ample opportunities of becoming acquainted with the geology of the country, considers that the greenstone which encloses the greater number of the veins in that locality can only be regarded as a diorite. Bustamante, on the contrary, calls it syenite. This rock, which at some points presents many of the characteristics of chloritic slate, overlies a blue argillaceous slate which occasionally comes to the surface, and closely resembles that forming the enclosing rock in the deepest portions of many of the Mexican mines. Quartz veins are exceedingly numerous in the neighbourhood of Zacatecas, and have generally a direction approaching north-west and south-east. The Cantera vein is remarkable, not only on account of its variation in direction at different points in its course, but also for its prominent outcrop, which may be traced on the surface over a length of more than three leagues. This outcrop, which sometimes stands at a height of a hundred feet, and is from forty-five to sixty feet in width, throws off a branch towards the north, which is known as the San Martin vein; whilst the principal lode, turning towards the south, takes the name of the Del Muerto, and finally makes an intersection with the Quebradillas. This vein, which has a dip of 35° towards the south, is for a long distance enclosed between a greenish slate on its foot wall, and sandstone on the hanging wall, but finally enters the green slate, which thus constitutes the enclosing rock on either side. The principal workings on this vein, which is at this point about 36 feet in width, produced large quantities of ore, yielding by amalgamation from 0·0010 to 0·0012, or from 33 to 39 oz. of silver per ton; but the workings having been badly secured, fell in some years since, and caused the abandonment of the mine.

The San Bernabé vein was first opened by the conquerors of Mexico in 1548, and is said, in common with the San Alvado, to have been worked by Cortez. The eastern extension of this vein, which dips to the south, and of which the direction is nearly east and west, has produced large quantities of ore in the concessions of Malanoche, Rondanera, Loreto, and Peregrina; but the most productive mines of Zacatecas, in 1843, were those of San Clemênte and San Nicolas, of which the workings were commenced in 1836, to the east of the mines above mentioned. In the various workings of the old mines, the width of this vein was from twelve to thirty feet, but in the San Clemênte and San Nicolas it rarely exceeds six feet, although the selvages of clay on the walls, which frequently have a considerable thickness, are so impregnated with argentiferous matter as often to admit of being worked with as much advantage as the lode itself.

The most important vein of Zacatecas is the Veta Grande, which has been worked over an extent of nearly 2,500 fathoms. The first extensive operations on this lode were undertaken in 1765, by a

M. Laborde, a Frenchman. The general direction of the vein is north 60° west, with an inclination of about 35° towards the south, and like the Veta Madre of Guanaxuato, it is divided into bands, which sometimes have an united thickness of seventy-five feet, but of which the average width may be taken at about forty feet. Of this width about twelve feet are occupied by country rock, dividing the lode into three bands. The gossans, or colorados, usually extend to a depth of forty fathoms, and contain native silver and chloride of silver; the ores below the water level consist of various sulphides of silver, associated with a little blende, galena, and iron pyrites. A *bonanza*, or bunch of ore, discovered in this vein, and worked from 1828 to 1838, yielded a net profit of above $9,000,000 to the proprietors of the mines.

According to Bustamante and Burkart, the Veta Madre produced from 1790 to 1833, 3,902,252 marks, or about 2,500,000 lbs. of silver.*

Where first worked by the Bolaños Company, the vein-stuff, as extracted from the mine, was so generally productive, that only one-sixth had to be rejected as not paying the expense of reduction. Gradually, however, the vein became so much impoverished, that not quite two-thirds could be treated with advantage. During the former period the proportion of silver extracted by fusion was one-fifth of the whole production, whilst, during the latter, ores sufficiently rich for this method of reduction were very rarely met with.

The average produce obtained from the ores of the Veta Grande at the *Hacienda* de la Sauceda from 1804 to 1839, was as follows :—

1804 to 1808	. . .	0·0025 = 81 oz. per ton of 2,240 lbs.
1820 „ 1824	. . .	0·0021 = 68 „ „ „ „
1825 „ 1832	. . .	0·0019 = 62 „ „ „ „
1839	. . .	0·0017 = 55 „ „ „ „

It must, however, be remarked that the produce obtained by no means represents the actual richness of the ores treated, since from the large quantities of antimonial silver present, the patio process failed to extract nearly the whole of that metal, and this loss is estimated by Duport at nearly two-fifths of the total contents of the argentiferous matter subjected to amalgamation. The Veta Grande, however, like all the principal veins of Mexico, begins to diminish in richness at depths, from the surface, varying between 75 and 150 fathoms. Another important vein in the district is that of the Tajos de Panuco,

* The Spanish mark equals 3,550·5 grains.

on which open workings were commenced in 1548, and extended over a length of above three hundred and fifty fathoms. The silver from the Veta Grande contains but a very small proportion of gold; that from the San Bernabé often affords from 0·001 to 0·003 of this metal.

The following table, from Duport, will afford an idea of the produce of the mines of Zacatecas—

				Marks.	lbs. troy.
From 1st June,	1548, to 16th September,	1810	.	67,317,937 =	42,161,224
„ 16th September,	1810, „ 1st June,	1818	.	2,296,472 =	1,438,484
„ 1st June,	1818, „ „	1825	.	2,107,350 =	1,319,833
„ „	1825, „ 31st December,	1832	.	3,532,769 =	2,212,573

The operations of the English Company were suspended in 1838, after which time the produce of the mines continued gradually to diminish, and in 1842 some of them were let out to buscones at a *partido*, or share of one-fourth, which in 1846 had been increased to one-third.

Fresnillo.—The Cerro de Proaña is situated fourteen leagues north-west from Zacatecas, and consists of an elevation of about six hundred yards in length, which does not exceed three hundred feet in height above the level of the surrounding plains. This hill is composed of a compact argillaceous rock overlying, at a certain depth, a blue slate containing bands of white quartz. In these rocks there exists a considerable number of veins running nearly north and south, and generally dipping towards the west, but at such variable angles that the different veins often intersect each other in depth, thereby forming a species of network. The whole surface of the mountain is here covered by the débris of former workings, and large open cuttings are seen, forming more or less continuous trenches on the course of the different veins.

These mines are known to have been worked by open cuttings and otherwise, as far back as 1755, but about the year 1760 operations were commenced on a more extensive scale, and abundant returns obtained over a considerable extent of ground. Mining was subsequently carried on by some merchants of the city of Mexico, afterwards by the State of Zacatecas, and later under the auspices of the Central Government.

Real del Monte.—The mines of Real del Monte are situated about sixty miles due north from the city of Mexico, in a district containing numerous bands of porphyry of evidently different ages. To the north-east of Real del Monte the porphyries are covered by columnar basalt, and at a still greater distance, in the same direction, by metamorphic slate. The rock enclosing the various argentiferous veins of this locality is a decomposed porphyry, in which the presence of hornblende is announced by numerous greenish stains. The principal veins of Real del Monte run nearly east and west, whilst the cross-veins course almost north and south, the inclination of the former being to the south, and of the latter towards the west. The principal east and west vein of the Real del Monte is the Biscaina, usually about fifteen feet in width, but there are numerous others, particularly near the town of Pachuca, which have nearly the same direction, whilst these are crossed by the Santa Brigida, and others.

The partido system has prevailed among the mines of Real del Monte from a very early period, but differs somewhat in its arrangement from that of the other mining districts. Here the working miner or *barretero* receives a certain portion, frequently an eighth, of all the ore he raises, and in addition is paid a daily sum equal to about two shillings. From the Real del Monte Company having been the first of the large associations organised in this country for working mines in Mexico by the aid of British capital, some notice of its history and progress may not be uninteresting.

Real del Monte Company.—But little is known of the mines of Real del Monte, prior to the year 1749, except that they had yielded considerable quantities of silver from irregular and detached surface workings, and had at last become almost entirely abandoned from the influx of water, as the excavations increased in depth. At the above period, Don Pedro Terreros, a merchant of Queretaro, joined a practical miner named Bustamante, in a general *denuncio* of the district, by which they obtained possession of its two principal veins, La Biscaina and La Santa Brigida, on the condition of effecting their drainage by means of a horizontal gallery.

For this important work, a point was chosen sufficiently down the slope of the northern descent of the valley to ensure its entering the principal mines of the Biscaina vein at the depth of one hundred fathoms from the surface; but as the distance necessary to obtain this difference of level was nearly 1,500 fathoms, the work, although commenced in 1749, was not completed until 1759. Bustamante did not live to see the result of his great work, but Terreros persevered to reap the reward; for, having by this adit freed the mine from water, he extracted at comparatively small cost, up to his death in 1781, the large amount of fifteen millions of dollars, having been previously ennobled by the King of Spain, under the title of Conde de Regla.

His successor, the second Conde, continued the working of the mines, but not to equal profit with his father, who, having exhausted the upper portions of the veins, rendered dry by the adit, left his son the more difficult task of contending with the water under that level. This drainage was effected by malacates, which, raising the water in skin bags to the level of the adit, were for some time sufficiently effective, but gradually, as the mine became deeper, the difficulty and cost of drainage with such imperfect machinery also augmented. In the year 1801, the twenty-eight malacates then at work, occupying twelve hundred horses, with four hundred men, and costing $250,000 per annum, were not found sufficient to keep down the water to fifty-four fathoms below the adit, to which depth the workings on the Biscaina vein had attained in the mines of Santa Teresa and Guadalupe; and consequently, although these mines were then producing at the rate of $400,000 annually, the drainage was suspended, and their deeper workings abandoned. After this the workings were limited to a higher level; and on the hitherto unexplored extensions of the vein, and up to 1809, when the second Conde died, the mines of San Ramon with some others continued to yield about $300,000 per annum.

From this period the produce of the mines gradually decreased, and the War of Independence having commenced, their working was entirely suspended in 1819; the total produce since the death of the first Conde having been $10,000,000.

After the recognition of the independence of Mexico by Great Britain, the attention of English capitalists became directed to the mines of that country, and, at the suggestion of the late Mr. John Taylor, an association known as the Real del Monte Company was formed for restoring and draining the mines belonging to the Regla family.

In July 1824, Captain Vetch of the Royal Engineers, the first commissioner of the Real del Monte Company, arrived at the Mines, which he found in a state of utter ruin; most of the shafts had fallen in, leaving their former sites only to be detected by immense hollows overgrown with brushwood. A still more serious evil was the destruction of the great adit, which having in many parts so gone to ruin that it no longer carried off the water, it consequently rose to a great height in the mines. All the machinery in the large reduction works was gone, the population had become very scarce, and the town a collection of ruins. The chief inducement of the new Company to resume the drainage of these deep mines, being the advantages they expected to derive by the substitution of steam-power for the imperfect and costly one of horse machines raising water and ores in skin bags, a body of miners and mechanics, with steam-engines, pumps, and other machinery, arrived at Vera Cruz in May 1825, under the charge of the late Colonel Colquhoun of the Royal Artillery.

The rainy season commenced shortly after, attended by its usual scourge, the yellow fever, and soon made sad havoc among both English and Mexicans. Colquhoun, however, persevered through all difficulties, and by May 1826 the engines had arrived at the mines. In the meantime the district of Real del Monte had been carefully surveyed, the great adit cleared and restored, many of the shafts had been repaired down to adit, and buildings, workshops, and stores were rapidly rising around the mines. From this period the work of clearing and restoration progressed steadily, until by the end of 1829 the drainage had been effected to the depth of fifty-four fathoms under adit. The annual cost of pumping did not exceed $30,000, being an immense saving as compared with the large sum of $250,000 which the twenty-eight malacates formerly employed for this purpose had cost the second Conde when at the same depth he abandoned the lower workings.

It, however, soon became evident that the drainage at the distant points of San Cayetano and Dolores was not sufficiently effective for working the richest portions of the vein in the mine of Santa Teresa: a new vertical shaft was consequently sunk, and a more powerful engine erected. An engine of fifty-four inch cylinder having been erected, and assisted by the smaller ones at Dolores and San Cayetano, this portion of the Biscaina vein was worked for some time with considerable profit, and to the depth of 235 fathoms from the surface, or 120 fathoms under adit. At this point the water having so increased as again to overpower the engine, a still larger one of seventy-five inches was erected at Dolores. The reward of this expenditure was two bunches of rich ore, the one discovered on the Santa Brigida vein near Acosta, and called La Luz; the other at San Enrique, on the Biscaina vein near Dolores.

Up to the end of 1847, however, the general result of working the mines had been decidedly unfortunate to the English adventurers; for although they had profited by three rich bunches of ore at Terreros, Acosta, and Dolores, and had produced $10,481,475 worth of silver, the outlay on all the undertakings of the Company had also reached the amount of $15,381,633, leaving a loss of nearly five millions of dollars as the result of the twenty-three years they had held the mines.

The deep workings were now 120 fathoms under the great adit, or sixty-one fathoms below the point at which they had been abandoned by the second Conde, and the difficulty of drainage had so increased, both from the augmented quantity of water, and the greater height to which it was necessary to raise it, that three powerful steam-engines, which were discharging two thousand seven hundred gallons per minute, at a cost of $90,000 per annum, could barely stem the coming water of the mine. To show the difference of the cost of steam drainage as compared with the plan of the country, becomes at this point interesting. The English Company, at the commencement, had easily effected with two small engines, and at a cost of $30,000, what the Conde de Regla had been obliged to relinquish in 1801 with twenty-eight malacates, and at an annual cost of $250,000; but with the increased depth, and greater volume of water, three pumping engines expending $90,000 were barely able to maintain the drainage, while to replace them would have required at least one hundred and eighty malacates, employing seven thousand horses, with upwards of two thousand men, and an expenditure of not less than two millions of dollars per annum.

With this increased difficulty of drainage, seeing their rich bunches of ore all worked out, and a debt of five millions of dollars still outstanding, it is not surprising that the energy and perseverance of the English adventurers were at last exhausted. Towards the middle of 1848, Don Manuel Escandon and Don Nicanor Beistegui were induced by Mr. Buchan, the manager of the mines under the original Real del Monte Company, to take up the enterprise on terms which, although not returning to the English adventurers much of their lost capital, at least relieved them from all further responsibility.

After having carefully examined the position of the enterprise, this gentleman came to the conclusion that the concern had hitherto been worked, as well on too limited a scale as with too expensive an establishment; but particularly that without any effective attempt to render the poorer and more abundant ores available, or to make new discoveries on the higher and still virgin portions of the veins, every effort had been directed to the search after rich ores in depth, which, when at last discovered, did not repay the large amounts expended to find them. With reference to this subject Mr. Buchan remarks:—"Experience had convinced me that to render an extensive mining enterprise secure, it should mainly depend on the poor and abundant ore of its veins for the current cost of exploring them, so that the richer bunches, which would occur in a regular and systematic process of working, might be found without any forced effort or outlay, and thus become more profitable. It was further clear that as certain costs, such as general management, drainage, rents to owners, &c., were unavoidable and nearly the same under any scale of operations, that a larger return of the poorer ores must be obtained, in order to support them, and lastly that a perfect system of economy in every branch of so large an establishment, was most essential to its success." *

To carry out these views, he commenced by arranging the entire system of accounts on such a plan that every week's result, in each mine and reduction work, might be clearly shown, and the economy of the different departments thus fairly compared with each other. To reduce the excessive cost of drainage, he abandoned the very deep workings on the Biscaina vein, and only maintained the water to sixty-five fathoms under adit by one large steam-engine, while at the same time the extraction of poor ores was facilitated, and increased by additional shafts, winding machines, and internal rail-roads. Conjointly with these operations the eastern and yet virgin portions of the Biscaina vein were selected for the site of new trials, in high ground above water level, and another trial was commenced at Pachuca in the Rosario mine. Here the Company had already worked and incurred a considerable loss by extracting ores from the old mine, but finding that the famous vein of Xacal would intersect that of Rosario, to the eastward of all former trials, it was determined to take advantage of an adit, already considerably advanced, to examine so promising a point. After driving this adit some sixty fathoms, they had the good fortune to meet with the expected intersection of the veins, from which a considerable extraction of ore was at once commenced.

It is a peculiarity of the mineral veins of this district, that while those which run in an easterly and westerly direction produce ores readily reduced by the usual amalgamation process, practised to so great an extent in Mexico, the ores from the north and south veins have a different mineral character, and in many cases will not yield their silver by this process. Trials having, however, proved that they could be advantageously reduced by a modification of the well-known barrel system of Freiberg, and the great mass of the poor ores being of this character, it was determined to adopt barrel amalgamation on a very large scale. For this purpose, two new works were erected at San Miguel and Velasco, whilst those of Regla and Sanchez were enlarged and modified.

In the haciendas of San Miguel and Regla, which are at a distance of twelve miles from the mines, water-power is alone used to drive the machinery, blow the furnaces, grind the ores, and revolve the barrels; but at those of Sanchez and Velasco, built at the mouth of the valley descending from the mines, steam is employed as an auxiliary power; so that in 1855, besides the powerful pumping engine of seventy-five inch cylinder, which drained the mines, there were, at the reduction works, two smaller rotatory engines and eighteen water-wheels of different sizes, which drove 110 wet stampers, sixteen large arrastres, and three edge mills, all employed in grinding ores; besides revolving sixty-four large barrels in which the prepared ores were amalgamated. In the hacienda of Regla were eight blast furnaces for smelting rich ores; and in San Miguel, Velasco, and Sanchez, thirty-six reverberatory furnaces for drying and roasting the ores preparatory to amalgamation in barrels. We are informed by Mr. Buchan that a great increase in the reduction works has

* Report of the Real del Monte Company, 1855.

been made since 1855, by the erection of the hacienda of Loreto, which, situated in the midst of the Pachuca mines, has already the power of reducing yearly 55,000 *cargas* of ore by the patio process, and is being gradually increased, so as to be enabled to treat 100,000 cargas annually.*

The machinery employed by the Real del Monte Company having been much increased since 1855, the following are now in operation:—

Steam Engines for Drainage.				
1	of 75 in. cylinder on the	Dolores	Shaft.	
1	of 54 „ „ „	Acosta	„	Real del Monte.
1	of 30 „ „ „	San Patricio	„	„
1	of 85 „ „ „	San Juan	„	Pachuca.
1	of 30 „ „ „	San Nicolas	„	„
1	of 30 „ „ „	Corteza	„	„
1	of 18 „ „ „	Rosario	„	„

Total drainage — 7 steam-engines.

Rotary Engines.		
1	San Juan	Shaft, Pachuca ; winding.
1	Rosario	„ „ „
1	San Pedro	„ „ „
1	Velasco hacienda ; driving barrels.	
1	Sanchez „	„
3	In workshops, turning lathes, blowing, &c.	

Total rotary — 8

Grand Total —15 steam-engines.

Water-wheels.			
3	Loreto	reduction works ;	one pumping and two working stamps.
1	Guerrero	„ „	wet stamps.
2	Aviadero	„ „	„
1	Sanchez	„ „	driving barrels.
1	Velasco	„ „	„
2	Peñafie	„ „	driving wet stamps.
6	San Miguel	„ „	two wet stamping, four driving barrels.
11	Regla	„ „	one „ ten working arrastres, &c.
2	Regla smelting works ; blowing and stamping.		

Total 29 water-wheels.

The present grinding machinery amounts to 350 stamp heads, 24 water-power, and 50 mule-power arrastres, and 80 amalgamating barrels ; which reduce yearly—

	Cargas.
By the barrel process	206,000
„ patio „	106,000
Total	312,000

* The carga weighs 300 lbs.

The following summary of the operations of this Company for 1860, which was one of the most favourable years, the produce being good, and the amount of dead-work small, is of great practical interest :—

General Results of Mining Operations by the Real del Monte Company, in the districts of Real del Monte and Pachuca, in the year 1860.

General expenses of management	$50,170
Cost of draining the two districts	167,934
Cost of extracting ores from various mines	647,338
Cost of reducing ores in different haciendas	841,606
Duties on silver, paid to the Mexican Government .	173,587
Freight of ores from mines to reduction works, including cost of repairing roads	186,503
Convoys of silver to the coast, or mint of Mexico . .	14,877
Agencies, Commissions, &c.	7,109
Total cost on current working of the mines	2,089,124
Total produce, 277,396 cargas of ore, from which were extracted 423,394 marks of silver, value	3,710,891
Profit on current working	$1,621,767

The above profit was applied as follows :—

Re-invested in discovery works in different mines . .	$181,052
Re-invested in enlarging and improving works for the reduction of ores	73,120
Purchase of forests for fuel	31,000
Cost of maintaining a force of 150 cavalry and 50 infantry, necessary for the security of the districts during the civil war	60,000
Paid as dues to part owners of mines	353,070
Paid as dividends to the Shareholders of the Company	923,525
Total . .	$1,621,767

Table of stores consumed during the year 1860 :—

From forests belonging to the Company—		
Timber	$ 30,000	
Wood-fuel	200,000	
Charcoal	60,000	
		$290,000
Salt	$150,000	
Quicksilver	100,000	
Iron and Steel	50,000	
		300,000
Carried forward		$590,000

Brought forward		$ 590,000
Barley and Straw	$ 100,000	
Tallow and Oil	40,000	
Gunpowder	15,000	
Sulphate of Copper	14,000	
Sacks and Cordage	18,000	
Lime and Bricks	10,000	
Litharge	13,000	
Leather and Hides	15,000	
Sundry stores	45,000	
		270,000
Total		$ 860,000

TABLE *showing the details of Silver Ores reduced by the Real del Monte Company, in the districts of Real del Monte and Pachuca, from May* 1849, *when the present Company was first formed, to the end of the year* 1865.

	Ores reduced by smelting.		Ores reduced by Barrel amalgamation.		Ores reduced by Patio amalgamation.		Total each Year.			
To Dec.	Ores.	Silver.	Ores.	Silver.	Ores.	Silver.	Total Ores reduced.	Total Silver produced.	Total Value of Silver produced.	Mean Produce of Silver per monton.*
	cargas	marks.	cargas.	marks.	cargas.	marks.	cargas.	marks.	dollars.	marks.
1852	7,108	45,671	281,629	221,827	21,975	19,412	310,712	286,910	2,508,655	9·00
1853	2,903	15,358	141,208	131,518	37,040	29,063	181,151	175,939	1,537,796	9·71
1854	2,386	14,913	152,614	160,900	37,982	31,318	192,982	207,126	1,811,822	10·73
1855	2,690	23,612	181,353	217,193	38,010	46,868	222,053	287,673	2,375,503	12·90
1856	6,011	48,666	209,053	243,041	40,490	58,843	261,554	350,550	3,081,663	13·40
1857	4,926	44,942	219,326	238,041	50,400	63,183	274,652	346,166	3,039,019	12·50
1858	5,056	49,582	217,461	218,291	48,355	53,638	270,872	321,511	2,824,831	11·80
1859	4,813	52,057	226,775	283,112	44,013	51,434	275,601	386,603	3,404,459	14·00
1860	4,698	47,442	222,498	314,745	50,200	61,207	277,396	423,394	3,710,891	15·20
1861	4,162	42,397	212,480	263,990	63,947	87,545	280,589	393,982	3,782,399	15·70
1862	4,203	47,518	209,861	310,906	60,412	73,968	274,476	432,392	3,445,222	14·00
1863	3,543	32,983	194,007	217,204	76,920	88,370	274,560	338,557	2,984,351	12·30
1864	3,500	29,067	205,850	229,946	105,740	142,697	315,090	401,710	3,432,107	12·40
1865	1,921	19,273	170,600	186,535	97,642	144,055	270,163	349,863	3,044,572	13·00
	57,920	518,481	2,844,805	3,237,249	779,126	951,596	3,681,851	4,702,326	40,983,290	12·77

* The *monton* varies in the different mining districts, but, in Real del Monte and Pachuca, is 10 cargas, or 3,000 lbs. The mark of silver is 8 Spanish oz. of 443·8 gr. each.

PRODUCE *and* **PROFIT** *of the Silver Mines worked by the Real del Monte Company, in the districts of Real del Monte and Pachuca, Mexico.*

	Value of Silver produced.	Profits paid.		Duties on Silver to Mexican Government.	Cost of draining Mines.
		As Dues to Part Owners.	In Dividends to Shareholders.		
Four Years, to	dollars.	dollars.	dollars.	dollars.	dollars.
Dec. 1852	2,508,655	155,373	......	101,109	215,541
1853	1,537,796	152,681	256,250	66,015	69,344
1854	1,811,822	199,371	307,500	82,566	83,707
1855	2,375,503	194,511	461,250	108,604	86,815
1856	3,081,663	276,652	820,000	140,441	115,886
1857	3,039,019	241,553	461,250	138,375	107,286
1858	2,824,831	233,294	410,000	130,860	128,177
1859	3,404,459	364,858	666,250	158,939	120,777
1860	3,710,891	448,905	871,250	173,587	167,934
1861	3,782,399	433,963	820,000	175,359	156,627
1862	3,445,222	341,018	334,500	159,620	143,075
1863	2,984,351	178,936	557,500	138,466	174,135
1864	3,432,107	279,377	580,000	159,437	178,856
1865	3,044,572	136,815	......	141,064	212,713
	$40,983,290	$3,637,307	$6,545,750	$1,874,442	$1,960,873

Total dividends to Shareholders of Real del Monte Company . .	6,545,750
Paid as dues to part owners of Mines	3,637,307
Duties to Mexican Government	1,874,442*
Total profit of the Real del Monte and Pachuca mines, 17 years	$12,057,499

Mr. Buchan, to whom we are indebted for the foregoing statistical information, remarks :—

"That no dividends were paid to shareholders of the Company in 1865, must not be attributed to any failure of the mines themselves ; but that during the very unsettled state of Mexico, our expenses were greatly augmented by the increased price of materials, and the loss incurred in keeping up a considerable military force for the security of the district. Contributions and forced loans to different governments have for several years past been exceedingly heavy ; but with the hope of their speedy repayment, these sums have been carried to a 'Suspense Account,' until the amount became so large as to determine the Company to suspend dividends, and dedicate all their share of profits to the liquidation of this debt.

"All the accounts I receive from Mexico assure me that the state of the mining negotiation is as promising now, as at any former period.

* Legal dues, not including forced loans.

"The great formation of ore in the Rosario vein of Pachuca, which, since its discovery in 1850, has yielded 25 millions of dollars, still promises a steady continuance of its produce; and although by underlie south, and extension south-eastward, this orey ground is now passing gradually out of the old mine of Rosario into the neighbouring setts of San Pedro and Guatimotzin, to the benefit of the owners of these latter mines, yet this will in no way affect the Company, whose interest is equal in all.

"The mine of Xacal, on the same vein, and adjoining Rosario to the west, which in former times was so famous for its richness, and the chief inducement for the drainage of the Pachuca district, has hitherto proved a great disappointment, by being found poor in its lower workings. But the works of discovery which have been steadily prosecuted into new ground, are now opening out what appears so rich and extensive a body of ore, as promises to entirely change the character of this mine. Many of our other mines are also in good produce; and if the unsettled state of Mexico does not interfere with our mining operations more than it has hitherto done, the coming year promises to be a very profitable one in Real del Monte, but more particularly so in the Pachuca district."

NEVADA.—Although the discovery of silver in this region can only be said to date from 1859, its extraordinary production has already rendered it more famous for its mineral wealth than localities in which this metal has been for centuries continuously mined in large quantities. This abundance of mineral wealth has attracted a numerous and industrious population to a country before but thinly inhabited by tribes of wandering savages; and flourishing towns have already sprung up in a desert which, from its situation and inhospitable character, seemed for ever to defy the progress of civilization and the arts.

The two principal mining centres of Nevada are Virginia city in Storey County, and Austin in Lander County; and, although numerous veins are being more or less extensively worked in other portions of the State, the mines in the vicinity of these towns have hitherto been more productive than those of any other mineral region.

Great Comstock Vein.—The range of the Washoe mountains, in which the Great Comstock Vein is situated, is separated from the eastern slope of the Sierra Nevada by a continuous meridional depression, in which are the deep basins of the Truckee, Washoe, and Carson valleys. Its shape is irregular, but its general direction is from north to south. In a southerly direction, it gradually slopes down to a smooth table-land, traversed by the Carson river, beyond which the Washoe mountains become merged into the more elevated Pine-nut range. Towards the west, the Washoe hills descend rapidly, and finally sink beneath the detrital beds of the Washoe and Truckee valleys, but are connected with the Sierra Nevada by two low granitic ridges, stretching across the northern and southern extremities of Washoe valley. To the north-east, this range passes into a very extensive, and but little explored, mountain region; whilst to the south-east it abruptly disappears below one of the basins of the Carson river. The entire width of this range is not above fourteen miles, whilst its length is not yet determinable, on account of the scanty knowledge possessed of the northern portions of the State. The culminating point of the Washoe range is Mount Davidson, the elevation of which, as determined by Whitney, is 7,827 feet; and at its foot are situated Virginia city, and the principal mines on the Comstock lode.

The aspect of the Washoe mountains is exceedingly barren, as is also the view from Virginia, over the hilly country to the east. The air is, however, extraordinarily pure and transparent, so that every ravine and declivity on the sides of mountains a hundred miles distant is readily distinguished. At the time of the discovery of the Comstock vein, the Washoe mountains were covered by scattered and stunted trees, of nut-pine and cedar; but these have long since disappeared, and Virginia now depends for her supply of wood on the slopes of the Sierra Nevada.

The enormous consumption of wood for fuel, and of square timber in the mines, is, however, rapidly causing the destruction of these forests; and the time is, consequently, not distant when the mines and reduction works of Virginia must derive their wood from greater distances, and chiefly from near the Truckee River, which is about thirty miles from the mines, and to which a railway, in connexion with the Central Pacific Railroad, is projected. Mount Davidson, the prominent central point of the Washoe range, consists of syenite, which is here composed of two kinds of feldspar, orthoclase and oligoclase, associated with hornblende, mica, and occasionally epidote. Metamorphic rocks adjoin the syenite on the north and south, and are intersected by dykes of that rock, which of itself sufficiently proves its later origin. These metamorphic rocks differ materially in their lithological characteristics, but may be divided into three distinct groups, the most recent of which belongs to the triassic epoch. These are immediately preceded in age by a series of micaceous and quartzose slates, frequently containing bands of limestone; below which is a third series, chiefly consisting of hornblendic rock, with interstratified layers of quartzite, grey slate, crystalline limestone, and specular iron. These rocks form the hills which flank American Flat to the west, as well as those between Silver City and Carson, and are generally capped by an overflow of porphyry. They constitute the *ancient series*, and partially preceded, and were partly contemporaneous with, the gradual upheaval of the Sierra Nevada and the entire chain of the Cordilleras. The *recent series*, which is volcanic and eruptive, belongs to the latter part of the tertiary and beginning of the post-tertiary periods.

The first of these in point of age is a species of dioritic porphyry, to which Richthofen has applied the name of *propylite*. This rock has the peculiarity of exactly resembling many ancient rocks in appearance, whilst in reality it is of very recent origin. It occupies a prominent position among the enclosing rocks of the Comstock vein, and likewise encloses a considerable proportion of the largest and most productive silver veins in various parts of the world. Among these may be mentioned the silver veins of the Carpathian Mountains, those of Zacatecas, and other localities in Mexico, and probably, also, many of those in Bolivia. This rock is composed of a fine-grained paste, generally of a greenish, but sometimes of a red, grey, or brown colour, with embedded crystals of oligoclase, and columns of dark-green fibrous hornblende, which is also the colouring matter of the base itself. A peculiarity of this rock is its ferruginous character, when decomposed by weathering. Geologically, it is an eruptive rock, but has been accompanied by vast accumulations of brecciated matter, which are sometimes found regularly stratified. Several different kinds of volcanic and eruptive rocks followed the outbreak of propylite; but of these, trachyte is the most important, not only as taking a prominent part in the formation of a large extent of country, but also on account of its intimate relations with the formation of the Comstock vein. Its essential characteristic is the predominance of glassy feldspar, which, along with hornblende and mica, is embedded in a paste of a peculiarly rough texture, caused by the presence of an infinity of microscopic vesicles.

Eruptions of basaltic rock, of considerable magnitude, have taken place in various parts of the great basin; but in the neighbourhood of the Comstock vein they have not made their appearance to any important extent. Volcanic and eruptive agency appears to have gradually declined in the whole region, leaving the last trace of its active existence in the still boiling waters, and daily increasing silicious deposits, of Steamboat Springs.

The Comstock vein runs nearly in the direction of the magnetic meridian, along the eastern slope of the Mount Davidson range, a little above the slope on which are built the towns of Virginia, Gold Hill, and American City. The outcrops extend in a broad belt along the foot of the mountain, and immediately at the back of the three towns. The course of the vein, as far as it has been hitherto explored, appears to be more or less modified by local circumstances, passing the ravines in concave bends, and enclosing the foot of the different ridges in convex sweeps. These irregularities are of considerable importance, as they would seem to influence the ore-bearing character of the lode. The length to which the Comstock vein has been traced with certainty is somewhat over nineteen thousand feet, while its total extent is probably at least twenty-four thousand feet. The most extensive operations have been carried on between the Ophir Mine, north, and the Overman, a distance of about eleven thousand feet; whilst in other parts the workings have been of a very superficial character. Several of the mines are worked to a depth of six hundred feet; but the shafts of the Hale and Norcross, Chollar Potosi, and Gould and Curry, have reached a depth of above eight hundred feet.

The Comstock vein, at a depth of from four to six hundred feet below its outcrop, has a width of from one to two hundred feet; but contracts in some places, so that its two walls come into close proximity with each other. At this depth, both of its walls descend, with an easterly underlie, at an angle varying from forty to sixty degrees. Upwards, from an average depth of five hundred feet, the western wall rises to the surface with the same inclination; whilst the eastern assumes a vertical position, and subsequently turns off with a westerly dip. The vein consequently expands towards the surface in the shape of a funnel, as shown in Fig. 39, which represents, on a scale of 240 feet to one inch, a section made by Messrs. James and Stretch, Mining Engineers of Virginia, through the Chollar and Potosi shafts.

This increase in volume is especially produced by the intervention, between the vein-matter, of large masses of country rock, detached from the walls, but which have usually moved a short distance only downward, by sliding from their original positions. The number and bulk of these *horses* increase towards the surface, where some of them have a length of nearly a thousand feet, and in many cases a width of above a hundred. The vein-matter filling up the spaces between these intervening masses of country rock is generally, near the surface, far inferior in width to that of the horses lying between it. The width of the mineral belt in which these branches come to the surface, and there form a scattered outcrop, is usually above five hundred feet.

The Comstock lode is, on the western side, accompanied by a number of smaller veins, the outcroppings being visible on the surface, and some of which appear to be of considerable size. The western

Fig. 39.

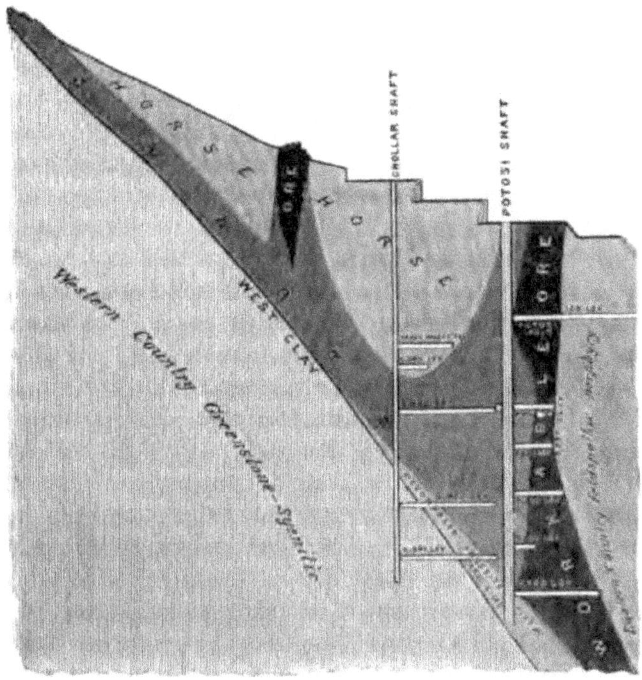

Section of Comstock Vein.

(Looking North.)

boundary of the main vein is defined by a continuous clay selvage, or flucan, lying on the smooth foot wall, and separating the vein-matter from the country. On the eastern sides, the adjoining country rock is impregnated with matter similar to that composing the vein itself; and consequently, the well-defined east wall has often not precisely the same relative position with regard to the entire vein, and, by cutting through what appears to be the east wall, another or succession of others of a similar character are discovered beyond it.

The enclosing rocks which accompany this vein vary somewhat in different portions of its course, although on the eastern side they invariably consist of slightly-differing varieties of propylite, or compact porphyry. On the western wall, the composition of the country presents greater differences. From the Best and Belcher Mine to Gold Hill, it is formed of syenite, which is, in some places, separated from the selvage of the vein by a fine-grained crystalline rock, of a black colour, partaking of the nature of aphanite, but of which the mode of occurrence is at present obscure. The outcrops of the Comstock vein do not form one continuous line, but rather consist of detached parallel ranges of brownish quartz, ordinarily protruding above the surface of the ground, and sometimes forming bold crests, which in the aggregate constitute a broad, interrupted belt. The porous nature of this quartz, originating from the decomposition and removal of fine particles of disseminated ore, and its brown colour, caused by the presence of metallic oxides, indicate the ore-bearing character of the vein in depth. A minute examination also reveals the occurrence of finely-disseminated metallic gold and silver, and occasional spots of the chloride and sulphides of the latter metal.

The vein-matter of the Comstock lode is exceedingly varied in its character; its chief constituents being fragments of the enclosing rock, clay and clayey matter, quartz, sulphide of silver, and other minerals. The shape and extent of the fragments of country rock are very various. They are, however, generally of a lenticular form, and differ in their dimensions from large "horses" down to the smallest brecciated fragments. Clay forms, in continuous sheets from north to south, the eastern and western selvages, which are sometimes from ten to twenty feet in thickness. Other sheets of this substance divide the horses from quartz, or the different bodies of quartz from each other; and where the vein-matter is so thin that the two clay bands come nearly together, the selvages have often a united width of from fifty to sixty feet.

The quartz of the Comstock lode is very rarely solid, and consequently its removal seldom requires the intervention of gunpowder; it is usually much fractured, and in many places the effects of mechanical or chemical action are so great as to give it the appearance of crushed sugar. It almost always occurs in this condition when enclosed between two clay walls, and in the immediate vicinity of rich masses of ore. The principal silver ores are stephanite, vitreous silver, native silver, ruby silver, horn silver, and polybasite, with which are associated small quantities of exceedingly rich argentiferous galena. Besides these are found native gold, iron and copper pyrites, blende, and carbonate and phosphate of lead; the two latter only occurring in very minute quantities. These ores are seldom crystallised; and consequently, specimens which would in other mining districts attract no attention, are regarded in Virginia as great curiosities. Quartz is, in reality, the only gangue of the Comstock vein. Carbonate of lime but seldom accompanies it, whilst the other carbonates are of exceedingly rare occurrence. Sulphates abound in the waters issuing from the mines, but the only one forming an essential constituent of the vein is gypsum, which is sometimes found in large crystals.* Sulphate of baryta has never been observed, and small specimens of stilbite and chabasite are only met with in the northern portion of the vein.

The ore is differently distributed in the northern and southern portion of the lode, the passage between the two methods of occurrence being very gradual. In the northern part, the ore is concentrated in elongated lenticular masses, of which the greater axis is nearly ver-

---

* An examination of the water issuing from the Comstock vein, in the Ophir Mine, January 12th, 1865, afforded Mr. G. Attwood the following results:—

Heat of water, 70° Fahr., the air near being 62° Fahr.; in Seventh Gallery, 25 feet below where water was taken, and 400 feet below the surface, it was 48° Fahr. Flow of water estimated at from 150 to 200 gallons per minute; the total amount of water taken from mine being 300 gallons per minute.

One imperial gallon contained 14·84 grains of mechanically suspended matter.

Both water and suspended matter were apparently free from any trace of the precious metals.

Specific gravity at 60° Fahr., 1·0007.

Carbonic Acid in an imperial gallon, 23·30 grains.

Fixed Matter " " " 28·02 "

	Composition of Fixed Matter.
Carbonate of Lime	4·10
" Magnesia	2·82
Sulphate of Lime	10·01
" Potassa	0·65
" Magnesia	2·93
" Soda	2·67
Carbonate of Iron	1·82
Chloride of Sodium	0·60
Alumina	Trace
Silicic Acid	2·20
	27·80

tical, but dips towards the south, and sometimes also to the east, their width varying from fifteen to fifty feet. In some cases, several of these adjoin each other in such a way that the most westerly one extends further north than the one situated next to it towards the east, and this again further than its next eastern neighbour. The great value of the mines on the southern portion of the vein consists in the continuous character of the ore-bearing ground, which extends for an uninterrupted distance of above fifteen hundred feet. The vein is by no means productive throughout its entire width, but the ore is concentrated in continuous sheets, the principal of which is very near to, and parallel with, the eastern wall. Its widest places have a thickness of about fifty feet; it generally commences at a depth of from one hundred and fifty to two hundred and fifty feet from the surface, and is at many points still worked in the lowest levels of the mines. Besides this very extensive eastern body of ore, there is another in the Gold Hill Mines, further to the west, which extends from the outcrop down to a depth of two hundred and fifty feet. A similar body has been worked in the Yellow Jacket, Crown Point, and Belcher Mines, and was remarkable from its southern portion being very rich in gold. It is, however, a well known fact, that the richness of the ores from the Comstock vein has in general diminished, although the total yield of the district has been more than kept up by the larger amounts which are now daily passed through the mills. When the vein was first opened, ores affording from one to seven hundred dollars to the ton were of frequent occurrence, and considerable shipments were made of parcels yielding from two to three thousand dollars per ton. Such ores are now but rarely met with, and the general average yield of all those treated will probably not much exceed thirty dollars to the ton. The cost of extraction has, however, been greatly reduced, and the methods of reduction much improved; and therefore ores which formerly could not have been treated with advantage now afford highly remunerative returns. The aggregate amount of ore now daily extracted from the Comstock vein is about twelve hundred and fifty tons.

During the early period of the workings on the Comstock vein, the relative proportions of gold and silver yielded by the ores were found to change as a greater depth was obtained, the yield of gold being greatest near the outcrops, and gradually diminishing in the deeper portions of the lode. Recently, however, the proportion of gold has again been on the increase, and this is found to be the case, not in any one particular mine only, but throughout the whole extent of the lode.*

The various phenomena connected with the occurrence of silver ore in the Comstock vein have been summarised by Richthofen as follows: †—

1st. The ore is, in the northern part of the vein, concentrated in chimneys dipping to the south; in the southern part it forms continuous sheets of great length, but which are comparatively narrow.

2nd. These deposits of ore are enclosed in the eastern, and sometimes also in the middle portions of the vein; the western branches are either barren or poor.

3rd. The richest and largest deposits have been found at those places where the outcrops, including those of the western branches, were most prominent.

4th. In the northern part the vein is, at the levels explored, invariably poor where it passes a ravine; but in the southern part the ore continues in the ravines.

5th. The richest portions of the lode are south of each ravine crossed by the vein.

6th. All the chimneys in the northern part are at those places where the walls, after close contact, rapidly diverge, and cause the vein to expand.

---

* The following assays from parcels of crushed ores worked in barrels, by Mr. G. Attwood, show the relative proportions of gold and silver in the rock from the Comstock Mines:—

Second Class ore from the Ophir Mine, June 16th, 1863.

Silver, per ton	71·92 oz. . . .	$93·49
Gold „	2·79 „ . . .	57·66
	Value . . .	$151·15

Second Class ore from the Gould and Curry Mine, May 12th, 1864.

Silver, per ton	81·16 oz. . . .	$105·50
Gold „	2·58 „ . . .	52 70
	Value . . .	$158·20

Second Class ore from the Savage Mine, May 12th, 1865.

Silver, per ton	76·18 oz. . . .	$99·03
Gold „	1·57 „ . . .	32·45
	Value . . .	$131·48

† "The Comstock Lode, its Character, and the probable Mode of its Continuance in Depth," by Ferdinand, Baron Richthofen. San Francisco, 1866.

7th. All the principal accumulations of ore are at those places where there was most room in the fissure for the deposition of quartz, and they are therefore generally rare where an unusual number of horses obstruct the vein.

The first discovery of silver in Nevada appears to have been made in 1857, by two brothers of the name of Grosh, in a quartz vein now held by the Kossuth Gold and Silver Mining Company, on which they had a claim. Shortly after the discovery, one of the brothers accidentally wounded himself with a pick, from the effects of which he died; and the other brother went to California, where he died early in 1858, which probably prevented the valuable nature of their discovery from becoming generally known. In the meantime, placer mining was carried on to a considerable extent in various localities, principally in Gold Cañon. In 1857, a man named Kirby, and others, commenced placer mining in Six Mile Cañon, about half a mile below where the Ophir works now stand, and worked at intervals with indifferent success until 1859. On the 22d of February, 1858, the first quartz claim was located in the Virginia Mining District, on the "Virginia Croppings," by James Finney, generally known as "Old Virginia," from whom the city of Virginia takes its name. This may be considered the first location of the Comstock lode. The discovery of rich deposits of silver ore was not made until June 1859, when Peter O'Reilly and Patrick McLaughlin, while engaged in gold washing, on what is now the ground of the Ophir Mining Company, and near the south line of the Mexican claim, uncovered a rich vein of sulphide of silver in an excavation made for the purpose of collecting water to use in their rockers in washing for gold. This discovery being on ground claimed at the time by Kirby and others, Comstock was employed to purchase it, and Comstock's name has thus been given to this great lode.

From this discovery has resulted the almost miraculous growth of the district. Claims were at once taken up on the vein for miles in extent; an unparalleled excitement followed, and miners and speculators rapidly congregated in the hope of obtaining a share of the reported wealth, while prospectors were busily examining almost every part of the country in search of silver ores.

The following table, from the report of the State Mineralogist for 1866, gives the names of the various mining claims on the Comstock lode, as far as its continuity has been ascertained; also, the length of the individual claims, length of each claim explored, percentage of explored and unexplored ground, depth of the lowest workings, and other information.*

NAME.	Length of Claim in feet.	Length explored in feet.	Per cent. of Claim explored.	Per cent. unexplored.	Depth of lowest Workings.	REMARKS.
					feet.	
Utah	1,000	300	30	70	260	Engine removed; not working.
Allen	925	300	32	68	200	Not working.
Sierra Nevada	1,959	400	25	75	650	
Union	500	5	1	99	80	Explored by tunnel; not working.
Ophir North Mine	1,200	400	33⅓	66⅔	549 (Ophir North Mine, Mexican, Ophir South Mine)	Explored through Ophir, "Mexican Shaft." (Ophir North Mine, Mexican, Ophir South Mine)
Mexican	100	100	100	...		
Ophir South Mine	200	200	100	...		
Central	150	150	100	...	620	
California	300	300	100	...	428	Explored by tunnel and winzes.
Central, No. 2	100	100	100	...	869	Explored by whim on White & Murphy's claim, and by the Latrobe tunnel; not working. (Central, No. 2, Kinney, White and Murphy)
Kinney	50	5	10	90	369	
White and Murphy	210	210	100	...	369	
Sides	500	200	40	60	500	Not working.
Best and Belcher	250	250	100	...	469	Engine removed; not working.
Gould and Curry	1,200	921	100	...	900	
Savage, Old Shaft	771	771	100	...	614	
,, Curtis ,,	...	...	...	...	448	
Hale and Norcross	400	400	100	...	783	
Chollar Potosi	1,434	700	50	50	923	
Bullion	940	450	47	53	803	
Exchequer	400	...	...	100	540	
Alpha	278½	278½	100	...	680	
Apple and Bates	31½	31½	100	...	Average 650 feet. (Apple and Bates to Burke and Hamilton)	
Imperial Alta	118	118	100	...		
Bacon	45	45	100	...		
Empire North Mine	55	55	100	...		
Eclipse	30	30	100	...		
French	20	20	100	...		
Empire South Mine	20	20	100	...		
Plato	10	10	100	...		
Bowers	20	20	100	...		
Piute	20	20	100	...		
Winters and Küstel	30	30	100	...		
Consolidated	21	21	100	...		
Rice Ground	18½	18½	100	...		
Imperial, H. and L.	65⅔	65⅔	100	...		
Challenge	50	50	100	...		
Confidence	130	130	100	...		
Burke and Hamilton	40	40	100	...		
Yellow Jacket	943	943	100	51	560	
Kentuck	93⅔	93⅔	100	...	460	
Crown Point	540	540	100	...	400	
Belcher	940	940	100	...	850	
Segregated Belcher	160	160	100	...	500	
Overman	1,200	700	60	40	711	
North American	2,000	...	...	...	800	Not working.
Baltimore American	2,000	500	25	75	300	Not working.

North of the Utah, locations have been made on what is supposed to be the Comstock lode, but the developments are unimportant; the same remark applies to that portion of the vein south of the Overman. As far as is at present known, these two claims limit the productive portions of the vein, and include a length of nearly four miles.

* This table commences with the claim on the extreme north of the vein.

The length given as belonging to the Best and Belcher, and Gould and Curry Companies, is the amount of ground claimed by each. The actual length of ground between the Sides and the Savage Companies, is only one thousand one hundred and forty-three feet. The lengths given for the Hale and Norcross, and Savage Companies, are measured on the croppings. Owing to the divergence of the north line of the Savage and south line of the Hale and Norcross, to the eastward, and the direction in which the vein dips, the length of their claims on the lode, in depth, is constantly increasing. Six feet of ground is in dispute between the Apple and Bates, and Imperial Companies.

There are consumed annually by the Virginia Companies about 22,650 cords of wood, at an expense of $16 per cord, and a total cost of more than one-third of a million of dollars, and they also use about 15,504,120 feet (board measure) of timber and scantling, all of which must be transported long distances in wagons, at a cost of about $40 per thousand feet. Thus, for wood and timber alone the total annual expenditure is at least one million of dollars.

Work commenced in earnest upon the Comstock lode about five years since, and its total yield has been about $65,000,000.

The following was the production of the Gould and Curry Mine from the incorporation of the Company in June 1860, to Nov. 30th, 1866:—

Dates.	Ore worked, &c.	Bullion, &c.	Average Yield.
	Tons.		Per Ton.
From July 1, 1860 to Dec. 13, 1860	140½	$22,004·82	$156·62
„ Dec. 14, „ „ Dec. 13, 1861	300	44,221·44	147·40
„ Dec. 14, 1861 „ Nov. 30, 1862	8,442½	842,538·80	99·80
„ Dec. 1, 1862 „ Nov. 30, 1863	48,745	3,902,912·64	80·07
„ Dec. 1, 1863 „ Nov. 30, 1864	66,477¾	4,798,124·90	72·18
„ Dec. 1, 1864 „ Nov. 30, 1865	46,022¾	2,026,172·57	44·02
„ Dec. 1, 1865 „ Nov. 30, 1866	60,417½	1,690,952·25	28·00
Total	...	13,326,927·42	
From Tailings	...	300,143·76	
Worked, Tons	230,546	$13,627,071·18	$59·02

On hand, December 1st, 1866 . . . 4,249½ tons.
Total produce . . . . 234,795½ „

It has been estimated that five or six other Companies have taken out more than a million dollars each, and about twenty have each taken out small sums.

Richthofen estimates the total yield of the Comstock vein, up to the end of 1865, as follows; thus making the produce of silver from this source during three years, equal to about 23 per cent. of the whole production of the world during that period :—

The quantity of ore hoisted during the quarter ending 30th September, 1865, was 71,000 tons, or about 284,000 tons per annum, but this was considerably exceeded in 1866.*

Year.		Total.		Silver.		Gold.
1862 . . .	about	$ 4,000,000	about	$ 2,500,000	about	$1,500,000
1863 . . .	„	12,000,000	„	8,000,000	„	4,000,000
1864 . . .	„	16,000,000	„	11,000,000	„	5,000,000
1865 . . .	„	16,000,000	„	11,250,000	„	4,750,000
Total produce 1862 to 1865		$48,000,000		$32,750,000		$15,250,000

The aggregate amount of water daily pumped from the several mines cannot be ascertained, since no record has, in most instances, been kept. Nearly every mine has its pump, which is in most instances idle during a large portion of the twenty-four hours, but in the deeper mines it is kept constantly working. The Best and Belcher, and Hale and Norcross, each, during some part of the summer of 1865, pumped 15,000 gallons of water per hour. The Gould and Curry has a pumping capacity of 25,000 gallons per hour.†

The chief difficulties attending the working of the Comstock vein are occasioned by its immense width, and the friable and clayey nature of its constituents. In order, therefore, to be enabled to remove the ore, and at the same time keep open the necessary workings, the whole width of the lode has to be timbered with rectangular beams of pine, generally 10 in. × 12 in., which are put together in bays, about eight feet from centre to centre, in which the vertical supports stand perpendicularly over each other, from bottom to top, whilst the cap-pieces of one set, which form the foot-pieces of the next, extend across the vein from one wall to the other. The spaces between the timbers are filled in with attle when no longer required to be kept open for mining purposes or ventilation. The expansive force of the

* Tons of 2,000 lbs. each.

† The American gallon is equal to 0·83311 imperial gallon.

clay selvages is, however, under the influence of moisture, exceedingly great; and it is by no means uncommon, in wet situations, to see heavy beams, 12 in. × 14 in., broken like match-wood, or bent so as to obstruct the levels. The subdivision of the Comstock vein into a large number of claims of very limited extent, has been productive of much unavoidable expense; occasioned not only by the multiplicity of shafts and the extra amount of machinery thereby rendered necessary, but also further augmented by the additional expense of greatly-divided management, and a series of ruinous and vexatious lawsuits, due to disputed claims and alleged encroachment of rights.

In order to relieve the various mines on the Comstock lode from the constantly increasing expenses of drainage and of hoisting the ores to the surface, it has been recently proposed to bring in a deep adit, sufficiently wide for a double line of railway, from the Webber Cañon, a distance of nearly four miles. This proposed gallery, which is known as the "Sutro Tunnel," would intersect the lode at a depth of one thousand nine hundred feet below its outcrop; and besides effecting the drainage of all the mines to that level, would cross-cut several veins in its course, and afford means of transport for the ores to Carson River, where water-power can be obtained, and wood procured at a comparatively cheap rate. Intervening cañons, about three-quarters of a mile apart, afford facilities for sinking four different shafts to the level of the proposed tunnel, and from these the work would be extended in both directions, as well as from its mouth in the Carson valley. These shafts would respectively require to be sunk to the following depths, viz., 443, 980, 1,360, and 1,436 feet; the cost of the tunnel is estimated at $1,983,616. It is calculated that under favourable circumstances this great level could be completed within three and a half years after its commencement; but, although the rock through which it would have to be driven is, generally speaking, of a not unfavourable character for the prosecution of such work, it is more than probable that a considerably extended time would be required for its execution. A franchise has also been granted to a company to construct a railway from Virginia to the Truckee River, with a branch from thence to Carson city. The length of the road from Virginia to the Truckee will be forty-five miles, and its maximum gradient seventy-two feet per mile. This road, complete and ready for traffic, including rolling stock, is estimated to cost $3,774,000, whilst it is stated that its gross income would exceed $2,000,000.

With the exception of those on the Comstock vein, some of the most important mines of Nevada are comprehended within what is known as the Reese River Mining Region, for much important information relative to which, we are indebted to voluminous notes furnished us by Mr. A. Blatchly, Mining Engineer, of Austin, who has devoted much time and attention to the study of the mineral deposits of that portion of the State in which he resides.

Reese River Mining Region.—The extensive mineral country known as the Reese River Mining Region, is situated in a great mineral belt which extends three hundred miles north and south, by two hundred and fifty east and west, and comprises the whole north-eastern portion of the State of Nevada. The face of this plateau, which is elevated about five thousand feet above the level of the sea, is covered by broken and detached ranges of mountains, whose highest peaks rise to an altitude of ten thousand feet. Owing to the broken nature of these ranges, the valleys lying between them are connected with one another by low passes, generally forming good natural roads, and furnishing easy grades for the construction of railways. Although numerous streams rise in the mountains, some of sufficient volume for driving mills, yet they all sink and disappear on reaching the sandy valleys below. North-west of this region lies the Humboldt valley, which contains a large amount of arable land.

On the hills and mountains a small variety of pine grows abundantly, but the valleys are entirely destitute of timber, and only covered with sand and a small shrub known as "sage brush." Many of them, in close proximity to the mines, contain vast deposits of nearly pure salt, and, consequently, the price of this substance may be considered as merely nominal throughout the whole country. This district lies between longitude one hundred and fourteen and one hundred and eighteen degrees west, and latitude thirty-seven and forty-one degrees north.

At some period, generally subsequent to the cretaceous epoch, igneous agencies have been active, and probably three-fifths of the whole country are covered with rocks of volcanic origin. The other portions of the surface, where exposed, are composed of granite, syenite, gneiss, slate, and limestone; the two latter being frequently fossiliferous. Triassic fossils occur in many localities, and have been clearly identified; others much older, probably Silurian, have been found near Austin. The country has, however, been too recently discovered to admit of any but imperfect geological explorations. The great majority of the metalliferous veins are in granite, syenite, and slate; the limestone enclosing but comparatively few. Nearly all of the valuable metals are found in this region, such as gold, silver, copper, lead, iron, zinc, antimony, &c. At present, owing to the high price of transport, gold and silver mines are the only ones that can yield profitable results.

Reese River District.—This district is situated on the western slope of the Toiyabe range of mountains, which extends north and south for the distance of one hundred miles, and occupies nearly the geographical centre of the State of Nevada. A number of subordinate districts are situated on this range, and the majority of the mines worked in the country are found on its eastern and western slopes. In this region silver was first discovered, and here the mines have been more fully opened, and a greater number of mills erected, than in any other locality. Austin, the largest town in this part of the country, containing three or four thousand inhabitants, is built in the centre of the district. Nearly all the ores met with, at the surface, consist of chloride, iodide, and bromide of silver associated with native silver; whilst below the water level, ruby silver, stephanite, polybasite, antimonial silver, argentiferous galena, silver fahlerz, xanthocone, &c., besides a great variety of combinations more interesting to the mineralogist than valuable to the miner are found.

The first attempts at working these ores were unsuccessful; but since the introduction into the country of the process of roasting with salt in reverberatory furnaces, the results obtained have been satisfactory, although dry crushing and working the furnaces by hand render the process very costly in a country where labour costs at least four dollars per day. Sixty dollars per ton of 2,000 lbs. is the rate now charged at the *custom mills,* a return of eighty per cent. of the fire assay of the ore being guaranteed.

This district, though small in extent, six miles north and south, by one and a half east and west, contains a remarkably large number of silver-bearing veins. Over five thousand different branches have been discovered and recorded in the district, nearly all of which are visible at the surface; and ninety-five per cent. of this number contain silver, though frequently not in paying quantities. The vein-systems are remarkably numerous, besides which a complicated series of faults renders their study interesting. Six apparently distinct systems have been observed, and the relative ages of four of them satisfactorily determined. The oldest and by far the most numerous veins have a strike north-west and south-east, magnetic, the variation being sixteen degrees east, with a dip of forty-five degrees to the north-east; many of the richest veins belong to this system. The second system has a strike north seventy degrees west, and south seventy degrees east, with a dip of fifty degrees to the north. The third system has a strike of north twenty-five degrees west, with a dip of seventy degrees to the west. These three systems have all well-defined walls, accompanied by slickensides and flucan. The veins of the fourth system strike north and south, and stand perpendicularly. Two other systems are believed to exist, one with a strike east and west, and a dip of forty degrees to the north; the other running north-west and south-east, and dipping thirty degrees to the south-west; the relative ages of these have not been determined.

The mineral belt extends the whole length of the district, by nearly two miles in width. All of the richest mines are in this belt, which runs nearly parallel with the Toiyabe mountains. Owing to the recent discovery of these mines, and the disadvantages incident to new countries, no deep or extensive explorations have yet been made; about four hundred feet being the greatest depth yet attained by any incline following the dip of the veins. Many of the mining operations have been conducted with a very moderate degree of skill, and are consequently of little value. The following description embraces a few characteristic mines on each well-established system of veins, commencing with the oldest.

FIRST SYSTEM.—The *Oregon*, like all the veins of this system, has a strike north-west and south-east, and a dip of forty-five degrees to the north-east; its average thickness is about one foot. This was one of the first veins opened in the country, and has yielded a considerable amount of ore; the average produce of the rock worked has been over a hundred dollars per ton. An incline has been sunk to the depth of four hundred feet, and drifts run, on each side, for over a hundred feet. This vein was irregular and broken near the surface, but for the last hundred feet appears to be more regular. It contains the ores usually found in the district, such as chloride of silver, ruby silver, and stephanite, associated with large quantities of manganese.

North Star.—This mine has been opened to the depth of three hundred and forty feet, and drifts driven to the eastward for two hundred feet. Its average thickness is about eighteen inches, though in some portions it is three feet in width: the composition and yield of the ores are similar to those of the Oregon.

Revenue.—The thickness of this vein between the walls is two feet; the ore is found in streaks of from three to ten inches. The ores in this vein are rich, the yield by assay of the pure mineral having been over five hundred dollars per ton, whilst the yield by working in the mill has not been above two hundred. Larger pieces of native silver have been taken from this mine than from any other on Reese River.

North River.—This vein, so far as it has been followed down, has increased in thickness; at the surface it was only six inches wide, but at the depth of a hundred feet it is over a foot in thickness, and in some portions even eighteen inches. The ore in this mine resembles that of the Revenue. The yield of the ore worked has been about two hundred dollars per ton; nearly all of the veins of this system are double, consisting of two or more foliations, usually from two to four feet apart.

SECOND SYSTEM.—The strike of these veins is north seventy-five west, and south seventy-five east, and the dip fifty to the north. These veins are usually large; from two to eight feet thick.

Whitlatch Union.—This is one of the largest veins in the district, being from four to eight feet thick; it has been opened to the depth of a hundred and twelve feet, and drifts driven on each side for one hundred feet. The ores so far found belong to the surface class, and their yield has been about a hundred dollars per ton. This vein was divided by a fault, and much labour expended before its continuation was again found.

Savage.—This mine has been more fully opened than any other in the district, and hence it has produced more ore. An incline has been sunk to the depth of three hundred feet, and two levels opened; the lower one for a distance of six hundred feet, and the upper for about four hundred. The ores are antimonial with small amounts of ruby silver.

THIRD SYSTEM.—The strike of these veins is north twenty-five degrees west, and south twenty-five east, and their dip seventy degrees to the westward. All their ore is cased in greenstone with a large amount of clay, and they usually carry a considerable body of water. The ore is not so generally diffused throughout the veins as in the two older systems, but is found in separate deposits, and the thickness of the vein is not so regular.

Whitlatch Yankee Blade.—The thickness of this vein is from two to four feet; it has been opened to the depth of three hundred feet, and drifts driven to the distance of seventy feet. The ores are similar to those of the older systems, except that they contain larger amounts of arsenic; the average yield has been about a hundred dollars, though a number of tons have produced three hundred dollars per ton.

The Confidence is almost a fac-simile of the Whitlatch Yankee Blade.

FOURTH SYSTEM.—These veins strike north and south, and stand perpendicularly; they are less metalliferous than those of the older systems, and are more spotted, many portions being entirely barren. They all, however, contain gold in sufficient amounts to constitute a portion of the total value of the ore. So far as is known, this is the latest, or one of the latest of the known systems in the country; consequently it has been less disturbed by faults than any other. One of the veins, which has been opened to the depth of a hundred feet, has a thickness of about two feet. The average yield of its ores is not known, but some samples have afforded by assay a hundred and fifty dollars per ton. The average yield of the sulphides taken from below the water level, was nearly double that of surface ores.

Amador District.—This district adjoins that of Reese River on the north, and is on the same mineral belt. The country rock is slate, and the veins, though large, are not so rich or numerous as in Reese River.

No veins have been found passing from the granite into the slate, and none between the two formations. The usual strike is north-west and south-east, and the dip about forty degrees to the north-east. Many of the veins show evidence of great dynamic action, their walls being often polished as smooth as glass. The Amador, Rough and Ready, and Corral Mines have been opened to depths varying from two to four hundred feet; the average thickness of the veins being from four to six feet. These veins are capable of producing a large amount of ore, but, so far, have not proved sufficiently rich to leave a profit to the mine-owners after paying sixty dollars per ton for reduction.

Ravenswood District.—This district lies about eighteen miles north-west from Austin; the country rock is slate, and the veins are very numerous and rich in copper and lead, but rarely yield over forty dollars per ton in silver, which will not, at the present scale of charges, pay the expenses of working.

Cortez District.—Cortez is sixty miles north of Austin, and but a short distance from the Humboldt River. Wood, water, and grass are comparatively abundant; the country rock is slate, granite, and limestone. There are many known veins in this district, the principal being the Nevada Giant.

Nevada Giant.—This crops to the surface for the distance of two and a half miles, its thickness being from fifty to two hundred feet, with a direction nearly north and south, and dipping to the east. The vein contains many deposits or chimneys showing at the surface large quantities of valuable ore, which principally consists of disseminated stephanite.

Washington District.—Forty miles south of Austin is Washington, which contains a large number of veins, yielding argentiferous galena: they are generally rich in lead, and assay from twenty to sixty ounces of silver to the ton of ore; the country rock is slate and limestone.

Union District.—This district is sixty miles south-west from Austin on the western slope of the Shoshone range of mountains, which are generally well covered with wood. The enclosing rock is syenite, the veins are small, rich, and numerous; in the slate they are larger, less productive, and fewer in number, while the value of the few found in limestone has been in no way determined. Only one vein in this district has been opened below the water level, and in that, sulphide of silver was found. Hence all the ores worked in this neighbourhood have been chlorides. The general direction is north-west and south-east, with a dip of forty degrees to the north-east.

The Pleiades.—This mine has been opened to the depth of two hundred feet, and drifts driven on each side for a distance of seventy or eighty feet; the thickness of the vein varies from two to four feet; the ores are similar to those found near Austin, but contain rather more lead; their average yield has been nearly one hundred dollars per ton. There are many other similar veins in the district, such as the Clipper, Idaho, Shaw, Silver Moon, &c.; some being rich in gold, as the Franklin and Shamrock.

The Great Eastern.—The strike of this vein is north and south, with a dip of about sixty degrees to the west. It is composed of a number of different bands, varying from ten to one hundred feet in thickness, with an aggregate width of from three to four hundred feet. It crops to the surface for a distance of over ten miles, and passes through different country rocks, such as slate, limestone, and porphyry, but it is only productive in the latter. In the Great Eastern claim a tunnel has been run through two of the strata, one thirty-five feet thick, and the other about ten. The larger stratum, out by the tunnel, afforded assays of forty dollars per ton; the smaller one yielded some samples producing a hundred dollars per ton.

Smoky Valley District is situated seven miles south-east from Austin, on the eastern slope of the Toiyabe range of mountains; the country rock is slate and granite; many small rich veins are found in the granite, but the principal lodes are in the slate. Those which have a direction east and west, and a dip of about forty degrees north, are known as the Mammoth and Smoky Valley, have a thickness of from twenty to forty feet, and run parallel, about one hundred yards apart, for a distance of over three miles. An incline has been sunk on the Smoky Valley, to the depth of two hundred feet, but the average yield has not yet been determined.

The Twin River District is situated on the eastern slope of the Toiyabe mountains, about fifty miles south from Austin; the country rock is slate and granite; all of the valuable veins are found in the slate, or at the point of junction of the slate and granite. They are large and numerous, many of them having a thickness of from twenty to forty feet; their general direction is nearly north and south, with a dip of seventy degrees to the west.

The Murphy is the only vein that has been opened and worked sufficiently to prove its value; it is twenty feet thick, with a paying streak of from five to seven feet in thickness. Many other veins are of equal or greater size, and present equally favourable indications.

The Vanderbilt is nearly seventy feet in thickness, with a foot wall of granite, and a hanging wall of slate, and can be traced on the surface for a distance of over a mile. The ravines cut the veins at right angles, to the depth of nearly two thousand feet; thus affording great facilities for opening mines by means of adits driven into the vein on its direction. This district has been recently discovered, but bids fair to become an important one; wood, water, and salt are abundant.

Mammoth District is seventy miles south-west from Austin; the veins in this locality are very numerous, regular, and uniform in direction, dip, and thickness; being but little disturbed by faults. Their general strike is north-west and south-east, and their dip forty degrees to the north-east; the average thickness is about two feet. None of the veins have been opened to any considerable depth, and all the ores, so far worked, have been from the surface. A large amount of ore can be taken from the backs, that will yield about forty dollars per ton. This district has not been discovered sufficiently long to admit of any but superficial openings being made, but it promises to become an important mining country.

San Antonio District.—This district is situated about a hundred miles south from Austin. It is an almost perfect counterpart of the Reese River district. The vein systems are equally numerous, but their relative ages have not been ascertained. The surface ores have the same composition, and are of about equal richness, although the veins are larger; the country rock is generally slate. No water is found within a mile and a half of the mines, and then only in small quantities; nine miles from the mines, water is met with in sufficient abundance to supply a mill, and wood can be procured within six miles of the water.

The Liberty.—This mine has been opened to the depth of two hundred and fifty feet without finding water. The thickness of the vein is from four to eight feet; the run is west-north-west and east-south-east, and the dip forty-two degrees to the north. So far as yet opened on, the ores are chlorides and iodides; more horn silver is found in this mine than in any other in the country. The yield of the ores, selected for working, has been over three hundred dollars per ton.

Las Animas.—This mine has not been opened as fully as the Liberty, which it very much resembles, only that the vein is thicker. Want of wood and water has greatly retarded the development of this district.

Silver Peak is one hundred and forty miles south from Austin. A large amount of exfoliated ore, which has fallen from the backs of the veins, is found at the surface; some of these ores have been worked, and good results obtained: the country rock is granite, slate, and limestone. Salt is abundant, and wood and water moderately plentiful. In addition to the foregoing two great mining regions of Nevada, there are numerous others which are as yet of minor importance, but which are being steadily and rapidly developed. It would, however, be impossible to enumerate even the names and positions of the different veins which have been discovered in this State.

Other Mining Districts.—In Esmeralda County, where there are some important veins, there are three distinct hills in which the principal mines are situated.

Silver Hill, in which are the Esmeralda ledge; the Winnemucca, Falls of the Clyde, St. Louis, Utah, Antelope, Red White and Blue, Cedar, Greenback, Lily of the West, Locomotive, and many others, on some of which, shafts have been sunk 300 feet, and rich ore taken out; about twenty levels have also been run into the hill, some of them from 500 to 600 feet in length: no water of any consequence has been met with. Middle Hill contains many promising veins, but sufficient work has not been done on them, to determine their true characters. Last Chance Hill, in which is the Wide West ledge, the Del Monte, Golden Age, Empire, Crocket, Ætna, and many others. Considerable amounts of the precious metals have been taken from them, but during the last twelve months the same amount of work has not been done on mines in this district, as in the previous year, owing to litigation and insecurity of title. In this district many hundreds of tons of boulders from the surface have been broken by miners and worked in the mills, generally paying well. Aurora is the county seat. During the past year, mines in the Bodie District, about twelve miles west from Aurora, have been worked with profitable results. Two large mills have been erected in the district, and are working ores which pay from $50 to $100 per ton. Montgomery, Blind Springs and Hot Springs Districts, about forty miles south-east from Aurora, have also been discovered within the last two years. Lake District, near Walker Lake, has also been recently discovered. Many large veins, with prominent croppings, are being worked, and some ore rich in both gold and silver has been taken out. Columbus, Silver Peak, Red Mountain, Cottonwood, and Minnesota Districts, about seventy-five miles south-east from Aurora, have also been discovered during the past two years. The veins are large and well defined, being from one to four feet wide, and can be traced for several hundred feet, the croppings being generally prominent.

The Montezuma Mine, in Humboldt County, is situated in Trinity District, fifteen miles west of Unionville. The Montezuma ledge runs in an east and west direction, and dips north at an angle of seventy degrees. The principal country rock is a metamorphic slate. The vein is ten feet thick, well defined, and has a clay selvage on each side. The ore principally consists of oxide of antimony, carbonate and oxide of lead, and arsenical pyrites. So far as yet explored, this vein contains but little refuse. The ore yields, by mill process, without roasting, an average of seventy-five dollars of silver per ton. On this vein two shafts have been sunk, each thirty feet in depth, and drifts have been extended to an aggregate length of eighty feet. The distance from the mine to the Humboldt River where at a moderate cost good water-power can be obtained, is four miles, over a good natural road. The work done, thus far, has been by way of exploration only.

The Montana Mine is situated n the Sacramento District, eighteen miles south of Unionville. The lode is in slate and limestone. It runs north and south, and pitches west seventy degrees.

The Sheba Mine is near Star City. Its ore principally consists of sulphide of antimony, brittle silver ore, and antimonial silver, and is found in deposits which are distributed irregularly through a stratified belt, or ore channel, about a hundred and fifty feet thick, which lies between quartzite and slate. In the development and working of this mine, three thousand feet of levels and drifts have been run at a cost of $75,000. The aggregate yield has been about $70,000; and the average produce per ton, $140.

The De Soto Mine is situated immediately south of the Sheba. The vein is four feet thick, runs in a northerly direction, and has clay selvages and polished walls; the country rock is slate. Upwards of a thousand feet of tunnel have been run. About two hundred tons of ore have been taken out, which averaged nearly $100. The ore closely resembles that of the Sheba.

The Yosemite Mine is situated two miles south-east of Dun Glen. The formation in its vicinity is slate and limestone. The vein is two feet thick, and has clay selvages and striated polished walls. It runs north and south, and stands almost vertically; a shaft has been sunk to the depth of fifty feet, and from this about fifty feet of drifts have been run. Three hundred feet of a working tunnel have also been run. Several small faults occur in the vein, which give it a broken appearance. The ore is a black sulphide of silver, containing a small proportion of carbonate of copper. It is exceedingly rich, some of it assaying as high as $13,000 per ton.

The Gem of the Sierras is situated in Sierra District, five miles from Dun Glen, in a limestone formation. The vein is twenty inches in thickness, runs in an easterly and westerly direction, and dips 70° south. A considerable portion of the gangue is calcareous spar. The ore consists of sulphide and chloride of silver, mixed with a little carbonate of copper; and the parcels worked have yielded at the rate of $175 per ton.

The Tallulah Mine lies a mile and a half west of Dun Glen, and comprises several ledges running north and south, and dipping west. The enclosing rocks are slate, syenite, and porphyry. A level has been extended five hundred feet, cutting at an average depth of a hundred and eighty feet, a well-defined vein separated from the enclosing rock by selvages and polished walls. The ores chiefly consist of antimonia, sulphide of silver, with a little native metal, and after selection yield about $150 per ton.

The Pride of the Mountain is situated in the Winnemucca District, twenty miles north of Dun Glen. The vein runs north and south, pitches east at an angle of 45°, and is about fourteen inches thick. It is well defined and continuous, and has clay selvages and striated walls. The country rock consists of a soft metamorphic slate, and much of the gangue is calcareous. In making the incline, forty tons of ore were taken out which, without selection, yield $80 per ton by the pan process.

The Manitowoc Mine lies two miles south of Unionville, in Buena Vista District. The vein is two feet thick, runs north and south, and dips west at an angle of 45°. The country rock is slate. The ore consists of sulphide of silver and xanthocone containing a small proportion of copper, and is easily worked by the common pan process.

Devil's Gate District is situated in the north-west portion of Lyon County, and is the oldest district in it. The lodes in the most northerly portion are auriferous in their character, many being well defined. The most prominent veins, however, are the Wide West Twin, and Buckeye. Lying south are the Daney, and Charles Cany Companies. The Daney Company has erected permanent works, and ore has been met with in several places in the mine, but not sufficient in amount to keep in operation the ten-stamp mill which the Company has erected. There are 34 mills in this county, principally employed in the reduction of ore from the Comstock vein.

There are several veins in Nye County, which in the aggregate produced during the year 1865 about $100,000 worth of bullion; this principally consisted of silver yielding only a small proportion of gold.

In Washoe County there are no mines worked to any extent, but it contains several reduction works, principally occupied in the amalgamation of Comstock ores.

According to the Report of the State Mineralogist, there are now in the State of Nevada no less than 116 distinct reduction works, provided in the aggregate with above 2,200 stamp-heads.

CHAPTER XV.

CENTRAL AMERICA AND SOUTH AMERICA.

GUATEMALA — MINES OF THE CENTRAL AMERICAN MINING COMPANY — MINING DISTRICT OF ALOTEPEC — PRODUCE OF SILVER—SOUTH AMERICA — MINES OF PERU—ANNUAL PRODUCTION OF SILVER—BOLIVIA—MINES OF POTOSI—THEIR PRODUCTION OF SILVER—CHILI—MINES OF COQUIMBO—ANNUAL PRODUCTION OF CHILI—NEW GRANADA—SANTA ANA MINES—TABLE SHOWING PRODUCTION OF SILVER IN VARIOUS COUNTRIES.

CENTRAL AMERICA.—Comparatively little is known of the geology of this country, except that the predominating rocks are granite, gneiss, and mica slate, and that the abundance of igneous rock bears witness to extensive volcanic action. Silver mines are situated in various parts of Central America, but the only ones of which we have any authentic information are the following:—

Mines of the Central American Mining Company.—The mining district of Alotepec is situated in about 14° 40′ of north latitude, and 88° 58′ of west longitude; being a portion of the Department of Chiquimula in the Republic of Guatemala.

The mountain of Alotepec forms part of the great chain which runs towards Honduras, in which the best silver veins of Central America are found. As a mining district it appears to have been known more than a hundred years ago, and a period of great prosperity occurred about seventy years since. The veins are found in porphyritic rocks, and occasionally pass into sandstones and limestones, which appear to have been uplifted by the porphyry. Their general direction is from east to west in the sandstone and limestone formations, and south-east and north-west in the porphyry. The mineral wealth of the district principally consists in silver, lead, and copper. The silver is found both with lead and copper; also as a sulphide of silver, and in the state of chloride. Lead is found as sulphide and carbonate; the copper is in the form of pyrites, green and blue carbonate, and as an oxide. There is also a great abundance of iron ore in different parts of the mountains. The rocks supply abundance of lime for mortar, building-stone of various kinds, clay for bricks and tiles, and an inferior kind of sand is found in the ravines. The firestone in the neighbourhood is not good, but it may be obtained from Tuitiapa, and fireclay at Esquipulas and near the city of Guatemala.

The number of veins and mineral deposits in the mountains of Alotepec cannot be less than thirty-eight or forty, which the late Mr. Floresi divided into five groups or divisions, viz.—

1st. The mines of Don Manuel Molense.
2nd. Those of Don Cruz Iriarte.
3rd. San José, San Rafael, and Santa Rita.
4th. Anderson's Hope and El Tajo.
5th. Taylor's Hope, &c. &c. &c.

The first group comprises the mines of San Pantaleon, Santa Rosalia, Socorro, and Santa Fé. These mines are on the north side of the mountain, looking towards the Rio del Valle, and are surrounded by a fine forest, chiefly of pine and oak. The pasture land enclosed is sufficient for about 100 animals during the greater portion of the year. There is a supply of water sufficient for stamps, &c.; and about two and a half miles from the mines, is a piece of land called "La Vega de San José," having the advantage of extensive water rights, and on which very convenient reduction works have been constructed: the German barrel process being that adopted. Before their purchase by the present Company, the mines had been worked at different periods, but very unskilfully. The vein of San Pantaleon is that which has yielded the best produce. The veins of Santa Rosalia, Socorro, and Santa Fé have been worked at different times, and produced moderate quantities of ore of *good ley*. They are well situated for deep cross-cuts, and can be worked and drained without the necessity of a shaft, requiring only such openings from the surface as may occasionally be wanted for ventilation.

To the second group belong San Carlos, Rosario, San Miguel, San José de Atutilca, and other mines. The veins, although in general not very wide, are promising; the ores are rather mixed, and principally consist of compounds of copper, lead, sulphur, and silver, generally better adapted for smelting than amalgamation. The mines of this group are also well situated for adits, and are not more than a league from the Vega de San José. In the third group are the mines of San José, San Rafael, Santa Rita, and San Domingo. San Rafael and San José appear to have been worked extensively, but they do not present such facilities for deeper levels as the other mines. The fourth group comprises the mines of Santa Catalina or Anderson's Hope, and El Tajo. Mr. Floresi considered them to be neither regular lodes, nor beds, but a reunion of several small veins. The ores of El Tajo form an excellent flux in the smelting of other ores. The fifth group consists of Taylor's Hope and adjoining veins. Taylor's Hope is about six miles from the reduction works.

The rivers in the immediate neighbourhood of the mines allow of the reduction establishment being worked entirely by water-power; the forests are capable of supplying charcoal and wood to any extent, and very few places can furnish a larger variety or a greater abundance of timber than this district.

The silver produced by the Central American Mining Company has been chiefly obtained from the mine of San Pantaleon, but recently, considerable quantities have been raised at San Carlos. Of late years also, some ore has been extracted from San José de Atutilca.

It will be observed by reference to the annexed tabular statement that the production of these mines has considerably fallen off since 1863, but discoveries are expected to result from the exploratory works now in progress, and it is hoped that the returns for the present year may again increase.

STATEMENT OF SILVER PRODUCED BY THE CENTRAL AMERICAN MINING COMPANY, FROM 1858 TO 1865.*

		oz.	oz.
1858	Produce of ore sold . . .		18,187·80
1859	" " . . .		62,623·45
1860	" " . . .		67,825·95
1861	" " . . .	45,508·05	
	" of bar silver sold .	80,579·94	
			126,087·99
1862	" of ore sold . . .	34,662·45	
	" of bar silver sold .	21,686·19	
	" " " .	65,897·00	
			122,245·64
1863	" of ore sold . . .	4,955·25	
	" of bar silver sold .	12,795·84	
	" " " .	109,446·29	
			127,197·38
1864	" of ore sold . . .	2,923·95	
	" of bar silver sold .	64,762·96	
			67,686·91
1865	" of ore sold . . .	1,768·20	
	" of bar silver sold .	27,354·58	
			29,122·78

Total produce . . . . 620,077·90 oz.

SOUTH AMERICA.—The silver mines of that portion of South America which constitutes the republics of Peru, Bolivia, and Chili, are next in importance to those of Mexico and Nevada, and would, had they been more favourably situated, probably be capable of affording a larger annual amount of silver than even the mines of Mexico. The great elevation of many of the argentiferous districts of South America is, however, a great drawback to their value, since nothing but the extreme richness, or the great abundance of the ores, could afford a sufficient inducement to undertake the working of mines in such desolate and inhospitable regions.

PERU.—The mines of the Cerro de Pasco are the most celebrated of Peru; the principal ores worked being of the description known as *pacos*, which are analogous to the colorados of the Mexican miners, and consist of ferruginous earths containing varying amounts of silver.

In order to form an idea of the enormous quantities of these argentiferous gossans, which nature has deposited in the calcareous hills of this district, it may be stated that the bed of silver-bearing oxide of

* Furnished by Mr. J. Phillips.

iron of Pasco or Yauricocha, had been worked, without interruption, since about the commencement of the seventeenth century; and that although, during the first twenty years previous to the commencement of the nineteenth, they had produced above five million marks of silver, very few of the workings then penetrated to a depth of above a hundred feet below the surface.

The metalliferous deposit of Yauricocha crops out on the surface for a length of 2,500 fathoms, and a width of 1,200 fathoms. M. de Rivero considers the pacos of Santa Rosa, one of the most productive mines in the district, to be a deposit and not a true vein, since they run parallel with the general formation of the country, and the gangues have no crystalline or drusy structure.*

These mines were accidentally discovered by an Indian in 1630, and were, for a long period, regarded as the richest in any portion of the American continent. They have, however, been badly worked, and, many years since, one of them fell in upon the workmen, of whom three hundred were killed, from which circumstance the mine has acquired the name of *Matagente*, or "Kill-people." The town of Cerro de Pasco is 13,673 feet above the sea, and when the condition of the mines is prosperous, sometimes contains 18,000 inhabitants; according to Tschudi, the two principal argentiferous veins of this district are the Veta de Colquirirca and the Veta de Pariarirca. The former of these runs in nearly a straight line from north to south, and has been traced for a length of 9,600, and over a breadth of above 400 feet. The second takes a direction from east-south-east to west-north-west, and is supposed to intersect the other under the market-place of the city. Its known extent, in length, is 6,400 feet, and its width 380 feet. Steam-power was first introduced into these mines in 1814, by the celebrated Richard Trevithick, but the acid waters of the veins acted so rapidly on the pumps, that they were very quickly destroyed, and in 1832 only one of the engines remained at work.

In addition to the district of Cerro de Pasco there are various others in Peru which have produced large quantities of silver. The principal of these are those of Caxamarca, Pataz, Huamanchuco, and Hualgayoc. In the Cerro de San Fernando alone, included in the latter district, there were in 1840 no less than 1,700 *bocaminas*, or mine openings. There are also numerous silver mines in the southern

* Ann. des Mines (3), f. ii. 169.

districts, but the amount of metal produced is small in comparison with the richness and extent of the veins.

The total amount of the silver produced from the principal mines of the Cerro de Pasco from 1784 to 1827, was 4,962,929 lbs. troy.

The total annual production of the silver mines of Peru is estimated at 299,000 lbs. troy.

BOLIVIA.—The mines of Potosi, which once formed a portion of the viceroyalty of Buenos Ayres, are now included in the Republic of Bolivia, and have, since their discovery in 1545, yielded almost fabulous amounts of silver. In this locality thirty-two principal veins, besides numerous smaller ones, have been worked in an isolated mountain called *Hatun-Potocsi*, or Great Potosi, the summit of which reaches an elevation of 16,000 feet above the level of the sea. From the time of the discovery of these mines, up to 1571, when the process of amalgamation was introduced, the ores were treated exclusively by fusion. The Spanish conquerors of the country, being military men, were but little skilled in metallurgical operations; and having been unable to effect the fusion of the mineral by the aid of bellows, adopted the primitive process employed by the natives for the treatment of ores obtained from the neighbouring mine of Porco, which had been in operation long previous to the conquest. For this purpose, according to Humboldt, small portable furnaces, called *huayres* or *guayres* were established on the mountains in the neighbourhood of Potosi, wherever they could be fully exposed to the action of the prevailing winds. These furnaces consisted of cylindrical vessels of refractory clay, pierced with numerous holes, in which the silver ores were introduced, together with galena and charcoal, in separate layers. The air, which entered the holes before referred to, caused the fuel to burn with great intensity; and when the combustion became too active, and the consumption of charcoal consequently very rapid, the furnace was removed to some locality less exposed to the wind. Early travellers who visited the country, speak with enthusiasm of the effects produced by these fires, more than six thousand in number, which, every night, lit up the mountains in the neighbourhood of the mines. The galena necessary for the operation of smelting was obtained from a neighbouring mountain called *Huayna-Potocsi*.

The argentiferous products obtained from the portable furnaces were re-melted in a fire kept up by means of copper blow-pipes, from six to seven feet in length, and of which from ten to twelve, used by as many different persons, were employed at the same time.

It will be readily conceived that the loss of silver experienced by this primitive process must have been exceedingly great.

The period of the greatest productiveness of the Potosi mines was the century which immediately followed their discovery, their average annual yield from 1545 to 1556 having been about $11,600,000. Shortly after the commencement of the seventeenth century their production began to decline, and at its close their annual yield had receded to between three and four millions of dollars. The annual yield of the Potosi mines was estimated by Chevalier, in 1845, at from 48,000 to 60,000 lbs. troy. Although the produce of the ore has considerably decreased, in proportion as greater depths have been attained, the mines of Potosi are far from being exhausted, and there can be no doubt but that, if intelligently worked on a large scale, under the protection of a reliable Government, they might be, at least to a great extent, brought back to their former state of prosperity and productiveness. According to Whitney there were in 1852, in the province of Potosi, above 1,800 abandoned silver mines, and only 26 at work; and in the remaining mining districts of the country there were no less than 2,365 abandoned mines, and only 40 in course of working.

The total amount of silver produced by the mines of Peru and Bolivia, from the earliest period up to 1845, was estimated by Chevalier at 155,839,180 lbs. troy.

CHILI.—Domeyko, who has described the mining districts of Chili, divides the rock formations of that country into three distinct groups, viz *

1st. Secondary stratified, prior to the upheaval of the Andes.

2nd. Igneous eruptive masses, of the period of the upheaval of that chain.

3rd. Tertiary beds, posterior to that epoch; generally speaking, the veins affording gold and copper belong to the second group, whilst those of argentiferous copper, containing these metals in combination with sulphur, arsenic, and antimony, are usually included in the first. The gold veins are principally enclosed in granite, and those of copper, uncombined with silver, arsenic, or antimony, are chiefly found in diorites, porphyries, and eurites, or in some other eruptive igneous rock. Chloride of silver and the native amalgams are, in most

* Ann. des Mines (4), t. ix. 22.

instances, met with near the point of junction of rocks belonging to the first and second classes.

The mining districts of Chili may be divided as follows:—

Mountains north of the valley of Huasco—This is the richest silver district of Chili, but also contains valuable mines of copper and gold. The most productive copper mines of this section are those of Carrisal.

Districts lying between Huasco and Coquimbo—In this region are the rich groups of copper veins of San Juan and La Higuera, which annually supply large quantities of copper ores of a high percentage produce. The mines from which these are obtained, are situated in dioritic rocks. On a line between Arqueros and Agua Amarga, which represents the course of junction of the first and second groups, there are numerous veins affording metallic silver, chloride of silver, and native amalgam.

The third district lies between the valleys of Coquimbo and Aconcagua, where the granite extends far inland, and the gold-bearing veins present a greater development. The whole of the granitic district is more or less auriferous, and on its borders are numerous veins affording copper ores.

The fourth district lies to the north of Aconcagua, where, as in the foregoing, the granite is traversed by auriferous veins; and mines of silver and argentiferous copper ores are worked above the level of the various ravines existing in the stratified rocks forming the elevated chain of the Andes.

The usual gangues of the copper veins are quartz and hornblende; whilst carbonate of lime and sulphate of baryta accompany the ores of silver. Gold is commonly associated with quartz and sulphide of iron. The most abundant ore of silver is the chloride, together with bromide of silver and the native metal. The chlorides are found in the usual ferruginous earthy deposits, called pacos and colorados by the miners of South America. In addition to these, there is a great variety of sulphides and arsenides of silver. The ores usually contain from 100 to 250 oz. of silver per ton; but it is a remarkable fact that the blendes and galenas occurring in the rich silver regions of Chili, as a rule, scarcely contain a trace of that metal.

The most important silver mines of Chili are those situated in the neighbourhood of Copiapo. All that portion of the country lying above the parallel of Valparaiso is rocky and sterile, excepting three tongues, or narrow bands, varying from three-fourths of a mile to one mile in width, extending inwards from Coquimbo, Huasco, and

Caldera. All the remainder is a desert, and in it, at distances of from thirty to forty leagues from each other, are the various mining districts. The mines of Coquimbo and Huasco chiefly afford copper, whilst those of Copiapo are rich in silver.

The principal workings are those in the vicinity of Chañarcillo and Tres Puntas; the first, sixteen leagues south, and the second, thirty to the north-north-east of Copiapo. The mines of the former locality were discovered, in 1832, by a muleteer, and were worked with large but gradually diminishing returns until 1836, when the veins were found to have been cut off by a stratum of tough limestone, called in that country a *mesa*, or table. On this discovery being made, the mine proprietors of the district became generally discouraged; but one of their number, more enterprising than the others, having sunk to a depth of 266 feet through the unproductive rock, found on the other side a rich deposit of silver ore. Several of these barren strata have since been intersected by sinking, and it has been invariably found that the veins are rich between them, and that the largest accumulations of ore are met with near the planes of contact of the limestone with the adjoining rocks. The first mine discovered in this district was that known as the Descubridora. The three principal mines of the Tres Puntas are La Buena Esperanza, La Salvadora, and the Al Fin Hallada; whilst in the district are some twenty other more or less productive and profitable workings, together with a great number producing little or nothing.

The development of the mineral resources of Chili has been more recent than that of the other South American States; but its comparatively flourishing political situation, and the internal quiet which it so long enjoyed, have enabled the workings to be established on an extensive scale, and has, within the last few years, led to a considerable increase in the amount of silver annually produced. Under the Spanish dominion, the production of silver was inconsiderable, and in 1800 the annual yield was estimated by Humboldt at only 18,300 lbs. troy. Since the discovery of the rich mines of Copiapo, however, in 1832, the production of silver has very much increased. The total yield of silver, up to 1810, was estimated by Chevalier at 804,000 lbs. troy, and from 1804 to 1845 at 1,803,636 lbs.

The silver exported for the eight years from 1834 to 1841, both inclusive, was, according to the returns of the British consuls, based on the confessedly defective information furnished by the Chilian Government, as follows:—

	Marks.		Marks.
1834	164,935	Brought forward	915,417
1835	231,988	1839	148,089
1836	163,158	1840	141,621
1837	219,482	1841	140,123
1838	135,854		
Carried forward.	915,417	Total . .	1,345,250

Mr. Danson estimates the total exports of silver from 1804 to 1848 at $38,555,205.* Whitney considers that the production of the country from 1846 to 1853 was probably about 1,750,000 lbs.; making the entire yield of the mines of Chili, up to that time, 4,357,656 lbs. troy. We are without any authentic returns of the produce of the Chilian mines since that period.

New Granada.—*The Santa Ana Mines* are situated in the Province of Mariquita, State of New Granada. They contain deposits of various argentiferous ores, chiefly consisting of silver-bearing pyrites mixed with native silver, ruby silver, and various sulphides. This locality also affords argentiferous galenas and blendes. The ores are enriched by a process of stamping and dressing previous to being submitted to barrel amalgamation. The mines have been worked to a depth of 120 fathoms, and the quantity of ore raised in 1864 amounted to 1,570 tons; which, after being reduced by concentration to 453 tons, yielded 78,281 ounces of silver. The cost of grinding and amalgamation, in 1861, amounted to $43·63 per ton; the loss of mercury being 5·72 lbs. per ton of concentrated ore treated. The loss of silver was stated in that year to have been only 5·33 per cent.†

The following is a statement of the silver produced from the Santa Ana Mines, from 1852 to 1864, both inclusive:—

Year.	oz.	Year.	oz.
1852	57,169	Brought forward.	675,940
1853	31,403	1859	140,509
1854	55,009	1860	84,771
1855	84,415	1861	81,044
1856	129,389	1862	93,436
1857	158,519	1863	112,474
1858	160,036	1864	78,281
Carried forward.	675,940		1,266,455

The following table gives the approximate yields, in pounds troy, of the principal silver-producing countries of the world, at the commencement of the present century, and for the years 1850 and 1865. In cases where the return for the year indicated could not be obtained, the produce for the nearest year for which they could be procured has been substituted. The quoted produce of the various European countries,

* Quarterly Journal of the Statistical Society of London, March 1851, p. 40.

† It is difficult to understand how the loss of silver should be so small with so large an expenditure of mercury.

and of the United States of America, may be taken in each instance as a sufficiently close approximation; but the figures relating to Mexico, Central America, and South America, must be regarded as estimates only. A large proportion of the precious metals produced in those countries is annually exported without passing through the hands of the Government officers, and consequently the most reliable information that can be procured is but little to be depended on. No systematic investigations have been made on the spot by competent persons since the date of the writings of Duport and Chevalier.

TABLE SHOWING APPROXIMATE YIELD OF THE PRINCIPAL SILVER-PRODUCING COUNTRIES.

	1800.		1850.		1865.	
	lbs. troy.	Ratio per cent.	lbs. troy.	Ratio per cent.	lbs. troy.	Ratio per cent.
Russian Empire	58,150	2·5	60,000	2·1	58,000	1·5
Scandinavia	141,000 (Scandinavia to Spain)	6·0 (Scandinavia to Spain)	20,400	0·7	15,000	0·4
Great Britain			48,500	1·7	60,500	1·5
Hartz			31,500	1·1	28,000	0·6
Prussia			21,200	0·7	68,000	1·7
Saxony			63,600	2·2	80,000	2·0
Other German States			2,500	0·1	2,500	
Austria			87,000	3·1	92,000	2·2
France			5,000	0·2	18,000	0·4
Italy			...	...	*25,000	0·6
Spain			125,000	4·4	110,000	2·8
Australia, New Zealand, British Columbia, and Nova Scotia	...	...	10,000	0·4	9,500	0·2
Chili	18,300	0·8	238,500	8·4	299,000	7·3
Bolivia	271,300	11·6	130,000	4·6	136,000	3·3
Peru	401,850	17·2	303,150	10·7	299,000	7·4
New Granada	5,000	0·2	13,000	0·5	15,000	0·4
Brazil	1,200	...	675	...	1,500	0·4
Mexico	1,440,500	61·7	1,650,000	58·4	1,700,000	42·3
United States	...	...	17,400	0·7	1,000,000	25·0
Total	2,337,300	100	2,827,425	100	4,017,000	100

* Obtained from the island of Sardinia, where it is found associated with galena.

CHAPTER XVI.

TREATMENT OF SILVER ORES BY AMALGAMATION—PATIO PROCESS, &c.

PATIO PROCESS—MAGISTRAL—SALT—MERCURY—LIME—COPPER PRECIPITATE—COMPOSITION OF ORES—ROUGH STAMPING—FINE GRINDING—RASPAR—LOSS OF GOLD—THE PATIO—INCORPORAR—TREADING OF TORTA—WASHING—STRAINING AMALGAM—DISTILLATION—LOSS OF SILVER—LOSS OF MERCURY—CHEMICAL REACTIONS OF THE PATIO—RESULTS OF THE PATIO PROCESS—AT GUANAXUATO—FRESNILLO—REAL DEL MONTE—VIRGINIA CITY—AMALGAMATION BY HOT PROCESS—ESTUFA AMALGAMATION.

It has been found after numerous trials that the ores of silver, with the exception of argentiferous galenas, do not generally admit of mechanical concentration, and they are consequently, after careful selection, in most cases, subjected to metallurgical treatment. The difficulty of treating ores of silver by mechanical means, arises from the fact of the greater portion of this metal being finely disseminated in the veinstone in the form of various brittle sulphides, which, on the pulverisation of the ores, become so finely divided as to float off in suspension in the water employed for concentration. Various carefully conducted experiments made on this subject by Berthier, on samples of silver ores obtained from the different districts of Mexico, go to show that under favourable circumstances, nearly one-half the amount of silver originally present, is lost by even the most careful process of washing that can be applied to them. It must also be borne in mind that, even had the results obtained by mechanical preparation been more favourable than they have been generally found to be, the supply of water in the districts affording a great proportion of the ores of this description, is exceedingly limited, and that the inconvenience and expense attending the dilution of the argentiferous mineral by a large quantity of silicious and earthy matter, is less than the cost and trouble that would be entailed by their concentration.

Patio Process.—The method of extracting silver from its ores, so long employed in the mines of South America, and known as the *patio process*, was discovered in 1557 by Bartolomé Medina, a native of the town of Pachuca, in the neighbourhood of Real del Monte. It is difficult to understand by what course of reasoning a man totally unacquainted with chemical science could have been led to the discovery of a process, of which the *modus operandi* is, even now, to a certain extent, a disputed question, and of which the efficiency does not admit of being at once tested by means of a simple experiment; but which, on the contrary, requires weeks, and, under certain circumstances, even months, for its completion. Although, however, this process requires a considerable period for the full development of its results, the operation of reduction commences almost immediately, and we can therefore only suppose that Medina, being aware of the affinity of mercury for silver, and having mixed this substance with silver ore, sulphate of copper, and common salt, found that a certain portion of the silver had entered into combination with mercury. By keeping this mixture for some time, and occasionally testing the amount of silver taken up by the mercury, which could be readily ascertained by taking a weighed portion of the amalgam and driving off the quicksilver by heat, it would be found, that, for a certain period, the proportion of silver gradually increased, but subsequently remained without change. It is therefore probable that some simple series of experiments of this kind may have conducted him to the discovery of a process which has been of such vast importance, not only to Mexico, but to the world at large, and has so materially affected the total production of silver. A Peruvian, of the name of Carlos Corso de Leca, discovered, in 1586, the method of reduction by iron, *el beneficio de hierro,* which consists in adding to the torta small pieces of iron, by which the reduction of chloride of silver is effected, attended by a corresponding saving of mercury. This process does not, however, appear to have been ever extensively employed.

The next modification in the process of amalgamation was introduced in 1590 by Alonzo Barba, which consisted in conducting the operation in large copper vessels heated by means of a fire placed beneath them. This process, called *el beneficio de cazo y cocimiento,* effected a considerable saving of mercury, attended by a corresponding loss of copper, since the chloride of silver is reduced at the expense of the vessel in which the amalgamation is carried on. This process, by which the reduction of the chlorides is readily effected, but which is not equally applicable to sulphides, was introduced into Europe in 1784 by Baron de Born, an Austrian mining officer, by whom its use in the Hungarian mines was recommended, and from which ultimately sprung, in 1790, the barrel process of Freiberg. It would, however, appear from a work on Metallurgy by Schlüter, printed in 1738, that a process of amalgamation in barrels, or rather vertical tubs, was in use at Kongsberg, previous to that period.

Not having had an extensive practical experience in the extraction of silver from its ores by this method, we have availed ourselves of the descriptions given of it by Humboldt, Duport, and other competent authorities, as well as of data contained in various foreign journals, and in a paper by Mr. J. Napier, jun.* We have also had access to notes made by various friends long engaged in different large reduction establishments in Mexico, and who have furnished valuable statistics relative to the cost of the different operations.

The materials necessary for the reduction of the ores of silver by the patio process, are *magistral*, common salt, and mercury; but in addition to these, sulphate of copper, precipitated copper, and copper and zinc amalgams are occasionally employed.

Magistral.—This is manufactured from copper pyrites, or raw magistral, of which mines occur in many parts of Mexico, but particularly in the district of Tepezala, about twenty leagues south-east of Zacatecas, and sixty from Guanaxuato, from which a large supply is obtained.

The following estimations of copper, made by Napier, show the average percentage of that metal contained in ores from this district:—

Copper per cent.	
No. 1=13·00	=10·32 mean percentage of copper.
„ 2= 7·47	
„ 3=13·75	
„ 4= 9·00	
„ 5=12·50	
„ 6=10·50	
„ 7= 8·60	
„ 8= 9·40	
„ 9= 8·73	

The copper ore, when brought to the works, is first reduced to a coarse sand by dry stamping, and then ground to a fine powder in arrastres. The ground ore is removed from the arrastre to an enclosure, where the water, with which it has been mixed during the process of grinding, is allowed to evaporate; it is then left exposed for a long

* "On the Mexican Method of Amalgamation," by James Napier, Jun., late Chemist and Assayer to the Guanaxuato Mint, Mexico. *Mining and Smelting Magazine*, vol. i. p. 101.

time to atmospheric influences, as it is generally believed to afford a larger proportion of sulphate of copper by roasting, if previously exposed for some months to the action of the air. The furnaces in which the calcination is effected are called *comalillos*, and have a double hearth, of which the roof is almost flat, with a fireplace at the side.

About eight arrobas, or two hundred pounds, of ground ore, with which a few handfuls of salt have been previously mixed, are charged on each hearth. The heat is then gradually raised, and the ore kept constantly stirred during from six to eight hours, when the doors are closed, and the furnace allowed to cool. When sufficiently cold, the doors are again opened, and the charge raked through holes in the bottom of the furnace into arched recesses beneath, prepared for its reception. The percentage of sulphate of copper formed, from an ore of given tenure in copper, depends, to a great extent, on the skill of the workman, and the care bestowed on the operation.

The following table gives the results obtained from the roasting of different parcels of copper ores at the various reduction works at Guanaxuato, as determined by Napier:—

Name of Hacienda.	Sulphates per cent.		Total percentage of Sulphates.	Copper not in the state of Sulphate.		Percentage of Copper in Ore before calcining.
	Copper.	Iron.		As Sulphide.	As Oxide.	
San Joaquin .	40·99	9·73	50·72	4·50	2·11	15·30
„ Nicolas .	20·50	12·38	32·88	2·50	0·23	7·83
Granaditas . .	34·37	6·95	41·32	3·78	2·47	14·00
Salgado . . .	24·64	7·40	32·04	...	2·50	8·00
Pardo . . .	33·18	6·75	39·93	3·00	3·50	12·80
Pastita . . .	31·62	9·05	40·67	0·70	0·15	8·75

In the above table the amount of sulphate of iron is given, as well as the proportion of sulphate of copper, since it has been found that sulphate of iron, as well as the former salt, may be considered an agent in the reduction of the ore, although its action is neither so rapid nor so complete. A small portion of the copper estimated as sulphate will also be in the state of chloride, produced by the chemical changes resulting from the decomposition of the common salt added to the charge. When the ores treated contain either oxide or carbonate of copper, it is usual to add to them a certain amount of iron pyrites, which, by supplying sulphur, assists in their conversion into sulphates. The sulphate thus obtained, being in an anhydrous state, becomes heated on the absorption of water, and this circumstance is taken advantage of for the purpose of making a rough estimate of the quality of prepared magistral, and determining the proportion it will be necessary to employ.

For this purpose the amalgamator takes a small quantity of the calcined ore in his hand, and then gradually inserts it into water, judging from the degree of heat developed, of the quantity of sulphates contained in the parcel. It is also considered by some amalgamators advantageous to employ the magistral as soon after its calcination as possible, since by absorbing moisture its action is said to become less energetic, and a larger amount to be required. The quantity of water, however, which could be absorbed from the atmosphere by the magistral, is so small, in comparison with that contained in the argentiferous mud with which it is incorporated, that the moment they become mixed the whole of the anhydrous sulphate present must at once become fully hydrated; and it is therefore difficult to ascribe the belief that it is necessary to employ freshly calcined magistral, to anything but prejudice on the part of those who entertain the opinion. That such is in reality the case, appears to be evident from the fact that the whole of the sulphate of copper derived from the operation of parting at the various mints, is purchased for the purpose of being employed in lieu of magistral, and that preference is now given to this hydrated salt by the more intelligent amalgamators.

Salt.—In addition to the salt imported from the sea-coast, a very large proportion of that employed in the mining districts of Mexico is obtained from various lagunes situated at more or less considerable distance from the mines. Large quantities of impure salt derived from this source, and forming an efflorescence on the surface of the ground during the dry season, were formerly employed under the name of *saltierra* for the purpose of amalgamation. The cost of transporting large quantities of such an impure material, added to the great increase, in bulk, of the tortas, caused by adding the amount necessary to furnish the required quantity of chloride of sodium, has, however, caused its use to be nearly abandoned; the salt is therefore now generally concentrated by lixiviation and evaporation before being brought to the mines.

The principal localities from which saltierra was formerly derived, and where salt is now manufactured for mining purposes, are Salinas, and Peñon-blanco, there being in both localities, in addition to the saline incrustations before referred to, springs holding chloride of sodium in solution. The following analysis, made by Berthier, of the saltierra from Peñon-blanco, gives the composition of the material formerly employed instead of salt, and shows how large a proportion of its constituents must have been totally inert when introduced into the torta:—

Chloride of Sodium	19·00	soluble in water.
Sulphate of Soda	2·20	
Carbonate of Lime	13·60	insoluble in water.
„ Magnesia	1·60	
Oxide of Iron	9·80	
Clay and Sand	46·20	
Water and Organic Matter	7·60	
	100·00	

The amount of chloride of sodium contained in the purified salt from Peñon-blanco is usually from 80 to 85 per cent.; the remainder, for the most part, consisting of sulphate of soda.

The following table gives the composition of four samples of salt supplied by the district of Salinas, analysed by Napier:—

	No. 1.	No. 2.	No. 3.	No. 4.
Chloride of Sodium	96·623	91·141	90·422	86·853
„ Magnesium	0·008	2·538	2·520	0·044
„ Calcium	0·114	1·574	1·310	0·125
Sulphate of Potash	Trace	3·141	3·556	0·029
„ Soda	3·255	...	...	12·949
„ Lime	...	1·606	2·192	...
	100·000	100·000	100·000	100·000

The purest description of salt employed in Mexico is that brought from the sea-coast, which often contains as much as 95·50 per cent. of chloride of sodium, but its great cost prevents its general employment in the reduction works of the country.

Mercury.—Nearly the whole of this metal, of which the consumption in the Mexican mines is very large, is imported from Europe and California, although it has been found in various localities in the empire, particularly at Mazapil and the Gigante, near Guanaxuato. These mines are not, however, now worked, although considerable quantities of quicksilver have, at various times, been obtained from them. The district of El Doctor, 150 miles north of the city of Mexico, has also furnished a certain amount of this metal.

Lime.—This substance cannot be regarded as an essential in the patio process of amalgamation, since it is only employed when too large a proportion of magistral has been added to the torta, and is then used for the purpose of decomposing the excess of sulphates. Wood ashes are also sometimes made use of for the same purpose.

Copper Precipitate.—Instead of using lime for the purpose of counteracting the effects of any excess of sulphate of copper which may have been added, precipitated copper is employed in many of the haciendas, and acts by the reduction of the metallic chlorides. The use of copper precipitate in the process of amalgamation by the patio was first introduced by Mr. Louckner, who also, in conjunction with Mr. Mackintosh, obtained a patent for the employment of copper amalgam in the torta, with a view to reducing the loss of mercury. This patent was, however, readily evaded by the use of precipitated copper, which, by combining with the mercury, produced the same effect.

Composition of Ores.—The ores subjected to patio amalgamation differ somewhat in their composition in the various mining districts. The following analysis gives the composition of an ore of more than average richness, from the district of La Luz, Guanaxuato:—

Silver	1·04
Iron	4·71
Copper	0·55
Sulphur	6·79
Carbonate of Lime	8·25
„ Magnesia	3·26
Silica	75·00
	99·60

The ores of Real del Monte vary considerably in their composition, but often contain manganese, antimony, and lead; and are consequently difficult of reduction by the patio process of amalgamation.

A sample of ore from the Santa Brigida vein, analysed by Mr. Rogers, afforded him the following results:—

Silver	0·25
Sulphide of Copper	0·40
„ Zinc	2·30
„ Lead	2·82
Peroxide and Sulphide of Iron	7·50
„ of Manganese	5·30
Carried forward	18·57

Brought forward	18·57
Alumina	8·00
Carbonate of Lime	1·45
„ Magnesia	1·60
Silica	68·00
Antimony, Tellurium, traces of Gold, Potash, and Soda	2·38
	100 00

An average sample of the ores worked in the district afforded the following result:—

Sulphide of Silver	0·15
„ Iron	26·52
„ Lead	2·07
„ Arsenic	0·10
„ Zinc	5·00
Sulphate of Iron	0·25
„ Lime	0·43
Peroxide of Manganese	3·54
Carbonate of Lime	4·18
„ Magnesia	0·96
Silica	50·00
Moisture	6·80
	100 00

In the mining districts of Mexico, as well as in Nevada and other localities producing silver ores proper, there are immense accumulations of veinstone containing in the aggregate vast quantities of silver, but of which the yield is not sufficiently high to admit of their being treated with profitable results. Numerous plans have been proposed, and various machines invented, with a view to the concentration of these ores by washing, but, as before stated, none of them have hitherto been found capable of extensive practical application.

Rough Stamping.—The ores to be subjected to the process of patio amalgamation are usually first crushed dry, to the state of coarse gravel in a stamping mill, and subsequently reduced by porphyrisation in the arrastre to the necessary degree of fine division. The former machines generally consist, in Mexico, of eight wooden lifters or stems, shod at their lower extremities with iron, and set in motion by cams, worked by a water-wheel, or more frequently by a team of mules. The ore, as fed to these *morteros* or stamping mills, is in pieces of about the size of the fist; and, as it is broken, falls into sieves formed of hides perforated with small round holes, and fixed in an inclined position before the battery: the portion of the ore which passes through these sieves is removed to the arrastres to be further ground, whilst the coarser particles, remaining on the skins, are again thrown back into the mill. In the majority of the reduction establishments of Mexico this work is entirely performed in mills worked by relays of mules which are driven at a rapid rate, and frequently replaced by a fresh team. Each *molino* requires eighteen mules, which are successively harnessed to the machine in sets of three. An apparatus of this description will, in the course of twenty-four hours, reduce about five tons of ore to a state suitable for treatment in the arrastre.

Fine Grinding.—The arrastre or *tahona* employed for this purpose is constructed as described, page 168: but is paved with great care and is very strongly put together. The bottoms are constructed of hard porphyritic stones about thirty inches in length, placed vertically, and the interstices carefully filled with *cabecilla*, which is the residue remaining after the washing up of a torta. The sides are formed of either wood or flagstones, which stand about two feet above the level of the floor. Their diameter in the haciendas of Guanaxuato is 4½ varas, or 12 feet 4 inches, arrastres of this size being called *arrastres de marca.* The *voladoras*, or mullers, are of porphyry, and have a length somewhat less than the radius of the arrastre, with a thickness of about sixteen inches. In each of them are bored two holes, into which are driven wooden pegs for attaching the chains or straps of raw hide by which they are connected with the arms traversing the vertical shaft. Each arrastre is provided with four voladoras, and is worked by a team of two mules.

In certain districts, as at Real del Monte, basalt is sometimes employed for mullers, but, although sufficiently hard for this purpose, it has a very close grain, and consequently, when once it has become smooth, it passes over the ore without causing the grinding effect produced by porphyry, which being coarser in its texture, retains a good rubbing surface to the last. As soon as the bottom of an arrastre has been put in, a new voladora is set to work to grind cabecilla, to which a certain quantity of water has been added, and by which the interstices between the stones are gradually filled. This is continued with one muller during the first day, and on the second another is added, with which the operation is carried on until the end of the third day, when another grinding stone is attached, and the treatment of poor ores may be commenced. After the expiration of four or five days, the fourth stone is put on, and the surface of the grinders and of the bottom of the arrastres, having now attained their normal condition, ores of the usual degree of richness may be charged into the arrastre, and fine grinding carried on in the usual way.

Extraction of Gold.—In districts such as Guanaxuato, where the ores contain, in addition to silver, minute quantities of gold, the latter metal could often not be advantageously separated from the former if obtained together in the form of an alloy; but by keeping the arrastre constantly charged with a certain quantity of mercury, or with an amalgam of silver or copper, the gold is so concentrated in the resulting amalgam, as to afford highly profitable results. This method of effecting the concentration and extraction of gold appears to have been long employed in some of the mining districts of Mexico, but Humboldt states, that at the time of his visit to Guanaxuato in 1804, it had not been introduced into that neighbourhood.

At Guanaxuato, where the ore is more finely ground than in any other district in North America, an arrastre is charged with from six to eleven quintals of *granza* or coarse sand from the stamping mill, to which are added about ten gallons of water, which is sufficient to bring it to the state of a thick mud; and on the amount of water thus added, will very much depend the degree of fineness to which the ores can be reduced. If the arrastre be a new one, or one from which the amalgam has previously been removed, from five to ten pounds of silver amalgam are introduced. For this purpose some amalgamators prefer a very dry amalgam, whilst others employ a larger proportion of mercury; but it appears to be generally admitted that a tolerably dry amalgam is to be preferred, since, if it contained a large quantity of mercury it would be liable to run into the crevices of the bottom, and thus cease to be of any advantage to the operation. When, on the contrary, the amalgam made use of is moderately dry, it not only spreads itself over the surface of the bottom, under the influence of the grinding action of the voladoras, but is also believed to possess a stronger affinity for gold, and to form with it an amalgam more readily than pure mercury would under similar circumstances.

The arrastres used in the haciendas of Guanaxuato are in most cases charged each morning at four o'clock, when, as before stated, a barrel of water, containing about ten gallons, is introduced at the same time with the ore; at nine o'clock another barrel, or sometimes a barrel and half is poured in, and at twelve o'clock one barrel, at three o'clock three barrels, and at four, five barrels are added. The quantity of water used, will however somewhat depend on the nature of the ores operated on. As the operation of grinding progresses, the amalgam by degrees accumulates in the crevices in the bottom of the arrastre, and every alternate morning a small sample or *tentadura* is taken from the amalgam in the bottom of each arrastre, cleaned well by washing, and its condition carefully examined. Its dryness or moistness is judged of in accordance with its behaviour when pressed by the thumb against the side of the jicara containing it, and from the result thus obtained is estimated the amount of mercury, if any, that is required to be added to the arrastre previous to the next grinding. The usual amount of mercury added is about half a pound every second morning, although this will in a great measure depend on the richness of the ores that are being worked, but as a general rule the amalgam should not contain above twenty per cent. of gold and silver. The amalgam is usually removed from the arrastres every three months, but in some instances they are cleaned up at even longer intervals. At the expiration of twenty-four hours, when the grinding is completed, the *lama*, or slime, is baled out into a barrel, in which it is removed to reservoirs, formed in masonry, from which a portion of the water becomes evaporated by exposure to the sun and air, and leaves the mass in a fit condition for subsequent treatment in the patio. In some establishments, instead of the lama being transported in barrels to these reservoirs, it is baled into launders by means of which it is conducted to the proper receptacles; whilst in others it is tapped from a plug hole at the bottom of each arrastre directly into these launders. When the lama is dipped out in a batea, a plate of iron, or some other metal, is laid on the bottom of the arrastre for the purpose of preventing any of the rich amalgam from being scraped up by the batea and becoming mixed with the slimes; after this operation, which occupies at most about half an hour, is completed, the arrastre is charged with a fresh quantity of granza and the process of grinding is again proceeded with, as before described. The mules, by which the machine is worked, are changed every six hours, the arrastres being generally arranged in a double row on either side of a long shed or *galera*.

The augmentation of weight which takes place during the operation of grinding, and due to the wearing away of the voladoras and bottom of the arrastre, usually amounts to from eight to ten per cent. The bottom will often continue in good repair during twelve months, but the grinding stones or mullers seldom last beyond a month, and are sometimes worn out considerably within that time.

Raspar.—The removal of the amalgam from the arrastres is called the *raspando* or scraping, and takes place more or less often in accordance with the quality of the ores under treatment. The arrastres are, however, seldom cleared of amalgam more often than once in three months, and in some instances only once in six months. This is done by removing, with a hooked iron scraper, all the substances which have accumulated between the stones forming the bottom of the arrangement, and which consist of a mixture of coarse fragments of gravel, finely ground ore, and an amalgam of silver and gold. If the bottom of the arrastre has been entirely worn out it is removed, and every stone well scraped and cleaned, after which a new bottom is put in as before described.

The substance collected either by scraping out the interstices between the paving of the arrastre, or by cleaning every portion of stone forming part of the old bottom, is next carefully washed in bateas in a tank filled with water. For this purpose, a portion of the stuff to be washed is placed in the wooden bowl, and a little fresh mercury added to it, for the purpose of collecting the finer particles of amalgam, and preventing them, as much as possible, from being floated off on the water. In this way the principal portion of the amalgam is collected in the bowl, whilst some of the smaller particles, mixed with the lighter earthy impurities, become deposited in the bottom of the tank, from which they are subsequently removed for the purpose of being re-washed on an inclined table, called a *planilla*. The amalgam, after being collected and cleaned, is first freed from a portion of its mercury by straining through a leathern or canvas bag, and then retorted and sent to the Government Assay Office, where it is assayed and melted into bars, and then forwarded to the Mint, for the purpose of being converted into coin.

Loss of Gold.—The yield of gold obtained by this method of treatment is considerably less than the total amount contained in the ores, as indicated by assay; the loss experienced being generally believed to vary from 25 to 40 per cent. on the assay produce. Various circumstances contribute to produce this deficit in the gold. In the first place, there is always a loss of finely-divided amalgam during the process of washing up the various substances obtained by scraping the bottoms of the arrastres. Secondly, the silver subsequently extracted by amalgamation in the patio, invariably contains a small proportion of gold; and thirdly, the *polvillos* remaining from the washings of the *tortas*, and which principally consist of argentiferous iron pyrites, also retain a certain amount of gold. These polvillos, or *relaves*, are subjected to a process of roasting in a reverberatory furnace, and a second grinding in the arrastre, after which they are a second time subjected to the process of patio amalgamation.

Loss of Mercury in the Arrastre.—It was formerly believed that by the process of grinding the ores of silver and gold with mercury, those portions only of the metals which exist in the metallic state are obtained in the form of amalgam; but this is evidently not the case, since there can be no doubt that more or less of the sulphide of silver is always reduced to the metallic state at the expense of a corresponding amount of mercury, which is itself converted into sulphide. It is also generally well known to *azogueros*, or amalgamators, that to obtain a given weight of the precious metal by this process, a nearly equivalent quantity of mercury must be sacrificed, and this could by no means be accounted for, on the supposition of its uniting only with the free gold and native silver present in the ores.

The following figures are given by Napier as the result of an experiment made at one of the reduction works of Guanaxuato, and go to show that the loss of mercury is mainly due to its combination with sulphur, derived from the reduction of sulphide of silver:—

The amalgam added to an arrastre weighed 70 lbs., and was composed of 14 lbs. of silver combined with 56 lbs. of mercury.

The mercury added, exclusive of that in the amalgam, weighed	330 lbs.
Mercury in amalgam	56 „
Plata Mixta, gold and silver obtained, including silver added in form of amalgam	84 „
Weight of amalgam which should have been obtained	470 lbs.

The amalgam actually produced only weighed, however, 400 lbs., and consisted of 84 lbs. of gold and silver, and 316 lbs. of mercury, showing a loss of 70 lbs. on the total quantity of quicksilver introduced into the arrastre. The alloy obtained, consisted of 18 lbs. of gold, and 66 lbs. of silver; and as the gold, being in the metallic state, must have united directly with the quicksilver without entailing any loss of that metal, the deficit may be regarded as equal to the weight of the silver taken up, the slight excess of loss observed, being readily accounted for by mechanical loss in washing, and the escape of mercurial vapours during the subsequent process of retorting the amalgam. The ores of Guanaxuato contain scarcely any native silver, gold being practically the only metal present in the metallic state, and consequently the loss of mercury can only be ascribed to the reduction of sulphide of silver by mercury, and its gradual conversion into the sulphide of that metal.* When copper amalgam, instead of an amalgam of silver, is introduced into the arrastre, the copper gradually disappears, and is replaced by silver, the loss of mercury being at the same time less than under ordinary circumstances. When the ores to be treated do not contain a sufficient amount of gold to render its extraction a profitable operation, they are ground in the arrastre without the addition of mercury; and in some localities, as in Zacatecas, the grinding is not so long continued, and the ore is consequently reduced to a less finely divided state. In the locality last named, an arrastre of similar dimension to those employed at Guanaxuato, grinds ten quintals in the course of thirteen hours, but the resulting lama is much coarser, and it is probable that the less satisfactory results generally obtained in this district may, in a great measure, be attributed to that circumstance.

The Patio.—The patio is a large court-yard, generally paved with flagstones, of which the joints are carefully cemented in order to prevent the loss of mercury which would otherwise take place. This flooring has given to it a slight inclination, in order that any water falling on it may the more readily run off. In some cases, however, as at the hacienda of Regla, near the Real del Monte, a wooden flooring is employed instead of a stone one; and the patio, comprising an area an acre and a half in extent, is carefully covered with a wooden floor, on which a thousand tons of argentiferous slimes, mixed with thirty tons of salt, three tons of sulphate of copper, and eighteen thousand pounds of mercury, are constantly spread in different stages of the process of amalgamation. Wooden floors were also employed in the various reduction works near Virginia City, into which the patio process was introduced, but as the climate of Nevada was not favourable to this system of amalgamation, its use has, for the present, been discontinued. The following woodcut, Fig. 40, represents the patio at the Gould and Curry Works, near Virginia.

The ground slimes, on their removal from the arrastres or tahonas,

* The equivalent of silver being 108, and that of mercury 101, sufficiently explains why the loss of mercury should about equal the weight of silver taken up by that metal.

are deposited, in an almost liquid state, in walled receivers, called *cajetes* or *lameros*, where a portion of the water is removed by evaporation, and where it is allowed to accumulate until there is a sufficient quantity to form a heap or torta, which at Guanaxuato usually consists of sixty montones.* When the amount of lama necessary for a torta

FIG. 40.

PATIO AT THE GOULD AND CURRY, NEVADA.
(*From a Photograph.*)

has been collected in the cajete, it is carried out into an enclosure formed on the patio, about thirty feet in diameter, generally made by laying on each other square beams of wood, kept in their places by large stones, and made tight by filling the joints either with clay or horse dung. Into this the lama is introduced, until it forms a layer of about a foot in thickness, and is allowed to remain until by

---

* The weight of the monton varies in different localities—

In Guanaxuato a monton usually contains	32	quintals
„ Real del Monte, Pachuca, and Tasco .	30	„
„ Zacatecas and Sombrerete	20	„
„ Fresnillo	18	„
„ Bolaños	15	„

the evaporation of the water, it has gained the consistency of a rather thin mud. This condition being arrived at, the amalgamator proceeds to *ensalmorar*, *i.e.* from three to five per cent. of salt is added in accordance with its quality, and the nature of the ores under treatment. It is, however, well known, that the larger, up to a certain point, the proportion of salt employed, the more rapid will be the action of the torta, although many amalgamators never employ above three per cent. of this substance, notwithstanding that an additional two per cent. would have the effect of completing the operation at least six days earlier; but the time thus gained is not found to compensate for the extra expense entailed. When the salt has been added to the torta, it receives the first treading, or *repaso*, after which it is allowed to stand until the following day, when the whole of the salt will be found in a state of solution, and thoroughly and regularly mixed with the lama composing the heap.

Incorporar, &c.—The day after the salt has been thus mixed with the lama, the addition of magistral and mercury takes place. For this purpose the torta is, if necessary, brought to the proper consistency by the addition of water, and the magistral thrown evenly over its surface by means of wooden shovels. The proportion of this reagent to be added varies, to a certain extent, in accordance with its richness in sulphate of copper; but in the case of employing magistral of the usual strength, something less than one per cent. is generally found sufficient. As soon as the magistral has been spread over the surface of the torta, it is again trodden by mules for about an hour, when the mercury necessary for the completion of the operation is generally added, the quantity required being from 3½ to 4 lbs. for every mark of silver supposed to be contained in the heap. The introduction of mercury is effected by making it run through a linen cloth in such a way that its particles may be divided in the state of minute globules, and great care must be taken that the torta be not too wet, since in that case the mercury will be liable to collect in large masses. The lama should not, on the other hand, be too dry, as the mercury would then become very finely divided, and a considerable loss, both of that metal and silver, takes place in the washing up of the torta. The exact consistency to be given to the metalliferous mud, in order to obtain the best possible result, can only be determined by practice; but it should be in such a condition that the feet of the animals treading it may pass readily through it, and yet leave behind them distinct prints of their hoofs. After the addition of the mercury the torta is again trodden for about four hours, in order to effect its intimate mixture throughout the whole mass. When crystallised sulphate of copper is employed in lieu of magistral, from 7 to 9 lbs. are added for each ton of ore contained in the torta.

When the magistral and mercury have been added to the torta, and it has received the first treading, chemical action at once commences, and it becomes necessary that the azoguero should closely watch its operation, by taking frequent samples or tentaduras; the colour and general appearance of the mercury being the chief guides by which he is enabled to judge of the progress of the operation. Shortly after the *incorporo*, the azoguero takes a sample collected from thirty to forty different places, in the torta, and washes it carefully either in a jicara or in a horn spoon, similar to that sometimes employed for testing samples of gold quartz in California, and, after removing the earthy particles, carefully examines what remains, which consists of *polvillos*, or metallic sulphides and mercury. The latter at this stage of the operation contains but little silver, and its colour and state of division afford the only indications of the more or less satisfactory working of the torta. If the mercury be found divided into minute globules, or if its natural colour has been but little changed, except that it has acquired a slightly yellow tinge, it is considered a proof that a sufficient amount of magistral has not been added. When, on the contrary, the mercury is of a deep grey, or leaden hue, it is evident that there has been too large a proportion of magistral introduced into the torta, which is said to be *hot*, and it may be found necessary to add a little lime in order to prevent an undue loss of mercury. When the heap is in good working order, the surface of the mercury presents a distinct light grey appearance, and although it is of course desirable to at once introduce such a proportion of magistral as will immediately throw the torta into good working condition, it is better that the amount of this ingredient should be too small, than that it should have been added in excess. When the magistral has been added in proper quantity the appearance of the tentadura will, on the day after the repaso, be found to have considerably changed. The mercury, if now pressed with the thumb against the side of the jicara, or bowl, is found to contain silver amalgam, and what, at the first trial, appeared as *desecho*, or broken-up mercury, has now become *limadura de plata* of a whitish colour and in the form of thin scales, which, when rubbed, are found to consist of dry silver amalgam, or *pasilla*. When this makes its appearance shortly after the addition of magistral and mercury to the torta, it is a proof that the former has been added in proper proportion, and that the operation is progressing favourably.

To make a tentadura, a fair sample of about eight ounces, taken from different parts of the torta, is placed in a jicara, and slowly washed so as to remove the lighter portions only, leaving in the bottom the limadura de plata, the mercury with its *lista* or tail, and a portion of the heavy sulphide of iron. A little water is now taken in the jicara, and a peculiar motion given to it so as to arrange its contents in the following order: the limadura occupies the upper portion of the bowl, next come the sulphides contained in the ores, and last of all the mercury and amalgam, in the form of a large globule. As the most important indications are to be obtained from the condition of the limadura, this is first examined by holding the bowl in an inclined position in the right hand, whilst with the thumb of the left hand it is rubbed against the side of the vessel. Whilst this is being done, its colour is carefully observed, as well as the facility with which it can be converted into amalgam, and the consistency of the amalgam so produced. The metalliferous portions of the ore are generally passed over as not affording any information relative to the progress of amalgamation, but the globule of mercury at the bottom is examined with regard to its colour and the amount of amalgam it contains. The latter is determined by pressing it with the thumb against the side of the bowl. Three tentaduras are usually made on each torta daily; one in the morning before commencing to tread, another after it has been trodden for some time, and a third after the repaso has been completed. In selecting samples for the purpose of making a tentadura, it is necessary to take portions, not only from the surface of the heaps, but also from the interior, since the top from being exposed to the action of the sun and air is always in a more advanced condition than the middle of the heap.

The treading of a torta has the effect of stimulating the action of the magistral, and is repeated, every alternate day, as often as the tentaduras indicate a necessity for doing so. Formerly, the mercury was not all introduced at once, and after from fifteen to thirty days, according to the season, &c., it was found to be no longer in a liquid state, but had been wholly transformed into a dry amalgam from which quicksilver could no longer be obtained by pressure between the finger and thumb. A further addition of mercury, amounting to three-twelfths of the total quantity, was now made, which in the course of about ten days was, in its turn, converted into dry amalgam, when the last twelfth was added; and this was not, in most cases, entirely converted into solid amalgam. If, however, this took place, more mercury was added, until the further action of the torta had no longer the effect of converting it into solid amalgam, when the heap was said to be *rendido*, or to have yielded the whole of the silver which could be obtained from it. It is, however, now usual to add all the mercury immediately after the introduction of magistral.

If in the course of the operation it be observed that after repeating the repasos no augmentation takes place in the quantity of limadura and solid amalgam, the torta is said to be *cold*, and an additional amount of magistral is introduced, the process of amalgamation being subsequently continued until the desired effect has been produced. When, on the contrary, the mercury is covered by a dark grey coating, and the limadura is replaced by desecho and finely-divided mercury, the torta is said to be too "hot," and an addition is made of a little lime or wood ash, the treading being also suspended until it has been ascertained, by repeated tentaduras, that the torta has again recovered its normal condition. The azoguero never has, however, recourse to the introduction of lime or ashes except in extreme cases, since these reagents have the effect of retarding the operation, and decreasing the yield of silver, without effecting the revivification of the mercury already uselessly expended.

The amalgamators of Guanaxuato, when they are well acquainted with the nature of the ores under treatment, do not hesitate to work their tortas rather hot, and consider that by doing so they not only save time, but also obtain a larger yield of silver, without incurring a greater loss of mercury. At Zacatecas and Fresnillo, where the ores contain considerable quantities of mixed sulphides, it is customary to employ a larger proportion of magistral, particularly when a notable amount of galena is present. From this circumstance the mercury frequently presents an appearance which would cause much uneasiness to an azoguero of Guanaxuato, but when the torta shows symptoms of becoming too much heated, it is allowed to remain some days without treading, and after a time again falls into good working order without the addition of either lime or ashes. When the action of the torta has almost ceased, and nearly the whole of the silver which the process is capable of extracting from the ore, has been taken up by the mercury, the limadura becomes weak, and on being rubbed with the thumb shows but little solid amalgam. As soon as, on examination, it is found to be free from amalgam, and runs together in globules in the bottom of the jicara, the operation is generally considered finished, and the torta is said to be "rendido."

In some cases, however, the limadura may show signs of a torta being finished, when in reality such is not the case; and for this reason the ground sulphides or polvillos must also be examined by extending them over the interior surface of the jicara, and rubbing with the finger the small metallic globules with which they are mixed. If these readily unite into a large globule of running mercury, there can be no doubt that the torta is rendido; but if, on the contrary, they yield dry amalgam, such is evidently not the case, and the operation is further continued.

The amalgamators of the present day, however, do not entirely depend for their guidance on results obtained by washing, but also take an average sample from the torta, which being assayed, the total amount of silver contained in it can be readily calculated therefrom. Another weighed quantity of the same sample is carefully washed and the mercury and amalgam collected, which, on being assayed, afford a result from which may be calculated the total amount of silver which has been removed by amalgamation. In most instances, also, the mercury, instead of being added to the torta at different periods, is now all introduced immediately after the addition of the magistral.

Repasar.—The treading of the tortas is effected by means of mules or horses, the former being most frequently employed, and is repeated every alternate day until the operation is completed. The mules used for this purpose are tied together four abreast and blindfolded, one mule for every two montones of ore being required for the effectual treading of a heap. The operation is directed by a driver, who stands in the centre of the torta and guides the animals by means of a long halter, causing them to first tread at the edge, and gradually diminishes the radius of the circle described. In this way the circle becomes slowly diminished, and the thorough treading of the whole mass is thereby insured. This work, which commences at six in the morning, is generally completed about one or two o'clock in the afternoon; and in addition to the treading, each torta is turned over twice a week by means of wooden shovels. This operation is commenced immediately after the completion of the day's treading. In some instances, instead of entirely relying for the incorporation of the mass on the action of the feet of the animals, they are made to drag behind them a framework on wheels, which acts in the same way as the ordinary mortar mill. When this is employed it is attached to a long wooden arm revolving on a spindle in the centre of the torta, and in order to allow of the radius being gradually diminished, the arm is provided with slots, in which the central pin readily traverses; thus admitting of the circle described by the wheels being increased or diminished at pleasure. This arrangement is represented, Fig. 41.

FIG. 41.

PATIO AT GUANAXUATO.
(*From a Photograph.*)

The animals employed for the repasos are kept exclusively for that purpose, and, when they have finished treading, are at once taken to a large cistern, prepared for that purpose, and carefully washed. They, however, often lick themselves, on leaving the torta, probably for the sake of the salt contained in the mixture adhering to them, and consequently, when they die, a ball of amalgam is frequently found in their stomachs. These pieces of amalgam sometimes weigh many ounces, and are always exceedingly hard, and contain but a comparatively small proportion of mercury.

Washing.—When the operation of the torta is completed, and the whole of the silver which the process is capable of extracting has entered into combination with mercury, it is rendido, and a portion of fresh mercury, called a *baño,* is in some districts added to the heap; but this is not usually employed in the haciendas of Guanaxuato. The next operation is the separation of amalgam from the various earthy and metalliferous constituents of the torta by a process of washing, which, at Guanaxuato, is conducted as follows:—The *lavadero,* or washing apparatus, consists of three circular tanks, or *tinas* B, C, and D, Fig. 42, built close together in a circle, and con-

FIG. 42.

WASHING APPARATUS EMPLOYED AT GUANAXUATO.
(*From Tilmann.**)

structed of stone slabs, carefully cemented, in order to prevent loss of mercury. The depth of each of these tanks is 5 feet 4 inches, and its diameter 9 feet 6 inches. They are made to communicate with each other by means of an oblong opening, 8 inches in height, and 10 inches in width; of which the first is placed at a height of 8 inches,

* From "Bergbau und das Amalgamations-Verfahren in Guanajuato in Mexico, vom Königl. Preuss. Berg-Referendar E. Tilmann," Münster, 1866.

and the other at a distance of 30 inches, from the bottom of the tanks. In addition to these, the last tank is provided with two separate discharge holes; the first at a height of six inches from the bottom, and the other, which is only opened for the purpose of cleaning up, is situated close to the bottom. The diameter of the upper opening is about four inches, and that of the lower one inch.

In the middle of each tank is an upright wooden shaft, carrying four arms, furnished with wooden teeth, acting as agitators; the whole being set in motion by a central shaft A, provided with a spur wheel, working in pinions on the tina shafts; the central shaft, passing through the upper flooring, is turned by means of mules, attached to an arm fixed horizontally for that purpose.

The pinions giving motion to the agitators in the second and third tanks are a little larger than that working the stirrer in the first, and consequently their motion is somewhat slower.

The tank B, into which the metalliferous slimes from the torta are first charged, is called the *tina cargadora;* whilst the last D, from which they are run off after passing through C, is called the *descargadora,* or discharger. Before being taken to the lavadero, the torta is first divided into several parcels, each of which is softened by the addition of water, and subsequent treading, and then carried to the washing house in large bateas, dusted on the inside with dry horse-dung, in order to prevent loss. About three montones of lama are now measured, by means of large wooden bowls, and gradually introduced into the first tank, water being at the same time run in, and the machinery made to revolve rapidly by driving the mules at a gallop.

When the whole of the lama has been introduced, the speed of the machinery is gradually reduced, until the mules, which are specially trained for the work, move only at a gentle walk; whilst the azoguero from time to time dips out a portion of the slime, and washes it in a jicara, for the purpose of ascertaining if it still retains an appreciable amount of mercury, or whether it is sufficiently free from quicksilver and amalgam to safely admit of running off the earthy particles in suspension. When the washings of the samples taken from the tinas afford only minute metallic traces, the plug at some distance above the bottom of the descargadora is removed, for the purpose of discharging the slimes; and as soon as they have been run off, the plug is replaced, and the operation continued until the whole of the torta has been washed up. At Guanaxuato, the weight of the torta usually amounts to about 60 montones, although as many as 80 are occasionally treated at one time.

In addition to the amalgam which remains in the bottom of the tinas, there is also a considerable quantity of the heavier constituents of the ore treated. This residue, or *cabezilla*, contains a large proportion of amalgam, which is obtained by a subsequent washing. For this purpose it is removed in wooden bowls to a tank, called the *pila apuradora*, and thrown into large bowls or bateas. The *batea apuradora* varies from three to five feet in diameter, and floats on the surface of the water contained in the tank. The person using the batea leans over the side of the tank, and, with one hand on each side of the bowl, gives to it the peculiar washing motion, taking up a small quantity of water, which, after circulating round the edges of the vessel, is finally discharged, carrying with it a certain portion of the cabezilla. The deposit of finely-divided mineral remaining with the amalgam in the washing apparatus is, at Guanaxuato, generally about one-eighth of the total weight of the torta; and the relaves, resulting from its treatment by washing in bateas, are subsequently re-ground in arrastres. By this means they are made to yield a certain quantity of amalgam rich in gold, but are not generally a second time subjected to patio amalgamation.

The amalgam thus obtained is carried to the mercury-house, or *azogueria*, where it is deposited in a large stone trough; and as soon as the whole amount produced by a torta has been collected, a large quantity of pure mercury, together with a little water, is added. The mass is now well stirred by hand, for the purpose of causing the separation of impurities which gradually come to the surface, and which are, from time to time, wiped off by means of a woollen cloth. A small quantity of clean water is added after each removal of the impurities, and the operation repeated until the surface of the amalgam presents a bright uniform appearance; when, after being carefully wiped, it is ready for removal to the *manga*, or strainer.

At Zacatecas and Fresnillo the treatment of the ores in the patio is very similar to the process employed at Guanaxuato; but they are generally much less finely ground, and the washing up of the tortas is not similarly conducted. At Zacatecas, an arrastre of the same dimensions as those used at Guanaxuato is made to grind ten quintals of ore in the course of thirteen hours; and this difference in the fineness of the division of the lama in the two localities would lead to the conclusion that this circumstance may, to a certain extent, account for the less satisfactory results obtained at Zacatecas and Fresnillo. The azogueros of these districts, however, maintain that a more complete grinding of the ores would not sufficiently augment the returns to pay the extra expense incurred.

Instead of transporting, as at Guanaxuato, the lama containing the amalgam, in a nearly dry state, directly from the patio to the lavadero, the azoguero, as soon as he considers the torta to be rendido, adds a quantity of mercury, weighing about eighty per cent. of the amount previously employed for the extraction of silver; and, after giving it a repaso, it is carried to the washing house.

The washing is conducted, in the principal haciendas of Zacatecas and Fresnillo, in a single circular cistern of stone, nine feet in diameter, and seven feet in depth; and of which the bottom is generally made of a single stone, about ten feet in diameter, and a foot in thickness. Two of these tinas are placed side by side, in such a way that one vertical shaft, turned by mules, communicates motion to both; but no other connexion exists between them. The speed of the agitator is greater than that at Guanaxuato, and about two and a half montones of lama are passed through each cistern in the course of an hour. The violent agitation caused by the rapidity of the motion given to the arms, together with the great speed with which the slimes are passed through the apparatus, causes a considerable amount of amalgam to be carried off during the operation; in order to recover which, it becomes necessary to re-wash, by means of the planilla, the heavy residues collected outside the discharge orifice of the tina. The amalgam remaining in the bottom of the circular tank is deposited in an almost pure state, and does not generally require concentration by hand washing. The residues chiefly consist of iron pyrites and other sulphides, forming metalliferous sands, containing more or less silver, according to the nature and richness of the ores originally treated. These, when sufficiently rich, after being previously roasted in a reverberatory furnace, and again ground in an arrastre, are often a second time subjected to the patio process of amalgamation. This second treatment of the residues is found to consume a large quantity of quicksilver, and to afford only about one-half the total amount of silver which they contain; although some azogueros are of opinion that the loss of quicksilver is considerably reduced, and the yield of silver proportionately increased, by mixing them with from three to four times their weight of crude ore, as usually prepared for the patio. It is, however, probable that this mixture of fresh ores may only have the effect of so complicating the calculation of the result obtained, as to render it difficult to estimate, with any great degree of accuracy, the produce of the roasted residues.

Instead of effecting the washing in circular cisterns provided with agitators, this operation, in the districts situated nearest to the city of Mexico, is usually conducted in a wooden tank, which at one extremity is pierced with holes, which are placed at different heights from the bottom, and admit of being closed by plugs, whilst a constant stream of water is admitted at the other end. After this cistern has become nearly filled with water, the lama to be washed is thrown into it, and briskly stirred with shovels. When the ore has thus become well incorporated with water, the holes are successively opened; thus drawing off, at first, the lighter earthy matters, and subsequently the heavier metallic sulphides, until the amalgam remains in the bottom, in a state of considerable purity. After escaping from this box, the slimes pass for a distance of from sixty to eighty feet over inclined riffle boxes, by which a portion of the amalgam and mercury, which would otherwise be lost, is retained. This method of washing is generally considered more expensive, and to be attended with a greater waste of amalgam, than those previously described.

Filtration.—When the amalgam has been purified from the last adhering particles of mineral, by wiping with flannel, it is filtered through a cone-shaped bag, called a manga, Fig. 43, of which the upper portion is covered with leather, whilst the lower consists of strong, closely-woven canvas. This is hung by chains or cords from a stout beam, and when the mixture of mercury and amalgam is introduced, its weight causes a large portion of the quicksilver to escape through the meshes of the sail-cloth in a liquid form, and to fall into a vessel placed beneath it for that purpose. The amalgam, which is allowed to remain in the manga during a greater or less time, in accordance with the quantity operated on, finally assumes the appearance of fine sand, and is then ready for conversion into bricks, previous to distillation. This amalgam usually contains mercury to the amount of from five to five and a half times the weight of silver present. The proportions differ, however, in accordance with the quantities operated on; the relative amount of silver being greater when the weight of the mass is very considerable. The amalgam at the upper part of the filter is also always more argentiferous than that lying near the middle of the bag, whilst that at its lower extremity frequently does not contain above one-seventh part of that metal. In some cases the manga is made sufficiently large to contain from two to three thousand pounds of amalgam at a time; and when the weather is dry, and large quantities of mercury have passed through it, the apparatus frequently becomes highly electric, giving off sparks very freely to any conducting body that may approach it.*

The filtration of a charge usually occupies about two hours; and when the mercury has ceased to drip from the bottom of the bag, the manga is emptied on a table covered with leather, and the amalgam beaten into triangular bricks in iron moulds having the form shown, Fig. 44.

FIG. 43.

MANGA, OR STRAINER.
(*From Tilmann.*)

FIG. 44.

MOULD CONTAINING BRICK OF AMALGAM.
(*From Tilmann.*)

These bricks, or *bollos*, are each from three to four inches in thickness, and so shaped, that when six of them are placed together, they form a circular cake, leaving a round hole in the centre for the escape of mercurial vapours during the process of retorting.

Retorting.—This operation, by which the separation of mercury and silver is effected, is conducted by the aid of a large iron or copper bell, which is placed over the amalgam, and around which is kindled a charcoal fire. A circular tank of masonry is constructed below the floor of the burning-house, through which a stream of water is constantly caused to flow; and in this is placed an iron tripod, covered by a round plate, having a hole in its centre for the escape of mercury. On this plate are piled the bollos of silver, to such a height

* Duport, p. 269.

as to reach to within a short distance of the top of the bell, which, when placed over them, leaves a space of about an inch between its sides and the column of amalgam. When thus arranged, the bell (*capellina*) is lowered over it, and the bottom secured, either by lute or a water-joint, constantly supplied by means of a pipe. Unburnt bricks, or *adobes*, are now built around the arrangement in the form of a hollow wall, leaving an annular space between them and the bell, of about eight inches in width. This is filled with charcoal, which is ignited, and as the temperature increases, the mercury becomes volatilised, and, passing into the chamber below the floor, is condensed, collects in a liquid form, and escapes by an iron pipe into a proper receptacle. The fire is thus kept up during about fifteen hours; after which the apparatus is allowed to cool, and, when sufficiently cold, the bell is removed, either by a windlass or by means of simple blocks, as shown, Fig 45.

FIG. 45.

LIFTING THE CAPELLINA.
(*From Tilmann.*)

This silver, which is found to have assumed a porous structure, and a beautiful frosted appearance, is called *plata piña*, and is placed in leathern bags for removal to the smelting house, where it is assayed, and run into bars. The silver obtained by the patio process of amalgamation is in most cases very nearly pure, being generally above 990 fine; and in many cases, as at Guanaxuato, almost absolutely pure silver is obtained.

In some localities, the arrangements for retorting by the capellina are slightly varied from those above described, as shown, Fig. 46, in

FIG. 46.

CAPELLINA.
(*From Tilmann.*)

which the amalgam is supported beneath the bell B, on a stand A, enclosed in a cast iron vessel C, kept cool by means of a current of water constantly flowing beneath the bottom, and through the annular cavity D. The condensed mercury escapes, as soon as deposited, by means of a wrought iron pipe, into a proper receiving vessel. In some cases, the charcoal is retained in its place by means of a circular iron grating.

The interior measurements of the bell are usually as follow: height, 3 feet; diameter, 18 inches; thickness of metal, 1½ inches. The charge of amalgam is about 2,000 lbs., affording 400 lbs. of silver; the consumption of charcoal per charge is 500 lbs.

Loss of Silver.—The loss of silver by this process of amalgamation is considerable, but varies in different localities, in accordance with the nature of the ores operated on, and the degree of fineness to which they are reduced by grinding. At Guanaxuato, the average loss may be estimated, on docile ores, at from 10 to 14 per cent. At Fresnillo, the results of assays made during a year on ores containing a considerable quantity of galena, pyrites, and blende, as compared with those actually obtained from the patio, showed a deficit equal to 28 per cent. of the assay produce. According to Duport, the loss experienced on the ores from the Veta Grande, at Zacatecas, which contain a large amount of antimonial sulphides of silver, averaged from 35 to 40 per cent. of the produce, as indicated by assay. A portion of this loss is, however, mechanical, occasioned by particles of amalgam being carried off by the water employed for washing the lamas, after amalgamation; and a more efficient system of separation would, consequently, have had the effect of reducing the amount of silver so carried away. In some establishments, and particularly at Guadalupe-y-Calvo, the sulphides resulting from the ordinary process of washing in the lavadero are subsequently treated on shaking tables, and the results obtained are stated to be satisfactory.

Loss of Mercury.—It has been long established as a principle among Mexican azogueros, that, in order to obtain a given amount of silver by the process of patio amalgamation, it is absolutely necessary to sacrifice an equal weight of mercury. To this deficit of quicksilver they apply the name of *consumido;* whilst any excess of loss above this amount, and which is considered to be due to want of care, and mechanical causes, is called *perdida.* The total loss of this metal may be consequently divided into two elements, of which one is constant and the other variable, and to which different names are applied.

All calculations are made, in Mexico, with reference to the production of a mark of silver weighing eight Spanish ounces (3,550·5 gr.); so that, in case of the total deficit of mercury being twelve ounces per mark of silver, an azoguero would divide the loss as follows:—

Consumido	8 ounces	3,550·50 gr.
Perdida	4 „	1,775·25 „

It is, however, evident that this principle is not of universal application; since metallic silver, which occurs in considerable quantities in certain ores, combines directly with quicksilver, forming an amalgam of which the weight corresponds with the united amounts of the two metals weighed separately. The total loss of mercury varies in accordance with the nature of the ores, the method employed for washing the contents of the torta, and the greater or less proportion of native silver present. In many cases this loss does not exceed ten ounces per mark of silver, whilst in others as much as twenty-four ounces of quicksilver are expended for each mark of silver obtained.

The average loss may probably be taken to vary from ten to sixteen ounces per mark of silver extracted. The time necessary for working a torta varies, according to circumstances, from fifteen to forty-five days.

Fine Stamping.—At Real del Monte, where the Freiberg process of amalgamation in barrels is extensively employed, the ores are for this purpose reduced by wet stamping. The arrastre, although the slimy nature of the ore ground by it is well suited for patio amalgamation, yields a bad return for the mechanical power employed, and the slimes produced are not well adapted for the barrel process, for which fine sands are found preferable. The great augmentation of weight and bulk arising from the gradual wearing of the grinding-stones is also an objection to this apparatus, and it has consequently been found advantageous to grind the ores destined to be treated by the Freiberg process in ordinary stamping mills. Into these the ore is gradually fed by a hopper, a small stream of water being at the same time introduced, which, displaced by the successive falls of the heads, carries with it all the finer particles of ground ore which float over an inclined plane, whose height regulates the fineness of the grinding. The ground ore is subsequently conducted into large tanks, in which it becomes deposited; the water finally passing to a pump, by which it is elevated and returned to the stamps coffer, to again commence its duty as a sorter and carrier of the reduced ore. Thirty stampers, when driven with a velocity of from sixty to eighty blows per minute, grind weekly 100 tons of hard quartz to an exceedingly fine sand. The consumption of stamp heads, where such mills are employed, is necessarily very great, and to effect the annual reduction of 35,000 tons of ore at Real del Monte, not less than 60 tons of cast iron are expended; but as new heads can be obtained at iron works in the immediate vicinity of the mines, they are readily replaced at a moderate cost. In some localities in which water power is abundant, the ores are sufficiently reduced by the stamping mill to fit them for treatment in the torta without a preliminary grinding in arrastres.

Roasting.—The minerals destined for being worked by patio amalgamation are, in Mexico, seldom subjected to any preliminary treatment, with the exception of grinding; but in the case of highly-pyritous ores, they are sometimes partially roasted, for the purpose of removing the excess of sulphur. At Zacatecas, certain kinds of ore, after being broken into small lumps, are roasted in heaps, by mixing them with wood and covering the pile, which is surrounded by a wall of loose stones, with a layer of charcoal. This operation occupies but a few hours, and, after its completion, the ores are ground in arrastres, in the usual way. In the districts of Tasco, Sultepec, &c., where metallic sulphides are particularly abundant, the ores are, after grinding, generally roasted in the reverberatory furnaces employed in the preparation of magistral. The fuel employed for this purpose is wood; but although the roasting of a charge frequently occupies as much as twelve hours, but a comparatively small proportion of the sulphur is thus eliminated. The *marmajas*, or concentrated sulphides, obtained by washing on the planilla, are also roasted in the same way.

Chemical Reactions of the Patio.—The general opinion entertained by the various authors who had, previous to Sonneschmid, written on the subject of patio amalgamation, appears to have been, that in the different argentiferous ores, the silver was covered by various substances, such as sulphur, arsenic, and antimony, and that this covering prevented its forming an amalgam with mercury. The salt added to the torta was supposed to possess the property of removing these impurities from the surface of the silver; but this "clearing action" was thought only to be developed in presence of a sufficient amount of magistral, properly moistened, and which produced this effect through the agency of the heat produced. They also believed that for each mark of silver extracted an equal amount of mercury must necessarily be lost, and that any further expenditure of quicksilver in the progress of the operation was due to mechanical causes.

To Sonneschmid, who published his work entitled "*Tratado de la Amalgamacion de Nueva España*," in 1825, belongs the credit of first presenting a rational explanation of the nature of the reactions which take place during the process of patio amalgamation. This author, who, from his knowledge of chemistry and his long practical experience, was well fitted for the task which he undertook, refuted by unanswerable arguments the notions which had hitherto been entertained; and by means of a close examination on the one hand, of the various phenomena which present themselves during the progress of the operation, and by the aid of the light then recently thrown on the subject by the progress of chemical science on the other, propounded a theory which, with slight modifications arising from a more advanced state of chemical knowledge, is that generally entertained at the present day. According to Sonneschmid, that portion of the silver which exists in the ores in a native state is alone capable of uniting directly with mercury; and if, in grinding with this metal any ores which do not contain silver in the metallic form, a small quantity of amalgam be obtained, it is produced by the action of some substance which in presence of mercury has the property of reducing the silver existing in a state of combination. These compounds, as well as the native metals, are susceptible of conversion into "muriate of silver," under the influence of "muriatic acid" liberated by the action of the sulphuric acid of the magistral on a solution of common salt. The muriate of silver thus formed may be destroyed by the addition of alkaline earths, but the silver will then be converted into an oxide which has no longer the property of forming an amalgam with mercury. Further, that as certain metals have the peculiarity of separating others in a state of purity from the acids with which they are combined; mercury performs this part with regard to silver, by taking from it the muriatic acid by which a portion of it is destroyed, whilst the remainder forms an amalgam with the liberated silver. This reduction of silver by the action of muriatic acid on metallic mercury, together with the direct action of the same on that metal, are the two causes occasioning the loss of quicksilver; the direct action of the acid manifesting itself whenever it becomes necessary to make a further addition of magistral. The mercury lost remains in the residue, either in combination with muriatic acid, or in the metallic state; the former representing the deficit known as *consumido*, and the latter forming that portion of the loss classed as *perdida*.

It will be observed that according to this theory, the salt and sulphate of copper act only in furnishing the acids which they are respectively supposed to contain, and it remained for future observers, aided by a further development of chemical science, to point out the influence exercised by the sulphate of copper, as well as that of the common salt, as a solvent for the chloride of silver formed. Karsten first called attention to the fact that the addition of magistral caused the production of chloride of copper, by the aid of which the transformation of the sulphides of silver into chloride is chiefly effected, but without supporting his statement by any confirmatory experiment. The same chemist also pointed out the importance of the presence of a solution of salt as a solvent for chloride of silver, which is thus brought into intimate contact with mercury, at the expense of a portion of which it is decomposed, thus liberating the silver, previous to its entering into combination with the remainder. About the same period, Boussingault confirmed the statements of Karsten with regard to the formation of chloride of copper, and proved, beyond dispute, that this salt is abundantly produced during the process of patio amalgamation. The whole of the mercury by which the decomposition of chloride of silver is either directly or indirectly produced, appears to be converted into calomel, since no traces of the higher chloride have ever been discovered among the products of amalgamation by the patio.

The essential ingredients constituting a torta are salt, magistral, mercury, and sulphide of silver. Salt and the sulphate of copper in the magistral react on each other, giving rise to the production of chlorides of iron and copper, and sulphate of soda. The chloride of copper in its turn acts on the sulphide of silver, producing chloride of silver, which is dissolved in the excess of salt added to the torta; and the silver, finally reduced to the metallic state by a portion of the mercury which is ultimately converted into calomel, whilst the reduced silver enters into combination with the unattacked mercury, forming an amalgam. It has also been shown that the lower chloride of copper, formed by the action of sulphide of silver on the higher chloride, is dissolved in the solution of salt, and acts on another portion of sulphide of silver, also converting it into chloride, which is subsequently reduced by the mercury, and finally converted into amalgam. Boussingault has further proved that the copper of the magistral is ultimately to a great extent transformed into sulphide; sulphide of mercury is likewise occasionally found in the torta, and has, by some chemists, been supposed to be the result of the action of calomel on sulphide of silver, by which sulphide of mercury on the one hand, and chloride of silver on the other, would be produced. It is, however, probable that this substance may, in many cases, have been formed by the direct decomposition of sulphide of silver by metallic mercury, since it is well known that under certain conditions this action takes place. Messrs. Bowring and Uslar, both of whom were practically acquainted with the patio process of amalgamation, have contended that chloride of silver is not necessarily formed during its operation; but the various phenomena which they have brought forward in support of this view of the question, appear to be far from conclusive, and are all easily explained by the chloride theory, which is now almost universally received.*

* Some chemists are of opinion that the chlorination of the mercury is, at least partially, effected by the higher chlorides of copper and iron, and that the lower chlorides of these metals, in their turn, assist in the reduction of chloride of silver.

Cost and Results of Patio Amalgamation.—The results obtained by this process and the cost of the various operations will evidently depend, not only on the nature of the ores, but be also, more or less, influenced by numerous local circumstances connected with each particular district in which it is employed. Under such circumstances it would be impossible to furnish the various items of expense under any general heading, and we shall therefore give the results of this operation as obtained from the books of some of the most important establishments in which it is employed.

TABLE *showing the result of* 11 *tortas of Ore from the Mines of Cata and Secho, reduced in the hacienda of San Joaquin, Guanaxuato, Mexico.*

No.	Date, 1863.	Weight of Lama.	Salt.	Magistral.	Mercury.	Silver produced.	Mercury		Total loss of Mercury.	Days in Operation.	Number of Treadings.
							Perdida.	Consumido.			
		mon. qtls.	ar.	ar.	lbs.	marks.	lbs.	lbs.	lbs.		
1	May 13.	81 20	573	95	3,200	870	1	461	462	15	8
2	June 9.	80 02	480	117	3,100	848	196	436	632	21	12
3	July 2.	72 21	432	109	2,721	780	100	402	502	23	10
4	„ 23.	66 30	379	93	2,450	634	43	335	378	17	9
5	Aug. 14	67 29	306	84	1,936	553	11	292	303	22	10
6	Sept. 20	75 29	329	70	2,529	719	73	379	452	25	9
7	Oct. 9.	77 07	293	68	1,711	508	143	276	419	36	15
8	„ 30.	57 18	285	48	1,920	566	117	299	416	30	14
9	Nov. 25	79 00	480	60	2,839	816	151	427	578	32	15
10	Dec. 23.	80 12	400	56	2,548	736	96	403	499	38	16
11	Jan. 14.	44 28	270	33	2,238 } *	1,251	31	361	392	32	15
„	„ 24.	36 30	216	32	1,818 }		36	293	329	38	17
		821 02	4,443	865	29,010	8,281	998	4,364	5,362	27†	12½†

* One torta divided into two parts.
† Average.

Statement, *continued, showing the result of* 11 *tortas worked in* 1863, *at the Reduction Works of San Joaquin, Guanaxuato, Mexico.*

	Quantities.				Costs.				Produce.			Remarks.
	Ores.		Containing									
			Silver.	Gold.	Ores.	Working.	Raspa.*	Total.	Silver.	Gold.	Total Value.	
No.	cargas.	arrs.	marks.	grains.	dollars.	dollars.	dollars.	dollars.	marks.	grains.	dollars.	
1	770	13	1,028·58	38,817	4,816·54	3,182·88	....	7,999·42	869·90		7,247·75	Two of the arrastres used for grinding these tortas were charged with 4 lbs. of silver amalgam, and 41½ per cent. of the gold was obtained. (Nos. 1–3)
2	748	11	1,019·81	35,672	4,798·54	3,184·16	....	7,982·70	848·26		7,081·23	
3	718	04	929·37	39,807	4,358·04	2,814·18	....	7,172·22	780·15		6,513·15	
4	622	02	843·92	32,909	4,124·19	2,545·61	....	6,669·80	633·62		5,291·51	Two of the arrastres used for grinding these tortas were charged with 10 lbs. of copper amalgam; and each time it was found free from copper, some more of the same amalgam was added. Gold obtained = 62 per cent. (Nos. 4–11)
5	621	02	662·86	16,702	2,705·52	2,420·17	....	5,125·69	553·00		4,705·52	
6	691	05	919·74	24,696	4,128·60	2,752·52	....	6,881·12	718·92		6,061·17	
7	716	04	739·58	21,530	2,992·60	2,729·39	....	5,721·99	507·83		4,238·61	
8	526	04	743·10	32,323	3,484·22	2,164·74	....	5,648·96	565·59		4,722·00	
9	744	00	1,016·81	41,358	4,814·55	3,206·97	....	8,021·52	816·41		6,682·40	
10	747	00	960·10	27,276	4,467·94	2,951·49	....	7,419·43	786·12		6,144·66	
11	780	13	1,545·80	48,202	8,248·03	3,304·94	....	11,552·97	1,251·50		10,443·59	
								1,057·28				
	7,687	10	10,409·67	359,292	48,938·77	31,257·05	1,057·28	81,253·10	8,281·30		69,071·59	The salt employed contained about 85 per cent. of chloride of sodium; and the copper ore, used for preparing the magistral, 20 per cent. of copper. Loss of mercury perdida 3·44 per cent. Total loss of mercury per mark of silver 10·36 oz. *In the whole of these tortas copper amalgam was employed.*
	1st Raspa								145·98	47,443	2,538·24	
	2nd ,, ...								177·26	42,065	2,626·66	
	3rd ,, ...								159·84	19,439	1,828·35	
	4th ,, ...								298·37	37,958	3,448·97	
	5th ,, ...								173·59	22,552	2,083·16	
	6th ,, ...								219·45	33,562	2,711·60	
	Sundries								9·16	392	82·36	
									9,464·95	203,411	84,390·93	
	Loss								944·72	155,881	...	The loss of silver was 9·08 per cent.
	Total								10,409·67	359,292		
	Total Cost of 11 tortas								...	...	81,253·10	
	Profit								...	...	$3,137·83	

* The *Raspa* is that portion of the precious metals which is obtained by grinding with mercury in the arrastre.

TABLE *showing the results obtained at the Hacienda Nueva, belonging to the Fresnillo Company, during the years* 1840, 1841; *and including the first nine months of the year* 1842.*

Date.	Montones.	Silver.		Value.	Cost of Treatment.
		marks.	oz.	dollars.	dollars.
1840	31,995	147,851	3	1,293,675·12	664,274·13
1841	35,291	222,022	0	1,942,692·50	731,346·90
9 months of 1842	28,324	167,377	3	1,464,552·50	504,460·50
	95,610	537,250	6	$4,700,920·12	$1,900,081·53

These 95,510 montones = 85,366 tons of ore, produced 537,250 marks of silver, about 8,974,000 oz. troy; which gives a mean produce obtained by the process, of 0·0014 of the weight of the ores operated on.

The cost of treatment, per monton of 2,000 lbs.; the cost per monton, exclusive of the value of mercury expended; the average loss of mercury; and the average yield of silver, were as follow:—

Date.	Total Cost of Treatment, including Mercury.	Total Cost of Treatment, exclusive of Mercury.	Ounces of Mercury lost, per mark of Silver.	Mean Produce of Silver per Monton.	
	dollars.	dollars.	ounces.	marks.	oz.
1840	20·76	14·45	14·064	4	5·00
1841	20·72	13·46	12·312	6	2·25
9 months of 1842	17·02	11·75	11·875	5	7·25

Mean result of Patio Amalgamation at Real del Monte, 1864-5†:—

Regla hacienda, reducing yearly	51,300 cargas.
Loreto " " "	54,430 "
Total yearly	105,730 cargas.
Mean assay of ore thus reduced	15·5 marks per monton.
Mean produce	14·1, or 9·0 per cent. loss.

The mean cost of reducing these ores was—

Coarse crushing in dry stamps, and subsequent fine grinding in arrastres	1·9 dollars per monton.
Manipulation in Patio	4·5 " "
General expenses of management	1·2 " "
Repairs	1·2 " "
	8·8
Sulphate of copper (2 dols. per monton)	3·2
Salt (1·6 quintals per monton)	6·5
Quicksilver (11 oz. per mark, silver)	6·5
Total . . .	$25·0‡

* From Duport. † Furnished by Mr. Buchan.

‡ At Loreto, to this must be added the cost animal power in grinding.

Ore from Ophir Mine, Comstock, worked at Ophir Works, Washoe. Average cost per ton of working during eighteen months, ending June 1864.

PATIO

*From December 1st, 1862, to June 1st, 1864.**

	Labour.	Wood.	Salt.	Sulp. Copper.	Mercury.	Castings.	Material.	Horses.	Total.
	dollars.	dollars.	dollars.	dollars.	dollars.	dollars.	dollars.	dollars.	dollars.
Crushing .	2·68	1·85	...	...	...	0·85	0·22	...	5·60
Beneficiating	3·82	0·19	5·95	0·55	2·85	...	0·07	1·56	14·99
Washing up.	1·48	0·09	0·17	0·10	0·80	...	0·02	...	2·66
Total Cost .	7·98	2·13	6·12	0·65	3·65	0·85	0·31	1·56	23·25

AMALGAMATION BY HOT PROCESS.—This process for extracting silver from its ores is much less employed in Mexico than in some portions of South America, where the ores are more generally found suitable for this method of treatment. The only ores which can be advantageously worked by this process are such as contain a large proportion of native silver, or in which that metal occurs in the form of chloride, iodide, or bromide.

The ores worked in the *cazo* are almost invariably of the description known as colorados, which are, generally speaking, coloured red by an admixture of oxide of iron. These, after being roughly stamped in the usual way, are subsequently treated in the arrastre, but, as they are afterwards concentrated by washing, care is taken not to carry the grinding to such an extent as would cause a large portion of the finely-divided silver ore to be carried off in suspension by the water. This concentration is effected by means of the inclined plane, called a planilla, before mentioned as being employed for treating the residual matters resulting from the washings of the torta in the patio process of amalgamation. By this means the ore is reduced to about two per cent. of its original weight, and the lighter portions, thus removed by water, may, if found sufficiently rich, be subsequently treated by the patio process.

The cazo is a vessel formed either of curved blocks of stone, or of wooden staves, like those of a barrel, and of which the bottom is made of copper.

The dimensions are usually as follow:—diameter at top, 3 feet,

* Furnished by Mr. W. W. Palmer.

3 inches; diameter at bottom, 2 feet; depth, 18 inches. The bottom, which, as before stated, is of copper, has, when new, a thickness of 2½ inches, but becomes gradually thinner by use. This is retained in its place by a groove running around the interior of the vessel, near its lower extremity; all the joints being carefully luted with clay, with which the sides of the apparatus are thickly plastered, and which is kept in its place by an exterior wall of unburnt bricks. The copper bottom of the cazo rests on the wall of the hearth, thus forming the roof of a fireplace which has neither fire-bars nor chimney; and is provided with but one opening, which serves, at the same time, for the introduction of the fire, and the escape of the products of combustion. The fire is lighted, and a sufficient amount of water poured into the vessel to form, with the ore subsequently added, a very liquid paste. When the temperature of this mixture has reached the boiling point, and it has become strongly agitated by ebullition, salt is added, in proportions varying from five to ten per cent. of the weight of the ore operated on. It is, however, necessary not to introduce the salt until the contents of the cazo are in active ebullition, since it would otherwise form, with the ore, a compact mass, adhering firmly to the copper bottom, from which it could not be removed without emptying the apparatus.

As soon as the salt has been added, a workman, who squats on the side of the cazo, continually stirs its contents by means of a wooden agitator, with which he constantly rubs the copper bottom; and at this stage the first addition of mercury is made. The amount of that metal employed is carefully regulated according to the richness of the ore under treatment, and should never exceed twice the weight of the silver it contains. At first, one-fourth only of this quantity is added, and, about a quarter of an hour after its introduction, the workman takes a sample, by means of a bullock's horn attached to a wooden handle, with which he scrapes the bottom of the boiler so as to obtain a small quantity of the heaviest portions of the ore and amalgam. By washing this in a horn spoon, he afterwards removes the lighter constituents of the mixture, and exposes the amalgam, which, if the operation is progressing favourably, should present the appearance of finely-divided granules, of a light lead-grey colour. The amalgam in this state is called *polvo*, and it is known by experience that it then contains one-third of its weight of silver, or, in other words, that about two parts of quicksilver are united with one part of silver.

More mercury is subsequently added, and other samples taken, until it is found that the hardness and state of division of the amalgam begin to change, when the operation is considered to be terminated; but, before stopping, the workman makes another trial, called a *prueva en crudo*. For this purpose he washes a portion of the amalgam in such a way as to entirely remove all traces of mineral, and, after adding a little clean mercury, and rubbing the mixture with his fingers, he observes whether the quicksilver thus added becomes solidified. Should this be the case, he introduces a further portion of mercury, and continues the operation; since he has thus learnt that this metal has not been added in sufficient quantity to extract the whole of the silver which the process is capable of affording. When, on the contrary, the mercury introduced retains its fluidity, the liquid contents of the cazo are dipped out into reservoirs, whence they are subsequently removed, to be added to the ingredients of a torta; whilst the solid deposit of ore, which contains the amalgam, is stored in wooden cisterns, from which it is afterwards taken, for the purpose of being washed in large bateas. Before washing this deposit, an amount of mercury is added to it nearly equal to that which has been employed in the cazo, in order to produce a less dry amalgam, which, becoming united in a mass, is no longer so liable to be carried off in suspension with the mineral and earthy residues. The exact consistence which should be given to this amalgam, in order to avoid loss, is a matter of considerable importance, since, if too dry, a portion of it is readily carried away by the water; if, on the other hand, the amalgam be subjected to the process of washing in a liquid state, it is liable to be projected over the edge of the batea by the oscillation necessary for the removal of the various metallic sulphides with which it is more or less mixed. The cazo, which is the apparatus described by Alonzo Barba as that employed in his time for the amalgamation of silver ores, by the aid of heat, has, in the district of Catorce, been much enlarged, and, under the name of *fondon*, is extensively employed in some important metallurgical establishments.

The diameter of the copper bottom of the fondon varies from 5 feet 6 inches to 7 feet 6 inches; and, instead of the necessary friction being produced by the action of a wooden stirrer, worked by hand, it is obtained by means of an upright shaft, provided with cross-arms, to which are attached rectangular blocks of copper, set in motion by a mule, harnessed to a prolongation of one arm. This apparatus may therefore be regarded as an arrastre, in which the paving and stone voladoras are both replaced by metallic copper; and beneath the bottom of which is a fireplace, similar in all respects in its construction to that built below the ordinary cazo. In one of the sides of the fondon is an orifice on a level with its bottom, which, during the working of a charge, is closed by a plug; the removal of which allows its contents, both liquid and solid, to be drawn out into tanks, in which the heavier matters are allowed to settle, previous to being washed.

The weight of the charge, which for the cazo seldom exceeds 100 lbs., is in the case of the fondon increased to from 1,200 to 1,500 lbs. The time necessary for working this amount is six hours, being the same as that employed to work 100 lbs. in the ordinary cazo. The fuel employed consists of the wood of the palm-tree, which, from its small density, burns rapidly, and produces a large amount of flame. The amalgam obtained by washings is treated precisely like that resulting from the patio process; but the silver produced in this way invariably contains a little copper, which, at Catorce, is removed by cupellation with lead, in a furnace called a *galeme*.

The slimes separated from the amalgam by washing are, together with the residues from the cazo, treated by the patio process. In order to prevent adherence of the mercury or amalgam to the copper bottom of the apparatus, the workmen take care to always employ a less amount of quicksilver than would be necessary to form an amalgam with the whole of the silver present; but this is of comparatively little importance, since the whole of the residues of the operation are re-treated in the way above described.

By this process, the silver existing in the native state, as well as the chlorides, iodides, and bromides of that metal, is readily reduced; but this is not the case with regard to the sulphides, and it consequently becomes necessary, in order to obtain the silver which they contain, to have recourse to the supplementary treatment by the patio. In working such residues, however, the addition of magistral is not required, since they contain a sufficient amount of chloride of copper to convert the whole of the sulphides of silver into chloride.

The loss of mercury experienced during the treatment of silver ores in the cazo or fondon is extremely small, as at the close of the operation a weight of amalgam is obtained which, deducting the silver it contains, corresponds with the quantity of mercury originally employed; but this amalgam, in addition to silver and mercury, contains a little copper, and the total loss, which is purely mechanical, may be taken as being between two and three per cent.

By this process, the chlorides and other analogous compounds of silver are evidently not reduced, as in the patio, by the action of metallic mercury, but by the copper furnished by the bottom of the apparatus; and even if it be admitted that this reaction gives rise to the production of the higher chloride of copper, which has, under certain circumstances, a chlorinising action on mercury, this could not take place in the presence of the excess of metallic copper furnished by the bottom, which would at once transform into the lower chloride any of the higher chloride of copper which might be produced. If, in treating ores by this process, the quantity of mercury added be so great as to be attended with the adherence of the amalgam to the copper bottom, the operation is found to proceed very slowly, and a great loss of mercury is the result; as, under these circumstances, the chlorides, iodides, or bromides, present in the ore, being cut off from direct contact with the metallic copper, are reduced at the expense of quicksilver. The most important condition necessary for the economical working of the cazo is to keep its bottom constantly free from any adherence of quicksilver or amalgam; and when the amount of mercury added does not exceed twice the weight of the silver present, there is no danger of any inconvenience arising from this cause. With even twice this amount of mercury, Duport states, he was enabled to work without inconvenience; but the moment that proportion was exceeded, the amalgam attached itself firmly to the copper plate, and a large loss of mercury was the result.

Although this process of amalgamation is only adapted for the treatment of colorados, which contain chloride and other analogous salts of silver, it has sometimes been applied to the reduction of the negros, in which the silver exists in the form of sulphides. Under these circumstances, it becomes necessary to make an addition of magistral, which causes a most destructive action on the mercury present, and which is, apparently, not modified by the presence of the bottom of metallic copper, since this loss of quicksilver often exceeds four times the weight of the silver obtained.

At Catorce, the poorer ores, after being previously concentrated by the planilla, were, according to Duport, in 1843, treated in the cazo, at a total cost of one dollar six reals per carga of 300 lbs.

The richer class of ores, on the other hand, which it was not necessary to wash, but which required fine grinding and great care in working, was operated on in the fondon at an expense of two and a half dollars per carga.

The loss of mercury was estimated at two per cent., and the silver obtained contained about one per cent. of copper.

ESTUFA AMALGAMATION.—In some of the colder and more humid districts of Mexico, a modification of the patio process has been employed. The ground ore, instead of being exposed in the open air, on a paved court-yard, as in the ordinary patio process, is placed under a shed, and the usual method of patio amalgamation proceeded with, until the operation is about half completed. The ore is then removed into a sort of room, termed an *estufa*, or stove, which has under it a fireplace, six or eight feet long, so connected by side flues with small chimneys as to elevate the temperature of the room containing the ore. Here it is exposed to a gentle heat, and allowed to remain during two or three days, when it is again removed, and the reduction completed by the ordinary method of patio amalgamation. By this process, the time required for the reduction of the ore is less than by the patio, and the yield of silver greater; the loss of mercury, on the other hand, is more considerable.

CHAPTER XVII.

TREATMENT OF SILVER ORES BY AMALGAMATION—BARREL PROCESS.

FREIBERG—BARREL AMALGAMATION—WHEN INTRODUCED—COMPOSITION OF ORES—CHLORINATION—AMALGAMATION—DISTILLATION OF AMALGAM—REFINING—CONSTANTE—GRINDING CRUDE ORES—CALCINING WITH SALT—SIFTING AND GRINDING—AMALGAMATION AT CONSTANTE—TREATMENT OF AMALGAM—MELTING AND REFINING—TREATMENT OF RESIDUES—COST OF TREATING ORES AT CONSTANTE—COST AT REAL DEL MONTE—THE BARREL PROCESS IN NEVADA—METHOD OF CONDUCTING, AND COST OF OPERATION.

THE first works erected in Europe for the treatment of silver ores by amalgamation appear to have been those described by Schlüter as having been put up at Kongsberg, for the purpose of treating the stamped ores of that district. This apparatus consisted of eighteen small cylindrical vessels, arranged in a circle, in which the ores were mixed with mercury and kept in a state of constant agitation by means of a vertical spindle in each tub, the whole being worked by a large horizontal toothed wheel placed in the centre. It was not, however, until the latter part of the century that the attention of mining engineers on the continent of Europe became particularly directed to the process of amalgamation. In the year 1780, the Baron de Born suggested to the Austrian Government the propriety of adopting this system in the mining districts of Hungary; and, at his solicitation, some experiments were instituted at the Glashütte Works near Schemnitz. Although these trials were not followed by the introduction of this system of amalgamation into the Hungarian mines, they, nevertheless, gave rise to many valuable discoveries, of which the Saxon Government, which had deputed a commission to attend on De Born, availed itself in the erection of the works at Freiberg.

FREIBERG.—The first works were erected at Freiberg in the year 1790, under the direction of M. de Charpentier, but these were destroyed by fire shortly after their completion. The existing amalgamation works, commenced immediately after the destruction of the former, were completed in 1794, and finally closed about the year 1856.*

The amalgamation of silver ores was perhaps at one time more economically conducted at the Halsbrücke works, in the vicinity of Freiberg, than in any other European establishment.

Composition of Ores.—The usual constituents of the ores treated, were sulphur, antimony, arsenic, silver, copper, lead, iron, and zinc, which were more or less mixed with various earthy minerals; besides sometimes containing traces of bismuth, gold, nickel, and cobalt. In selecting these ores, they were so assorted as not to contain above four per cent. of lead or one per cent. of copper, as from combining with the mercury added, these metals gave to the amalgam produced a spongy consistency, and thereby rendered the treatment difficult and expensive. The different ores selected for amalgamation varied in produce from 15 to 200 oz. of silver per ton, and formerly the mixtures were so arranged that the charges of the furnaces should contain from 75 to 80 oz. per ton. Latterly, however, it was usual to work the poorer and richer ores separately, as it was found that the loss of silver in the residues was thereby considerably diminished.

The mixtures of the poorer ores afforded, on an average, from 30 to 40 oz. per ton, whilst the amount of silver in those of the richer ores varied from 90 to 130 oz. per ton. It is essential that all mixtures of ores should contain a certain proportion of sulphide of iron for the formation of sulphates, the presence of which is necessary to the success of the operation of roasting: the quantity of sulphide of iron present should, generally speaking, be about twenty-five per cent. If the amount of pyrites naturally occurring in the ores was not equal to this proportion, addition was made either of that mineral, or of crude sulphate of iron. Sometimes, however, the ores at Freiberg contained more iron pyrites than was necessary to the success of the operation, and in such cases it was found advantageous to subject the more sulphurous of them to a preliminary roasting without addition of salt, and thus reduce the average amount of sulphur in the mixture to the right proportion.

Chlorination.—The ore, properly selected, was laid on a large floor forty feet in length by twelve in width, and on the top of it was

* The ores formerly treated at Freiberg by amalgamation are now, to a great extent, smelted with galena, and the silver extracted by crystallisation and cupellation.

thrown about ten per cent. of common salt, let down from an upper room by means of spouts placed in the floor for that purpose. The heap thus made up of alternate strata of ore and common salt, was well mixed, by being carefully turned over, and then passed through a coarse sieve. It was subsequently divided into small parcels or charges, weighing from 4½ to 5 cwt. each. The salt employed for this purpose was supplied by the Prussian salt mines. The mixture of ore and salt was now roasted in reverberatory furnaces, provided with fume flues for the reception of the pulverulent matters mechanically taken over by the draught. The prepared charge had now to be spread on the bottom of the hearth and gently heated, for the purpose of expelling the moisture, which, to a greater or less extent, it invariably contained. During the process of drying, usually occupying from twenty to thirty minutes, the charge required to be kept constantly stirred with a long iron rake. The lumps formed during this operation must also be broken down by means of a beater provided with a long iron handle. On the temperature being subsequently raised, white fumes were given off, and in about two hours from the commencement, the whole mass had become redhot. The charge was likewise occasionally turned, so that every particle of ore might be equally exposed to the action of the fire, and during the whole time the mass required to be diligently stirred with the rake. The fire was then left to burn down, and the combustion of the sulphur promoted by constant stirring. This went on without intermission, until the interior of the furnace had become dark red, and a sample taken from the mass no longer evolved any odour of sulphurous acid. During this process the ore increased considerably in volume, and the particles cohered so loosely together as to offer but little resistance to the movements of the rake.

After this the heat was again raised during about three-quarters of an hour; the sulphate of iron, formed by the oxidation of pyrites, thus reacted on the common salt, causing, in the presence of peroxide of iron, the evolution of chlorine and hydrochloric acid gases, which, coming in contact with the sulphides of silver, rapidly converted them into chlorides. Chlorides of the other metals present were at the same time formed, together with sulphate of soda. When this roasting was terminated, the charge was raked from the furnace into an iron barrow and removed to an adjoining floor. The ore was subsequently raised to an upper story for the purpose of being passed through a set of sieves, with the view of separating the finer powder from the agglutinated lumps. The latter were broken down to a proper size, and a portion re-roasted, by adding a small quantity to each of the subsequent ordinary charges. The remainder was mixed with from two to three per cent. of salt, and calcined in the usual way. The finer particles, which passed through the sieves, were, on the contrary, ground between heavy millstones, by which they became reduced to the state of an impalpable powder.*

After roasting, the ores, besides various earthy salts, chiefly consisted of peroxide of iron, basic sulphate of iron, the chlorides of iron and copper, and a certain proportion of oxide and sulphate of copper, sulphate of lead, oxides of antimony and zinc, and a small quantity of various metallic sulphides in addition to sulphate of soda, and the excess of common salt employed. The different compounds of silver originally present in the ores were thus converted into the chloride of that metal, with the exception of traces of metallic silver, and perhaps, also, of minute quantities of sulphide and oxide of silver. The charge suffered in roasting a considerable diminution in weight, generally amounting to about ten per cent.; this loss being chiefly due to the escape of sulphur, chlorine, and the volatilisation of common salt, zinc, antimony, arsenic, and the chlorides of iron and copper.

Amalgamation.—The amalgamation of the roasted ores was at Freiberg conducted in twenty wooden casks, arranged in four rows, and turning on cast iron axles secured to the ends by means of bolts. These barrels, which were internally two feet eight inches in length, two feet eight inches in diameter at the ends, and two feet ten inches in the middle, were made of pine wood three and a half inches in thickness, and strengthened by iron hoops and binders.† On one of the ends of each tun was placed a toothed wheel working in a pinion keyed on a shaft receiving its motion directly from a water-wheel. The general arrangement of these barrels is represented, Figs. 47, 48.

Above each of the tuns so arranged, was placed a wooden box C, Fig. 47, into which was thrown the roasted ore.

At the bottom of this was a spout terminating in a hose *h*, made of strong canvas, finishing with a cylinder of tin plate, for the purpose of introducing the powdered ore into the different barrels B. Each

* The crude ores were not crushed at the works, but at the mines, where they were often enriched by mechanical treatment.

† At Constante, and at the different works in Nevada, the barrels are perfectly cylindrical in form.

cask was furnished with a circular opening *a*, five inches in diameter, fitted with a wooden plug, through which was bored a small hole

FIG. 47.

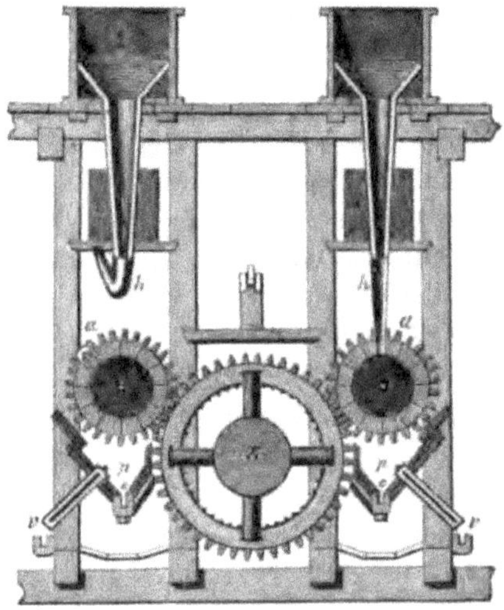

AMALGAMATING BARRELS.
(*Sectional Elevation.*)

FIG. 48.

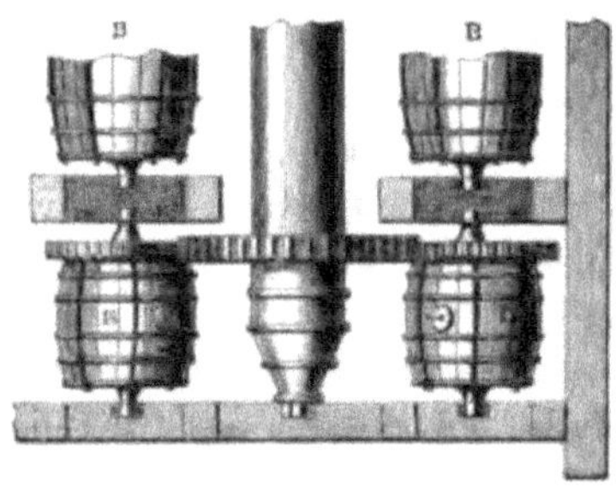

AMALGAMATING BARRELS.
(*Plan.*)

provided with a pin, made of hard wood, for the purpose of running off the argentiferous mercury at the termination of the process.

Below the tuns, and a little above the level of the floor, were placed triangular troughs destined to receive the residual matters at the termination of the operation. Before charging the barrels, 3 cwt. of water were run from the vessels E, exactly holding that quantity, into each; after which 10 cwt. of finely-ground and sifted ore were introduced through the hose *h*. Each cask should also contain from 80 to 100 lbs. of wrought iron, cut into fragments of about an inch square and three-eighths of an inch in thickness, which, in proportion as they become dissolved by the action of the substances with which they are associated, require to be replaced by fresh pieces. As soon as the barrels had been charged, and the bungs firmly secured in their places by binding screws, the apparatus was thrown into gear, by a screw acting on a sliding pillow-block, and made to rotate with a rapidity of from twelve to fifteen revolutions per minute. At the expiration of two hours the barrels were in succession stopped for the purpose of examining the state of the metalliferous paste which they contained. If the charge was too firm, a little water was added; but if, on the contrary, it was too soft, a small quantity of ore was introduced. When this had been attended to, five cwt. of mercury were drawn off into each cask, and the tuns, after being securely closed, again thrown into gear and kept constantly revolving for about sixteen hours, at the uniform rate of thirteen turns per minute.

During the first eight hours of this period they were, at Freiberg, twice examined for the purpose of ascertaining whether the paste was of the proper consistence; for if too thick, the mercury becomes very finely divided, and if too thin it remains at the bottom, and does not become sufficiently incorporated with the various constituents of the charge. In the first case it is necessary to add a small quantity of water, and in the second a little roasted ore. After the introduction of mercury, the temperature becomes considerably raised by the chemical changes constantly going on, so that, even in winter, it sometimes reaches 104° Fahr.

At the expiration of eighteen hours the amalgamation was in this establishment ordinarily complete, and the tuns were then filled with water, and again made to revolve, during from one and a half to two hours, with a velocity of only six or eight revolutions per minute. By this means the mercury was separated from the slimes with which it was mixed, and became collected in one mass at the bottom of the tuns. When this union of the globules of mercury had been accomplished, the different casks were successively thrown out of gear, and stopped with the apertures uppermost. The small peg in the bung was now removed, and in its place was inserted an iron pipe, to which was attached a small hose with a screw and clasp, for the purpose of closing it when required. The cask was then so turned that the plug should be immediately over the spout *o*. The hose being put into the iron tube *p*, the mercury was allowed to run off into the gutter *v*, by which it was conducted to a receiver prepared for that purpose. This period of the operation was closely watched by the workmen, who, the moment any of the earthy matters began to flow from the orifice, at once closed it tightly. The barrels were now turned with the apertures *a* upwards, the small hose plug removed, and the large bung loosened by a few taps with a mallet. The barrels were subsequently turned mouth downwards, the bungs withdrawn, and the muddy residuum discharged into troughs situated immediately under them, from whence it flowed into large washing vats, or tinas, placed on the ground-floor below the barrels. In the course of fourteen days 180 tons of mineral were treated in this establishment, every ton of which required an expenditure of 3 lbs. of metallic iron, and 8·95 oz. of mercury, so that every pound of metallic silver produced was obtained at an expense of $\frac{85}{100}$ths of an ounce of quicksilver.* The loss of silver experienced amounted, on an average, to from seven to nine per cent. of the total amount present, as indicated by assay, but the latter figure may be taken as most nearly approximating to the mean result.

During the first two hours that the casks were set in motion, before the introduction of mercury; the chlorides contained in the roasted ore were thus reduced to the state of minimum chlorination, the saline matters dissolved by the water present, and the particles of chloride of silver exposed. If, instead of this, the mercury had been immediately introduced into the barrels, it would, by reacting on the sesquichloride of iron, &c. have become partially converted into calomel, which not being again reduced, during the subsequent stages of the operation, would have resulted in a considerable loss of that metal. This loss is, however, avoided by the action of metallic

* Winkler states the loss of mercury at Freiberg to have averaged during five years 1·41 loth, or $\frac{3}{4}$ ounce nearly per centner of ore, assaying 3 to $3\frac{1}{2}$ oz. of silver; and 3·57 loth, or $1\frac{3}{4}$ oz. per mark of silver produced.

Subsequently, however, a great reduction in the loss of mercury was effected. In 1853 the amalgamation master stated the loss was then scarcely $\frac{1}{2}$ oz. per mark. We cannot, however, vouch for the accuracy of this assertion, and our own experience would lead us to somewhat doubt its correctness.

iron, since the protochlorides thus formed are without action on metallic quicksilver. The chloride of silver contained in the roasted ores is, in the Freiberg process, decomposed by agitation with metallic iron, the chlorine combining with it to form protochloride of that metal, whilst the reduced metallic silver becomes subsequently dissolved in mercury. The chlorides of lead and copper which may be also present, are reduced at the same time as the chloride of silver, and enter into the composition of the amalgam produced.

Treatment of Residues.—The residues conducted to the washing vats before mentioned, were mixed with an additional quantity of water, and kept constantly stirred by agitators attached to iron arms worked by an upright shaft in the centre of each vat, which received its motion from a small water-wheel. These vats were furnished with openings, at various distances from the bottom, through which the tailings, held in suspension by the water, could be successively drawn off into tanks, in which they were allowed to settle. When these residues contained more than four and a half ounces of silver per ton, they were removed to a drying floor, and subsequently re-roasted with from fifteen to sixteen per cent. of iron pyrites, and from five to six per cent. of common salt. These calcined residues were sifted in the usual way, and then, without being re-ground, subjected to amalgamation in barrels for a somewhat shorter period than was customary in the case of ordinary ores.

The mercury collected in the bottom of the different washing vats was drawn off every five or six weeks, and from the large proportion of base metals which it contained, it was treated apart from the ordinary amalgam produced in the usual manner. The mercury and amalgam obtained by tapping the barrels, were afterwards filtered through close canvas bags in the ordinary way. The amalgam which was retained in these bags consisted of a mixture of six parts of mercury and one of an alloy composed of about eighty per cent. of silver, and twenty of a mixture of copper, antimony, zinc, lead, and some other metals.

Distillation of Amalgam.—The amalgam, after being well pressed, was subsequently heated in iron retorts placed in suitable furnaces, and the mercury separated by distillation from the non-volatile metals which were obtained in the solid form. Three retorts were latterly employed for this purpose, and into each were introduced, on iron dishes, 350 lbs. of amalgam; usually resulting in the production of about fifteen per cent. of retorted silver at the close of the distillation, which generally occupied ten hours. The base metals contained in the alloy of silver thus produced, were, with the exception of a certain proportion of copper, removed by a process of refining in a large iron crucible, which was conducted in the following way.

Refining.—The crucible was first placed in the furnace and made red hot, when the lumps of silver were successively introduced and brought to a state of fusion. Powdered charcoal was then thrown on the surface of the fused metal, and the crucible temporarily covered with a thin plate of iron. This, after the lapse of a few minutes, was again removed; and the impurities which had risen to the surface, were, together with the unconsumed charcoal, skimmed off by means of a perforated ladle. More powdered charcoal was then thrown on the fluid metal, and the scum removed as before. These operations were repeated, with occasional stirrings of the metallic bath, until the surface of the metal had become bright and clean. This process occupied from six to eight hours, and when completed the metal should be malleable and dissolve completely in nitric acid, to which the addition of an excess of ammonia should impart a clear blue colour free from turbidity. The silver was afterwards cast into ingots of a semi-hemispherical form, and in that state forwarded to the Saxon Mint. The dust removed from the furnace flues was, at Freiberg, after being sifted, mixed with, and treated as, ordinary silver ore. The slags and sweepings from the various melting operations, were crushed and afterwards fused with carbonate of soda and nitre, by which means the silver was obtained in the metallic state. The water run off from the tanks in which the residues from the tinas were allowed to settle, contained, in solution, a considerable amount of common salt and sulphate of soda, together with small quantities of sulphate of iron, and various other soluble salts.

BARREL AMALGAMATION AT CONSTANTE, SPAIN.—The ores treated at Constante are obtained from the mines of Hiendelaencina, and contain silver in various states of combination, but principally in the form of antimonial sulphides disseminated in gangues, chiefly consisting of sulphate of baryta, together with a small proportion of quartz, accompanied by considerable quantities of carbonate of iron, which chiefly occurs in the richer portions of the veins.

In addition to the sulphides of antimony, arsenic, &c., in combination with sulphide of silver, the ores contain iron pyrites and uncombined sulphide of antimony, with small quantities of galena and sulphide of copper. The proportions of these constituents vary, however, with almost every parcel of ore received into the works. The mineral, as delivered at the establishment, is likewise more or less mixed with micaceous slate derived from the rocks in which the lode is enclosed; and the poorer ores usually contain much more of this substance than the richer varieties, to being mixed with which, they generally owe their impoverishment. Immense quantities of such ores, too poor to be amalgamated with profit, were formerly wasted at the mines; but this loss might, to a certain extent, have been avoided by employing a better system of extraction, and greater care in the selection of the ore.

Grinding and Roasting Crude Ores.—The ores as they are brought from the mines are immediately taken to cylindrical Cornish crushing mills, and ground and sifted through circular sieves of wire gauze, having ten holes to the linear inch. Each parcel is now laid apart and weighed in presence of two parties; one of whom is appointed by the mines from which the ores are purchased, the other on the part of the reduction works. As soon as the mineral has been weighed, it is removed to the stores where the several parcels are piled one on another heterogeneously, and from whence the ore is taken as it may be required. The furnaces employed for the calcination of the ores with salt are, at Constante, eight in number; six of them having revolving hearths worked by machinery similar to Brunton's calciners, whilst the remaining two are hand furnaces of the ordinary reverberatory description. The mechanical calciners employed in the establishment make from three to four revolutions per hour, and have movable hearths fourteen feet in diameter. Each of these furnaces requires an expenditure of about half a horse power to turn it, and is provided with a single fireplace consuming from 120 to 140 lbs. of pine wood per hour. An improvement on this apparatus has been effected by Mr. W. West, who employs two fireplaces, and thus more evenly distributes the heat over the surface of the hearth.

This improved calciner is represented, Figs. 49, 50, in which A is the doorway of the calciner house; B, a window in ditto; C, cast iron hopper through which the ore is fed; and D, three cast iron fluke or agitator frames built in the masonry of the arch. The revolving table E, on which is spread the mixture to be calcined, has a slightly conical surface, and is made of the best firebricks set on end in a cast iron shell. The lining of the furnace F, in which the calcining table revolves, should also be built of refractory material. The fireplaces G, are situated on either side of the furnace, after traversing which, the products of combustion make their escape by the flue, H, to the chimney.

After calcination, the ore passes through the cast iron spout I, into the chambers J, in which it is deposited. The opening K, beneath the furnace, is for the purpose of allowing space for working the worm wheel and pinion communicating motion to the revolving table. The foot-block, carrying the perpendicular shaft, is supported by the block of stone L, and the furnace is tightly braced by the girders M.

Fig. 49.

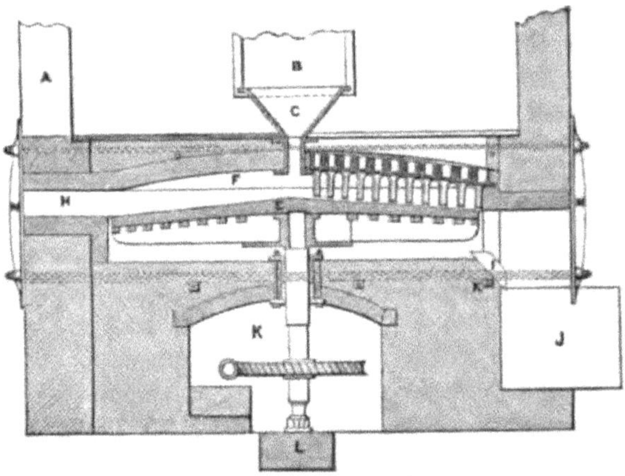

Revolving Calciner.
(*Vertical Section.*)

The mixture of mineral and salt is made as intimate as possible, especially for the mechanical furnaces, since in them the charge is but little disturbed by the rakes: they are charged with ore and salt by means of the iron hoppers placed immediately over the centre of each of the hearths. For the supply of the hopper a heap of about fourteen quintals of ore, with from five to six per cent. of salt, is, from time to time, prepared upon the platform on the top of the furnace, and a few shovelfuls thrown in occasionally, as required; taking care, however, always to have enough in the hoppers to prevent the escape of acid vapours through them from the furnace. The time during which the mineral remains in the apparatus, and the quantity calcined per hour, must necessarily depend on the rapidity of motion given to the revolving hearth, and the angle at which the iron stirrers are fixed. The average amount passed through each furnace in twenty-four hours is about eighty-four quintals, or three and a half quintals per hour; or for every revolution of the bed, nearly one quintal is discharged from the furnace. Compared with the German roasting furnace, the mechanical furnaces are found less efficient for the treatment of rich

FIG. 50.

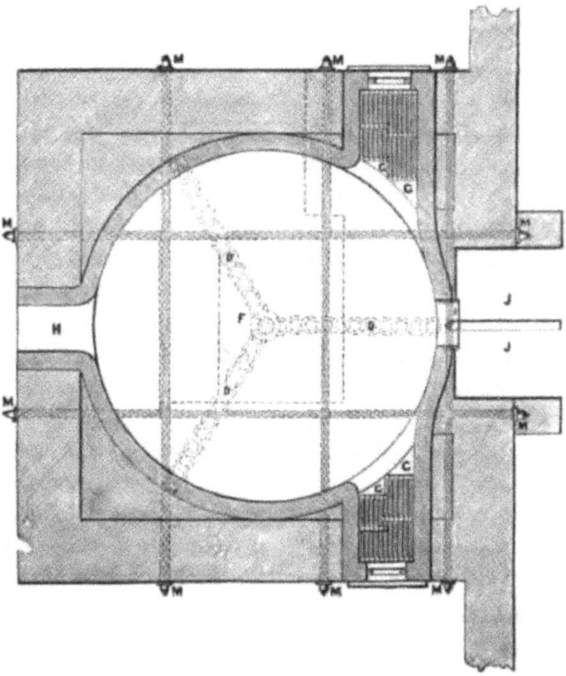

REVOLVING CALCINER.
(*Horizontal Section.*)

ores; particularly when they are charged damp and contain much sulphur, in which case the excessive production of lumps becomes a serious inconvenience. But in the treatment of the class usually brought to the works, they possess the advantage of calcining a larger quantity in a given time, and they require no further attendance than is necessary for supplying them with ore and fuel. The management of the fires is also a matter of importance, since should they be forgotten, and the heat become lowered, the mineral, from continuing to pass at the same rate through the furnace, cannot be properly calcined ; and in order to raise the temperature, after having been neglected, the workmen sometimes charge the grate with fuel to such an extent as to overheat the ore.

Of the three hand furnaces used at Constante one is very old, and only employed for drying salt before grinding, and for calcining sweepings, and other refuse matters, containing silver. The other two are similar in form to those of Freiberg, and are worked in much the same manner. They are chiefly employed for the calcination of such ores as contain 9 oz. and upwards per quintal. A charge for these furnaces weighs about 540 lbs., and consists of about 495 lbs. of dry ore, 40 lbs. salt, and 5 lbs. moisture. A smaller proportion of salt may be employed in the calcination of very poor ores, but it is seldom less than six per cent. ; for the richer minerals it is necessary to add a larger proportion of salt, frequently as much as 15 per cent. When a charge is introduced into the furnace, it is evenly spread over the surface of the hearth by means of an iron rake, and for the space of half an hour scarcely any fuel is thrown on the grate, whilst the mineral is constantly stirred, in order to evaporate the moisture and to prevent the formation of lumps. The fire is then gradually increased, and the ore, which by degrees becomes so heated that the sulphurous matters enter into ignition, is stirred uninterruptedly with the rake, so as to expose continual fresh surfaces to the action of the air. The charge is likewise turned, in order to, from time to time, equally expose every part to the action of the fire. After the lapse of about two hours the mineral has become fully heated, when the fire may be left to burn down for about an hour. It is then again urged for nearly three quarters of an hour longer, so as to cause the sulphates produced by the oxidation of metallic sulphides to react on the salt, which, in the presence of metallic oxides, evolves chlorine, which combines with the silver and other metals present. The whole operation, from the introduction to the withdrawal of the charge, occupies four hours, during which time from 140 to 160 lbs. of wood are consumed. The metallic sulphides, contained in the rich ores operated on in the furnaces, do not amount to more than from 9 to 10 per cent., whilst in the poorer ores the proportion is often considerably less.

Sulphide of iron is a necessary ingredient in silver ores to be submitted to this process of amalgamation, and during the roasting process is oxidised and partially converted into sulphate which, reacting on the salt, evolves the gases necessary for converting the silver into chloride. The proportion of sulphide of iron requisite for this purpose appears to be variable as regards different ores. At Freiberg at least 20 per cent. was considered indispensable, whereas at Constante good results have been repeatedly obtained with only 8 per cent., even when operating on rich minerals. The silver ores of that neighbourhood are but little accompanied by sulphides, and arsenides of other metals, and the pyrites found is very poor in silver and easily oxidisable. The comparative purity of these minerals may account for their ready calcination, for in the case of ores containing large proportions of sulphides, arsenides, &c., a great excess of chlorine is required for the purpose of effecting their complete decompostion.

In the hand furnace, as much as 14 per cent. of salt was formerly added, but with ores containing 9 oz. of silver per quintal 6 per cent. has sometimes been found sufficient. Separating the richer from the poorer ores, and treating them apart, has been found very advantageous here, as well as at Freiberg. The calcination of the ores with salt is the most important of the operations connected with this process of amalgamation, as on it, in a great measure, depends the nature of the results obtained from the barrels; since, in whatever way the operation may be conducted, the silver extracted will be commensurate with the amount of chloride formed in the furnace. The success of the calcination is, therefore, judged of by the proportion of chloride of silver contained in the roasted ore. This is ascertained at Constante by digesting for some hours a small weighed portion of the roasted mineral with warm dilute ammonia; it is then thrown on a filter, the residue well washed, and finally dried and assayed for silver. It is obvious that the weight of this metal obtained indicates the quantity remaining uncombined with chlorine. Another method, in some respects preferable to the process with ammonia, is to treat the roasted mineral with a strong solution of common salt. For this purpose a few grammes of the calcined ore, just as it is drawn from the furnace, are thrown on a filter upon which is poured a hot saturated solution of salt, until the liquor, which filters through, no longer affords a white precipitate of chloride of silver on being largely diluted with cold water. The residual ore is then dried and assayed for silver, as in the former case. It has been suggested that the crude mineral, which is at present sifted through an eight or ten-hole sieve, would be better if ground a little finer, but a certain degree of coarseness is necessary in order that the oxygen of the air and the gases evolved in the process of calcination with salt may become freely diffused throughout the charge. If the mineral be very finely ground previous to calcining, the porosity of the charge is greatly diminished, and consequently the calcination is found to proceed more slowly; besides which the formation of lumps is thereby facilitated.

Fig. 51.

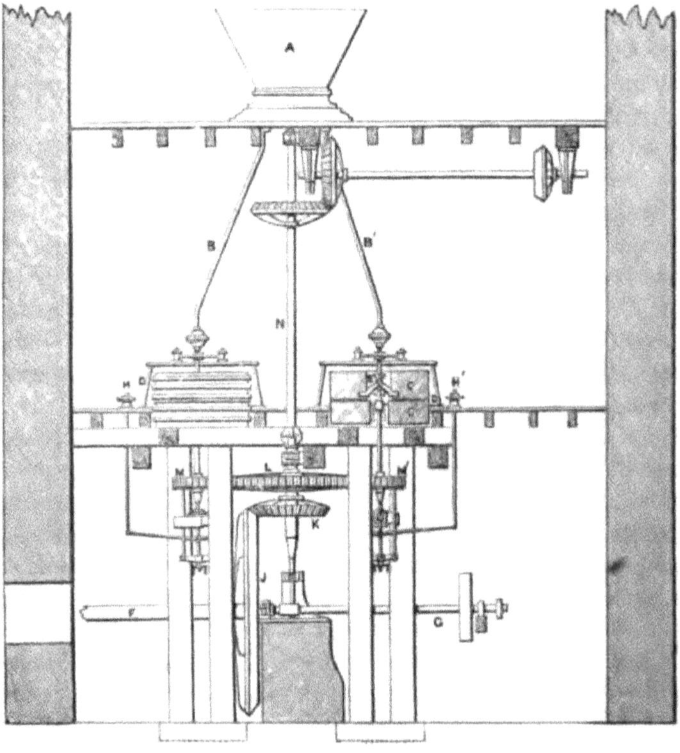

HORIZONTAL MILLS.
(*Constante.*)

Sifting and Grinding Roasted Ores.—The calcined ores before being submitted to amalgamation in the barrels are first sifted through a circular sieve of sixty holes to the linear inch, and the portion which does not pass through is then very finely ground, in order that every particle of silver which it contains may be exposed to the action of mercury; the portion passing through the sieve, amounting to 40 per cent. is taken directly to the barrels for amalgamation. The coarser portion of the ore, which is allowed to accumulate in the furnace-house, is, when required, removed and passed between a pair of cylinder mills from which it falls into a revolving sieve of sixty holes to the linear inch; the coarser ore escaping from this sieve is then raised by an elevator, and dropped into the hopper of a second pair of smooth cylinders, from whence the mineral falls into another sieve of the same degree of fineness as the first. The hard coarse particles, which refuse to go through this second sieve, are finally ground in horizontal mills of French burr stones. The arrangement of four of these mills, of which there are eight in the establishment, is represented, Fig. 51, in which one pair of stones is shown in section. Into the circular hopper A is introduced the stuff to be ground; B B′ are small pipes of sheet iron for delivering the stuff between the surfaces of the runner C, and the bedstone C′; D casing enclosing the runner into which the ground material is delivered; E hole in centre of runner; F driving shaft with continuation G for belt pulley; H H′ regulating screws for elevating the runners C; J driving wheel; K crown wheel; L wheel giving motion to pinions M M′; N vertical shaft for driving supplementary apparatus. Four pairs of stones are driven by the wheel L. The surface of the runner is parallel with the bedstone from the periphery to within one-third of its diameter; the line of the lower face of the runner then feathers upwards in order to receive the feed.

The following particulars afford sundry details relative to this apparatus:—

Diameter of stones	4 ft. 2 inches.
Thickness of bedstone	12 inches.
„ runner	14 „
Gauge of stuff in hopper, about . . .	100 holes to square inch.
„ „ on delivery	3,600 „ „
Number of revolutions	100 per minute.
Quantity of stuff ground per 10 hours.	1 ton per pair of stones.
Horse-power employed, about . . .	5 „ „
Revolutions of sizing sieves	23 per minute.
Diameter „ „ . . .	30 inches.
Length „ „ . . .	108 „
No. of holes per sq. inch in sizing sieve	3,600.
Character of runner	French burr.
„ bedstone	Compact quartz, moderately hard.
Duration of runner	Average, 18 weeks.
„ bedstone	„ 22 „
When dressed	Every third day.

In place of fine sifting and carrying the remainder of the calcined ore directly to the mills, and there crushing and grinding the whole to a fine powder, it might be desirable to first remove the hard lumps of ore, which are always produced in the operation of roasting, by passing the mineral through a sieve of about the same fineness as that employed in the mills for grinding the crude ores.

The lumps, which would be separated from the calcined mineral by the sieve above mentioned, are found to contain a considerable proportion of silver not converted into chloride, which is owing to the circumstance of these lumps being chiefly formed at the commencement of the operation, so that the inner portions escape the action of the gases evolved at a later period. These lumps should, therefore, be crushed, and submitted to a second roasting, either alone or mixed with the ordinary charges of crude ore. In the hand furnaces a much smaller proportion of lumps is produced than in the mechanical ones, owing to the constant stirring to which the mineral is subjected in the former.

Amalgamation.—The total number of barrels employed is sixty, each being, internally, three feet four inches long, and two feet six inches in diameter. The barrel department is divided into three sections:—No. 1, contains twelve barrels; No. 2, contains twenty-four barrels; and No. 3, twenty-four barrels. All of them can be driven by water power; those of Nos. 1 and 3 can likewise be worked by steam. The barrels are placed at a height of about twelve feet from the ground-floor. Immediately over them, and projecting through the floor above, are fixed iron hoppers for receiving the mineral to be amalgamated, which is introduced into the barrels by means of leathern hose, with which the whole of the hoppers are provided. The average weight of a charge for each barrel is thirteen quintals; but the hoppers are capable of holding a still larger amount. These latter are charged by gangs of men, each of whom carries a sack of mineral, weighing about a quintal. In the barrel-house No. 3 a railway is laid down between the hoppers, by means of which they can be regularly and quickly filled with the requisite quantity of ore. The internal shape of the barrels is, when new, cylindrical; but, after being in use for some time, their dimensions are increased by the wearing away of the inside, near the middle.*

* In the amalgamation works of Nevada the barrels are made of 2-inch planks, and internally lined with 4-inch blocks of pine, similar to an internal wooden pavement. These blocks are so arranged as to cause the wear to take place across the

The amount of water introduced into each barrel varies with the nature of the ore, but the usual quantity is about 320 lbs.; and the iron contained in each amounts to 100 or 150 lbs. Considerable wear and tear of the barrels is caused by using large scrap iron of every kind for this purpose; and its action is less effective than would be the case with iron in smaller pieces.

The charge of ore and water having been introduced, the barrels are set in motion, and made to revolve at the rate of from eight to ten revolutions per minute during two and a half hours, in order that the ore, water, and pieces of iron may become completely incorporated. They are then stopped, and the state of the pasty mass examined. If this be too soft, or too stiff, more mineral, or additional water, is added, as the case may require. Should the paste be found of the right consistency—that is, just sufficiently stiff to allow of being formed into a ball in the hand—the mercury is poured in; the weight of that metal introduced being four quintals to each barrel. The loss of quicksilver is rather diminished than augmented by employing large quantities, since its fluidity is less affected by its combination with silver. After the introduction of mercury, the barrels are driven at the rate of from eighteen to twenty turns per minute, for a space of sixteen and a half hours, at the end of which time the amalgamation is considered to be accomplished. The barrels are now filled with water, for the purpose of rendering the paste liquid, and collecting the globules of argentiferous mercury into one mass for drawing off, and kept slowly revolving during a further space of two hours. In discharging the barrels, the mercury is first drawn off into the trough fixed beneath each row of casks, and thence conducted to an iron vessel, in which is collected the quicksilver run off from all the barrels; and any earthy matters which may escape with the mercury are carefully cleaned off the surface with flannel cloths. The fluid metal is subsequently run into canvas bags, which retain the solid amalgam, whilst the more liquid mercury filters through, and is received into an iron tank, situated beneath. During this operation, which lasts upwards of an hour, the barrels are continued in motion; because the whole of the residues having to pass through the vessel in which the quicksilver is collected, before they can arrive at the washing vats, cannot safely be discharged until the mercury has been run into the filters.

grain, and whenever a lining has become worn out, it can be readily replaced; the adoption of this form of construction has resulted in a considerable economy.

The process of amalgamation includes three operations :—

1. The barrels are charged with ore, water, and iron (without any mercury), and made to revolve, at the rate of ten turns per minute, for two hours, or until the mixture has become thoroughly incorporated, and is of the consistency of thick paste. This being accomplished, the mercury is introduced.

2. The casks are immediately afterwards put in more rapid motion, viz. eighteen to twenty turns per minute, and continued at this speed for about sixteen and a half hours; at the end of which period the complete amalgamation of the silver is supposed to have been effected.

3. In order to collect the argentiferous mercury into a mass for drawing off, it is necessary to reduce the consistency of the paste contained in the barrels. For this purpose they are filled with water, and driven slowly, at eight or ten turns per minute, for the space of two or two and a half hours. The amalgam is then discharged, and subsequently the residues; the barrels are discharged every twenty-four hours. The average richness of the ores treated may be taken at about 4½ oz. per quintal.

Treatment of Amalgam.—The solid amalgam collected in the canvas bags above mentioned is treated in a very simple form of distilling apparatus, for the purpose of separating the mercury from the silver. The amalgam to be distilled is moulded into a cylindrical form upon an iron tripod supporting a perforated disc, depending from which, and fixed in brickwork, is an iron tube, dipping into a vessel of water placed beneath. Over the cylinder-shaped pile of amalgam is placed either a copper or cast iron bell, and perfect contact with the plate is ensured by carefully luting the joint. A circle is then made with loose bricks, raised around the bell at a short distance from it, and the space between filled with charcoal. The heat afforded by its combustion volatilises the mercury, which is quickly condensed and is collected in the cold water supplied to the cistern beneath. About 2,000 lbs. weight of amalgam are usually operated on at a time, nearly forty-eight hours being required to complete the distillation; and as many as forty sacks, weighing, in the aggregate, eighty arrobas, of charcoal are consumed during the operation.*

As may be supposed from the form of the apparatus, a portion of amalgam fuses, and falls into the cistern below; which, however, may

* This apparatus is merely a modification of the Mexican capellina.

be readily separated by filtration from the fluid mercury. This generally amounts to 60 or 80 lbs. in weight. The quantity of crude silver yielded by 2,000 lbs. of amalgam is generally about 290 lbs., or 14½ per cent. of the amalgam operated on. This silver has a brownish-white colour, is exceedingly porous, and may be readily broken in pieces under the hammer.

Melting and Refining.—The porous silver obtained from the distillation of amalgam is melted, at Constante, in a species of cupola, called a *cras.* When the metal is uncontaminated by impurities which impair the malleability of the resulting bars, the cras may still be employed for melting it, although a loss of silver must result from exposing it, at so high a temperature, to the action of a powerful blast. But when, as is most frequently the case in amalgamation works, the silver to be melted contains matters which impair its malleability, the removal of these is readily effected by this apparatus. The amount of impurities required to impart the property of brittleness to fused silver is, nevertheless, very small, and chiefly consists of lead, sulphur, antimony, and iron. These bodies may be readily got rid of by cupellation with lead, an operation, however, which, for this purpose, is attended with considerable trouble and expense. Melting the silver in black-lead crucibles appears to be, therefore, preferable. It may be thus purified by repeated additions of powdered charcoal, skimming and stirring, and be finally obtained in a perfectly malleable state. Instead of employing black-lead crucibles, large iron pots, capable of melting from 500 to 600 marks at a time, were used at Freiberg, and found to answer very satisfactorily. By fusion in large wrought iron crucibles, the silver may be obtained free from all impurities impairing its malleability, and rendering it unfit for the coining press.

Treatment of Residues.—The residues, on being discharged from the barrels, are conducted into large vats, in which revolve upright stirrers, fixed on four radial iron arms. The mud is retained in these vats for several hours, and kept in continual movement by the stirrers; in order that the particles of amalgam, disseminated in the residual matters, may subside to the bottom, and be afterwards collected, a constant stream of water flows into the vats during the whole time of washing. On being discharged from the vats, the mud flows directly into the river, in the bed of which it accumulates until it is carried off by a freshet.

COST OF TREATING ORES AT CONSTANTE.

Cost of working Mechanical Furnaces—

Wood for each furnace per week	940 rs.*
Salt, 6 per cent. 3,528 lbs. at 14 rs. per quintal	494
Splitting wood	19
Labour for each furnace	184
	Rs. 1,637

Ore calcined per week, 588 quintals in each furnace; 1637÷588=2·8 rs. per quintal.

Hand Furnaces—

Each furnace calcines 210 quintals of rich ore per week.

„ „ consumes 294 arrobas wood	294·0 rs.
„ „ „ 12 per cent. salt=2,520 lbs.	353·0
Labour	242·6
	Rs. 889·6

889·6÷210=4·23 rs. per quintal.

Hence cost of calcining in mechanical furnaces is . . 2·8 rs. per quintal.
„ „ „ hand „ . . 4·23 „ „

Average cost of roasting, 3·2 rs.

Section of 24 Barrels—

Wear and tear	800 rs.
Iron consumed, 5 arrobas	120 „
Mercury, reckoning the loss at 5½ oz. per mark of silver, or 454 lbs. at 5·62 rs.	2,551
Labour	1,157
	Rs. 4,628

Ore amalgamated per week by 24 barrels,
2,352 quintals; 4,628÷2,352=1·96 rs.
Incidentals . . . . ·04

Cost of amalgamating 2·00 rs. per quintal.

Summary.

Cost of crushing, per quintal	0·95rs.
„ calcining „ „	3·20
„ amalgamating „ „	2·00
„ distilling amalgam, and melting into bars	0·80
Sundry labour and materials	3·00
Total, exclusive of salaries, &c.	Rs. 9·95

or about 45*s.* 6*d.* per ton for ores containing on an average 4½ oz. of silver per quintal.

* Reals Vellon = 2½*d.*

The quantity of ore which 60 barrels will reduce per week is 5,880 quintals.

Weight of mineral which all the furnaces will calcine in the same time	4,058	„
Viz. Six Mechanical Furnaces	3,528	„
Three Hand „	530	„

These works have consequently the means of reducing upwards of 1,800 quintals of mineral per week more than the present number of furnaces can, when in full work, calcine. Forty barrels would therefore be apparently sufficient to amalgamate all the mineral that can be roasted, but, as the supply of water is irregular, it is advantageous to have extra barrels, so that whilst the calcination is carried on without interruption, the ore accumulated during the dry season may be readily reduced when the supply of water is plentiful.

Notes relative to cost, &c. at Constante:—

Cost of firewood per 100 lbs., 10*d.*
„ mercury per lb., 1*s.* 2*d.* including carriage.
„ salt „ 100 lbs., 3*s.* „ „
Average cost of carriage of ore from mines to work, about 3*s.* per ton.
Cost of ordinary labour per diem, 1*s.*
Estimated loss of mercury per mark of silver, 5½ oz.
„ „ silver per cent. on assay produce, about 12.
The length of time a wooden barrel will last in regular work, 6 months.
Miller's wages at horizontal mills, 9½*d.* per ton of ore ground; cost, including wear and tear, 2*s.* 3*d.* per ton.
At Miner's crushing mill, usual cost, including labourers and wear and tear, about 3¾*d.* per ton.

The sifting of the calcined ore is done by contract at the rate of ¾*d.* per quintal of fine powder. This fine powder usually amounts to 35 or 40 per cent. of the calcined mineral.

REAL DEL MONTE, MEXICO; MEAN RESULTS OF BARREL AMALGAMATION, 1864-5.*

Velasco hacienda, reducing	107,700	cargas yearly.
Sanchez „ „	48,550	„
St. Miguel „ „	49,600	„
Total reduced in the three haciendas	205,850	cargas yearly.

The mean assay of the ore thus reduced was 13·0 marks per monton.
The mean produce . . . . 11·3 „ „
Mean loss . . . . 1·7, or 13 per cent.

The mean reduction cost in the three works was as follows:—

* Furnished by Mr. Buchan.

Grinding by wet stamps	2·20	dollars per monton.
Drying, sifting, and roasting	2·75	„ „
Amalgamation in barrels	1·10	„ „
General expenses of management . . .	1·20	„ „
Repairs to furnaces and machinery . .	1·55	„ „
Total . .	$8·80	
Fuel (wood, 21 quintals per monton) .	3·70	„ „
Salt (2 quintals per monton)	8·30	„ „
Quicksilver (4·7 oz. per mark of silver) .	2·80	„ „
Total per monton .	$23·60	

To this must be added, for auxiliary steam-power, Sanchez $2
„ „ Velasco $3

Barrel Process as conducted at the Ophir Works, etc., Nevada.—*Drying the Ores.*—The ore is first dried on a kiln composed of twenty parallel flues 12 in. × 12 in., covered by cast iron plates, half an inch in thickness.

Crushing.—The rock is stamped dry, in batteries with four discharges in each coffer, through brass wire screens of 1,600 holes to the square inch.

Roasting.—It is then roasted, 1,300 lbs. at a charge, in reverberatory furnaces 8 ft. 6 in. × 9 ft. in the hearth; salt is added from twenty minutes to an hour and a half after the furnace is first charged. The time required to roast a charge varies from 4½ to 6 hours; about 4¾ hours is the average time necessary for second class ores, and the usual quantity of salt added is 5½ per cent. One hour before the charge is drawn, from 1½ to 8 per cent. of carbonate of lime is added in order to decompose a portion of the sulphates and chlorides of copper, zinc, &c., to prevent loss of quicksilver during the amalgamation, and also to produce an amalgam of greater purity. The ore when in the furnace is continually stirred, and is turned three times during the roasting: 1stly, two hours after the furnace is charged; 2ndly, before the limestone is added; and, 3rdly, when the limestone has been in about 35 minutes. Mr. G. Attwood, the former manager of these works, states that he found, that by a careful addition of limestone all the chlorides and sulphates of copper, &c. in excess, can be decomposed.

Screening.—The roasted ore is put through a bolt with a screen of 1,600 holes to the square inch, and then elevated to the barrels.

Amalgamation.—The barrels are charged with one ton of ore, and run with water and 450 lbs. of iron during three hours. It is found that with a large amount of iron in the barrels, upwards of 4 per cent. more silver is obtained than with the usual quantity, of 10 per cent., of that metal.

From 350 to 400 lbs. of mercury are now added, and the barrels allowed to run, at twelve revolutions per minute, during 12 or 13 hours, when they are filled up with water and drawn off, after being again run for two hours.

The amalgam obtained is strained through a stout canvas conical bag, and the tailings washed in a settler 15 ft. in diameter, passing from thence through a series of sluice boxes into a flume about 600 ft. long and four feet wide provided with riffles.

The amalgam yields about one-sixth of its weight of bullion, averaging 650 parts of silver in a thousand; the most impure samples assay about 375, and the best 992 thousandths.

Distillation.—The amalgam is distilled in circular retorts 4½ ft. long and 10 in. in diameter, set on an arch of brickwork, with three dampers to direct the flame towards any part where the heat may be required.

Returns from Ophir Ores, worked at the Ophir Company's Reduction Works, Nevada, for the Months of June, July, August, September, and October, 1865.*

Quantity. tons.	lbs.	Class.	Total Value.	
1,998	1,160	3rd	$121,512·71	
101	940	1st	49,450·51	
2,100	100		$170,963·22	$81·41 Average per Ton.
Returned 130 bars; weight 11,732 lbs. Valued at .			$158,774·20	$75·60 Return obtained.
Loss			$12,189·02	7·12 per cent.

Total loss of Quicksilver 2,176 lbs., or 2·96 oz. to each lb. of Bullion.

Returns from Ores extracted from Mexican Mine, Virginia City, and Empire Mine, Gold Hill, worked at the Mexican Company's Mill, at Empire City, in July and August, 1865.

	Quantity. Tons.	lbs.	Value in Gold.	Per Ton.	Value in Silver.	Per Ton.
	137	1,525	$7,585·17	$55·06	$12,753·80	$92·58
Bullion produced . .			$6,237·21	$45·27	$12,225·64	$88·74

Produce of Gold	82·25 per cent.
„ Silver	95·82 „ „
Value of Ore	$20,338·97 = $147·64 per ton.
„ „ Bullion	$18,462·85 = $134·02 „ „
Produce	90·74 per cent.

* Communicated by Mr. G. Attwood.

Experiments made by Mr. G. Attwood in order to determine the loss experienced on the precious metals in the operations of roasting and amalgamation of Comstock Ores.

One thousand pounds of Black "base metal" ore, from the Ophir North Mine, roasted for 4½ hours with 5·50 per cent. of salt, and 2·50 per cent. of limestone, weighed 1,080 lbs. It lost 4·99 per cent. in value, and the mixture gained 3 lbs. in weight—

Assay value, silver	$43·43
„ „ gold	50·22
Total	$93·65

Again, 700 lbs. "base metal," North Mine ore, from the Ophir.
300 lbs. first class „ „ „ „

Total 1,000 lbs., roasted 5¼ hours with 7 per cent. salt, and 6 per cent. limestone, weighed 1,123 lbs., lost 6·72 per cent. in value, and 7 lbs. in weight. Twenty-one tons of the same ore, after being roasted, assayed

Silver, per ton	$99·97
Gold „ . . .	92·80
	$192·77 = $4,048·17 value of parcel.

Value of bullion returned . . . $3,915·57
Loss in amalgamation 3·27 per cent.

The loss experienced during barrel amalgamation is, however, generally greater than the above, as the samples were in this case taken out of the barrels before being drawn off, the amalgam washed out by hand, and the residue dried and assayed. The average loss on working the ores from the Comstock vein in barrels is 13·50 per cent. Ophir ores work better than Savage, Chollar Potosi, &c.

Composition of Ores.—The following analyses of ores from the Ophir Mine will serve to show the character of the rock usually treated at the different mills in the vicinity of Virginia City.

	1st Class.	2nd Class.	3rd Class.
Gangue . .	63·38	80·70	95·75
Silver . .	2·78	0·89	0·10
Gold . . .	0·05	0·03	0·00
Lead . .	4·15	4·04	0·40
Sulphur .	7·95	3·05	1·04
Zinc . . .	14·45	5·51	0·48
Copper . .	1·59	1·43	0·30
Iron . . .	5·46	3·46	1·55
Antimony .	0·08	trace.	trace.
	99·89	99·11	99·62

The analysis of an outside chip of a bar of bullion, obtained by barrel amalgamation, from the ores of the Comstock vein, gave the following results:—

Gold	1·58
Silver	41·51
Lead	39·01
Copper	17·04
Zinc	0·56
Iron	0·17
Total	99·87

Assay of samples from flues of Roasting Furnaces at the Ophir Reduction Works, August 5th, 1864.

		Value.
No. 1 contained	Lead 28·02 per cent.	
„ „	Silver, per ton 60·14 oz.	$ 78·18
„ „	Gold „ 1·21 „	25·01
	Value	$103·19
No. 2 contained	Lead 24·66 per cent.	
„ „	Silver, per ton	$122·80
„ „	Gold „	62·63
	Value	$185·43

COST OF REDUCTION OF ORES BY BARREL AMALGAMATION AT THE OPHIR WORKS, 1865.

Labour, of every description, per ton	$ 9·50
Wood, at $5 per cord	6·00
Salt, 4 per cent. at 3 cents. per lb.	2·40
Quicksilver, 1 lb. at 64 cents.	0·64
Shoes, Screens, Shovels, Belts, Tools, &c.	0·75
Castings, Scrap Iron, Timber, &c.	0·65
Charcoal, Assay office expenses, &c.	0·20
Total	$20·14

These ores assayed about $80·00 per ton. Ores assaying over that yield cost from $20·14 to $27 per ton, according to the amount of salt required, quicksilver consumed, and lime employed in furnaces.

Each furnace requires four men, two on each shift, as the charge is constantly stirred, and about a cord of wood is burnt in 24 hours.* The usual charge, for $80 ore, is about 1,300 lbs. which is roasted during 4½ hours.

The chief cost of the barrel process is roasting, labour, and dry stamping. The cost of amalgamation is only about $3 per ton.

The cost of labour in Nevada may be taken at $4 per diem.

* The roasting is conducted in furnaces entirely constructed of ordinary red bricks.

CHAPTER XVIII.

TREATMENT OF SILVER ORES BY AMALGAMATION—PAN PROCESS.

STAMPING—COMMON PAN—VARNEY'S PAN—WHEELER'S PAN—HEPBURN AND PETERSON'S PAN—SEPARATORS—WORKING IN PANS—RETORTING—ARRANGEMENT OF REDUCTION WORKS—TREATMENT OF ROASTED ORES IN PANS.

SHORTLY after the discovery of silver mines in Nevada it became evident, that owing to the prevailing high prices of labour, firewood, and other materials, none of the processes employed in other countries for the reduction of silver ores, could be rendered available in that locality for the treatment of rock assaying from $20 to $80 per ton: it consequently became necessary to have recourse to some method of operating which would dispense with roasting, as practised in the ordinary barrel process, on the one hand; and the frequent manipulation, and great expenditure of time involved in working by the patio, on the other; and to endeavour, by the introduction of direct amalgamation, to work the poorer description of ores at a profit. Many deposits of ore of extraordinary richness have been discovered in the Comstock vein, and the ores from these it has been generally found most profitable either to ship to England, or to work by the barrel process. Amongst such ores may be instanced a lot of 80 tons, shipped from the California claim, which yielded on an average $2,200 per ton. But the main deposits vary in assay from $35 to $70 per ton, and it is the treatment of these ores which furnishes the largest proportion of the silver obtained from the district.

The silver ores of Nevada are worked but to a limited extent in reduction works belonging to the mines themselves, but more commonly on what is termed "custom work" at a fixed price per ton of ore of 2,000 lbs. The price charged varies according to whether or not a percentage amount of the assay value of the ore be guaranteed. If the ore be worked without guarantee, it is the interest of the mill-owner to pass as large a quantity as possible through the mill, consistently with the maintenance of a respectable character for the quality of the work done, since at any time when the supply of ore from the mines may slacken, an opportunity arises for working over the tailings, which always remain the property of the mill. As at the first working of the mines the mill power was insufficient for working the ore as rapidly as it was raised, its produce was only roughly estimated, and consequently not unfrequently overvalued, but a more satisfactory method is now generally adopted in the district. As soon as the ore is brought out of the mine it is deposited on the pile or floors in parcels of from two to three hundred tons, every tenth waggon-load being reserved for dry stamping, so as to allow of careful sampling. The crushed ore is forwarded with the parcel to which it belongs, a small charge being made for crushing. The small sample retained by the mine is assayed, and from it the gross assay value of the whole parcel is determined, and the charges by the mine against the mill made accordingly.

Ores at the mines are usually assorted into three classes. The first consists of those whose assay value is over $90 per ton of 2,000 lbs. As these contain but a small proportion of free silver, or silver in the metallic state, but have in their composition a considerable amount of sulphur, in combination with "rebellious metals," such as antimony, zinc, lead, copper, and iron, they are reserved for treatment by calcination and subsequent reduction in barrels by the Freiberg process.

The second class consists of ores of the assay value of from $40 to $90 per ton. The third class ranges from $20 to $40 per ton ; the second and third classes are worked by the pan process. These ores usually contain, in value, about one-third gold to two-thirds silver. Ores of the first class are crushed by dry stamping, those of the second and third are crushed wet. The ores are prepared for stamping by being crushed into fragments of about a pound in weight by Blake's crushers.

Stamping.—For wet crushing, stamps are used of from seven to nine hundred pounds per head, including the stem, and are driven at the rate of seventy blows per minute. They are fed by an attendant whose duty it is to regulate the supply of ore, water, and quicksilver, when that metal is used in the battery for amalgamating the free gold present. Amalgamation in the battery requires careful attention, principally to avoid the too rapid addition of quicksilver, which should be supplied in very small quantities only.

To amalgamate the free gold in a battery, the quantity of quicksilver to be used is about one ounce weight to each ounce of gold present; this is sufficient to collect the gold and form a dry amalgam. If, therefore, a mill will stamp 24 tons of ore in 24 hours, and the ore contains an ounce of gold per ton, it will be necessary to put into the battery an ounce of quicksilver every hour. When, in addition to gold, the rock under treatment contains metallic silver, the amount of mercury added must be proportionately increased. More than 80 per cent. of the assay value of the gold in the ore may, by careful manipulation, be thus obtained. The gold amalgam accumulates in the corners and crevices of the battery box, between the dies, on the breast of the mortar, over which the crushed ore is washed into the settling cisterns, and is even found in considerable quantities adhering to the shoulders of the stamp shoes. The amalgam thus obtained is very hard and heavy, and is commonly so rich in gold, as to be worth as much as ten dollars per ounce. The crushed ore is taken off from the mortar by a supply of water, equal to the run of a three-quarter inch pipe to each set of five stamps, through screens in the back and front of the box. These screens are made of thin Russian iron perforated with holes punched by sewing-needles, with the points cut off, and set in dies as closely as consistent with the maintenance of sufficient strength to bear the necessary concussion. The needles employed are usually those known as Nos. 5 and 6.

Settlers.—The troughs by which the crushed ore is conveyed to the settlers are provided with gates or stops in order to allow of the successive filling and emptying of the different tanks. These are made of wood usually about ten feet in length by eight in width, and three feet in depth. Here the ore is allowed to settle, and the water is run from tank to tank, and not allowed finally to escape until it has become tolerably clear.

As the water flowing from the settlers still contains much fine clayey matter, it is led off into one of a series of tanks which are successively filled, and after being again allowed to settle, the clear water is run off. This settling is much expedited by the use of two or three ounces of alum to each thousand gallons of water contained in the tank. It must be added in solution to each cistern of foul water, as soon as it has become filled, and sufficient time must be allowed for settling before the clear water is discharged. When the cistern is sufficiently full of mud it is run off, and the tailings dried for further treatment. Ores of the assay value of $80 per ton produce tailings of the value of $100 per ton, and in such quantities as to be equal to 20 per cent. of the total assay value of the ore.

Of the amalgamating pans employed in the reduction works of Nevada, it may be said that their modifications are almost endless. Much ingenuity has been expended on many of them, but the best are those of Varney and Wheeler, and that of Hepburn and Peterson. These makers have, however, all obtained patent rights, and supply their various amalgamators to the different reduction establishments at a fixed price; which includes the necessary licence for using them.

Common Pan.—There is, however, a more simple form of apparatus usually known as the common pan, with which results can, by careful working, be obtained almost as good as from those of the above makers. The common pan, Figs. 52 and 53, is a round wooden or cast iron

FIG. 52.

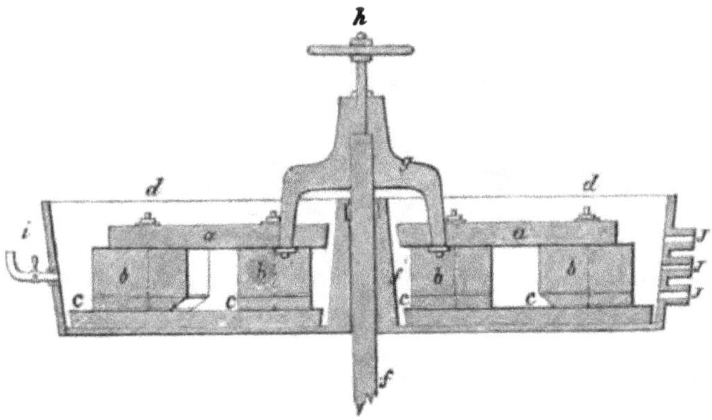

COMMON PAN.
(*Vertical Section.*)

tub, 6 feet in diameter, and about 2 feet in depth, with a flat bottom. A false bottom of 1½ inch iron is inserted into this, and a hollow pillar in the centre admits the passage of an upright shaft, which is generally worked by gearing, beneath the pan, capable of communicating to it from 15 to 20 revolutions per minute. To the wooden arms *a* are attached the blocks *b*, also of wood, to which are fastened the iron shoes *c*, by means of the bolts *d*, passing up through the arms. Each shoe has also an iron pin, about an inch in length, which fits into the wooden block and keeps the iron facing steadily in its place.

On the shaft *f*, passing through the central pillar *f'*, is the yoke *g*, which, being fitted with a sliding key, can be raised by means of the screw *h*; and the ends of the yoke itself being attached to the wooden cross arms, the mullers will be raised at the same time. This arrangement for raising the mullers is not, however, very important, since they are usually allowed to grind with their full weight. Steam is introduced into the pulp by the pipe *i*, the discharge being effected by means of the apertures J. The false bottom is made one inch less in

FIG. 53.

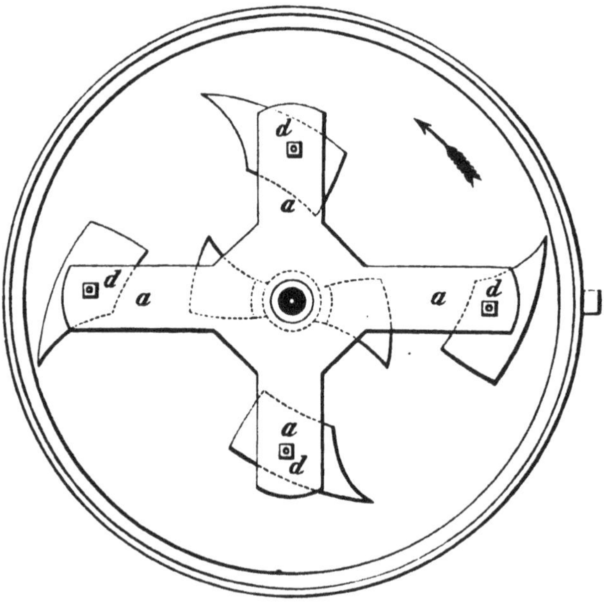

COMMON PAN.
(*Plan.*)

diameter than the bottom of the pan itself, and has an aperture in the centre an inch larger in diameter than the base of the pillar, in which the vertical shaft works. To fasten the bottom in its place, and prevent the mercury from finding its way under it, strips of cloth, about two inches in width, are lapped around the edge of the false bottom, as well as applied against the sides of the pan. A little iron cement is then poured in, and the bottom secured in its place by means of well-dried wooden wedges tightly driven between the two layers of cloth. These wedges, which are driven quite close to each other, must be somewhat shorter than the thickness of the false bottom; thus leaving a space above them which is subsequently covered with a paste of iron cement, that is allowed to set before using the apparatus. About one horse-power is required to work this pan, which will amalgamate from one and a half to two tons of ore in the course of 24 hours.

Varney's Pan.—A drawing of this apparatus to scale is given Plate VII.: fig. 1 is a Vertical Section of this amalgamator; fig. 2, a Plan of the parts beneath pan; fig. 3, Elevation of the amalgamator complete; fig. 4, View of interior of amalgamator; fig. 5, View of one-half the lower dies with wood in slots; fig. 6, View of under side of one-half of muller with shoes attached; figs. 7 and 8, Stand for gear on vertical shaft; and fig. 9, Pillow-block for the driving shaft.

The body of the amalgamator consists of a pan or tub A, figs. 1 and 3, with cover B, through which is an opening for the introduction of the pulp to be ground and amalgamated. The pan is supported on suitable framework, shown in fig. 2. From the centre of the pan and extending from its bottom, to which it is cast, some distance above the cover stands the vertical tube D, through the interior of which is a hole passing vertically through the pan, in order that the shaft C may work through it. On the bottom of the pan, and secured to it by bolts *e*, is fixed the lower muller *a*, consisting of a circular iron plate having a round hole *d* in its centre, considerably larger than the base of the tube D. This die may, if desired, be made in sections.

That portion of the hole through the muller not occupied by the tube D, is so filled with wood as to present a plain surface from the tube to the circumference of the muller. The diameter of this muller is somewhat less than that of the interior of the pan, by which means a space *a'* is left to be filled with quicksilver. Above the lower muller is the upper one *b*, of like general form and size, having twelve shoes *c*, the form and relative positions of which will be understood by supposing a plate of the diameter and thickness of the lower muller attached to the under side of the upper one, and sawn into twelve equal parts on lines drawn from the circumference of the plate to the outside of the tube D. The saw must also be supposed to be held inclined at an angle of about forty-five degrees, thus forming radial grooves from the inner to the outer opening.

Each shoe is fastened to the muller by a bolt, or a wrought iron rivet, cast into the shoe and riveted into a counter-sink on the upper side of the muller, as shown at *f*, fig. 1; the bosses and recesses *j*, keep the die in its place. In the lower muller are radial slots, similar to those in the upper one. These slots may be either inclined laterally or be made vertical. The slots in the lower muller are filled with wood, so as to grind on its end, in order that it may be kept slightly worn, in advance of the wear of the die; thus furnishing a cavity for the admission of pulp between the surfaces, by which the grinding capacity of the machine is greatly increased.

Over and around the tube D, but not in contact with it, is placed the larger tube E, exactly perpendicular to the lower face of the upper muller, and having around its lower extremity the flange V, upon which rests the ring *h*, which is cast with, and forms a part of, the upper muller. This is connected with the muller by means of six curved arms *i*, two pairs of which are much nearer together than the others, and the space between them is filled by a projection from the periphery of the flange V, for the purpose of carrying with it the upper muller when the flange makes a revolution. To the shaft C is fastened the large tube E by the feather *k*, and set screws *l* in the hub G. The shaft C passes through a Babbet metal bearing at *m*, and through the boss F of the driving wheel, in which is a feather sliding vertically in the shaft. The shaft is stepped, by the ordinary method, into the vertical sliding box H, which is itself held in the laterally adjustable box O.

The step box rests upon an iron bar, one end of which is supported by a screw bolt *w*, fig. 4, and the other is held by a bolt and hand wheel *x*, figs. 3 and 4, by which it can be either raised or lowered; raising or lowering the upper muller at the same time.

Within the body of the pan are suspended three curved plates *r*, figs. 1 and 4, extending from near the surface of the upper muller upwards, and stretching in length from the inner side of the pan around to a point near the outside of the large boss, opposite that from which they started.

The lower edges of the curved plates are bent inwards, as shown at *s*, fig. 4, forming flanges. The inner ends of the curved plates are secured rigidly to the ring *q*, of sufficient diameter to surround and clear the tube E; the whole being suspended by a rod attached to each plate, passing through the cover and hand wheels J, by which it may be adjusted. The outer ends of the curved plates slide vertically in grooves in the projections *t*, cast upon the inner side of the pan. The operation of this apparatus is as follows: The space *a'* about the periphery of the lower muller is filled with quicksilver, and the pan nearly filled with pulp, of the proper consistency to flow easily; the shaft C is now made to revolve at a proper speed, from sixty to eighty revolutions per minute, by which the upper muller is rotated. The pulp between the mullers, by means of the centrifugal force developed, is made to pass out through the radial channels between the dies, as well as between the grinding surfaces of the upper and lower mullers; also into and over the quicksilver, thereby causing amalgamation.

The outward motion of the pulp has the effect of keeping the quicksilver entirely away from the grinding surface, thereby obviating what has often proved a very serious difficulty—viz. the grinding of the mercury.

The rotation of the upper muller causes the pulp in the pan to revolve with it. This current is met by the cuneiform projections and curved plates, and thereby turned towards the central opening in the upper muller. The radial slots between the shoes, running from the central opening to the outward one, allow currents of considerable size to pass with great velocity; and the pulp filling these slots, being continually thrown outwardly, tends to produce a vacuum. By this the pulp in the body of the pan is set in motion, causing a rapid and abundant flow downwards at the centre, and upwards along the inner surface of the pan. The pulp is thus made to circulate, until complete pulverisation of the quartz and amalgamation of the metals have taken place.

Wheeler's Pan.—This apparatus, which in size and certain other respects closely resembles that of Mr. Varney, is represented Fig. 54; A being the pan, with the dies *a*, in their several places; whilst B represents the rotating muller, fitted with its shoes *b*, removed from the pan, and turned bottom upwards. The upper muller is, like that of the pan last described, driven by means of a hollow cone, which passes over the central pillar, and is connected with the vertical shaft by means of a sliding key.

As in the case of the other pans, the distance between the mullers is regulated by a screw, fitted with a hand wheel. The shoes *b* are secured to the upper muller, either by bolts and nuts, or more frequently by projections passing through inclined oblong holes in the rotating plate, to which they are firmly secured by means of wooden wedges. The dies *a* are laid on the bottom of the pan, and kept in their places by the ring *c* in the centre, and on the sides by the inclined ledges *d*, under which their ends are wedged. The dies, like the shoes, are one inch thick, and bevelled on the edges in the same direction; so that, when put together, grooves are formed between them, as shown in the drawing. On the upper side of the outer edge of the muller are inclined ledges, which, in connexion with those, *d*, cast on the pan, create an upward current in the pulp; whilst guide plates, somewhat similar to those of the Varney Pan, which slide into grooves at *e*, convey it towards the centre. This pan stands on a cast iron framing, and is driven by mitre wheels from beneath.

FIG. 54.

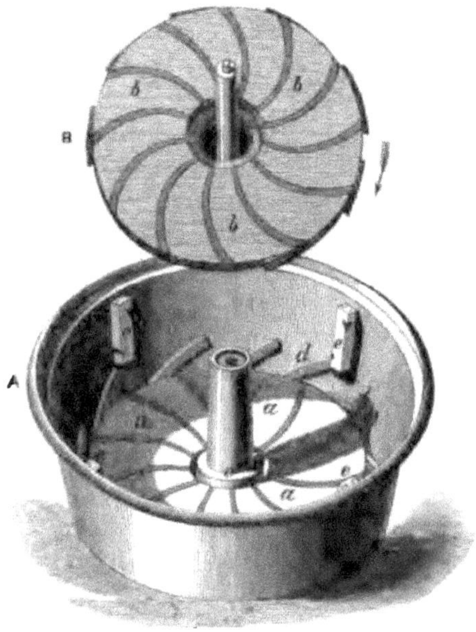

WHEELER'S PAN.

From the dies and bottom not being cast perfectly true, the grinding surfaces are often, at first, a little uneven, and consequently the grinding planes should not at once be brought into too close contact.

The runner of these pans requires to be lifted at least once a week, for the purpose of removing the amalgam which accumulates around the central pillar, and thus prevents the pulp from passing freely between the grinding surfaces. This pan, like that previously described, is generally made four feet in diameter at bottom, and requires from two and a half to three horse-power to work it efficiently. It usually makes about sixty revolutions per minute.

Hepburn and Peterson's Pan.—This pan differs mainly from the foregoing, as will be seen by the annexed illustration, Fig. 55, in the

FIG. 55.

HEPBURN AND PETERSON'S PAN

shape of the bottom, which is inclined towards the centre, or shaped like an inverted cone. The shoes are bolted to this cone, and the corresponding dies fastened to the bottom. When the pulp is thrown into this apparatus, and the mullers set in motion, that portion of it which finds its way between the grinding surfaces is thrown towards the circumference, from whence it again descends by gravitation to the centre, and passes between the mullers. A constant and active circulation is thus established without the aid of curves or wings; which have sometimes been found an impediment in starting similar machines, after the sand has become packed from stopping. Under all ordinary circumstances, however, this or any of the other well-constructed amalgamating pans may be readily started, without either removing or thinning down the pulp, by simply elevating the muller, by means of the screw and movable nut with which they are now generally provided. The charge for this pan is about 1,400 lbs. and the time required for working it is from two to four hours, in accordance with the fineness of its state of division and other characteristics. When the ore has been sufficiently reduced and amalgamated, the pulp is, after dilution with water, discharged into another pan, called a *separator*, and the amalgamating pan immediately re-charged, without stopping the machine. After the pulp has been run off into the separator, it is further thinned down with water to such a consistency as will allow the mercury and amalgam to settle, whilst it still retains sufficient plasticity to hold the coarser particles of ore in suspension in water. The condition of the pulp is readily ascertained by placing the hand in it during the process of separation. If it be in a proper state of dilution, the mercury and amalgam will gradually precipitate, and at the same time no perceptible difference will be felt in the consistency of the pulp situated near the bottom and that at the top of the vessel. When, however, too large a proportion of water has been added, the coarser particles will be felt to distinctly separate from the slime, and strike against the hand when placed near the bottom of the separator. In working these, or other similar machines, the charges are generally so regulated that only one charge, from the two pans, working in conjunction with a separator, may be ready to operate on at a time; thus taking, in each case, one-half the time for effecting the separation that is consumed in reducing and amalgamating. Some amalgamators, however, prefer to occupy the same length of time in effecting the separation that is required for amalgamation; and in this case the separators require to be of larger dimensions, or to be more numerous, since both pans are run off together.

The Hepburn and Peterson Pan is much employed in the reduction establishments of the Pacific Coast, and, in addition to being an excellent amalgamator, is also a good grinder; but it has the disadvantage of requiring the expenditure of from four to five horse-power for its efficient working. The charge of the Wheeler Pan is not only less than that of the Hepburn and Peterson Pan, but its grinding power is also less considerable. This pan usually makes between fifty and sixty revolutions per minute.

Separators.—These differ more or less in their details, but generally consist of a large wooden tub, having a considerably greater diameter than the pans, and provided with a cast iron bottom. Arms and mullers are attached to a shaft working through the centre of this bottom, as explained when describing the construction of the common pan. In this case, however, the mullers are sometimes made of mere blocks of hard wood, the object being simply the agitation of the pulp for the purpose of concentrating at the bottom the quicksilver and amalgam run off from the pans. The mullers in the separator are only allowed to make from ten to twelve revolutions per minute.

Working in Pans.—The reduction process simply consists in treating the pulverised ore in cast iron pans in such a way as to cause the amalgamation of the gold and silver it contains. The same principles are to a great extent involved in this process as in the Mexican patio; but, by intelligent modifications of the treatment, as much is accomplished by the former in a few hours as can be effected by the latter in as many weeks. Although the improvement on the old Mexican process already made has been very great, much yet remains to be accomplished. In order to the most complete and perfect separation of the metallic from the earthy constituents of the ores, it is first necessary that they should be reduced to an impalpable powder by grinding. This is but imperfectly done by the stamping mill, and much is left to be accomplished by the pans. The friction of the pan should not, however, be more than sufficient to insure the perfect mixture of the ingredients which it contains, in such a way as to promote a rapid series of chemical changes, resulting in the decomposition of the constituents of the ore, and the combination of the precious metals with mercury, at the least possible cost of power and material.

With this view, from twelve hundred and fifty to fifteen hundred pounds of ore, from the tanks of the stamping mill, are put into the Varney or Wheeler Pan, and the grinding muller gradually lowered until the whole mass has become reduced to an impalpable powder. This is usually accomplished in about an hour. Loose steam is then turned on until the temperature has been raised to 200° Fahr.; but care is at the same time taken not to render the pulp too liquid by the accumulation of condensed water. The muller having been slightly raised, to prevent too great an amount of friction between it and the dies, quicksilver is gradually added in the form of a fine shower, by pressing it slowly through a canvas bag. The quantity of quicksilver used varies, according to the richness of the ores, to from ten to fifteen per cent. of the weight of mineral operated on. Amalgamation is further promoted by the addition to the pulp, immediately after introducing the quicksilver, of sulphate of copper and a small quantity of sulphuric acid.

For second class ores, two pounds of sulphate of copper, in solution with an equal quantity of sulphuric acid, and three pounds of salt, may be advantageously employed.* An endless variety of substances has been used for this purpose, since at one period every amalgamator prescribed some new specific for avoiding imperfect amalgamation; but those above enumerated have alone maintained a permanent character for efficiency.† Much, however, yet remains to be accomplished by a more careful study of the modifications rendered necessary by the varying constitution of the ores operated on. The running of the pan is continued for three hours and a half, the heat being maintained at from 180° to 200° Fahr. At the expiration of this time, water is run into the pulp to render it sufficiently liquid to flow off, through a valve in the bottom of the pan, into the agitator or separator. The pan is then roughly washed down, and, with as little delay as possible, recharged with ore, as before. A Varney Pan four feet in diameter is capable of working six charges in twenty-four hours, or from 7,500 to 9,000 lbs. of ore. Once or twice a week, or at the finishing of any particular parcel of ore, the muller is taken out, the shoes and dies removed, and all the amalgam adhering to the working parts, or deposited in the crevices, carefully scraped off. A notable accession to the product is thus obtained, especially as, at the same time, the mortar bed of the stamps is likewise cleaned out.

In the separator the pulp is mixed with a large quantity of water, and a regular steady supply kept up, so as to carry off the lighter particles of earthy matter, at first from holes in the upper part of the pan; but as the separation proceeds, the discharging point is gradually lowered, until eventually nothing but the heavier pyrites and liquid amalgam is left. The amalgam is drawn off from the bottom, and the pyrites then scooped out, and, after being further washed in another

* Dr. Oxland, who has had considerable experience in the treatment of silver ores by the pan process, informs us that he has obtained as good results with sulphate of copper alone, as with the addition of salt and sulphuric acid.

† It is scarcely necessary to notice the various absurd ingredients which have occasionally been employed in Nevada with a view of facilitating amalgamation, such, for instance, as tobacco juice, decoction of sage bush, and of oak bark; since any success which may have attended their use must manifestly be attributed, rather to a fortuitous combination of circumstances, than to any direct action of the materials themselves.

separating pan, to remove the last traces of amalgam, it is reserved for final treatment by calcination and reduction in barrels. The amalgam is now carefully washed in clean water, dried with flannel, and finally removed to the amalgam room, where it is strained through thick conical bags of canvas, twelve inches in diameter at the larger end and two feet in length.* After the bags have drained for some time, they are beaten with a round stick to cause a further quantity of the mercury to run off. The hard dry amalgam is finally removed from the bags, and weighed into store. The mercury run off from the bags is technically known as "charged quicksilver," and, after being mixed with retorted mercury, is returned to the pan room for further use. Charged quicksilver is preferred to the pure metal, as with it amalgamation is found to proceed more rapidly.

Retorting.—The amalgam is finally handed over to the assay office belonging to the mill, and the separation of mercury is effected by exposing the amalgam to a red heat in a cylindrical cast iron retort, about twelve inches in diameter and three feet long, mounted on an arch of firebrick, and placed within another arch, from the crown of which the smoke is carried off to the chimney. The retort is fitted with a stout cover, carefully adjusted like the stopper of a coal-gas retort. From the upper part of the end, a two-inch iron pipe carries off the volatile matters. This is so fitted to the downcast pipe, four feet in length, that, by T-pieces and stoppers, every facility is afforded for cleaning out the pipes. The downcast pipe is so fitted within another pipe, 3½ to 4 inches in diameter, as to constitute a Liebig's condenser, into the bottom of which cold water is supplied; the heated water flowing off from the top. The downcast pipe opens into a small bottomless chamber, immersed sufficiently low in a tank of water to keep it air-tight, but in such a manner as to prevent accidents from the absorption of water into the heated retort.

This retort is provided with several cast iron semicircular trays, which slide easily in and out; these are divided into two parts by a transverse partition. Before the weighed charge of amalgam is put into the tray, it is coated with milk of lime, or a thin wash of clay,

* The washing of the amalgam is generally effected in a vessel called a cleaning up pan, provided with four arms furnished with shoes like those represented, Figs. 52 and 53. In some cases, however, the matters escaping from the separators are now run off over blankets on which a certain proportion of the undecomposed sulphides is caught, and this is subsequently re-treated either by barrel amalgamation or otherwise.

and not unfrequently a sheet of paper is also placed over the bottom. By these precautions the retorted amalgam is prevented from adhering to the iron, and much trouble avoided. The charge having been placed in the retort, the cover is carefully luted with a mixture of clay and wood ashes, made up into a thin paste. The fire is then lighted, and the heat slowly and steadily raised, until the retort is of a bright red colour, and is so maintained until the mercury ceases to distil over. The retort is now allowed to cool gradually down, and when cold the retorted silver is withdrawn and weighed, as is also the mercury obtained, as a precaution against any possible loss of quicksilver from hidden leaks in the retort. The retorted amalgam is broken up, melted in plumbago crucibles, and cast into bars or ingots of "bullion" of from one thousand to fifteen hundred ounces each. These are assayed and valued, the value being marked on the bars, which are then ready for the market. The quality or "fineness" is marked in thousandths, thus—gold 24, silver 841, making together 865 thousandths; leaving 135 parts in a thousand, which principally consist of copper; but no notice is taken of this, as it is of no money value in the sale of the bar.

The retort employed at the mills near Virginia for the distillation of silver amalgam is represented, Figs. 56 and 57, of which the first is partially in section, and the second is a longitudinal section.

The ash-pit A is beneath the fireplace B, which communicates, by means of flues *a*, with a chamber *b*, enclosing the cast iron retort C, from which the products of combustion are conveyed by the flues 1, 2, 3, through the arched cavity *c*, to the chimney *d*.

By dampers covering these flues the draught may be controlled so as to heat the retort according to the requirements of the case. The pipe D carries the vaporised mercury to the vertical pipe E, in which it is condensed, by the action of a stream of cold water passing upward from the bottom through the Liebig's condenser F. The condensed mercury collects in the reservoir G, from which it is drawn off into bottles through a bent tube at the bottom. Any vapours escaping from the retort door are conveyed into the flues by the hood *e*, of sheet iron. The arrangement of the cover of the retort is shown at *g*, and a portion of the semi-cylindrical tray, used for charging the retort, at *h*; the position of the iron plates and braces for binding the brickwork is represented by the letters *f*.

The best results obtained by the pan process rarely amount to 75 per cent. of the assay value of the ore; the average will scarcely exceed 65 per cent. The barrel process, being more expensive, cannot be employed in Nevada except on ores of the first class. The tailings from the pan process, after having been exposed to the action of the atmosphere for a few months, may sometimes be again advantageously worked over, thus increasing the total produce to about 85 per cent.; but it is only under favourable circumstances that this can be done.

Fig. 56.

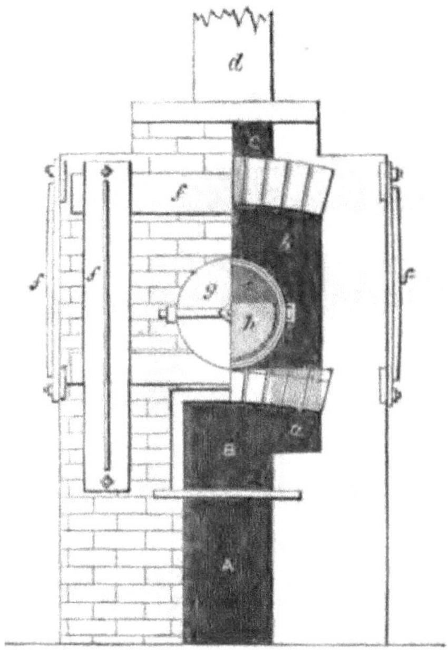

Retort.
(Front Elevation.)

The cost of working from $45 to $50 ores by the pan process is, in those portions of the State of Nevada in which water-power can be obtained, nearly as follows:—

Stamping wet, through No. 6 screens	$1·50	per ton.
Milling, including loss of mercury, &c.	5·00	„ „
Total cost, including wear and tear . .	$6·50	„ „

The loss of mercury amounts to from $1\frac{1}{4}$ to $1\frac{1}{2}$ lb. for each ton of ore containing silver to the amount of from $35 to $50 per ton.

Arrangement of Reduction Works.—The usual arrangement of crushing and amalgamation works for the treatment of silver ores by the pan process, where water-power is available, will be understood by reference to Plate VIII., which represents a transverse sectional elevation of an establishment in Nevada, in which Wheeler's Pans are employed. The water-wheel A communicates its motion, by means of toothed segments around its periphery, to a pinion shaft on which is

FIG. 57.

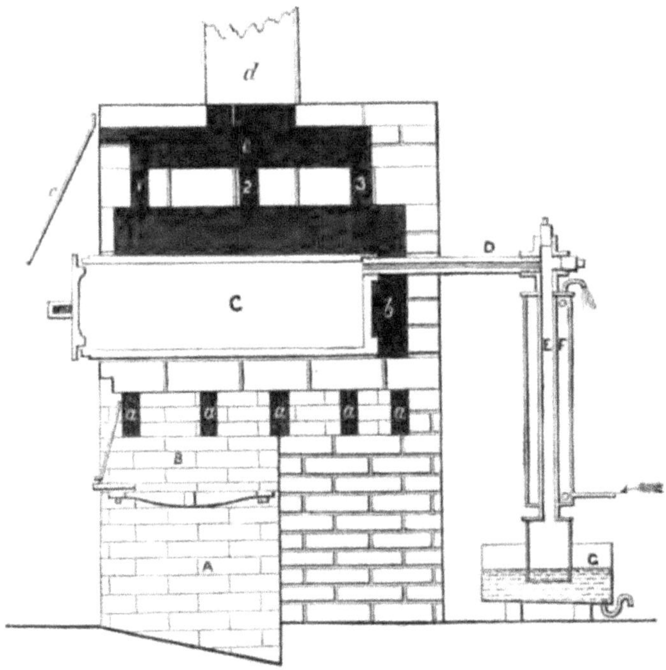

RETORT.
(*Longitudinal Section.*)

the drum B, which, in its turn, transmits the power, by means of broad composition belts, to the whole of the machinery employed in the establishment. The dimensions of the second pulley C, and that on the shaft D, are so calculated as to cause each stamper to be raised from 70 to 80 times per minute. The stops *d* are employed for supporting the stampers when not in action, and are for that purpose slipped under the bosses or tappets on the iron stems, when raised to the full extent of their course by the cams keyed on the shaft set in motion by the pulley D. The tightening pulleys E are for the purpose of keeping the different straps in a proper state of tension. The stampers F discharge the pulverised ore, through the grates or screens *f*, into the spouts *g*, which conduct it to the receiving tanks G, G′. The hand wheel H is employed for opening and closing the valve *h*, by which the supply of water to the wheel can be either regulated or cut off. From the amalgamating pan I, the *slums* are run off, through the spouts *i*, into the separator K, which is provided with the overflow *k*. The cleaning up pan, L, with the other pans and separators, receives its motion from belts driven by pulleys on the shaft O. The pipe M affords the necessary supply of water, whilst N is the steam pipe by which the heating of the pulp is effected. In the drawing, the pan is represented as having a false bottom, for the purpose of heating the pulp by the introduction of steam, but in practice it is generally now found more convenient to blow loose steam directly into the pulp.

The hand wheel P is for the purpose of regulating the tightening pulley E. This mill has twenty stampers, twelve Wheeler Pans, six separators, and two cleaning up pans.

AMALGAMATION OF ROASTED ORES IN PANS.—In some of the mining districts of Nevada, and particularly in the neighbourhood of Austin, where the ores consist of various compound sulphides of silver, containing a considerable amount of antimony, the ordinary pan process, as practised in Virginia, cannot be advantageously employed. The ores from this part of the State consequently require roasting before being subjected to amalgamation, and then, when worked in the pans, afford better results than those obtained from the ores of the Comstock vein treated in their raw state. Each battery of five stampers will crush (dry) four tons of ore daily, through a wire gauze screen of 40 holes per linear inch. One thousand pounds of this crushed ore is roasted with 8 per cent. of common salt; the time occupied in the furnace by each charge being, on an average, six hours. Varney's Pans are most commonly employed, and are charged with from 800 to 1,000 lbs. of roasted ore, which occupies five hours in working.

A mill of ten stampers, with all the necessary furnaces, pans, and appliances, will treat eight tons of ore in the course of twenty-four hours, with a total consumption of about ten cords of wood. The following figures, relative to the treatment of roasted silver ores by pan amalgamation, give the results of an experiment made at Virginia city on ores from the Comstock vein, but it is stated that the loss of silver in the neighbourhood of Austin, where the ores contain little or no gold, seldom exceeds 7 per cent. of the assay value.

Results of an Experiment showing Loss of Metal by Amalgamation of Roasted Ore in Pans.

Value of ore in gold	$112·85, in silver	$180·37 . . .	$293·22
„ Bullion	97·43, „	162·99 . . .	260·42
„ loss „	13·60 per cent.	9·06 per cent.	11·18 per cent.

Loss of quicksilver greater than in barrels.

CHAPTER XIX.

TREATMENT OF ARGENTIFEROUS ORES AND PRODUCTS BY SOLUTION AND PRECIPITATION.

AUGUSTIN'S PROCESS—ROASTING WITH SALT—LIXIVIATION AND PRECIPITATION—ZIERVOGEL'S PROCESS—ROASTING—SOLUTION OF SULPHATE OF SILVER—PRECIPITATION OF SILVER BY COPPER—VON PATERA'S PROCESS—ROASTING WITH COMMON SALT—SOLUTION OF CHLORIDE OF SILVER IN HYPOSULPHITE OF SODA—PRECIPITATION BY SULPHIDE OF SODIUM—TREATMENT OF SULPHIDE OF SILVER.

THE different processes by which silver is obtained by the *wet way* from the various ores and metallurgical products containing that metal are all of recent invention, and belong to the latest period in the history of metallurgy. These methods have now, in many cases, supplanted the older processes of liquation and amalgamation, and may be often advantageously adopted for the treatment of argentiferous compounds; particularly when the amount of lead present is small, and the proportion of copper large. They all possess the advantage, over amalgamation, of entailing no loss of mercury, and in the promptness and completeness with which the metal may be extracted. They are also, from requiring less time and fuel, and in being attended with a smaller loss of the various metals contained in the substance under treatment, less expensive than fusion with lead ores. The several wet processes are likewise more expeditious, and require a smaller amount of fuel than the old method of liquation; besides which, they effect a much more complete separation of the copper and silver.

AUGUSTIN'S PROCESS.—This method of treating argentiferous compounds was first introduced in 1849 by an officer of the Mansfeld Copper Works, at the Gottesbelohnung Works, near Eisleben, in Prussian Saxony, where, after being retained for a short time, it was superseded by the cheaper and still more simple process of Ziervogel. Augustin's method of extracting silver from its ores is dependent on the following circumstances:—

1st. That the silver contained in ores of that metal may be converted into chloride of silver by roasting them with a proper admixture of common salt.

2nd. That a solution of common salt will dissolve chloride of silver in quantities depending on its temperature and state of concentration.*

3rd. That the silver contained in an argentiferous solution of chloride of sodium is precipitated in the metallic state by copper. At Freiberg this system is employed for the extraction of silver from a regulus or copper matt, containing about 70 per cent. of copper and 0·0042 of silver, besides a certain amount of iron, antimony, and arsenic, with other impurities. In order that this matt may be properly roasted, it is first ground to a very fine powder and bolted through sieves of wire gauze.

Roasting.—The furnace employed for this operation is of the ordinary reverberatory description, the fuel employed being pit coal, and the weight of the charge treated four hundred pounds. One workman attends to each furnace, and the fire, which at first is kept low, is gradually raised, care being at the same time taken to keep the powdered matt constantly stirred, in order to prevent caking, and that every portion may be equally exposed to the full temperature of the hearth. At the termination of eight hours the operation begins to approach completion; the bright glow, indicative of the presence of sulphur, disappears, and sulphurous acid is no longer evolved.. The charge is now withdrawn from the furnace, and, after being allowed to cool, is ground between burr stones, passed through a fine bolt, and subjected to chlorination.

Roasting with Salt.—The roasted matt, in which, at this stage of the operation, the copper and iron chiefly exist in the state of oxides, whilst the silver has either been converted into a sulphate or reduced to the metallic state, is now roasted in charges of three hundred pounds weight, in furnaces similar to those employed for the first operation. After being for a short time exposed to a low temperature, common salt, to the amount of 5 per cent. of the weight of the charge, is introduced, and the roasting continued, with the usual amount of

* At a temperature of 32° Fahr. the amount of chloride of silver dissolved by a solution of common salt is almost inappreciable. At 50° Fahr. a solution of salt takes up chloride of silver amounting to 0·0017 of the weight of chloride of sodium present, at 64° its dissolving capacity has increased to 0·0024, and about 212° to 0·0068, of the amount of salt in the brine.

stirring, for about three hours. By this means the decomposition of the chloride of sodium is effected through the agency of the sulphuric acid of the metallic sulphates; and, by the combination of chlorine with the silver present, nearly the whole of that metal becomes converted into chloride. The charge is now withdrawn from the furnace, and is ready for the process of lixiviation.

Lixiviation and Precipitation.—The lixiviation of the matts thus prepared takes place in an upper story of the establishment, and is conducted in a series of tubs ranged in a line along one of its walls. The construction and form of these vessels will be understood by reference to Fig. 58, which represents one of the lixiviating tubs with the portion nearest the spectator removed. Upon the bottom *a* is

FIG. 58.

LIXIVIATING TUB.

first laid a wooden cross *b*, on which rests the perforated false bottom *c*, on the top of which is again arranged a layer of straw *d*; above this is placed a filter of linen cloth, made tight against the sides of the tub by means of a hoop, and on this is deposited the roasted matt to be lixiviated; the filtered liquor being drawn off by means of the tap *d'*. These tubs are three feet nine inches in height, two feet eight inches in diameter at top, and two feet four inches at bottom.

Eight of them are charged at the same time, each with eight hundred pounds of the prepared matt; and a stream of hot brine is directed, through a perforated cover, into each, by means of suitable pipes arranged for that purpose. The chloride of silver being thus dissolved in the hot solution of chloride of sodium, is carried by it through the filter, and flowing off by the taps *d'*, is conducted through a wooden gutter to a covered tank, in which the particles of ground matt, carried off in suspension, are allowed to settle. The liquors from this settling tank are now conveyed to a series of three tubs, which, like those already described, are all furnished with false bottoms and filters; being also so placed one above the other that the liquor escaping from the tap of the first will flow into the second, and from thence into the third and last vat. In the bottom of the two upper tubs is placed a layer of cement copper from six to seven inches in thickness, whilst on the filter of the last is laid a quantity of scrap iron. On admitting the saline liquor into the first of these tubs, a large proportion of the silver which it contains is precipitated in the metallic form at the expense of the copper, which, by combining with the chlorine of the chloride of silver, is itself in turn converted into chloride. The liquors escaping from this tub are received into the second of the series, also provided with a thick layer of cement copper, by which the last traces of silver are precipitated. The liquid, which has been thus freed from silver, but has now become highly cupreous, falls directly into the lowest tub, containing scrap iron, by which the copper is deposited in a form suitable for the precipitation of silver in the upper tubs during succeeding operations.

The brine flowing from the last tub, and deprived both of its silver and copper, is now pumped into a proper receiver, and, after being boiled, may be again used for lixiviation. In this way the hot brine is passed through the lixiviating tubs until a plate of bright copper does not become coated with silver when held for some time in the liquors escaping from them. The residual matters remaining in the tubs, and which chiefly consist of oxide of copper, are then removed to give place to fresh charges, but before being treated for copper are assayed, in order to ascertain the amount of silver which they still retain. Should they be found to contain more than a quantity corresponding to 0·0003 of the weight of matt operated on, they are again roasted and lixiviated; but if, on the other hand, the proportion of silver be less than that stated, they are at once fused for copper.

The cement silver, in the form of a crystalline powder, is about once a week removed from the tubs in which it has been precipitated; and after being treated with dilute hydrochloric acid, for the purpose of removing any traces of copper, is thoroughly washed with clean water. When sufficiently washed, the metallic sponge is pressed into balls, thoroughly dried, and taken to the Saxon mint, where it is purified and fused into bars. This process is at present only employed for the extraction of silver from matts in which that metal has, in conjunction with copper, become concentrated by repeated roastings and fusions. It may, however, under certain conditions, be found directly applicable to some of the various ores of silver.

ZIERVOGEL'S PROCESS.—Shortly after the adoption of Augustin's process at the works belonging to the Mansfeld Company, the cheaper and still more simple method of converting the silver into sulphate, and subsequently dissolving it out by hot water, was introduced by Hüttenmeister Ziervogel, and since the year 1857 the whole of the argentiferous matts worked in the establishment have been treated according to this plan.

The efficiency of the method of Ziervogel depends on the circumstance, that when a finely-powdered matt, consisting of the sulphides of copper and iron containing a certain proportion of silver, is, with proper precautions, roasted in a reverberatory furnace, the iron and copper first pass into the state of sulphates, which are afterwards transformed into oxides. The sulphide of silver subsequently undergoes a similar transformation, and, if the roasting were continued, would ultimately be reduced to the metallic state. If, however, the operation be arrested at the proper stage, the copper and iron will have become transformed into oxides, whilst nearly the whole of the silver exists as a soluble sulphate readily removed by water; which thus affords a means of separating that metal from the other constituents of the charge, which are, for the most part, insoluble in that menstruum. From the argentiferous liquors thus obtained, the silver is afterwards precipitated by means similar to those employed in the method of Augustin; but when a solution of the sulphate is effected by the use of water, in place of dissolving the chloride by means of hot brine, nearly the whole of the silver originally present in the sulphides treated may be obtained in the metallic state.

Roasting.—The matt, after being ground between a pair of millstones, four feet in diameter, made of the granite of the Hartz, is bolted through a circular sieve, of from 1,400 to 1,500 apertures to the square inch, and then carefully roasted in a reverberatory furnace, specially adapted to the purpose.

This furnace, which is provided with two distinct hearths, placed one above the other, has an exterior length of nineteen feet, and a width of thirteen feet; its total height being about fifteen feet. The two hearths on which the roasting is conducted are each ten feet long by eight feet wide, and are built of good firebrick, of which all the parts of the apparatus subjected to a high temperature require to be constructed. The fireplace is provided with a grate, from which the flame passes across a firebridge over the contents of the lower hearth, and, ascending a perpendicular flue, the heated gases are conducted, in a tortuous direction, through a number of channels over the arch of the upper chamber. In these flues are deposited the fine particles of matt mechanically carried over by the draught, and which are, from time to time, removed through suitable openings, for the purpose of being subjected to metallurgical treatment. From these horizontal flues the gases finally pass off into the chimney, whilst the upper hearth, being heated both from above and below, is in the condition of a muffle, through which none of the gases of the furnace are allowed to pass. This hearth is, therefore, well adapted for effecting the calcination of ores when they cannot be brought to a high temperature without danger of fusing. In the bottom of this hearth, passing through the arch of the lower one, is an aperture, closed by an iron plate, through which the charge can be raked into the lower bed of the furnace. When the roasting on the lower hearth is completed, the charge is raked through another opening, also covered by a plate, into an iron waggon, which is run into an arched tunnel beneath it.

The ground matts from the mill are mixed with about 15 per cent. of the residues remaining in the tubs, after the process of lixiviation; and from 500 to 600 lbs. of the mixture is charged upon the upper hearth of the furnace, where it is exposed to a gradually increasing temperature, and kept constantly stirred during about seventy-five minutes. The portion of the charge most remote from the fire is now brought forward towards the bridge, and any lumps which may have been formed are carefully broken with an iron rod. The roasting is continued, as before, during another period of seventy-five minutes; and at the expiration of two and a half hours from the first introduction of the charge, an addition is made of from 20 to 25 lbs. of ground lignite, in a perfectly dry state. This is mixed with the pulverised matt, by a stirring which occupies about ten minutes, when the plate is removed from the hole in the bottom of the muffle, and the whole of the contents of the upper chamber are raked through it, and spread evenly over the surface of the lower hearth. The heat applied is, at first, moderate; but at the expiration of little more than an hour, during which time the charge has been constantly stirred, and the powdered lignite has become consumed, the temperature is considerably increased.

At the expiration of about ten hours from the time of first charging, the workman, who, particularly during the latter stages of the operation, has kept the contents of the hearth carefully stirred, withdraws a sample, for the purpose of determining whether or not the roasting has become sufficiently advanced. This is done by taking, with a small iron ladle, a spoonful of the ore from different parts of the hearth, and, after placing it in a white earthenware saucer, dropping on it a little pure water, which is allowed to percolate slowly through the edges of the sample. In this way the water takes up any soluble salts which may be present in the roasted matt, and, from the colour assumed by the solution, a correct judgment can, after a little practice, be formed of the condition of the charge.

The liquor which thus escapes from the sample of roasted mineral should present a slightly blue appearance, but be without any shade of green: the addition of a few grains of common salt should, moreover, produce a copious white precipitate of chloride of silver. When these conditions have been satisfactorily fulfilled by the sample taken, the operation is considered finished, and the charge withdrawn. Brushwood, which makes a strong fire, with a long flame, is the only fuel employed in the roasting furnaces at the Mansfeld Works.

The success of this process for the extraction of silver manifestly depends on the degree of facility with which the operation of roasting may be controlled, so as to be enabled to seize the exact period at which the several metallic compounds are in the precise condition required. The sulphate of copper should be, as far as possible, converted into an oxide, whilst the whole of the silver ought to exist in the form of a soluble sulphate. Should the roasting be arrested before this point has been attained, a large amount of copper will be found to remain in a soluble state; whilst a portion of the silver still exists in the form of an insoluble sulphide. If, on the contrary, the roasting be carried too far, the sulphate of silver will have become reduced, leaving that metal in the metallic state; which, being totally insoluble in the hot water employed for lixiviation, will remain with the copper, and become commercially lost. Long practice and much observation are required on the part of the workmen employed in this process, and, with a view of increasing their efficiency, a scale of premiums has been instituted for any more than ordinary success in the work performed.

This system of rewards has been particularly successful at Mansfeld; for, although the process has not itself been in any way modified since its first introduction into the works, yet the skill of the workmen has, within the last few years, increased, in so marked a degree, that the results now obtained are much more satisfactory than those formerly yielded by this method of treatment.

Lixiviation and Precipitation.—The roasted argentiferous matt is now taken to the lixiviation department, which consists of a large room, in which a number of vessels are arranged (as shown in the following woodcut, Fig. 59), and so placed that the liquors flowing from one are immediately received in the next which follows in the series.

FIG. 59.

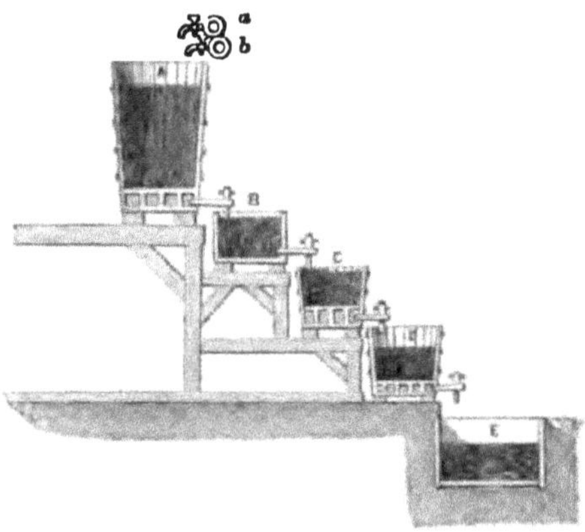

ZIERVOGEL'S PROCESS.
(Arrangement of Apparatus.)

The powder to be operated on is divided into parcels, weighing 400 lbs. each, which are placed in the vessels A, two feet six inches in diameter, and of about the same height, provided with filters and false bottoms; twenty-two cubic feet of liquor from a previous operation, together with about three cubic feet of fresh water, both heated to a temperature of 160° Fahr., are run into each of the upper tubs through the pipes *a*, *b*. A little sulphuric acid is also employed for the purpose of preventing the inconveniences which are found to accompany the presence of basic salts. This fluid, soon permeating the ore in the tubs A, takes up the sulphate of silver, and any other soluble salts present, which, passing through the filter, are carried in solution into the tank B, thirty feet in length, and eighteen inches square, divided into two parts. In this reservoir the liquors enter the first division, and, after allowing the matters held in suspension to settle, the solution flows over the partition, and from thence through ten taps into as many tubs C: in the bottom of each of these are placed 10 lbs. of cement copper and 250 lbs. of coarse copper bars, by which the larger proportion of the silver is precipitated in the metallic form. The fourth vessels D, of which there are five, also contain metallic copper, and in them are precipitated any traces of silver which may have escaped precipitation in the tubs C. From these last tubs the spent liquors flow off into the lead-lined cistern E; from which they are subsequently raised by steam pressure into another leaden cistern above the level of the first series of tubs A, heated to a temperature of 160° Fahr., and passed over a fresh charge of roasted matt, introduced into the series of dissolving vessels A.

About two and a half hours are required to dissolve out the sulphate of silver contained in each charge; and at the end of that time the residual contents of the dissolving tubs are transported to an adjoining room, where an assay sample is taken. Should the results of this assay show that the amount of silver remaining is less than 0·00036 of the weight of the material operated on, the residues are placed aside, for the purpose of being fused for blistered copper; but if, on the other hand, they contain more than this proportion of silver, they are re-roasted by the workmen, without any further payment for labour. When, on the contrary, the assay shows a less amount of silver in the residues than that above stated, the roasters receive a bonus of the value of 12 per cent. on the excess of the precious metal extracted.

The finely-sifted matt, after being withdrawn from the furnace, is allowed to remain about eight hours before being introduced into the lixiviating tubs, and thus becomes cooled down to about 160° Fahr. before charging. When placed in the tubs, hot water is admitted from *a*, until it begins to escape from the taps at the bottom. The water is then turned off, and hot liquors from a previous operation are introduced from the leaden cistern by the pipe *b*, until the liquid flowing from the cocks at the bottoms of the tubs no longer affords a precipitate of chloride of silver on the addition of a weak solution of common salt. The final liquors collected in the vessel E, when they have become too highly charged with sulphate of copper, are brought in contact with scrap iron, and thus afford a supply of cement copper, which may be subsequently employed in the tubs C and D.

The process of Ziervogel is, however, adapted to the requirements of comparatively few localities, since the presence of certain impurities, and particularly of any considerable amount of either arsenic or antimony, gives rise to the formation of insoluble salts, which materially interfere with the extraction of silver. In the Freiberg works, where the process was for some time experimented on, it was found that the presence of these substances so far interfered with the results obtained, that a notable amount of the silver present in the concentrated matts, invariably remained in the insoluble cupreous residues.

As might be anticipated, by far the largest proportion of the silver is deposited in the first precipitating vessel, from which it is from time to time taken for the purpose of being purified and melted into bars. The principal impurities with which it is associated are the sulphates of copper and lime; together with a certain amount of metallic copper derived from the cement copper employed as a precipitant. The two former are removed by repeated washings with hot water, whilst the latter is partially dissolved out by treating the finely divided silver with dilute hydrochloric acid. The precipitate is subsequently refined in a furnace constructed for that purpose, and affords bars containing about 980 thousandths of silver.

According to Lamborn, who carefully examined this process at the Mansfeld works, the cost of treating one hundred weight of copper, usually containing nearly ½ lb. of silver, at that establishment, was as follows:—

By Liquation	10 thalers.
„ Amalgamation	5½ „
„ Augustin's method	4½ „
„ Ziervogel's „	2½ „

The amounts of silver remaining in the Mansfeld copper after treatment by the several processes are the following:—

After Liquation	$\frac{1}{10}$th of one per cent.
„ Amalgamation	$\frac{1}{17}$th „
„ Augustin's method	$\frac{1}{17}$th „
„ Ziervogel's „	$\frac{1}{84}$th „

Von Patera's Process.—This method of extracting silver from its ores consists—1st, in roasting them with an addition of common salt until the whole of the silver has been transformed into chloride; 2nd, in dissolving out the chloride of silver by means of a cold dilute solution of hyposulphite of soda; 3rd, in precipitating the silver in the form of sulphide by the addition of polysulphide of sodium; and 4th, in reducing the precipitated sulphide of silver to the metallic state by exposing it in a muffle, at a high temperature, to the ordinary influences of atmospheric air.

The solution in hyposulphite of soda of the silver contained in argentiferous ores was first suggested in a paper published by Dr. Percy in 1848; and a translation of this having reached the Austrian chemist, it resulted, in 1858, in the introduction, at Joachimsthal, by Von Patera, of the process which now bears his name. The ores from that district are remarkable for the diversity of their constituents, and in addition to silver frequently contain various compounds of copper, lead, bismuth, iron, nickel, and cobalt, associated with sulphur, arsenic, and antimony. The veins in the vicinity of Joachimsthal, though less productive than formerly, still afford a certain amount of argentiferous ore of extraordinary richness, since the average yield of the whole quantity delivered at the works may be taken as affording about 2 per cent. of silver. Smaller quantities are not unfrequently worked containing from 5 to 6 per cent. of that metal, and as much as 15 per cent. of silver has sometimes been extracted from a parcel of ore.

The fuel employed consists of lignite, coal, charcoal, and wood; the first of which is cheap and the second expensive, while the two last are becoming scarce, and growing every year higher in price. The price of labour varies from a shilling to one and sixpence per diem.

Roasting.—The ores, which are prepared partly by hand picking and partly by concentration on shaking tables, are, on being brought to the works, subjected to a process of roasting in a furnace of a somewhat peculiar construction. This apparatus, instead of having the long narrow hearth, broad firebridge, and short wide fireplace, usually employed for roasting sulphurous ores, has a hearth 9 feet 9 inches across, and measuring but 6 feet from the bridge to the flues leading into the chimney. The grate, which is only six inches in width, is four-fifths the length of the longer axis of the hearth, from which it is divided by a sort of firebridge, consisting of an iron tube covered with clay, and pierced with from ten to twelve small openings on the side furthest removed from the fuel. A small boiler, set in brickwork near the furnace, supplies low pressure steam, which can, when required, be introduced into the tubular bridge, and allowed to escape in numerous jets over the surface of the roasting ore.

The mineral to be operated on is introduced into this furnace in charges of four hundred pounds, and the heat slowly and cautiously raised, in order to prevent agglomeration of the particles. During this stage of the operation no steam is admitted, but, as soon as the charge has arrived at a red heat, the tap is turned, and as much steam blown into the hearth as can be safely introduced without so far reducing the temperature as to materially check the activity of the various chemical decompositions which it is desired to effect. At the expiration of four hours from the time of charging, the operation is usually completed; and the ore, after being withdrawn and allowed to cool, is taken to a mill, in which it is ground to a fine powder, with the addition of from six to twelve per cent. of common salt, and two to three per cent. of sulphate of iron. A charge of this mixture, weighing three hundred pounds, is now introduced into a furnace similar to that above described, and is spread evenly over the surface of the hearth. This is raised to a red heat, and the steam admitted as before, care being taken to keep the contents of the apparatus constantly stirred. The temperature is now gradually increased, and at the end of from ten to sixteen hours, according to the nature and richness of the ore, the operation is complete.

The addition of sulphate of iron to the partially desulphurised ore is for the purpose of effecting the necessary decomposition of chloride of sodium, in case a sufficient amount of metallic sulphates should not be otherwise present. The introduction of aqueous vapours is found to facilitate the chlorination of the silver, besides greatly assisting in the condensation of the fumes and vapours in the chambers interposed between the furnaces and the chimney through which the products of combustion finally make their escape. If this recovery of the substance carried off by the draught were not carefully attended to, the loss of silver so caused would amount to about 10 per cent., and the economical treatment of argentiferous ores, by this process, be thus rendered impracticable. The roasted and finely-divided ore, containing silver in the state of chloride, is now taken to the lixiviating room for further treatment.

Lixiviation with Water.—The apparatus employed for the purpose of solution and precipitation will be understood by reference to Fig. 60, which represents a vertical section of the whole arrangement.

In addition to chloride of silver, which is insoluble in water, the

Fig. 60.

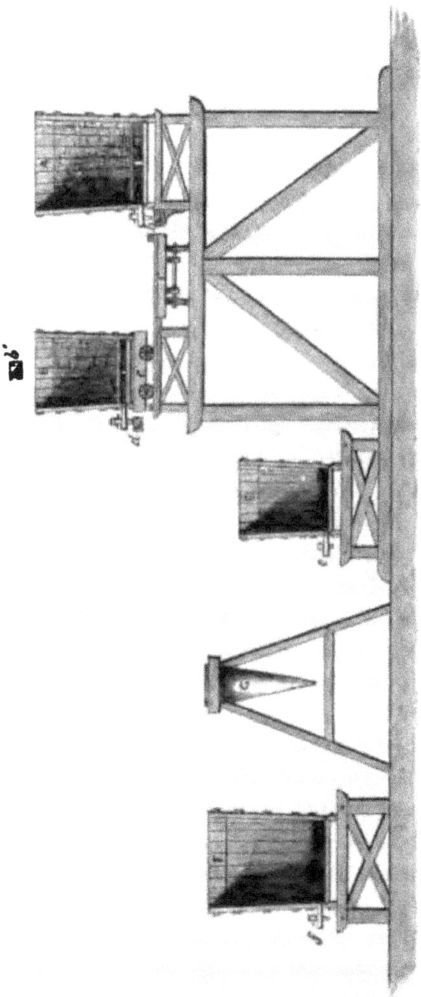

Von Patera's Process.
(*Arrangement of Apparatus.*)

ores contain a certain amount of copper, zinc, nickel, cobalt, iron, &c., which, being present in the form of sulphates and chlorides, are readily dissolved in that menstruum. Into each of the tubs A, in the first series, are introduced four hundred pounds of roasted ore; and boiling water is allowed to percolate through the several charges during a period of six hours. By this means all the soluble salts enter into solution, and passing through the filter *a*, are conveyed by the trough *b* into suitable tanks, in which they are precipitated by lime-water, and, if found to contain a sufficient amount of silver, are subsequently treated by fusion with lead ores in a blast furnace.

The liquors falling into *b* are from time to time tested by sulphide of ammonium, and, as soon as no further precipitate is obtained on adding to a sample a few drops of this reagent, the operation is considered to be finished, and cold water is passed through the tubs for the purpose of reducing the temperature of the residues; which must not, until quite cold, be subjected to the action of the solution of hyposulphite of soda.

Lixiviation with Hyposulphite of Soda.—The pulverised ore remaining in the several vessels A, which has been thus freed from all the different salts soluble in hot water, is now transferred to the tubs B, which, like the first, are furnished with filters and false bottoms. Seven of these are employed at Joachimsthal, placed on a level with the tub A, between which and the vessels B is a small railway on which is the car *c*. The tubs B stand on a low truck *c'*, which can be run from the position shown in the woodcut on to the waggon *c*, and afterwards made to traverse, either backwards or forwards, parallel with, and in close proximity to, the line of tubs A. The vessel B, after receiving a charge of two hundred pounds of the residual ore from one of the tubs A, is taken back to its place and there treated with the liquor by which solution of the silver is to be effected.

This consists of a cold aqueous solution of hyposulphite of soda, brought from a tank by means of the trough *b'*, and allowed to percolate slowly through the mass. In this way the chloride of silver is taken up in the form of a double salt and passes through the filter, in the bottom of the tub, into the trough *d*, by which it is conveyed to the precipitating tubs E, F.

The time necessary for the completion of the operation is more or less influenced both by the richness of the ores and their state of mechanical division; the richest samples, containing 15 per cent. of silver, requiring as much as forty-eight hours before becoming sufficiently impoverished; whilst the poorer ores, affording about 1 per cent. of silver, generally require but twelve hours for their treatment. In the case of ores not containing above 7 per cent. of silver, one chlorination and lixiviation is found sufficient, but when richer ores are operated on it becomes necessary to have recourse to two distinct processes of lixiviation, together with an intermediate roasting with salt and sulphate of iron. The lixiviation is known to be complete when the liquors dropping from the tubs no longer afford any traces of a precipitate on the addition of a few drops of sulphide of ammonium, and the residues are then removed, and, after being dried, fused in a blast furnace for copper.

Precipitation of Silver.—The liquor flowing through the filters in the tubs B, are conducted by the trough *d* into the vessels E, F, of which there are ten—six holding 40 gallons each, and four of the capacity of 80 gallons. The precipitant here employed is a polysulphide of sodium, produced by fusing common soda-ash with sulphur, and subsequently boiling the product, dissolved in water, with sulphur in a finely divided state. The solution thus obtained is taken in large stone jars to the precipitating tubs, and poured into the argentiferous liquors so long as a precipitate is produced by the introduction of an additional quantity. The contents of the tubs, after being well stirred, are allowed to settle, and a sample of the clear liquor having been taken in a test-tube, a little of the solution of sulphide of sodium is added.

If a dark-coloured precipitate be formed, it shows that a portion of the silver still remains in solution, and a further supply of the alkaline sulphide is required in the precipitating vessels. If, on the contrary, the addition of polysulphide of sodium has not the effect of producing a dark precipitate, it becomes probable that too large an amount of the sulphide may have been added to the argentiferous liquor. In order to ascertain this fact, some fresh liquor, holding the double salt of silver in solution, is added to a sample taken from the tub under examination. Should a precipitate of sulphide of silver appear, fresh argentiferous liquor must be carefully added to the tub until no further reaction is observed. When this point has been attained, all doubt as to whether the whole of the silver has been precipitated, on the one hand, and that no excess of the precipitant has been employed on the other, is removed by the addition, to one sample, of a few drops of a weak solution of common salt, and, to another, of a small quantity of acetate of lead.

If no precipitate of chloride of silver be produced by the addition of chloride of sodium, it is a proof of that metal having been completely removed; and should no discoloration take place on the addition, to the other sample, of a solution of acetate of lead, it shows that no excess of the precipitant has been added.

The exact neutrality of the residual liquid is essentially necessary to the success of this process, since the liquors from which the silver has been thrown down are employed in succeeding operations. It is evident therefore that the presence of sulphide of sodium would convert a portion of the silver into an insoluble sulphide of that metal, whilst any chloride of silver allowed to remain in the hyposulphite solutions would diminish their solvent properties, in a proportionate degree with regard to that salt. This process of precipitation, which would appear to be both delicate and complicated, is for each tub readily accomplished in the course of fifteen minutes by two workmen; and experience enables them to perform this operation with such facility that they never fail in obtaining the result desired.

Six hours are now allowed for the flocculent precipitate to settle at the bottom of the tubs, after which the clear liquor is syphoned off into a reservoir beneath the floor, and the black slimy sulphide drawn off by the taps *e*, *f*, to be placed in a filter-bag of close canvas.

It may be remarked that, instead of any loss of hyposulphite of soda taking place during the working of this process, an actual increase of that salt is the result. This is occasioned by the oxidation from exposure to the air, of the sulphide of sodium employed as a precipitant; and consequently the solutions containing this solvent have occasionally to be reduced in strength by the addition of water.

The spent liquors from which the sulphide of silver has been precipitated are afterwards pumped from the tank beneath the floor of the establishment to another above the level of the row of tubs A, from which they are drawn off, as they may be required, for the lixiviation of a subsequent charge of roasted ore.*

Treatment of the Sulphide of Silver.—The pasty sulphide of silver as drawn off from the precipitating tubs is placed in conical canvas bags G, supported on wooden frames, and allowed to drain. After standing in the filter until it has ceased to drip, the pasty mass, together with the enclosing bag, is placed under a screw press, and the remaining moisture expressed as completely as possible. The

* A pound of crystallised hyposulphite of soda in solution in twenty pounds of water, is capable of dissolving out, at 58° Fahr., an amount of chloride of silver corresponding to 0·358 lb. of metallic silver.

The present wholesale price of hyposulphite of soda is about 16*l*. per ton.

precipitate is now removed from the bag, dried, and, after being replaced in the filter, is washed with hot water for the purpose of removing the adhering soluble salts, of which sulphate of soda is the chief ingredient. The sulphide of silver, thus purified, is again dried, and afterwards heated to redness in a muffle, through which a current of air is allowed to circulate. In this way the sulphur is almost entirely burnt off, and at the expiration of about two hours the entire mass has assumed the metallic condition.

This metallic residue is now fused, in charges of about 300 lbs., in large plumbago crucibles, and any traces of sulphur, which it may still retain, removed by the addition of metallic iron, with which it forms a ferruginous sulphide readily skimmed from the surface of the metal. A small quantity of a mixture composed of wood ashes and bone-ash is now thrown on the surface of the metallic bath, and this, on being carefully scraped off, leaves the fused silver in a condition suitable for casting into ingots. The silver is thus obtained at a total cost of 9*s.* 9*d.* per lb. or about 6*s.* less than the cost by the old method of fusion with lead ores.* Bars produced by this process usually contain from 980 to 985 thousandths of silver.

* Bodeman.

CHAPTER XX.

CONCENTRATION OF THE PRECIOUS METALS IN METALLIC LEAD—SMELTING.

PRELIMINARY OBSERVATIONS—SMELTING AURIFEROUS SILVER ORES FOR MATTS—EXTRACTION OF THE PRECIOUS METALS IN BATH OF FUSED LEAD—CONCENTRATION OF SILVER IN MATTS, AND FUSION WITH ROASTED LEAD ORES, WITHOUT ADDITION OF IRON—REDUCTION OF UNROASTED LEAD ORES BY METALLIC IRON—CASTILLIAN FURNACE—REDUCTION OF PARTIALLY-ROASTED LEAD ORES BY METALLIC IRON—RESULTS OBTAINED AT WILDBERG.

THE amount of the precious metals extracted from their ores by the process of smelting, even including the silver obtained from the treatment of argentiferous galena, is small as compared with the annual production by amalgamation. This mineral, however, although, without exception, containing a certain proportion of silver, cannot be for that reason regarded as a silver ore; since the value of the lead which it affords is generally far in excess of that of the silver; and, consequently, galena must be considered as an ore of lead, affording variable quantities of the former metal.

In the various processes which have been adopted for the extraction of the precious metals from their ores by smelting, advantage is taken of the affinity which lead possesses for them when in a fused state; and consequently it performs, when in that condition, a similar service to that rendered by mercury at lower temperatures. From the great facility with which the sulphides of silver are converted into an impalpable powder, which, by floating off on water, becomes commercially lost, the mechanical concentration of silver ores is a very wasteful operation; and hence the solubility of sulphides of silver in other fused metallic sulphides is generally made use of as a means of concentration. The gold present in the ore is also concentrated in these fused metallic sulphides.

This observation, as far as it relates to silver ores proper, is also to a great extent applicable to argentiferous galenas in which the sulphide of silver, at least evidently to a great extent, exists in the form of a mechanical mixture, and consequently it is not generally advantageous to carry their mechanical concentration to a very advanced stage. From this circumstance, the processes employed for the metallurgical treatment of galenas rich in silver, differ materially from those made use of for smelting ordinary lead ores, and consequently the peculiarities of treatment adopted in some cases, in which the amount of silver present almost entitles them to be regarded as ores of that metal, will be noticed at some length. The details of the various methods for the reduction of gold and silver ores are, to a greater or less degree, modified in accordance with the resources of the districts in which they are employed, and consequently the processes adopted in different localities are so exceedingly numerous and complicated, that even a brief reference to all of them would occupy far more space than is at at our disposal for that purpose. We shall, therefore, confine ourselves to a description of some of the more important methods of treating these ores, as employed in various large and well-conducted establishments, and of such as can, at the same time, be taken as types of the several systems which they represent; although, in a more or less modified form, they may have been adopted in other localities. The presence of gold in an ore of silver in no way modifies its treatment in the furnace, since the former metal invariably accompanies the latter, and is ultimately separated from it by the process of parting.

Smelting Auriferous Silver Ores for Matts, and Extraction of the Precious Metals by Bath of Melted Lead.—The following description refers to this process as employed, some years since, for smelting argentiferous ores in Lower Hungary, and is given as a type of the system it represents.* The ores from the mines of Schemnitz and Kremnitz contain both silver and gold; those smelted from the former locality being generally more auriferous than those obtained from the latter. At the mines these ores are partially in the form of *Scheide-erz*, or cobbed ore, and partly in the state of slime, or *Schlich*; the latter being again classified into silver ores, containing more than two loths of silver per centner, or 20 oz. per ton; and pyritous ores, generally yielding much less than that amount.†

* A valuable paper "On the Smelting of Silver Ores," as then practised on the Continent of Europe, by the late Mr. John Henry Vivian, F.R.S., was published in "Records of Mining," Murray, Albemarle Street, 1829.

† Loths of 271 gr. and centners of 123·80 lbs. avoirdupois.

The ores are, at the works, subdivided into three classes, viz.:

a.—Those containing less than three loths per centner.

b.—Those yielding from three to five loths per centner.

c.—Those containing more than five loths per centner.

This classification enables the operations at the smelting works to be conveniently regulated, as the matts obtained from the fusion of the poorer varieties are, after roasting, smelted with those containing a larger amount of silver, and a matt is thus produced, which, after being in its turn subjected to several successive roastings, is again smelted with still richer ores. The various operations at the smelting works succeed each other in the following order:—

A. *First Fusion—Roharbeit*—The charge consists of poor ores of the average yield of one loth of silver per quintal, or 10 oz. per ton. Slags from third fusion, with limestone, as flux.

Products.—Crude matt, or *Rohlech*, containing from three to four loths of silver per quintal; which, after repeated roastings, is fused in the second operation. The slags produced are subjected to no further treatment.

B. *Second Fusion—Reich-roharbeit*—The charge is made up of ores of an average produce of two and a half loths of silver per centner. Roasted matt from first fusion; slags from third fusion; limestone.

Products.—Rich crude matt, containing from eight to ten loths of silver per centner, and which, after roasting, is passed into the third process. Slags of no value.

C. *Third Fusion—Frischarbeit*—The charge consists of rich ores; roasted matts from second and third fusion; limestone. ***Metallic lead added in tapping pan.***

Products.—Argentiferous and auriferous lead, subjected to cupellation; rich matt (*Frischlech*), which is roasted and re-smelted; and slags, which are employed in fusions A and B.

D. *Cupellation* of lead obtained from tapping pan.

A. *Crude Smelting.*—The furnace in which the first fusion is effected is called a *Hohofen*. It is 18 feet 6 inches in height, and receives its blast through two tuyeres, supplied with air, either by bellows, moved by water-power, or from a blowing-machine, formed of an oblong box, provided with the necessary valves, in which a piston is made to traverse. The width of this furnace is 2 feet 9 inches, and its depth at the tuyeres 3 feet 3 inches; whilst the back wall slopes in such a way that at the top, or charging place, the internal depth is four feet five inches. Over the top of this furnace arched flues or chambers are constructed, for the purpose of collecting any fine particles of ore that may be driven over by the blast; which are occasionally removed through openings closed by iron doors. The tuyeres are placed exactly in the angles, and their direction is so adjusted that the blasts from them cross each other at a distance of about two feet from the back wall of the furnace. These tuyeres are made of wrought iron, and project about three inches into the furnace; the nozzles being covered with refractory clay to secure them from the action of the fuel and slags. The tuyeres have a very trifling inclination, and one of them is placed somewhat higher than the other; the lower tuyere being situated about two feet above the top of the breast stone. The well, formed in the bottom of the furnace for the reception of the fused matts, communicates with a breast pan, on each side of which is a tapping hole leading to two pans sunk in the floor of the establishment. The bottom of the furnace and lining of the breast pan are composed of brasque, which, after having been well rammed in by proper beaters, is subsequently cut out into the required form. The material operated on chiefly consists of pyrites, and stamped silver ores of very low produce, to which are occasionally added some low quality cobbed ores. These are charged in about the following proportions :—

Stamped pyrites ore about 70 parts; low class silver schlich (*a*) about 25 parts; poor cobbed ore 5 parts. This mixture is so composed that its average yield of silver may be something over one loth per centner, or 10 oz. per ton. The gangue, being chiefly silicious and argillaceous, is exceedingly difficult to fuse, and consequently requires a large proportion of flux, particularly in the first operation; in the subsequent processes the fusion is greatly assisted by the addition of roasted matts. The mixture consists of about 120 centners of ore, the same amount of slags from the third operation, and from 20 to 30 centners of limestone. The ores, fluxes, and charcoal are thrown into the furnace from an upper floor, and the matts collect in the well at the bottom. The slags flow off in a constant stream over the edge of the breast pan, and are thence taken away as being of no value.

As soon as the well and breast pan have become full of fused matts, they are tapped off into a float on the level of the floor, and usually contain from three to four loths of silver per centner, or from 30 to 40 oz. per ton. The furnace is kept in fire for about a month, when it is blown out for repairs, and during that time usually smelts about 130 tons of ore. Four men are employed at each furnace, and are paid in accordance with the amount of ore smelted. The crude matt is broken, and, after undergoing three successive roastings in heaps, is treated in operation B. For the purpose of being roasted, the matt is laid, in pieces of about the size of the fist, on a layer of wood; a little charcoal being mixed with the broken matt. Each roasting occupies from a week to ten days.

B. *Second Fusion—Reich-roharbeit.*—This operation is generally performed in the *Halbhohofen*, which is 11 feet in height, and at the tuyere, 2 feet in width by 3 in depth; at the top it is about two inches wider, and, from the inclination of the back wall, about nine inches deeper. This apparatus has only one tuyere. The high furnace is also employed for this purpose when new, and before its internal dimensions have become too much enlarged by the erosive action of the fused matts and slags.

The charge chiefly consists of poor washed silver ores (*a*) containing from two to three loths of silver per centner, of some cobbed ore of about the same produce, and a small quantity of pyritous slimes, so that the average yield may be about two loths per centner, or 25 oz. per ton. The relative proportions of these substances in the charge are nearly as follow:—

Washed silver ore about 70 parts, cobbed ore 20 parts, pyritous slimes 10 parts. To every hundred centners of this mixture are added from 40 to 50 of roasted crude matt, from 50 to 60 centners of slags from operation C, and 15 to 20 centners of limestone. The matt produced by the fusion of this mixture contains from 8 to 10 loths of silver per centner, or from 81 to 102 oz. per ton, whilst the slags are thrown aside as useless, unless there should not be a sufficient amount on hand, from process C, to serve as flux; in which case a portion of them may be reserved for that purpose. This furnace burns out in fifteen days, and in that time smelts about 40 tons of ore, together with a due proportion of slag and roasted matt. The fused sulphides obtained by this operation are roasted in precisely the same way as the matts from the first fusion, and then form one of the ingredients of the charge in process C.

C. *Third Fusion—Frischarbeit.*—This is conducted in the same furnace as the preceding, and the ore worked during a campaign, extending over a week, is about 16 tons. The mixture operated on consists of schlichs and the richest cobbed ores in the following proportions:—schlich about 40 parts, cobbed ore 60 parts. To every hundred centners of this mixture are added from 30 to 40 centners of roasted matt from the third fusion C, from 20 to 25 of that from the second B, and the same amount of limestone. From four to six centners of lead, in accordance with the richness of the ores, are also charged into the float in the course of each shift of eight hours. The matt from the furnace is tapped into the float on the top of the metallic lead, and well stirred, in order that the largest possible amount of the gold and silver contained in the fused sulphides may be made to combine with that metal. From its greater specific gravity the lead collects at the bottom of the pan; whilst the lighter matt floats on the surface, whence it is removed in the form of flat cakes in proportion as it cools. As soon as the whole of the matt has been taken off, and the lead begins to appear, the furnace is again tapped, in order that the metal may not become oxidised from exposure to the air, and in this way an additional quantity of the silver and gold is taken up by the lead at each successive tapping. The whole of the lead is not introduced into the float at the commencement of the operation, but at different periods during the progress of the shift of eight hours; at the expiration of which time the enriched lead is ladled out into moulds, and the next tapping is made into the float on the other side of the breast pan.

The amount of silver and gold present in the lead thus obtained obviously depends on the richness of the ores treated, but usually varies from 40 to 60 loths per centner—from 408 to 613 oz. per ton. The matts from this fusion contain about 14 loths of silver per quintal, or 143 oz. per ton; and, after being repeatedly roasted in small heaps, are added to the charge in a subsequent operation. The slags contain about one-fourth of a loth of silver per centner, 2½ oz. per ton, and are employed as a flux in operations A and B. The copper contained in the ore continues to accumulate in the matts until a regulus containing from thirty to forty per cent. is obtained, when it is removed for the purpose of being subjected to a special treatment for that metal.

D. *Cupellation.*—The cupellation of the rich lead, which is effected in a large circular cupelling furnace, with a marl bottom and a movable iron dome, will be described when treating of the extraction of silver from argentiferous lead.

The foregoing is a description of the various operations by which the precious metals were some years ago extracted from auriferous silver ores at Kremnitz, but we are not aware to what extent they may have since been modified.

CONCENTRATION OF SILVER, IN MATTS, AND FUSION WITH ROASTED LEAD ORES WITHOUT METALLIC IRON.—This process was extensively employed at Freiberg previous to the introduction of Augustin's method of extracting silver by means of a solution of salt. At present, the matts from certain descriptions of ore, after being so concentrated as to contain about 70 per cent. of copper and $\frac{42}{100}$ths per cent. of silver, are roasted with salt, and subsequently lixiviated with brine, as described page 409. This process of smelting was in principle very similar to that employed in Hungary. The separation of the metallic constituents of low produce ores was in this, as in the former case, effected by the production of matts; these, after repeated roastings, were smelted with richer ores containing lead, and the resulting argentiferous lead subjected to cupellation.

The blast furnace employed in Saxony for this purpose differed materially from the Hungarian, as its height, from the bottom of the brasque to the charging hole, did not exceed 9 feet. Its width at the top was 2 feet by 2 feet 9 inches in depth; but as it gradually expanded in descending, it was considerably larger in the vicinity of the tuyere and breast pan.

The ventilating channels, situated beneath the furnace and breast pan, were covered by slabs of gneiss, on which was placed a layer of broken slag, about six inches in thickness, overlaid by a bed of clay, which was well rammed, and had an inclination towards the front. When the furnace had been constructed on this foundation, the bottom and breast pan were formed by ramming in, with proper beaters, successive layers of a brasque composed of two parts of fireclay and one of powdered charcoal or coke dust, and afterwards cutting it out to the required form.

The breast was supported by a flat stone or cast iron plate, and was terminated, on one side, by an inclined plane of earth, over which the slags continuously flowed off; whilst on the other was an iron plate set on edge, in which was a slot for the tap hole, beneath which, on the level of the floor, was a float for the reception of the fused matt. The tuyere was of cast iron, placed in the middle of the back wall, and projecting from it about three inches; its degree of inclination depending on the nature of the ores to be operated on. The blast was supplied either by a blowing machine or a pair of leathern bellows set in motion by a water-wheel, and in the vicinity of each furnace was a trough of water, for the purpose of cooling the various tools employed.

Crude Smelting—Roharbeit.—The materials selected for this operation were silver ores of rather low produce, containing little or no lead, and less than five loths of silver per Saxon centner—about 45 oz. per ton. To these was added an equal weight of pyritous ores yielding only a quarter of a loth of silver per centner. This mixture was so proportioned that the resulting crude matt might contain about five loths of silver per centner; and the amount of matt produced was from 40 to 50 per cent. of the total weight of ore operated on. With the ores thus mixed, was smelted a little more than their united weight of slags from the fusion with lead. These slags, besides acting as a flux, usually contained from an eighth to a quarter of a loth of silver per centner.

In charging the furnace, the coke or charcoal had to be evenly distributed over the surface of the material which it already contained, whilst the ore was chiefly thrown near the back wall; care being at the same time taken to keep the upper part constantly clean, and a good nose of infusible slag around the end of the tuyere. When the ores contained blende, it was found desirable to volatilise a large proportion of the zinc, and with this view a high temperature was kept up during the whole progress of the operation. As however the use of a strong blast would entail the loss of a large proportion of any lead which might be present, ores containing that metal should, as much as possible, be excluded from all mixtures to be subjected to crude smelting. The various substances, in proportion as they became fused, collected in the bottom of the furnace and from thence passed into the breast pan, in the bottom of which the heavy argentiferous matts accumulated, whilst the lighter silicious slags floated on the surface, and, flowing over its edge, ran down the face of the inclined plane at the side.

When the pan had become sufficiently full of matt, a clay plug was removed from the tap hole, and it was drawn off into the float; in proportion as its surface became sufficiently cold, it was thence removed, in the form of discs about three inches in thickness. A smelter, one assistant, and a slag wheeler, relieved every twelve hours, were required to conduct the operations of each furnace.

The coarse matt, thus obtained, was broken into pieces of the size of an orange, and laid in heaps for roasting. These heaps were about four feet in height, six in width, and from twenty to twenty-five feet in length. They were placed under cover of a large shed; and as the matts contained a sufficient amount of sulphur to carry on combustion when the requisite temperature had been once attained, but little fuel was required for the operation. A layer of wood was first placed on the floor of the roasting shed, and over this was spread a little coal or charcoal, on which the broken matt was piled. Each heap, in the first roasting, continued on fire during about fourteen days, when it was opened, turned, and laid on a fresh bed of fuel, care being taken to place the most completely roasted pieces on the top and sides of the pile. Each heap was afterwards subjected to a third roasting, conducted in a similar way; except that, a large portion of the sulphur having been by this time expelled, a larger amount of fuel became requisite, and the time required for the operation was less considerable.

Smelting with Lead Ores—Bleiarbeit.—The ores subjected at Freiberg to this operation were classed as follows:—Silver ores free from lead, and containing above nine loths of silver per centner—about 90 oz. per ton; silver ores containing not less than 16 per cent. of lead; and lastly, all lead ores containing silver. The proportion of argentiferous galena was such that the whole mixture afforded from 30 to 35 per cent. of lead. These ores, after being well mixed, were roasted in a reverberatory furnace, until all smell of sulphur had ceased to be evolved, after which they were agglomerated in order to fit them for working in the blast furnace.

The furnace employed for this purpose precisely resembled that used for crude smelting, except that the dimensions of the hearth were somewhat larger. The tuyere also required to be kept more inclined than during the first fusion; and more particularly so, when the ores contained blende, since in that case the portions of the furnace in the vicinity of the hearth required to be kept at a high temperature. In order to prevent loss of lead it was also necessary to regulate the blast and the supply of fuel, in such a way as to keep the top of the furnace always dead, and the nose of the tuyere at a dull red heat.

To the mixture of calcined ores from the reverberatory furnace were added from 60 to 70 per cent. of roasted matt from the operation of crude smelting, and a small quantity of cupel bottoms and other furnace products containing lead. The average produce of the rich lead thus obtained was about two marks per quintal, or about 300 oz. per ton. The plumbiferous matt, *Bleistein*, obtained from this operation, which floated on the surface of the metallic bath in the tapping pan, was taken off in the form of thin cakes, and subjected to repeated roastings in heaps, after which it was either smelted by itself, or with the addition of poor copper ores. As, however, the ores invariably contained a small amount of copper, the products were in either case argentiferous lead, copper matts, and silicious slags; the slags both from this operation and from the fusion with lead ores being employed as a flux during the crude smelting, whilst the copper matt or *Kupferstein* was re-roasted and treated for that metal.

The furnace employed for this fusion was kept in blast about six days, and during that time smelted about seven tons of calcined ore, and from three to four tons of roasted matt. The argentiferous lead, *Werk-blei*, was formerly treated by cupellation.

Various modifications have of late years been introduced into the processes employed at Freiberg for the treatment of silver ores, and more particularly so since the suppression of barrel amalgamation, and the introduction of Augustin's process. A writer in the *Revue Universelle des Mines* states that, in 1863, nearly twenty-five thousand tons of ore were treated by fusion at the various works in the vicinity of Freiberg; about half these were lead ores, of which the poorest contained from 15 to 30 per cent. of lead, and the best from 30 to 80 per cent. The whole of the lead was present in the form of galena, which was associated with ordinary iron pyrites, arsenical pyrites, blende, quartz, and carbonate of lime. The ordinary tenure of these ores was about 40 per cent. for lead, and 48 oz. of silver per ton. In addition to lead ores, various argentiferous minerals, containing about 32 oz. of silver per ton, are smelted with plumbiferous ores at Freiberg. It is, however, considered necessary that these should not contain above 6 per cent. of copper, since ores containing more than 6 per cent. of that metal are treated apart; and very poor silver ores are enriched by fusion in reverberatory furnaces with a mixture of slags from the blast furnace. The matts thus obtained are called *Rohstein.*

Previous to smelting, the ore is roasted in a double-soled furnace, of which the upper compartment is heated in the same way as an ordinary muffle.

The mixtures are composed as follow :—

Roasted Ore	60 cwt.
Rohstein	20 ,,
Slags	100 ,,
Limestone or fluor spar	2½ ,,

In order to smelt this quantity of material, from 24 cwt. to 27 cwt. of coke are required, or from 40 to 45 per cent. of the ore operated on. The blast furnaces employed have each two tuyeres; and, at a height of 4 feet 6 inches above them, are divided, from front to back, into two parts by a brick division, nine inches wide, which is continued up to the charging hole. The height of the body of the furnace is about 12 feet 6 inches; the depth of the canal, which communicates with the breast pan, is 15 inches below the nozzles; the width of the back of the furnace is, at the tuyeres, 5 feet 6 inches, width of the breast at same level, 3 feet 5 inches. The depth of the furnace at this level is 3 feet 7 inches, and the distance between the tuyeres 23 inches.

Smelting is conducted with a dull charging hole, and a nose of from four to five inches in length is kept on each tuyere. In the ordinary way of working the furnace, it is charged with one measure (20 lbs.) of coke, and alternately, with two, and four, measures of the usual mixture, each measure of which weighs about 60 lbs. If the nose should become too short, four measures of mixture are added to one of coke; but if, on the contrary, it should become too long, the proportion of coke is augmented.

Three workmen are employed at each furnace, viz., a smelter, an assistant, and a man who wheels away the slag, &c. &c. Each furnace is tapped four times in the course of twenty-four hours, and at each tapping 4 cwt. of metallic lead are obtained, containing variable quantities of silver, and 2 cwt. of argentiferous matts, yielding 20 per cent. of lead, besides 10 per cent. of copper. In addition to this, 73 per cent. of the entire weight of the mixture charged is obtained in the form of slags, yielding from 5 to 6 per cent. of lead, and a small quantity of silver. These slags usually contain less than 30 per cent. of silica, and are, consequently, highly basic. Each campaign lasts about ten weeks. The lead is desilverised by crystallisation, whilst the matts, after being roasted, are re-smelted with an admixture of blast furnace slag and fluor spar, thus affording a copper matt containing 30 per cent. of that metal. All the slags from the fusion of ores, as well as those obtained from the treatment of matts, are subsequently treated for the purpose of extracting from them the last traces of metal; and at the same time effecting the fusion of ores, poor in silver, which contain neither lead nor copper. These are generally pyritous and arsenical, and a portion of them is first roasted until it contains only about 5 per cent. of sulphur, and is then charged into a reverberatory furnace with a slag bottom; the charge is composed as follows:—

Roasted Ore	5 cwt.
Raw „	5 „
Lead Slags	20 „
Total	30 cwt.

When necessary, from 100 to 200 lbs. of quartzose sand are added to this mixture. At the expiration of 2½ hours the whole charge is in a state of fusion, and the furnace, for a few minutes, is fired very sharply. In this way a matt is obtained which accumulates at the bottom, where it is allowed to remain, whilst the slags are removed, either by tapping, or by being drawn off by an iron rake. As soon as this has been done, a new charge is added, and the operation is repeated; the matt being tapped off only after the fusion of the third charge. The matt thus obtained from the three charges usually weighs from 1 to 1½ ton, and contains all the useful metals; whilst the slags, on the other hand, are exceedingly poor: this matt contains from 4 to 5 per cent. of copper, from 8 to 10 per cent. of lead, and from 45 to 60 oz. of silver per ton. This matt is subsequently broken into coarse fragments, roasted in heaps, and afterwards smelted in the blast furnace with roasted ores.

It may be remarked that, although the processes of smelting employed at Freiberg are doubtless well adapted to the peculiar conditions existing in that locality, they could only be adopted, with any degree of advantage, in districts affording cheap labour, with fuel at a reasonable price.

Reduction of Unroasted Lead Ores by Metallic Iron.—The process of treating lead ores by metallic iron is chiefly employed for smelting galenas containing a considerable amount of silicious gangue. The reduction of galenas rich in lead, of which the matrix is chiefly calcareous, and which generally contain but a small amount of silver, is often effected by first roasting on the hearth of a reverberatory furnace, and a subsequent fusion in the same apparatus.

In this case the metal is obtained by the double decomposition which takes place between the undecomposed sulphide of lead and those portions of the ore which have, by roasting, been converted into oxide and sulphate of lead. In this way the decomposition of one equivalent of sulphide of lead, and two of the oxide of the same metal, give rise to the production of an equivalent of sulphurous acid, and the liberation of three equivalents of metallic lead—

$$PbS + 2PbO = SO^2 + 3Pb.$$

In the same way, the fusion together of one atom of sulphide of lead and one of sulphate, results in the formation of two equivalents of sulphurous acid, and the liberation of two of metallic lead—

$$PbS + PbO, SO^3 = 2SO^2 + 2Pb.$$

The presence, however, of a very small proportion of silicious or argillaceous gangue renders the application of this principle extremely difficult, since when contained in the ores to the extent of only from 12 to 15 per cent., no metallic lead can be obtained in the reverberatory furnace by these reactions. As before stated, lead ores containing a large amount of silver cannot be advantageously enriched by mechanical treatment beyond a certain moderate percentage; and it is consequently usual, in smelting such minerals, to fuse them either in the raw state, or, after a partial roasting, with an admixture of metallic iron. The iron in this case, by combining with the sulphur of the galena, liberates the lead, and sulphide of iron is produced. When ores only partially roasted are operated on in this way, the intermediate reactions are of a somewhat more complicated character; but the final results, as far as regards the liberation of lead, are the same.

At Clausthal, in the Hartz, the ores usually contain about 30 oz. of silver per ton, and the furnace mixture consists of hand-selected and washed ores, to which are added certain secondary products, and a small proportion of granulated cast iron.

The charges are composed as follows :—

Hand-picked and washed ores, containing 55 per cent. of lead, 34 parts; old cupel bottoms, saturated with litharge, 4 to 5 parts; impure litharge from cupel, 1 part; slags from a previous fusion, or from the treatment of roasted matt, 39 parts; granulated cast iron 4½ parts.

The fusion is conducted in a blast furnace, varying from 18 to 20 feet in height, and having a width at the boshes of about 3 feet 6 inches, Figs. 61, 62, and 63: Fig. 61 being a vertical section at right angles to the tuyeres; Fig. 62 a section through one of the nozzles; and Fig. 63 a horizontal section above the breast pan.

The casing walls are of common masonry, but the interior lining *a* is of firebrick; the bottom *b*, and breast stone *c*, are of sandstone, the breast pan itself being supported by iron plates *d*. The brasque of which it is formed extends under the front wall of the furnace into the interior, and a communication is thus established by which the

Fig. 61.

Claustnal Furnace.
(*Vertical Section.*)

Fig. 62.

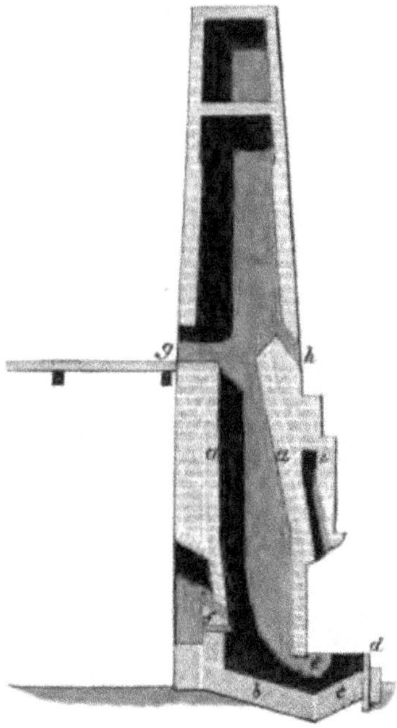

Clausthal Furnace.
(*Vertical Section through Tuyere.*)

Fig. 63.

Clausthal Furnace.
(*Horizontal Section, through Tuyeres.*)

metal and liquid slags can flow into the pan *e*; the tuyeres *f* are placed in the back wall, and have a slight inclination downward, and also towards each other. At top, on a level with the charging hole, the form of this furnace is circular; at the level of the tuyeres it is a parallelogram, with truncated angles; and at the bottom, a square. The distance between the back and front walls is, at the tuyeres, four feet, and the width, two feet six inches. The diameter of the charging hole is two feet.

This furnace is fed through the back by the opening *g*, and the small aperture *h* enables the workmen to instantly perceive the appearance of any flame which may escape at the top; it being essential, in order to avoid an undue waste of lead, to keep the charging hole constantly dead. The arrangement of the flues and condensing chambers is seen, Figs. 61 and 62. The side flue *i* is connected with the projecting arch or mantle, and is for the purpose of carrying off any arsenical or other vapours that may arise from the breast pan *e*. In the back wall of the furnace are small iron doors *k*, for the convenience of cleaning out the various deposit chambers and flues. On each side of the breast, on a level with the floor of the establishment, is a float or tapping pan *l*, into which the liquid metal is from time to time run out; whilst the slags flow off in a continuous stream from a notch in the iron plate, supporting the brasque which forms the breast.

The ores are chiefly charged along the wall in which are placed the tuyeres, whilst the fuel is principally spread in the vicinity of that which is opposite to them. The blast, passing through the tuyeres, and coming into immediate contact with the liquid slags in the body of the furnace, so cools them as to form a tubular elongation or nose. This is so managed by the smelter as to extend from five to six inches beyond the tuyere. When the basin and hearth have become full of matt and metallic lead, a plug of clay is removed, and their contents are run off into one of the floats *l*, where they are allowed to remain until the matt begins to solidify; when it is removed in discs, as before described, and the metallic lead ladled into moulds ready for desilverisation.

The matts thus obtained consist of sulphide of lead, associated with any other metallic sulphides which may have been originally present in the ore; together with sulphide of iron, resulting from the decomposition of galena by that metal.

The matts so produced are laid aside for subsequent treatment whilst the slags, except such as accidentally contain lead, either in he form of shot or in combination with silica, are thrown away as useless. Under ordinary circumstances a sufficient amount of rich slag is produced to serve the purpose of flux in the furnace mixtures; but when such slags are not obtained in sufficient quantities, poor ones have to be employed in their stead.

The matts are thus allowed to accumulate in the works, until a sufficient amount to enable their special treatment to be proceeded with has been got together; when, after being broken into pieces of a convenient size, they are roasted in heaps, each containing from 50 to 100 tons.

The first roasting occupies from three to four weeks, at the expiration of which period, the fire having burnt out, the pile is turned over, and the fragments which are found to be sufficiently roasted are picked out for the purpose of being smelted. The remainder, after this selection, is subjected to a second roasting, at the termination of which the heap is again picked over, and the residue subjected to a third roasting. In this way the insufficiently-roasted fragments remaining from one heap are made to form one of the constituents of another roasting, until the whole has become sufficiently desulphurised to allow of its being advantageously fused in the blast furnace.

The roasted matts are smelted in a small furnace called a *Krumofen*, which is much employed on the Continent for the treatment of substances requiring a moderately high temperature for their fusion. This furnace is supplied with air through a single tuyere, around which a nose, of from three to four inches in length, is allowed to grow. The bottom and breast are formed of brasque, the tapping being accomplished by the removal of a plug of clay from a channel communicating with the forehearth, which allows the fused metal to flow into a float sunk below the level of the floor. The charging takes place at the opening at top, and the fuel made use of, both in this furnace and in that employed for the first fusion, is coke; although charcoal or a mixture of coke and charcoal was formerly employed.

The mixture treated in the krumofen is constituted as follows:—Roasted matt, 32 parts; rich slags, 30 parts; cupel bottoms, 4 to 5 parts; impure litharge, 2 parts; reducing cinder, 2 parts; granulated iron, 1 part.

From this second fusion, as from the first, the results are matt and argentiferous lead. The matts from the second fusion are treated as before, and the same series of operations is continued until the fourth fusion. The sulphides which then result are known as copper matts, and, after numerous successive roastings, are smelted for coarse copper, from which the silver is generally extracted by liquation.

Castilian Furnace.—Reduction of Partially-Roasted Lead Ores by Metallic Iron.—This furnace, which was first employed for the treatment of Roman slags in the neighbourhood of Carthagena in Spain, is now used, not only for the reduction of various furnace products and argentiferous galenas of low produce for lead, but also for smelting, with the addition of plumbiferous matters, the rich silver ores imported from abroad.

This apparatus has a circular form, is generally about 2 feet 8 inches in diameter, inside measure, and is constructed of arched firebricks, so moulded as to leave no unnecessary spaces between the joints. Its usual height, from the floor of the works to the charging hole, is about 8 feet, and the thickness of the masonry the depth of one brick, or 9 inches. The bottom and breast are formed of brasque, supported in front by a curved plate of cast iron, furnished with a lip for running off the slags, and provided with a perpendicular slot, in which is situated the tapping hole. The details of this apparatus will be understood by a reference to Figs. 64, 65, 66, which respectively represent an elevation, a vertical section, and section at the top of the breast pan.

Around the top of the cylinder of brickwork A, is a hood of masonry B, supported on a cast iron framing, resting on four iron pillars C, in which is the door D, for feeding the furnace, and the outlet E, by which the various products of combustion escape into the flues. The lower part of this hood is fitted closely to the body of the furnace, whilst its top is closed by an arch of bricks turned on edge and set in fireclay. The hood B is built of ordinary non-refractory bricks set in lime. The bottom F is made of a brasque composed of one part of fireclay and two parts of coke dust, slightly moistened and well beaten in to the level of the breast pan G, which stands nearly three feet above the floor of the smelting house.

When the bottom has been solidly beaten in up to the required height, it is hollowed out so as to form an internal cavity communicating freely with the breast pan, which is itself hollowed out to a depth slightly below the level of the internal basin. The blast is supplied by three water tuyeres H, 2½ inches in diameter at the smaller end, 5½ inches at the larger, and 10 inches in length. Into these are introduced the nozzles of sheet iron, by which the blast is supplied by means of a fan, or ventilator, making about 800 revolutions per

Fig. 64.

Castillian Furnace.
(*Elevation.*)

Fig. 65.

Castillian Furnace.
(*Vertical Section.*)

Fig. 66.

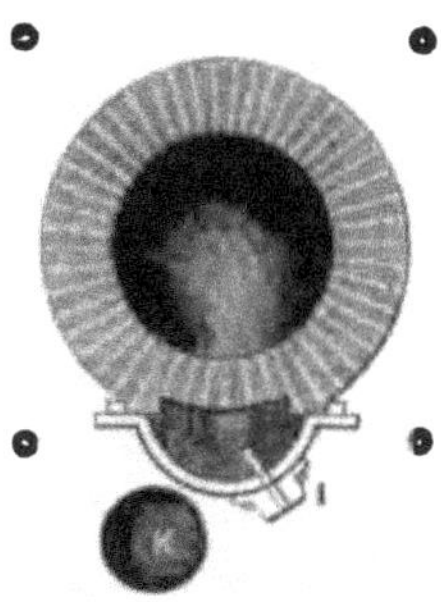

Castillian Furnace.
(*Horizontal Section.*)

minute. The blast is generally conveyed to the nozzles through brick channels formed beneath the floor of the building.

This furnace has not only the advantage of smelting a large amount of ore in a given time with a small expenditure of fuel, but also, from the thinness of its walls, the masonry does not become so intensely heated as to cause its rapid destruction. When any portion of this apparatus becomes burnt through, the damage may be generally repaired, either by plastering the outside with clay, or, if necessary, introducing a few new bricks. The Castillian furnace can therefore frequently be run from six to eight weeks before being finally blown out for repairs.

The ores treated in this apparatus may contain from 30 to 50 per cent. of lead, and require to be roasted either in heaps, in kilns, or in reverberatory furnaces, and are then generally smelted with an admixture of slags and limestone. In charging, the ores and fuel are supplied in distinct strata, and care is taken to so dispose the coke that the brickwork may not be exposed to the corrosive action of the slags. In order to allow of the free escape of slags the breast is not continued much below the level of the hearth, which, for the purpose of preventing the cooling of the scoriæ, is kept covered either by cinders or coke dust. From the breast, the slags flow constantly off by the lip I, into cast iron waggons, where they consolidate into masses having generally the form of truncated pyramids, of which the larger base is about two feet square. As soon as a sufficient amount of metal has accumulated in the bottom of the furnace, it is let off into a lateral float K, by removing the clay stopper of the tap hole, situated in the slot L of the breast pan; and, after allowing the matt to cool, it is taken off in flat cakes, and the still liquid lead cast into moulds.

The matt consists of sulphide of lead, more or less mixed with sulphide of iron, produced by the decomposition of imperfectly roasted ore by that metal; and, if the ores treated originally contained copper, a certain proportion of sulphide of copper will be also present. These matts are subsequently roasted in heaps, and afterwards smelted in the same furnace with an admixture of slags and limestone. The products of this fusion are argentiferous lead and matts, which after being subjected to repeated roastings, and being again passed through the furnace, contain so large an amount of copper as to be regarded as copper matts; and are sold, under the name of "regulus," to be treated for that metal.

The slags in the waggons are allowed to solidify, and, when sufficiently set, the casings are turned over, so that the blocks readily drop out. In addition to the facility for transport thus obtained, one of the great advantages derived from this method of manipulation arises from the circumstance that, should the furnace at any time run off either lead or matt without its being detected by the smelter, the greater portion of it will be found collected at the bottom of the blocks of slag, from which, when cold, it can readily be detached.

As before stated, in working these, like all other blast furnaces employed for smelting lead ores, great care must be taken to prevent the appearance of flame at the charging hole; since, provided the slags be sufficiently liquid, the lower the temperature at which the fusion can be effected the less will be the loss of metal experienced through volatilisation. In addition to great attention being paid to the working of the furnaces, it is essential, in order to obtain the best possible results, that the establishment should be provided with long and capacious flues, in which the condensation of the fumes may take place before arriving at the chimney. These flues should be built at least three feet in width and six in height, so as to admit of being readily cleaned out. They are sometimes made of very great length, since in one of the large establishments in the north of England their flues are now extended to a length of above seven miles, and a considerable amount of deposit takes place, even in the latter portions of its circuit.

In case of working finely pulverised ores in blast furnaces, it is essential that, after roasting, they should, before being withdrawn from the furnace, be agglomerated into masses, which are subsequently broken into fragments of the size of the fist, and then mixed with the fluxes before described. If the charge of a blast furnace contains much fine ore, or there be much coke dust in the fuel, the draught is affected, and the working of the apparatus becomes seriously deranged.

Each of these furnaces requires two smelters and an ore tender, who are relieved every twelve hours, during which time about three and a half tons of roasted ore, independent of slags and other fluxes, are passed through it, with a consumption of from 18 to 20 per cent. of coke. At the Wildberg Smelting Works in Prussia, where the ores raised consist of a fine-grained argentiferous galena, disseminated in a silicious gangue very difficult to smelt, and containing a considerable amount of spathose iron, the charge was, in 1859, composed as follows:—Roasted ore, containing by assay 42·8 per cent. of lead, 100 parts; slag from previous operations, 42 parts; limestone, 7 parts;

granulated cast iron, 8 parts.* The results obtained were about 39 per cent. of work lead, slags to about double the weight of the lead obtained, and 5 per cent. of lead matts, containing a certain amount of silver and copper. The roasted ores, at Wildberg, require 20 per cent. of coke for their treatment in the blast furnace.

Cobbed and other lead ores which have not been subjected to mechanical concentration may, before being smelted, either alone or with minerals containing silver, be conveniently roasted in kilns consisting of rectangular chambers 10 feet by 8 feet, having arched roofs, and provided with proper flues for the escape of the evolved gases, as well as with a wide iron door for charging and withdrawing the ores operated on. Each of these chambers will contain from 25 to 30 tons of mineral, and in order to charge it, a layer of faggots and cord wood is laid upon the floor, and this, after being covered by a layer of raw ore two feet in thickness, is ignited; care being at the same time taken to close, by means of loose bricks, the opening of the doorway to the same height. When the first layer has thus become well ignited, more ore, mixed with a little charcoal or a few small billets of wood, is thrown upon it; and when this layer has, in its turn, become sufficiently heated, another stratum of ore is added. In this way more ore is from time to time thrown on the top of that already in the kiln, until it has been filled to the spring of the covering arch, when the opening is closed by the iron door, and the operation proceeds regularly and without further trouble, until a large portion of the sulphur has been burnt off. This generally happens at the expiration of about four weeks from the time of first charging: the kiln then cools, the loose brickwork is removed, the roasted ores broken out with picks, and, after being mixed with scrap iron and the other necessary fluxes, they are passed through the blast furnace.

The following were the results obtained at the Wildberg Smelting Works during three months in 1859:—

Roasting:—

	Ctr.		£.	s.	d.
Roasted in kilns	10,679	cost per ton .	0	6	9
„ in reverberatory furnace	3,321	„ .	0	14	6

700 tons at an average cost of 9*s.* per ton.

---

* The prices of materials delivered at the works were then as follow:—

	£.	s.	d.	
Granulated cast iron	3	18	0	per ton.
Coke	2	3	4	„
Limestone	0	15	0	„

Smelting:—

	ctr.			Lead. ctr.		Silver. oz.
Smelted	11,240	ores	containing	4,835	. . .	6,125
„	308	„	„	147	. . .	161
„	453	fahlerz	„	} 357	. . .	1,235
„	534	calcined dross . . .	„			
	12,535	ctr.	„	5,369		7.521
			which produced	4,886		7,405
			showing a loss of	483*	= $3\frac{7}{8}$ units.	116 †

Total Cost, at Wildberg, of treating 1 *ton of Ore, containing* 42·8 *per cent. of lead and about* 11 *oz. silver.*

	£.	s.	d.
Roasting	0	9	0
Smelting	1	7	1
Calcining	0	2	9
Crystallising	0	8	0
Reducing	0	2	3
Refining	0	0	9
	£2	9	10

* In addition to the lead lost in smelting, about two units were volatilised in the process of roasting. The Wildberg ores, however, contain copper, antimony, and other impurities, and, consequently, the losses experienced in calcining and desilverising the hard lead, and converting it into soft marketable metal, are very considerable. The total loss on the assay produce of lead may consequently be taken at about 11 units.

† The difference of silver subsequently obtained from matts; the total annual yield being slightly above the amount indicated by assay, although a certain quantity always goes off in the market lead and in the matts sold as copper regulus.

CHAPTER XXI.

EXTRACTION OF THE PRECIOUS METALS FROM ARGENTIFEROUS AND AURIFEROUS LEAD OBTAINED BY SMELTING.

CONTINENTAL PROCESS OF CUPELLATION — REFINING SILVER OBTAINED FROM CUPEL—ENGLISH SYSTEM OF TREATING ARGENTIFEROUS LEAD—CALCINATION —CONCENTRATION OF SILVER BY CRYSTALLISATION—PATTINSON'S PROCESS—FRENCH PROCESS—REFINING ENRICHED LEAD—COSTS AND RESULTS OF DESILVERISING—LIQUATION.

Cupellation.—The argentiferous lead obtained by the treatment of ores of that metal, or the fusion of silver ores with roasted galena, or some other plumbiferous material, is either directly subjected to the process of cupellation, or the silver is previously concentrated in a small portion of the lead, by a series of crystallisations in a set of large cast iron pots or kettles.

The process of cupellation is, as before stated, dependent on the property possessed by lead of becoming oxidised when strongly heated, and at the same time exposed to the air; whilst the silver with which it is united is not so affected, and consequently becomes gradually concentrated in that portion of the lead which still remains in the metallic state. It results, from this difference in the behaviour of the two metals, that, when the operation has been continued for a sufficient length of time, the lead becomes entirely oxidised, whilst the silver remains in the metallic form. In order that the oxidation of the lead should proceed rapidly, and without interruption, it is necessary that the temperature to which the alloy is subjected should be sufficiently elevated to cause the fusion of the litharge produced. The surface of the fused alloy naturally assumes a convex form, and the fused oxide of lead constantly flows into the annular space existing between the edges of the metallic bath and the surface of the vessel in which it is contained. If, therefore, a depression be made in the edge of the containing vessel, so as to form a channel, the level of which can from time to time be lowered by scraping the bottom by means of a pointed iron bar, the whole of the litharge may be thus drawn off without the escape of any of the unoxidised argentiferous lead.

The furnace commonly employed for this purpose on the Continent of Europe, where the lead to be operated on is often subjected to cupellation without any preliminary concentration of the silver, is

FIG. 67.

CUPELLING FURNACE.
(*Vertical Section.*)

FIG. 68.

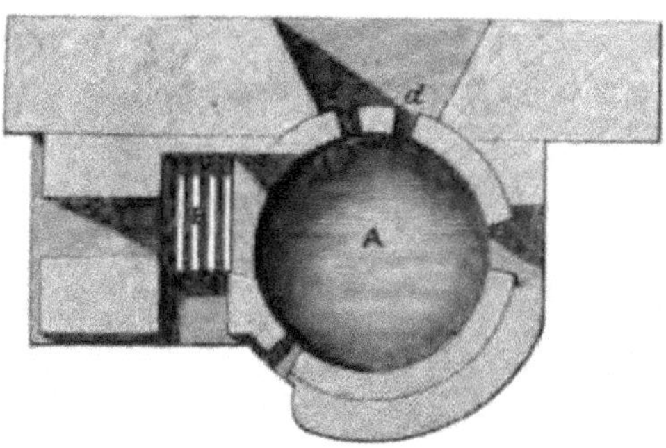

CUPELLING FURNACE.
(*Horizontal Section.*)

represented, Figs. 67 and 68, of which the first is a vertical section and the second a section at the level of the tuyeres.

This apparatus is a reverberatory furnace, consisting of a circular hearth from 9 to 10 feet in diameter A, sloping from all sides towards the centre, built of bricks *b*, set on edge on a layer of broken slags *c*.

On this is laid a bed of marl, *a*, which is firmly beaten in, when in a damp state, and renewed after each operation.* This bed of marl, in point of fact, constitutes the cupel, which is heated by means of faggots of brushwood burnt in the fireplace B. The roof of this furnace consists of a sheet iron dome C, which may be suspended by chains from the crane D, by which it can be removed and again placed in its position over the cupel. This dome is internally plastered with clay.

The cupelling furnace has five openings: one through which the flame from the grate enters the hearth; two, *d*, through which the nozzles pass supplying the blasts to the surface of the metallic bath, for the purpose of oxidising the lead, and which also assist in carrying the resulting litharge towards the annular space before referred to: the aperture E is employed for the introduction of the discs of lead to be cupelled; and F is that through which the fused litharge makes its escape from the furnace. At the commencement of the operation this last opening is closed by the edge of the layer of marl; but, as the cupellation proceeds, it is from time to time cut down so as to keep the channel constantly at the level of the metallic bath. The litharge thus flowing from the apparatus accumulates on the floor of the smelting house, where it solidifies, and from whence it is removed as may be found convenient.

Before commencing a cupellation, it is necessary to prepare the cupel; and for this purpose, after lifting the iron dome, the old cupel, which has become thoroughly impregnated with litharge, is broken up and removed, in order that it may be passed through the blast furnace. The brick bottom of the apparatus is now moistened with water, and successive layers of finely-ground marl are well beaten in whilst in a somewhat damp state. The iron covering is replaced when the cupel has become sufficiently dry, and all the joints are well secured by luting them with clay.

The furnace is now charged with 160 quintals (about eight tons) of lead, which, to prevent injury to the bottom, is laid on a bed of straw; the fire is lighted, and the metal rapidly begins to melt. As soon as the fusion of the discs is completed, the bellows are slowly set in motion, and the surface of the bath becomes covered with a dark-coloured powder, consisting of oxide of lead, associated with various impurities. These pulverulent matters, the first of which are known as *Abzugs*, and those which follow as *Abstrichs*, do not enter into fusion;

* When good marl for this purpose cannot be obtained, a mixture of clay and lime, or clay and wood ashes, is employed.

but the refiner now and then throws a shovelful of coal-dust on the surface of the bath, and, by the aid of a billet of wood, fixed crosswise on the end of an iron bar, draws the impure oxides towards the hole through which the litharge escapes, and finally on to the floor of the works. After the expiration of a short time, fused litharge begins to make its appearance; but that at first formed, being impure, from the presence of other oxides, is usually laid aside, and not mixed with the purer descriptions which soon follow; these are generally sold for glass-making and other purposes, in preference to being again reduced to the metallic state. The litharge produced during the last period of the cupellation invariably contains a considerable amount of silver, and, after being reduced to the metallic state, forms a portion of the charge worked in a subsequent operation.

The blast is now slightly increased, and the oxidation proceeds rapidly; small flaps, or valves, being frequently fitted to the ends of the nozzles, for the purpose of checking its strength, and distributing it more evenly over the surface of the fused metal. The operation is continued in this way until almost the whole of the lead has been converted into oxide; and the silver, retaining only traces of that metal, remains in the cupel, in the form of a metallic cake.

At the moment the oxidation of lead entirely ceases, a phenomenon known as the *brightening* takes place, and the operation is then known to be terminated. During the whole period of cupellation, the metallic bath is observed to present a more brilliant appearance than the brickwork of the furnace itself, and its temperature is in reality greater; since it not only participates in the heat developed by the combustion of the fuel employed, but also absorbs nearly the whole of that resulting from the oxidation of the portion of lead which is being constantly converted into litharge. As soon as the oxidation of the lead ceases, this source of heat is at once withdrawn, and the temperature of the bath of metallic silver rapidly descends to that of the brickwork of the furnace; losing at the same time the brilliancy of appearance which it before possessed.

On the other hand, at the instant the last portions of lead become oxidised, an extremely thin pellicle of litharge remains on the surface of the metal, which, rapidly decreasing, exhibits a series of brilliant prismatic colours. This exceedingly thin film of fused litharge finally disappears, leaving the surface of the metal uncovered. These successive rapidly-changing phenomena are called by the Germans, the *Blicken*, and by the French, the *Éclair*.

As soon as the operation is thus perceived to have terminated, the refiner throws water into the hearth, and removes the solidified cake of silver, which usually still retains a sufficient amount of lead to render its further purification necessary, by a process to be shortly described.

In some establishments, however, where the marl of which the cupel is composed is of good quality, the process of refining is conducted in the same apparatus. For this purpose the blast is continued during fifteen or twenty minutes after the appearance of the phenomena above described; and some small billets of wood, which are introduced through the litharge door, are kept burning over the surface of the metal. The plate thus obtained contains about 950 thousandths of silver.

The amount of silver resulting from each operation manifestly depends on the weight and richness of the lead operated on; and at Kremnitz a charge, consisting of about four or four and a half tons of auriferous silver lead, formerly produced from 1,900 to 2,800 oz. of silver, containing a certain proportion of gold.

At Clausthal, the treatment of 160 centners of ordinary lead, equivalent to about eight English tons, affords 56 marks of silver, about 450 ounces; 118 quintals of litharge, 21 quintals of cupel bottoms, and 15 quintals of abstrichs. The lead obtained in the same establishment from the fusion of roasted matts is more argentiferous than that directly produced from ores, and yields about 62 marks of silver per charge of 160 quintals.

The Continental cupelling furnace is not always provided with a chimney, but is usually placed under a large hood of masonry, which serves to carry off the smoke escaping from the charging hole and other apertures. Each operation, including the time necessary for preparing the cupel, occupies about thirty hours, and is attended with a loss of lead amounting to from 10 to 12 per cent. of the weight of metal subjected to cupellation. In some localities, coal is the fuel employed in furnaces of this description; but wood is much preferred, when it is to be obtained at a moderate price, since it affords a clearer and more oxidising flame, and can be managed with greater facility. At Clausthal, where wood is employed, the diameter of the furnace is 10 feet; the fireplace, 6 feet 6 inches in length, and 1 foot 6 inches in width. The metallic dome has, in that establishment, a diameter of 9 feet 10 inches.

Refining.—The purification of the silver obtained by the process above described is, on the Continent, frequently effected in a small reverberatory furnace, of which the bottom is composed of bone-ash, tightly rammed, whilst in a damp state, into an iron ring, and afterwards so hollowed out as to contain the bath of fused metal. The cupel, which must be thoroughly dry, and ought therefore to be prepared some time beforehand, is, whilst the furnace is still cold, so supported on bricks against abutments prepared for that purpose, as to form the bottom of the apparatus. It is charged with about one cwt. of the impure silver to be operated on, and the firing is continued until a bright red heat has been attained; the silver, which has by this time become fused, being exposed to the oxidising influences of the flame. In this way the lead contained in the alloy becomes oxidised, and the resulting litharge is absorbed by the cupel, of which the temperature is sustained until the oxidation of all but the last traces of lead has been produced. When this point has been attained, the surface of the fused metal becomes exceedingly brilliant, and reflects, as in a mirror, all the irregularities of the interior of the crown.

The bottom of the cupel is now pierced by a pointed iron bar, and the silver is run out into moulds, previously heated on a ledge of the furnace. In order to prevent the spirting, or "vegetation," of the bars, they are covered, whilst cooling, by a piece of dry wood, kept down by a weight; and in case of any irregularities making their appearance on the surface of the ingots, they are subsequently removed by hammering. This operation altogether occupies from four to five hours, and the resulting bars usually contain from 997 to 998 thousandths of silver. The actual loss of silver is almost inappreciable; but the diminution in weight experienced, on the crude metal from the cupelling furnace, is from 2½ to 5 per cent.

English System of treating Argentiferous Lead.—The lead obtained by the different processes before described, in addition to silver, contains various impurities, such as tin, copper, and antimony, which, when the metal is subjected to direct cupellation, are removed in the form of "abzugs" and "abstrichs;" but, when the previous concentration of the silver by crystallisation is resorted to, they materially interfere with the operation, and require to be removed by the process of calcination.

Calcination.—This consists in keeping the fused lead exposed at a cherry-red heat to the oxidising influences of the gases passing through a reverberatory furnace, in which the calcination is effected. By this treatment the antimony, copper, and other impurities become oxidised, and, rising to the surface, are skimmed off, and removed by means of an iron rake. The length of time necessary for the purification of hard lead obviously depends on the nature and amount of the impurities with which it is associated; and, consequently, some varieties will be sufficiently softened at the expiration of twelve hours, whilst in other instances it becomes necessary to continue the operation during several days. The time necessary for sufficiently softening the argentiferous lead obtained from the Castillian furnace, when working ordinary ores, is about thirty-six hours.

The hearth of the furnace in which this operation is most frequently conducted consists of a large cast iron pan, about 1¼ inch in thickness, which may be 10 feet in length, 5 feet 6 inches in width, and 10 inches in depth. The fireplace, which is 20 inches in width, has a length equal to the width of the pan, from which it is separated by a bridge 2 feet in width. The height of the arch, at the bridge end, is 16 inches above the edge of the pan, whilst at the other extremity it is only 8 inches. All the angles of the casting are rounded in order to prevent breakage from expansion, and the softened lead is, when required, drawn off into a float by means of a hole bored in the bottom, near its outside edge. This, when closed, is stopped by means of a turned iron plug kept in its place by a weighted lever.

The charge of this furnace, which is about 11 tons, is first fused in a large iron pot, set in brickwork at the side, and is subsequently ladled into it through a sheet iron gutter prepared for that purpose. The amount of coals required for the calcination of a ton of ordinary hard lead is generally somewhat less than 3 cwt., and the cost of wages usually amounts to about 1*s.* per ton. The softened lead is cast into pigs, and is in that form taken to the crystallising pots.

In some smelting works the hard lead is calcined in an ordinary furnace of the reverberatory description, into which a slag bottom has been run. This usually rests on a layer of brickwork, supported on old railway bars, in such a way that, in case of any leakage taking place, the lead flowing through may be readily collected from the chamber formed beneath the hearth. When this furnace is employed, the calcination takes place at a higher temperature than in the iron pan, and consequently the operation only occupies one-fifth the time required in the latter; the consumption of fuel is about the same, but the loss of lead probably greater.

Concentration of Silver by Crystallisation—Pattinson's Process.—This process is founded on the circumstance, first noticed in the year 1829, by the late H. L. Pattinson, of Newcastle-on-Tyne, that when lead containing silver is melted in considerable quantities in suitable vessels, allowed slowly to cool, and at the same time kept constantly stirred, at a temperature near the melting point of lead, metallic crystals begin to form. These sink to the bottom, and, on being removed, are found to contain much less silver than the lead originally operated on. The still fluid portion, from which the crystals have been thus removed, will at the same time be found to be proportionately enriched.

This operation is usually conducted in a set of from 9 to 12 pots, which, if worked by hand, each contain 6 tons of metal; or, if cranes be employed, are 5 feet 4 inches wide and 2 feet 6 inches deep, and contain 10 tons of argentiferous lead. Each of these pots is provided with a separate fireplace, the heat from which is made to pass around it by means of a wheel flue, which can be closed at pleasure by a damper; the products of combustion finally escape into a large arched flue parallel with the line of pots.

We will suppose that the lead under treatment contains about 20 oz. of silver per ton, and is introduced into pot No. 5, Fig. 69. This metal when fused is carefully skimmed with a perforated ladle, and the fire at once withdrawn. The cooling of the metal is now hastened by sprinkling water on its surface; and whilst the temperature is being thus lowered, it is kept constantly stirred with a chisel-pointed iron bar, called a slice. All those portions which become solidified, and adhere about the side of the pot, are also removed and forced under the surface of the metal, in order that they may again become melted. Under this treatment, crystals soon begin to make their appearance; and as they fall and accumulate at the bottom, they are removed by means of a large perforated ladle, in which, after being well shaken, they are first allowed to drain over the pot whence they have been taken, and afterwards carried over to the next pot (No. 6) to the left of the workmen. This operation is continued until about two-thirds of the lead originally present in pot No. 5 has been transferred in the form of crystals to pot No. 6, at which period the lead remaining in pot No. 5 will contain about 40 oz. of silver per ton, whilst that transferred to No. 6 yields only 10 oz. The rich lead in the bottom of No. 5 is now ladled into the pot No. 4 next on the right.

In this way a fresh supply of calcined lead is constantly introduced, the resulting crystals passing continually to the left of the feeding pot, whilst the enriched lead, remaining in the bottom, is ladled into the pot on the right. Each pot in succession, when it has become filled with metal of the proper produce for silver, is in its turn crystallised; the poor lead passing to the left, and that which has become enriched to the right in the series. It is evident that by this means the crystals obtained from the pots to the left of the feeding pot gradually become deprived of their silver, whilst the rich lead passing to the right is continually enriched. The final result, therefore, is, that at one end of the line of kettles the lead contains but little silver, whilst at the other extremity it becomes exceedingly argentiferous.

The desilverised or *market lead* obtained by this process should never contain above 12 dwt. of silver per ton, and is frequently much poorer, whilst the rich lead is sometimes so concentrated as to yield 600 oz. per ton. This rich lead is passed to the refining furnace for cupellation.

The ladle employed, when manual labour is made use of, is 16 inches in diameter, 5 inches in depth, and pierced with ½ inch holes. When cranes are employed, the ladles are 20 inches in diameter, 6½ inches in depth, and are pierced with holes ¾-inch diameter: thickness of iron, ½ inch; length of handle, 9 feet 4 inches. The large *baling ladles* used for turning back the bottoms, are 14 inches in diameter and 8 inches deep, and have a handle 7 feet long.

Two crystallisers are employed in working each pot, and one fireman every twelve hours is required for each set. By the use of cranes a ten-ton pot can be worked as quickly, and at the same expense for labour, as a six-ton pot by hand ladles.*

Fig. 69 represents a plan, and Fig. 70 an elevation, of a set of Pattinson's pots, fitted with cast iron cranes arranged according to the most approved system. Nos. 1, 2, 3, 4, 5, 6, 7, 8, and 9, are working pots, and No. 10 the market pot, out of which the desilverised lead is ladled into moulds; and which, from only receiving the crystals from No. 9, and not having a bottom of enriched lead left in it, has only two-thirds the capacity of the other pots.

A long ash-pit A extends the whole length of the set, and is partially covered by the iron platform B, supported on iron pillars. The fireplaces *a* are provided with iron doors.

* With cranes, two men can work a ten-ton pot in about two hours.

When, during the operation of taking out crystals, the perforated ladle becomes chilled, it is heated to the proper temperature by being dipped into the pot of hot lead into which they are turned over.

Fig. 69.

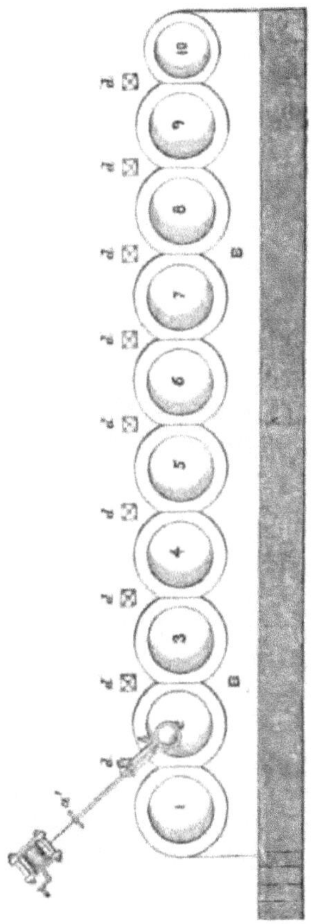

Plan of Crystallising Pots.

Fig. 70.

Elevation of Crystallising Pots.

Fig. 71 represents an elevation of one of the pots and the crane, winch, and chain, by which the ladle, when full of crystals, is withdrawn.

In order to work by the aid of this arrangement, the potman sinks the ladle sidewise to the bottom of the kettle, and having turned it over so as to be full of crystals, he attaches a hook to the cross handle a', of the ladle, Fig. 69, which is then withdrawn by the other workman turning the winch.

In doing this, the iron shank slides over the roller *b*, at the end of the crane *d*; and as soon as it is withdrawn from the fused metal, the first workman, who guides the handle during the operation, slips it into one of the cheeks *c*, at the back of the crane, where it becomes firmly secured. The ladle, full of crystals, is thus suspended over the pot from which it has been withdrawn, and after being allowed a

FIG. 71.

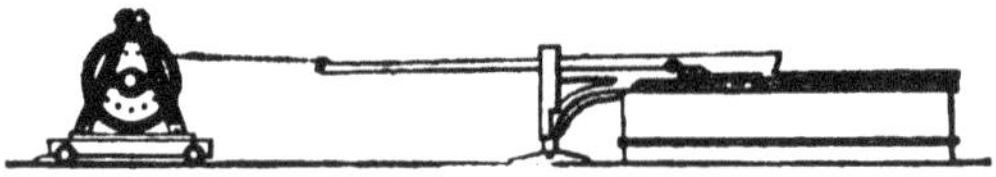

ELEVATION OF POT AND CRANE.

short time to drain, it receives a few shakes by jerking the iron handle. The crane is now swung round, the shank slipped out of the catch, and the crystals deposited in the next pot on the left. This is continued until the necessary amount of crystals has been withdrawn, when the rich lead remaining in the bottom is taken out, in the same way, by a ladle without perforations, and turned over in the next pot on the right. In some establishments the lead remaining in the bottom of the rich pot (No. 1) is further concentrated by allowing it to cool to the crystallising point, and then pressing it with the convex side of one of the large perforated ladles. The still liquid alloy is thus made to enter the bowl through the holes with which it is pierced, and is taken out with a smaller unperforated dipper. The lead thus obtained will evidently be richer than the crystals remaining in the kettle.

The following memoranda relative to the Wildberg Smelting Works afford some practical data respecting the costs incurred, and results obtained, in the desilverisation of argentiferous lead in six-ton pots by hand ladles:—

Crystallising from July 1858 to May 1860. Cost of coal, delivered, 40*s.* to 45*s.* per ton. Average assay of calcined lead, 28 oz. of silver per ton. Lead concentrated to 340 or 370 oz. of silver per ton. Assay of market lead, from 7 to 9 dwt. per ton. Number of pots employed in crystallising, 9. Market lead obtained, 30,032 Prussian centners. Rich lead cupelled, 2,486 Prussian centners. Weight of coals consumed, 10,807 ctr., or about 7 cwt. per ton of market lead.

Cost on one ton of market lead—

	Th.	sgr.	pf.	£.	s.	d.
Wages	3	7	3	0	9	9
Coals	5	3	10	0	16	4
				£1	6	1

When worked regularly so as to leave a bottom of one-third the weight of their total charge, the richness of each pot in a series will be found to be about double that of the kettle next it to the left. Assays of the contents of each of a set of nine pots, in which the calcined lead worked, contained 21 oz. 9 dwt. 8 gr. of silver per ton, gave the following results :—

	oz.	dwt.	gr.	Remarks.
No. 1	219	16	0	Bottom of No 1, or rich lead, gave 358 oz. 8 dwt. per ton.
„ 2	129	8	0	
„ 3	79	8	0	
„ 4	41	1	8	
„ 5	21	9	8	Lead fed into No. 5 pot.
„ 6	11	4	0	
„ 7	4	5	0	
„ 8	2	0	0	
„ 9	0	18	16	
Market Pot . .	0	9	0*	

French Process of Crystallisation.—Instead of effecting the crystallisation of argentiferous lead in a series of iron pots or kettles, and then removing the crystals formed by means of ladles, worked either entirely by hand or with the aid of cranes, a process has been recently introduced by which manual labour is almost completely dispensed with. The apparatus employed for this purpose essentially consists of two cast iron vessels, the first of which is called the melting pot, and the second the crystallising pot. The former has the same capacity as the latter, and is so set that its bottom is at a higher level than the top of the other. This melting pot is provided, on the side next the crystalliser, with a discharge pipe, which can be tightly closed by means of a slide valve.

The crystallising apparatus consists of an ordinary cast iron pot provided with a vertical stirrer. This pot has, at opposite sides of the bottom, two discharge pipes fitted with slide valves; and each heated by a small separate fire to prevent its becoming obstructed by the

* Cast into moulds and sent into the market as soft lead.

cooling of the metal. Beneath each of these pipes is placed a pot for the reception of the liquid alloy which, on opening the valves, drains from the crystals.

The stirring apparatus consists of two wrought iron shafts working vertically in the centre of the pot; of these one is solid, and supported on a step cast on to the pot, whilst the other consists of an iron tube enclosing the former. Each axle has, at its upper extremity, a mitre wheel, and, as the outer shaft is shorter than the inner one, another mitre wheel is made to work horizontally between them in such a way as to cause the two shafts to revolve in contrary directions. To the lower end of each is connected an iron stirrer, provided with knives, and almost touching the sides of the pot, so as to protect them from any incrustation of lead. The object of this stirrer, which is set in motion by a belt from a small steam-engine, is to promote throughout the mass the production of the uniform temperature necessary for the crystallisation of the metal; and at the same time to so compress the crystals formed, as to cause them to separate readily from the liquid alloy.

It is evident, that, with the formation of increasing quantities of crystals, the friction of the stirrers becomes greater; and when a certain amount of crystals has accumulated, the friction increases to such an extent that the power of the engine is insufficient to continue the motion of the shafts. For this reason the engine employed should not be too large; or an arrangement may be made for causing the strap to slip when the proper accumulation of crystals has taken place. These conditions may be so adjusted as to suit any system of crystallisation; but when the alloy is to be reduced to one-third the weight of the lead operated on, the apparatus must be brought up by the friction as soon as two-thirds of the lead have become crystallised. The pots are heated by a suitable fireplace, and above those into which the liquid alloy is run is a crane by which the enriched lead is lifted out, by means of iron eyes cast in the metal, and brought back to the melting pot for the purpose of being further enriched.

To use this apparatus, such a quantity of original lead must be melted as corresponds to the capacity of the crystallising pot, and as soon as it is fused it is run into it, and the operation of stirring commences. The formation of crystals is effected by lowering the temperature in the usual way, and, as soon as a sufficient amount has been formed, the lateral valves are opened, and the enriched alloy is run into the receiving pots.

Lead, of the same richness in silver as the crystals remaining in the crystalliser, is now melted in the melting pot, in sufficient quantity to make up, with them, another charge. This is tapped in upon the crystals, the mixture again crystallised, and a certain quantity of liquid alloy obtained as before. These operations are repeated, until a concentrated rich alloy, ready for cupellation, is produced, on the one hand; and, on the other, desilverised crystals, which, after being run into moulds, are ready for market.

This process can be continued with unbroken regularity, as soon as there is accumulated a sufficient amount of each class of lead to make, with the crystals remaining in the crystalliser, a full charge for that pot. We are not aware whether this process is found more economical than the ordinary one in which the crystals are removed by means of ladles and cranes.

Refining.—The cupellation of argentiferous lead is in this country conducted on a hearth composed of bone-ash, forming the movable bottom of a reverberatory furnace. The cupel or *test* is contained in an oval iron ring, usually six inches in depth, and generally about four feet in its greater, and three feet in its lesser diameter. In order to better support the bottom of the test, the frame is provided with cross-bars, 4½ inches wide, and half an inch in thickness. This framing, or *test ring*, is most frequently made of wrought iron bars held together by rivets, but in some cases it is formed of cast iron, and is then, including the bars across its bottom, cast in one piece. In order to prepare a test, the frame is filled with bone-ash, well beaten in layers, after having been slightly moistened with water, containing a small quantity of pearlash in solution; the presence of a minute proportion of that salt having the effect of giving consistency to the cupel when heated.

After the framing has been thus filled with moistened bone-ash, solidly beaten down, the centre is carefully scooped out with a small trowel, until the sides are left 2 inches in width at top, and 3 inches at bottom, whilst the thickness of the sole itself is about 1¼ inch. At the front or wide end of the test, the bone-ash border is allowed to stand for a width of six inches, and an opening is cut through the bottom; which, by communicating by means of a channel with the fluid litharge in the annular cavity, formed between the cupel and the edge of the metallic bath, allows the fused oxide of lead to run off as fast as it is produced.

The test, when thus prepared, is kept several days to become thoroughly dry, and when required for use is placed in the refining furnace, of which it forms the bottom. Figs. 72, 73, and 74 represent respectively an elevation, a horizontal and a vertical section, of the refinery most commonly employed.

The size of the fireplace A varies with the other dimensions of the apparatus, but is usually nearly square, and in a furnace of ordinary

FIG. 72.

ELEVATION OF REFINERY.

FIG. 73.

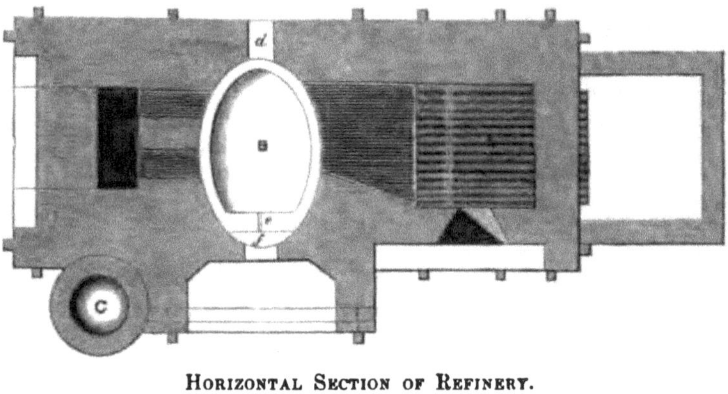

HORIZONTAL SECTION OF REFINERY.

size, may be about 2 feet by 2 feet 4 inches. This is separated from the body of the furnace, by a bridge of from 14 to 18 inches in width, so that the products of combustion pass directly over the surface of the cupel, and from thence escape by two separate apertures, into the main flue.

The test B, when sufficiently dried, is placed in the refinery, of which, as before stated, it forms the bottom; being closely jammed by means of the wedges *a*, of which there are four, resting on two iron bars, against an iron ring *b*, firmly built into the masonry of the furnace. When first lighted, it is necessary to regulate the fire with great care, since, if the cupel were too suddenly heated, it would be liable to crack and exfoliate. As soon, however, as it has become properly annealed, it is heated to incipient redness, and its cavity nearly filled with the rich lead, to be operated on. This has been previously fused in an iron pot C, provided with a fireplace and a gutter *c*, through which the melted lead is ladled into the cavity of the test.

FIG. 74.

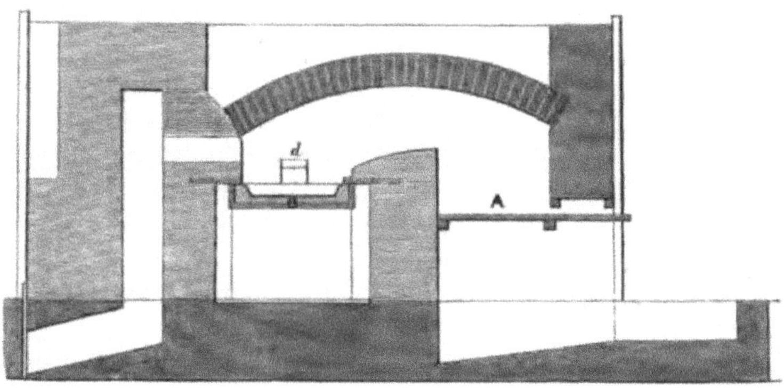

VERTICAL SECTION OF REFINERY.

The liquid metal when first introduced into the cupel becomes covered by a greyish dross, but on further increasing the temperature the surface of the bath uncovers, and ordinary fused litharge begins to make its appearance. The blast is now introduced through a nozzle entering at *d*, and the fused litharge is by this means driven from the back of the test up towards the breast; where it passes over the *gate*, *e*, and, falling through the aperture *f*, between the bone-ash and the iron frame of the cupel, is received in a small shallow cast iron pot, running on wheels, and provided with a long handle.

Some refiners, instead of feeding the test with rich lead in a fused state, prefer to introduce it into the furnace in the form of pigs. In this case the apparatus is provided with one or more iron-lined openings *g*, called pig holes, through which the pigs of metal are introduced. The blast, which is usually supplied by means of a fan, thus not only sweeps the oxide along the surface of the fused metal towards the breast, but also supplies the oxygen necessary for the formation of fresh litharge.

In proportion as the surface of the metallic bath becomes depressed through its constant oxidation and the continual removal of the resulting litharge, additional metal is supplied from the melting pot C, so as to raise it to its former level; and in this manner the operation is continued until the lead in the bottom of the test has become so much enriched as to render it necessary that it should be tapped. When the lead obtained from the rich pot affords about 600 oz. of silver per ton, this operation is usually performed every eight hours, during which time 32 cwt. of metal have been introduced into the cupel, and six cwt. of enriched alloy remain in the metallic state. The removal of the concentrated argentiferous lead is effected by carefully drilling a hole in the bone-ash forming the bottom of the cupel, and running it off into a pot on wheels, which is placed under the test frame for its reception. The reason for thus removing the rich lead is to prevent too large a quantity of silver being carried off in the litharge; which is the case when lead containing a large amount of that metal is operated on. When the rich lead has been thus drawn off, the tapping hole is closed by a pellet of wet bone-ash, and another charge immediately introduced into the test.

As soon as the whole of the rich lead has been subjected to cupella tion, and has thus become further enriched, the argentiferous alloy is itself similarly treated. The brightening of the silver at the moment of the separation of the last traces of oxidisable lead indicates the precise period at which the operation is terminated; and the blast is then turned off and the fire removed from the grate. The plate of silver is now allowed to set, and as soon as it has become sufficiently hardened, the wedges are removed from beneath the test, which is lowered upon a small iron waggon and taken away to cool. The silver is subsequently detached; and any adhering particles of bone-ash or litharge removed by scraping with a wire brush.

A refinery of the usual dimensions will work off 4 pigs (4 cwt.) of lead per hour, and consumes about 6 cwt. of coal per ton of lead operated on.

The expenses, in this country, of refining one ton of rich lead containing 600 oz. of silver, in a locality where coal costs 10*s*. per ton, are as follow :—

Refiner's wages	4s.	6·0d.
Coal, 6 cwt.	3	0·0
Engine, wages	1	9·0
„ coal, 3·1 cwt.	1	6·6
Pearlash	0	3·5
Bone-ash, 17·5 lbs.	3	3·4
Repairs	0	7·0
Total	14s.	11·5d.

The plate thus obtained usually contains from 997 to 998 thousandths of silver.

The following statement gives the fuel consumed, and results obtained, in 1858, at a large English establishment for the treatment of argentiferous lead.

Cost of crystallising 2,838 tons of soft lead and 2,019 tons of hard lead containing 114,738 oz. of silver, including expenses of improving, reducing, and refining. The pots employed each contained 10 tons of lead, and were worked by means of cranes :—

Average assay	23 oz. 13 dwt. 3 gr. per ton.
Average allowance* . .	7 „ 10 „ 2 „ value, £2 1s. 3d.

Coal consumed 7 cwt. 16 lbs. (at 14s. per ton) per ton of lead.

Crystallisers paid per piece 1s. 3d. each per pot of 10 tons. Refiners paid 30s. per week. Reducers 4s. per shift, to run 60 pigs from pot dross, 40 from litharge, or 25 from hard dross. Improvers 21s. per week of 6 days or 5 nights.

---

* The allowance made by the seller of argentiferous lead to the buyer, for the purpose of covering the expenses of desilverisation, is calculated according to what is called the Newcastle Scale, which is as follows :—

Newcastle Scale of Deductions on Desilverising Lead.

Lead under and not exceeding	Deducted.
10 oz. per ton	5½ oz.
20 „ „	6½ „
30 „ „	7½ „
40 „ „	8 „
50 „ „	9 „
60 „ „	9½ „
80 „ „	10 „
100 „ „	11½ „

In calculating the quantity of silver in lead, no fraction less than $\frac{1}{10}$th of an ounce per ton is reckoned. The surplus over the above allowance is paid for at the London price of the day, less ¼d. (one farthing) per oz. for carriage and other charges.

	Total cost. £.	s.	d.	Cost per ton. £.	s.	d.
Potmen's wages	2,227	14	9	0	9	2
Labourers at pots	115	15	1	0	0	6
Labourers	167	14	9	0	0	8½
Coal and coke, crystallising . . .	895	11	4	0	3	4
Reducing	260	9	0	0	1	1
Improving	300	9	9	0	1	3
Refining	366	6	5	0	1	7½
Landing and delivery	269	13	10	0	1	1½
Castillian furnace	121	5	10	0	0	6
Tools, Repairs, and Materials . . .	650	9	0	0	2	9
Salaries	378	11	0	0	1	7½
Rent, Taxes, and Furnaces	441	19	6	0	1	10
Gas	88	19	6	0	0	4½
Sundries	53	5	3	0	0	3
	£6,338	5	0	£1	6	1½
Loss of lead*	80	0	0	0	0	4
Silver in market lead .	1,007	0	0	0	4	2
	£7,425	5	0	£1	10	7½

LIQUATION.—The process of extracting silver from argentiferous copper by liquation is still employed in some localities, although it has been now generally supplanted by the cheaper and more efficient systems of treatment by the wet way. In the Upper Hartz, however, it may yet be seen in full operation, as the Ziervogel and other wet processes, as well as the ordinary methods of treatment by barrel amalgamation, do not appear to be applicable to the complex ores, of that district, containing lead and silver.

This process is based on the circumstance that when copper containing silver is alloyed with a certain proportion of lead, and afterwards heated above the melting point of the latter metal, but below the temperature at which copper enters into fusion, the lead becomes liquid and drains or sweats out, carrying with it the greater portion of the silver, whilst impure copper remains behind in a cavernous or spongy form.

It has been found by experience that, to conduct this operation successfully, the lead should be present in the alloy formed, in the proportion of eleven parts of that metal to three of copper, and that for every part of silver present about five hundred parts of lead should be employed. In the Hartz, according to Lamborn, black

* The actual loss of lead is greater than that shown, but there was the usual trade allowance of 14 lbs. on every ton of silver lead weighed into the factory, which thus reduced the deficit to that above stated.

copper containing one-sixth per cent. of silver can be treated with advantage by liquation; but when only one-eighth per cent. of this metal is present, its extraction does not pay the expenses incident to the operation.

This process is not however generally applicable to the extraction of silver from ores in which that metal forms the most valuable and important constituent; and since it has been often described with much detail in various German and other treatises on metallurgy, we refer those who desire information on this subject to the authors in question, rather than attempt to describe an operation of which we have had no practical experience, and relative to which we possess no special information. The process of liquation will be found described in the works of Villefosse, Kerl, and others.

CHAPTER XXII.

TREATMENT OF ARGENTIFEROUS GALENA AT PONTGIBAUD.

PREPARATION OF LITS DE GRILLAGE—ROASTING—PREPARATION OF LITS DE FUSION—SMELTING IN CASTILLIAN FURNACE—IMPROVING OR CALCINING—CRYSTALLISING—REFINING—REDUCING—RE-SMELTING RICH SLAGS—ROASTING MATTS—TREATMENT OF CALCINED DROSS—TREATMENT OF LEAD CINDER—TREATMENT OF LEAD FUME—LOSSES OF LEAD AND SILVER—SUMMARY OF COSTS.

THE method of smelting employed at Pontgibaud affords an example of the treatment of highly silicious lead ores rich in silver.* These ores occur in large veins of quartz and feldspar traversing gneiss. The average produce of the ore, as extracted, scarcely exceeds 6 per cent. of lead, and consequently very large quantities must be passed through the different washing processes in order to obtain the amount of mineral, averaging about 50 per cent., which is annually smelted in this establishment. As much as possible, however, of what is

* The gangues of the Pontgibaud ores are similar in composition to those of many of the silver-bearing veins of Mexico, Nevada, and other parts of the American Continent. We shall consequently describe, with considerable detail, the various operations conducted in that establishment, since the system there employed is well adapted for the treatment of argentiferous minerals containing a large amount of silica, wherever fuel and lead ores can be obtained at reasonable prices.

The mines of Pontgibaud, Puy-de-Dôme, France, have at various periods afforded large quantities of argentiferous galena, but were never so productive as at the present time. The re-working of the concessions was commenced by a local company in 1825, and the operations were continued under the management of French engineers until the year 1852, when the property was transferred to an Anglo-French Association, under the management of Messrs. John Taylor & Sons, of London. We were at that period for some time occupied in re-modelling the smelting works, and introducing into them various modern appliances, but great improvements have been since made, and more particularly in the apparatus employed for roasting the ores and their preparation for the blast furnace.

The various ameliorations introduced into the system of treatment at Pontgibaud are, to a great extent, due to Mr. W. Hutchison, the present manager of the Smelting Works, to whom we are indebted for the drawings of the different furnaces, and for very copious and admirably arranged notes, affording the practical results of the several operations as now conducted.

called *massif* or cobbed ore is carefully selected, in order to avoid exposing it to unnecessary mechanical loss. Recently the proportion of massif to washed ore has become much greater than formerly, particularly since the discovery of a new mine yielding ores very rich in silver. The effect of this has been to render the ores more refractory, since the assay of hand-picked ores for lead is seldom higher than 40 per cent., whilst the proportion of silicious gangue is much greater than in the washed ones.

It is to the uniformly silicious nature of the Pontgibaud ores, together with the impurities contained in the work lead obtained, that many of the difficulties experienced in smelting them are due, and which have rendered necessary the adoption of the special processes employed at this establishment. These difficulties are further increased, particularly in the matter of cost, by the remoteness of the locality in which the mines are situated; Pontgibaud being at a great distance from any centre of industry from which fuel and fluxes can be obtained at moderate prices.

All the ores are delivered at the smelting works in a state of fine powder; that is to say, the coarsest will pass through a sieve with apertures of 4 m.m. in diameter. As many as seven varieties are received monthly from the different mines belonging to the company. They vary considerably in richness, both as regards lead and silver, and the amount of gangue which they contain; this gangue is *always silicious*, although generally associated with small quantities of sulphate of baryta, arsenical pyrites, iron pyrites, blende, &c.

The produce of each mine is sampled on the 1st of each month, and immediately delivered to the smelting works; where the operations are so conducted that all the ores received during one month may be converted into pig lead before the next month's deliveries take place. This system, besides its convenience, has the advantage of enabling the smelter to check the calculated produce by the actual monthly returns. Each sample of ore is tried by two assayers, one on the part of the mines and the other on that of the smelting works; if their results differ to the extent of 1 per cent. each repeats his assays. In case of a constant difference, a sample is sent to a professional assayer, and the result he obtains is considered final; but this course is seldom resorted to.

All the assays are made in an iron crucible, and when properly conducted yield results quite as high as those obtained by the humid way; a circumstance probably owing to the impurities in the lead button compensating for the slight loss by volatilisation.

It will be necessary to bear this in mind, in comparing the losses of lead at the Pontgibaud works, with those experienced in other establishments where ores of a different nature are treated, and where the assays are, generally speaking, less carefully executed.

In the treatment of these ores nine distinct operations are necessary, viz.:—

1.—Preparation of *Lits de Grillage.*
2.—Roasting.
3.—Preparation of *Lits de Fusion.*
4.—Smelting in Castillian blast furnace.
5.—Improving.
6.—Crystallising.
7.—Refining.
8.—Reducing.
9.—Re-smelting rich slags.

In addition to the above, the routine of the establishment renders four supplementary operations necessary, viz.:—

a.—Roasting matt.
b.—Treatment of calcined dross.
c.—Treatment of lead cinder.
d.—Treatment of lead fume.

1. *Preparation of Lits de Grillage.*—Although the ores do not differ materially as regards the nature of their gangues, they vary considerably in richness; and consequently also in the proportion of earthy matters present.

It has, therefore, been found important, before commencing their treatment, to prepare a uniform mixture of the whole sampling.

On this depends the regularity of the subsequent operations, and, in a great measure, their economical working.

As it is impossible to thoroughly mix the whole weight of the various parcels of ore (often amounting to upwards of 300 tons), a *lit* of twenty tons, or a little more than the quantity usually roasted per diem, is prepared by weighing out, and spreading in thin layers, one above another, the exact proportion of twenty tons, which each parcel bears to the total weight delivered.*

The "lit" being finished, the charges are made by successively cutting down with a shovel the pile of stratified ore; and in such a way that every ton of the mixture removed shall have nearly the same composition as the entire mass.

Experience has proved the advantage of this arrangement over that

* Tons of 1,000 kilos.

of charging the hoppers direct from the several heaps in the ore magazine.

The following will serve to show the kind of ore comprised in an ordinary monthly sampling :—

	Dry ore. kilos.	Assays. Lead per cent.	Assays. Silver per M. kilos.*
A.—Washed ore	134,504	56½	1·100 grammes.
B.—Massif	37,520	40	0·725 ,,
C.—Washed ore	21,960	47½	1·137 ,,
D.—Washed ,,	9,393	66¾	1·650 ,,
E.—Massif	41,378	47	2·300 ,,
F.—Washed ore	29,515	49	1·206 ,,
G.—Washed ,,	26,528	66¾	0·380 ,,
Total	300,798		

To this mixture of ores are added the matts resulting from the previous month's smelting in the blast furnace, which are, after being ground and roasted *dead* in a reverberatory furnace, treated exactly as ordinary ores.

The total weight of matt mixed with the ores in the above instance was 35 tons, containing 14 per cent. of lead, and 400 grammes of silver per ton of 1,000 kilos.

For preparing a lit de grillage of 20 tons, the proportion required of each of the above parcels (wet weight) was as follows:—

Ore A.—8,094 kilos.	Ore E.—2,454 kilos.
,, B.—2,174 ,,	,, F.—1,780 ,,
,, C.—1,374 ,,	,, G.—1,594 ,,
,, D.— 570 ,,	Matt.—1,960 ,,

The average amount of moisture contained in these ores was 6 per cent.

It will be observed that the proportion of roasted or calcined matt in the above mixture is about 10 per cent.; but this proportion constantly varies from month to month. The object of adding it to the lits de grillage is, that its oxide of iron may serve as a flux in the subsequent operation.

In some cases, *i.e.* when the ores are more than usually quartzose, 10 per cent. of matt is found to be insufficient for this purpose, and ground *scories de forge*, or mill cinders, are added as a substitute: not unfrequently the previous month's production of matt does not

* The average produce of these ores for silver will be found to be about 39 oz. per English ton.

amount to 10 per cent., and then also iron slags are employed. As a rule, 10 per cent. of matt, or 15 per cent. of mill cinder, is sufficient, but it often happens that these proportions must be considerably exceeded.

It would perhaps appear preferable to add iron slag directly to the mixture prepared for the blast furnace, as is done in some other works; but repeated experiments have led to the adoption of the method now employed; since its value as a flux in roasting, by the Pontgibaud system, is almost as great as its subsequent utility during the operation of smelting.

Two men are employed in the preparation of the roasting mixture; they are paid two francs each per day, and in that time prepare the mixtures, and charge each furnace with eight tons of ore. The cost of this operation is 0·25f. (2½*d.*) per ton.

2. *Roasting.*—The ores are roasted in very large reverberatory furnaces worked from both sides. There are three of these at Pontgibaud, but two only are in constant operation; all have exactly the same form and dimensions; their great width, as well as their great length, is a most important feature as regards economy of fuel.

FIG. 75.

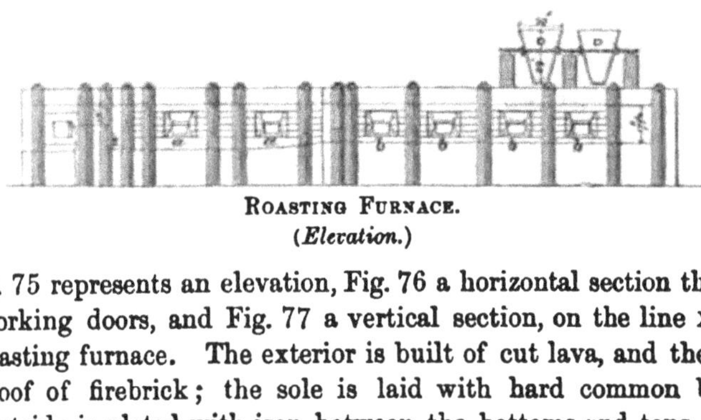

ROASTING FURNACE.
(*Elevation.*)

Fig. 75 represents an elevation, Fig. 76 a horizontal section through the working doors, and Fig. 77 a vertical section, on the line X Y, of the roasting furnace. The exterior is built of cut lava, and the sides and roof of firebrick; the sole is laid with hard common bricks. The outside is plated with iron between the bottoms and tops of the doors *a*, *b*, as shown by the horizontal lines. The doors *a* nearest the fireplace are a little smaller than the others. The fireplace A is divided from the fusing hearth B, by a firebrick bridge 20 inches in width; the ore being admitted into the hearth C, through the hoppers D. The bottom E, beneath the lining of common bricks, is composed of a mixture of sand and slag well beaten in. The tap hole is shown at *c*, Fig. 77. This apparatus requires but little repair.

When working, this furnace contains six tons of dry ore and matt, divided into three charges of two tons each, severally occupying about one-third the surface of the entire sole. There are six doors on either side, two of which correspond with one or other of the charges, and enable the workmen to turn or advance the ore when required.

FIG. 76.

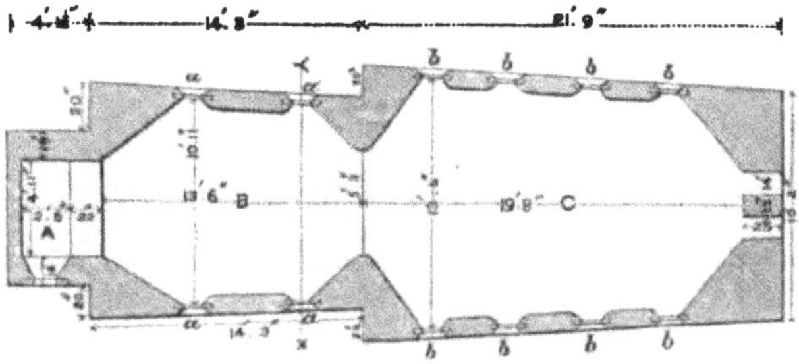

ROASTING FURNACE.
(*Horizontal Section.*)

FIG. 77.

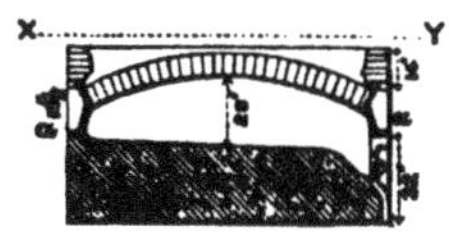

ROASTING FURNACE.
(*Vertical Section.*)

The different parts of the furnace occupied in succession by each charge may be distinguished as follow :—

1st.—Drying bed, immediately under the hoppers.
2nd.—Desulphurising or oxidising bed, widest part of furnace.
3rd.—Agglomerating bed, next to fireplace.*

The first two are on the same level, the third about 20 c.m. lower than the others.

The peculiar form of the agglomerating or fusing bed has for its object the equalisation of the temperature over that portion of the furnace in which the greatest heat is required.

The ore arriving on this bed is fused and run out in the form of

* The agglomeration of the ores at Pontgibaud is in reality a fusion, without reduction.

a liquid slag. At intervals of six hours a charge of melted ore is withdrawn, and the other charges in the furnace are advanced a stage; whilst a fresh charge is let down through the hoppers upon the drying bed. The time each charge remains in the furnace is consequently 18 hours. Eight tons of ore and matt are thus roasted in each furnace in the course of 24 hours, with a consumption of about 2,000 kilos. of coal, and 6 per cent. of lime. The consumption of iron slags averages 7 per cent.; but, whatever the proportions of this flux, or of lime, may be, the quantity of ore charged remains constant—that is to say, 1,800 kilos.

Four men are employed at each furnace, per shift of twelve hours; the foreman is paid 2·20f. per day, the others 2f.

The general system of roasting in this furnace will be understood from the foregoing description; but, in order that it may be fully comprehended in all its various details, it may perhaps be necessary to explain the mode of working more minutely.

Let us, for this purpose, suppose that the usual regularity of the operations has been uninterrupted during the night, and that at six in the morning we accompany the men to their work. We shall find the bed next the grate empty, the charge having, about two hours previously, been run out upon the floor, on one side of the furnace. The charge in the middle bed having been roasted dead, is heaped up in the throat ready for being advanced into the agglomerating bed, which is still at a red heat, although the fire has been allowed to burn down in the grate. The foreman begins by throwing a shovelful of coals on the fire to create a blaze and light up the interior, so that the men may see their work. All hands then commence busily advancing the ore with long paddles. Two men advance it upon the agglomerating bed, and pile it up as near the bridge as they can; whilst two others push forward the ore from the drying bed into the middle or desulphurising hearth. In the latter, the ore is spread evenly over the sole, and two or three shovelfuls of slaked lime are afterwards scattered over its surface; especially on the side next the fire, to prevent the formation of a crust of partially-agglomerated ore very difficult to calcine.

The time required for advancing the two charges is about forty minutes. A new charge is now let down from the hoppers D, and spread over the drying bed with a rake. The doors are then all closed, the grate charged with coals, and the fire increased until the furnace has acquired a bright red heat.

In about three quarters of an hour the ore in the middle bed has become sufficiently hot to scintillate when stirred, and to give off sulphurous acid vapours. Two men, one on each side, now commence turning over the charge with paddles, which they do repeatedly, first forwards towards the fire, and then backwards towards the flue; taking care that the whole of the ore is turned, and that fresh portions are constantly exposed to the action of the heated air. From time to time a shovelful of slaked lime is thrown in and worked up with the ore to keep it "dry;" especially on the side next the fire, where it is most liable to clot. The operation of turning is continued without interruption until the charge in the agglomerating bed is ready to tap, when, during the time of tapping, &c. there is an interval of nearly half an hour; but it is afterwards renewed and continued until the expiration of six hours, or at least until the ore has been roasted dead. When the mixture of ores is good, *i. e.* when it is moderately rich in lead, and contains at the same time a good deal of oxide of iron, the charge in the agglomerating bed requires but little working. It then melts easily, and in about two hours and a half after the firing commences it is ready to draw. But, should the mixture contain an excess of silica, it is difficult to get the ore into a liquid state. Part of the charge attaches itself to the sole, and another portion is drawn out, after great trouble, in a tough pasty condition. A great loss of lead, and considerable waste of fuel, are the consequences. For this reason it is advantageous to add oxide of iron to the ore, and the cheapest way of doing this, at Pontgibaud, is in the form of iron slags, although their cost is 27f. per ton.

Assuming the charge worked to be easily fusible, it is only requisite to paddle it once towards the bridge; about three-quarters of an hour after beginning to fire. It is also necessary, just before tapping, to rake over the bottom, to be certain that none of the ore is sticking to it, and that the whole charge is perfectly fluid. When this is found to be the case, the tap hole is unstopped, and the charge run out upon the floor; where it is prevented from spreading beyond certain limits, by a small dam or ridge of ore and sweepings, &c. reserved for that purpose. No lead is reduced in this process, but a certain quantity of very rich sulphide of lead is generally met with at the bottom of the charge. This is particularly the case when the ore is rather rich in lead, and has been imperfectly roasted.

The bulk of the charge of roasted ore is composed of a clean black slag containing from 30 to 40 per cent. of lead. The whole of the sulphate of lead formed in the middle bed is subsequently decomposed by the silicic acid present. As soon as the charge has been run out, the tap hole is examined, and any adhering ore is cut away with a long chisel; after which it is again stopped. The bridge and sides are then looked at to ascertain whether they require repairs; since holes are often eaten out by the melted ore, which require to be stopped with clay after almost every charge. The fire is now suffered to burn down, to allow of clearing the grate of clinkers. The damper is at the same time partially closed, and preparation is made for the advance of another charge, when the time for doing so shall have arrived. Charge thus succeeds charge at regular intervals of six hours: the loss of weight in roasting amounts to about 10 per cent. of the quantity charged.

The loss of metal by volatilisation is extremely difficult to estimate, as it is scarcely possible to obtain a fair sample of the roasted ores. Several experiments, undertaken with this object, have fixed the loss of lead at from 2 to 3 per cent. of the total quantity present. The loss of silver is still more difficult to determine, and no result which can be depended on has yet been obtained.

The cost of roasting ore per ton is as follows (the dry ore per charge being 1,800 kilos.):—

Coal,	280 kilos. at 35 f.	9·80 f.
Lime,	60 „ at 24 f.	1·45
Scories de forge,	70 „ at 27 f.	1·90
Labour		2·90
Tools and repairs		0·80
Sundries (including superintendence)		2·90
		F. 19·75 = 15*s*. 9.6*d*.

3. *Preparation of Lits de Fusion.*—The lits de fusion are usually composed as follow:—

Roasted ore	10,000 kilos.
Scrap iron	1,000 „
Limestone	1,600 „
Fluor spar	300 „

The above figures give the average quantities of flux in the furnace mixtures. They are, however, modified with the nature of the ore; the proportions of limestone and fluor spar varying most considerably. Two men are employed at this work, and receive 2f. each per day. They prepare a lit and a half in that time—15 tons consequently the cost is 0·27f. per ton of roasted ore, and 0·25f. per ton of crude ore.

4. *Smelting in Castillian Furnace.*—There are two of these at Pontgibaud, but it is seldom that more than one is in blast at a time. Fig. 78 represents a front elevation of one of these furnaces, which are constructed of cut lava, and are very inexpensive to build.

FIG. 78.

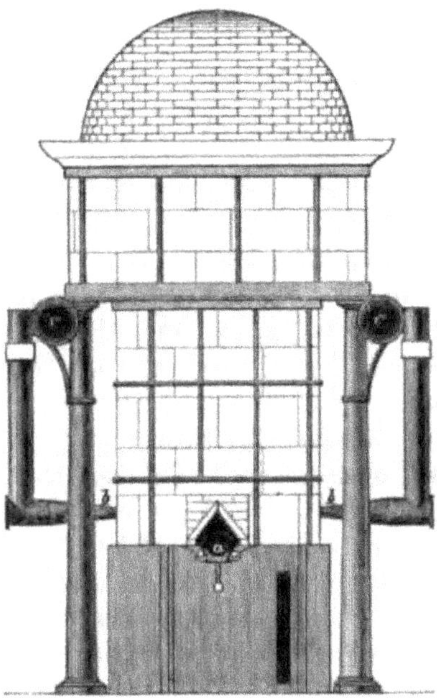

CASTILLIAN FURNACE, PONTGIBAUD.
(*Front Elevation.*)

Their height from the slag-overflow *a* to the charging door is 5 feet, internal diameter 35 inches; diameter of tuyere 3 inches; pressure of wind about 4 inches of water. These furnaces are supplied with the blast by the nozzles *b*, of which there are three, connected with the main *c*; water tuyeres are not employed in the Pontgibaud furnaces.

The mode of charging is similar to that employed for other furnaces of the same kind.

The ore is distributed around the sides, the coke in the middle and against the breast. The furnace is kept constantly full, and particular care is taken not to let the flame appear above the charge; it being considered important to keep the top as dark as possible. A large breast pan, capable of holding 20 pigs at a time, is preferred, but it is sometimes difficult to maintain it of that size.

From 14 to 16 tons of ore are smelted in 24 hours, with a consumption of one ton of coke, or about 7 per cent. of fuel.

The quantity of lead obtained in the same time is from 100 to 120 pigs, or from 5 to 6 tons. From 7 to 10 per cent. of matt is also produced.

It is found that the production of a certain quantity of matt cannot be prevented. Indeed its presence is regarded as being in no way prejudicial to the working of the furnaces, unless it be formed in too great an excess. When very little matt is produced, the slags are generally rich in lead. Sulphide of iron appears to act on the silicate of lead as a powerful reducing agent. Whenever oxide of iron does not abound in the ores smelted, the presence of matt alone does not prevent the slags from becoming rich. The presence of a large quantity of oxide of iron is indispensable to the production of poor slags, since without it the oxide of lead remains combined with silicic acid, and cannot be separated therefrom.

It has been found by analyses of poor slags that those most easily freed from lead contain at least 40 per cent. of oxide of iron. This base may be however, in part, replaced by lime, especially if fluor spar be at the same time added. Yet, although by this means poor slags can be obtained, they are never so poor as when oxide of iron is present in slight excess; the amount of lead volatilised is also considerably increased. The proportion of slags produced is from 65 to 70 per cent. of the ore smelted.

The slags formed under the most favourable circumstances do not contain less than 2 per cent. of lead. When they exceed 3 per cent. they are re-smelted in a furnace of similar construction to those already described, but situated in another part of the works.

The slags, as they flow from the furnace, are received into cast iron waggons, which, when full, are drawn away to the waste heaps on a small tramway constructed for that purpose. The waggons employed at Pontgibaud, of which Fig. 79 is a side view, Fig. 80 an end view, and Fig. 81 a plan, are very convenient in form, and but little liable to break. The depth of the pan is 20 inches, and its width 21 inches.

These have been in constant use for the last five years, and have scarcely ever needed repairs, except to the wheels and axles.

FIG. 79.

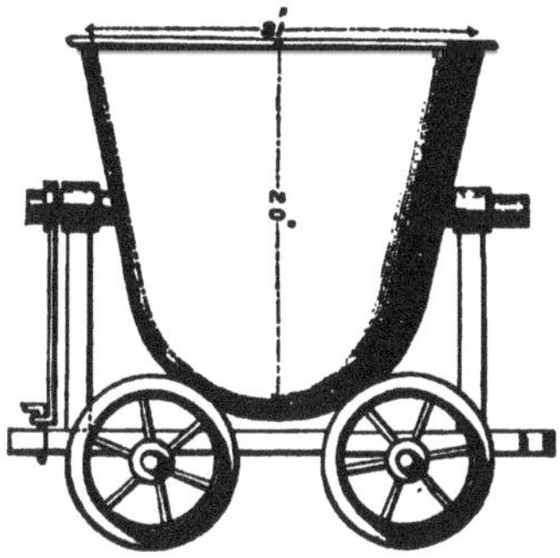

SIDE VIEW OF SLAG WAGGON.

FIG. 80.

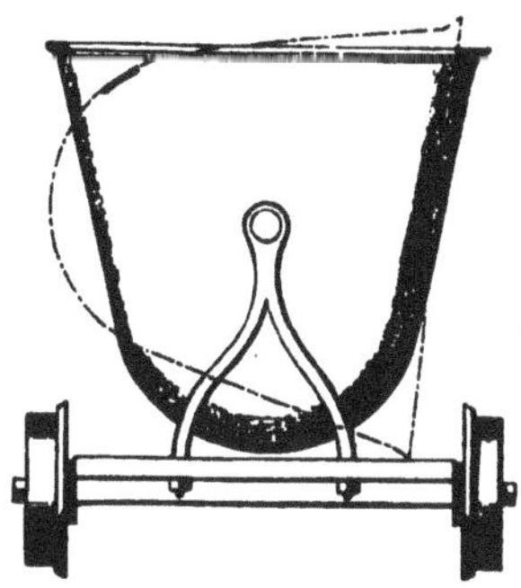

END VIEW OF SLAG WAGGON.

FIG. 81.

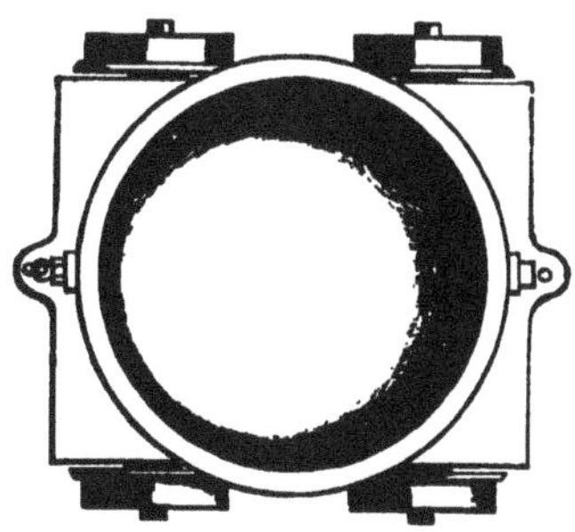

PLAN OF SLAG WAGGON.

The men employed at this furnace per shift of 12 hours are:—

1 Foreman	paid	2·50 f.	per day.
1 Charger	„	2·20	„
3 Trammers	„ each	1·80	„

The costs per ton of *roasted* ore are as follow:—

Iron	110 kilos at 95f.	10·45 f.
Limestone	160 „ at 20f.	3·20
Fluor spar	30 „ at 15f.	0·45
Coke	70 „ at 48f.	3·35
Labour		1·85
Tools and repairs		0·75
Sundries (including superintendence)		3·35
		F. 23·40 = 18*s.* 8·6*d.*

The cost per ton of *unroasted* ore is therefore 21·06f. or 16*s.* 10·1*d.*

The cylinders of the blowing machine are 1·34 m., or 52 inches in diameter.

Length of stroke, 52 inches.

Number of strokes per minute, 12.

The lead obtained from the Castillian furnace contains nearly all the silver originally present in the ores smelted, excepting a small proportion combined with matts, or retained in the slags. The usual assay of matt is from 15 to 20 per cent. of lead, and 400 to 500 grms., or from 12 oz. 17 dwt. to 16 oz. 2 dwt. of silver per ton; the average assay of the lead is about 3 kilos. = 96½ oz. per ton. The whole of the silver in the matt, and a portion of that in the slags, is recovered in the subsequent operations; but a small fractional part of that metal is nevertheless unavoidably lost. This loss amounts to 10 grms., or 6½ dwt. per ton of slag, or 0·568 per cent., according to assay, of the total quantity contained in the ores.

A certain amount of silver is also volatilised with the lead, but how large a proportion is, from this cause, entirely lost cannot be accurately ascertained. That it is, however, exceedingly small is probable, from the known properties of silver, and the small amount found in the fumes collected in the flues and condenser. The proportion of silver thus volatilised or mechanically carried off, and again recovered, in all the different processes, including cupellation, amounts to only 0·470 per cent. of the total quantity, according to assay, contained in the ores. The loss of lead in smelting ores in the blast furnace amounts to about 17 per cent. of the total quantity contained in them.

It has been ascertained that about 5 per cent. of all the lead is retained in the slags, and about 12 per cent. carried off in fumes. Two per cent. is, however, afterwards recovered from slags by re-smelting, and about 3½ per cent. from the fumes. The actual loss, therefore, in the operation is equal to 11¾ per cent. of the total quantity of lead contained in the ores.

It will be seen from the foregoing that the system of roasting and smelting at Pontgibaud has undergone very important alterations since the publication, in 1851, of Rivot and Zeppenfeld's "*Description des Gîtes Métallifères &c. de Pontgibaud*," which appears to be still regarded by many continental engineers as a description of what is being done at the present time. In proof of this it may be stated that in a lengthy paper on the Metallurgy of Lead, published in the "Revue Universelle des Mines," so recently as 1863, the engraving of a roasting furnace shown in Rivot and Zeppenfeld's work is reproduced as though it were still in use; whereas, in point of fact, it had been demolished ten years previously.

It is, however, in the treatment of the argentiferous lead obtained that the system now employed differs most essentially from that in use in 1851. At that period, the whole of the lead obtained from the blast furnace was immediately cupelled in a large German cupelling furnace, and the silver separated and refined in the usual way. The litharge produced was afterwards submitted to a complicated mechanical preparation in order to render it fit for sale; the whole, or very nearly the whole, of the lead thus converted into oxide being sold in that state. The small quantity of metallic lead sent to market was obtained, after great loss, by the reduction of a portion of the litharge, and was of very inferior quality. At the present time it would be extremely difficult to find a sale for so much litharge as the Pontgibaud works could now produce, as the yield of the mines has been enormously augmented. There is, however, never any difficulty in disposing of pig lead.

In the method employed at Pontgibaud since the works have been under the direction of Messrs. John Taylor and Sons, the object in view has been to convert the whole of the lead into metal of first-rate quality, and to obtain at the same time as complete a separation as possible of the silver: this is accomplished by means of Pattinson's process. The advantages of this method have been long appreciated both in England and on the Continent, and it is now generally adopted, either in combination with the old continental method, or with some modification of it suitable to the locality and the nature of the ores treated. The principal advantages of Pattinson's process, as compared with the old Pontgibaud method, are the following:—

1st.—Direct production of metallic lead.

2nd.—A greatly diminished loss of metal.

3rd.—A higher yield of silver.

In the treatment of the argentiferous lead obtained from the blast furnace, four distinct operations are necessary, viz.:—

Improving or softening.

Crystallising.

Refining.

Reducing.

5. *Improving or Calcining.*—The whole of the work lead produced at Pontgibaud must be purified before it can be treated by Pattinson's

process, and this is done by exposing it at a low red heat to partial oxidation in a reverberatory furnace specially adapted for that purpose. The chief impurity contained in the lead is antimony; the others are sulphur, iron, arsenic, and copper. All are in relatively small proportion, but are still in sufficient quantity to render the lead *hard*. The accompanying drawings, Figs. 82, 83, and 84, show the arrangement and dimensions of the furnace employed.

Fig. 82.

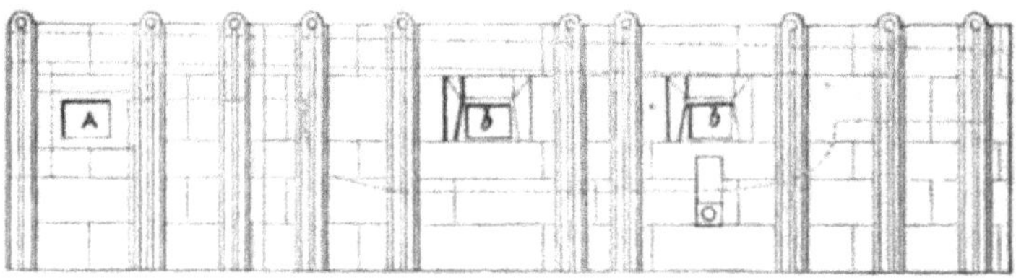

Improving Furnace.
(*Elevation.*)

Fig. 82 is an elevation; Fig. 83 a horizontal section at the level of the top of the pan; and Fig. 84 a vertical section through the tap hole. The fireplace A is separated from the pan B, by a bridge 3 feet 3 inches wide, and the furnace is provided with two doors *b*, through which the dross may be removed. In principle this resembles the ordinary softening furnace with its cast iron pan, but its greater size and solidity of construction render it much more economical than the furnaces usually employed for the purpose.

On reference to the drawing, it will be remarked that the pan is not only much larger than those commonly employed, but has also a rounded form; the object in giving it this shape being to diminish the tendency to crack, to which all square-sided pans are so liable. Another essential feature in the construction of these furnaces is to make them perfectly lead-tight, in case the iron should break. This is most effectually done by setting the pan on a bottom of well-beaten brasque two feet in thickness, resting on a solid foundation of masonry. The sides of the furnace must be either of thick iron plates or of large cut stones. In either case the space between them and the pan should be at least a foot wide, and well filled with hard beaten brasque.

The lead is tapped from the pan through a small hole *a*, three-fourths of an inch in diameter, bored in the bottom of the pan, and communicating with a thick cast iron tube *b'*, fastened to it by means of stud-bolts screwed into about half the thickness of the metal. Before charging, the hole in the bottom is plugged by a long

FIG. 83.

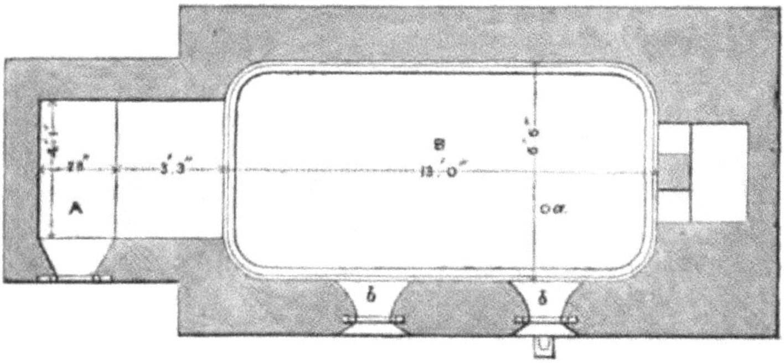

IMPROVING FURNACE.
(*Horizontal Section.*)

pointed bar passed through an opening *c*, Fig. 84, in the roof, corresponding with the tapping hole, and placed vertically over it. This bar will not generally stop the hole quite tight; especially after the furnace has been working a long time. The tube is, therefore, partly filled with bone-ash, firmly rammed in; a bar having been previously

FIG. 84.

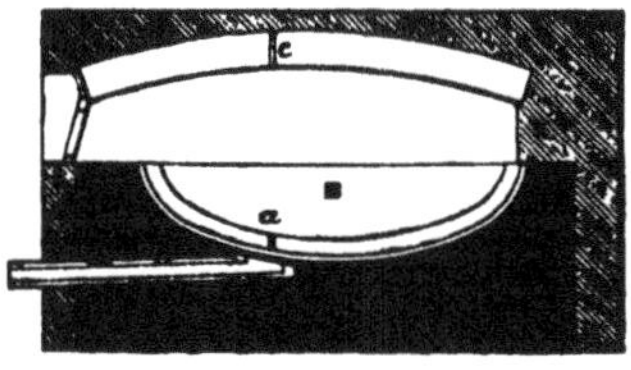

IMPROVING FURNACE.
(*Section through Tap Hole.*)

placed in the tube in such a way that the channel left, after its withdrawal, shall correspond with the hole in the pan. This horizontal bar is even more necessary than the vertical one; the use of the latter being to take off the pressure of the lead in the pan, and regulate the flow of metal in tapping. The horizontal bar is put in and withdrawn by the aid of a sledge; in much the same way as, though more easily than, a tapping bar at the blast furnace.

Two of these furnaces have been erected at Pontgibaud; one for common work lead, the other for the hard lead reduced from calcined dross. The former has been almost constantly in use for upwards of five years; and although the pan is now cracked, the furnace is as tight and serviceable as ever.

Both improving pans were originally lined with bricks, as shown in the drawings, Figs. 83 and 84, to protect the iron from corrosion by the oxides formed on the surface of the metallic bath. This precaution is now thought to be unnecessary; all that is required being to avoid overheating the furnace, and the consequent fusion of the dross. It is also found that a dull red heat is the best temperature for calcining Pontgibaud lead; and at that point the oxides neither melt, nor exert any corrosive action on the pan, especially if a little lime be from time to time added. The usual charge of a pan without lining is about twenty tons. The brick lining diminishes its capacity by about one-fifth. A charge of twenty tons of common work lead requires sixty hours to become sufficiently soft for treatment by Pattinson's process, the whole time necessary for the operation, including charging and discharging, being three days.

Three men are employed in filling and emptying the pan, and are paid 2f. each per charge. The pigs of lead are introduced through one of the working doors by means of a long charging bar, and the charging is effected with great ease and rapidity. Except for charging and discharging, scarcely any labour is required, as the firing is attended to by one of the men working at the Castillian furnace.

An ordinary month's work at this furnace is as follows:—

Work Lead in. Tons.	Soft Lead out. Tons.	Percentage of soft Lead obtained.	Dross. Tons.	Coals consumed. Tons.	Lime used. kilos.
139·150	131·528	94·7	8·675	11·560	554

The small consumption of coal is partly due to the employment of cinders picked out from the imperfectly burnt ashes at the pots, and mixed with the coal; their cost per month being equal to a boy's wages, viz. 20f. per month. The cost of calcining one ton of blast furnace lead is—

Coal, 83 kilos. at 35f.	2·90f.
Cinders	0·15
Lime 7·5 kilos. at 24f.	0·18
Labour	0·45
Sundries	0·60
	F. 4·28 = 3*s*. 4·8*d*.

Cost on ton of ore 1·90f. = 1*s*. 6·2*d*.

The drosses resulting from the calcination of the work lead contain, besides the various impurities, a large proportion of lead, partially in the form of oxide, and partly in the metallic state. These drosses are subsequently treated in the reducing furnace.

The lead reduced therefrom is very impure and exceedingly hard, and, as it contains a considerable proportion of silver, 1,400 grammes, 45 oz., per ton, it is again calcined in the ordinary way. The hard lead obtained in the treatment of the lead cinder left as a residue in the reduction of litharge and pot dross is also calcined in the same furnace.

The hard lead contains a large amount of antimony and other impurities very difficult to separate, and consequently the process of softening in this case becomes long and costly. The average time required for calcining 20 tons of hard lead is about four weeks. The usual quantity treated per annum, with results and costs, is as follows:—

Hard Lead in. Tons.	Soft Lead out. Tons.	Percentage of soft Lead obtained.	Coal consumed. Tons.	Lime consumed. Tons.
148·845	96·978	65·1	99·900	5

Cost per ton of Hard Lead.

Coals, 665 kilos. at 35f.	23·27f.
Lime, 33½ „ at 24f.	0·80
Labour	0·43
	F. 24·50 = 19*s*. 7·2*d*.

Cost on ton of ore smelted 1·03f. = 9·6*d*.

The dross skimmed from this hard lead yields on reduction about 55 per cent. of a very hard lead, assaying 600 to 700 grammes, 19 oz. 5 dwt. to 22 oz. 10 dwt., of silver per ton; which is generally mixed with the ordinary hard lead and treated in the same way. In the statement of costs, all the hard lead, of every kind, is included. Occasionally, when a sufficient quantity has accumulated, it is worked separately. It then gives a dross which on being reduced yields an extremely hard lead. This, whenever it contains too little silver to pay the costs of extraction, is immediately disposed of for making certain alloys containing a large quantity of antimony. But this seldom happens, as it is only after repeated calcinations and reductions that a hard lead is obtained too poor in silver to pay for again working over. The proportion of poor hard lead produced at Pontgibaud is therefore exceedingly small.

6. *Crystallising.*—At Pontgibaud there are twelve pots in one set—eleven ten-ton pots, and one six-ton, or market pot. The system of working is by *thirds.* The ladles used are 20 inches in diameter, and 6 inches deep, and of the ordinary English pattern. The cranes employed are also of the usual form.

The average assay of the work lead is, as before stated, about 3,000 kilos., 96½ oz., of silver per ton. It is charged in the tenth pot.

The usual assays of the whole series of pots, tops and bottoms, are as follow:—

No. of Pot.	SILVER PER TON.				Remarks.
	Top.		Bottom.		
	grammes.	oz. dwt. gr.	grammes.	oz. dwt. gr.	
1	15	9 15	—	—	Poor Lead.
2	30	19 7	60	1 18 14	
3	60	1 18 14	120	3 17 4	
4	120	3 17 4	220	7 1 11	
5	230	7 7 21	400	12 17 5	
6	400	12 17 5	720	23 3 0	
7	700	22 10 3	1,200	38 11 16	
8	1,150	36 19 12	1,800	57 17 12	
9	1,850	59 9 16	2,900	93 4 21	
10	3,000	96 9 4	5,000	160 15 8	Charging Pot.
11	5,200	167 3 22	8,500	273 6 1	
12	8,500	273 6 1	16,000	514 9 1	Rich Lead.

In working the rich pot, the whole of the bottom is not ladled out; it is found to be more advantageous to ladle out the liquid only, and leave the crystals behind. When the ordinary quantity, or about two-thirds, of the lead has been turned into the eleventh pot, the remaining one-third consists of a mixture of crystallised and uncrystallised alloy. The latter, being much richer than the former, is separated as completely as possible; and this portion only, amounting to a little more than half the bottom, is sent to the refining furnace.

The work of removing the liquid is readily effected by means of what the French workmen call a *panier*, which is made of a piece of sheet iron, pierced with numerous small holes, turned up and fastened with rivets in the form of the frustum of an inverted cone. It is provided with two handles for putting it into and taking it out of the pot. By its use, a well is readily formed in the middle of the crystals, which facilitates the draining of the liquid metal from the surrounding mass, and allows of the lead being easily ladled into moulds. The right moment for introducing the panier, and ladling out the liquid, is easily determined by practice. When it is desired to take out much liquid metal, the pot is, on approaching the bottom, worked thin; but when the contrary is required, the work of stirring is continued until the crystals have become thick. In all cases, it is necessary to remove the whole of the liquid lead, otherwise the crystals left behind may be too rich.

The proportion of rich lead, viz. 18·2 per cent., cupelled at Pontgibaud is necessarily large, as the original lead is itself comparatively rich in silver. It is, therefore, very important to concentrate the rich alloy as much as possible before taking it to the refinery, where it is necessarily exposed to considerable loss from volatilisation.

Experiments made by Mr. Hutchison, with the object of enriching lead to a much higher degree than is usual, have demonstrated the impossibility of doing so beyond 2 per cent. of silver; and this degree of concentration is only attained after repeated and very careful crystallisations, and by at last drawing off a small quantity only of liquid alloy. When the converse of this operation is tried—*i.e.* when lead, enriched in the cupelling furnace so as to contain about 8 per cent. of silver, is fused in a pot, and cooled down in the ordinary way, the portions which first solidify are much richer than the liquid drained from them; the latter, after repeated drainings, invariably containing about 2¼ per cent. It therefore appears that the remarkable property of crystallisation, discovered and utilised by Pattinson, arrives at its turning-point when the lead has acquired a richness of from 2 to 2¼ per cent. of silver.*

In the ordinary way of working, it is remarked that in proportion

* Mr. Hutchison remarks: "I have never seen any explanation of the reason for stopping the concentration at from 400 to 600 oz. per ton. We are generally told it would not be economical to push the concentration further; but this is not altogether true, as further concentration would certainly effect a saving of a part of the lead now volatilised during cupellation."

as the concentration advances, it becomes more and more difficult to obtain the same degree of enrichment per pot or per ton of lead crystallised which is possible with poorer lead. An ordinary month's work at the pots may be tabulated as follows :—

CHARGED.			OBTAINED.			
Calcined Lead. Tons.	Reduced Lead. Tons.	Total. Tons.	Market Lead. Tons.	Rich Lead. Tons.	Coals consumed. Tons.	Wages. f.
135·000	63·000	198·000	130·000	23·400	61·000	960

Four pairs of men are generally employed, whose time is divided into twelve-hour shifts. Four, and sometimes five, pots are worked by each pair per shift. The crystallisers are paid 0·60f. each per pot, and the stokers 2f. per shift.

The cost of crystallising per ton of market lead produced is as follows :—

Coal, 470 kilos. at 31f.	14·57f.
Wages	7·40
Wear and tear of pots	1·70
Tools and repairs	0·60
Sundries, including superintendence	4·00
	F. 28·27 = 22s. 7·4d.

Cost of crystallising per ton of ore, 12·39f. = 9s. 10·9d.

The loss of lead in the process of crystallisation proper is trifling, as the losses incidental to the process chiefly occur in the cupellation of rich lead and the reduction of drosses, and will be indicated under their respective headings. There is, however, a certain loss of silver in the market lead sold, since it invariably retains about 15 grammes, 9 dwt. 15 gr., of silver per ton; but this quantity amounts to only 0·533 per cent. of the total weight of silver contained in the ore according to assay.

7. *Refining.*—The ordinary English furnace is employed at Pontgibaud for the cupellation of rich lead. The operation is conducted in the usual way, except that the tests are deeper than those generally used. About four tons of rich lead are passed in twenty-four hours; but a certain quantity, amounting to one-fifth, is tapped out about every eight hours, or whenever the lead in the cupel has attained, by concentration, a richness of about 8 per cent. of silver. The bottoms of enriched lead thus accumulated are cupelled, as usual, at the end of the operation. About 15 tons of rich lead are usually worked at one time, and a plate of silver, weighing from 240 to 250 kilos. (7,720 to 8,042 oz.), is obtained. When cleaned, the silver is tapped at the

back of the test into moulds, and afterwards melted down in large black-lead crucibles. It is then cast into ingots of from 20 to 25 kilos. each, suitable for the market. These ingots contain 999 thousandths of silver.

The cost of cupellation per ton of rich lead is as follows:—

Coal, 290 kilos. at 35f.	10·15f.
Bone-ash 17 „ at 275f.	4·67
Pearlash 0·17 „ at 1,765f.	0·30
Repairs	0·30
Refiner's wages	8·23
Sundries, &c.	3·80
	F. 27·45 = 21*s*. 11·5*d*.

Cost of refining per ton of ore smelted, 2·27f. = 1*s*. 9·8*d*.

The loss of lead in refining is about 7 per cent. of the weight of lead worked, or 1·252 per cent. of the total work lead obtained from the blast furnace. The loss of silver volatilised with the lead vapours, although very minute, is probably greater during cupellation than in any of the other processes. Its amount cannot be determined with accuracy.

8. *Reducing.*—The furnace employed for reducing the litharge, pot dross, and calcined dross, is similar in form to the Welsh reverberatory furnace, but has only four working doors, two on the back side, and two on the fore side.

Its principal dimensions are as follow:—

	m.	ft.	in.
Height of furnace	1·75 =	5	8·8
„ from fire-bars to top of bridge	0·52 =	1	8·4
„ „ bridge to crown of arch	0·25 =	0	9·8
Width of fireplace	0·75 =	2	5·5
Length „	1·35 =	4	5·1
Width of bridge	0·60 =	1	11·6
Length of sole	3·70 =	12	1·6
Average width of do.	2·80 =	9	2·2

In the reduction of litharge and pot dross the operations are conducted in the usual way.

The average cost of reducing one ton of litharge and pot dross is—

Coal, 140 kilos at 35f.	4·90f.
Wages	1·15
Tools and repairs	0·40
Sundries, including superintendence	1·00
	F. 7·45 = 5*s*. 11·5*d*.

Cost on ton of ore, 1·73f. = 1*s*. 4·6*d*.

Nearly one-third the weight of market lead produced is skimmed off the different pots as dross, and passed through the reducing furnace. This large proportion of dross is due to the richness of the lead worked, and the consequent repeated crystallisations to which it must be submitted. The proportion of litharge reduced is nearly the same as that of the rich lead refined. The total weight of lead reduced from pot dross and litharge, and returned to the pots, is equal to nearly one-half the market lead made.

9. *Re-smelting rich Slags.*—The slags are smelted in a blast furnace of similar construction to those employed for smelting the ore. About 260 tons are smelted per month, and are derived principally from the ores actually worked during that time. Their average assay for last year was 3½ per cent. of lead.

The slags, after passing through the furnace, are thrown away, but still retain about 1¼ per cent. of lead. A very large proportion of the lead they contain is volatilised, but part of it is afterwards recovered in the flues, though in what proportion it is impossible to ascertain. Only 1¼ unit was obtained last year as pig lead (assay 750 grammes of silver per ton), and yet it was more than sufficient to pay the expenses of treatment; the fume collected in the flues of itself affords a fair profit. At present the slags are far too poor to make it advantageous to melt them over again, and it is probable that as the slags produced direct from the ore are gradually obtained poorer, this process will either be abandoned altogether, or only employed when the accumulation of rich slags may render it desirable.

The costs of smelting one ton of slag are the following:—

Coke, 100 kilos.	4·80f.
Smelter's wages	0·90
Tools and repairs	0·45
Cartage and breaking	0·77
	F. 6·92 = 5*s.* 6·4*d.*

Cost on ton of ore, 6·10f. = 4*s.* 10·6*d.*

SUPPLEMENTARY OPERATIONS.

a.—Roasting Matt.—The matt produced in the blast furnace is returned to the ore magazine, and mixed with ores in the "Lits de Grillage," as already explained; but before being mixed, it is ground in a mill to a coarse powder, and calcined in one of the reverberatory furnaces employed for roasting ore. A charge of matt weighs 2½ tons; each charge remains in the furnace double the time allowed for ore.

Every twelve hours a charge is withdrawn, and a fresh one introduced. The matt is worked on the bed next the fire, and as soon as a charge has become sufficiently hot, which takes place after about half an hour's brisk firing, it is, uninterruptedly, turned with paddles, during the whole time. Rapid oxidation of the metallic sulphides then commences; and as sufficient heat for calcination is thereby maintained, the fire in the grate is allowed to burn down, but not to go out, since in that case too much cold air would enter the furnace, and lower the temperature of the charge.

When the charge has been properly calcined it becomes almost black, contains very few lumps, and emits scarcely any sulphurous fumes. It is then drawn through the working doors, by means of iron rakes, and is thence removed to the ore magazine.

The cost of roasting one ton of matt is as follows:—

Coals, 150 kilos.	5·25f.
Labour	3·30
Grinding and cartage	1·00
	F. 9·55 = 7s. 7·6d.

Cost of roasting matts on ton of ore, 1·05f. = 10d.

b.—Treatment of Calcined Dross.—The drosses skimmed from the work lead, and from the hard lead in the process of improving, are treated in the reducing furnace, and the residues smelted in the blast furnace. The object of this preliminary operation is to separate all the metallic lead by eliquation, and to reduce as much as possible the amount of the material to be treated in the Castillian furnace. It has been found that this is best effected by working it in small charges mixed with a certain proportion of fine coal. Five tons, divided into four charges of 1¼ ton each, are usually worked in twenty-four hours. The charge is turned and frequently paddled to facilitate the drainage of the lead from the mass, which acquires, after a short time, a rather pasty consistence. The cinder drawn out on the floor at the end of each operation is subsequently smelted in the manner described under the head of "*Treatment of Lead Cinder.*" About 56 per cent. of hard lead is thus obtained, with a consumption of 30 per cent. of coal.

The cost per ton of stuff is as follows:—

Coal, 305 kilos. at 35f.	10·68f.
Wages	2·22
	F. 12·90 = 10s. 3·8d.

Cost on ton of ore, 0·68f. = 6·5d.

c.—Treatment of Lead Cinder.—These residues include the cinder from the reduction of the pot dross, calcined dross, and litharge. They are smelted in the blast furnace, with about twice their weight of common slag; no other fluxes are necessary. The coke employed as fuel, together with the carbonaceous matters contained in the cinder, effects its complete reduction. None but the usual precautions are necessary in smelting this cinder. Particular attention must, however, be paid to the charging, and to the proportion of slag added, otherwise there will be great risk of choking the furnace.

The quantity of cinder smelted per annum, with results, is as follows:—

Cinder smelted. Tons.	Lead. Per cent.	Slag employed. Tons.	Coke consumed. Tons.	Lead produced. Tons.
119·340	38·9	240·000	19·980	46·440

or 85·26 per cent. of total lead contained in stuff smelted.

The above quantity was smelted in twenty days, and cost for

Coke	959·00f.
Smelter's wages	404·00
Cartage	214·80
	F. 1,577·80

or per ton of cinder—

Coke, 16·7 per cent.	8·00
Wages	3·40
Cartage	1·80
	13·20 = 10*s.* 6·7*d.*

Cost on ton of ore smelted, 0·45f. = 4·3*d.*

d.—Treatment of Lead Fume.—Roasting.—Owing to the peculiar nature of the fumes collected in the flues at the Pontgibaud works, it has been found impossible to smelt them advantageously alone, as is done in various other establishments. Several methods have been tried and abandoned, but the best hitherto devised, and that which is now adopted, is to mix with the fume a certain proportion of silicious ore, and fuse them together in a common roasting furnace. The fused mass thus obtained, has the appearance of a clean black slag, and closely resembles ordinary roasted ore. It is subsequently smelted in the blast furnace in precisely the same manner as already described when treating of the smelting of ores.

The fume and ore are intimately mixed in the following proportions before being introduced into the furnace :—

Fume	60 parts,	assay 62·7	per cent. lead.
Ore	40 „	40·0	„ „
	100		

This mixture is divided into charges of 2½ tons each, and treated in exactly the same way as ore which has been roasted dead. It is charged *à la pelle* through the working doors of the furnace, upon the middle bed, where it is left undisturbed until the preceding charge has been melted and run out from the agglomerating bed. The charge on the middle bed is then immediately advanced towards the fire and piled up near the bridge; care being taken to move the mixture of ore and fume as gently as possible, otherwise considerable loss may occur from the fine particles being carried away by the draught. The whole of this charge having been advanced, and a new one introduced through the doors of the middle bed as before, the fire is urged so as to melt the mixture as quickly as possible, which is accomplished in from two to three hours. Five charges, or 12½ tons, can thus be passed in one furnace in twenty-four hours, the loss of weight in roasting being about 15 per cent.

The same number of men are employed as in roasting ore, but, instead of being paid by the day, they receive one franc each per charge. The consumption of coal is 17 per cent., and of lime 3 per cent. of the weight of stuff roasted.

The cost of roasting one ton of a mixture of fume and ore is as follows :—

Preparation of mixture	0·25f.
Coal, 170 kilos. at 35f.	5·95
Lime, 30 „ at 24f.	0·70
Labour	1·30
Cartage	1·00
	F. 9·20 = 7*s*. 4·3*d*.

Cost of roasting fume on ton of ore, 0·40f. = 3·8*d*.

Smelting.—The roasted stuff is broken and made into lits de fusion in much the same way as ordinary ore, but the proportion of fluxes added is much greater than usual.

The lits de fusion for fume and ore are composed as follow:—

Fume and ore	10,000 kilos.
Iron	1,200 „
Limestone	3,500 „
Fluor spar	300 „
	15,000 kilos.

The above quantity is usually smelted in twenty-four hours, with a consumption of 9 per cent. of coke.

The following are the costs of smelting one ton of the mixture of fume and ore in the blast furnace:—

Preparation of lits de fusion			0·40f.
Iron	120 kilos.	at 95f.	11·40
Limestone	350 „	at 20f.	7·00
Fluor spar	30 „	at 15f.	0·45
Coke	90 „	at 48f.	4·32
Labour			2·02
			F. 25·59 = 20s. 5·6d.

Cost per ton of unroasted mixture, 21·77f. = 17s. 4·9d.
Cost of smelting fume on ton of ore, 0·95f. = 9·1d.

The quantity of fume collected annually in the flues is about 154·900 tons, averaging 56·8 per cent. lead and 132 grammes, or 4 oz. 5 dwt. silver per ton. The richness of the fume varies considerably in different parts of the flue, but in general the percentage of lead increases, whilst the proportion of silver diminishes, with the distance from the furnaces. The lead obtained from fume by the process described, amounts to 78·57 per cent. of the quantity found by assay, or 3·67 per cent. of the total weight contained in the ores treated.

When it is considered how large a proportion of lead is lost by volatilisation in the form of fume by every known method of smelting lead ores, it evidently becomes a matter of importance to condense as large a proportion as possible of the metal thus driven off in order to reduce this loss to a minimum. Particular attention is now being devoted to this subject at Pontgibaud, and considerable improvements have been introduced with a view of recovering a larger proportion of fume than has been hitherto found possible.

Losses of Lead and Silver.—From 100 parts of lead contained in the ores treated, 85·75 are obtained either directly from them, or indirectly from slags or fumes, viz.:—

Direct from ores	80·04 per cent.
From fumes	3·67 „
„ slags	2·04 „
Total	85·75 „

In desilverising the lead thus obtained, a loss of 3·25 per cent. is experienced, the total weight of poor lead produced for sale being 82·50 per cent. of the quantity contained in the ores.

The loss in desilverising is distributed as follows :—

Refining	1·25 per cent.
Improving and reducing	2·00 „
Total	3·25 „

The loss of lead in the three principal divisions of the Pontgibaud process is therefore—

In roasting	2·50 per cent.
„ smelting	11·75 „
„ desilverising	3·25 „
Total	17·50

The percentage losses on the total quantity of silver contained in the ores are *—

In slags	0·568 per cent.
„ Market lead	0·533 „
Total	1·101

The process now employed for the extraction of the silver is not only much superior to the old Pontgibaud method, but is even more perfect than the best methods of assaying at present known, since, in the large way, from 3½ to 4 per cent. more silver is obtained than the assays indicate.

Of 100 parts of silver produced—

98·82	are obtained direct from the ores.
0·64	„ „ from the slags.
0·54	„ „ „ fumes.
100·00	

* These losses are indicated by the assay of the slags and market lead, since the amount of silver annually obtained is, nevertheless, considerably in excess of the weight determined by assay.

The quantities of lead and silver sold from the Pontgibaud Smelting Works for the years ending June, 1865, and June, 1866, were as follow :—

			Value.
1865	Lead 1,391 tons Silver 124,230 oz.	. . . .	£61,582
1866	Lead 1,550 tons Silver 145,280 oz.	. . . .	69,420

Summary of Costs.

		Cost per Ton of Ore smelted.				Cost per Ton of Lead produced.				Cost per Kilo. of Silver produced.			
	f. c.	f. c.	£	s.	d.	f. c.	£	s.	d.	f. c.	£	s.	d.
Preparation of "Lits de Grillage"	0·25	21·45 =	0	17	1·9	48·94 =	1	19	1·8	16·78 =	0	13	5·0
Roasting Ore	19·75												
,, Matt	1·05												
,, Fume	0·40												
Preparation of "Lits de Fusion"	0·25	22·71 =	0	18	2·0	51·82 =	2	1	5·4	17·77 =	0	14	2·6
Smelting Ore	21·06												
,, Fume	0·95												
,, Lead Cinder	0·45												
Improving { Ordinary Work Lead	1·90	2·93 =	0	2	4·1	6·69 =	0	5	4·2	2·29 =	0	1	10·0
Improving { Hard Lead . . .	1·03												
Crystallising		12·39 =	0	9	10·9	28·27 =	1	2	7·4	9·70 =	0	7	9·1
Refining		2·27 =	0	1	9·8	5·18 =	0	4	1·7	1·77 =	0	1	5·0
Reducing { Pot Dross & Litharge	1·73	2·41 =	0	1	11·1	5·50 =	0	4	4·8	1·88 =	0	1	6·0
Reducing { Calcined Dross . .	0·68												
Smelting Slag	...	6·10 =	0	4	10·6	13·92 =	0	11	1·6	4·77 =	0	3	9·8
		70·26 =	£2	16	2·4	160·32 =	£6	8	2·9	54·96 =	2	3	11·5

N.B.—General Expenses are not included in the above statement.

CHAPTER XXIII.

SMELTING SILVER ORES IN MEXICO.

ROASTING—FUSION—CUPELLATION—VASO—GALEME—ÑUFLA.

In Mexico, only the richer varieties of silver ore are smelted, by far the larger proportion being treated by the patio process; whilst in some few of the mining districts, as at Real del Monte, barrel amalgamation is extensively resorted to.

Roasting.—The ores destined for smelting are, at Zacatecas, and in some other localities, subjected to a process of roasting in heaps, which is effected by surrounding the mineral, broken into large lumps, with a layer of charcoal, retained in its place by an open wall of rough stone built in a circular form. The openings in this wall admit of the passage of the necessary amount of air, and the operation is completed in the course of twenty-four hours, with an expenditure of charcoal amounting to one-half the weight of the ores operated on.

At Nieves the ores are roasted in circular kilns four feet six inches in diameter, and of about the same height. These are formed of a hollow wall of adobes or sun-dried bricks, and are without a roof, the walls being so constructed that the area of the openings is nearly equal to that of the brickwork between them. Into each of these kilns are charged 2,000 lbs. of roughly-broken ore, intermixed with one-half its weight of dry wood; the operation requires a week for its completion; but this method of roasting can only be employed during the dry season.

Fusion.—The fusion of the roasted ore is effected in a small blast furnace, having the following dimensions: height to the charging hole 4 feet 6 inches, and depth from the front to the back wall 15 inches, width at top 11 inches, and at bottom only about 9 inches.

The aperture through which the fused materials make their escape is about 2½ inches in diameter, and is situated at the bottom of the furnace, whilst the copper nozzle through which the blast is supplied is placed about 9 inches above it. The breast, which is built of firestone, is taken down whenever the furnace becomes choked, or when it is found necessary to re-line the interior with a fresh coating of refractory clay; which is usually required at the expiration of a week from the time of first getting the apparatus into blast.

In front of the furnace, and below the aperture through which the various fused matters make their escape, is a breast pan 10 × 13 inches, in which they accumulate, and from which the lead and other fused matters are from time to time tapped into a basin, situated at a still lower level; whilst the slags are removed from the breast pan whenever any portion of them becomes sufficiently solid.

The blast is supplied by bellows, set in motion by cams, fixed in a horizontal axle connected, by toothed gearing, with a vertical shaft, to which a mule is attached. A couple of these furnaces are usually built side by side under a hood of masonry, open at the top for the escape of metallic fumes and the products of combustion. In front of each, is a series of bins containing the ores to be smelted, which are mixed in various proportions with the different fluxes employed. The fuel made use of is, in most instances, charcoal, prepared either from pine or green oak.

This furnace, which was first introduced into the country by the Spaniards, and appears to have undergone but little modification during the last three centuries, is that still almost universally employed in the different native establishments, although furnaces on the model of those used in the metallurgical works of the continent of Europe have replaced them in the larger haciendas, conducted under the superintendence of Europeans.

The materials employed as fluxes, or for the purpose of supplying the lead necessary for the extraction of silver, are *tequezquite*, or native carbonate of soda, collected during the dry season from the beds of certain lagunes; *greta*, or litharge, frequently very impure, and chiefly derived from the treatment of the lead ores of Mazapil and Zimapan; *temesquitate*, or the slags which float on the lead bath of the furnace known as the "ñufla," in which silver is extracted by a process of scorification; *crasas*, or the slags obtained during the progress of previous operations; and *fierros*, or the impure litharge, which floats on the surface of the lead bath during the earlier stages of the process of cupellation in the test furnace with a movable dome: this name is also applied to the matts obtained during the operation of smelting, which, together with cupel bottoms, and other materials containing lead, are added to the charge during succeeding operations.

The ore, after having been previously roasted, is placed in hutches before the furnaces, from which it is taken to be mixed with the various fluxes and furnace products constituting a charge.

At Sombrerete, where the rich ores are chiefly composed of quartz, iron pyrites, and the sulphides of silver, the furnace mixture was, in 1842, according to Duport, constituted as follows:—

Ore	37½ lbs.
Tequezquite	8 "
Temesquitate	8 "
Cupel bottoms	8 "
Fierros	12½ "
Litharge	50 "

The fusion of these ingredients produced a pig of lead weighing from fifty to fifty-eight pounds. The ores from La Cañada, which contain a larger proportion of lead, required a less amount of litharge, and somewhat less of the native carbonate of soda.

The campaign of a blast furnace begins on the Sunday evening, and extends to the morning of the following Sunday, at the expiration of which time the bad quality of the materials employed renders it necessary to suspend operations for the purpose of making repairs. After getting the apparatus into blast, 300 lbs. of lead ore are first passed through it, and of which the yield of metal is not calculated in the results obtained. As soon as the preliminary charge has been fused, the mixture of ore and fluxes is thrown into the furnace, with alternate charges of charcoal, as often as its contents descend sufficiently below the level of the charging hole.

The smelter, who has charge of two furnaces, takes care to keep the eye constantly open, and for this purpose frequently introduces an iron bar, with which he gently raises the slags and fuel which occupy the lower portion of the apparatus; he also attends to the proper regulation of the blast, and the proportion of fuel to be employed. When a sufficient amount of lead to form an ingot has accumulated in the breast pan, the blast is stopped, and the eye of the furnace is closed by a plug of clay; after which the dam, between the breast and receiving basins, is pierced, and the fused metal and matt are allowed to flow into the latter, when the eye of the furnace is again opened, and the operation continued until enough lead to yield another ingot has been produced.

As soon as the contents of the tapping pan have become sufficiently cooled, the matts are removed from the surface of the bath of lead, and at once passed through the furnace with the next charge, after which the metallic lead is ladled into a convenient mould. The foreman is assisted during this work by a man who charges the two furnaces, and by another who attends to the preparation of the mixture of ore and fluxes; he is relieved every twelve hours by another smelter and his assistants.

The quantity of charcoal consumed during the production of an ingot of metal varies from fifty to seventy-five pounds; and from eight to twelve are produced in the course of twenty-four hours, according to the nature and richness of the ore treated. When the minerals operated on contain a considerable amount of lead, each furnace will sometimes smelt as much as a ton of roasted ore in the course of twenty four hours, with a consumption of about 55 per cent. of charcoal; but such results can only be obtained under very favourable circumstances.

Cupellation.—The furnace usually employed for cupelling the argentiferous lead, resulting from the foregoing operation of smelting, is called a *Vaso,* and differs but slightly in its construction from many of those used for the same purpose on the continent of Europe. The hearth of the vaso is not, however, renewed after each working, but is employed for the cupellation of successive parcels of lead, until the test which, when new, is three feet in thickness, has become worn through. The bottom of the furnace, or *cendrada,* is composed of three parts of wood-ash and one of clay, well mixed together, and carefully beaten in.

In the largest description of cupelling furnace, the greatest diameter of the cendrada is 4 feet 6 inches, and of the smaller one, 4 feet; whilst the depth of the cavity for the reception of the metal is about 5 inches. The fireplace varies in its dimensions according to the nature of the fuel employed; requiring to be larger where the wood of the palm tree is made use of, than for furnaces in which pine is alone consumed. It is, however, in all cases situated very close to the edge of the cupel; but as this has itself a considerable diameter, it follows that towards the close of the operation the metal is at so great a distance from the fuel that the heat produced is far from being economically applied. The blast is furnished by bellows worked by two men, who relieve each other alternately; the bellows communicating with a movable tuyere capable of being depressed, in proportion as the bottom of the cupel itself becomes lowered. The blast thus applied drives before it the oxide of lead towards an opening in the opposite side of the hearth, and of which the level is lowered, in proportion as the depth of the metallic bath becomes less. These furnaces are not provided with chimneys, the products of combustion making their escape by a long low opening, situated opposite the fireplace, and on a level with the edge of the hearth, which also serves for the introduction of the ingots of metal to be cupelled. In order to prevent injury to the workmen from the action of volatilised oxide of lead, these furnaces, like those employed for smelting ores, are placed under large hoods of masonry, which effectually carry off the smoke and metallic vapours, so that the refiners are but little subject to diseases incidental to exposure to lead fumes. Although this apparatus is that still most commonly employed by Mexicans for the cupellation of argentiferous lead, the larger establishments now make use of the ordinary cupelling furnace fitted with a movable iron dome.

The *planchas* or ingots of argentiferous lead are taken from the smelting furnace to the vaso, which is capable of working off about two thousand pounds of lead in the course of twenty-four hours. The working of this furnace is conducted by a refiner and two workmen, who attend to the bellows, and are relieved every twelve hours by another foreman, and his two assistants who supply the blast. The fuel employed is usually pine wood split into small pieces, of which some six or eight hundred pounds weight are consumed in the course of twenty-four hours. In this furnace the process of refining is not generally carried so far as to allow the silver to brighten, but as soon as the metal remaining in the cupel begins to assume an iridescent appearance, the blast is arrested, and the fire withdrawn. The silver obtained by these means is, in the majority of cases, the property of individuals who sell it without its being assayed, and whose interest, consequently, is not to remove the whole of the lead; the resulting plates, therefore, usually contain from 970 to 985 thousandths of silver. In addition to lead, the silver obtained by this process generally contains a small amount of antimony, and requires to be refined, with an addition of pure lead, before it becomes sufficiently soft to admit of its conversion into coin.

The cost of smelting ores in Mexico is in all cases exceedingly high, but varies considerably in accordance with the nature of the power employed for supplying the blast. When, as is usually the case, mules are made use of for working the bellows, the expenses for power and manual labour are excessive, and at Zacatecas the costs under this head alone amounted, in 1842, to no less than $36 per ton, including the wages of the men employed for the cupellation of the resulting argentiferous lead: charcoal generally costs about 2¼ reals per arroba of 25 lbs., and these several expenses, added to the value of the litharge lost during each operation, made the total cost, at Zacatecas, of treating a ton of ore by this system, about $133, or 26*l.* 12*s.* per ton. The high price of smelting ores in Mexico is not, however, the only objection to the more general application of this process, since the loss of silver by the imperfect processes employed appears in all cases to be very considerable; varying, according to the nature of the ores and the skill of the workmen employed, from 15 to 25 per cent. on the assay value. The quantity of ore daily smelted at Zacatecas was estimated by Duport, in 1842, at from five to six tons only.

At Sombrerete, where the ores are generally rich, and where a larger proportion of them is, consequently, treated by smelting, the cost did not generally exceed about 13*l.* per ton; whilst at Nieves, which is at a more convenient distance from Mazapil, from whence the chief supply of litharge is obtained, and where the ores themselves contain a considerable amount of lead, the total expense of smelting a ton of mineral, together with that of refining the resulting work lead, was estimated at 6*l.* 6*s.* In some districts, in which water power is unusually abundant, the treatment of the ores is effected at an even less cost than the above; but such cases must, nevertheless, be regarded as altogether exceptional. The amount of silver obtained in Mexico by smelting, as compared with the total produce of the country, was estimated, in 1842, as being about one-tenth, but is now much less.

Galeme.—In some localities, a smaller, and more rudely-constructed apparatus than the vaso is employed for the cupellation of work lead obtained from the blast furnace. This arrangement, called a *galeme*, is constructed by marking out on a floor of well-beaten clay a space 2 feet 3 inches long, and 1 foot 8 inches wide, which is enclosed by a wall of stone, about 6 inches high, supporting a stone slab, or a large brick, forming the top, and covering the whole space. At one end is placed the fuel, consisting of pine wood, cut into small fragments, on which a current of air (supplied by bellows, worked by a lever) is directed, by means of an iron nozzle; whilst sundry small apertures at the other extremity allow of the escape of the products of combustion. Before charging the furnace, it is heated for some hours, in order to raise the temperature of the masonry to the proper point, and to so vitrify the hearth as to render it, to a great extent, impervious to litharge. An ingot of lead, weighing from forty to fifty pounds, is now introduced, and an aperture left in the side is partially stopped with clay, so as to allow the litharge to flow off; care being taken to lower its level in proportion as the surface of the metallic bath becomes depressed. The lead, thus placed in close proximity to the burning fuel, becomes rapidly converted into litharge, and the cupellation proceeds at the rate of about an ingot per hour, although the loss of that metal is considerable, and a deficit on the silver is the result. The galeme is the only means of cupellation employed in the mining district of Charcas, and is also made use of at Catorce, for refining the impure silver obtained by the treatment of silver ores in the cazo.

The Ñufla.—This furnace is probably the most primitive apparatus employed in any country for the extraction, by the dry way, of silver from its ores; and is in principle merely a scorifier, in which the cupellation of the remaining lead is subsequently effected.

The sulphides of silver sometimes occur in so large a proportion, with regard to the gangue with which they are associated, that if finely ground and thrown on a bath of metallic lead kept at a proper temperature, the silver combines with the lead; which, becoming partially oxidised, unites with the silicious and earthy impurities of the gangue, forming a slag, which may be readily removed from the surface of the metal before commencing the operation of cupellation. This apparatus, which is much employed by the native miners of Sombrerete, consists of a cupel formed of a mixture of ashes and clay, contained in a large coarse earthen dish; enclosed between walls of sun-dried bricks, and covered by a dome of somewhat refractory clay, in which numerous holes are pierced. The whole of the interior of this arrangement is filled with charcoal, on which a blast is thrown by means of a nozzle of baked clay; and, although the whole of the heat is applied from above the surface of the lead, it quickly melts, and the scorification of the ore, thrown on its surface, commences. When the workman considers that the bath of lead has, by the introduction of successive additions of ore, become sufficiently charged with silver, he cleans off the silicious slags, and commences the cupellation of the residual lead. For this purpose he makes an opening at the level of the metallic bath for the escape of litharge, and continues the operation, at the same time gradually lowering the level of the exit for litharge, until a button of silver alone remains in the bottom of the cupel.

CHAPTER XXIV.

ASSAY OF SILVER ORES AND BULLION.

ARGENTIFEROUS GALENA—ASSAY OF SILVER ORES PROPER—SCORIFICATION—CUPELLATION—ASSAY TABLE—ASSAY OF SILVER BULLION.

Assay of Silver Ores.—In the assay of ores of this metal, the object sought is first to obtain the silver present in the mineral in the form of an alloy with lead, which is subsequently passed to the muffle and cupelled, with proper precautions.

Argentiferous Galena.—The assay of argentiferous galena is, in this country, usually conducted in a wrought iron crucible. The vessel employed for this purpose is made of a piece of plate iron, of good quality, turned up in the form of a crucible, and carefully welded at the edges; the bottom is closed by a large iron rivet, securely welded to the sides, and the whole finished by the hammer on a properly-formed mould. To make an assay in a crucible of this description, it is first placed in the assay furnace, and heated to dull redness; and when it has become sufficiently hot, 400 grains of the pulverised ore, intimately mixed with its own weight of soda-ash, about 30 grains of pearlash, and from 8 to 10 grains of charcoal powder, or lamp-black, are introduced by means of a long copper scoop. With certain varieties of ore, the addition of a small quantity of common salt, or fluor spar, is found to be beneficial for the production of a thoroughly liquid slag; fluor spar being particularly advantageous in the case of highly silicious ores. On the top of this, is placed a thin layer of dried borax; and the crucible, which, for the introduction of the mixture, has been withdrawn from the fire, is at once replaced in the furnace. At first the contents of the pot boil somewhat violently, and therefore, in order to avoid loss, the crucible should be made of sufficient capacity to prevent any portion of the mixture being projected over its sides. At the expiration of from eight to ten minutes, the ingredients in the crucible will be observed to be in a state of tranquil fusion; and the pot must now be removed from the fire, and its contents briskly stirred by means of a small iron rod, flattened at the end in the form of a spatula. Any matters adhering to its sides are also scraped downward into the bottom of the pot, which is replaced in the furnace, and, after being closed with an earthen cover, is, during three or four minutes, heated to full redness.

The crucible is now seized, by a strong pair of bent tongs, on that part of its edge which is opposite to the lip; and, after being removed from the fire, its contents are rapidly poured into a cast iron mould, having internally the form of an ordinary egg cup. The sides of the pot are now carefully scraped down with the chisel-edged bar before referred to, and any adhering particles of lead and slag are obtained by sharply striking the edge of the crucible against the top of another cast iron mould, similar to that into which the assay was first poured. When sufficiently cold, the contents of the mould are readily removed by merely turning it over; and the metallic button, after being separated from the adhering slag, is carefully cleaned by means of a hard brush, and weighed, in order to determine the percentage yield of lead. When a metallic shot has been obtained in the second mould, it must be freed from adhering slag, and weighed with the larger button. The alloy thus obtained is cupelled, in order to determine the amount of silver which it contains.

Assay of Silver Ores Proper.—Ores of silver, in which that metal exists in the form either of oxide, sulphide, or chloride, in a gangue principally consisting of silica or of carbonate of lime, are usually fused with a mixture of litharge and carbonate of soda, to which a small quantity of finely-powdered charcoal is added; and by this means a button of alloy is obtained, which is subsequently treated by cupellation.

The proportion of litharge to be employed for this operation must be varied in accordance with the circumstances of the case, as the resulting button of alloy should not be too rich in silver, since, in that case, a portion might be lost in the slags; neither should it, on the other hand, be too poor, as the cupellation would then occupy a long time, and a loss through absorption be the result. In ordinary cases, where the silver principally exists in the form of chloride and sulphide, and the quantity operated on is 400 grains, a button of alloy weighing about 200 grains will be a convenient amount for cupellation: such a result may generally be obtained by the addition of 300 grains of litharge, 400 grains of carbonate of soda, 150 grains of borax, and from 7 to 8 grains of finely-powdered charcoal. The whole is to be well mixed, and introduced into an earthen crucible, of which it should not occupy more than one-half the capacity. Ordinary French pots are best adapted for making all assays in which large quantities of litharge are made use of, as they resist its action better than any of the pots usually made in this country.

The crucible is now placed in an assay furnace of the usual form, care being taken to withdraw it from the fire as soon as a thoroughly liquid and perfectly homogeneous slag has been attained; since the fused mixture would otherwise be liable to cut through the sides of the pot, and thus spoil the experiment. When it has sufficiently cooled, the crucible is broken and the metallic button obtained, which, after being properly cleaned, is passed to the cupel. When a great degree of accuracy is required, it is always best to break the pot, and extract the button of alloy, as above described; but when numerous assays have to be made on ores of nearly the same tenure, the assay is sometimes poured into an iron mould, and the crucible is employed for making other fusions. In this, and all similar cases, it is, of course, essential to ascertain, by previous experiment, the proportion of silver contained in the lead obtained by the reduction of the litharge, in order to obtain the necessary data for calculating the requisite deduction to be made from the results afforded by cupellation. When, however, very poor litharge is made use of, the resulting lead contains so small an amount of silver that, for some commercial purposes, its presence may be disregarded: generally speaking, however, the assayer, on the receipt of a fresh supply of that reagent, ascertains, by means of careful assays, the proportion of silver which it contains, and makes the necessary correction on each assay in which it is employed.

Argentiferous minerals containing a considerable amount of copper may be generally assayed by this process, since the amount of that metal which enters into combination with the lead produced is comparatively small, and the resulting button of alloy admits of being readily cupelled by the addition, when necessary, of metallic lead. When the mineral to be assayed contains a large proportion of metallic sulphides, the addition of charcoal, or any other reducing agent, becomes unnecessary, as litharge readily attacks all the simple and complex metallic sulphides, oxidising their constituents, with the exception of the precious metals, which form an alloy with the lead set free. The slags resulting from this operation contain the excess of litharge added, and the button of alloy produced is subjected to cupellation. The proportion of oxide of lead to be added to ores of this description varies in accordance with their composition, but it should in all cases be present in decided excess, since, should the sulphides not become completely decomposed, the whole of the silver will not be concentrated in the resulting button of alloy. For the successful assay of pure argentiferous iron pyrites, as many as 50 parts of litharge are required, whilst for mispickel, blende, copper pyrites, grey cobalt, and sulphide of antimony, from 15 to 20 times their weight may be employed.*

It must, however, be remembered that earthy and silicious gangues usually constitute a large proportion of the bulk of the ores operated on, and consequently these excessive amounts of litharge are, in practice, seldom requisite. One of the chief objections to this method of assay is the large amounts of lead that are produced for cupellation, since pure iron pyrites affords 8·50 parts of this metal, whilst sulphide of antimony, and grey copper ore, yield from six to seven parts.

This inconvenience may be obviated by effecting the partial oxidation of the sulphides, either by roasting or through the aid of nitre, by the skilful use of which a button of almost any required weight may be obtained. If this reagent be employed in excess it determines the oxidation of the various metallic and other oxidisable substances present, not always excepting silver itself. When, however, the mixture at the same time contains an excess of litharge, and nitre has not been added in sufficient quantity to effect the decomposition of the whole of the sulphides present, reaction takes place between the portion of sulphide undecomposed and the oxide of lead added. This gives rise to the formation of a button of metallic lead, which, combining with the silver, affords a button of alloy suitable for cupellation. The amount of nitre required to be employed for this purpose necessarily depends on the nature and richness of the ore operated on, but it must be borne in mind that 2·5 parts of nitrate of potash are sufficient to completely oxidise the constituents of iron pyrites, and that 1·5 and 0·70 parts, respectively, are, in the case of sulphide of antimony and galena, sufficient for this purpose.

When the ores contain a large proportion of sulphides, it is generally found most desirable to conduct the assay on the mineral after calcination. The roasting of the pulverised ore is best effected in a shallow scorifier, or earthen dish, into which a weighed quantity of the mineral to be operated on, (generally 400 grains) is introduced, and then carefully roasted in the muffle of a cupelling furnace. For this

* Berthier, Traité des Essais par la Voie Sèche, tome ii. p. 827.

purpose the scorifier and its contents should be first placed in the mouth of the muffle, and kept constantly stirred with a thin bent iron rod; care being taken to commence the operation at a low temperature, since, from their great fusibility, such ores would be otherwise liable to agglutinate. As the calcination progresses, the scorifier may be gradually pushed further into the muffle, and thus subjected to successively increasing temperatures; as soon as sulphurous vapours are no longer evolved at a full red heat, the scorifier and its contents are withdrawn and allowed to cool. The ore, when sufficiently cold, is carefully removed from the earthen dish, and mixed, on a sheet of glazed paper, with the fluxes requisite for effecting its fusion, and the reduction of the quantity of lead necessary for cupellation. When the amount of mineral operated on is 400 grains, there should be added soda-ash 400 grains, borax 200 grains, litharge 400 grains, and charcoal 10 to 12 grains. The whole is now introduced into an earthen crucible, fused with the usual precautions, and the resulting button of lead passed to the cupel.

Scorification.—This is a simple and convenient method of assaying ores containing the precious metals, when large quantities of metallic sulphides are present. The process consists in subjecting the finely-pulverised minerals, mixed with granulated lead and placed in a saucer-shaped earthen vessel or scorifier, to the action of a bright red heat in an ordinary assay muffle. A portion of the lead is thus converted into litharge, which, as fast as it is produced, combines with the various silicious and earthy constituents of the veinstone, forming slags, in which the other metallic oxides produced are taken up, whilst the silver and gold form an alloy with the lead remaining at the close of the operation. The scorifiers employed for this purpose should be made of well-baked close-grained fire-clay. It is necessary that they should be compact in their structure in order to resist the corrosive action of the litharge, and that they should be capable of withstanding sudden changes of temperature without breaking.

A number of these scorifiers corresponding to that of the assays to be made are selected, and into each are introduced 100 grains of powdered raw ore, intimately mixed with from five to eight times its weight of granulated lead, and a small quantity of dried borax. In all cases, however, the lead should be added in excess, as the resulting slags are thereby rendered more liquid. The granulated lead used for this purpose should, if possible, be almost entirely free from silver, but this is difficult to obtain, and when it cannot be procured it becomes necessary to estimate beforehand the amount of silver contained in the lead employed, and to make a corresponding deduction from the weight of the button afforded by cupellation.

The scorifiers, after being duly charged with the ore, lead, and borax, are taken to the furnace and introduced into the muffle, which has been previously brought to a full red heat. Their introduction at first considerably reduces the temperature of the furnace, and some pieces of charcoal should be placed in the opening of the muffle for the purpose of again raising the heat to the proper point. The muffle door is now closed, and in the course of a few minutes the lead enters into fusion, whilst white vapours are observed to rise from the assay, and the formation of litharge rapidly takes place. In proportion as the borax fuses, and the quantity of litharge increases, the contents of the scorifier soften; and as the temperature becomes more elevated, they enter into fusion, whilst the lead accumulates in the centre, in the form of a large metallic globule.

When the assays have reached a bright red heat, which is usually the case in from ten to fifteen minutes from the commencement of the operation, the stopper of the muffle is removed; and the current of air, which now enters, causes the oxidation of the lead to proceed more rapidly. In proportion as the litharge accumulates, the slag formed, by its combination with the earthy, silicious, and other matters contained in the ores, increases in quantity, and gradually extends itself over the whole surface of the lead. The door of the muffle is allowed to remain open about fifteen minutes, at the expiration of which time it is again closed, and the temperature is raised for about five minutes to full redness, for the double purpose of rendering the scoriæ as liquid as possible previously to pouring, and also to facilitate at the same time the reunion of any disseminated globules of metallic lead.

The scorifiers are now withdrawn by means of proper tongs, and their contents rapidly poured into moulds. When sufficiently cold, the buttons of lead are detached from the adhering slags by being hammered on a small anvil, and are then passed to the cupel. When this operation has been successfully conducted, the resulting buttons of alloy contain, practically, the whole of the precious metals present in the ore. It is, however, essential that the slags should be perfectly and uniformly liquid at the time of being poured into the moulds, for should they either be pasty or contain imperfectly fused lumps, a portion of the mineral will remain unacted on, and small metallic buttons may either be enclosed in the unfused part, or remain attached to the scorifier.

When, in spite of the temperature of the muffle and the other conditions of the process having been carefully attended to, the slags do not become sufficiently liquid, it is necessary to introduce an additional quantity of borax, and in some cases a little nitre may be added with advantage. Sometimes, although rarely, it is found necessary to stir the slags with an iron rod, for the purpose of dividing any lumps that may have been formed, and to incorporate them with the more liquid scoriæ.

This method of assay is applicable to all kinds of argentiferous and auriferous minerals, of moderate richness, containing large amounts of metallic sulphides; and, from its convenience and freedom from causes of error, it is very generally employed in establishments in which such ores are subjected to metallurgical treatment. When, however, very poor ores have to be operated on, the ordinary method of fusion with litharge is to be preferred, since larger quantities can thus be dealt with, and more accurate results consequently obtained.

Cupellation.—The cupellation of the buttons of argentiferous lead is conducted as described when treating of the assay of auriferous compounds, but as silver is, at high temperatures, more volatile than gold, the heat requires to be more carefully regulated than is necessary in the case of gold ores. In making all cupellations it is necessary to bear in mind that a cupel is only capable of absorbing about its own weight of litharge, and consequently a test should always be employed a little heavier than the button of alloy to be subjected to the operation.

The results obtained are also, to a certain extent, influenced by the temperature at which the cupellation has been conducted, and consequently all assays are liable to a small amount of error. If the muffle be too strongly heated, the silver becomes perfectly refined, but experiences a small amount of loss, through sublimation and the absorption of the cupel; whilst, on the contrary, when the temperature has not been sufficiently elevated, the button is liable to retain a small portion of lead. These two causes of error, existing at the same time in all cupellations, are found, in practice, to often nearly neutralise each other; although, in order to obtain uniform results from the same alloy, it is necessary to employ various minute precautions, both with regard to the temperature of the muffle and the condition of the cupels employed. The more important of these precautions have been specified when treating of the assay of gold ores, and will be found in detail in all works on the assay of minerals by the dry way, but a small amount of practical experience will be far more advantageous than any mere verbal instructions.

When, however, the amount of lead employed has been sufficient, the cupel is perfectly dry, is made of fine and well-prepared bone-ash, and the cupellation is conducted at a full cherry-red heat, the results obtained will, in almost all cases, be found of a satisfactory character. If the resulting buttons of silver be large they should not be abruptly withdrawn from the muffle, but be gradually drawn towards its mouth, since their sudden removal might cause them to "spirt," and a loss be thereby entailed. In the case of a very large button being obtained it is sometimes found advantageous to cover it, immediately after brightening, andbefore its removal from the muffle, by another cupel kept hot for that purpose.

When it has sufficiently cooled the metallic button is seized, laterally, between the jaws of a pair of strong pliers, and tightly squeezed, for the double purpose of loosening it from the cupel and detaching any adhering litharge. The button is then cleaned by the aid of a stiff brush, and weighed in a delicate assay balance. When, in addition to silver, the mineral under examination contains gold, the button obtained on the cupel is first weighed, and its weight noted; it is then flattened, dissolved in nitric acid, and the gold also weighed; the difference of the two weights thus obtained corresponds to the amount of silver present in the assay.

The weight of mineral employed for making an assay is, to a great extent, regulated by the amount of silver which the ores are supposed to contain. In Cornwall, for assays of argentiferous galena, the quantity operated on is often one ounce avoirdupois. In the mining districts of Nevada, two hundred grains are commonly made use of, and the contents of the crucible are often poured out into an iron mould. Scorifications are not easily conducted, in the common muffle furnace, on much above one hundred grains; but for assays of an ordinary silver ore by fusion, four hundred grains are conveniently employed.

For commercial purposes, the silver contained in any given mineral is, in this country, estimated in oz. dwt. and gr., one ton of 2,240 lbs. avoirdupois being taken as the standard of unity.

TABLE *showing the weight of Silver to the ton of Ore corresponding to the weight in grains and decimal parts of a grain, obtained from 400 grains of Mineral.**

If 400 grains of Ore give Fine Metal,	One ton of Ore will yield	If 400 grains of Ore give Fine Metal,	One ton of Ore will yield
gr.	oz. dwt. gr.	gr.	oz. dwt. gr.
0·001	0 1 15	0·200	16 6 16
0·002	0 3 6	0·300	24 10 0
0·003	0 4 21	0·400	32 13 8
0·004	0 6 12	0·500	40 16 16
0·005	0 8 4	0·600	49 0 0
0·006	0 9 19	0·700	57 3 8
0·007	0 11 10	0·800	65 6 16
0·008	0 13 1	0·900	73 10 0
0·009	0 14 16	1·000	81 13 8
0·010	0 16 8	2·000	163 6 16
0·020	1 12 16	3·000	245 0 0
0·030	2 9 0	4·000	326 13 8
0·040	3 5 8	5·000	408 6 16
0·050	4 1 16	6·000	490 0 0
0·060	4 18 0	7·000	571 13 8
0·070	5 14 8	8·000	653 6 16
0·080	6 10 16	9·000	735 0 0
0·090	7 7 0	10·000	816 13 8
0·100	8 3 8	20·000	1633 6 16

ASSAY OF SILVER BULLION.—The assay, by the dry way, of silver bullion comprehends three distinct operations. First, the accurate weighing of a given quantity of the alloy to be operated on; secondly, the cupellation, with due precautions, of this weighed portion with a proper amount of metallic lead; and, thirdly, the re-weighing of the pure silver thus obtained, when the loss of weight will correspond to the amount of alloy which has been removed. The furnace used for this purpose should be provided with the means of very accurately regulating the temperature; and is therefore generally constructed of a wrought iron shell, internally lined with firebrick, and has sliding doors arranged at each of its openings, by the aid of which the several apertures can, at the pleasure of the operator, be easily contracted or enlarged.

The quantity taken for examination is usually in this country

* For the method of using this Table, see page 235.

a representative of the troy pound, which is subdivided into ounces and half-pennyweights, that being the lowest denomination to which assays of silver bullion are reported. It is evident that the assay pound may be represented by any actual weight chosen by the assayer, but from 10 grains to 1 gramme, about 15·44 grains, is the quantity most frequently employed by English assayers. An assay pound of 10 grains, with weights corresponding to the ounces and half-pennyweight, is very convenient for silver assays. The old assayers made their calculations in ounces, pennyweights, and grains, but it is more convenient to work by the decimal system, and, when trade estimations are required, to convert the decimal into trade expressions.

By this method pure silver will be called 1,000, and English standard, which contains in the pound 11 oz. 2 dwt. of silver, with 18 dwt. of alloy, will be 925 in the thousand. Assayers therefore often speak of such an alloy as being 925 fine, and this expression is constantly employed in the different American mints. All excess of alloy over the English standard is, in this country, called "worseness," and Mexican dollars, which are composed of a mixture of 10 oz. 16½ dwt. of silver, with 1 oz. 3½ dwt. of alloy, would be reported as "worse" 5½ dwt. The true decimal expression of such a mixture would be 902·7, or worse 5 dwt. 8 gr.; but, as trade reports are only made to the half-pennyweight, it would be reported W. 5½ dwt.*

On the other hand, certain Indian rupees are composed of 950 parts of silver, united with 50 parts of alloy. This is equal to 11 oz. 8 dwt. of silver, combined with 12 dwt. of alloy, and hence their trade report would be "better" 6 dwt.

The first step to be taken in making an assay of silver bullion is to flatten out, in the form of a thin disc, the cutting taken from a bar. The edges of this are carefully cut off, and from the centre are prepared two assay pounds, which are wrapped in pieces of sheet lead, amounting to about one-half the weight necessary for effecting their cupellation. The amount of lead necessary for this purpose increases in proportion with the amount of alloy present in the specimen under examination, but even fine silver requires, according to Makins, three times its weight of that metal to ensure a satisfactory result. English standard silver will require six times its weight, and coarser varieties a proportionately larger amount. The estimation of the quantity of

* Makins, "Manual of Metallurgy," p. 172.

lead required is a matter to be determined by the experience of the assayer. It should, however, be as free as possible from silver, and the amount of that metal in the lead employed must be deducted from the results obtained.

The several weighed portions of the bars of bullion to be assayed, after being carefully wrapped in lead foil, are arranged in the compartments of a divided tray, having nearly the dimensions of the bottom of the muffle, so that the place of each cupel may correspond with its position in the furnace during the operation of cupellation. During the preparation of the different assays, the heat of the furnace must be got up, and a number of cupels placed in regular order in the muffle, so that they may become heated to the proper temperature. When the muffle and cupels have attained a uniform bright red colour, and the fuel in the furnace is in a compact state and free from cavities, the muffle door is closed by pieces of charcoal. This is done by commencing with large pieces, which are followed by a layer of smaller ones, and so on, until the orifice is about two-thirds built up.

The remainder of the lead necessary for cupellation is now introduced into the cupels by means of proper tongs, and, when it has become fused, the assays, wrapped in the necessary amount of lead foil, are placed in their respective cupels. When they have been all placed in their proper positions, the assayer completes the closing of the mouth by means of small twigs of charcoal, and, shortly afterwards, removes some of the upper pieces for the purpose of admitting a current of air, by which the starting of the cupellations is effected. This makes itself apparent by the metallic bath becoming uncovered, with the exception of certain small patches of oxide of lead, which circulate from the centre towards the edges. When the working has been thus fairly set up, the adjustment of the draught, by means of the various furnace openings, must be carefully attended to, in order to maintain a steady circulation from the centre towards the circumference, where the litharge, as fast as it is produced, is absorbed by the bone-ash of the cupel. During this operation little or no fume should be apparent, as the whole of the lead should, as far as possible, be converted into oxide, and absorbed by the cupel. In this way the globule of fused metal goes on diminishing in size, until finally, after the expiration of from twenty minutes to half an hour, the whole of the lead and base metals have become oxidised, and the phenomenon of brightening takes place.

When the operation has been skilfully conducted, the "going off" of the assays will commence with the front row, and gradually pass back, from row to row, to the last. When, on the contrary, the working off takes place irregularly, or commences at the far end of the muffle, it is an indication that the management of fire has been unskilfully conducted, and the resulting assays will turn out unsatisfactorily. It now only remains to remove the "mouth coal," or charcoal in the muffle door, which must, by means of a rake, be done quickly and completely; and the door of the muffle is fitted in its place. The whole of the openings in the furnace must be now closed, and the apparatus allowed to cool, during from one-half to three-quarters of an hour. At the expiration of this time the furnace is opened, and the assays taken out into a divided iron tray.

If the buttons obtained appear rounded on the top, or have a slight depression in the centre, and can be readily removed from the cupels, it is an evidence of the operation having been properly conducted; when, on the contrary, the buttons adhere firmly to the cupels, or throw out projections near the bottom, they are not fine; and if, in place of being convex and nearly spherical on their upper surfaces, they exhibit a flattened appearance, it shows that the cupellation has been effected with the addition of an insufficient amount of lead.

It now only remains to clean and weigh the assays, and to compare them with a well-ascertained standard of comparison consisting of weighed quantities of silver, of which the degree of fineness has been previously determined, and which have been cupelled in the same furnace, and at the same time, as the unknown alloys. It will be found that, in all cases, a loss has been experienced, which is partly due to volatilisation of silver, and partially to absorption by the cupel. The amount of this loss will depend on the conditions under which the cupellations have been effected, and will be in a great degree influenced by the temperature which has been employed. The standards, or proofs, subjected to the same conditions as the assays themselves, will necessarily experience a corresponding loss, and afford data for correcting the results indicated by the balance.

In establishments where large numbers of assays of silver bullion are daily made, the process of Gay-Lussac for estimating silver by means of a standard solution of chloride of sodium is extensively employed. As, however, this operation is rarely performed by the metallurgist, and comes rather within the province of the professional assayer, we refer for a description of it either to the work of the inventor of the process,* or to an article, chiefly translated therefrom, contained in Mitchell's "Manual of Practical Assaying."

* "Instruction sur l'Essai des Matières d'Argent par la Voie Humide," par M. Gay-Lussac. Publiée par la Commission des Monnaies et Médailles. Paris. 1832.

APPENDIX.

A.—VOLATILITY OF GOLD AND SILVER.

It has been long known to Metallurgists, that both gold and silver are, under certain circumstances, to some extent volatile; but Napier has shown that when an alloy of these metals is kept in a state of fusion at a high temperature, they are very distinctly so. By collecting the metallic vapours escaping from a crucible containing from twenty-five to thirty lbs. of melted alloy (gold coin), the results obtained in two instances were respectively as follow:*—

Vapour collected. grains.	Pure Gold in Vapour. grains.
1.—4·80	4·50
2.—4·40	4·10

Deposits obtained from top, middle, and bottom of a chimney thirty-five feet in height, attached to a small furnace used for fusing an alloy of silver and copper (silver coin), gave the following results:—

	Top. per cent.	Middle. per cent.	Bottom. per cent.
Metallic Silver	3·30	9·19	29·95
Oxide of ,,	7·18	5·21	0·17

Deposits were also examined from the top, middle, and bottom of a chimney attached to a furnace in which an alloy of silver containing a considerable portion of gold was melted, with the following results:—

	Top.	Middle.	Bottom.
Metallic Silver	29·380	39·160	48·750
Oxide of ,,	1·982	3·140	0·032
Gold	2·120	2·640	4·250*

* Quarterly Journal of the Chemical Society, 1857.

Makins has corroborated these results by experiments on deposits obtained from a flue attached to a muffle in which assays of an alloy of gold and silver had been made. 1,000 grains of this deposit gave—

Gold	0·087
Silver	0·763*

The lead carried off in the form of fume, during the metallurgical treatment of argentiferous galena, is invariably found to contain a certain proportion of silver, but the lead resulting from its re-treatment is always much less rich in silver than that obtained directly from the ores.

The following results, obtained from samples of fume taken at different points along the course of a flue leading to the stack of a lead-smelting establishment, in which the work lead contained, on an average, twenty-six ounces of silver per ton, show the relative volatility of the two metals when subjected to the heat of a Castillian furnace.†

From top of Flue.		Lead.	Silver per ton.	From bottom of Flue.		Lead.	Silver per ton.
No.		per cent.	oz. dwt. gr.	No.		per cent.	oz. dwt. gr.
1	Near Castillian Furnace .	49	2 9 0	1	Near Castillian Furnace .	53	2 9 0
2	„ Reverb. „ .	20	3 5 8	2	„ Reverb. „ .	59	2 9 0
3	100 ft. in advance of No. 2	70	3 5 8	3	100 ft. in advance of No. 2	63	3 5 8
4	„ „ 3	44	3 5 8	4	„ „ 3	61	2 9 0
5	„ „ 4	48	2 17 0	5	„ „ 4	49	2 17 0
6	„ „ 5	47	3 5 8	6	„ „ 5	64	2 1 5
7	„ „ 6	46	3 5 8	7	„ „ 6	40	3 6 5
8	„ „ 7	40	2 1 5	8	„ „ 7	58	1 12 5
9	„ „ 8	42	3 5 8	9	„ „ 8	62	2 17 0
10	Throat of Refinery . . .	49	22 17 8	10	Foot of Chimney . . .	66	3 5 8

B.—MINERAL STATISTICS OF VICTORIA FOR THE YEAR 1866.‡

Number of Quartz Miners employed in the different districts :—

Ballarat	2,005
Beechworth	2,941
Sandhurst	4,118
Maryborough	2,292
Castlemaine	2,648
Ararat	874
Total	14,878

* Quarterly Journal of the Chemical Society, 1860.

† The lead obtained from re-smelting slags is also, unless it occurs in the form of lead matt, relatively much poorer in silver than that obtained directly from the ores.

‡ Mineral Statistics of Victoria for the year 1866 : Melbourne.

Number of steam engines in operation during 1866 :—

Alluvial mining engines, 480 ; aggregate horse-power, 9,981.

Quartz mining engines, 510 ; aggregate horse-power, 9,231.

Number of stamp heads, 5,437.

Very full returns of the yield of gold from quartz veins have been obtained for the year 1866. It is not practicable to give an account of the yield from all the quartz put through the mills in the various districts, but accurate information has been received relative to 861,468 13/20 tons, which gave 452,895 oz. 7 dwt ; or an average of 10 dwt. 16·2 gr. per ton :—

Mining districts.	Tons crushed.	Total produce. oz.	dwt.	Yield per ton. dwt.	gr.
Ballarat . . .	238,503½	58,157	3	4	21
Beechworth . .	130,519 11/20	118,495	19	18	3·7
Sandhurst . .	244,807½	118,743	10	9	16·8
Maryborough .	79,552⅗	44,967	14	11	7·3
Castlemaine . .	124,374½	85,662	3	13	18·5
Ararat	43,711	33,868	18	15	11·9
Totals	861,468 13/20	459,895	7	10	16·2

The prices paid for treating quartz ranged from 4*s.* to 1*l.* 10*s.* per ton.

Quantity of gold exported during the year 1866 as returned by the Customs Department, 1,479,194¾ ounces.*

Returns show approximately the gold obtained from quartz veins and alluvial workings during the year 1866 to have been as follows :—

From quartz veins	521·017	ounces
,, alluvial workings	958·177¾	,,
Total Gold exported . .	1,479·194¾	,,

C.—ST. JOHN D'EL REY MINING COMPANY.

The quantity of mineral raised from the mines, and the quantity of ore stamped during 1866, were as follow :—

	Tons.
Mineral raised	107·087
Ore stamped	60·685

The quantity of killas and other inferior mineral rejected at Morro Velho during 1866 was 45,931 tons, or 43 per cent. of the quantity raised.

The total produce of gold from the 23rd March, 1866, to the 23rd March, 1867, was 622,129 oitavas.

The net profit on the working of the mines from 23rd March, 1866, to 23rd March, 1867, was 109,407*l.* 15*s.* 8*d.*

The average yield of the ores at Morro Velho, for the year ending 31st December, 1866, was 9·780 oitavas per ton of ore stamped. By re-

* In addition to the above, 407,394 ounces of New Zealand gold were shipped from this colony during the year.

stamping with killas, and grinding (in arrastres), the refuse afforded in addition, 0·525, giving a total yield per ton of ore stamped during 1866, of 10·305 oitavas.

D.—DON PEDRO NORTH D'EL REY GOLD MINING COMPANY.

Stone treated and Gold returned for twelve months ending December 1866.

MAQUINE.		BAWDEN'S MINE.		DAWSON'S MINE.		TOTAL.	
Ore. tons.	Gold. oitavas.	Ore. tons.	Gold. oitavas.	Ore. tons.	Gold. oitavas.	Ore. tons.	Gold. oitavas.
12,779	70,348	4,787	11,754	106	35	17,672	82,137

	£	s.	d.
Value of 82,137 oitavas of gold at 8s. 7*d*.	35,250	9	3
Cost	20,162	8	5¾
Profit	£15,088	0	9¼

The returns made and profits realised from these mines during the first four months of the year 1867, have been as follow:—

	Gold produced. oitavas.	Profit. £	s.	d.
January	7,026	1,119	19	5
February	12,416	3,358	0	4
March	20,056	6,133	14	5
April	24,066	7,702	14	6
Total	63,564	£18,314	8	8

E.—RETURNS MADE FROM THE ANGLO-ITALIAN GOLD MINES SINCE 1863.*

The Val Toppa Gold Mining Company.

	oz.	Value. £	s.	d.
1864	509·275	1,798	18	9
1865	574·575	2,032	14	5
1866	1,400·925	4,957	15	8
Total since 1863	2,484·775	£8,789	8	10

Val Toppa has yielded upon an average 1 oz. 5 dwt. of gold per ton of ore.

The Vallanzasca Gold Mining Company.

	oz.	Value. £	s.	d.
1864	381·650	1,105	14	10
1865	740·475	2,291	14	9
1866	1,746·925	4,966	16	3
Total yield of Gold since 1863	2,869·050	£8,364	5	10

Vallanzasca has yielded upon an average 15 dwt. of gold per ton of ore.

* Furnished by Mr. J. C. Goodman.

The Pestarena Gold Mining Company.

		oz.	Value. £	s.	d.
1866	January, Gold received . . .	776·350 . .	2,504	9	8
	August ,, . . .	815·375 . .	2,638	0	8
	October ,, . . .	556·650 . .	1,806	9	8
	December ,, . . .	658·125 . .	2,176	17	9
	Total . .	2,806·500	£9,125	17	9
1867	January, Gold received . . .	265·850 . .	554	19	9
	May ,, . .	1,308·975 . .	4,293	17	8
	June ,, . .	1,154·950 . .	3,820	16	7
	Total . .	2,729·775	£8,669	14	0

	£	s.	d.
1866	9,125	17	9
1867	8,669	14	0
Total . .	£17,795	11	9

The Pestarena ore has yielded 2¼ oz. of gold per ton.

F.—RETURNS OF GOLD AND SILVER BULLION ASSAYED IN THE UNITED STATES DURING THE YEAR 1866, ON WHICH THE GOVERNMENT DUTY OF ONE-HALF PER CENT. WAS PAID.*

	Bullion assayed.
California	$49,020,250
Colorado	219,860
Idaho	535,105
Missouri	815
Nevada	15,272,546
New Jersey	13,688
New York	7,295,803
Oregon	4,785,231
Pennsylvania	4,044,218
Rhode Island	2,211
Utah	60,278
Washington	139,533
Total value	$81,389,538

* The duty is only paid on bullion assayed for the first time.

INDEX.

N.

T.

R. CLAY, SON, AND TAYLOR, PRINTERS, LONDON.

Milton Keynes UK
Ingram Content Group UK Ltd.
UKHW011818231023
431197UK00003B/86

On Time

Appointments, Schedules, Calendars, Deadlines

G.V. Loewen

Strategic Book Publishing and Rights Co.

Strategic Book Publishing & Rights Co., LLC
USA | Singapore
www.sbpra.net

ISBN: 978-1-68235-532-9

Contents

Time is a game played beautifully by children.

— Heraclitus

Chapter One

Introduction Section A: The Quotidian – Ontic Facticality

> This takes some time. Lose your time, go ahead, enter into the game, follow the words and perceptions of a memory that takes shape in front of you as well as inside you. You yourself can experience the sense of time. (Kristeva 1996:196).

Time. I can have it, I can give it. It can be taken from me or it can be allowed for me. I can save it and I can lose it. I can make up for its loss, or I can waste it. I can arrive when it is right, or be somewhere when it is wrong. I can even stop it, or it can run on so quickly that I could never catch up. More obscurely, a stitch in it saves nine. It flies and yet drags, but mostly it simply passes. It could come again, or it might never come at all. I am a child of it, but I also end up quite out of it even so. It can weigh heavily, or it can go unnoticed. It is money and it is free. We can have it down, but at some point it will be up.

And it can be marked. What follows is a phenomenology of *marked* time. In a world where everyone has the time for something or other, or yet does not have the time for any specific thing, marking time is of the utmost. The marks and remarks that we place upon the temporal skein of being adjudicate mightily our sense of place, identity, and even our meaning of consciousness. Being there, in the existential sense, is famously a function of being *in* time as much as it is being in the world. Heidegger quite rightly declares that being, to a great extent, *is* time. We are certainly historical beings, even if we have not a clue regarding the details of this or that history. Indeed, our knowledge of History, with a capital but also perfunctory 'H', is mostly immaterial to our life within it. History, so stated, is really someone else's, and not my own. I have a biography. Cultures have a history. One can study history but I would never have the vanity to study myself in the same manner.

Perhaps. Nevertheless, we construct an avid and picayune history of the self by marking time. Appointments are set, met or fulfilled, missed and have to be reset. The euphemistic 'rain check' is always a possibility, as metaphoric rain falls in everyone's biographical forecast. Schedules are made up of appointments, like sentences are constructed from words and syllables. Sometimes schedules entire have to be reconstructed. A longer term, heavier weather pattern may set in and we have to batten down the hatches for a while. Illness, divorce, job loss are the most common sources of the schedule change. We do not wish to appear as a drowned rat. Further up the scale of marking are the calendars. Their 'hallmark' is that they, like scripture, may be interpreted to hold a chronology of dates and times that will suit any sensibility, or none at all. The festival has its home just here, but so does the attempt at sanitizing the sacred in the 'holy day', in some places referred to as a 'bank holiday', as if the accounting metaphor can overtake the spirit of the thing.

But it is the deadline that animates all three of these other forms of marking time. At some point, our time *will* be up. There are a variety of means by which the dress rehearsal for death is accomplished. Most of these are minor, and involve the penalty of stigma, shame, or perhaps merely a slight embarrassment, as if we would look down in the face of finitude, or cast our glance away, not daring to meet the eyes of our shadow at the moment it cares to step in front of our face. Missed appointments, especially of the medical variety, could incur a fine and a longer wait to reconnect with the person so sought after. As well, illness or other discomfort remains unaddressed. Perhaps we might lose our chance at an opportunity of some other kind, career, romance, or even recreation. Well, we say, all of that can be replaced. Just so, in actual fact, none of it can. The job, love interest, or even activity can be *substituted*, but not replaced, as each of these places, persons and things, as well as all that flows from this missed timing, will inevitably be different. Our fantasies run along these viscous rails. What if *she* and I had gotten together? That is, rather than *her*. What if I had chosen this other job? What if, in the course of this activity I had met yet some other, or realized some potential in myself I never knew existed? Such is life. Or might I have had a rather different life in the larger sense if this other schedule had been my own? And I certainly would be a different person if I had adhered to this other calendar rather than the one I have always used. Perhaps I do not work well under pressure. The sense of the deadline does not motivate me, or if it does, it creates anxieties regarding its fulfillment. Telling me that something *must* be done by this or that time or else does not impress me, and I am like most North Americans in my disdain for any kind of authority at all, whether work, the state, church or text, even spouse, though this last, perhaps ironically, is the most weighty upon us in this culture. We know what we have to lose, in a sense, whereas most feel like the state can be lost or at least, get lost, simply because we identify its existence with happenstance of the current regime, to our collective peril. The church is already long gone for the vast majority of us, so much so that we cannot, collectively or otherwise, even recall why it used to be so important. Work is something that one does only because one has to. The identity relation between vocation and work is at best, strained in modern society. 'Good times' tend to be off work hours. 'Thank God its Friday' is an apt, though ironic expression of this sensibility. God hails from a time out of time, and no benevolent God would ever have forced us to work in this way. Indeed, we are dimly aware that the modern work life of capital was precisely what killed the old God, that is, if He didn't do Himself in first.

So the time which is our own, in which we find ourselves and perhaps have the time of our lives, must somehow be marked off from general time, the time of institutions certainly, but also the time in which others dwell. This in-dwelling, this historicity writ small, characterizes the subjectivity of our desire. It strains against its own subjectitude of course, and it is this tension which constitutes 'lived time'. It may be bad timing on our parts to have to confront this otherness inside the self, but it must be done. The fact that we are willing to work on it, without respect to other labors, suggests that we value our time enough to commit to bracketing both the objective oppression of social life as well as the subjective suppression of what hurts us in our own life experience. The two are related, but not always as intimately as may be first thought. It isn't, in the end, anyone else's fault but our own if we waste the time we are given with the trivial, the dull, the repetitive, or yet the frisson of false scandal.

The confrontation between myself as an object in the world, the experience of subjectitude that I understand and live within due to this relationship with the world of objects and others as both subjects and objects, as well as my fragile sense of being myself *in* the world, a being both in time and place, is precisely where marked time occurs. We will explore each of the four major means of marking time in turn, from that which is the most gentle, the appointment, to that which animates the entire structure at an experiential level, the deadline. In between, the biographical calendar of the schedule and the cultural calendar of history will carry our analytic forward to a point where we might imagine that because we already know ourselves to be in time, to be historical beings through and through, that we might even be said to be identical with time itself. If so, then we carry around with us and within us not only our own life and times, but the history of the species as a whole.

1.1 The Definite:

History has a history. Not to obfuscate, but we know that each idea, even if it overtakes itself and renders itself obsolete, comes from somewhere other than itself, where it rests of the moment. As do we. Ideas have careers just as we have biographies. Interpretations change over time, often radically. We know only what we know, and we are aware that much has been lost to the 'sands of time', or some other sentimental sediment. All of this is patently old hat. Though it may seem trite to state, rather unctuously that "...any account of the *concept* of time would have to allow one to explain and endorse any temporal presuppositions built into the term 'concept'..." (*Wood 1989:4*), it is at least true that there have not always been calendars with all that this implies, and that the only real deadline our primordial ancestors faced was the final moment wherein realization was made that life, or what had just passed for it, was done. But ever *since* history began its own history, our kind have lived with and within the ambit of the four phenomenological markers set out above. And it is not so much the concept of time that is of interest to us here, but rather the conception of it that comes out of it being marked in the manner that it is so. The historical careers of the appointment, the schedule, the calendar and the more existential career of the deadline will be of only passing interest to us. Such investigations tend to get caught up in precisely the fabric that must be unwoven from itself. The coteries of culture and the keepsakes of kindred clash with a phenomenological understanding. For it is, if not to the things themselves, to the structures of culture and personhood that we must attend if we are to bring to light the meaningfulness of marking. It must be seen as deep enough, as we are regularly referring to animals who 'mark' their territory, as if these creatures were somehow less evolved versions of the nation state. In the wild, the lion stakes his claim, in the suburbs, one's neighbor's pet. Somehow much less profoundly, the latter is yet indescribably closer to us. However disappointing this may be to all those who iron john their way through social life, or run with wolves, or perhaps even imagine themselves a hero of some or other sort, its facticality provides both a bland blandishment to personal fantasy as well as marks the territory of our phenomenology. Yes, we are more than dogs pissing into the wind, but we are not the jaguar of the night, and never can be.

In the effort to mark off some time for ourselves, we have, in modern North American society, tended to construct an amusement park within which the soul is to gain a polished presentiment. This ludicrous luster lasts only as long as does the hallowed holiday. Dogs replace wolves, plastic supplants iron. It is generally a demographic feature that such movements have even arisen, and those generations that follow may rightly disdain them and all that they appear to represent. Even so, the existence of attempted alternatives to the quotidian, while not escaping the mundane – indeed, perhaps they bring it to the forefront, as will be suggested below – do provide examples of the intense desire, even need, to mark time as apart from how it is marked objectively. In other words, we do search for a different conception of what time is, or what it can be. We do question the time we are given, and wish to make the most of it. It is surely not quite our own fault that the charlatanry of a Barnumesque culture overtakes us now and again. The one who takes the sucker may yet himself be taken. It all depends on the context and the desires found within. Nothing about time is in fact 'self-evident', as Heidegger notes early on in his rehearsal for his masterwork, asking what makes time 'appropriate' for dividing reality into domains of existential 'function'. (cf. Heidegger 1992:6 [1925]). The conventional understanding of time allows it to be marked in a yet more self-evident manner. But these marks remark upon themselves, and through them, phenomenologically, can be understood the reason, and not only the reasons, whereby such an understanding, however conventional, takes hold and never leaves us. If 'experience, apprehension and determination' can be designated by the methodological sense of phenomenology (cf. ibid:85), or yet it can be characterized as the scientific study of the intentional apriori (cf. ibid:86), and that such noesic intentions are directed towards the noema, 'intended in its intention' (cf. ibid:94), we can duly report that there exists no wide and abstract gulf between the transcendental and the 'unity of a real human being' after all (cf. ibid:101). Indeed, not only ourselves as aspects of 'Being-the-World', more self-absorbed but also more recognizably beings-in-the-world, fall within the marked circles of ongoingness and lived time, but "The world is wholly immersed in time." (Puech 1973:46 [1951]). It can only become a world if it is so immersed. For the world has time in a manner that persons have biographies and cultures have histories.

This is no mere geological junket, the cosmos writ into the local formations, so standard that they are reiterated uncounted times over in the entirety of the universe as it can be known. No, rather the world in its worlding is a work of time more than space. For not only does its evolution from a charred chunk of metals and minerals to a thriving and of late, throbbing entity full of life and the threat to life occur given a generous enough amount of time, the world also heals itself throughout that same period. How many mass extinctions have there been? How large will the current one, ongoing - in our own time, itself a scurrilous child of the time we ourselves have taken to mark time into a subjection of our own subjectivities - become? The time that belongs to the world extends itself backward into the mere earth and the solar system, and forward into the indefiniteness of the infinite cosmos.

Even so, the time the world has is translated into the history we give ourselves. Geology helps us mark our place in that very cosmos, and our human career, itself extended now some seven million years into 'the past' while not daring to look much more than a mere seven in the other direction – and we can pause just here to wonder if our interest in palaeoarchaeology in particular is somewhat of a decoy; it is easy to have 'a past' and everyone, as is said, 'has one' – and provides for us the dates of birth of our ancient ancestral lines. It begins to help us paint the portrait of our selfhood and species, shared and individuated alike: "A man's relation to time, understood thus, may be taken as a task or as foreordained destiny. In some situations one can assume a correct or wrong attitude towards time, while in others one must accept this time as fate." (Wilhelm 1973:227 [1951]). The gravity of cosmic time does not translate well into the more focused and scrutinized mass of a history merely human, but ironically, and perhaps necessarily, we effect this translation by virtue of the specific weight of our personal biographies, for it is we who must live on in the face of the unknown future and as well the vast and knowable, but still mostly unknown, past. Just as the concept of god is an interlocutor between past and future, the concept of self has much more recently become the translator of the cosmic and the historic. The operations that emanate from such a position make up the quotidian. In saying this, however, it is very much not the case that such things, events, encounters and what-have-you should be viewed as trivial. Here, and there too, the gods are also present: "The in-order-to and for-what (the daily meals, the habits of writing and working, sewing from time to time, playing from time to time) are not just arbitrary, free-floating modes of being-occupied at the table and tarrying for a while at it, but rather ones which are defined in the awhileness of their temporal particularity from out of historical everydayness." (Heidegger 1999:75 [1923]). Whether in Marx, Nietzsche or here, in Heidegger for the first time, the table marks itself down as a place where things can be set down with civility and within civilization. It is a place of ordering, and also of order once made. Seated round it, in prayer or conversation, the one directed upwards to Being, the other directed across at beings, the table is a metaphoric and metastatic center of living though it is just as often passed over in life. There is a 'table of values', old and new, in Zarathustra, and each is of its own time. The commodity fetish is introduced by the example of the table, advisedly no doubt, in Capital. And just here, before the hammer, the table appears as the way in which beings equate themselves unto Being. Even so, we must remain cautious. Even if function and social reality demonstrate the metaphor of Being and beings, "...it is a mistake to take the requirements of a certain sort of civilized life as proof of some deeper truth about Time itself." (Wood 1989:322). Likewise, it is a similar injunction against both personalizing time or personifying it, in life or myth alike, to remind ourselves that the social world also worlds itself, and in a different way than does that existential. It is certainly yet more ordered, which is one of the major pints in favor of studying marked time phenomenologically, and it is as well, more aloof to the concerns of individuals. Akin to its own history, social reality imposes upon us *its* time, a time which can never be fully our own or owned by us. In that, capital-T Time may have more bearing here and not so much in the realm of ontology. For it is the event, as known by the living, the always temporary victors over the history of others, that sediments itself, clogging our arteries: "Their stark but ineluctable historical weight remains and haunts any discussion of the past. In what sense is it meaningful to suggest that such primal reality can be 'defined' by the individual or be affected by his choice of history?" (Natanson 1970:102-3). The idea that at certain times we have the choice to make, wherein others we are 'fated' to act as we in fact do, muddies the water with yet another kind of sediment, this time, a subjective one. These sentiments may also be cultural in import – certainly, they are more and more stereotypical and mass-marketed – but they nonetheless set up what perhaps is a conveniently false dichotomy between lived time and the time in which we live. The former is of choice, the latter, of destiny.

For neither open-endedness nor ultimate closure overtakes time. The former may elevate intent far above its more pedestrian underpinnings, while the latter assumes that there is a cosmic order that cannot be known in its entirety. Everything comes to an end, even universal processes. We cannot say, for instance, if cosmological constants take a different form, or at least, rest within altered parameters, in other universes that might yet be, that may exist alongside our own, or have come before. Just as there was always another choice that could have been made –

for the moment, we can safely disregard the social reality of the moralizing 'should' or the 'would', oddly wilful and yet will-less simultaneously – fate, famously, the 'weight of circumstance', is also subject to alternative interpretations, even if in the moment of its advent it appears to brook no positive alteration. And just as can intent and outcome notoriously disagree, this disconnect, once again, so often bemoaned by moralizers of all stripes, provides for us a patent clue to understanding the diversity of choice and fate in time. Indeed, it gives us far more than this. A solid, human and working definition of time itself can itself be constructed: "The riddle of time is the riddle of the beginning. We know that there can be no true beginning. Something has always gone before. In the beginning lies the whole past. The beginning is the past. Yet we say that we begin something, that we make a new beginning, And we call this long list of beginnings, time." (Van Der Leeuw 1973:325 [1949]). Each choice we think we make, each fate we imagine we undergo, starts something other than what it might have. We become something other as well. Not only does making a new start confer upon us the privilege of our shared humanity – it enacts it, puts it into play, gives it some time to think about itself and its would-be likenesses – it reenacts the primordiality of a beginning forever lost out back behind not only history, but also touching the time before there could *be* time. Of late, we have of course pushed back the notion of human time into the depths of the cosmos and unto the steps of creation itself. But this is not time as we can know it. Indeed, we can understand the beginning of this our version of the universe only by marking the first sight of the Big Bang on our current calendars. It actually occurred at the moment time began and thus falls itself outside of any temporality. To behold creation in a moment is to reduce the responsibility of living within it as it is. To take it all in within the trice that it itself took to commence its journey is to foreswear the responsibility of our small portion of being a fellow traveller with creation. It is somehow typical of the technical mindset to desire this moment and heave it up above all others. For this is the beginning of all things, we are told. And the idea of the 'true beginning' still has a hold over us. What Van Der Leeuw says in so many words is that the search for the grail of any historical or primordial beginning is one tinged with both cowardice and irresponsibility. Vanity might be added to this incomplete list. To see the Big Bang gives us the view we imagine a God would have had. Its sexual connotations, ludicrous and yet also somehow typical of those responsible for its frame, innuendo their way into our vulgar consciousness. All of the matter that will make up this universe ejaculated into the void in a few moments. The birth of the cosmos, let there be light.

It is easy to overlook the awe of such a moment, but it is also easy to aggrandize it, to personify it, to anthropomorphize. Simply put, we do not know what it is or how it occurred. Somehow, this ignorance – which is, of course, the hallmark of the reality of no true beginnings after all – is intolerable for us. On the side of the light, this kind of vanity pushes us to do better, and sometimes, even to be better. But in the shadows, it allows us to imagine ourselves as far more important than we might actually be, both at the level of the individual and the species. The push to view cosmic creation has its roots not in the modern sciences – these provide only the techniques for making such an attempt – but in ancient religions. We still have not gotten our revenge for Babel, but we have not yet forgotten it. In time, given enough time, we will own this act and turn the tables on the dead gods of all eras and creeds. For though all such gods *are* dead, yet even this is not enough for us. We want to rediscover their graves and spit on them, nay, dig them up and bury them again and again, or cast their immortal remains to the cosmic wind.

Partly what faces us is simple ignorance. The future is also part of marked time, and indeed much of what is to follow in our substantive chapters concentrates on how we mark something that has not yet occurred. The point of appointment, arrow of schedule, the cycle of calendar, and the immanence of the deadline chart the future as it could become, and us with it. The cult of prediction, grown over the past four centuries or so to a religion of its own novel vintage, is a testament to this fetish. Yet it is no mere fetish. It has become an entire language. Even so, it is in fiction and not science where this language speaks to us most deeply. For in the narrative we imagine we can know both past and future alike. The novel is the recently promoted romantic god. More than an allegorical journey, more than a satire, what the nineteenth and twentieth century literary form bequeathed to us is almost modernity itself: "By tracing the beings and things situated in time, the novel becomes a journey to the end of memory." (Kristeva 1996:167 [1994]). One of the subjective reasons why change is sometimes so slow in coming in certain regions of human affairs, that is anything serious, is that we have the tendency to 'remember' the future as if it were only a memory. This attitude rejects change as a matter of course, but fools itself into imagining that things are both changing – which they are, in any case – and that this kind of change is best because things are still working – which they may or may not be, pending context. There is no ethical evidence that supports this version of cowardice, but the novel is used to shore it up. Narrative makes the world into a story wherein characters can take their place as those who change for us, or who are altered. Choice and fate have truest reign in fiction, because someone, after all, did write the thing in the first place. There *is* both a beginning *and* an end. A watch implies a watchmaker, and the novel doubles over its start and finish, because it also has to be read, something we absolutely cannot do with our own lives or those of any of our contemporaries. Children suffer the most under this regime of ethical error, because adults of all stations often presume to read a young person's life off before it has really begun. This is accomplished either by the vicariousness of attempting to live again our own lives through our children's, or have our children live the life that somehow was denied us. These two tangents alone could explain much regarding the lack of change in the wider world.

So, however penetrating the insights that the novel or other narrative form supplies us, it is also an act of cowardly escapism. It presumes to take time out of time, the world out of the world. The novel *novels* its way along as a form of parousia. It is otherworldly and because of its wordiness, for our modern culture, it has also supplied the supplication we need to assuage our incomplete attempt to avenge ourselves against the failure of Babel. God never wrote anything down. This also modernity tells us. Only we have the story in our heads and can know it. God needs neither knowledge nor story. He just Is and what He hath wrought remains what Is. And hence our pending advantage. We *do* have the time – time, which he never gave himself, at least in Western beliefs – to eventually overtake His works. His death is but a footnote. The real triumph is making humans into gods but as well, and perhaps even more stridently important, remaking His creation into that of our own.

To write our own story is to have killed the gods and only part of that narrative can be said to rest in science. Literature, high or low, takes its place in the contemporary pantheon of all too human idols. This said, we also know that we cannot, nor should, return to the time of the Gods. The appearance of a God on earth in both East and West was the beginning of the end of religion. It was the half-way house to humanity as we have come to know it, prosthetic, to be sure, but also still prodigal. But our return to the house of our parents is also part of the vengefulness. We not only stride over the threshold and announce our success, we make sure that no one survives our visitation. With the Gods dead by our own hands, we take our rightful place as the future of existence. This allegorical act is the means to attain the seer of accurate and reliable predictability in all things. God was the only being who had knowledge of both the beginning and the end. Eschatological thought, linear time, and indefinite life were all born in and borne on this knowledge. But in focusing too tightly on godhead and divinity, in working to extend our lives and in becoming immortal, we have forgotten about the world.

It is thus, Heidegger relates, because being has been predefined as making the pure presence of something (cf. Heidegger 1962:48-9 [1927]). Hence the destruction of the ontological tradition clears the space of being for an understanding thereof. For being as we know it is not only within time, it is time, though not quite time 'itself'. It is also true that we live in the moment even if we do not live for it, but this is not an equal truth, as it were: "For if it be, it is divided into past and future. The present hath no space." (Augustine, in Gale 1968:42). The somewhat rattled sense that time does not really exist because of this and like phenomena allows us egress from the weight of the world and of life. Living on in time extends our sense of selfhood in two directions at once. Yet these apparent opposites share their goal of running away from the present moment, of absconding with presence pure or otherwise: "Without temporal extension there would be no objects… And the concern to get to the bottom of our common-sense understanding of time is nothing more than an attempt to bring relief to those who, like St. Augustine, find themselves at sea when they try to get a reflective grip on time." (Wood 1989:57). If each station along the way to understanding the relationship between time and being has a self-concealing faculty (cf. ibid:156), all the more necessity is placed on this destruction. At first glance, there seems little enough of 'common sense' to any of this, either the history of metaphysics or a metaphysical history. Even so, the idea of extension *via* both memory and anticipation – and each has the other riding shotgun for it; the past and the future are constructed by this team effort – borrow their impetus from something closest to us and indeed, both common and sensible, and that is, the body: "...the inclination is thus strong to tie both inner time and the kinaesthetic field to objective space." (Larrabee 1989:391). Larrabee cites sayings such as 'leaving one's past behind one' or 'look forward to this or that' as evidence that our language is infused with this sort of analogy. And is it only an analogy? "Since we measure time-consciousness by seeing our actions in space, we can think of our whole life as one long walk through space. We complete a journey co-extensive with our conscious life, and our entire history unfolds in measurable time." (Lampert 2012:126-7). The convenience of this is unmistakable, and to a great extent, unavoidable. If time is to be extended into what does not, in the strict sense, exist – the past has existed but is now gone, the future has not yet occurred – then we must at east embody temporality, if not time itself. We are the basis for any extension of time as an *object*. Objecting to the pure present through memory and anticipation, we find in ourselves the subjection of pure presence. We have 'our own internal time' which may itself be investigated (cf. Koselleck 1985:247), but we also know that its measure is not the only one available to us, nor to history. Herder's sensibility that 'every changing thing' has its own internal measure of time relaxes the hold any pure presence might have had over us. But this presence is not vanquished completely. It still presents to us itself as a goal, beyond and somehow also construing the other two senses, that of 'clock time' and that of immanence (cf. Larrabee 1989:374-5). *Erlebnisse,* or 'lived experiences' are the stuff of immanence and temporal objects. Though this being said, other kinds of objects extend themselves through time by virtue of the fact that they are used to measure it. The body measures time only obliquely. We are conscious, growing older, of the entropy of intimate things. Mercifully gradual in most cases, nevertheless an appointment, diagnosis, test and operation have a similar sensation to them as replacing the batteries of an alarm clock, or charging up a phone. Both kinds of experiences are lived, though the body is to be lived *through* and the objects of the world, and perhaps other persons as well, are to be lived merely *with*. The withness of others and other things is often more comforting to our immanential sensibilities than the 'throughness' of the body. For the latter is always conscious of itself through its own self-consciousness, and we are, willy-nilly, made self-conscious of this. Indeed, we are also often told in this day of self-esteem, that being self-conscious in *front* of others, or because we are *behind* them – yet more images of bodily extensions through space and not time – is something to be overcome, akin to pure presence. Gender, for instance, is seen as very much a performance, and not as a thing. Hence there is an art to it more so than a science. These ideas, so contemporary and politic at once, have their genesis in more ancient understandings. Not to say that their roots undermine their present reality. Indeed, contrary to the politic mutterings of all those who live only in the fashionable now of would-be things, histories provide support for ideas. The representing of a history allows the idea to not only question itself, it allows history itself to unfold before us in the present. The great diversity of performances, theater, and manners in which the game of social life is played and enacted, gendered or otherwise, have their advent in the ability to understand time in different ways: "... we might speak of a game among three opposing conceptions, the first represented by a circle, the second by a straight line, the third by a broken line." (Puech 1973:40 [1951]). For us, time is more of a tube than anything else. Part of its torus overlaps with what has been – evidenced in the realms of human theater where the performance alters but slowly – and part moves along with less regard for its pedigree. Nonetheless it retains part of its cyclical structure. A cycle and an arrow at once, 'tube time' is the most realistic conception of temporality. Within the skein of its lengthening snake, the broken lines of disconnected and disjointed aspects of human life are also represented. Each of the major conceptions of classical time is a reduction of the reality of being in time.

Even so, the fact that at some point there were conflicting interpretations of what time actually was points us in the direction of understanding diversity 'itself'. Looking 'backwards' today means something quite different then doing what appeared to be the same thing yesterday. In this way, 'anisotropy' as applied to time can be understood more than as simply a logical construction. It "...would consist of an *intrinsic* dissimilarity of the past and future directions: a difference that would be manifested in some time asymmetry within our laws of nature." (Horwich 1988:37, italics the text's). This is saying a great deal at once. One might imagine that due to shifts in historical outlook, the appearance of history overtaking timeless being, the world born from earth, what has been and what could have been conjured from the dust and ash of the fallen - the dead first memorialized perhaps some three hundred thousand years ago are suggested as being concomitant with the advent of our current version of humanity in the archaeological record, for instance, as well as suggesting that mourning is the birthstone of all memory, as in Durkheim – time itself and in principle contains this difference. Succession alone will not cut it here (cf. Lampert 2012:89-90). If Kant prefers the simultaneity of space and Hegel that of place, neither kind of time held within these contrasting visions allows for that difference to be played out simultaneously, as the strong version of anisotropy wants to maintain. If pure presence, 'instantaneous subjective simultaneity' by human definition, without respect of any temporal construct, necessitates the sharing of either space or place or both, then the idea of objects 'alongside' does present to our senses a contrast with temporal succession (cf. ibid:4). Each of these attempts to provide some definition to that which is both inexistent – it has not yet ever been but it might be – and that which is non-existent – it has been but is no longer – does help us to fathom how anisotropic time could exist simultaneously, precisely, 'alongside' itself. What the past and future share is their inability to be present, both at once and singly. But their inclinations do intrinsically differ from one another even so. The present thus becomes a transitional state, a kind of *Sattelzeit* as momentary as is the sudden realization that things, in general, have changed and all around us. (cf. Tribe, in Koselleck 1985:x). The 'valency' of such a term allows it free play over any limen (cf. ibid:xii). Understanding is both an historical and an experiential act that occurs in time and through time. It has time as its object, or more precisely, the aspect of time that is ever-changing and very much is, change 'itself', and it takes time to accomplish. It shares little with pure presence, in other words, for it is neither snap judgement nor intuition of essence. It has nothing of the *Augenblick* or the *Wesenschau* about it. It is hermeneutic through and through. By virtue of this sleight of historical hand, what is no longer extant can be made present, can attain the presence of the present (cf. ibid:xiv).

But contemporaneity is not simultaneity. There is clearly no one concept of time, and the very idea contains a 'hidden complicity' (cf. Wood 1989:12-3). Just as what we find ourselves doing in time, or having the time in which to do something, anything, there rather appears to be different kinds of time 'out there'. Classically, we sell our labor power to the owners of various operations within capital for wages, but all of this occurs because time itself is also a commodity. In the most literal manner possible, time and money have been equated, and the means by which they are brought together in this joint merger is labor. Yet this is but one conception, though a dominant one. Against this, or rather, over against it, we have also developed contending versions of time, mostly of the more fantastic variety coming as they do out of the romantic counter-movements to materialisms or positivisms. More to the point, however, are the differing conceptions of time that different kinds of role players who must interact within it have of it during this or that interactive social context.

For instance, all of us wait for things in this life, aside from its end point. We spend what seems like an inordinate amount of time doing so. We are impatient, notoriously, as well as sing the praises of being its very opposite. Patience too might well be a commodity, and a rare one. But "...waiting is not simply a barrier to service but is rather the very condition of its subjective value." (Schwartz 1975:33). The longer we wait for something, the higher that something may be esteemed. It is not always so, of course, but 'value' here can cut both ways. We are 'conditioned' to incline ourselves in the direction of waiting out of the desire for the service or object waiting might produce. This is no mere behaviorism. We may just as likely disdain the service rendered if the wait-time to attain it does not match other cultural indicators. A fine restaurant can expect its patrons to add the longer wait into their dining experience, whereas a fast food joint could not. Time is experienced differently in diverse contexts. The idea that that there should be a 'thing itself' at the back of this experience is something that places the onus on the one doing the analysis. There is, in other words, no evidence at all of a time outside of the time in which people live. This does not mean, of course, that measured time is somehow irretrievably subjective. No, it is both. An hours wait at a four star restaurant is not the same as that in a pizza place. We know that ahead of time, and plan accordingly to either find some other activity with which to indulge ourselves or avoid the situation entirely. It is true that pending age and source of power, clocks may run slowly or more rapidly. Near the speed of light, things of the sort happen as well due to other, more cosmic, causes. But in general, all of the objective aspects of time can be corrected *to* the cosmic order. Even so, by its very position as arbiter of temporality, the cosmos and its value are also subjectively understood and waited upon. There is an indefinite aspect to the infinite that will never avail itself to us no matter how long we are willing to wait. By this same sense, we can safely call this aspect 'objectivity' because no meaningful wait-time accrues to it.

In studies of cognitively impaired persons as well, time is experienced quite differently. The tendency is twofold: either there are things or conditions that have always been or have been for an indefinitely lengthy period of time, or things and conditions that have just occurred (cf. Minkowski 1970:392). There is no middle term and no way to express any degree of time having passed. Things simply are or are not. Children also betray this kind of dichotomous thinking about time. This is one of the chief reasons that young persons of all stripes share a common impatience with all things. Learning to wait, that is, developing a different and differing sense of how time passes, is one of the marks of adulthood in our society. This itself has been the case for a long period of time, and we sometimes imagine it to always have been so. But the penchant for getting somewhere as rapidly as possible, completing tasks in a 'reasonable' amount of time - or if the task be quotidian or repetitive, the faster the better – is a hallmark of our modern condition. Given that "... even one's method of reading history has a history that needs to be explained." (Wood 1989:6), and thus we can begin to ascertain why we rationalize our doings with those of our ancestors by examining the way we experience time in our *own* time.

If the days pass in a 'dreary succession', as they do with those who are marginal to our normative mental sensibilities (cf. Minkowski 1970:186), then time 'itself' becomes a drag. It is both uniform and monotonous. But time itself could not be other than that in any case. The doings of the day are what make time livable or unlivable for us, and that should also suggest that we ourselves are the source of temporal conceptions of all kinds. Everyone experiences the dull wrack of entropy that characterizes parts of a human life. Being ill, working in a tightly controlled institution, forcing ourselves to tolerate those we actually do not, queuing up during holiday travel are all common enough conditions that lend themselves to mental marginality. Yet we are still active, and time spent in this way is still a means to an end, like most jobs or most line-ups. Given that our 'natural attitude' is completely unnatural, conceptions of time let alone history have nothing to do with things 'themselves' and everything to do with our actions and experiences in and of the world (cf. Heidegger 1992:113 [1925]). Scheler did not of course mean that we were merely more sophisticated animals. What comes 'naturally' to us is that which surpasses all instinct. The casual expression 'second nature' betrays this relationship, even if it also betrays the laziness inherent in all casual speech. Since it is also true that every language as well as our very being is historical by definition, we should not be surprised that 'making history' is not the common lot (cf. ibid:271). We are already our history, both in terms of our own historicity – the lived experience of being in time – and by being objectively historical beings – we live and have lived in this or that recorded time, even if we are judged to have been impotent regarding it. All of this attains an integration that we unreflectively judge as 'natural' simply because it is experienced in the same manner as we imagine all others experience it. But whether we qualify this understanding by replacing the term with cultural, historical, psychological, social, or even 'subjective', the mere fact that we have to work so diligently to do so and to remind others to attempt to do so is proof that the natural attitude *is* just that. It is, in other words, so fully integrated into our culture that it no longer passes *for* culture. It is a social fact. Nonetheless, like all such facts, it does not always have our complete support or loyalty: "The full historical fact, the 'integral past', is properly an Idea in the Kantian sense, that is to say, the *never attained limit* of an ever more extensive and complex effort to integrate." (Ricoeur 1965:24, [1955] italics the text's). Like the much disdained and disheveled idea of a 'continuous history', Whiggish at best, *The* past is akin more to a god or, for moderns, even a culture. Given the polyglot 'nature' of the most nation states, culture is in fact just as much in question as is nature. This state of affairs which is neither state nor affair was first called to mind by the discarding of the idea of integral history. And the manner in which this was accomplished had very much to do with the recognition that the diverse conceptions of time we experience in our own lives were also experienced, in different ways, in the past. We could now ask, for the first time, whose past, which past, and what past? Written history, that of the victors or otherwise, became only one standard, or lost its ability to be a standard at all. Yet history does not lose its force because it is now many things. If anything, it gains in the suasion it has over us, hermeneutically *via* the confrontation with the tradition – and now, traditions – and phenomenologically *via* the lack of immediate guarantee that any reduction can bracket all which must be present in order for any Neo-Kantian idea to take semblance or form. This new sophistication suggests that "… historical time is not simply an empty definition, but rather an entity which alters along with history and from whose changing structure it is possible to deduce the shifting classification of experience and expectation." (Koselleck 1985:271). And it is just these classifications that are experienced subjectively without respect to their ability to become 'ideas' in any sense.

This said, there are dominant sources of temporal definition that go beyond mere timepieces. There are those whose time is viewed as more valuable than that possessed by others. The encounter between differing values and valuations of time occurs daily, and is also something experienced as quite 'natural', even for some, 'ideal'. Transporting this across time, back into history - as if the past was a present day option, not quite living, but not quite passed either – gives us the sense all the more that the manner in which we do things in the present has a gravity to it that should not, or even cannot, be questioned. The Doctor's office is a tired exemplification of the steep hierarchy accrued to the value of time. We may speak of 'time zones' in a new way here, wherein different social contexts time is not only experienced divergently, the standard of timekeeping itself is altered. Yet this is not quite historical in the larger sense, for one can question even the Doctor, who either apologizes to some degree or does so, these days, *ahead* of time, before the question can be pointedly raised. Indeed, one marker of social station is the ability to manipulate time in a way that others of lower social standing accept and even honor. The apology for waiting overlong can be effected only by those upon whom we have waited. These persons themselves may not even have a higher status than we in general, but in forcing us to wait, they have raised the stakes regarding their usual status. At the very least, they have forced us to deal with them in a novel manner, even if it means having to fire them.

But to pin all of this on history is to do more than equivocate or apologize or even act. For it places the space of human action at a distance from the actors, as if 'the tradition' were a force of nature. Politically, all neo-conservative movements take this tack, transparent and simplistic though it is. More distressing by far is the general acceptance that history can offer 'proof' of something, anything, in the present world. Like the death of god, the studied disregard we have of the historical world is pronounced by our deference to the past. If God served as an interlocutor between past and future then His death might well mean that these two necessary aspects of human time have ceased to speak to one another. It certainly seems to be the case: "History is the expired history that the historian recaptures as *truth*, that is, as objectivity; but it is also the history in process that we are experiencing and making." (Ricoeur 1965:24, [1955] italics the text's). Something past its expiration date is general indigestible. What gave it life has passed on. Religion, in any transcendental sense of the term, is like that for the vast majority of people, even, and perhaps especially, for all those whose regular church attendance is seen as a mark of faith. While certainly a mark of community, either insincere or authentic or perhaps even both depending on the day or ritual in question, faith today is very much like history and for that matter, time as well. Divergent, set to conflicting ends, used against itself without end. Making history thus may be taken in this doubled over sense of *la brisure*. It is easier to do archaeology, perhaps. We are reconstructing something by ourselves in our own time. No one has told us how it must go or how it had gone, as in the written historical record. No doubt artifacts have their own textual quality, and hermeneutics does not stop when the final page of this or that tome is turned. But every kind of knowledge that is still respected in our world is so because it remains enthralled to the rather slavish servitude we render unto its history. This is a rare example where slavery is convenient for the one enslaved, for it brackets away our need to question the way things are in the present. The shelf life of these kinds of commodities, however indigestible in practice, far exceeds their 'best-before' dates. So much so that unless we are strict and simplistic functionalists, we could very well question the very idea of when and for whom these ideas were 'best', and before what? What occurred and when and to whom, that this or that idea, Kantian or no, ran out of time?

No, it is more clear that history, let alone the history of time, is conceived along rather different lines. The meaning of Being of *Dasein* is temporality, and hence what structure it has, that which makes *us*, must be interpreted as modes of the temporal (cf. Heidegger 1962:38 [1927]). This temporality also *understands* Being, as if time is the language in which Babel can be rebuilt. It must be 'brought to light' as the 'horizon' for all such understanding (ibid:39), and thus it is to time that befalls the Fall itself as well as we the fallen. Ideas, history as integrative and continuous, culture as homogenous, thinking as individual and living as biography are all rendered superfluous, or, at least, secondary, to this new device. All that once was definite has been displaced.

1.2 The Finite:

So much so that we can now state that both the beginning and the end are relative to time served, or time pressed into the service of Being, or yet further, Being expressed as time. Not only through the lived time of beings, not simply due to the world as a place wherein time occurs and recurs, but that the happenstance of history in the making *is* ontology. This more radical sensibility has its own history, but it has its genesis in the recognition that the now torrid pace of certain aspects of cultural change may be experienced over the course of a single human lifetime. This *is* something we take to be quite new, and thus our own. It may be unwanted or even tragic, as when elderly persons discover that they no longer live in the world as it is, or it may be welcomed, though in perfunctory and manufactured fashion, as when young persons discover that the market caters to them and them alone. We live longer than any of our ancestors ever did, and the pace of change in many, though hardly all, quarters of human existence has also stepped up significantly. This combination allows for history to not only lose its previous status as integral and integrating – if anything, it is history, i.e. the checkered careers of various ideas, that promotes most of the conflict present in the world today – it also rudely shoves time outside of itself. The fashion for fantasies of all kinds - but most noticeably, nostalgia - in our entertainment fictions, is testament to this dislocation and how we struggle to bear it up. Time is no longer a guarantor of much of anything. It might not even be able to 'heal' us, in a time-honored fashion. Indeed, nothing can be so honored because time has lost its ability to honor anything. The concern about the demise of this version of earth's biosphere reflects only secondarily an environmental concern or even a concern regarding what kind of future we may have to live in. More than either of these, the climate topic is also a function of nostalgia, of *lost* time.

The presence of the absence of the future is one somewhat circumlocuted way in which to express this kind of backward glance. This is what takes hold in fantasy. It is no mere Rousseauism. I am not about to pack up and move to a Pacific atoll, though it is always tempting to do so, and my home city could be characterized as a large, expensive, and increasingly busy and congested version of that same ideal in any case. No, it is rather that we do not wish to bear the responsibility of having *any* future. We think it should simply come to us, serve us in its presence, simply by becoming present at the appropriate time. What is now should end in its proper time, and what was to come is no longer awaited but rather fully here. The temporalization of ontology is something that has appeared as part of our present, but it was, at one time, only something about a possible future: "Finiteness is synonymous with temporality, and is so in a precise sense which is exemplified in varying degrees by living creatures. Not only are living creatures datable in time like lifeless material phenomena, they also require time in order to live." (Plessner 1973:250 [1951]). Our objective status is just as novel as our 'much vaunted' subjectivity and experience. Grasping the moment means putting an end to it. Living for the day entails that we forget that we are doing just that. The motto, nay, the slogan of all those who do so without doing so should warn us that this too is a fantasy. Living in the moment is what all of us do in any case. We date ourselves in this way as undatable, and indeed, who would 'go out' with us if all we were ever able to do and think about was the moment? We would be seen as children or worse, not 'marriage' material in the least. So the ability to find ourselves in time takes on more of an historical sense rather than an existential sensation. Running on towards death is something that moderns confront. We quite simply have the time to do so, and for the first time.

The simple combination of living longer and the world running on without our consent – and note too that it runs apace, the worlding of the world is no longer a stolid stroll or even a jog – has allowed this new definition of being to appear. It is horizontal because it approaches the edge of life in a way that cannot be observed ahead of its time. But it also uses the metaphor of the horizon because for a much greater length of time than ever before in human history this edge recedes in front of our approach, no matter how rapidly we move. This gives us the impression that we run on towards death. In previous eras, death appeared beside us and took us down. We didn't move toward it, much less run. Now we are almost eager to confront it, or at least, possess the sense that part of this confrontation is willed by us and thus has some semblance of control about it: "His knowledge of it, his life in the face of death, avails him nothing. But his having laid bare his own finiteness means a confrontation with it, which limits it for him, which makes it questionable and fragmentary. The knowledge of his finiteness reveals the contrary possibility." (ibid:252). What is this possibility? No less than the infinite. But since it is no less, and can never be so, it is to the cosmos that infinitude is attached.

So, while our human and even historical horizons betray ultimately our equally human finitude, the corresponding realization that things are much less limited in this manner than before calls into question the ends thought previously to have final hold over us. Living longer not only exhibits to us the possibilities held within our lifespan and those of others – and we mourn all the more forcefully its sudden and truncated loss due to this extension as well; hence the pushing back of the definition of what humanity is to the moment of birth and for some, even before this – but it also allows us to see just the slightest bit more of cosmic processes. This extended view cannot be underestimated. The very idea of 'possibility' is something recently renovated. Its gentrification, dressing it up with propagandistic fantasy, is only one side of the story. It is not true, for instance, to imagine that with a university degree the world becomes one's oyster. Or that the university has something for everyone. Or that it is the home of wisdom. But no matter. Each of us by our very existence retains the possible for most of his or her life. The very definition of what human life is has been radically altered. It no longer finds itself confronting death in the same way, nor does it seek to make life merely a way-station on some greater journey. Rather, it searches out the possibility of making itself worth dying for.

In doing so, we notice a number of essential features. Life still passes, but now we are concerned not so much with this passage but whether or not it passes us by. We have dropped the ethics of the otherworld into our own. This has not occurred without some translation, of course. The time of the gods which was no time and which could not be experienced as part of history – its temporality was expressed in the timeless narrative of myth wherein events held succession in them but metaphorically – was overtaken by the radically subjective time of our inner ethical life. Here, biographical history, memory and desire construct a new kind of narrative: "We are directly aware of inner time, and its principal feature, *succession*, is indisputable." (Wood 1989:62, italics the text's). Wood reminds us that even if we suffer abnormative breaks with the reality of succession, we are nevertheless borne along with it. Minkowski has already stated that those with severe mental diagnoses lose this very sense. It may be indisputable, but it can go unrecognized. And this sometimes by choice. But it is to be suggested on top of this that the possibility for its subjective loss resides in the facticality of paying so little attention to it in normative contexts. We ignore the succession of time as experienced, and call upon it only when there is some dispute as to what occurred or may have occurred. Perhaps this is one of the chief reasons why detective fiction remains perennially popular. Very often it is the succession of events that proves to be the source of the mystery. Solving it in fantasy absolves us from looking too closely at the reality of intersubjective and also conflicting understandings of personal history: "For in becoming intelligible, history would ultimately cease to be historical. We would eliminate the actors who make it; we would have a history wherein nothing happens, a history without events." (Ricoeur 1965:90 [1955]). Even if we are 'actors of our own ideals', we are certainly comfortable with professional actors portraying these ideals in entertainment fiction. Here, the ideal not only of the solution to a puzzle – what occurred and why and how, when and where, the usual interrogative suspects – is one thing, but its resolution is sometimes quite another. Knowing all of this, how everything went, might not mean being able to do anything about it going forward. Another ideal, that of 'closure' and all that *it* suggests to us, might be outside the realm of possibility, at least for now. For closure hails from the previous metaphysics and it maintains an ambiguous presence in our own. We would prefer, perhaps, foreclosure, which is something more concrete and also much more likely given a set of preceding conditions. Succession itself is demonstrated by the ability to tie one thing to the next, and indeed, to be able to think 'the next'. If succession really is indisputable, we would presumably never have closure in any final sense in any case.

The finite version of succession is based upon our own experience of time. To shore this up, the time of nature has of late become the basis for historical time. There is a simple compare and contrast going on here. But there is more to it than just that: "The progressive rationalization and profanization or secularization of history is accompanied by a corresponding rationalization of the concept of time." (Plessner 1973:236 [1951]). It is one of the great historical ironies that Christian eschatology held within it the seeds of its own demise. Demythology itself is heralded by the advent of a God on earth, a ludicrous idea outside of the mystery cults of the Eastern Mediterranean, of which Christianity was but one of many. But the appearance of such a being makes the earth into a world. And demythology, however progressive, makes the world into a social world. The worlding of the world, now horizontal, flattened with the fullness of finitude, is a direct result of the otherworld stooping too low to haul itself back up again. With this fall comes crashing down the remainder of the heavens.

Well, almost. We still have not yet viewed, as we alluded to above, the moment of creation. But it will come, in time. In another now patent irony, the first moment is actually the last. The first *shall* be last after all, and we can prove at least that. Once overtaken the Big Bang will provide not so much closure to the cosmic riddle but rather foreclose on the question of origins. This follows the logic of demythology exactly: "... events lost their historically secured character to the extent that they had been previously established and carried forward in an annalistic mode of writing." (Koselleck 1985:250). In a word, instead of myth *being* history there was now a history of myth. The past could become radically 'other' to the present, and just as importantly, Koselleck reminds us that it was now possible for persons to have new experiences, and new even in the hermeneutic sense (ibid). The idea of the new is itself new. Whether or not this is an improvement, the relation to which all marketing today seeks to convince its markets, becomes a matter for jurisprudence. But what had been solely the purview of ontology – transfiguration, the limen, the resurrection, the ascension, amongst many others – becomes in our time part of the facticality of the possible. It is true that some of us shun new experiences like the plague, but that does not effect the principle involved. With the ever pregnant next moment, the possibility of new experiences alter our ontology on the ground, as it were: "Interpretation is consequently founded in the structure of Dasein. All hermeneutics, all elucidation of the various possibilities of interpreting must refer back to this basic structure and so to the constitution of the being of Dasein." (Heidegger 1992:300 [1925]). And of course we *care* about this condition. All conflict arises from it, so in uncaring, in the absence of concern, lies death and the completion of Dasein's project, a finished work that can never be experienced. Heidegger cites Dilthey as the thinker who brought the historical 'into view' in a way that ontology could be given its new structure and interpretation (ibid:17). Such '"...works out Dasein's historicality ontologically..." (1962:62 [1927]), and not only as the structure of the being of Dasein but also "...the ontical condition for the possibility of historiology...". (ibid).In other words, being can now be studied as part of the material relations of worldly facticality. Its 'ontic facticality' can be worked out, resolved, even, but at the very least, given its ownmost possibility.

To underscore this shift in thinking about being and world one need only pursue the question of time. History, however Whiggish, must admit to not only succession but also difference. Discontinuity, rupture, discursive breaks, punctuated equilibria and the like are always options within the ambit of the new interpretation, but paradigms and regimes of truth are concomitant: "...there is no doubting the hermeneutic importance of the asymmetry between past and future; the future is the horizon of possibility in the *strong* sense. And it is a horizon that is essentially *finite...*" (Wood 1989:364, italics the text's). At the personal level this is presumed to be correct. But at that cultural, the very presence of a past that is understood historically allows for a corresponding future which is at least indefinite, as we will see below, as well as the sense that any thrown project is, in its very thrownness, part of something larger than itself. The indefinite overtakes the finite, and we will also explore in the second section of the introduction, how the idea of indefinitude has a similar relation to that finitude given such oblation in existentialism. If 'Being through time' had been the manner of understanding both beings and their ontology since the beginning of Western thought, the historical fact of time being now understood as an elemental part of the new physics allowed for a new interpretation of being, human or otherwise (cf. ibid:254). More so, it is 'presence' that is set up over against process, for instance, the language of becoming, appearance, thought, and 'the ought'. The definition of physical time as 'continuous' actually aids the discovery of temporal ontology in another way; there is a state to state identity between a moment in time and the condition of any possibility, physical and otherwise. The nature of becoming, or of thought, lies in the presence of what must be and then, what cannot be (cf. Horwich 1988:134). That this is a homology only leads to an overfull reductionism, but as an analogy it is most fruitful. Even our sense of human freedom may be said to rest on the declension of the moment to moment. Possibility is, once again, ever-present in the manner in which Being was ever thought to be. Possibility, in other words, has that same kind of 'is-ness' about it that characterized discussions of essence for over two millennia. So it is plausible to contend, "Free will is largely the capacity to change rhythms of expectation in time, to control intervals." (Lampert 2012:131). This interval thus is to philosophy what identity is to science.

And we live our life according to intervals. Essentially so, for it is only in the difference between this time and some other, either past or to be past, do we find both history and humanity alike. We cannot identify with anything else, so the scientific sensibility is lost on us at any personal or experiential level. We can note sameness and difference across categories, but whether in biochemistry or neuroscience, psychopathology or high energy physics, there is a range of events that tend toward some kind of mathematical essence, but never demonstrate it. There are intervals in science too, of course, but they can be operationalized more clearly than those of lived time. Yet the task of science is not to suggest the subjectivity of experience but to state the identity of conditions, one moment to the next. Whether cosmically or infinitesimally, the great chain of this kind of being demonstrates the extension of nature in a manner corresponding to - once again, by a stronger analogy than a too stringent homology – the extension of human history and still further and more personally, biographical longevity. The spectrum of intervals in the sciences extend beyond human experience, but its center tends to have our sensibilities in mind. The 'human scale' is one way of speaking about this more or less benign bias. We are told that Newtonian mechanics, though not a true description of events, nevertheless 'holds' within the realm of human activity. Or at least, so much so that we can avoid the ever-present possibility of a car wreck, for instance, or a missed flight. This holding, this attachment to our ongoingness that parts of the scientific experience itself holds onto is no doubt our modern version of the god who has an abiding interest in human affairs.

The human interval is thus crucial on at least two fronts: one, it allows us to understand the language of the cosmos as both attached to *and* detached from our subjectivity and from our history, but as well, two, it allows us to do the same for *and* to one another. Because in the midst of any two intervals there is a limbo, a kind of liminality which awaits all those who must travel from one moment to the next, as defined by human events and relationships, encounters and confrontations. Waiting out these intervals is an obvious exemplification of such a condition: "...because suspension of activity in deference to another entails forfeiture of alternative activities and associate rewards, deferential waiting comes sharply into view as a functional equivalent to sacrifice." (Schwartz 1975:42). Marking the hours wherein both intervals must be experienced and awaited, mechanical devices of ingenious though at first very unreliable design began to appear in Europe at the beginning of the fourteenth century, Milan in 1309, for example, and Cluny by 1340 (cf. Cipolla 1967:40ff). But the very fact that such hours must now be marked is the inevitable expression of both linear temporality but also the experience of it. Time thought in this manner was absolutely new, though its own history takes us back to the advent of eschatological thought. The overtones of the previous understanding of temporal relations were still present, and they remain so, from a sociological perspective, to this day. 'Sacrifice', however quotidian – and of late, tempered by the appearance of digital clocks and their 'smart' accessories; and indeed, is this not a recapitulation of the original appearance of the timepiece in public and private hands alike? – is still the lot of those who traverse the intervals. Intervallic time is a kind of absence of history, if not that of time itself.

No mere waiting, however, can describe the full picture: "Time, like money, is valuable because it is necessary for the achievement of productive purposes; ends cannot be reached unless an appropriate amount of it is 'spent' or 'invested' on their behalf." (Schwartz 1975:45). Metaphor aside, we live these expenditures and investments by passing from one interval to the next. We live in the hope of its possibility, as well as in the shadow of its doubts. These become our personal dreams and our self-doubts alike. Desire might be given a working definition along these lines as the drive to join intervals together, to overcome their differences and to stop time from taking them away from us. One's definition of 'productive' may vary widely. Playing a digital game on one's mobile phone while waiting to see one's doctor might be construed as productive given the age of the patient, for instance. Within each limen then, possibility does not desert us. We 'fill the time' until we can 'make it'. Rather perversely, perhaps, we can also make it in order to simply fill it. Retirement tends to produce this further condition, and it is viewed by the rest of us as characteristically 'unproductive'. Even so, this is mostly *ressentiment* speaking, or more gently, mere resentment. But the fact that we desire to pass from one interval to the next even if merely to 'see how things turned out' – more darkly perhaps, this can also be a reason to live on in the face of the option of suicide or worse – is tantamount to admitting to ourselves that in spite of the finite character of human existence, we desire to see time pass after all.

In the midst of this desire, in the expression of our possibility over against the old-world idea of ontology, we mark finite time in a way that not only juxtaposes various idealistic conceptions of events but has a mind to make them more and more similar to one another. If "...a possible event can happen at various times; an actual event happens at a particular time; a necessary event happens at all times." (Lampert 2012:38), then their interchangeability is to a certain extent, limited. But this somewhat 'Sesame Street' rendition of Kant's sensibilities regarding the logic of events betrays a deeper intent. The 'singularity' of the time-line is seemingly vouchsafed by their détente. Yet one can make the possible into the actual, and given enough impetus either way, this actuality can become an apparent necessity, especially given the current sensibility that nothing at all is ultimately necessary, even my personal death. All events are conditioned by the temporal context of their history and their enactment. Certainly, if one event that used to be necessary is no longer, that would require other events to become necessary in its stead, like my indefinite life requiring an alteration of my physiology and cognitive abilities. So perhaps what we *can* say about this simple logic of event and circumstance is that all three modes of temporal experience, intervallic in their possibility and alteration, are necessary to understand our relationship to objective time, such as it may be.

In displaying our affections for making the possible into the actual, with the desire to make the most valuable actuals into those perennial if not absolutely necessary in some idealistic sense, we encounter the difference, again, intervallic, between the inner thoughts of the actor and the 'temporal character' of the worldly device with which our decisions must come to terms (cf. ibid:186). In doing so, we thrust the present into the future, decisively, perhaps, but also without the realm of the absolute. What is finite is only what has been. The dead *have* buried the dead, but they have not done the same with the hatchet by which those who once existed and made decisions self-same as do we, even if they in turn were not our own, were finished.

Part of the lived ideal of the finite is the idea of 'lived synchronism'. (cf. (Minkowski 1970:293 [1933]). It characterizes an 'appropriation of ambient life' and is affective in nature. 'Syntony' is weakened by pathology, but Minkowski, in a very prescient move, shuns the definition of the 'normal' person as being either too ideological or too clinical or both. Perhaps

Heidegger's conception of 'averageness' is all the more accurate considering the difference between the finite and finitude (cf. Heidegger 1962:69 [1927]): "That which is ontically closest and well known, is ontologically farthest and not known at all; and its ontological signification is constantly overlooked." True, we displace finitude by way of the finite. In a similar manner, we do not discuss our absolute values, if we indeed have any at all, with just anyone. These *Wertrationales Handeln* that follow along from such are generally never of the order of either vision or vocation. Rational actions directed to an absolute value, from Weber, is almost an archaism. Generally, this may well be a good thing, given our experience with fascism. In their stead, and not necessarily in a means-ends relationship with them, are the *Zweckrationales Handeln*, or rational actions proceeding from finite goals. Such actions are *ad hoc*. Quite literally, they are directed to a specific purpose, and though this logic assumes rational action and not rational actors, at least, not exclusively, most importantly, it also does not assume rational *goals*. If finite goals appear as ontical elements in a landscape limited by specific and time-sensitive horizons, their accomplishment will depend on a kind of existential telescoping of not only focus, but will: "Having understood means nothing other than being this temporally particular understanding." (Heidegger 1992:259 [1925]). This specificity lenses itself through the 'world of concern', and this is how the world in its entirety is 'encountered' (ibid:195). Both goals and actions in this stripped down version of necessity or yet need can be defined by 'remotion', which refers to 'temporally particular nearness' to myself regarding elements of the world at large (ibid:225). Such a remotive quality is made diffuse by absolute value. In turn our goals, if we attempt to direct them afar in this manner become dissolute. No, the most focused and determined acolyte of any cause metaphysical or ethical still must choose between a number of front and center options, it is simply that he or she defines the ends in a manner of différance. Heidegger underscores the importance of the 'average' and the finite by reminding us that "*Everydayness does not coincide with primitiveness* but is rather a mode of Dasein's Being..." (1962:76 [1927] italics the text's).

Thus there is no sense that this concentration on the finite at the expense of finitude should suffer us an existential loss. To allay the anxiety that might arise, or might have arisen, from such a shift in thinking about *what* one must do in order to live on – the problem of the absence of why in modernity slides into its first new base squarely on the basis of the what – the concept of remotion designates a value. At once it suggests that "Time is not really a dimension of its own; it is more the negation, or the freedom, or the mobility of, spatial dimensions." (Lampert 2012:86). Speaking of Husserl, Wood also suggests that "... the language of temporal predicates belongs to the realm of the constituted and cannot properly apply at all to the constitutive ground itself." (1989:105). What is constituted includes finite goals and rational actions directed towards them. The 'ground' is the space, and perhaps also the time, of absolute value. This is what is missing in the everyday living on of Dasein as being in the world. Indeed, one might be stretched to offer some other definition of what it means to be in the world without the absence of absolute value and thus any ultimate why, including the understanding of finitude. Since 'average' action of 'normal' actors takes place in a remotive sequence and has always in its mind what is finite – the end of my action might correspond to the end of the horizontal appearance of this or that desired goal; that is, when I stop I have attained it – it is also the case that this landscape, ontic and perhaps even hyletic does not apprehend itself as a veil, covering over something more fundamental than it itself. This would contradict the sense that what is everyday, yet not primitive, is an elemental aspect of the Being of Dasein. Put another way, remotion relativizes or at least differentiates our ability to not only decide what part of the finite should be acted towards, but also the *how* in which this is to be effected. In relation to any possible ground from which such motives may spring, "Once temporal differences arise, the condition of immediacy and unity that would make signs unnecessary is lost, and the possibility of a prelinguistic immediacy seems to vanish." (ibid:123).

Needless to say, living on towards only the finite obscures the completion of Dasein's thrown project. Death loses its ontological import and becomes an outcome only to be avoided as long as possible. Such an outcome is characterized amongst all the others, including the promise and premise of an indefinite life. Perhaps this is why we are so enamoured of the lack of 'sting' in it that Hamlet was apparently astonished by. We hope this to be in fact so. Indeed, our birth carries with it the converse sting of a longer and longer life. Unlike that of the bee or wasp, the stinger of birth remains attached to its source, its venom slowly and inexorably drying up, but nevertheless, every last drop of it makes its way into our body. And we are made exquisitely conscious of this fact only through the base contemplation of the finite. For here we confront our limitations, rather than encountering our limits. This latter is reserved for the more reflective contemplation of finitude, which is easily characterized as a release, a pulling out of the stinger of birth, finally and forever.

So the reflexivity of remotion applies also to our bodies as objects, stung and stung again. Nostalgia for a time before time, that is, in human terms, before we were born, thrown into the worlding of the world without our consent, understands itself as being able to will backwards: "Reference backwards is consciousness's way of referring to its own body. Reversed time-order matches the spatial order of the body's already-thereness." (Lampert 2012:116). Before executing any action directed to a finite goal, we may well take stock on what we have accomplished thus far and the means by which we have done so. One salient question is always, and already, that of how much time does it take to do this or that versus some other thing? The 'already-thereness' of any body, and of anybody, contains within it all of the time it has taken to progress this far. Entropy is also contained in this equation. But remotion, the temporal nearness of an object, including a goal or a state, is reflected on in this manner only as a phase of the overall consideration we give it. It cannot hold us like either an absolute value or an essential or elemental object might, for it remains, even though briskly and keenly desired, simply another step. In pathological conditions, however, the idea of a finite goal or observable end is lost: "Our synthetic view of time disintegrates, becomes transformed into a succession of similar days unfolding in a boundless sadness and monotony. But with most of us these are passing states." (Minkowski 1970:187 [1933]). Surely it is not the case that only with the loss of will and desire we see clearly the reality of our condition? No, the pathological sensibility merely transfers over to the absence of will and desire the same focused intensity the rest of us have applied to the finite. In confronting our impotency, we generally change tacks. This is painful, without doubt, and may take up yet more time than we had originally bargained for, but nevertheless it is accomplished or it is not. If not, we adapt yet again. But some of us are transfixed on the point of that adaptation, seeing in it only the impossibility of attaining anything at all. It is a subjective form of nihilism that animates all still- births. Indeed, avoiding the sting of birth is in fact a desire, and one by which the pathological consciousness maintains its steadfast detachment from the world as it worlds along.

But it is not quite as simple as that. Given that all of us experience the moment of despair unto death, and lose our perspective on life because of it, if only in passing, we are made aware of the 'nullity' of human action and that the finite is somewhat of a sham after all. Lining up one's achievements, especially as one grows older, has less and less charm to it. Not only is the available time to add to this list on the wane, one begins to question the point of doing so. What *meaning*, in other words, lies in the accumulation of posterities that one can oneself never enjoy? In the moment of reflection, in which sincere doubting plays only a cameo at first, we are thrust toward ourselves in a way that is perilously close to the recognition of finitude: "Primordial and authentic coming-towards-oneself is the meaning of existing in one's ownmost nullity." (Heidegger 1962:379 [1927]). If temporality is indeed 'primordially finite', finitude suddenly is exposed as the bas-relief of what we had for so long considered to be merely finite. The facticality of 'time going on', to be taken more as 'carrying on' than ongoingness, now appears to be deeper than we had surmised. Or is it precisely because the absolute value of Time has been disposed of in the same manner as has all other such values?

Back to the problem of a continuous and integrated history. If time as an absolute element of Being cannot be approached in lived time, and is only encountered in a completed project, in the end of Dasein and thus also the end of experienced time as something lived, then the anguish surrounding the loss of action directed toward the finite, the recounting of accomplishments over the counting of days seems itself a little insincere. For we have already contented ourselves with jettisoning the value of these acts and their outcomes with reference to anything essential. Indeed, we might not have felt entirely comfortable, in our modern guise, in considering them at all if we were motivated by a value larger than ourselves. 'Megalomania', while not a new term, nevertheless has a new stature for our times. We would rather speak of self-indulgence or even egotism. Both of these reference the individuated consciousness of a finite being, not the extended and objectivizing consciousness of a being directed to, and by, its own finitude. If the latter were still in force in any serious way – rather than appearing as part of the myth-invoking narratives of entertainment fictions; the hero may still well be linked to the oversoul of humankind, for instance, and part of his or her journey is even so, still one of self-discovery that this is the case, and it is *this* aspect to which we are drawn, unlike our ancestors – we would have to admit to the possibility that will and desire were seconded, sub-contracted to some other kind of Being: "The idea of 'integral history' is therefore a limiting idea; any dialectic is oversimplified and overburdened with the criss-crossing of the longitudinal motivations proper to each series and the transversal interferences from one series to another." (Ricoeur 1965:188 [1955]). A series of goal-directed actions, that is. Yet is it not the case that in contemplating actions, in phantasm, as Schutz refers to it, we make ourselves as aware as possible of the conflicting adumbrations of x and y-axis variables? Our thesis, in this dialectic of the everyday, involves stating the case as it is. The anti-thesis is our action to adjudicate it in our favor, to change it, and the synthesis is the goal accomplished. Only within an integral history, understood here as something that denotes continuous and elemental time, the time of Being as played out by beings in the world, does any synthetic approach the standard of an Aufheben. Yes, it is correct to say that we conserve some elements while cancelling others of both the current state, the present, as well as whatever changes we then make, which are soon part of the past as well as what has been changed in the world immediately around us – others are of course quite another matter – and thus what is conserved may be said to be 'uplifted' into a new state, unlike either of its co-constituents. This new present however, never attains 'presence'; it is not a superluminal form. It is simply what is 'next'. It itself may be a mere link in a chain that carries itself forward, not as a thrown project, but one that is calculated and daydreamed in some systematic manner. It is a scheme, not a mission.

The absence of an integrating idea, an absolute value to human history as either lived or as studied or both, engenders what we take to be the finite, and pushes us away from finitude. Authentic being in the world does not shy away from the latter. But even here, is it realistic to say that finitude is a *goal* of Dasein? It is certainly one condition of it; I am finite in the existential sense and in the sense that I am historical in my very being. Rather, it may well be better taken that it is our goal to bracket finitude from our ownmost being. It is owned, but it also owns us, in the *lingua franca* of the modern world. Wandering with one's shadow no longer takes the high road. We seek the brightest light of constant action, even activity in lieu of action, in order to demonstrate to, rather than merely suppress, our shadow self that its sylph has but a passing place in our project. The very idea of a 'project', suggests plans, scheme, and actions of this sort and this sort alone. Work as vocation aside – this too may be a decoy – we 'spend' our time working or working to avoid working. Indeed, we are often astonished at the efforts young persons expend in avoiding delegated tasks. It is cliché to acknowledge the parental injunction to 'spend less time and effort avoiding work and more time working' aimed in a partly resentful arc at our children. Young people, in their partial socialization, have not quite been convinced of the idea that an absolute value can be attached to a finite goal. We should not be convinced of this either. The fact that we make the effort to push this quite worn peg into an ill-fitting hole "...emphasizes *a very profound dislocation of the phenomenon of time, with a prevalence of the past*, which, as we know, represents the most static aspect of lived time." (Minkowski 1970:284 [1933] italics the text's). Maturity in the hermeneutic sense is very much in opposition to the social and interpersonal ideal of a mature adulthood. In the latter, we are adepts at making the finite seem like the absolute. There is no 'beyond' of which to justify or even speak. 'Idle talk', notoriously characterized as being 'of the day' and 'of fashion', does not speak of it, and cannot do so. We might rather refer to it equally aptly as 'idol talk'. The marketplace may direct us to the future, but entertainment pushes us backwards, into the static past. The tribe even more so. Whether the 'old days' are bad or good is immaterial. Culture memory is loosely based on the bias of that personal. For after all, it is groups of fellow humans who write and produce the fictions by which we are drawn into a false consciousness of what can be lived, and indeed, what time it is: "In these conditions, memory intervenes only insofar as it is static. It thus undergoes a complete deformation in relation to the perspective of lived time, imposes itself in a mechanical manner, and finally usurps the characteristics of the present." (ibid:340). The religious overtones of worship, ritual, and sacrifice are thus maintained by the modern idolatry we willingly genuflect with regard to fantasy and fiction. One does not needs authentic memory to avail oneself of such narratives themselves taken out of the space of memory, of lived time. Their temporality is, in other words, *integral*. Even sporting events, where the outcome cannot be known in advance and scripts are relatively loose, must climax in the same manner as before. Teams may vary, but the structure of play and the goals are ever the same. This too is a ritual affair wherein supposedly great sacrifices must be made. It is myth writ small. It is heroism of the passing and the petty, though at a personal level there can be much suffering nonetheless. But there again, the 'why' is missing. There is no absolute value or ultimate end in any kind of fiction, even the charming allegory of sport.

One of the chief attractions of fantasy of all kinds is that the viewer, the reader, the one in attendance can witness both the beginning and the end, can be as a god. The time of these events is taken out of lived time. This is why such phenomena are commonly referred to as 'an experience', as if experience can be bracketed and uplifted in a dialectical manner from being-in-the-world as ongoingness: "Endings in a novel confer a kind of liberty that life stubbornly denies us: to come to a full stop that is not death, and discover exactly where we are in relation to the events leading to a conclusion." (Sontag 2007:223). There will be another Open Championship next year, after all. There is always another novel. Ironically, the very name has been superseded by the fact that the novel is not only not a new form of literature, it is, in its plot device and goal, nothing new at all. The idea of ending without having to commit to our own demise is certainly attractive. It is a major way in which we effect the transposition of finitude into the finite. Given that "The passage of the past into the present does not have a linear character. [and] ...this present is not destined to become entirely past..." (Minkowski, op. cit:165), we have to come to grips with the facticity, and not the facticality, that what is forgotten is not at all the past. It is simply what is *not*, and not even what is 'no more'. This is a relationship that exposes a piece of ontology to us, or better, *at* us. The recording and archiving of every piece of fiction as commodity and as consumer item betrays the desire to make sure nothing *is* forgotten. If one's own personal memory fails, we can consult the archive. It is no coincidence that the well-used on-line dictionary-encyclopedia Wikipedia has copious accounts of popular culture 'events' and personages and relatively sparse mention of anything to do with capital-C 'culture'. If the devil is truly in the details, our devil resides squarely in the round and ever deepening hole of popular culture, its oxymoron highlighted by the avid interest we maintain in keeping up its supposedly fragile ability to exorcise finitude from being.

Only something outside of mortal memory, old-fashioned at best, barbaric at worst, could withstand the idea that the devil now performs its own exorcism. To do otherwise would place us backwards into the time of non-sense, the time not of rational activity or action, but rather non-rational *acts*, always and already thus directed to an absolute value. Even if our existence is finite in the brute sense, "Man's knowledge of this fact as a fact raises him above mere finiteness; which thus comes to his consciousness as a fatality, as something contrary to his essence, an accident, despite its naturalness and matter-of-courseness." (Plessner op, cit:249). It is disturbing, perhaps, that in entertaining fantasy *and* reality too seriously, we rail against very gift that does so raise us above both.

1.3 The Indefinite:

The question of the future dominates our concernfulness within the world of beings. Previously, such care was directed as well towards the other world, not so much regarding its character or its future, as it was both static and timeless, but with regard to our fate within it. Now that both heaven and hell are earthbound, their two poles flooding the world with moral greyscale, we have a dual set of concerns that are at once, singular. The objection, the sense that the future of the world and its species are paramount, is at one hand. The subjection, the sense that I must suffer for the world to have any future at all, lies at the other. In spite of the presence of a nostalgia industry – whose chief function may be to allay concern about the past by fraudulently reconstructing it at every turn so that we might direct our gaze forward - it does appear that we are mostly future-oriented in our care, "...except for bouts of regret and self-congratulation. But why is this? Why is deliberation biased with respect to time?" (Horwich 1988:2). Well, one somewhat pat response is that we imagine there is a certain probability of control within our grasp. The past is been and done. In our temporal mechanics and metaphysics both, there is no going back. This knowledge may well be another impetus for the fetish we exhibit with regard to nostalgia. However that may be, what is to come, by definition, has not occurred. We can, given careful and even concernful planning influence it towards the good, or, at least towards our desires.

But there is more to it than just this casino-like aspiration. There is something as well to be said about the lingering aspects of sacred thought: "Being incipient refers to something that is not yet determined in this or that sense, not yet determined in the direction of this or that end, and not yet determined appropriate for this or that representation. This means that many eventualities – within reason, of course – are still possible." (Gadamer 2000:17 [1996]). This set of indeterminacies, or rather, what we hope to be a suite of merely undetermined but still determinable frequencies, implies a more sophisticated response to the question of the indefinite. Senses, ends, and representations may be said to gather the symbolism of the sacred together in a new way. In our probabilistic universes, there are still 'glad tidings'. Something incipient has barely begun. It is nascent, perhaps a renaissance, but at the very least, a new start or yet a new day. Mark this; a *new* day does not mean the *next* day.

And we do mark it as such. Hence the resolutions to do better things, or, more uncommon, to be better people, or very rarely, to be better at being itself, that mark the turn of annual calendars. 'New' Year's day is the only day of the year – with the exception perhaps of personal birthdays, which actually mark biographical new years – wherein the idea of advent and incipience is formally acknowledged on any secular calendar. What is being so marked?

On the one hand, it is a stronger and more socially sanctioned remarking with regard to control over one's subjective destinies, the probability that this or that will befall us over the course of the coming year, the one that is now incipient. More tellingly, it is a recognition that another year in the 'duration of the ego' has in fact passed us by, though New Year's Eve is also formally marked, once again, with a kind of melodrama of subjective nostalgia, to this end and others. But why mark such spans of time? What value do they have for us? "It is *the value of the virtual duration of the ego*, and this duration is, as we know, directly related to the development of the personality." (Minkowski 1970:364 [1933], italics the text's). So not only are we aware that we have a slightly more compressed span of time with which to accomplish this or that kind of thing, experience this or that kind of event, or become this or that kind of person, we also have to mark what indeed we have done, experienced, or become, in the meanwhile. This is more difficult, and shades our concern for the future into the present, perhaps even into what has been. Our sensation of how we make sensible the alterations in our personal development is also compressed to the point of it being taken 'outside' time, in a sense. We are made more directly aware of the present even if we are deliberately celebrating both the past year and toasting the one to come. Who *am* I and what *have* I done are often pointed, sometimes, poignant, questions. But what *could* I do and who *might* I be are also quite serious, perhaps the more so given our understanding of the connections between personal development and the self in time.

Husserl reminds us that "The duration of sensation and the sensation of duration are different. And it is the same with sensation. The succession of sensations and the sensation of succession are not the same." (1964:31 [1905]). Within the first tandem, we are much more aware of time passing, the sensation of duration. Exactly how much time has passed must be measured by some other instrument than our senses, that is, the duration of sensation. Within the second tandem, it is the opposite; we are generally more aware of things following one another than our feelings or experiences regarding them, at least while they are ongoing. Certainly, one can reconstruct the succession of sensation later on, when one is no longer precisely feeling as one had felt 'at the time'. But Husserl almost immediately asks the question of how these durations are themselves constituted (ibid:42). Our experience of them is one thing, to be sure. But it is the object that is immanent, if not necessarily 'transcendent'. Immanence opens up a kind of lighted space of being, but it remains incipient, so to speak, whether or not such a space is part of the intentionality of consciousness and thus in part a form of subjectivity while also becoming a mode of being-there: "For Husserl, time-consciousness is (initially at least) a form of intentionality, and for Heidegger, temporality is a horizon, an 'opening-onto'." (Wood 1989:162). For both, Wood argues, temporality is an additional way to describe any 'scene' already present. But for Heidegger, as is well known, the *Vorhandenheit* of Husserl represents a false start. In a word, a person is not a thing. Fine. This incipient characterology of myself and others like me grasps hold of an opening in part because it flatters the very ego which is to be 'developed' over time, or within time and in the world .We are not things but we also do not wish to be taken for things. There has been quite enough of that, we rightly feel, throughout history. But there be the rub: the history of objectivity contains the history of objection but suppresses it, just as the biography of subjectivity contains that of subjection. It is with Heidegger that we are able to gain a certain lexical flex with these Diltheyan terms. Following a lineage from Herder and kindred thinkers, Heidegger continues apace the effort to bring consciousness into itself, into the lighted space of what is both always already and what is about to be, that is, once again, incipient though indefinite: "The past was henceforth no longer to be preserved in memory by an oral or written tradition, but rather was to be reconstructed through the process of criticism." (Koselleck 1985:142). From this beginning - now well understood and even abused in the perhaps gentle but yet disturbing sense that we often offer critique without option, and that it is always easier to tear something down than to replace it - to the more ambiguated and murky sensibility represented by an ontology that always seems to be verging onto an ethics: "… *the history of the concept of time, that is, the history of the discovery of time, is the history of the question of the being of entities.*" (Heidegger 1992:141 [1925], italics the text's). This is clearly not Stephen Hawking. Heidegger speaks of an 'unfolding' of the question of being. Time is the guide, even the 'clue'. The merger of ontology and ethics that one observes occurring in the canonical text from two years later also stretches our understanding of what can constitute critique. Or does it?

The presence of the term 'but', in other words, the objection of the future pressed in against the subjection of the past, the tidings of the new world, brave, glad, revolutionary, elysian, or what-have-you, confronting the evils of the old, is maintained in Heidegger. He still speaks a sacred language. This is no doubt one reason why he has of late been referred to as the 'last metaphysician'. Perhaps. But being is not all it seems to be. It can be just as well said of phenomenology at this point in its history that "The temporalization of history endowed with an interrupted perspective made it necessary to consider one's position, for this altered with and in the historical movement." (Koselleck, op. cit:145). One's 'position' is always limiting, but at the same time, unlimited with respect to possibility, simply because the change exhibited in the present – the French Revolution is always cited as the exemplar to this regard – strongly implied that the future would exhibit the same structure of experience, if not at all the same events, as that would be in contradiction to this new experience. Once again, a combination of the pace of change and the lengthening of the span of human experience created a new way in which revelation could be known. A phenomenology that seeks to merge ontology and ethics through time preserves the sense of both 'epiphany' – *ekstasis* – and revelation – the 'opening onto'.

That this is still seen to be part of the objection to the world as it has been or even as it is, if this latter can be adequately understood in its own time, denotes its sacred aspect. But the sense that that very world in its objectivity objects to our presence as critics and as potential revolutionaries presents a problem: "...subjective time-flow is never entirely independent of intentional references to the time-patterns found in objects." (Lampert 2012:22). Since the experience of succession – either that sensation or of duration or both – is also an experience of the 'time-line' of a particular object, as we do not understand time to be one thing. It is too trite to say that many things are happening at once. How does a *thing* 'happen'?

We *do* sort through time by way of intentional consciousness. It is abundantly clear, both from our own quotidian experience as well as the conflicts in the world at large, that we focus on one thing to the neglect of another, one person versus another. We know that this concentrated intentionally concernful gaze can produce peril for both ourselves and others, but nevertheless it remains necessary. No one can take in the whole all the time. That is, no one can be in possession of all time, as connoted by the things in the world. We assuage ourselves by reminding ourselves of this facticality, something about onticity that we cannot alter. But it more authentically is something that attaches itself to our ontology. It runs more deeply than a merely material relation, or an intersubjective reality. Its ethics assumes that, given enough people caring about enough different things, all the bases will be covered. There are plenty of people, but the problem lies in the equally factical issue of there not being a diverse enough number of things on our plate with which to be concerned. Most potential cares are screened out ahead of time, and thus cannot even attain incipience. And we are ourselves only partially to blame for this effect: "Ordinary motivational time can be glossed as a structure of asymmetry between past and future, in which the past is complete and unaffectable, and the future the scene for projection of one's freely chosen ends." (Wood 1989:15). What is 'ordinary' about this conception is that neither is the past aloof to change – it is being rewritten all the time pending the politics of the present, or more benignly perhaps, archaeological discoveries and the like – nor is the future a free-for-all. Subjection will continue to impress, our objection to it may well falter. But it is not to the extraordinary understanding of consciousness or for that matter, time, that we should turn to raise our awareness of the authenticity of the indefinite.

In arguing for the precise place of intentionality in consciousness, the source of 'motivation' and perhaps more darkly, the vehicle for the screening out of potential futures and possible events therein, Husserl reminds us that "…the form of time is itself neither the content of time nor is it a complex of new content added to the time-content in some fashion or other." (op. cit:40). This desired 'addition', as if all things could be accounted for over time and given enough time, is also mindful of the dilation effect adduced by the observation of relative motion. We are told that this effect, so important for the new physics, is symmetrical (cf. Lampert 2012:101). Clocks tick more slowly in motion. But as everything is in motion, clocks, and everything else, including one's heartbeat, appear to move more slowly to any observers ensconced within a different frame of reference. Oh well, we might shrug. We can still collect to any analysis all of the frames, no matter how relative, and proceed from there. In physics, this at least is a possibility. But in the social world, fraught as it is with an obscuring yet vital intersubjectivity, the frames of reference and *their* relative motion do *not* add up. No sum of experience can be produced. One's experience of time as a subject does not 'go toward' the experience of time as object; only can it maintain a relation with *some* temporal objects at a time.

And the arbiter of these objects, in our modern world, is the clock. While even 'clock time' given relative motion, can be altered in our experience, its pedigree as a kind of pseudo-sacred object both allays our discomfort with relativity of all types, as well as provides a focal point around which other kinds of objects are gathered. Especially, objects that are deemed to have some relationship to time. Think of doing one's laundry, teaching a class, working a shift, commuting, cooking and perhaps even eating. Even sexual intimacies are aggrandized or disdained along a temporal axis, though mostly this is to be taken in jest. The lineage of interest in the clock and its strange abilities – counting something that isn't really there, for starters – began as early as did the thing itself: "As a rule, medieval scholars were not interested in machines, but the clock, because of its connection with astronomy, was an exception." (Cipolla 1967:56). This may be profound, but it is also symptomatic of the 'gathering together' of other temporal objects around the one that aspires to measure them. It is as if the clock has replaced intentional consciousness, or at least, is now its proxy. It is more objective – one might well cut class or work if it were not for its 'presence' – and it is more demonstrative. 'Everyone' can now observe the passage of time. Who is this 'everyone'?

Those who wait upon the clock. In doing so, we have ceased to experience the passing of time as due to the actions and intentions of other people. The clock is most importantly an instrument not of social control, but of social decoy. Certainly we use it in evidence to support the case against others – *you* have made me wait because, etc. – and in this it ironically calls attention to the acts and intents of other people. But it does so in a way that reduces consciousness to as mechanical a relation as the device itself: "...waiting is at once disadvantageous because of the immanent costs unique to it and because it is instrumental to the accrual of costs outside of and having nothing to do with waiting as such." (Schwartz 1975:182). Such 'costs' may also be measured, often by adding up the time served. In doing so, we once again reduce the gravity of what counts against our indemnification and even what might hurt us. What can be counted can be recounted, in a dual sense. I can tell you about my losses, but only in such a manner as you recognize them as being potentially your own. This conception of joint loss or gain animates our collective future, but it also denies to it the authenticity of the becoming of beings. Time passes but our experience of it is not only measurable but also is thus capable of being lost and found, like any other thing. Our experiences of persons, especially those the more intimate, do not have the same kind of ability. They cannot be recounted, so instead they must be recanted. In doing this, our intentionality is baffled by precisely that which it seeks. The time of our lives was held within the world of revelation and not of remorse: "…lost time is immediately 'searched for' within a spatial imaginary and within the discontinuity of language, so that spatio-temporal continuity and its fragmentation are not an antithesis to pure time but its servant…" (Kristeva 1996:194). This recantation we are called upon to offer up to the memory of those who are 'lost' must rewrite our history with them. They can never be as they were. The onus is on us to somehow also change, and to commit the time of revelation only to memory. This is more than simply avoiding 'living in the past'. We must also overcome the finite quality of human relationships. Within the indefinite, we tarry along for a while through not memory, but reminiscence. It is not without some substantial risk to do so for overlong, of course. In doing so, however, we exercise the editing process, exorcising whatever demonic force that led to the appearance of the finite. Human finitude in general is of quite another order. Just because we must die does not mean this or that love had to end. They have nothing to do with one another. It is on this premise – rational enough on the face of it, but ignoring the mystery of the aspect of living on that is in fact a rehearsal for death – that the finite is displaced by the indefinite, though not vanquished.

Whomsoever has been encountered, loved and lost, reminds us that the otherness of the other is the source of finitude in life, and its parallel is our own existential demise, which proffers finitude in death. There is a direct relation between the scarcity of an encounter with a desired other, whatever the social scene that fills this temporality, from love to contract and back again, and their accessibility. This relation runs on multiple rails: "The parallel also follows the extremes of price. Too much waiting time renders the server inaccessible, no waiting time makes him a 'free' commodity. In most cases, however, service is accessible but scarce, accordingly, the person desiring it must wait." (Schwartz, op. cit:103). Any encounter with another human being that we desire in some manner has an immediate scarcity about it. It is as if the other knows at some level that she is being sought. Giving oneself freely is unheard of. It is more common by far to hold oneself aloof to any other, at least until the cost-benefit ratio may be ascertained. Human relations are completely calculated, even if they are not entirely calculable.

But the editing process of reminiscence, a kind of backward looking anticipation that is on the way to memory, allows us to become ambiguous with regard to what occurred. By the time our sense of what was undergone ascends into the space of memorialization, we can live with the 'uncertainty' which plays itself out behind us, as it were, like a 'kinetoscope'. (cf. Kristeva, op. cit:280). Though we may well attempt to 'relive' what is past through future encounters – from basic appearance, as in a similar looking sexual partner, for instance, to more profound aspects of being such as imagining the vision quest keeps returning to us in fragments – we know we are not 'swimming in the same river twice', as Schutz puts it. The sensibility we bring to memorialization is this time one that knowingly seeks the indefinite. It does not desire to fix any point, to monumentalize what is done. Rather, it seeks to keep itself open to what could have been done, what could have happened. The prevalence of popular song-writing on this topic is testament to its widespread social function; 'what if' she and I had stayed together, or gotten together, or never met'? etc. "The concepts here are oriented in terms of an irreversible temporal process, loading its agents with responsibility while simultaneously relieving them of it, for the process of self-creation is included within the properties of the prospective future." (Koselleck 1985:262). Perhaps it is more of a reloading. After all, one of the chief factors in disdaining the human encounter, especially the more intimate it may become, is the issue of responsibility. Freedom, ironically, is all the more free the closer to its being bereft of responsibility. The gendered state of the loading of responsibility onto and into dyadic human relationships is well known, and it is self-evident why women report, over many decades, that they feel much more free outside of marriage-like conditions, while men feel the less so. Time is itself experienced differently along major gender lines, both within and outside of intimate relationships. It would not be a stretch to imagine a social world wherein men are constantly seeking intimacy and women just as constantly seeking to avoid it. Yet we are told, somewhat stereotypically, that the very opposite is the case. I doubt it.

Either way, it is clear that a gendered state of temporality is part of the equation of the indefinite, for it makes the waters of experienced time murky and divergent. It allows for the process of reminiscence to accrue a sentimental sediment to itself, as if the way in which we recall what *was* is transformed into what 'should' have been, and not merely the bare empiricity of one 'could', amongst myriad others. Whatever happened was, in other words, *meant* to happen. This is surely a cop-out of epic proportions. Events are so transformed, yes, but people may well be transfigured. In another summary move, those to whom we have been profoundly indebted, desirefully attached and resignedly detached become either more or less than human, depending on how the end of their temporal subjectivity occurred. All of this too is part of *Erlebnisse*, but the idea that it can provide us with a pattern of consciousness forces us to concede that our own biographical work, recall, that kind of duration of the ego within which personality is supposed to be developing – though, it is of note, this statement is made quite blandly and without the judgement of value; what *kind* of personality is being developed here? - does so in serpentine ways: "The phenomenological data are the apprehensions of time, the lived experiences in which the temporal in the Objective sense appears." (Husserl 1964:24 [1905]). A great many experiences then must be built up and into such a sense, though there is no immediate understanding that these must also come from a great many people, others to self. We are indeed, 'apprehensive' about doing so, about including the other's perceptions. For just here, our self would be pushed over the edge of the auto-constructed indefinite that we strove so hard to attain. Reminiscence provides more than a safe harbor for the specific content of memory. It is a process by which one is absolved of responsibility, moral or otherwise. It must be so, we feel strongly, otherwise one could not live on. Almost all of us have committed the heinous act of betrayal. Rationalization during the moment, in particular, is not enough given enough time. No, we would rather simply forget it entirely, and the memorialization function of biographical edit accomplishes this on our behalf. We have 'apprehended' that which had escaped us; the very absence of memory as to what 'actually' occurred. Similar to the criminal who is now caught in his own net of designs, we desire to be apprehended in this way, as long as it is ourselves who track us down and pin us to this or that calling card. Another notch on one's belt, so to speak, is the best monument we can muster in many cases.

What Husserl speaks of here, however, is neither history, nor biography, nor the politics of the rewritten past. Rather, it is the 'essence' of time that must be studied and apprehended by a certain analysis of the data that are phenomenological in character (cf. also Wood, op. cit:55). Like the relationship which ended – and how do we speak of 'failure' here in any specific sense, when by definition something that has ended has failed, even due to mere and unavoidable entropy; it is clear that failure is a morally loaded term in these contexts – and is thus rewritten - not as if it had carried on but precisely the reason why it did not do so - it is plausible "...that the history of our understanding of time is the history of our inadequate ontological grasping of it..." (ibid:142) mainly because ontology 'itself' is about what is present and yet further, in its presence. The present, classically, has no time and cannot be used to define time simply due to its self-understanding as both here and not here at once. It is more than elusive due to the facticity of its being unavailable to us without it already being past. All reflection is a memorial project. And yet all of this is old hat. 'Presence' and its deconstruction proceed from this point, amongst others. What of the metaphysics of self? That is, the one who undertook to bury oneself in the other for all time, only to find out that being indefinite accorded the other rights beyond my desires. This alone puts memory out of court, for no single recollection, as well as no single person who does the recollecting, can do justice – perhaps we would rather say, *serve* justice, for after all, we are supposed to be 'apprehending' something or someone here – to the past: "Detached from the real subject, facts 'pass away'. There is past, and there is past that has been 'passed beyond', 'transcended'. Hence the resentment against the yoke of the past..." (Corbin 1973:xvi [1949]). Even if we have managed to get beyond this or that occurrence or encounter, if we recall it to ourselves, it remains within history, it is not yet part of the unknowable past, the black box of human doings that have receded from what we had known to what we can never know again. *This* is the key ingredient to successful living on, especially when it come to intimacy and love. Yet at the same time, this is what must be avoided at all costs at the cultural level, if we are not to both blindly and blithely live on in ignorance of what we are capable of doing to one another. It is almost if the person must forget her past but the social body to which she belongs must remember it. Where then is the cleavage between the territory of the forgettable and the unforgettable?

Since the present cannot avail us of itself, it is part of the primordial character of Dasein to know itself only through what it technically no longer is. We only know a past self. The corresponding aporia is faced down from the other direction, that we cannot know our own deaths and yet we are completed by them. Dasein "...can never establish itself as a fact which is present-at-hand..." (Heidegger 1962:376 [1927]), we are an 'is that is a having been', a 'thrown fact'. But thrown toward the future only to, in becoming part our consciousness, rebound upon itself and pull away back behind itself. On the enlightening side of this temporal fencing match, this is the basic reason why we are not things, as mentioned above. Being present at hand is a character of the object in the world of objects. On the shadier side, however, we are only insofar as we are not. We are the only existential object, so far as we know, that faces this odd predicament, which makes sense only if we give up on the idea that the present makes sense, that is, can be experienced in any direct manner. Yet "The horizontal functions of time and temporality are part of the solution, not the problem. Fundamentally they supply a way of describing the dimensionality of the 'horizon' of what for Dasein is its 'disclosure of Being'." (Wood, op. cit:154). Neither time nor being raise by themselves an ethics. Fortunately, any ethics is a product of both future-oriented contemplation and past-oriented reflection. An ethics, in other words, does not need the present. It presents itself, rather, by turning what had absconded with, or monumentalized, presence into action. Morals can only present to us *acts*, that is, the action of the past enshrined and made material, timeless and yet breathing our finitude in our collective face. But an ethics by way of a temporal ontology reaches both backward and forward at once to relieve morality of its overburden. We *are* thrown projects, projecting ourselves in a fragile arc away from presence and all that it would imply and impose.

And we *intend* upon doing so. Only in this way can life be lived for finite beings. It is through the construction of the indefinite that life becomes livable. That things end can now be taken as a matter of course. They must do so, otherwise there would be no change, the crucible and catalyst for life to recognize itself as still living and not already dead. So the ethics of any phenomenology rests within this project of apprehending the finite and committing to its ambiguation. That it does so under the guise of an ontology merely tells us that being *in our time* is restive and restless and not subject to the objection of metaphysics. If "...what the phenomenological account of temporality allows one to grasp is the intentional structure of a certain kind of consciousness." (ibid:325), then we must pay rapt attentiveness, even concernfulness, to not only the facticality of other kinds of measured time, but more importantly, other modes of being temporal. Phenomenology does not in fact have a monopoly on the temporal analytic, as Wood duly discusses. Rather, "The search for *time* becomes a search for a *volume* in which the drama of selves can be played out..." (Kristeva, op. cit:190, italics the text's). For selfhood is quite self-evidently not timeless. It must be 'played out' because it cannot be kept in. 'From now on', however ironic this turn of phrase has also suddenly become, "The problem of talking about Being and of talking about Time are the *same* problem." (Wood, op. cit:223, italics the text's). Since history is the most powerful argument against morality, it suggest the same relation holds between Time and Being, capital letters or no. Though the history of ethics does show that it cannot stand entirely alone against and aloof from metaphysics – their separation is never complete, and perhaps this is also a clue to the mystery of finitude and another opportunity for the indefinite to take perilous but necessary hold within human relations and the human condition more generally – nevertheless change as part of consciousness, a change that can be known and experienced as having been known, *this* change changes everything. Like the ambiguous depths of a body of water, the 'volume' in which life is played out as a series of imbricated selves demonstrates the *presence* of time in our lives. It is an ongoing present, and is never simply present simply because it is ever-present. This would be merely an impoverished attempt at poetics if it were not for the facticity of competing and conflicting temporalities. It is also not the case that these are addenda or attachments other multiple selves that inhabit and inhibit social role 'sets'. Though we do experience time differently depending on social context – and perhaps one of the most persuasive factors in reminiscence is the problem of having experienced the time of beauty as a form of timelessness; we have made it noble without recourse to either history or morality – it is not the case that we cannot recall what we have lived through simply because the next social context calls for us to wear a different role-directed hat. If anything, we need this constant and consistent comparison of how we have acted in this or that other role in order to keep the scripts of the social stage straight. 'Playing out' selfhood is mostly this kind of experience, and not one that takes its metaphors too seriously, as in a novel.

If we are somewhat and sometimes overly and even overtly self-conscious about our role-playing, then part of what is often felt to be an encumbrance on life allows for the perspective that inures us to the beauty of time both passing and yet to come. We look forward to things, events, people, and even change within ourselves as much as we regret what has occurred, or what we may imagine has *had* to occur. On the one side, a highly rationalized version of progress hampers this perspective, as all must be enthralled to the sense that things can, will, and must be 'better' than they were. And in general, if not in principle, they are. This is no return to a Churchillian colonialism. A glance at the quality of life indices will confirm a certain kind of 'progress'. But this is not what sways us at a personal level, nor does it constitute 'lived experience' in a phenomenological sense. The more sophisticated by far is historical consciousness, 'effective' at its best, and disdainful of all affects. Yet even here, the lived experience of the individual realizes itself, as Gadamer is wont to point out, in the overwhelming absence of personal control over history. We are not the judges of the world and what occurs within its ambit: "Progress and historical consciousness reciprocally temporalize all histories into the singularity of the world-historical process. Without resort to a Hereafter, world history becomes the tribunal of the world." (Koselleck, op. cit:253). Akin to the always already lost present, our inability to judge what occurs in its own time is not only a function of being children of our time and no other, which is also now a cliché, but more penetratingly, being part of a conscious process of being-changed. This is the effect of historical consciousness writ into a phenomenological reduction. The glancing ray of any ego is transformative to the object, yes, but it is often neglected that it is also transfigurational with regard to the ego, so called. For what now becomes present in its floating presence is apprehension, in a sense, the very opposite of ego. For we must take this term not as a simple denoting of a selfhood stripped of its hyletic limitations. In judgement, transcendental or otherwise, we express the ego in the form of both what seeks to overtake its object – apprehend in the 'always gets his man' sense – and in the sense that it remains unsure of itself in its ability to do so. We do not, in fact, always get what we want, nor yet even need, perhaps contrary to the popular song. And just as our actions directed toward representing something or someone that has just as likely slipped through our grasp more than once, "...the destiny of a civilization remains uncertain, it may or may not invent the answers which will make it survive, or it may stagnate; it may cast off its outdated values or fall into decadence." (Ricoeur 1965:88 [1955]). Exactly the same may be well said of ourselves.

Uncertainty in principle is necessary for change to occur. It may be ironic, though not quite paradoxical, that ambiguity flows both ways away from the present. The open-endedness of the future, that which is to come but come as it will, it cannot come as it is or as it would think it is, is balanced by the shortfall the half-remembered past offers back to us in turn. Whether or not Time within philosophy is counter to the study of time as part of philosophy (cf. Wood, op. cit:264), and though the 'Hereafter' as ceased to be, there is still a 'thereafter', or more accurately, a 'thereafterness': "Death exists for me only because there is an 'after it' in me, and I feel so bound to this after that my life draws all its meaning from it." (Minkowski 1970:146 [1933]). The sickness unto death is not the absence of health in the usual sense of falling ill. It commits us, rather, to the 'afterwards' of our demise, though in a palpably trepidatious manner, speaking of yet a third form of 'apprehension'. It is in the approach of finitude that the indefinite holds out the longest and brightest hope of its conscious temporalization.

1.4 Indefinition:

The attempt to define the indefinable may be referred to as the process of indefinition. Within this process, what is known to be finite and yet also participates in human finitude is confronted indirectly. We act as if we understand the situation; we are within the definition of it, to nod to Cooley, and thus we can also nod sagely to ourselves about it. Part of this is a sham, but another part is authentic to the human condition. At the very least curious about our fates – it would not do to append the term 'ultimate' to any of this, for who can say if any notion of the afterlife is the final state of being; could there not be yet another afterlife after this? – we take hold of them until bereft of consciousness. But by then, of course, only the observer is left, and consciousness might be less, more, or no more. If Durkheim is correct in questioning the idea that death should confer extra privilege or power even if something of ourselves continues, then we add to our curiosity a sense of puzzlement. What is the point of death? The meaning of it may be more lit in life than within its own dark ambit. We find purpose in dying very much in life. The revolutionary, perhaps, or the loyal comrade. The lover who sacrifices himself, the mother herself, and so on. All of this is pat, if oft taken all too seriously and aggrandized in entertainment fiction to the point of malingering.

But that is about dying, not death: "…today there is a pronounced tendency to endow time and death with an exclusively existential meaning – that is, to consider them solely in terms of human decision…" (Plessner 1973:248 [1951]). We wish to place something definite within the penumbra of the indefinite, to use the finite to define itself more clearly. Yes, there is an edge to all of this; it is edgy in its emotion, fraught perhaps with a latent anxiety or even desperation. More than this, we are speaking of crossing a threshold into a space where nothing can be seen. Dying is nothing when compared to it, simply because we do all of our dying while we are still alive. Dying is part of living, but death is something other. Its otherness comes not from being part of life, but from being set apart from it. Can it too, along with the actual process of dying, coming towards it, meeting it head onwards, be brought into what is still life without it becoming the foreground of a still life?

One manner in which indefinition makes its mark upon the end times as defined by our personal entropies is through the extension of what has been considered normative through to the edge of total breakdown. This occurs through our popular culture – one can consume entertainment until one's final breath; the television above the palliative care ward bed is testament to this – as well as by way of our intersubjectivity. In defining death back into life – for animals and plants, they are one thing, but not for human beings – we do risk leveling the culture and perhaps committing it too, aside from ourselves, to a premature burial: "This threat is expressed, among other disturbing effects, by the spreading before our eyes of a mediocre civilization which is the absurd counterpart of what I was just calling elementary culture." (Ricoeur 1965:276 [1955]). It is tragically ironic that this is the aspect of our society to which the rest of the world is both attracted and repelled. The reactionary Islamic groups rail against it, so much so that they have redefined themselves in some medieval phantasmagoria that cannot but fail to relate to almost anyone living today. Yet the vast majority of people in the ancient civilizations of China and India, for instance, desire this inauthentic 'expression' of the West. The reason is transparent: everyone knows it is a shallow façade representing nothing of profundity, and hence cannot be a threat to serious culture. This is why immigrants to the West continue doing whatever it is they have been doing since childhood while partaking in everything else we claim to offer them. There is no conflict between the shallow and the serious, the popular and the profound. They exist at utterly different levels of being, and even conjugate their own respective temporalities. Very much like life and death., they are hung, nevertheless together in a new kind of indefinite definition. They are made to resemble living and dying, which are already the same thing. So, 'culture' both anthropologically general and exclusively specific, merge into an altogether novel creature of modernity.

What is more, the creators of this mélange also understand it. It is consciously calculated as part of a deeper decoy game. The minstrel wishes only that his audience does not see him for who he really is, expose him for what he really does. Traditionally, he even appears to be of the same kind, the same culture as is his audience. And we do not need to stop there: black-face has simply given way to class-face, language-face, humor-face, and so on. But more importantly for us, the time-face on these carefully measured and controlled hours of distraction is a combination of rusticating in prime time and beating the clock itself. The studied irony of one's own place in time is magnified to the point of indefinition. We no longer know who is real or even what passes for reality. And we no longer need to know: "For there is no necessary relation between the true importance of a man and that imputed to him by his own time – that is, by the representatives of the cultural canon. In the course of time, 'leaders' and 'geniuses' are exposed as frauds, while outsiders, outlaws, nobodies, are found to have been the true vehicles of reality." (Neumann 1973:8 [1951]). Of course there is always a politics to these redefinitions, but if we find we can rewrite history without most people even noticing – and part of the purpose of the spread of 'mediocre' civilization (and by the by, with it a rather mediocre attempt at civility as well), is to dull one's cultural sensibilities by narrowing even basic historical knowledge to the point of irrelevancy – we could certainly be pardoned for imagining that we could do the same thing to the present.

The 'in' that popular culture and its time out of time has to exploit and take hold within comes from the tension that exists between our subjective experience of time, the temporality of *Erlebnis*, and the measured physical time of both the world and the cosmos beyond it. World time is encountered only when we either desire or are forced to communicate with someone far way from where we are. Cosmic time is generally encountered not at all. Indeed, in a courageous effort to stand against the tide of mediocrity and distraction, famous attempts have been made to generate interest in the indefinite nature of the infinite. It remains the case that Carl Sagan's documentary series 'Cosmos' (1981) – more recently given a worthy 'reboot' by DeGrasse-Tyson - is the most watched television effort of all time. This does suggest that we are quite willing to encounter the serious and even the profound if it is available. The cosmos can be entertaining in its own right, though that is manifestly not the point of such efforts. But in being entertained, the indefinition of the tension between subjective temporality and objective frames of measured time is assuaged. We feel these tensions daily, especially if we work outside of the home and are on a strictly monitored schedule: "Sometimes ego-time seems to me to go more quickly than world-time; we have the impression that time flows rapidly; life smiles on us, and we are happy." (Minkowski 1970:297 [1933]). Clearly he is not speaking about wage-slavery at this point. It is ironic that the *tempus fugit* of happiness is a hallmark of the good life, for we would, more rationally, wish that this kind of experience of time be as timeless as the original 'in-time' sensation of it appears to be. On the other hand, we have plenty with which to compare it: "Sometimes, on the contrary, ego-time seems to be slower than world-time; time drags on; we are morose, and boredom takes hold of us." (ibid). In another patent irony, those without work, however numbly it itself 'takes hold', experience this kind of time. Here we say that we have time 'on our hands', in close proximity to, but evidently of an entirely different order, than the experience of time being 'in our hands', that is, wherein time is of the essence and we must seize the moment of destiny, and yet it is ours *to* seize.

But what if all of this is part of the ongoing fiction we tell ourselves to explain not only why these different experiences both exist and seem to co-exist but also why we do not generally experience other kinds of time? If we bracket out this set of subjectivities, is it not possible that "...everyday experience does not exhibit the passing of time [ ] memory preserves before-after sequences rather than letting them vanish." (Lampert 2012:111). Perhaps before we can ask such a question, we need to separate the sense of the passage of time culled from reflective machinations from the sensation of lived time as a form of ongoing being in the world. Boredom in our culture is different from boredom *with* our culture. The latter is more a kind of anomie, or at least, is experienced as ennui. Being bored in everyday life has only the significance of having nothing to do. This sometimes attains the pre-moral understanding of 'unlived' time. 'Down time' is one casual expression for it, but even here, we feel we either need or deserve such a kind of time, wherein nothing is *supposed* to occur. In our culture of work, at least - which would include the domesticity of both child and elder care etc. – time should be made available to us where we do not have to live at all. This does not mean dying and then coming back to life when the school or shift bell rings, but rather that we 'take a break' from life whilst still alive. These expressions of discontent are commonplace. But the ability to be bored with our culture at large involves an expression of malcontent, which is why we tend to shy away from it. So we parse boredom, the stilled life temporality of transfixed unconsciousness, from the more reckless and perhaps even revolutionary sense that something is amiss with the way in which we live time itself.

Just as we cannot expect to approach all of our ideals at once, we cannot live in all kinds of time at the same time, as it were. Idleness in one part of our life may reflect productivity in another, just as within organizations and institutions (cf. Schwartz 1975:28). Depending on our druthers 'at the time', the value we place on this or that kind of experienced tempo, *pro tempore*, or tempest, alters in relation to what occurs, or what must not occur, within it. 'Taking a break' means choosing to wait to perform some other task or make some other kind of effort. We willingly do so, or we are forced to do so. Either way, it is also clear that "...a common willingness to wait for a service sustains its objective scarcity which, in turn, transforms itself [ ] into a subjective value." (ibid32). This is all the more the case if the service awaited is one we must ourselves perform. Commonly parodied in sexual theatre, 'delayed gratification' in fact occurs all over the intersubjective map. If Koffka is correct in stating that the perceived unit of time is 'determined by its sameness with regard to stimulation' (cited by Mabbott 1951 in Gale 1968:320) – or lack thereof, given our most recent example – then we should by a certain point in our lives have become past masters at both procrastinating and overworking. Indeed, if we take the principle of deserving our down time too far, both relaxation and labor begin to approach their poles. It is better then to not define them too closely, and to break them up. It is well known that short vacations are more relaxing than longer ones in reference to how difficult it is, stress-wise, to return to work after being away from it for instance, for an extended period. Leaving 'breaks' within the ambit of indefinition aids in their keeping the work life off balance, disallowing it any total control over the rest of life. Lest this begin to sound like a shoddy shill for self-help, we should immediately remind ourselves that people spend a great deal of time and effort planning and then executing their vacations as well. Going on holiday is also work, especially if there are younger children involved, or if one's own health is beginning to falter due to the aging process. Cramming in all of the sights one 'must see' serves the purpose of making one feel relieved to go back to work. Further down this ironic avenue, are those whose family lives are so stressful that it *is* work that is seen as the true break. It is also commonplace to observe professionals, especially women, to whom the majority of domesticity still befalls, much more relaxed and in control of themselves and those around them in the workplace. They live *for* work, versus those of us who live to work, and the better, work to live.

In the home life of such unfortunate persons, time itself breaks down: "But the 'disappearable' of time is not there, and how can you take hold of time, when it was yesterday? There it goes on inside of me, always farther behind, but where? Time breaks." (cited in Minkowski 1970:287 [1933]). If our experience of temporality becomes too one-sidedly subjective, we are liable to fall into this sensibility simply because we cannot pay attention to world time as if we ourselves were a chronometer. The nonsense regarding 'biological clocks' as applied to purely cultural habits and habitus is part of the attempt to rationalize our desire to remain normative, if only to manipulate others. More seriously, but still too casually, the 'doomsday clock', whose hands hover between 11:30 and midnight pending the political tensions of the day, is another attempt to illustrate the approach of an end-time, to give definition to that which is by definition, indefinite. So the concept of indefinition, while it can serve us well being applied to the so-called work-life balance, does us a collective disservice when it shows up in other realms such as reproduction and geo-politics. If Russell is correct that our sense of the past, the present and the future are a subject-object relation and the simpler earlier-later relationship exists only for objects in relation to one another (cited in Grünbaum 1968:341, in Gale), then we have a more general case by which indefinition is carried forward by epistemological concerns. Our experience of time, an aspect of our our subjectitude, is a condition of the encounter with the world and with objects. The character of our place in that self-same world, experienced this time by others to self, is one of an objectitude, given that our presence objects to their own and that we cannot thus be summarily dismissed as mere object. This is a deeply felt experience, as it must be, and has even been party to some analyses of the power of art or indeed, the aesthetic object 'itself'. Art objects to us in the same way as do others. It is not purely and simply an object in the landscape of objects, but an objection in the world of objections. Yet it is not personal; that is, art does not object to us as individuals, but rather to the cultural conditioning that makes us desire the normative life. These norms are objectifying – the usual example of feminine commercial attractiveness falls squarely within this category of subjectitude – but they are also desired by us. They do not, in other words, entirely of their own accord impose their superposition upon us.

The same may be iterated at the level of historical consciousness, or rather, the level to which an effective historical consciousness points: "...after the establishment of modern historical criticism and Darwinian theory, it would be naïve to suggest any longer that history represents either a *single* process or one with a demonstrable *direction*." (Toulmin and Goodfield 1965:286, italics the text's). Just as with the day to day, the divergent possibilities of temporal experience may either be allied with one another or amalgamated with one another to the extent that each allows the other some of its own experience.

Once again, the self-help discourse uses these metaphors regularly, speaking of 'balance' in all things. This attitude, first exemplified by certain aspects of Greek thought, has a face value to it that is undeniably sensible. Why over-reach oneself in a single direction at the expense of all else that could be done or could be experienced? What is being reflected here, however, is not the enduring influence of ancient ethics but rather the very recent and still discomforting understanding noted above. Indeed, "…it *constitutes the totality of Dasein from the start*, so that it is only on the basis of this totality that Dasein has the being of temporally particular parts, that is, of possible ways to be." (Heidegger 1992:313 [1925], italics the text's). 'The start' being, of course, the beginning of the metaphysics of modernity. Social role sets aside, it is clear that we now believe we can *be* most anything, and we rather fraudulently instill this in our children also 'from the start' and throughout formal education. The evidence to the contrary is suppressed or bracketed. Social mobility is still in the minority, and there is as much downward movement as there is upward. But privately we have a little more leeway, and this is why our experience of time in this aspect of being-conscious has within it the 'unlived' time of doing nothing without any ultimate commitment to *being* nothing, let alone the encounter with 'Nothing', the very much still *something* that emanates from the dark well of nothingness and the source of focused existential anxiety.

Doing nothing for the time being also allows us the pretense of being no one. There is no one else to whom we might have responsibility. The hobby was a form of this absence of social being for many decades, though it is currently on the wane in many of its forms mainly due to the increase in labor hours per household. Being no one stops short of being nothing, of course, just as our temporary absence from the social world of role sets of obligations falls short of a non-presence. If time 'belongs in all its aspects to metaphysics' as Derrida famously intones, 'naming the domination of presence' (cf. Wood 1989:372), then we seek, through our dropping out of sight for a time, to experience a kind of timelessness. The purely private person, if he is so consistently and with calculation, may be more than the 'idiot' that the Greeks referred to him as, as we understand this term to be more narrow than did our forebears. But the hobby or like activity does not 'privatize' our selfhood for a long enough period to allow us the full measure of irresponsibility and self-absorption the true idiot requires. While we may engage in idiocy – the effort and expense involved in many hobbies may well qualify us as irrational, at the very least – the idiot, like the neighbor invented some time later, is not a social role. Rather it itself is a form of indefinition, a blending of lack of personhood with the desire to remain a person to oneself. Like any entity or object, the turning inward of a person can 'show itself in itself from itself' (cf. Heidegger 1992:81 [1925]), and Heidegger suggests that we refer to such an appearance as a 'semblance'. It is an apt term, for it is only a semblance of the self that retires from itself and into itself by way of a treasured activity or more radically and spontaneously, an unreflective action that imagines itself as part of a wider ethics. We speak of someone who is 'honest to a fault', or even a kind of 'kindness that can kill'. It is also true to say to ourselves, that part of which seeks the succor of the purely private and the timeless, that we can become "Riveted to the present, [and] our assumed attributes can sometimes bar us from the horizon as much as our bad inclinations do." (Minkowski 1970:113 [1933]). We can easily be taken in by our virtues, especially, shorn of their actual effect in the world of others, if they in the meanwhile have taken on a moralistic feature, which is also something that by no coincidence tends toward ideals of timelessness. For moral principles writ historically into stone or like material within the self, speak as if they were something *outside* of time. The metaphor of their being received atop high mountains is transparent, as well as their oft cited source as being otherworldly. Aside from the social control function of such narratives, their picturesque quality descends unto us and not only makes us small, it makes us long to be in that very picture, to be pictured with them. Hence the drive to clamber back up the cliffs and peaks and take photos of oneself at the summit. The most striking paean to this pose must be Richard Strauss' 'Alpine Symphony', where the brief movement 'At the Summit' soars into transcendence. But the humanity of both the composer and the art is revealed when the mountain itself takes revenge upon the intrepid climbers, forcing them hurriedly off the top and back down the sides into the relative safety of the valleys and away from the winds of a storm both natural and existential.

Like the relationship between the sciences and the applied techniques of popular science, the relationship between art and hobby is one of distanciated and perhaps paternalistic kinship. Any heroic narrative, even if reduced to the everyday scale of a nature outing, has within it both the practice of a skill and the art of a vision: "The art of a writer is to find as much as one can in that story, in that sequence… [ ] A conviction of the potential richness of our existence *in time* is also characteristic of the imagination that is distinctively novelistic…" (Sontag 2007:214-5, italics the text's). The indefinition of the hobby or outing collects our focused intentionally and narrows its scope. It means to be a means to another end, but the overarching narratives that used to frame these ascending ends are recently mute, if not lost entirely. The vocationalism of the personalist Christian in the West, especially in the United States, dos not connect with the mythopoetic tradition. It has, like the hobby, privatized itself unto itself. This is not to say that it can do no good in the world. Its kindness, if it stops short of killing, is still beneficial. But its purpose is self-oriented nonetheless. Not in the sense of pure selfishness, the irresponsibility of the idiot, but one acts to save, or at least, salve one's soul through the faith of aiding others to self. Plessner suggests that with Christianity more or less an impotent force for cultural organization, time itself has begun to lose all of its meaning. This fits well with the efforts to annul time in the hobby and even in the vocation: "Consequently, nothing remains of 'time' but temporality, just as nothing remains of history but historicity." (op. cit:259). Only in our time then, can we turn inward and ironically regain the search for selfhood and for time. Proust is certainly a major benchmark in this radically modern shift away from umbrella narratives that define what time is and what it must be. We are, quite literally, out of time, and this too is reflected in the conditions we have constructed for ourselves with regard to our technologies of mass destruction and the erosion of our environmental envelope. Children of our own time, we have in turn annulled the resonance of any time that would both save us from any end imposed upon us from without. The death of the 'old god of morals' has placed the responsibility for the apocalypse squarely on our huddled shoulders. It is not the case, then, that the 'last myth' holds us back. It is rather our demythology of the end times that presents the gravest threat to our continued existence. For as long as a God made the judgement, it was one which not only could never occur in real human history, it was one that we ourselves shunned and worked to avoid, even personally. Neither option is now available.

In our time, which is both indefinitely outside of time and definitely within the shifting horizons of competing temporalities, we allow ourselves to daydream: "Perhaps because there once was another time and another experience in which time-thought-language *had not taken place.* [ ] regaining time would also mean causing it to return…" (Kristeva, op. cit:239, italics the text's). But the very notion of cause is also called into question by both the timeless affect of the introverted space of personal pursuit as well as the loss of the metaphysical conception of time. The 'constant conjunction' of modern causality does not attain the latter space nor does it obtain in the former. The hobby or the outing are said to 'make time for ourselves', and this is indeed a principle exhortation in all personalist self-help literature. Causing time to return is seen as the same thing as regaining the self. Just as faith has been privatized to the point of idiocy – who, in the twenty-first century *after* Christ could take seriously the evangelical pulpit unless they themselves were persuaded that they were mufti gods on earth – so too has time. Even the idea that 'time is money' stated near the historical beginning of this new sensibility pushes its metaphor to a narrowed no-exit alley from which only idiots egress. In the face of indefinition, the personalist 'ethics' of both salvation and wealth attempt to redefine time in their own image. But any ethic worth the lives ensconced in the wider human ambit of finitude and finiteness alike must have a more consciously reflective adumbration. Such a temporal ethic would have "…nothing to do with either hundreds or thousands of years, as it has nothing to do with in general with measurable time. It arises directly from the ethical élan which opens the future wide before us, renders it accessible to us in all of its grandeur, and which, in going beyond death, is revealed to us through its own persistence…" (Minkowski, op. cit:146).

Indefinition is both the call and response of an ethics that has found itself paradoxically both in its own time and out of time. But is this really as new as it seems? For any ethical act was always both something radical to the morals of the time and thus also something that took its time by taking itself outside of its time. It heeded not the date, not the hour, but acted only in the moment whose presence had overcome, through such an act, its own present.

Chapter One

Introduction Section B: The Mundane – Deontic Facticity

> Uncanniness reveals itself authentically in the basic state-of-mind of anxiety; and, as the most elemental way in which thrown Dasein is disclosed, it put's Dasein's Being-in-the-world face to face with the 'nothing' of the World..." (Heidegger 1962:321 [1927]).

The idea of the mundane should ideally be taken as one is directed to understand concepts such as the 'fall', 'temptation', 'authenticity' and 'inauthenticity' in Heidegger. Ninety years and more on from his seminal text wherein these ideas are discussed, it is, admittedly, still difficult to do so. Here, we have designated the quotidian to be that part of experienced time that gives itself over to us in the routine and the expected. By contrast, the mundane is that which is predicted and predictable but nevertheless marks itself off from anything extramundane. Thus the mundane, like the inauthentic of which it is a sibling, should be taken without value judgment, unlike the quotidian, which appears to have a more narrowly defined merit and indeed seeks to have this narrowness applied to itself as a rationalization for its persistence, as we have seen. Within the ambit of the mundane we discover human finitude. As well, we find ourselves living within time. The mundane also has the character of ongoingness in the basic phenomenological sense, and finally, it holds out the promise of overreaching itself in a nebulous manner, for it is no longer beholden to any definition that comes at it from extramundane sources. This concept, introduced in my 2017 book, can be called indefinitude. It was characterized there as having a 'sacral state of being', and it is seen as understanding itself as 'being-desiring-being-fulfilled'. More on this below.

But first, the idea of finitude will be discussed. Unlike the finite, which presses into us from without, finitude presents itself as an existential horizon which is already within us, built into us, so to speak, by the very nature of our thrown projects. If anything, we project finitude back out into the world of forms through both the social construction of the reality of objects and our interactions with them and others.

1.5 Finitude:

If the existential aspect of subjective time holds itself into the world as finitude, broaching the finite with its presence and non-presence alike, then its source is kindred with the source of human consciousness itself, the 'moment' of the social contract, itself lost to a mythical primordiality about which it is more important for us to think of as an aesthetic object than any historical event: "Time was determined by an event that emerged from the unconscious at the moment when it was given form…" (Van Der Leeuw 1973:333 [1949]), and can thus be properly seen as a 'possession' of burgeoning first order humanity, like a dance, song, totem or clan crest. These can be so grouped because in the consciousness which is both conscious of its own unconscious and thus is, by definition, not unconscious of itself on this score and others, both 'care and meaningfulness' are represented by such objects and aesthetic phenomena alike. Indeed, it would be somewhat arrogant for us to separate them in some more Cartesian cartography. Let us instead let them lie together, even if they are both outside of our time and can no longer figure in our modern social imaginaries. Just as the artist Emily Carr once discovered in her travels a damaged Raven rattle laying on top of a shaman's grave, its objectitude representing itself for a final time long after it had already encountered its fatal ipssissimosity, we should understand the primordial consciousness to have occurred before the subject-object relation took hold. It is this 'beforehand' that also marks such time as the time of finitude rather than finiteness. Facticality was also not present at this point in the human endeavor. Heidegger uses facticity, alongside Scheler, to refer to this 'basic structure of life'. (cf. Heidegger 1992:221 [1925]). Thus the corresponding phrase to ontic facticality could be characterized as deontic facticity. Also first introduced in my 2017 book, 'deontic facticity' describes events that are both mundane and concernfully circumspect with regard to ontology yet without being otiose. Aside from both health and illness, aesthetic objects and our experience of them as well as the scandal of art, even the 'evil of art', as per Ricoeur, alongside the evil of the congested and too-intensified human confrontation are also plausible examples. Expressing the day to day, they nevertheless bring finitude into the mundane sphere as the chief form *of* their expressiveness.

If we take a look at finitude from the ground floor, as it were, we are led to examples that occur only in situations of everyday crisis, like the demand rates on hospital emergency departments (cf. Schwartz 1975:118), or more generally, in situations where time is experienced as burdensome, 'gestalts' which are 'dissonant' or 'unbalanced' (ibid:168). These kinds of events of course do pass, even if 'in the moment' we are driven and focused by them to a much greater extent than the rest of what constitutes mundane time. They do help us understand the 'closeness' of time to Dasein, exposing our being in the world as *it* is before lighting up the more penetrating space of being thrown into the world as *being* is: "…if we can understand how everyday Dasein conceives of 'time' theoretically in terms of an understanding of time in the way which is closest to us…" (Heidegger 1962:472 [1927]), then we are inevitably to encounter temporality. Perhaps ironically, it was the gradual gradient of measuring devices that graded time and marked it down as one marks down the lessons of the day that aided this recompense of nearness. In a word, the clock brought time down to earth.

At first, the clock was ironically immobile. Its hands moved but it itself could not be (cf. Cipolla 1967:48). With the invention of spring driven mechanisms, however, the clock's portability and thus its mobility increased. More people were making them, and just as importantly, more were also buying them (ibid:49). But most profoundly, they were being carried around. They were part of which that was *closest* to us. All of this early evolution effloresced across major European centers in the mid sixteenth century (ibid:53). The pocket watch was a Baroque era craze, an emblem not only of wealth but of fashion (ibid:54). It was, in a sense, the 'smart' thing not only to know the time – how often does one get asked for the time today, for instance? – but to be the *bearer* of the time. To be, in other words, like a figure of legend, Death, or at least Saturn. By 1800 or so, London and Geneva were producing an extraordinary number of timepieces, by some counts more than eighty thousand a year (ibid:75). If Husserl is correct in stating that both "…Objectivity and Objective time as being constituted by our lived experience…" (Wood 1989:60-1) is the elemental sense in which temporal being constructs itself, then it is clear that through the use of personal and portable chronometers *Erlebnisse* took on a measurable and objectifying status. In one sense, time itself became objectified by the bearing of the burden of *keeping* time, keeping it to oneself, or keeping it on behalf of others. The measure of simple time became with the advent of capital, a measure of not only self-worth but also the merit of these others. One became not only part of time but also a timed part of life. This aspect of the mundane experience of the day to day, the facticality of the ontic world, was transformed into a facticity, one deontic in its import, by the presence of that which could mark what the present was made of: "Anything which, taken ontically, *is* in an average way, can very well be grasped ontologically in pregnant structures which may be structurally indistinguishable from ontological characteristics of an *authentic* being of Dasein." (Heidegger 1962:70 [1927], italics the text's). What if the timepiece grasps something here, 'letting something be seen' in a phenomenologically apprehensive manner? The averageness of an experience is, as we have noted above, subject to our objections along the line of temporality being experienced in a manner disturbing to us. But such a category only defined in this way would group both the uncanny and the otiose together. They are both close to us, no doubt, though the latter is by far ascendant in terms of measurable time, the time it takes to occur and the fact that it seeks to place us within the objective time of the ontic world even though it ironically fails to do so. Not unlike the Kairos, such a category of temporal experience "… has the aeon in it, but over it lies the eternity in total otherness. Originating in nothingness, it leads from promise to fulfillment and ends in eternity." (Plessner, op. cit:242). One can begin again with the stop-watch, for instance. One can 'time oneself' as well as place oneself in time. One can keep time in the performance of musical art or dance, or one can miss a beat, as does one's heart at the sight of the beloved. It is clear that Heidegger is quite correct to imply that what is commonplace and even 'average', once again, in this non-committal value-free pseudo-Weberian manner of speaking, is at least a bold clue, not to utter an extramundane transcendence as Peter Berger would have us believe, but to humane and lived Being and thus only thence to ontology.

The value and privilege of presence does not have to push us in the direction of vertical transcendence simply because it may also be seen as infinitely repeatable. Both my present and the present as a moment in objective time possesses this characteristic (cf. Wood 1989:117). Does presence thought of in this way annul the imposition of my own death as also a future that will become present in the latter but will never be present for me? One might refer to death as the non-presence of the present, or more technically, as the existential absence of a subjective presenting of oneself *to* presence. Yet it is not immediately clear what such language accomplishes with regard to the overcoming of one's own finitude. The present does indeed overcome it if we are also present to experience it 'as such.' Its being-present-to-hand is neither something that is conferred upon us as Dasein nor does it come to us in the form of an object. It's 'at-handedness' is also overcome by its actuating arrival. It is no longer something imminent, but rather has become a lighted space of immanence.

We might object that in recognizing this we are no longer experiencing the present at all. Some kind of object has passed in front of us, taking an aspect of our own immanentiality with it. Lampert suggests Bergson thought more or less along these lines; that past objects were still somehow extant and could be 'used' and that consciousness could directly perceive the past as such. (cf. Lampert 2012:140). This could make sense with regard to the differences between the finite and finitude if only the latter is understood ontologically, that is, with respect to some form of beinghood that alone understands its end to be its completion, unlike an object, for instance, which can place itself complete before us. Finitude, even if it is what takes us outside of time in its immanentiality, nevertheless has its own kind of temporality to it, and this means that "...'temporal' can no longer simply mean 'being in time'. Even the 'non-temporal' and the 'supra-temporal' are 'temporal' with regard to their Being, and not just privately by contrast with something 'temporal' as an entity 'in time' but in a *positive* sense." (Heidegger 1962:40 [1927], italics the text's). The temporality of being ends its isolated status. It charges it with not only immanence, it reflects in its presenting-to-itself the facticity of the imminent. It is always already ready in its at-handedness. Even as early as 1916 Heidegger was developing this point, one which had its roots in Herder and Dilthey; that the concept of time in history is fundamentally different from that of physics. (cf. Wood, op. cit:139). Following from that, acts, intents, even phantasms must also participate in a different kind of time than do mathematically constructed events: "Their noemata are temporally variable, in-between imagined and actual time." (Lampert, op. cit:187). Needless to say, even imagining a time to come takes its own time, very often, much longer in any measurable sense than does the moment of its actual appearance. But just here, might we not suggest that the idea of 'actual' is artificially telescoped to reflect only physical time? Perhaps it is rather that the actuational sequence, which includes its own end as experienced in a manner that might be taken metaphorically as a rehearsal for our own never-to-be-experienced completion as the imminence of human finitude, is as well something that metastasizes us from the mortal to the immortal. In setting upon any project of action our intent is to see it through to its completion. We begin it and we end it, and we experience both. So it is *not* the case that only a god can see the beginning and the end. It is more correct to say, as did many a god before us, that godhead *is* both the beginning and the end in its Being, which is something that we cannot be. This wider kind of Alpha and the Omega are not available to us, and indeed, this could be a negative definition of finitude, exposing to ourselves what it itself lacks.

But what we *do* possess are the starts and ends of all other kinds of being in the world as it is. These temporal sequences are enacted both in history and as history, and like the gods themselves, because of their very ability to be experienced as beginnings and endings, we can turn away from them at will: "History seems to be disposable in a dual fashion: for the agent who disposes of the history he makes, and for the historian who disposes of it by writing it up. Viewed in this way, both seem to have an unlimited freedom of decision. The scope for the disposition of history is determined by men." (Koselleck 1985:199). As soon as a god took an active interest in human affairs, it found itself within the ambit of human history. This could be understood as a god's fatal mistake, the only one it needed to make in order to ensure its own demise. Perhaps this is real reason why God died, and not so much the waning power of the belief of his would-be followers. For human beings never carry on indefinitely anything they begin. *All* things must pass, including the gods. Very much like the non-mathematically defined forms of being and experience, Being and Time have become projects which hold within them their own finitude.

In our own time, we have long since accepted the variable fate of decision, action, intent and desire, but "...if there are to be distinctions within the field of psychic phenomena, they must be distinctions with respect to the basic structure of this indwelling, distinctions in the way in which something is objective in these lived experiences." (Heidegger 1992:22 [1925]). We have never had occasion to admit that non-mathematical 'entities' or events are somehow less objective than their less variable counterparts. Not unlike the claim made about the past – it is no longer present but it maintains its presence – the whole structure of intentionality not only constructs the objectitude of others and the subjectitude of myself, but also apprehends the world of objects so that they are endowed with a meaning that in fact completes them, makes them *more* objective than ever they could be 'in themselves'. Their *Wesenschau* is included in their full presence. They have become, in a word, immanent and have lost their imminence as something approaching us or for that matter, as that we engage in our approach to them (cf. ibid:27 for the three basic discoveries of phenomenology to this regard). We 'live thematically' in this apprehension, and do not 'live directly' in perceiving an object (ibid:99). This understanding brings back into temporal focus the metaphorically inclined manner of perception to be found in cultures closer to the social contract than our own. There, we are often guilty of thinking that aboriginal time has 'no meaning', though we are mostly making a pejorative remark about the lack of concern for measured punctuality. 'Indian time' then is both venerated as a kind of Rousseauistic fetish – imbibing in hallucinogens is sometimes thought of as a way of experiencing this kind of 'dream-time', or 'the dreaming' but this is likely inaccurate – and derided as primitive or ignorant in some manner. Neither is correct. Instead, it is quite plausible that the 'logic' of mythological analysis annuls time and not the myths 'themselves' (cf. Wood, op. cit:351), which still must be narrated within time and with the intent of constructing an alternative temporality. Myth 'reunites' a culture with the time of its origins, themselves variable and subject to both 'liberation from time' but also to metaphor. (cf. Kristeva 1996:213). Indeed, the artist or writer is often thought to participate in his or her intentional acts in a similar manner as do pre-agrarians. This is not quite naïve. For instance, "…Proust's version of 'pure time, which captures the past and the present through a metaphorical coincidence, seems to be in accordance with Bergson's notion that the past coexists with the present." (ibid:316). Every present refers to itself and to its past. Through myth and its narration, a culture can both refer to itself as it is in the now and how it was 'back then'. And it is this relationship that explains the 'why' of a culture's continued existence.

We too have our myths, but they tend to focus rather narrowly and perhaps also morbidly on our culture's non-existence. One could speculate at length about the reasons for this eventuality, but suffice to say just here, that our conception of time, ever since it began to include its own null points at either end of its ascendant yet fallen arc, has projected human finitude into itself all along its linear being. We have not, in other words' lost time' but instead found it, and found it to be wanting: "Prognosis produces the time with which and out of which it weaves, whereas apocalyptic prophecy destroys time through its fixation on the End. From the point of view of prophecy, events are merely symbols of that which is already known." (Koselleck, op. cit:14). Prophets may be consistently disappointed, but they never lose their faith in the idea that the end will, sooner or late, arrive. One can always misinterpret symbols or even ignore them, but yet they remain. Hindsight is as clear in prophecy as it is in commonplace decision-making and the interpretation of daily life. It is also just as handy a rationalization. For prophecy is neither other-worldly nor is its subject matter any other world but our own. Its 'fate' so-called, is itself a metaphor for the variability of human decision-making and the congeries of our desires, for all these must come to an end. In myth, the sum total of human experience is both described and brandished.

Modern art reenacts myth without reproducing its specific cultural contents. Even when the subject matter is so directly focused on the temporality of lived time, the structural relationship amongst the elements of mythopoetic narrative are preserved: "Placed within a time that must be lost, *the characters turn into giant metaphors* that have the privilege of evolving within the duration of time while erasing it and replacing it with the narrator's recollections." (*Kristeva, op. cit135*). Any narrator of myth or yet more modest story must place his audience within the sphere of its action. She herself must also become part of the voice that reanimates the 'original' events. We need to feel like we are 'there', as with any narrative and character development. We develop along with the characters, and we are quite aware of their metaphorical relation to ourselves and to the world. There is no such thing as a 'literal interpretation 'of anything. This is an oxymoron that in fact does more by far than any pre-agrarian mythic consciousness to be the 'machine that suppresses time'. If our narrator fails in her resolve to place us within the action and intent of the characters, to share their motivations and feelings with us, then time itself is lost.

But it is not only the narrator's fault: "If time is lost, it is the fault of the characters, who wear themselves out by trying to define it too closely." (ibid). This indictment points us back in the direction of the problem of measured time, or mathematically defined temporality. Since the art of human decision is temporally variable, as well as are its outcomes, and since mathematics can only offer us a zero point and never an ultimate end or a beginning, defining such things with too much precision inevitably would mean the loss of time. Not only is such a practice a waste of time in the casual sense of the phrase, that one has lost time in doing so, but also that one loses time as a kind of experiential object, like an aesthetic object. But if we must speak of definition, *discourse* about it, we must avail ourselves of an idea of time that is itself temporalized: "The problem of their existential-temporal structure *cannot even be formulated* with the help of the ordinary traditional concept of time, to which the science of language needs must have recourse." (Heidegger 1962:400 [1927], italic the text's). Even the experience of becoming does not yet grasp the future of itself. Talking about what might occur is the finite version of speaking about what *will* be. This latter represences finitude in the world of forms while at the same time representing it in the world of discourse. Yet one might well parse out the differences between either an 'ordinary' conception of time – measured and subject to certain kinds of marking activities as will be seen below – and that 'traditional' – cyclical and subject to a different set of marks. Our ordinary conception of time in fact betrays little of that traditional. In our time, "…the future, truly understood, begins for me only beyond that point." (Minkowski 1970:82 [1933]). And it is in our conceptuality with regard to the future that animates our entire understanding of what time is *for*. For the future is where we will not only be - it is what is next - but it is also the time in which we will not be.

The mythopoetic finitude of that paradoxical presence of absence is reflected by the loss of time to a precision-making prophecy. Such an attempt may not at all be religious in content. But however it be cast, it is clear that "The End of the World is only an integrating factor as along as its politico-historical meaning remains indeterminate." (Koselleck, op. cit:8). Just so, if it is defined 'too closely' or yet populated by a cast of characters that are themselves too clear in their intentions and their desires as well as in other more commonplace social variables – the 'elect' – the clarity that the event is supposed to bring to us falls on its face. Too close a resemblance of the vital characters in any narrative to real persons tends to defeat the purpose and presence of metaphor. One has to be able to imagine oneself in the movement of the story, and if this or that persona who is already there trumps our description of the essence of ourselves in its gravity or depth, or distracts from it in its detail, we are lost to the time is proposes to reconstruct for us. There is a finality about the end time that cannot be duplicated in its approach by any metaphor. For "Final time begins in the midst of historical time. In the New Testament as elsewhere it is announced to the peoples by omens – Adunata and wonders. But it also sets its stamp upon time." (Van Der Leeuw 1973:348 [1949]). The impossible event wherein things are brought together in a way that finally exposes their true relations – akin to magic by which the basic principle of 'things once brought into contact or together, remain connected' – weaves every last thing into its adunatic tapestry. There remain no loose threads. But this is an end that is itself an adunatos. For there can never be an end after which there is nothing at all. There, the end of time presents itself as a summing up of that which has been. But once accomplished, time, if not history, continues to simmer along somewhere back behind the presence of the event. It is not so much on the back burner as on afterburners. It moves more rapidly than did historical time, simply because there is no longer the variability of human finitude as part of its content. Yet it remains.

Certainly one can say that 'before' such an event – not just before historically, as in, 'I'm waiting and waiting and nothing is happening', but also a 'standing before' – it is reasonable to impugn our standing by reminding each other of its ontic qualities: "The inauthentic temporality of everyday Dasein as it falls, must, as such a looking away from finitude, fail to recognize authentic futurity and therewith temporality in general." (Heidegger 1962:477 [1927]). Once again, it is notable that the idea of the future is what animates our conception of all aspects of time, simply because it is within the future and the future alone that exists the purpose of time, and being in time. But even this betrays a kind of eschatological drive. Its desires may be distracted, overcompensated, made into neuroses perhaps, or driven forth into that very future in a way comparable to always keeping poor drivers in front of one on the road. On top of all this, we are also to take what is clearly inauthentic in that it does not resemble the reality of human finitude as somehow no less valuable to our beings as the authentic turning towards and confronting one's own personal death. No less real, certainly, but no less valuable? Similar to the turning of one's back to another person which can still be seen as a form of 'ritual rejection' (cf. Schwartz 1975:177), the studied nonchalance in the face of the subjective non-experience of finitude could rather be seen as the clearest manifestation of the finite imagination. As well, precision, the fetish for making predictions based on probability relations, from the casino to the weather-map, may flow from this 'turning away' from an authentic relationship with futurity. It may also be viewed as a regression, or at least, an attempted one: "...if one talks to a child about the end of the world or about death, either these things will not have the slightest effect upon him or he will expect to see them occur immediately." (Minkowski, op. cit:363). But at the opposite end of the human temporal experience, the figures to which Tiresias is the apical ancestor have somehow overcome this lack of perspective. They have done so by engaging in the arts of both creation and re-creation, as well as perhaps the lesser devices of pure recreation. Either way, they have performed the opposite ritual to turning one's back. They have turned to fully face the future and not only that, embody it as the lived expression of human finitude as experienced. They are, in a word, old: "In the creative solitudc of the Great Old men, the limitations of the epoch are passed over; they have escaped the prison of time and the ego-bound consciousness." (Neumann 1973:17 [1951]). A kind of Gnosticism is granted them. But the 'them' in each cultural case is really a set of metaphors. Maturity, perspective, even wisdom such as that held within the pragmatism of sense now more common to those who are elders without being the aged, has allowed these figures egress from their own history. Thus we are to understand that human history as authentically turned towards provides the clue to its overcoming.

1.6 Living Within Time:

It does so precisely by eschewing the finite for the indefinite, the precise for the variable, plans for projects, and the consistent for the constant. If one can loosely characterize the evolution of cultural consciousness as a passage from an originating collective unconscious to a recognizably 'awakened' canon of some kind (cf. ibid:6) - though one can immediately question the sense that our primordial ancestors were unaware that they had become quite different from their animal cousins through the equally murky passage from instinct to an unconscious that could drive the production of culture - it was just such a canon that negated the passing of time. Living within time at first meant to be unconscious of its presence or its passage. One can straightaway agree with Augustine when he comments "For there was no 'then' when there was no time." (in Gale 1968:40).

But is that not the nature of the unconscious? Even the most public of its expression, the half-recalled dreamscape from which we are suddenly awakened, in a cold sweat perhaps, or enveloped by a kind warmth, depending upon the message meant for us and only us, does not speak of the 'then'. Rather, the 'when' is paramount, though this reference too is not precise. Our relationship with the individuated unconscious is very much kindred with our society's relationship with its cultural canon. Both must be brought out, or even brought about, the one by psychoanalysis or something like it, the other by critique. Though overlapping, these dual forms of introspective reflection both also pass through the Augustinian subject. By our own time, "...each psychic structure has its own way of placing the unconscious 'outside time' within temporal duration." (Kristeva 1996:326). Because the connecting link between the collective unconscious – if this is a conception that can be applied to modern cultures, polyglot and even cosmopolitan – and the canon as well as, writ small, between our waking, social being and the language of our unconscious mind is the imagination, it stands to reason that the "... *experience of the imaginary is the experience of time regained...*" (ibid:195-6, italics the text's). What was first placed outside of time – it's presence bracketed in a quasi-phenomenological manner – is not exactly lost, but rather archived, akin to all of the cultural canon that remains extant but is not exhibited. We can think, perhaps too easily, of a museum, a gallery, or a library as the material expression of the human brain. What is called to action, to wakefulness, and to work, is both a small portion of the canon along with all of its infrastructure. For the person, the daily meals and commute, the quotidian conversations at home and the workplace, for the archive, the cleaning staff, the physical plant, those who welcome visitors and aid researchers, its accountants and its security systems. All of this and more in the service of the canon, though indirectly, and its partial representation. Just so, all of our daily efforts preserve at least our potential to exhibit and express that part of the culture that lies within us, mostly subconscious but not necessarily subterranean.

And just like the canon, the vast majority of which is stored, saved for another day, the next exhibit or the next student seeking a source, time is itself mostly unnoticed by its live-in denizens: "Time is presented to us as an ever present *primitive* phenomenon, vital and very close to us, infinitely closer than all of the concrete changes that we are able to discern in time." (Minkowski 1970:18-9 [1933], italics the text's). Such changes include those that affect, or are effected by, ourselves. Of course, and in due course, there must be a kind of translation made between what lies in the cognitive archive and what can be expressed even by the richest imagination. Proust, amongst many others - but never so many as to call into question the imagination of this 'set' of canonical voices – cannot represent everything about his culture all at once, or even over the changing life-course. But what can be 'regained' is not only part of the time of his life, or our own, but as well the manner of coming making it our own; we come home to what is already always present. We realize that we are living not only in time, but *within* it: "When the world is thus regained in time, it is not surreal but placed far inside the imaginary and subjected to transubstantiation." (Kristeva, op. cit:224). What this process of coming home both to oneself and to the world of forms expressing the cultural canon into which one was thrown as part of its project - and from which one can be ejected if one's *own* projections do not tally closely enough to its temporal orders – implies is that time and being are never two things. Even so, the more distanciated they might become does suggest that they can be at odds with one another. We might feel, again, perhaps too easily, that we 'should have been born in a different time' if we find admiration for a specifically temporally related set of cultural figures, Berlin in the 1920s, perhaps, Vienna in the 1900s, or Paris in the 1870s, not to suggest that in the intervening decades these centers or others were suddenly dormant. More commonly though is to hear from others or feel in oneself the dissonance between who we are and the 'when' in which we *do* find ourselves living. Our level of maturity may be ahead or behind most others of the same age, for instance, a common enough experience for adolescents in our culture and one that is strongly gendered. So quite without phenomenology, without *Wesenschau*, it is simple to observe the intimacy of time and being. Its 'primitive' aspect lies not in the occluded primordiality of the R-complex or such physiognomic formations but rather in its proximity to us. It is not at an distance of any kind, evolutionary or otherwise, but rather is with us and within us in its immanence. This kind of time never 'comes to' us, it is already and always present. This is authentic presence, and it reminds us that any 'account of temporality' must be 'essentially participatory, and that we are "...temporal in our very being." (Wood 1989:326). Heidegger speaks of a 'double involvement', wherein consciousness must needs have 'its own essence' exposed to us by intentionality within the realm of lived experience. This is testament to the 'gulf' between us and the merely animal form of consciousness or being. The 'distinction between immanence' – just characterized by our innate yet absolutely human ability to live within time – and 'transcendence' nevertheless "...establishes the possibility *within* which the transcendent world [ ] can become objective at all." (1992:98 [1925] italics mine). Now in this sense we must be cautious about rendering what can or cannot be 'objective'. Living within time, bracketing both the finite and human finitude in general if not in principle, we can immediately turn down the path of lived time and the experience of its passage as part of our own subjectivity: "Subjective time is constituted in absolute, timeless consciousness, which is not an Object." (Husserl 1964:150 [1910]). There is immanence in perception, but the continuity that allows perception to make sense to us as part of a lived world of both forms, others, and events, must include something from our memory and this 'whole' must be taken as the 'now' (ibid151ff). This is clearly not transcendence in any way. And yet why not? How otherwise could what is past rejoin itself to what is present and support it with all its previous being? It takes its place 'alongside' what is occurring, and not alongside in the sense of the object world within which we are ourselves placed. It is not we who 'tarry' along in this space of shared time but rather, due to the ability of time to transcend itself, we are able to experience the entirety of a phenomena that objectively speaking might continue or last for minutes, perhaps hours 'at a time'.

If "...intentionality is a structure of lived experiences as such..." (Heidegger 1992:29 [1925]), then it is not our intent to 'coordinate' a set of 'psychic states' and then make aggrandized claims about their gestalt qualities. Neither is the understanding of the structural processes involved nor the events or experiences 'themselves' something that occurs all at once. Yet by means of intentionalities, that is, plural, we are also told that both immanent time is constituted which is also 'Objective', and so the flux of time-phases, 'pre-phenomenal and pre-immanent' *and* that this 'is' in a remarkable manner, constituting the experience thereof as both immediate and flowing. The flux is present in the flowing. It is no wonder at all that Schutz follows his teacher's lead here by referring to the analogy of the river. Changing yet continuous, the flux within the flow is the same thing with regard to our perception; fluvial displacement as temporal event cannot be taken apart, as might other overused but apt analogies such as the tapestry or even the book 'of life'. Immanence and transcendence, both available to us within the time of the living because they are inseparable as two 'intentionalities', provide for us a kind of aspirational matrix that once again, 'within' which *Erlebnisse* occur as gestalts and not as analyzed aspects of temporal eventuality. There is nothing, in other words, of the 'between' within them.

The abstract metaphor of the 'space of time' should not deter us. There is no 'illicit spatialization' occurring when speaking of "…temporal betweenness while still leaving it open whether there are irreversible kinds of processes." (Grünbaum 1968, in Gale 1968:326). Just as it 'takes time' to cross any amount of space, even though space and time are not directly related in this specific manner, so does the space in which time 'occurs' coincide with its occurring. One always is somewhere both in space and some-time within time. 'Somewhere in time' is a mere figure of speech to this regard. Even the more phenomenological expression living 'within' time suggests a 'spatialization' along these lines. How can one be 'in time'. Musicians are perhaps most aware of this phrase, but they must take it both more literally and more figuratively than the rest of us. On the one side, one can 'keep' time and thus abide within its rhythmic enclosure. On the other, one is kept *by* time, it encloses us and we may or may not be willing to reside within its arrhythmia. But all of this timekeeping, all of these sections of rhythm do not sustain the sense that time *is* space and vice-versa. Similarly, the classical imagery concerning chaos, the 'back side of God', or the life of hell, "...in the image of man plunged into pure time, into absolute change…" (Puech 1973:66 [1951]), are to be taken with a grain of salt. The more so today than ever, perhaps, as we do in fact find ourselves immersed in constant, though not radically absolute, change. Even so, the anguish of hellishness remains, especially for those who have aged out of the commonly constructed and targeted 'space' of fashionable time, wherein everything is geared towards one's desires and expectations. The elderly in our society find themselves living in an alien world, and one does not have to stretch the imagination to envisage a 'day in the life' of any older person, though resembling the very inverse consistency of that of Ivan Denisovich, is nevertheless no less like hell.

Living within time does not grant us an special dispensation concerning our relationship to time. Just as the fact that we make history by living within it does not allow us to shape history in our own image, or to take especial offense at the history that has already been made. The 'confrontation with the tradition' is something necessary for historical consciousness to become effective, but it is a studied, patient praxis of reflection and not a sudden stand-off 'between' times. No, time has rather a 'distinctive ontological function', which in turn means that temporal is simply 'being in time', which Heidegger immediately admits as being 'pretty obscure'. (1962:39 [1927]). It is a separate, though related, question as to how exactly time *has* acquired this 'self-evident ontological ability'. He tells us that it is unquestioned 'to this day'. This may be overdramatic, but nonetheless it is well taken in the wider sense that such things as are unquestioned in our own time may well have a lengthy pedigree of discursive aloofness behind them: "Historical time here sets its own dissimulating work, its disparity, against the assimilative quality of the understanding. The historian cannot elude the nature of time..." (Ricoeur 1965:27 [1955]). This, and 'within' which it has been supposed that the 'original otherness' awaits its confrontation with the selfhood of our own time and being. The ongoing work of interpretation, itself a kind of 'objectivity' that participates fully in the flowing flux of being in time and yet having to be in its own time at once, is never a guarantor of apprehension of any essential quality that is elusive precisely due to its 'inexperienced' state. We cannot be in the when of its occurrence. We must make it reoccur for us. Whether or not understanding is *so* assimilative that the ;gulf' between immanence and transcendence is thereby both recapitulated and yet also overcome, dialectically or otherwise, or gotten beyond, as in some kind of deconstructive effort, is itself an open question. To push the difference between the stuff of history and the discourse of the historian too far - which no doubt Ricoeur is not here doing – is to exalt mere change into the principle force of dissimulation: "Time itself becomes a title of legitimation open to occupation from all sides. Without a temporal perspective, specific concepts of legitimation would no longer be possible." (Koselleck 1985:259). Certainly. Even so, change is also a function of the simple passage of time. Entropy in the world of objects and in the animal consciousness remaining within the human experience - the latter contributing in some basic way to the breakdown of cognition - and nostalgia, reminiscence, the pulling back of all memorialization and stretching out and forward of all anticipation, specifically of the end of the need to look forward 'any more', all play a part in the 'disparity' of historical eventuality. But it is sage to note that the transposition, the bringing down to earth of a metaphysical principle of legitimation - one that, say, a hypothetical church may have had during the heyday of its monopoly over thought, if this was ever the case - does also confer on such an ideology a kind of regime function that desires to enhance itself at the very least through its 'assimilative' drive. It desires, in other words, to be God on earth, the being of the world. All dictatorships have this political represencing as their goal. Less petty are the socializing institutions of a so-called liberal society, wherein one's lived-in time is taken rather to be time served, and not at all regained.

But the historian's vocation is to transpose what is within another time into our own. Not of a piece, of course, but as an 'understanding', as Ricoeur suggested, that somehow remains relevant to our consciousness of what our own time consists. No mean feat, this 'effectiveness' encounters as series of dissimulative moments. Some of these take the form of aggrandizing distraction, witting or unwitting: "Theoretical consciousness determines the truth of phenomena; it situates them in a field of the infinite series of real and possible witnesses. It does so by undertaking to answer for what it represents as given, to give a reason for its presence, a reason that would be valid for anyone." (Lingis 1989:89). This is just the first bump in the road. In this, theory too desires to assimilate what is left of Being. Shunning metaphysics in principle thereby becomes a mere ruse. There is no longer an emperor, but his wardrobe remains. The assimilative consciousness of discourse also desires to restrain persons at the level of cultural imagination and ethical action: "Answering for what is given to it and answering to all coming and possible contestations, the theoretical subjectivity makes itself equivalent to any infinite series of real or possible subjects." (ibid). And what is more, we are generally content to have this take place. One aspect of it is surely the reliance on 'expertise', something that Weber famously warns us against as being contrary to human freedom in general and democracy in particular. Even if hardly anyone reads a discursive text, the direct product of the philosophical imagination, nevertheless, like fashion itself, the time of its production and the time it has created by being produced descend in fragments and figments to the mundane consciousness. Indeed, this descent, itself a refraction of the fall of Man, transforms what was quotidian into that which is mundane. It lends the world a manner of worlding itself that includes human subjectivity in its transit. But, "...this transformation of the will already subverts what I have called 'ordinary motivational time'. One is to will – not just accept, but *will* – what has been, and the fact that time will continue to pass over into the past." (Wood 1989:23, italics the text's). Nietzsche's revaluation of temporality notwithstanding, the gravitational pull of the will subverted here is more commonly understood as subjection, and not even subjectitude. It is one thing to 'will the past'. Like active versus passive reading of a text, one now has a real stake in history. Correspondingly, Nietzsche exhorts us to take that stake as homologous to the one which we also have in lived time, the time of our own lives. Becoming who we are involves just such a transformation of the generally *accepted* notion of the will.

One actively affirms the passing of time. Time is one of the beautiful shells and rocks on the tidal beach, its surf giving and taking away time after time. We sit on the sand without rancor or ruination. We will the surf's approach. We thrill at its imminent becoming and wonder with heightened sensation whether or not we will be inundated. But this is part of the play of life. It is the new presence of godhead as the world of change. There is no discourse held within the immediacy and inevitability of the wave-front. It *itself* is what assimilates, precisely by scouring the beach and exchanging its treasures for others. Can we also perform such an exchange with our own personal history, as well as that of our culture? *This* is the profound question that Nietzsche has posed to us.

Indeed, we may approach a positive response without even thinking about it. Minkowski reminds us that this 'lived synchronism' which is embodied in the combination of activity and becoming is something that we not only take for granted, but that we generally, unless hobbled by illness, *can* take for granted (cf. op. cit:337). It is to time as lived that generates the ability to live within time. This is so for "...neither the idea of measurable time in the domain of the normal nor the distortion of time in the psychopathological domain can extinguish the phenomenon of time as lived." (ibid:15). It is noteworthy that Minkowski places objective time and the most extreme departures from it as *both* outside of the mundane sphere. Yet this is eminently sensible, recalling Schutz's famous distinctions between the world of science and the world of mental illness, both distinguished fully from the everyday wide-awake world of social reality, which consists of the vast majority of human experience and interaction. Indeed, in a move that at first appears to be the very opposite of phenomenological analysis, the everyday world of form and of appearance is bracketed, not away from the investigation, but from all other elements radical to it, so it can serve as the object for the heart of the investigation. 'Social' phenomenology aside, what has been apprehended is the recognition that the search for essences best begins not with abstractions but with the effects that most of us live with and within most of the time. Lived time also 'creates the conditions of its own proliferation', as Cipolla has said about the spread of timepieces of all kinds (cf. 1967:104). Indeed, the core of temporality and what contains the *Erlebnisse* which animates Dasein is held within the ambient ambit of being's becoming itself, being's on the way to itself, which is completed only when there is no time remaining to live within. This onrushing which is really mostly ongoingness and bears no semblance of desperation or anxiety to it other than the anxieties of the everyday or the travails regarding an unknown future, is more accurately described by being 'pressed for time', that is, time as something other to oneself without which one lives in both relevant senses; one doesn't have enough of it, and one is living outside it rather than within its existential envelope (cf. Schwartz 1975:191 and references within).

Even so, the withinness of being-time is not entirely salutary to one's sense of well-being, whether of the inauthentic projection of social selfhood into a world that cannot recognize who we are to ourselves, or the more authentic self-recognition that this is the I who I am and I am moved by this, that I can understand myself and become a mature being in the hermeneutic sense. In our very self-knowledge we are put at risk in the Gnostic awareness that time is also a tragic theater of the absurd. This is not only a mere possibility alongside other lighter themes, nor is it something that occurs because of the others . It is rather, once again, more akin to Nietzsche's reminder that in saying yes to one joy we also say yes to all sorrow, for ..." time is anguish. Horror takes possession of the man who feels engulfed and crushed in it, century after century, throughout the interminable expanse of his successive rebirths..." (Puech 1973:67 [1951]). The ascent into Nirvana in Eastern systems acknowledges this aspect of living within time as a foremost issue for being to solve. In getting beyond the cycle of rebirth, we are freed from time itself, and this is a good thing. But in the West, timeless being is associated with godhead more directly, and one can only participate in it through grace, rather than by meditative work and leading by ethical example. In the very idea of grace is still, of course, the sense that time carries within *itself* the most grave risk to being. We begin to approach this risk, symbolized by both its feeling of gravity – it is something that draws us downward, as into the grave – and its graveness – its very graven imagery points in the same direction, beneath, below, barefooted being to clotted non-being – through the "...feeling of a *gap between one's own life and ambient becoming*, as well as a feeling of impotence and very often of distress, is found at the heart of the phenomenon of 'growing old'." (Minkowski 1970:312 [1933], italics the text's). While at the heart of existential entropy, Minkowski is quick to remind us that we at most times of life can experience these grave doubts about not only our ontic selfhood but about our ontological self-worth. Inhibition and the bitterness that reacts from it are all too common an occurrence in our society, and they may even devolve as far as real *ressentiment* in some cases or contexts. We find ourselves outside of our own time, though the objective space of the historical period in which we continue to live despite our inner protest and doubt concerning this connection, makes all the more clear to us the fact that we have dropped out, lost our place in time while maintain it in space. This is why Kristeva suggests so strongly that the margins of temporality become more singularly spatial: "...by avoiding time's two implacable imperatives, - death and change, which are also the imperatives of *desire* [ ] what we might call a 'timeless time' locates a series of sensations on the margins of time, that is, in space." (op. cit:189, italics the text's). She also notes that Proust himself likens this kind of space to a cathedral. It is an apt metaphor, for do we seek succor and solace in such a space when things are not going our way, or when the time it takes to accomplish something important in life simply will not be there for us. We have not exactly run out of time *per se*, but we have had it close in on us enough that other projects must be constructed or larger one's recalculated and resized. Indeed, we are immediately thrust from the being-within to the being-without. We feel the chill air of such a space wherein time is in competition with our being rather than an intimate and indissoluble part thereof, and we of it. What we *have* done is 'run outside of time', even if we have not quite run out of it.

1.7 Ongoingness:

In doing so, we become as the broken hammer. We *do* experience the absence of the meaning of our being. To recover ourselves in time, both before disaster truly takes hold, but just as importantly, to place ourselves back inside time and thus regain the time of our lives and not some other time, some other's or as a measured object, which are always present to 'tempt' us, in the Heideggerean sense off the term, outside of lived being, we must turn to ongoingness. But the experience necessary to do so is not immediately and without reflection available to us. Ordinary experience as well as the 'problematic that arises from it' are equally insufficient for an examination of the 'Interpretation of time'. (Heidegger 1962:352 [1927]). Beforehand the primordiality of time as a conception must be clarified. If not, Dasein 'covers itself up' with its own temporalizing, and this is a 'deviation of Dasein from itself' (Heidegger 1992:274 [1925]). This everyday deviation is in fact called falling. It is something that happens, a 'movement of being'. More tellingly, it is a constitutive structure of Dasein and one that is most constant. Dasein 'loses itself' in this seeming simplicity of falling. Though we are told time and again that such an elemental movement is neither vulgar nor base, but simply is, we are moved to take seriously the injunction that in losing ourselves, we must find ourselves again, and we cannot do so by virtue of relying on the 'Das Man' caricatures of what is uprootedness, no matter how 'solid' or 'everyday' they may be.

This does make sense. It is not a paradox. Why so? Ongoingness holds within it both the existential time specific to our own being and all of the modes in which we are to be, and have to be, to exist as a being-in-the-world-as-it-is. Even curiosity is discussed as a manner of falling and uprootedness, though it is one of the elemental roots of our entire existential evolution, and we would be nothing like ourselves, in our most authentic being, without it. Yet curiosity, the human ability to take an active and abiding interest in something that at the moment before had no hold over us whatsoever, is in fact part of the process of regaining authentic being. It does not have a purely ontological import by itself because it is always distractive to its own authentic presence as part of our essential beingness. It distracts us by making us attend to specific content, the 'about which' we are curious, and the 'manner in which' we can be curious about this or that something in the world, or this or that someone in the social world. We thus get carried into and onto the worlding of such worlds which are not our own and we thus lose ourselves in them. Though it is sometimes necessary to do just that – for, in regaining the being-time of withinness we must temporarily leave it be, leave it 'on its own' and also *to* its own devices, part of its very ownness, for *Dasein is part of the falling of time* – it then necessarily bequeaths to us a task of recovery and of rediscoveredness.

If "Our experience of temporal process is continuous [then] Any sub-divisions within it can be made only in terms of content. Such sub-division is always to some extant arbitrary and sometimes impossible." (Mabbot 1951, in Gale 1968:319). Such partitioning of time descends to us from the imagined acts of cosmic creation, seven days or some other series of marked intervals. As James famously pointed out, this is part of the great human egotism regarding our place in such a creation, as if God had need of "...the human imagination so that the world and ourselves could be." (Minkowski, op. cit:51). Rather, lived duration and succession and the experience of this as a continuity without partition or arbitrary marking off is connected not by creation, but by the 'principle of unfolding' (ibid:30-1). This too is an abstraction, as Minkowski readily admits. In order to experience ongoingness, however, we need not only to remark upon it in the forms we will discuss in the following chapters, but as well, simply mark the time by using whatever happens to be occurring 'within' it or that which we are participative in. But 'whatever happens' is a function of falling, of the happenstance of the movement of being whose mode of being is falling, and thus losing oneself. So ongoingness presents itself to us as the scene *in* which the fall occurs, but not the device *by* which it occurs. The latter is occasioned not by its happening to be ensconced in general ongoingness, the kind of temporality which, in its tempo markings, feels to us to be either too slow, too rapid, or 'just right' relative to the event – a good experience may not last 'as long' as we would like, for instance, while a negatively defined one almost always takes 'too long' to complete, though we must immediately qualify that our value judgments in either case are *also* a result of fallingness and the loss of being – but rather by the immanence of ambiguity by which ongoingness is characterized. Never knowing quite what is going to occur is part of the subject for both idle talk and curiosity. Predictions regarding the weather are only the most obvious example of this ulteriority of connectedness that masks the unfolding. Historical happenstance merely further occludes the matter. Heidegger goes so far to state that "Genuine historiology is nothing but the struggle against this movement of the being of Dasein in the direction of covering up by way of its own public way of having things interpreted." (1992:280 [1925]). Though one may wonder why everything is characterized as such a 'struggle' during the Weimar Republic - aside from the obvious material reasons; Hitler's notorious book was written at the same time as Heidegger's seminal volumes – nevertheless the 'intensity' of talking with one another is seen as a mark of the ability to cover over the more authenticating 'against one another' that the inauthentic Mitsein is meant to distract from. This might indeed involve a struggle of some kind. If breaking up time into little bits and pieces is both arbitrary and not always even possible, then we should be at pains to make good on whatever and whenever such could be the case. The continuity of time impels us toward death. This is one reason. The presence of time impels us toward thought. This, for us, is the more compelling reason. For thought in its turn engenders a self-recognition, which though it includes my own personal death, it also includes, more significantly, my own personal *lack*, that is, the very smallness of my being when understood authentically as part of the cosmic or even worldly horizon. We could thus speak of the continuity of time in a highly objective manner, without referring to its content: "Time-series delays successors, time-fullness delays decay in predecessors, and together they maintain the continuity of time." (Lampert 2012:37). This Kantian sensibility remains abstract, of course, but it does not partake in either of Mabbot's caveats. In Husserl's famous diagram of the relationship between decay and delay, demonstration of continuity is the chief goal (cf. 1964:49-51 [1905]). Retention is also modification. But all that is subsequent refers to the same starting point. Whether by the euphemisms of 'shading', 'rays' or 'sinking', such a protean primordiality is in fact not as original as it appears to be. The 'actual now' of consciousness must always be modified. There is no true beginning to our experience that can be lived and recalled. Nor is there an end that can be noted either before or after it occurs. This gives us the sense that within ongoingness, there is ironically a kind of space that Dasein must access or apprehend on its way back to being-found: "The operation of time, the dynamic that lets time pass, is not another time before or after any successive moment, but time's 'interior'." (Lampert, op. cit:66). Within this interior we also lose language, just as Husserl famously states that we do within the 'lived experience of actuality', whose 'primal source-points' and 'continuities of moments of reverberation' do not help us assemble the identity of time as being (cf. op. cit:100).

And the chronology of ongoingness is also a factor. If around the age of twenty-five a person can envisage the unity of a single year, and around forty several years in sequence, as life-projects take on more sophistication and one is geared toward understanding oneself as a different kind of person in the future or 'given time' (cf. Minkowski, op. cit:363), then personal development or even the development of the 'ego' or yet ego-consciousness must also play a part in reconciling the loss of being through falling to the order of a temporality that does not temporalize. At the same time, perhaps quite literally, we are gradually made aware by the simple verity that things do not always go our way no matter what amount of time – or the intensity of idle talk, the idleness of idol talk, the idolatry of talk itself or the being-with another in succinctly normative standards of interaction, courtship as if it were in court or even *tout court*, etc. – we put into them, that "The notion of meaning is not exhausted by that of development or sequence." (Ricoeur 1965:38 [1955]). Continuity in the abstract may be a focused goal of theory, and just as focused in its intensity as the arbitrary and 'even impossible' subdividing of time in order to mark its very continuity or connectedness, but it does not encounter the *being* of the meaningfulness of unfolding *or* temporality. What has been, retained and modified in its memory, and what is to be, 'protended' in its anticipation if you will, presents to us an antinomous affair of both being and time once again at odds with one another. For not only being falls, time as well may be said to 'experience' a fall of its own, and not only due to the presence of authentic being, as we suggested above: "For the antinomy of historical time is not the antinomy of sense and nonsense, as if meaning were only one alternative, but is rather the antinomy of the meaning of history itself." (ibid). Like the value judgement that we, after Weber and Heidegger, are not supposed to make within the process of either method or analysis, but rather must be made 'beforehand' – the very search for primordiality is itself both a value and a judgment, though one can question whether or not by the sheer presence of both there must necessarily be a combination of the two – what makes sense and what is merely nonsense prevaricates that authenticity of diverse histories and their relative meanings. Such cannot of course be simply collected in the manner of butterflies, ambiguous, delicate, captivating, even 'pretty' in the same way as some would judge the value of a young woman. The truth quality of the 'womanhood' of history, notoriously, 'his story' taking on the world of objects, including women, as authenticating his presence alone, must be abandoned to its own fall, as if in saving ourselves on the knife edge of a precipice we let go into the void some of our dearest possessions. History 'itself' has this meaningfulness not only because it is never any one thing, but that the very idea of what is sense and nonsense can shift dramatically over its course: "The fundamental experience of thinking here seems to be the essential unreliability of everything that shows itself sometimes this way and sometimes in another. In the very next moment it can be different again and no longer present itself in this way." (Gadamer 2003:39 [1990]). The implication of this condition, also itself as much an historical fact as an abstraction of description or a theoretical summary, includes the clue to our regaining of being within time as a 'constitutive structure' of human freedom. Since thinking can no longer allay our doubts, since thinking persists in its very ability to doubt and yet pushes us to also have faith *in* doubting, we begin to recover ourselves; we begin to break our fall: "Facts remain contingent, however much they can be grounded, they arise in the space of human freedom. To this extent, the past and the future are always accidental…" (Koselleck, op. cit:127). Insofar as the diachronous character of lived time presupposes change as its *structure*, one must shed the usual physicality of our metaphors regarding what can 'stand' alone, as it were, or how things 'stand' up, either to scrutiny or to change, or yet more pointedly, to time. What 'stands the test of time', as tired as is this epithet, is something that we supposedly admire. In principle, perhaps. But why even in this way? Most of what has perdured across a variety of definitional and historical shifts are things we might rather have let go but have found it challenging to do so. The 'destruction' of metaphysics was also, in the end, reconstructive. Nietzsche has in fact defeated us.

The mythopoetic moment, the time that is only the now, has at least since Augustine been placed under suspicion, if not outright erasure. It always had a cross upon it, and over the course of understanding the 'now' to have stood the test of its *own* time, that mark has been remarked and twisted round so that it now bears its 'cross-wise' over-strike as a matter of course. Not unlike that more startling remarking, the Buddhist swastika inverted in front of a Western mirror, or that swastika of the Greek geometric period given a quarter-twist, the mark of erasure, of a destruction that in its remnants provides the relic of a still older revolution, that of Christianity, also holds out a similar menace to the Judaic foundations of the West. In choosing the Greek mark over the Jewish, we had also chosen the destruction of the people who themselves were to be cast as metaphysical. Their time was then, our time was now: "Deconstructive delay starts as a critique of the concept of the now, but it ends as a substitute for the now and a solution to the problem of time." (Lampert 2012:152). A *final* solution? Hopefully not. 'The Jews' are timeless after all, given that the false category represents no real person. The 'eternal Jew' also perdures as much as he or she endures. And what can it mean to 'start' a delay, deconstructive or otherwise? If every inauguration has some delay, (ibid:155), then at the very start of 'things' there can be no perception alone and aloof to anything preceding it. Yet one more sense of what retention and protention share is of course back to the very 'thing' that we might have sought to destroy, the presence of the present, the umbilical now (cf. ibid:163). But it might as well be that the now also has a pretention about it, for it does stand aloof to our perception. Even if there had been no world, no reality prior to consciousness, the clue that consciousness is not at all what it would like to be lies in the unperceived 'nowness' of the present.

At the very end of his run-up to *Being and Time*, Heidegger speaks of the 'one world in which we are', that it must be discovered in its specific temporality, and that such movements as we do encounter are also within this time 'which we ourselves are'. (1992:320 [1925]). It is an almost poignant sentiment, though it leaves as much to be explicated as hoped. Only ironic in the light of what was then to be the future, and horrifyingly so, such an exhortation must have taken down the scaffolding of metaphysics only to find that the façade of what was left standing had rotted away, exposing the skeleton of an entire culture, a culture that could only wage death, at least for the time being. Heidegger speaks here of a 'movement' which is nature as well as our nature. This seems to link him with others in his lineage, including Hegel. And it may be that aside from the presence of the present which cannot be phenomenologically known but also is immune from destruction, that such a movement courses through us and makes us what we are: "Through this movement, self-consciousness becomes Spirit instead of remaining the poor, anecdotic singularity of one's own life. On the other hand, one may say that history becomes self-consciousness, because the order of history coincides with the introduction of the radical teleology of self-consciousness." (Ricoeur 1965:66 [1955]). My life is part of a purpose beyond its own perception and selfhood. Perhaps. But what of this purpose? What might it be? Is this the 'meaning' that we search for in the existential sense or is it something that is laid bare before us through the quasi-revelation of just such a history that has taken into itself the form of self-understanding we hermeneutically bring to our own living history? What could Spirit be but what animates all historical being, lends it its essence and promotes a certain kind of character, remarks upon it with a particular tempo of marks and markings? And the sum total of all these 'anecdotes', all this Apocrypha, from Eve down to Mary and beyond, is *that* what we are now, even if we cannot quite perceive it with that self-same knowledge of being?

It is a piece of too distilled wisdom to simply accept the following: "If the form of heaven be contemplated, the changes of time can be discovered. If the forms of men are contemplated, one can shape the world." (Grace, in Wilhelm 1973:224 [1951]). Astronomy and sociology combined undertake the truth for us. This is correct in so far as it goes. The 'heavens' do betray themselves to us, and the nature of time at the cosmic level is well understood when compared to its phenomenological structure. And it is a matter of course that if one studies society and history one gains insights into the 'human nature' and such could be used to work the world into another shape . 'Working for a better world' is supposed to be every good citizen's mantra after all. 'In time' we do see some progressive alterations, one's that can be vouched for almost across the cultural board. The pace is painstaking, no doubt. There is no 'now' that can be said to have been reached universally, as if the cosmos itself had been brought down to, or *back* to, earth and its ipsissimous wisdom was *also* now our own, like the nature of this movement we are supposedly interested in tracking down. But nonetheless we are prepared to go on simply due to the imagined opportunity of having a grain of this wisdom acceded to us, and the 'remarkable' character of all remarking and remaking: "'Remarkable' days are truly rare in our lives; all the same, each one of them is a 'new' day for us; it cannot help but be 'remarkable' in this sense, and this is how the succession of days brings us to constitute what we call 'perspective in time'. (Minkowski, op. cit:338). Here, both the diachrony of the 'truly remarkable' and the synchrony of the 'new' day gives us more than mere succession. Perspective obtrudes along the y-axis of my temporal perception. It cuts into the x-axis and points things out. In their intersection, the z-axis of depth is both pronounced – we hear things more clearly because our pronunciation of them is more and more correct 'over time' – and announced – we are pushed to rise above the previous, the 'what has been' in our lives, including our has been selves; we participate in an annunciation. It is this third dimension that time places into space that gives rise to the sense that time 'itself' still lies beyond our experience of it. It is the proverbial 'fourth' dimension, and what our three dimensional spatiality represents is truly no less than the interior of time. An interiority of being within time is held to be the *sous-rature* of temporal intersection, the ongoingness that is going on, with or without us.

1.8 Indefinitude:

Let us begin at the end: "This opening up of incompletion and suspension is perhaps the place where we can experience the sense that time is getting away from us. By searching for this state of dissolution, however, we are able to name it." (Kristeva 1996:332 [1994]). Being desiring being fulfilled. It is a dissolute 'state', for it is no state. One we do not desire and one that must be fulfilled by desiring such a 'state' to come to an end, or at least a halt. Calling something to a halt must needs using its *name*. And I have been called everything in the book. Many no doubt can say as much. In spite of this, or perhaps yet because of it, we are able to fulfill desire. If not all the time, then sometimes. If not in principle, then in practice. If not in the world, then in theory. If not to know the cosmos as ourselves, to know ourselves within the epic ambit of the cosmos. This *should* be enough.

We accomplish this through changing the mere repetition of myth to recapitulation. The narrative is shortened without being foreshortened. It is interpreted as against previous interpretation, and its metaphoric arc is bent low. There is, now, an end of the rainbow and one can approach it, like we have approached the creation: "Here we have the idea of primordial time, not as time very remote in the past, but rather as a prototypical time in which everything already happened which today does not begin anew but is only repeated. Primordial time is creative; it creates what happens today." (Van Der Leeuw 1973:332 [1949]). But if it creates, that is, in the present and not *has* created, past tense, then we are not merely repeating things as they were. Mythology reiterates. Myth recreates. Perhaps not itself, no, for the archetypes then would have much less cantor in many forms of contemporary analysis that travel far beyond the discursive boundaries of the studies of myth and religion. But if mythology, the allegory of cosmic creation, creates the primordiality from which history eventually emerges, it does so at first by repeating itself to the point that it can no longer contain its own understanding: "Cosmic time is repetition and *anakuklosis*, eternal return." (Puech 1973:41 [1951]). This is precisely why human time cannot participate in it. But we would not want to. For the allegory of the cosmos is more important to us than its reality. In indefinitude, we experience the indefinite horizon of what is far from us and can never be either reached or apprehended as well as the finitude of our condition as mortal, rather than cosmic, beings.

Yet this suits us. The indefiniteness of our condition is partnered with its finitude, as we have seen above. So indefinitude desires itself. It is being-desiring-being-fulfilled in self-understanding. Its 'docetism', so to speak, lies in its ability to forget what it has already desired and what *has* been fulfilled (cf. ibid:81). In negating *our* historical and worldly character, we have to forsake the desires of the past. This too at the level of culture. But what primordial time does for us today is provide not a backdrop to cosmic majesty, but the chant of the cosmic monastery. A kind of distant rumble that reminds us to never be utterly and somnolently satisfied with what we are or what we have become. Even the denial of primordial time found in Derrida and others can be construed as a kind of avoidance of the nameless morass of self-satisfaction (cf. Wood 1989:114). Drawing from Husserl, Derrida has been seen to reiterate, almost mythopoetically, "…the recognition that temporality fundamentally undermines and does not sustain the idea of presence, and the very possibility of the interiority by which subjectivity has been traditionally thought possible." (ibid:128). The world opens up the subject in a similar manner as does temporality open up presence. Both of these 'movements' may also be seen in Heidegger, which is why ontology and ethics often seem so indistinguishable in the relevant texts. Hence "The text is a privileged site for the liberation of time." (ibid:331). Not only can we observe the beginning and the end, like Gods, as mentioned above in the case of a narrative form or a novel, we can postpone the end, defer it and differ from it, as well as question the beginning. What occurred 'before' the beginning?

Even if there is no 'then' in primordiality, as Augustine above reminded us, the time before time cannot remain nameless once time has in fact begun. Paleontology is hooked up and into history. Nothing remains unwritten, and all can be thought of as a text. The 'world as text' idea sounds fashionable, but it itself is a recapitulation, a reinterpretation of what was at least the medieval viewpoint of the 'prose of the world' that Foucault famously discusses. But even in deferring the endpoint of things is not exactly indefinitudinal. Experiences are not continuous in any subjective sense other than through our native ability to live and live on as we must. There is no real contradiction between Husserlian synthesis and Derridean *Fragwurdigheit*. It is more a matter of what can be desired in this 'state' or other. If we cannot know where 'all this' is leading, or what my memory of an event actually 'means' beyond what I name it (cf. Lampert 2012:18), calling its shot again and again but making different shots. Like a golfer who finds himself on a different hole, if such a greeting card analogy be acceptable, one is oneself 'called upon' to make a different shot, indeed, to *take* a different shot at it. So primordiality is not, after all that, only the timeless ground of creation. Not at all: it is at least also the moment, and sequence of moments, that occur time and again in the subjectivity of living-on. The "…whole Order of Nature, not as something completed at the time of the original Creation, but as something still coming into existence…" was first given serious venue in one of Kant's early works (Toulmin and Goodfield 1965:159). The period before 1770 is often disregarded because Kant was experimenting with seemingly odd topics, such as redefining aspects of mathematics or meditating on Swedenborg. But just here is found to be a crucial idea: that what is, *is* becoming. That being is *still* and not stilled. That is, it is still going on, becoming itself by being something other to what it had previously been. If Vico, some thirty years prior to Kant's work in question may be given latent credit for this idea at the very 'beginning' of modernity, than it is to Kant and those after him that we must nod regarding the sense that even if creation 'did once have a beginning', it never ceases. (ibid).

Fast-forward to Deleuze, for instance, where past, present and future are given their own ontologies (cf. Lampert, op. cit:162ff). This understanding could only be possible by refuting the idea that the beginning was and only was, and was that way only once. Three separate definitions are held within each of these three separate time zones, as it were. The present is 'dynamic', the past 'diagrammatic', and the future 'recurrent'. All three are true at the same time, at once, that is, but not *in* the same time, let alone the same time frame. Though no aesthetic object, this set of ideas nonetheless has an art about it. Its 'scandal', even its' 'evil' in the sense that Ricoeur has justifiably understood the necessary and ethical power of art in the world and to our subjectivity, lies in its ability to remark upon the mythopoetic imagination while 'at the same time' do the same with the philosophical tradition: "This art no longer relates either consciously or unconsciously to any historical time; the solitary monologue of these 'extreme' works is spoken, as it were, into the void. And one cannot quite tell whether it is a monologue or a dialogue between man and the ultimate." (Neumann 1973:18 [1951]). Deleuze and others are perhaps the poorer cousins of the transcendental artists of whom Neumann speaks here. Poorer not in intellect, of course, but in subject matter. Yet what more profound object of thought could there be than the relationship that animates time and being? Does temporality dislodge being in the same way that ethics shakes loose morality? And what *is* loose morality but a recognition of the full presence of ethics in the world?

To participate in such a dialogue, ultimacy itself must be redefined towards the human perception of not only the cosmos, which is ultimately neither here nor there, but of the self-understanding concerning the presence of indefinitude as a 'constitutional structure' of human existence. The ultimate presents and represents the indefinite, even the infinite. We bring ourselves into the conversation, or are thrown into it, carrying the weighty satchel of finitude and within this, indeed giving much of its weight, the tools of the finite. And this dialogue, if it occurs, if it is to occur, is something new. While not exactly recent, it is relatively current, still in and of fashion, when compared with the human tenure on earth: "The concept of the primordial era is no truly eschatological concept; it is not a marginal time, but simply time. This view is supported by the fact that there is seldom a corresponding final time among primitive peoples. Primordial time and final time as eschatological concepts presuppose something that has not yet entered into our discussion: history." (Van Der Leeuw, op. cit:337). Like the concept of god, also absent in social contract societies, the idea of time as something that begins and ends is utterly foreign to human existence as it has always been. Or almost always. This should tell us something about ourselves. It is we, historical beings, who need these concepts, mythological as they remain. History is itself a function of the observation of human development. The advent of permanent settlements, the entropy and the renewal. The presence of something older than a single generation's tools and clothing. Buildings, monuments, temples, arcadia and stadia alike. And eventually, written records, archives. It is not at all a coincidence hat the first records we have are of mythic narratives and bureaucratic lists, the two poles of human consciousness. The 'ultimate', and what is of man already and always in dialogue. But no, not *always*, for the appearance of history in administrative records, transactions, oblatives and tributes, and the reappearance of myth *as* history are artifacts of the eschatological consciousness. And it was to be left to our own time to fulfill the desire contained within these earliest clay vessels, the will and want of the first tablets, and the call and response of the first codes, themselves dialogues between 'man and the ultimate', Mosaic in their romance but quite practical and surprisingly realistic in their sentiment. Thus from Ur to Paris runs an unbroken, if staccato and sometimes exiguous, thread: "Since then, revolution obviously no longer returned to given conditions or possibilities, but has, since 1789, led forward to an unknown future. The nature of this future is so obscure that its recognition and mastery have become the constant task of politics." (Koselleck, op. cit:46).

Indeed, one necessary virtue of the political in the face of the constraints and vicissitudes of history is the ability to stand aloof to the concerns of the day and see the bigger picture, if possible. This reaction occurs at the organizational as well as the global level: "In the face of urgent demand they exude an air of casualness and detachment. [ ] The longer the queue, the less attention it gets." (Schwartz 1975:78). In part this is a defensive posture. For the subject, the person responsible must tell herself both that panicking will not help her own emotional balance and trying to do too many things at once will accomplish none of them in the end. Objectively, one's audience must be assuaged, convinced that looks deceive, regarding urgency and the fact that everything is about to come undone, get out of control. At the political level these needs are all the more stentorian. 'The public' demands something of its leaders, but not always what one would think. Not necessarily action, in other words but the cool resolve to *be* cool in the face of desperate action. This is itself a mark of taking the time to be different than the shape in which the world might present itself to us. The Second World War vintage British slogan 'keep calm and carry on', of late turned to an advertising shill, betrays this sentiment. We may be being Blitzed, but there's no way we're going to give the enemy the satisfaction of us being moved to emotion because of it.

In all of this aloofness and detachment, there is an element which is common to another temporal setting which at first would seem to be the extreme opposite of a disturbing and desperate urgency. This is the time of prayer. In prayer, one looks forward to another time from the one in which one is currently placed. One detaches from the world for a few moments to address the other world, though the content of orison always maintains its link with the world. But precisely *not* the world as it is, but one to come. Not necessarily in any ultimate soteriological sense, but one wherein the future has already taken place, that one's prayers have been responded to in some manner. Detachment, 'keeping calm', has this same temporal displacement of the present world within it: "It is the presence of the factor of the future in prayer that distinguishes it from the other religious and mystical states, such as oration, meditation, or ecstasy." (Minkowski 1970:105 [1933]). These three particular examples which are either succinctly about the present, or, with oration, the content of which may be about the past brought back into the present indirectly, have more in common with other kinds of present-directed action in organizations and politics. It is almost as if one must place oneself in the future to act in the present. This apparent contradiction is resolved by the effects of one's actions in the present. These effects, at first, hail from the a future which has not yet been attained. In order to get there from here, one has to detach from what is actually in the here and now and then alter it so that it *becomes* the future before one's eyes, as it were. A similar effect occurs when we are directed to what we imagine to be past: "…history is history only to the extent that it has reached neither absolute discourse nor absolute singularity – to the extent that the meaning of it remains confused and entangled." (Ricoeur, op. cit:76). This embeddedness in the ongoingness of lived time is also an aspect of indefinitudinal thought. The meaning is not definite, not certain. So our actions therefrom and thereby can take on an improvisatory role. The past is not so clear-cut that it cannot become the future we *now* need it to be. This 'now' is pronounced, or even announced, by the shape of the day, whether in an emergency ward or in a government under fire. So the temporalities associated with indefinitudinal states arrest not their own possibilities but our attention to the task of removing the present from itself.

Neither amnesia nor anamnesis will avail us this task. Rather, a sense that a certain kind of time can occur at our beckoning aids us in displacing the present into a willed future, though again, one that is not willed, nor wielded, too precisely: "The notion of time, insofar as it is empty of mnesic images, must impose itself on the mind and attempt to fill up this void at all costs." (Minkowski, op. cit:378). Perhaps senility is not the only context where such 'fabulation' occurs? Not at all, for in imagining a relevant future in any scenario, we must 'fill up' the present, itself devoid of the images necessary to attain this or that future. The agent, the narrator, the actor, will have his mind 'transcended' and 'restructured' by 'creating something' (cf. Kristeva, op. cit:18). Creation always involves the imagination. It always fills an empty void before, and as, it begins its work. Improvisation within the hospital, government, classroom or myriad other social spaces fulfills the dictum admirably. If anything, senility or like conditions disallows anything else to occur, thereby rendering the special powers of the creative imagination to be nullified, their ability to temporally displace the subject and convince the object that what is happening is the exact remedy to the present situatedness of being – the prompt to be in the world as it *will* be – in the end lost to their own fecundity. Once lost, such a person "…extends the present in an unlimited way and thus removes from it [ ] everything that is new, everything that is *actual*, everything that is 'now' in it." (Minkowski, op. cit:380, italics the text's). Paradoxically, the attentiveness to the present so that it dissolves its own future in itself is symptomatic of all those who imagine the world to be what it is because this is either the best way it could be, or the only way. Perhaps these two senses are equally dangerous to the human future. Either way, senility is not merely a description of a medical condition that afflicts the aged. It is a condition common to all those who take history too literally and take their own present too seriously.

In 'premature senility' one has chosen the flux over the tone, using Husserl's later example (cf. 1964:171 [1910]). The 'tone' endures in time, but the flux itself has no time. One has, in any conservative movement for example in politics, or in the bureaucratic mindset in organizations, exchanged the timeless for the temporal. We search for the 'substance', Husserl argues, and thus "...our regard is directed toward the identical…" (ibid). But such a substance bears little resemblance to either the stuff of history or the action of the present. It cuts off the vital link between what has happened and what we imagine thus could happen, or happen 'again'. For the 'presenile' sensibility, anything that could occur is something that has exactly occurred 'before'. Remember, there is no then if there is no when. History itself is annulled by this condition, and so is the future. Koselleck notes that it was Nietzsche's colleague and friend Jacob Burckhardt who asked 'where in the past and in the present does life begin?' (op.cit:169). Life, that is, as in the distinctive comparison between past and present that allows the future to be imagined. It is precisely this feature of lived time that is lost in presenility, as well as in the better documented medical condition. It is willingly lost in the case of politics, perhaps pathologically and irresponsibly so in the case of bureaucracy. The latter find rationalizations for their ineptitude regarding lived time and their inability to participate in indefinitudinal contexts and conceptualizations, but the former make it into a cause. The former are thus far more dangerous to the human future than are the latter. And though it is one thing to celebrate the ability to airily detach oneself from the present and also perhaps from the history of this specific present-day context in order to overcome it and change it, in order to 'acutely' diagnose it, as Koselleck reminds us was the great virtue of Augustine as historian (ibid:99-100). It is quite another to imagine that such 'freedom of interpretation' meant, in principle, that "...the meaning of history lies beyond history itself..." (ibid). Yes, in the sense that the meaning of the past lies in the future, but a resounding *no* in that meaning is sourced in a world bereft of human history, and indeed, bereft of humanity itself.

At the same time, to relativize the past to the extent that anything at all becomes either plausible or rationalizable from the perspective of a stunted present, gifted only in that it senses that it is missing something, is to go too far down the queer Augustinian street in the opposite direction: "...it makes the *specificity* of ideological and religious organizations *unthinkable*. It transforms them into 'representations' or into 'reflections' of social structures. Put otherwise, it eliminates them as real factors of history: they become additions and secondary effects, precious insofar as, through their transparency, they shed light on what instigated them." (De Certeau 1988:119). Weberian ideal types analysis does have such a tendency, not that he didn't recognize this from the start. But what De Certeau adds to Weber's own caveat is the caution regarding any super-structural or epiphenomenal reading of history and society. Such organizations or regimes of truth, such elements of 'culture' or concepts placed in the aesthetic or ethical realms no longer have the ability to create *themselves*. This ability is, in fact, their most profound characteristic. Such 'ideals', as well as exemplars of ideal types, are also indefinitudinal structures due to their uncertain status in day to day life. Most of us have yet to hear of their advent, or at least disdain their influence. We do not, in short, believe that they have any other function than that represented by the historian of ideals or the sociologist of structures. Because of this disbelief – not to attain the certitude of faith but rather a certain faith in our ability to regain our imagination and thus also our improvisatory abilities from their respective fonts – we lose our patent human ability to look ahead. To combat this, we must rather regain our sense that "...we are always *in search*. In this way, the place remains an open one, and it is not closed off within the evolution of selves – it is '*time embodied*'. (Kristeva, op. cit:191). This embodiment is, as we have noted, an aspect of indefinitude. Not that regaining this sensibility, contrary to identity and to the flux but also in contradiction to our subjective expectations of sameness, themselves party to a pathological condition identified mainly in those who cannot continue to live in an ever-changing world, is a guarantor of creating the future out of any particular present: "What makes it hard to know the future is not the scarcity of present phenomenon that determine future events but rather the difficulty in discerning the future implications of what we do see." (Horwich 1988:82). This is certainly a large part of the story, but at the same time, if our imagination of possible futures is itself constrained before we begin to observe, this must be taken as an even more serious source of a presenile present-to-self. Why do we have such a difficulty in so discerning? Are there too many possibilities written into the deeds of the present? In principle, this may be the case. But we hardly identify even the majority of possibilities, given relative probability itself calculated by our prevailing social structures and attitudes, before we begin to act. At once we disregard in a double sense the fact that time 'times' itself along through the declension of its contrary temporalities. Time's 'tube', as mentioned above, is constructed from the combination of its cycle and its arrow. To place oneself in the crevasse that exists simply between these two understandings of time is to lose the reality of time itself: "Here we approach the great cleavage in the self-consciousness of mankind. On the one side, time takes a cyclical course, on the other it has a beginning before which there was nothing and an end with which it stops." (Van Der Leeuw, in Plessner 1973:233 [1951]). The identity held within the cycle appeals, ironically, to those who wish to foster, in a rearguard political action, eschatological time. More accurately than the metaphysical cleavage of which Van Der Leeuw speaks and for which we can place its advent with relative accuracy, there appears to be more of a representation of an indefinite but finite cycle bookended by a beginning and an end. Yes, it is fair to say that during the agrarian period, time's cycle continued unabated but with the addition of merely the idea that at one point the cycle started up – something that in social contract societies is not imagined much less posited – and at some point will cease. This is not at all as profound as the idea of linearity per se, but in fact linearity is *not* itself the forefront of eschatological thought in its infancy and in its transitional opposition to the penultimate primordiality of the cycle. Linearity as we understand it today is the product of the enlightenment. It is Vico and like writers and not Augustine who recast history in this more radical manner. But subjectively, it is a different matter. For in Augustine and others we *do* get the sense that the self, itself a new idea, has a history and one in which eschatology *could* take hold, and thus take hold of. It is the cycle of the same that entangles the soul. Enlightenment, albeit of a superluminal variety at first, occurs to the subject, the person, and the self. Social structure, the economy, politics are not subject to enlightenment, and cannot be. They are part of the world that will end. But the part of the self that does not end is precisely that part which linearity has overtaken. I *was* born and *will* die, and in the meanwhile, progress and am changed. I am not the same throughout my lifetime, and if I repeat the same activities for most of its brief duration, this has no bearing on the status of my *historical* spirit. It is here that Augustine in fact enlightens us, and the new history of humanity put forward might well be better taken as an allegory not for Man, but for people as persons.

We betray this antique insight, preferring to label it as merely antiquated, by being endlessly distracted by a linearity that in fact has no end to it, and also covers over its meek and petty beginnings: "By presenting us with a limitless number of nonstopped stories, the narratives that the media value [ ] offer a lesson in amorality and detachment that is antithetical to the one embodied in the enterprise of the novel." (Sontag 2007:225). Sontag also correctly notes that such entertainment fictions have displaced reading rather violently over the past half-century. Certainly the literacy rate for textuality has dropped off the usual maps. This was a danger that Augustine himself warned against. By taking too seriously the ways of the world as it is presented to us as social role players, we are liable to libel the soul of an adventitial self. The 'neighbor', in its spontaneity and lack of role affiliation and loyalty, sabotages both the social world *and* the sense that the self must be any one thing at any one time. It is the latter displacement that is more important.

What Augustine and Heidegger share mostly stems from the historical fact of their own displacement in a wider social world that was in radical crisis and breakdown. The Roman Empire and German Empires had collapsed, and the after-effects were swirling around their respective refuges. Both were altogether too apt moments to engage in the revolution of self-consciousness and the sudden shift in the apprehension of being. But what made both thinkers more than children of their respective, but kindred, times, is the indefinitudinal nature of that *kind* of time. We experience crisis still. We also must comprehend the changing self, and confront the mystery of what animates us and gives us reason and self-consciousness alike. These may not be eternal questions, but they are, for the time being, perennial. And this 'time-being' was inaugurated, it had its *beginning*, in the realization that consciousness does *not* do what the world does. And this thought was indeed the *first* thought, the first idea.

After this 'event', nothing could last forever. And indeed, in spite of various nation state's attempts to make time into a fascism of flattery (cf. ibid:119), or certain social movement's attempts to arrest time as the leaders of which would love to arrest their disaffected and changing youth, what we actually observe is unremitting change, both in ourselves and in the world. This does have, however, an ironic consequence at the level of theory: "Time *seems* like an abstract container, and seems to be eternal, only because it is universally the case that things change over time." (Lampert 2012:86, italics the text's). But is it not in the very nature of change to be uncontained? Thus time as indefinitudinal performs a gestalt of all specific changes, of the pace and cantor of change, and from its 'passion, grace and fire'. But it is still a performance, and not a real thing. Being too is performed in a similar way: "That there are 'eternal truths' will not be adequately proved until someone has succeeded in demonstrating that Dasein has been and will be for all eternity." (Heidegger 1962:269-70 [1927]). The fact that philosophers might 'believe' in this idea is hardly enough. No doubt, but I would doubt that any serious thinker does, in fact, believe in such, let alone of course Heidegger himself. Yet if both time and being are performed as if they were 'mere' vessels, however earthly and mutable, what can we draw from this phenomenon? Is there a narrative that the audience of being understands that the audience of time does not, or vice-versa? Are their messages the same in each case? What could constitute sameness given the limitations of a performance that is about, to its very would-be or feigned essence, what is differenced and thus what is not the same? Perhaps it is not something that is communicated to us by either time or being, themselves part of how we imagine ourselves to be in time. Rather, we are led to believe in both not only because they are a part of us, or yet constitute between them the idea of 'soul', but because they lend to us an ability that the finite and the definite tend to mute: "The atemporality of the unconscious adjoins the monumental apprehension of Being. The psychic absorbs the cosmic and is diluted in style. Such is the experience of the imaginary." (Kristeva, op. cit:192). Kristeva is speaking of Heidegger at this point. Is it enough to contend that the imagination, an uprising of the unconscious and an indicator of its desires, can by itself fashion a vessel that then takes on airs, detached and calm not unlike the actors in a crisis, and imagines of itself an ability to contain both time and being?

Like actors, temporalities can be read as denoting not so much the halcyon 'living in the moment' shibboleth but rather as the 'right time' for this or that to occur or to be contemplated. Hence the casual version of the expression 'kind of time'. It may go farther than this: "Perhaps eternity is to time as a person's life is to their or her action." (Lampert, op. cit:53). We may be able to use this loose analogy as we live, given that an entire lifetime cannot be grasped in any one phase of life, each having its own 'kind ' of time once again. But we cannot push it too far; eternity is by definition an open-ended conception, and time very much a vague generalization. A person's life is both finite and participates in finitude, and one's actions may be timed as only a tiny part of time in the more general sense. Yet the is-as relation may yet hold: "One in a sense reckons that death can come and thereby overlooks that this *indefiniteness*, whereby death can come at any moment, belongs essentially to its certainty." (Heidegger 1992:317 [1925]). Akin to any kind of time that still belongs to time, in that it must *take* time to occur - and thus our actions within it also take this same time – we feel that time must always be a factor in any deliberation, as well as the deliberation itself. The certainty of the time of death, in that it will come and have its specific time apportioned to it, overtakes the absence of specificity regarding its *timing*. From Prometheus onward, we are aware and unaware at the *same* time regarding the end of our time, which is also, for Dasein, the end of all time. So indefinitude as it accosts us regarding the future of our lived time and its necessary end presents itself as the uncertain certain, or carries along with it, for a time, at least, a certain uncertainty. Either way, the analogy between acts and time holds only if we grant that eternity is a working or workable conception with regard to the time we can know about objectively, and the times we have known about as subjects.

It is true that this conception still has some value for us: "Eternity is the only form in which the possibility of passing beyond becoming can be expressed, and this is because the passing has a temporal nature. It contains the infinite in itself at the same time…" (Minkowski, op. cit:110). This is so because it as well contains within it all that we thought was indeed finite for us. Just as we cannot recall every experience or act we have had occasion to live and live through, and that this is indeed in principle both a blessing in the Nietzschean sense, and a curse in that more generally historical sense that Santayana refers to, we also cannot be expected to understand that the gestalt of the finite may well provide the infinite with its capability of overcoming that which ends. Perhaps the infinite does not extend without end, as Minkowski cautions us, but rather acts as an umbrella conception for the intersection between what is finite – all things – and what possesses finitude – human consciousness. It is this intersection that, when contemplated, speaks to us not of itself as infinity, for that is something that cannot be known by any finite consciousness, but rather of infinitude, the cross-hairs of human perception attuned not to its own ends but to the way in which we speak to ourselves about how we must replace the precipice of the finite with grace of the life as lived.

Chapter Two

The Congestive: Appointments

Since all acts require a certain time in which action takes place or yet takes its place, the intersections that at once rehearse the reconciliation and overcoming of the finite are so numerous as to be both uncounted and perhaps uncountable. Only time remains, after the dust of action has cleared, and it is this time that may be measured and summed as a human life, and not the great diversity of acts that have been committed in the meantime, a *mean* time both as a simple average, and perhaps also as a sorrow, a hard bitten edgy and impoverished aspect of our life, the life of the soul and the soulful in life.

And that we mean these times to have meaning is also part of the condition we find ourselves placed in, or place ourselves in by our own volition. These times are less numerous than either the quotidian or the mundane, but insofar as they are part of the elemental constitution of the temporality of Dasein, they figure as both meaningful and as well as a meaningful kind of time wherein one can begin to apprehend what it is to lead *my* life rather than someone else's. This is not only a task of every thrown project, to come home to itself and to know itself as an authentic Dasein, but as well, to be able to act in accordance with one's own pedigree, one's constructed lineage of actions whereby one has attained this or that social station, these relationships and intimacies and not these others, and so on. All of this must both have a meaning and must have, at one time at least, also been meant. For no human act is without the existential ambit of intentionality. Certainly every one of us has experienced the faltering of what is meaningful over the life course. Even children and young people know the difference between what was of great value to them 'at one time' and how they feel about it today. The content of these shifts in meaning pending time served or the kind of time that has changed in the meantime, of course varies greatly depending on the phase of life one finds oneself in. Nevertheless, it remains clear that what is meant, and *how* it is meant to mean to others, is always *pro tempore*.

In this first of four focused 'substantive' chapters, I want to examine how time is telescoped or *reduced* by slotting actions, in particular, social encounters, into momentary times we oft refer to as appointments. What is supposed to come out of these moments, what is to be *produced* by them and why, is also discussed. Finally, how these moments participate in their own overcoming, in that we desire to think of them as most meaningful to us and others by granting them some sort of saving grace. The *redemption* of the appointment, so often derided, disdained, grudgingly submitted to, or yet avoided and postponed, rounds out our brief analysis of the kind of time that congests our lives, or even may seem to infest it with something contrived and hastily constructed.

2.1 Reduction:

Making an appointment immediately does two things to time: first, it makes something more or less imminent, places it on a horizon that can and will be known. This is an ontic vision, to be sure. This horizon is not that which 'fuses' with any historical tradition with which we must confront and also become conscious of. Even so, it approaches. Something wicked may be coming in our direction, or merely something stupid. Either way, we have agreed to this condition and we also agree to follow through on it. Second, it telescopes time into an encounter wherein time ideally has only the meaning of which the encounter itself is composed. Time loses itself in the timing of an appointment. It is reduced not only to its component syllable or sound, but as well it holds itself still for just long enough that the appointment or meeting be completed. It does not matter, at this 'point', what transpires or what comes out of the encounter. This is something to be thought of only in relation to the production of the appointment, its product. Between committing to possessing time as only a commitment to what occurs within the time allotted, we reduce being in relation to time in the same way.

Not without resistance. We know time is of value, or possesses some kind of merit in relation to how it can be used. We also know that an other's time may well be much more valuable than our own. The objective value of finite time cannot be underestimated, and the fact that many *overestimate* their contribution to this general value only adds to our sense that time is not only not our own after all, but that we have to race against the time other's possess in order to make our needs and desires known and thus potentially viable in the world: "This gives rise first of all to a movement of revolt and rejection: the Gnostic refuses to accept the world or to accept himself in his present state. More particularly it inevitably gives rise to a sense of revulsion against time, in extreme cases to a passionate striving to negate time." (Puech 1973:64 [1951]). We are all 'gnostics' about something or other, one's 'in the know'. But all of our gnosticating will not get us out of the appointment. It is our appointed time, and we have been appointed to it. Or yet we have appointed ourselves, and all of this in a quite pointed fashion. We can postpone things, take a 'rain check', whatever that may still mean in today's technological world, but at some point, the point of the whole thing is driven home to us. We can no longer avoid it. If we had sought to simply banish it forever we would not have agreed to the encounter in the first place. Indeed, there are more occasions where appointments are not made than the opposite. This must be the case given all the possible encounters we might have had over the life course with people we both have known or never knew at all. This is not only a trivially true point, for "...the word 'now' functions somewhat like a noun, we are seduced into regarding it as standing for a single entity whose varying locations are instants of time." (Horwich 1988:33). We meritocratize time by lending both credence and credential to *this* moment instead of all of the others. The potential that lays dormant and eventually fades into nothingness that is or could have been contained in all the other possible 'nows' cannot simply be shrugged off. It is through 'their' sacrifice that the chosen time gains all of its value. More so even than the fact that many of our interlocutors could have also said no to us, could have refused to 'see' us or entertain our visitation. Their loss, we might think. But of all the times that could have been, most notably and most noticeable at the reduced level of the appointment, surely we were not always right about our choices. We could not have always made the best effort regarding marking time into its specific content, and then to rest content with this maneuver. We cannot have retained all that would be necessary even to make a comparison amongst the appointments we did make and followed through upon, all the encounters we did experience: "A now-phase is thinkable only as the boundary of a continuity of retentions, just as every retentional phase is itself thinkable only as a point of such a continuum, that is, for every now of the consciousness of time." (Husserl 1964:55 [1905]). 'Necessary modifications' occur, and these are mimicked, if not structurally realigned, within the process of meeting the time and then the persons involved meeting one another. 'What was the last meeting about, I missed it?" is a commonplace phrase heard at administrative encounters, for instance. If Husserl is holding up a diagram of the y-axis of the now and the x-axis of the continuum, it looks no different to us than that of Saussure. Temporally speaking now, such a visual aid charts the intersection of two aspects of time-consciousness, neither of them necessarily 'internal'. Indeed, the deeper function of the appointment is to *externalize* the interiority of time-consciousness, to bring 'other minds' together on this point, at this point, without making a habit of it, so to speak. For no one really likes meetings. They not only involve one in the professionalized performance, any gap in which is liable to be libel in these political times, but as well they involve us more or less intimately with those who are also more or less strangers. Appointments are something to be 'gotten through', once again more or less successfully. It is a good day when no social encounter goes awry, but when one jams one's day full of such encounters the probability necessarily rises that something or other *will* go off the rails. In other words, that someone will not agree to making his or her internal consciousness of time public, fair and square, cards on the table. The inveterate social scientist might simply smile it away and suggest that this is yet another one of those very human things that make life 'interesting', but the rest of us are not going for it. Since "…at one moment we are aware of something happening, at the next, we are aware of it as having happened." (Wood 1989:73), we are also made very much aware that we cannot stop the train. Once you are on board, you are going where it's going, and everyone else as well. So it matters very much not only what kind of train one has booked onto, but where, exactly, its destination is and what kinds of spots one might encounter along the way.

Most appointments take too little time to develop any kind of sophistication to the social encounter. Even items of great import, like one's health, for instance, are matters for only a momentary discussion. It is common to note that buying a used car takes orders of magnitude more time than consulting a physician. Yet there will always be another car out there, and never another body. Courtship rituals may be truncated, often to our peril. Yet marriages may be extended, as well to our further and deeper peril. Because Husserl has identified the disconnect between 'perception' and its strict absence in the moment – and thus which Derrida later simply dismisses as a relevant conception along these lines – we are plunged into the moment without due regard for its momentousness. At what point does the decision to marry take place? To buy an expensive object? To acknowledge that one is ill? These are all afterthoughts, as it were: "What is *actually* perceived is not the now, but *the now as it passes away into retention*. And the now has no existence independent of its own becoming not-now." (ibid:94, italics the text's). By the time of Heidegger, we suddenly observe the moment in the high relief of tension and conflict (cf. ibid 258). Ironically, this affords us some relief as well. We are not the only one who would have wished things had turned out differently. If temporality is to be understood in 'oppositional terms', it participation in Being as a kind of *Aletheia*, a clearing of space, one cannot but suggest that the conception of the now as a mode of being-present has as its most important element the faith of the subjects who *are* actually present 'within' it.

Even so, retentional phases as structures of perception aside for the moment, it is also clear enough that this 'space' of time allows us both rationalizations – 'I got swept up in the heat of the moment'; 'I wasn't thinking' (that is, retention can also mask its presumed absence); 'Things happened too fast', and the like – as well as a manner in which to extricate ourselves later on. 'Sober second thought' is also a tired and jaded expression, but it does point up the sense that we are aware of our *lack* of awareness of the now. There are various measures we can take to avoid being taken unawares by the now, and we often avail ourselves of them; "Looking at the clock is based on taking our time, and is guided by it. What has already shown itself in the most elementary time-reckoning here becomes plainer: when we look at the clock and regulate ourselves *according to the time*, we are essentially *saying 'now'*." (Heidegger 1962:469 [1927], italics the text's). The *Aletheia* of temporality occurs consciously as if we have stepped into a forest clearing. The clock has created its own version of the 'crop circle', descending into our conscious path and flattening everything beneath it. It rises again so that we can observe its face, and in so doing, we step onto the freshly squashed foliage of an otherwise virgin glade. The sexual connotation of all of this is also transparent. The 'loss' of virginity, so fetishized since the agrarian period or even before in some horticultural regions at least, fashions 'Aletheia' into a feminine name. She has cleared the way for our entrance or at least, allowed us to clear her away in doing so. It is time. High time, if we are beyond the time which is 'right', however that may be defined cross-culturally. We are thus made aware of the appointment with a kind of destiny, but without the interiority of a conscious appraisal of its meaningfulness beyond that moment. It is as if we are able to become self-conscious about the content by which this now must be filled, but can at once scrupulously avoid the *post hoc* of any later efforts; the morning after, even the 'next' time is devalued.

All of this comes perilously close to a form of mania. Just as senility takes its own form in otherwise healthy persons, so too the manic condition apprehends us out of its own kind of time. But unlike our sexual analogy, Minkowski suggests that such focused and telescoped time "…is only instantaneous contact. It lacks penetration. There is no longer any lived duration in it. What is lacking in our manic patient is *unfolding in time.*" (op. cit:294). There is a preference for the 'grammar of the present' (ibid:296), and that Syntony is 'subducted', suggesting that a phenomenological analysis might reveal the structural intimacy between mania and depression, amongst other conditions. Certainly the fetish, in social contract traditions, is often accompanied with frenzies of various kinds, well-noted and also romanticized by early ethnographers, and in turn fetishized in a discursive manner by the likes of Jung and others. Yet the timelessness of such corroborree sometimes bears little resemblance to the experience within an appointment in our own times. We strain first to commit to it, especially if it entails wait-times on top of the internal time of the appointment itself, as well as enthralling us to extra chores associated with its outcome, like a kind of 'homework', whether this be going and getting medical tests, to adding some new and unexpected function to one's job role, etc. Thus the appointment can actually extend itself in a kind of virtual manner, altering the reality around us precisely because it forces us to alter our expectations and thus those of others due to theses additional sets of tasks. Like school homework for young persons, the surveillance mechanism of the extras associated with many appointments help others observe our standing and our progress. Perhaps even more than children, adults remain supervised in more tacit though admittedly, more diplomatic ways. Yet the cost of failure or unsatisfactory performance may be far higher, including a deteriorating prognosis to a lack of promotion or worse.

But the ellipses of the appointment, the resonance of the now, pushing along Husserl's x-axis in both directions, 'falling off', to be sure, and engaging us in our own fallenness as well, flattens out the temporality of Dasein. In our ordinary understanding, the 'pure sequence of nows' holds within it no sense of its origins or the fetish by which it came to be recognized. Indeed, "... the ecstatical character of primordiality has been leveled off." (Heidegger 1962:377 [1927]). Unlike Saussure this time, such moments or 'nows', while appearing to be in an endless succession and grasped only after the fact, also take on the 'membership' of the vertical, a 'series of repetitions'. (cf. Wood 1989:20). The 'running-off' or 'sinking-down' exhibited in Husserl's original diagram, reproduced in Wood (ibid:72) and elsewhere, simply refers to the experience of happening and happened, and the relationship between the two. This relationship, crucial to our understanding of time-consciousness, nevertheless does not tell us very much. After all, it is old hat to declare something as 'having just been', and to note the difference between reflection upon experience and the experience 'itself', in which no reflection, at least upon the current object or condition, is possible. But within the temporality of the appointment, we *are*, through a chronometric sleight of hand, able to combine these two senses. The appointment considers itself to be a now in its entirety, no matter how extended. It brackets itself, almost phenomenologically, from the surrounding world. All times outside of *this* time are 'hyleticized', so to speak. It exerts a kind of Kairotic Chronoscopy upon itself, excerpting it from the x-axis of succession and highlighting its y-axis verticality at the expense of both what had come before it and what may transpire later on. It can affect this temporal biopsy due to its 'punkt' character. Not only are we told, in making an appointment, of the exact measurable and more or less objective time when we are to appear, to 'keep' it, we are often told about how much time it will take. Many persons are wary of 'going over time' within appointments, mainly because others are imminent. So in this sense, at least, the y-axis cannot forever hold at bay the horizontal, the horizon of which ever approaches us. But if the appointment may be considered the ontic version of ek-stasis, what occurs within its interiority appresents an altered consciousness of which we must become aware.

Another way of putting it places us right back into Heidegger's sense of how time is 'leveled' by the unending sequence of nows. And yet such time may still be held, and kept, possessed and dispensed with, almost at will. The appointment is one perfunctory and punctuality-laden effort in doing so, perhaps the most superlatively specific effort we humans make: "Publicly, time is something which everyone takes and can take. In the everyday way in which we are with one another, the 'levelled-off' sequence of nows remains completely unrecognizable as regards its origin in the temporality of the individual Dasein." (1962:477 [1927]). But might we not suggest that the appointment is - kindred with the representing of primordial time or even historical events seen in post-contact cultures in Latin America amongst others; the Columbian conquest is played out again and again in ritual theater, for instance – a rehearsal for the punctuality of death. Something is to end. In the case of the appointment, the waiting for and anticipation of it. Also the time 'before' it occurs, replete with the usual anxieties, ranging from unknown illnesses to misgivings about one's job performance to date, to the almost anguish of the first date or yet the trepidatious confidence about the tenth. All of these situations, commonplace and everyday in the extreme, nonetheless both bring to the surface of human consciousness both the primordiality of origin – we would not *feel* like this or that if we had not made this appointment – and the anti-primordiality of the end of that self-same consciousness – the appointment radically and suddenly places us within its own temporality, the time-frame framed away from what 'ran on' up to it, like running on toward a punctual kind of death.

The 'what-is-just-coming' of the protention, imminence turned to immanence, eminently calling us forth to appear in its eminence, cannot be directly diagrammed accurately (cf. Larrabee 1989:380). Interaction with delays, for example, both predictable and unexpected, or even the sense that one can experience delay 'itself' as its own separate kind of time, makes what is to come all the more ambiguated (cf. Lampert 2012:45). In Heidegger's language, we might say that by understanding delay and its experience, we give meaningfulness to terms such as frustration, alarm, and anxiety (ibid:46). Yet in all of these, however commonplace, we dissect the future in an altogether unreasonable manner. Perhaps this is what we also feel, at a deeper level or shall we say, in a more interior space. We have not, in fact, the ability to distinguish the value of what has not yet occurred, let alone with certitude state what it is that in fact *will* occur. "This reasoning, against which one feels defenseless, represents a serious disorder in the general attitude toward the future. Here time is split into isolated elements." (Minkowski, op. cit:186). What may or may not 'appear', criticized by Heidegger as 'empty' (cf. 1992:89 [1925]), finds its advance guard of meanings already present in our subjectitudinal apprehension. Here, aside from splitting time into isolated *and* alienated elements, the very conception of apprehension is confused with itself. In order to grasp something we allow ourselves to be entangled within *its* grasp. We are not fighting with monsters here. Its only an appointment.

Even so, what is 'in time' in the Offentlichkeit of the everyday, can be neither objectively experienced – we have seen quite clearly how the future is mere fodder for the circus sideshow of our desires – nor subjectively apprehended – it has no formal and concrete meaning for us, and may never have, if we continue, after the fact, to allow our portentous protentions to get the better of us. This pretentiousness, the pretense of which makes us prematurely tense, confuses the future and present tenses of time-consciousness as a subject. This 'inner' character of the temporality of what is to come is a sham. Public time 'attaches' temporality to events that have not yet occurred (cf. Wood 1989:244). This is, in a sense, the essence of the 'appearance' of any appointment. What is to occur within the altered *punktus* of the appointment derails us well before its content is made completely known. It is this lack of knowledge about a future which is either already known in other quarters or can be known through this or that dialogic device, that we take as manipulative. It twists our reason and muddies, or perhaps even bloodies, the clear pond of the ongoingness and the flux: "...everyday concernful living gets lost among the objects of its concern and fails to see the horizontal structure that makes this 'content' possible. So we treat each 'now' as something 'present-at-hand." (ibid:245). In the apparently unending sequence of now-points, the verticality of reflection, just past or meditation on an event deep in our biographical history, is itself lost to the appointment, which is nothing other than the onticity of concernfulness, a stunt in which we are expected to then perform, a proposition rather than a proposal.

All is not quite lost, however. Concernfulness, which is an ethical substrate and not a phenomenological one after all, differs from concernful being, the ontological character of concernfulness. What is gained by this distension or dissolution in the intersubjective *Erlebnisse* of the social world and the once apprehended but stuttering ethical integrity of the interiority of consciousness, is to be found in the objectivity of discourse and cosmology: "...the construction of high-precision time-keepers presupposed the solution to basic problems of mechanics that were at the very heart of the scientific revolution." (Cipolla 1967:57). Given this, it was "Clockmaking [that] was the first industry to put into practice the theoretical findings of physics and mechanics (ibid:58-9). Huygens' pendulum clock, more or less perfected just before 1660, initiated the most radical punctuation point in the more leveled equilibria of time-keeper design and use. It is reasonable to suggest that our concerns distract us from our concernfulness, in a way that is related to how the socius distracts us from the neighbor. Even so, what the world is in its nature or its being is revealed as an object that transcends human concern and concernfulness alike. Only by cutting into it with the tools of a cut-up time can we discern how temporality functions at a level much more profound than one in which humanity normally operates. Certainly we should not engage in the assimilation of 'psychic reality to material becoming at any price', nor should we 'reduce Time to merely juxtaposed points' (cf. Minkowski, op. cit:17). Here he speaks of a 'kaleidoscope' of spatialized time. Adjusting the rolling lenses, overlapping them in different configurations, gives us a very different sense of the object 'at hand'. This at-handedness may indeed ingratiate itself to us to such an extent that we come to believe that time is 'present-at-hand' as was warned against just above. Bergson also issues a caution to this regard: "Spatial time, the time of our clocks, is a 'hybrid concept, resulting from the incursion of the idea of space into pure consciousness'. It is an experience of time that we have organized spatially, a homogenous *temps-cadran,* a sequence of segments. In reality there are no segments. Nor is time homogenous." (Van Der Leeuw 1973:325-6 [1949]). Bergson states that we can 'count seconds' because they are units of space. This offends common sense only in that we think we do not have a ruler marked out in seconds. But in fact we do. The clock is just such a ruler. In both Bergson and Heidegger then there is a transparent acknowledgement that we are temporal in our very being. Five minutes passes and we cannot be literally the same person or being that we were beforehand (ibid:326). Only in the most specific content can we affirm that there have been no serious alterations, as in my feelings for my beloved. But this too is as may be. For in a different, and perhaps much shorter span, such feelings even as these can be altered, sometimes radically. This kind of thing must be considered to be, from the clearing of lighted concernfulness, much more 'alarming' that any appointed contents.

In the appointment as well, we have a resonance of ancient ontology, wherein "Entities are grasped in their Being as 'presence'; this means that they are understood with regard to a definite mode of time – the *Present*." (Heidegger 1962:47 [1927], italics the text's). This includes the notion of 'waiting-towards', which is mainly how we conjure the present to consciousness, and thence set about apprehending it as a mode of actual being-there. We are not yet there but we are thereabouts, the thereness of being-there extends into the present that is yet but a presentification of what is awaited. Lampert adds: "The present includes non-presence. The now is the passing into the future that will be. The now includes in itself the time that is not now. The now is somehow not now." (2012:152). There is thus a kind of 'maintenance' of the now that fuses all three usual tenses of time together. The appointment highlights this fusion. It is the ontic correspondent of the fusion of horizons in hermeneutics. Confrontation with the tradition is replaced, or at least, displaced, by the confronting of the now-point and the others held within it, the doctor, the boss, the date. Even the positive and stentorian exhortation 'Now!' is not enough to fully apprehend the actual point intended. The *Augenblick* of the present is not at all identical with the being of presence. Therefore, being-present occurs as an antidote to the pretense of the appointment. If the scandal of ontology is that it defers ethics, then the scandal of the now is that seeks to differ from all that creates its limelit moment. As Barrett mentions, "Heidegger calls this basic temporality 'ek-static' temporality, for in experiencing the present we already stand beyond it." (in Gale 1968:357). Or perhaps, more ontically, just past it. Or again, for someone like Deleuze, "A moment does not pass out of the present in order to become past; its pastness is contemporaneous with its being present." (Lampert op. cit:11). This in turn suggests that past and present are 'two distinct structures of time' (ibidL12). How does this help us, though, in encountering the present as only a portion of the full presence of being-there and on top of this, as only a minute aspect of the being of the world, its worlding itself being graced with neither our presence nor our absence? In short, it presents itself to us as *unconcernful* being.

One way of parsing this is to simply return to Husserl's early formulation of the difference between our experience of a thing and its relationship to the world disregarding our apprehension of either: "For the temporal thing, we have the ordering into the temporal form and the temporal world on the one side, and on the other the temporal thing itself and its changing orientation with regard to the living now." (1964:79 [1905]). It is sage to note, however, that immediately preceding this passage we find a spatial analogy being used. This kind of language returns some years alter, highlighted in the following: "Every different temporal *position* in the pre-empirical flux of *images exhibits* a different temporal *position*. Otherwise, indeed, a thing which as such as its duration, a *filled* Objective temporal series, would not *appear*." (ibid:167 [1910], italics mine). If time really isn't space, at least, not exactly, what are we to take away from such expressions? If we *are* temporality, how do we negotiate the overwhelming, and perhaps also overweening, sense that our bodies are positioned in space and only seemingly secondarily are we 'within' time? We manage these ambiguities in the everyday world by making and keeping appointments. This is the easiest way to do so, in spite of the many issues surrounding the emotion and the existentiality of the appointment, as we have seen. Through this we accomplish the problematic 'beyondness' of which Heidegger has spoken. We have fused present and past with a view to doing the same thing in the future, thus bringing it too into the ambit of the now. This accomplishment comes not without a steep price, for we ourselves are reduced in our being to both an element in a spatialized object realm that must be 'on time' and not within it, and as well we reduce the time that being may be said to 'have' to a series of consequences, none of them directly temporal and yet all of them taking yet further time 'away' from us. Thus the appointment, and further to that the schedule, as will see below, produces in us the work of loss. But it too has a schedule to keep, as when one receives two weeks or so of 'bereavement leave', a barbarous injustice to the event experienced: "The time of mourning is reduced to a series of fragmentary and contradictory memories that cancel each other out before they are extinguished by indifference, which is cruelty's ultimate avatar." (Kristeva 1996:187).

2.2 Production:

The fullest presence of the now brooks no losses. It rather seeks to produce the new, even if the new is not so different in content than the old, as the official records of a million administrative meetings will attest. The likelihood of newness in the hermeneutic sense of the term is slight, but there is still no time to be lost through contemplating one's losses. This only magnifies the sense that things are losing themselves, that one is on the losing side, or that one *is* oneself a loser. The *Carpe Diem* of the full presence of being-there must telescope even 'the day' to a minute portion thereof. It enlists others to support this effort, and it thus represences our desires regarding potential transcendence as well as the keen sense that we should 'get this over with' as quickly as possible: "Simultaneity requires that other egos be given not only transcendentally, but also concretely. Roads, monuments, clock towers, and meeting rooms testify to the presence of simultaneous intersubjective experience." (Lampert 2012:6). Not only this, but that given each of these examples has its own career and pedigree, the character of these intersubjectivities changes over time, sometimes quite radically. By the 1260s or so the mechanical clock had been produced, if not perfected (cf. Cipolla 1967:39). Before c. 1300 clock towers did not exist. Rooms set aside specifically for meetings and only meetings are an invention of the 19th century, though both roads, or at least thoroughfares, and monuments have a much more ancient vintage. But the *Mitsein* of such contexts is not quite what it seems: "Being-with-one-another takes place in talking with one another and in concerns with what is said-in-the-talk. To this Being-with-one-another, the fact that talking is going on is a matter of consequences." (Heidegger 1962:212 [1927]). Something that is talked about becomes the 'talked-about'. There is a loss, once again, of genuine Dasein towards the entity being discoursed about. Always it is the 'about-which' that leads us astray. So the tower, a monument in itself, now harbors a device capable of reading time into space, of measuring the hours. The Horologe, or Horologium, the hour-log, and the like, reference this patent characteristic of the early time-pieces, clumsy and unreliable as they were for at least some three centuries after their advent. Empathy is necessary here, of all places, and we might refer to our intriguing but very much nascent ability to successfully move a collection of atoms across a couple of meters of space by way of quantum teleportation. Are *Star Trek* style transporters just around the corner? Not likely. So whatever the technology is or has been, we can feel our ancestors' pain. That is, if we choose to do so. The keen sense that something, that is, something about which one can talk, must be produced by the appointment, the meeting, the checking of the time on a tower or more likely, on one's phone, or by travelling apace down a roadway, is so strong that it pushes everything else out of its sullen way. Not that genuineness is impossible in 'talk'. But such must veer sharply away from its usual format, that of either 'idle talk' or of 'idol talk'. And our sense that something must come of this is not necessarily ditched with the movement towards authenticity: "It is the understood meaning of what is to be done. On this basis, it is always possible to look upon the history of work as saturated and carried forward by a history of the spoken word." (Ricoeur 1965:201 [1955]). Our 'garrulous' nature animates even our utensils and tools. The clock face chiming the hours, whether or not this sound in any way corresponds to the progress of the solar day, arrests our attention and sets us speaking. Time has spoken to us. The road is calling. The meeting room welcomes our presence as we enter, or perhaps it doesn't. The monument unbends its will and teaches us something of note. We may indeed be expected to perform some small ritual in return. The prayer before meetings was a well known item before the Second World War, and in some quarters this tradition is kept alive. An orison or speech in front of a memorial or other marker itself marks the time of the monument, or perhaps even the monumental. And one always utters a ritual farewell to those about to travel. 'Safe journeys' is a common phrase in most languages. It is both an exhortation and a salutation, a hope and a caveat. In short, each metaphoric item, that which marks the day, that which leads us to a new day, that which focuses the present day, and that which recalls the previous day or the past to presence, all surrender their common phenomenological identity to the manipulation of time through the appointment that produces something. What is being produced? Quite simply, the presence of something in the day *other* than the day itself.

Of course, all of this is contingent on our meeting or keeping the appointment made, perhaps long before. The 'order of arrival' principle is in full swing here. Servers may themselves wait as clients may be late, (cf. Schwartz 1975:92), and there is the small matter of how valuable we might imagine *our* time is, after all. For instance, "...orderly queues do not necessarily presuppose consensual devotion to the rule of 'first come, first served' but may give more direct expression to mutual restraint and accommodation between the more or less impatient." (ibid:96). If this is indeed so, the much vaunted intersubjectivity constructed by temporal representing is at the very least a performance, not all of which can be quite believed. At its best, it retains the civility of a group of performers who, because they themselves are working at it, have a right to expect that their social comrades in arms do the same. In fact, much social interaction may be expressed in this manner, and it has nothing directly to do with the presence of time as a measured and objectified present-at-hand. At its worst, it may degenerate into other kinds of ritual, violent and even deadly. The pitched battles between factions of European football fans is a well known sociologically analyzed ritual performance of this kind. There, and elsewhere, time is not of the essence, but it is still very much highly thought of, as it is '*time* to do something about *them*'. Whether or not we are paying rapt attention to 'the time', we are attending its presence. We make ourselves present according to its rule, as when a young student answers a roll call. Our very being-there is hitched up to the moment at which, and *by* which, we announce our own presence. But is this presence 'our own' after all? Heidegger questions the relationship between presence and the present: "…first, 'presence' is an ontological term; 'present' is a temporal term. The claim is that the temporal is determined by the ontological. Second, a definite 'mode of time' has been so privileged, that is, the present…" (Wood 1989:242). Very well. Such presentification via an appointment might bear little enough resemblance to the presencing of an existential act or even intent. One may only note the inattentiveness 'fully present' in one's students, in churchgoers, or even the crowds at a concert or a sporting event, to realize that being present can have nothing to do with one's presence in any consciously focused manner. This is not as ontic as it sounds: if the push has been to demonstrate that presence drives the present, this is clearly existentially ambiguous. One would have to argue that Dasein is presentification deferred by its own ability to presence itself, that is, 'making-present' – and how then is the present *made* present? By presencing being in the face of the '*Praesenz*' of the world? Or is it the world that worlds presence and we are simply carried along with it? – Being as a mode of being-present. There might be a regression here somewhere. But just here, and not there, temporally speaking. For it is in this 'justness', the present which has come to be because we are ourselves present within it and can thus experience its 'presence', suggests that we must always interpret Being as presence in the present.

But just as we produce the present by our presence, so too does the appointment reach forward and backward from its own time to produce other temporal forms: "…if memory is the only means of putting us in relation to the past, it seems equally as justified to affirm that memory produces the past as it is to say that it reproduces it." (Minkowski 1970:151 [1933]). One may make it a matter of taste to prefer the sense that memory serves what has been as its chief function or that what has been *only* is as such because we recall it, or can recall it, or are *willing* to recall it, etc. But there is more to it than one's petty predilections for either an objective past, an intersubjective one, or one yet solipsistic. Certainly the politics of writing and rewriting history are part of the issue. On top of this, subjective memory is notoriously diverse, from Roshamon to last Friday night. Archaeological methods have changed drastically over the history of the discipline, and new interpretations often have followed hard along with new applications of technology or more simply, new discoveries. What we look for in the past has a direct bearing on how we are to be in the present, and how present in fact *we* are just there. Making-present is clearly more than an ontological turn of phrase, or even a manner by which Greek or German Idealism, with all of their patent differences, can ground their metaphysics. In light of all of this, early on in *Being and Time* Heidegger issues a forceful caveat: "Not only, however, does an understanding of Being belong to Dasein, but this understanding develops or decays along with whatever kind of Being Dasein may possess at the time." (op. cit:37). We may still leave no stone unturned in our search for presence as what is produced by the appointed hour, but we can no longer imagine that one or another of these stones will divulge itself through a message carefully recorded on its back, announcing to the world of relative temporal contexts that *it* is the source of all presence in and to that world.

Heidegger says that it is the same with duration, the experience of objective time internalized, or yet the subjectitude that a specific temporality may hold over us in its objection to our presence: "The diversity of this duration is grounded in concern itself and in what has been placed under care for the time being." (1992:231 [1925]). I am the time, and *how* I am at this or that time 'yields a different duration'. This also makes eminent sense: we experience time based almost solely on our self-experience and this set of 'remotions' has an average everydayness about it, insofar as it is the 'closest' to us, the most familiar. Schutz takes this point up in his discussion of the 'stock of knowledge at hand' and that 'in hand', versus other zones of experience, that of intimacy, for instance, or that of the hinterland, containing all that which we have a bare sense of its existence, which is most things. Heidegger reminds us that we 'look and listen beyond' the near, and that someone who wears glasses is removed from these in a way that he is not removed from, in his example, a table at which this person is seated. Similarly, not the ground upon which I tread, but the friend towards whom I walk, is the nearer. It is not a matter of simple familiarity, but of desire, need, memory and anticipation. I cannot hold an authentic conversation with the pavement. For that matter, I also cannot engage in idle talk, for what it's worth. Even the inauthentic, that in which Dasein loses itself and participates in what is fallen, including itself, is nearer me than any specific physicality or prosthetic. Taken *tout court*, this tells us that what is produced by the timing of specific experiences and phenomena is presence, duration, and the nearest, three crucial elements of Dasein and also the world-as-it-is.

These constitutive structures are not essences in the traditional sense. They are interactive, mutable, even absent, and are part of becoming as much as they are of being. For Dasein, being and becoming merge in what is the nearest, in what has presence, and in what is experienced as duration, that is, what 'lasts'. It is not the length of time *per se* that is of issue, but how this or that is experienced in time that gives it its own temporality. This includes the 'what' of the time, as in, what is the time for? What is to come out of it? What occurs within it? Different from the how of existence, but not unrelated, is also the what which will occur; what emanates from this time as compared with some other time? And what kinds of traces does this time leave for the future to understand why and how it occurred, and can these be calculated? None of this can be assumed before an appointment of any sort begins or yet before it is said to end, for "…it remains to be shown why the present provides more information about its causes than about its effects." (Horwich 1988:80). This must be done if causation itself is to be thought of as adequate to its usual explanation. Reasoning backwards is more easily accomplished than its opposite, but in principle they should be equally difficult. On the one hand, we may know what occurred in the past, and of course cannot have this kind of precision with regard to what is to come, or what may come. But we are speaking here of reason 'alone', for the moment. The present is merely a hinge upon which the door of synthetic and analytic reason swings. Even if we are aware of what 'did happen', numerous other things could have. If we treat all of these as equally possible in hindsight, then the presence of the present is leveled out. It is merely where we are and nothing more. The future options, the possibilities to come, have the same ability to be identified and catalogued as do those 'from' the past. Indeed, only this or that *actually* occurred, and just so, only this or that *will* actually occur. Often these actualities are found to be related, but *some* of that is rationalization, and not so much reason. That is, whatever explanation we construct to account for what has occurred will accrue to itself what we understand to be the nearest to us, that with which we are most familiar as Dasein and not as a mobile object in the world of objects or as a locus for the extension of the senses.

Husserl speaks here of the 'now-consciousness' that is 'self-modifying. In doing so, in being able to be this or that way on the basis of content, such a "...consciousness preserves its objective intention." (op. cit:86). Acts and apprehension are also part of this equation. This self-modification prevents things from becoming 'hard', in the sense that Heidegger later on uses to describe the 'obviousness' of the world, its 'pale and inconspicuous presence' that undergoes a 'hardening' (cf. 1992:189 [1925]). Indeed, one might suggest that it is one of the existential functions of Anxiety to alert us to what is obstructive to us in the world, and thus that self-same world becomes the nearer for us, almost as if we have sense a danger or threat to our beloved or to ourselves. But if our self-consciousness is content dependent, or at least content interactive, then what does it mean to experience appointedness, or productiveness, or beginning or ending. A change in time that is not only our own but is Dasein in its ownmost being must also be experienced 'at' these times. How so? Such could only be noted reflectively after the fact, but by then it is 'too late' to explain to ourselves that something is about to happen and that I must adjust to it. Adjustment comes after any adjustment that must come. It is more clear that by the simple problem of illiterate iterability, our inability to read the present without it becoming part of our presence without us being present to it as well as to its own time that is presented to us, even made a present to us, that what the present is must *not* be 'content-independent' and in fact is not the site of repetition or simple succession (cf. Wood 1989:121). The 'ideal repeatability' that such a present takes into itself is experienced as such only as an hypothesis. This speculation is based on the fact that I cannot know the present as it occurs *in* itself, but only after it *has* occurred and in myself: "It is a universal law, therefore, that to each presentation is naturally joined a continuous series of presentations each of which reproduces the content of the preceding but in such a way that the moment of the past is always attached to the new." (Husserl 1964:30-1 [1905]). Nothing else can be experienced. Husserl immediately states that even fantasy is thus productive, in the sense that Schutz also later turns to his analysis of projects of action. Appointments are particularly illustrative of this function. This 'universality' also explains why meeting records betray much that is in fact the same. But even all of this is also content dependent and not exactly identical with what preceded it, *ad infinitum.* The present experienced by us is not iterability but sedimentation. It makes itself into experienced time, and only then does it hold out its additive function as becoming a part of lived time. How does it accomplish this? Through the relationship it builds between what it is as an ecstasis and what it encounters as the world and as beings: "Temporality already maintains itself ecstatically within the horizons of its ecstases; and in temporalizing itself, it comes back to those entities which are encountered in the 'there'." (Heidegger 1962:417 [1927]). Human freedom could be said to be contained, or at the very least, strongly implied, by such a statement. Indeed, Heidegger takes no pains to avoid this implication, as we find further down the page what is 'only' left to the discretion of Dasein. It seems like quite a bit at first. But ultimately, the facticality of existence has already disclosed itself as being-with objects and with the world. We have no choice about these fundamental constituents of our existence, and 'even' our thrownness acts here as more of a limitation than anything else.

This may be somewhat narrow. Another direct implication of this facticality, which also must be seen as a product of specific kinds of temporalizing, just as presence, duration and the nearest are general product of most temporal experiences, is meaningfulness: "The future, then, is that realm of the open out of which man temporalizes – that is, establishes himself meaningfully within time." (Barrett, in Gale 1968:358). This may appear to be trite, but it must be stated clearly that what is to have meaning for us is not only content dependent but is also time dependent if time is to be thought of as a 'kind' of how, of the way Dasein's being-with is in this or that specific time. The timing of this is of the 'essence', and not the objects or others to be discovered within it. Once again, "...time abundantly filled flies as we experience it but seems long in retrospect. Thus our experience of duration is determined by the order and meaning of its content." (Plessner 1973:261 [1951]). Time is also kindness, as in sleep, or perhaps yet mercy, as in a quick and painless death. Its 'kind-ness' then rests heavily upon the kind of facticities produced in our co-presence with it. The facticality of our existence, its already-always of the encounter with objects, others, and world, for instance, does not impinge as mightily on meaning as we are led to expect. Just as the line-up represents not a problem but its solution (cf. Schwartz, op. cit:86), such facticality is the source of what is open, what is to be opened, and what opens onto us.

We may, of course, not want what is waiting for us, or we may disdain the other who is waiting on us, be rendered a disservice by the one who waits upon us, and so on. What opens and what is opened are not of the same kind, but they may evoke the same kind of response in us. In our intersubjectivity, for instance, we may find that the making of appointments is destined to be relatively unproductive, given other constraints that may be levied by them: "Although waiting subtracts from the profitability of a relationship, it cannot be said that identical amounts of waiting entail identical costs." (ibid:136). Most often experienced as a delay of anticipated action, and thus as well a catalyst for the ramping up of both anticipation and potential resentment, waiting is a key form of the nearest, as it is something that occurs as part of average everydayness and is thus close to us. As well, it places us in the way of duration; we are forced to experience time as a delay, almost of itself, but certainly it is time delaying 'the time', as in the appointed hour etc. Waiting is merely the ontic term for this experience, and the one all of us have used. 'I'm waiting' as a response to the query 'what are you engaged in?' is surely one of the most common responses known in our modern age. It matters less what one is waiting upon, or who has made one wait, than the factical experience itself. But this experience does not access the entirety of the presence of delay, even if it presents both duration and the nearest to us as products of having made an appointment: "The important thing is that the period of delay is not a temporary situation whose resolution will bring a lasting situation; delay is the real condition of situations throughout their temporal duration." (Lampert 2012:16). We never escape delay in this sense, only is the manner that delay is experienced apart from its ubiquity altered. It could be seen as somewhat trivial to make this more general claim for delay, that is, any experience of the passage of time holds within it a 'delay' of whatever is to be the next experience. So what? But there is some value here: delay is also close to us, part of the nearest, and yet not ontical, not a facticality in the way waiting or 'waiting it out' clearly is. Rather, it is a facticity of Dasein, and is not vanquished by acknowledging the passage of time as 'something being delayed' or by filling up the time with other things. It is, in short part of the always-already, like the world which worlds itself without respect to beings: "'Time' is present-at-hand neither in the 'subject' nor in the 'object', neither 'inside' nor 'outside'; and it is *earlier* than any subjectivity or Objectivity, because it presents the condition for the very possibility of this 'earlier'." (Heidegger 1962:472 [1927], italics the text's). Delay taken ontologically is an aspect of the precondition of the earlier and the later.

While we measure our own pace by checking 'the time', making sure we are 'on time' for the appointment, or at least in 'good time' so that we do not keep others waiting, we bring ourselves closer to delay by allowing ourselves the amount of time it takes to do any or all of these record-keeping tasks. We bring ourselves nearer the earlier and the later at once. We aspire to be the first, and are concerned that we are not the second. Aphorisms from around the agrarian world and into our own time affirm the timeliness of punctuality, but some of their metaphors bring nearer to us the manner of being-time that is closest to the point at which delay is expected to stop delaying. This is the final aspect of what is produced by the appointment: the translation of ontological delay into the ontic mechanism of waiting. In so doing, our experience is pushed away yet again from the authenticity of temporal being and we are lost to mere concerns of the scheduled day.

2.3 Redemption:

Concernfulness, however, may be directed towards both object and acts through reflection. And such is all the more likely to occur to us during the ontical delay of waiting, that is if we are not distracted by the numerous accessories to the queue, all the more available to us through recent portable technologies. Even here, however, we may read something that makes us reflect on itself or some related thing. If so, we place in a single category of being-reflective both acts and contemplations: "When we live in acts of reflection, we ourselves are directed towards acts."

(Heidegger 1992:96 [1925]). Heidegger tells us that this 'peculiar feature of reflection' is evident in the correspondence between acts and the contemplation of objects. This harkens back to Husserl's intentionality, where contemplation and the object of contemplation are part of one another, 'included in one another'. Here, in this relationship which is more than an intimacy, akin to a shared consciousness but one in which I am the fullest source of what is conscious, can be found also an act which redeems the appointment from itself: "Time is favored time: the dividing lines have been made on the basis of life's experiences. Time is full, and its content is the myth – that is, the forms of life that lie heaped up for all time in the womb of the unconscious." (Van Der Leeuw 1973:329 [1949]). Appointed time is the least full, but nevertheless, because it introduces to us what is farthest and then brings it into the nearest, as ontological delay is brought into focus as ontical waiting, it always also presents to us the act of redemptive experience, wherein time is made full 'again', without the concern of mere angst, but rather within the concernfulness of anxiety as also an aspect of Dasein's ontological constitution.

Even the casual sense that we disfavor this or that activity, or that something or someone falls out of favor with us due to its or their own actions is both a clue and a clew. The one suggests to us that we have spent the fullest of times within this condition – the unconscious action of the farthest brought near through reflection and contemplation of objects, or others – and the second tells us that we can leverage our expectations of time and what is bequeaths to us through this very process. The one implies the other almost in an immanent fashion. Just as Heraclitus had to remind his acolytes that cooking participated in Being, so too are we, through the appointment, part of the redemption of being through time and being as time. This is so because the appointment, seen ontologically, is simply the current incarnation of the Kairos, a reset, however 'arbitrary': "God is manifested in time. Each of his acts marks a *kairos*, a solemn and decisive moment." (Puech 1973:47 [1951]). Thus we might imagine something being excised from the history of consciousness, taken out and replaced not by a temporal prosthetic per se, but by another form of being, just as alive, but of a different kind than what it has now replaced. And so too we are made differently, made into the difference between what is past and what is to come. This 'kairotic chronoscopy', should not be thought of as an act of a *deus ex machina*. It is Erlebnis that confers this act upon us, as in a hermeneutic experience, something that is truly new to us and thus we are altered by it in an existential manner. We no longer *are* the same. Mytho-poetically, Jesus becomes 'the new Adam', the beginning of a new world, just as his second coming announces its end (cf. ibid:48). It is not a coincidence that bells were rung to herald the new in all of its hoped for ontological newness, like coronations, the appointment of high officials, the accession of religious leaders, down to the common marriage between equally common folks as ourselves. Bells kept away storms, disease, and announced the ongoing presence of the glory of institutions, such as churches and monasteries (cf. Cipolla 1967:38). Bells alone, rung by human effort, and later the mechanical chimes of clocks – the placement of both in the tallest structure of the time, towers and steeples, is also no accident and cannot be put down to merely the physical effect of having them heard over a greater distance than if they were buried inside towns or behind low hills in shorter structures – *appointed the time itself as full*. No other act, no different thing or contemplation thereof was required. The appointment of the fullest time redeems both time and our being *as* time. In the annual cycle of the fullest, that which is farthest from us brought into that which has displaced it by usurping the nearest, what is in the now extends itself in both directions in the manner phenomenology has analyzed: "The present plays out yesterday's events and last year's events simultaneously. The present enacts the past as its own distant contemporaneity." (Lampert, op. cit:12). And precisely *not* now distant, as it was in the ontic reality of chronologies and archives. Time itself is reset, a Kairos has been pronounced upon it, and we are made different, like the twice-born or the one who has 'died many times' in order to become immortal.

Just as the past is representenced in the present and as the present through the arbitrary reset of a chronoscopic contemplation, so too what is to come is brought into its fullest possible presence before it can occur as either an act or the contemplation thereof: "The moment of vision occurs in the present, but *points* to the future in its projection of possibilities." (Wood, 1989:224, italics the text's). The Ek-static quality to the mode of being conferred upon us by a vision resonates in the translation the present makes of the now. Only afterwards may we be said to have vision, yet this possession is possessed, by definition, of *the* future and not even of 'its own' future, that is, something that might have been prognosticated by virtue of experiencing this or that specific vision. One is always pronounced a visionary, or appointed one. Here, appointment and anointment linger with one another, 'tarrying awhile', so to speak, in the presence of their combined beinghood. But the actuation of the vision is thereby lost: "The now emerges in the present and is submerged by it. But the present is not a not-now because of that. It keeps something of the 'now' in it. It is a now that is stretched out." (Minkowski 1970:36 [1933]). Since both duration and presence are experienced in the present, the present is also an aspect of the nearest. But it also clues us into, and clews us up to, the farthest, because we cannot consciously apprehend the present in the now, nor even in its nowness, that which attains the extension of the not-now in itself. The 'submergence' of the now makes it an other to both presence and to the vision. But within that process, so indistinguishable from the present as lived time, this other is 'delayed' into its authentic being: "Delay is the other in time." (Lampert 2012:13).

The present then redeems itself through not being beholden to the mere moment, the now unstretched. It can 'carry the moment' within it, 'keep time' or lend it to us, its respective others, through the very otherness that is the ontological equivalent to ubiquitous delay, the 'other in time' as Lampert has aptly put it. Just as in a specific vision there is no sense of either value or even meaningfulness - it is the mirror of the unstretched nowness; hailing to us from the unconscious, the collective consciousness, the collective unconscious, or some amalgamation of these, who can say? – such an experience, if it even may be called this, at a stretch, perhaps, is ironically one of the most limiting things a human being can in fact have occur. This is why, phenomenologically speaking, that the vision quest in traditional cultures must be kept to oneself, or at the very most, may be spoken of in circumlocutions when one becomes an elder, as part of the pedagogic apparatus for constructing the next generation of social beings. As Heidegger says, "'In the moment of vision' nothing can occur; but as an authentic Present or waiting-towards, the moment of vision permits us *to encounter for the first time* what can be considered 'in a time' as ready-to-hand or present-at-hand." (1962:388 [1927], italics the text's). The implication here is at first startling: the real experience of time is that of the occurrence of nothing. It is Anxiety and the full presence of the No-thing, or 'Nothing'. 'Nothing', conceived in this ethical manner, is not at all the same thing as nothingness. Nothing *is* a thing, but unlike any other thing that can exist. It is the otherness in Being, but it is, in spite of that, not non-being, not an ultimate form of Parousia. Time itself is redeemed, as we have stated, by understanding the appointment to be *about* nothing, and not even occurring. This is the 'waiting-toward' experienced ontically as simply waiting, for we do not know what will occur – hence its relative transposition of the Nothing – nor has it yet occurred – hence nothing in factical living on, has in fact occurred.

But after a time, a second implication arises: if the 'present-at-handedness' of the moment of vision is construed as at once being about the Presence-of-Nothing and thus being in its presence, 'it' not to be taken for anything or any specific thing, then 'somehow' what has been experienced by us is an actuation not of the nearest, but of the closest, that which thus can be completely and utterly overlooked: "The time which it has thus 'experienced' is understood within the horizon of that way of understanding Being which is the closest for Dasein; that is, it is understood as something which is itself somehow present-at-hand." (ibid:457). In the unstretched now of the visionary moment, what is envisaged then has nothing to do with anything else but itself, one's ownmost being experienced as authenticity, what *it* is, and nothing else. Without any accessory, let alone objectivizing prosthesis in which being loses itself and experiences not just itself but also its fallenness, I am as Dasein is: ipssissimosity. In time, this might be understood also as ipseity, as we will examine below, but for now, what is redemptive of itself in the temporality of the appointment is the present-at-handedness of Dasein.

Is there a third implication to the moment of vision recast in our contemporary temporality as the appointment, its quest now a waiting-towards that experiences itself not as a destiny per se, but as a commitment no less important? That which is closest to us acts only as that which is closest for us in its nearness. This at first seems paradoxical, as the nearest is made up of the average-everydayness of acts and the contemplation of acts having to do with something that is recognizable to the many through its *Offentlichkeit*. But if we consider that "...*there is in Dasein itself a characteristic inclination to nearness* – to nearness, which in its sense stands in a correlation of being with the present. But the present is *one* possibility of time itself." (Heidegger 1992:230 [1925], italics the text's), then we must accede to the sense that what is closest to us both 'emerges and is submerged by' what is nearest. It is the ontological equivalent of what Minkowski states of the temporality of the present and what it does to and for the 'now'. The closest is kindred with the now, the nearest, as Heidegger makes plain, with the present.

Speaking of Minkowski, Grünbaum reminds us that "... we must be mindful that there are tenseless senses of the words 'becoming' and 'now'. (in Gale 1968:331). Given that there are many other 'possibilities of time itself', the present should not necessarily be accorded pride of place as a latent function of our very language: "But conversely we must realize that some important *seemingly* tenseless uses of the term 'to exist', 'to occur', 'to be actual' and 'to have being or reality' are in fact laden with the present tense." (ibid, italics the text's). The tacit nowness of such phrases, used both casually and analytically, must serve as a caution, and is one of the themes of Heideggerean 'destruction'. A sociological example may help clarify this penchant for viewing the nowness of that which exists or occurs so studiously: the person who occupies a role status that governs access to valuable resources is important not of course in himself or herself, but in the very social position that they occupy. Thus, off campus, a professor is regarded as perhaps interesting or yet quaint, but not at all important. He or she has nothing to offer the wider world in its own terms., just as the present cannot offer the now its own vision without stretching it into terms which can be both presented as an act or object, or as a temporal space of contemplation and thus meaning. Just so, those who can force others to wait, stretching *themselves* out in time and delaying the moment of vision, whatever it may consist, have a value beyond themselves, just as does the present (cf. Schwartz, op. cit:16). Well and good. We experience this kind of disinclinativity daily. It may well be part of the 'slings and arrows', if viewed existentially, or the mere 'insolence of officials', if viewed ontically. Indeed, insolence, official or otherwise, may well portend more serious nativities to which we are the more disinclined. But once again, the delay function of the stretched out nowness of ourselves experiencing what the present is to itself, may well also be salutary to authenticity. All the more so, is this 'value-neutral' concept be oriented toward consciousness 'alone'? In another enlightening moment, Lampert suggests that "The delay is so essential that we might say that consciousness *is* the delay in the body whereby it knows itself." (op. cit:114, italics the text's).

The stretched now of Minkowski is also contained within the ambit of the observation that "...simultaneity allows things to take their time gradually, without speed, whereas succession requires fixed starts and stops. Paradoxically, simultaneity is gradual and succession is segmented." (ibid:208). We may of course ask, what things? In the vision, it is Nothing. And if this is the closest to us ontologically, the most authentic to Dasein's ownmostness - if not to its very-ownness, which would have to also include what is nearest and what holds presence and duration – then nothing else can occur in the unstretched now of the non-present present. Being 'it', apart from the children's game which is itself symptomatic of the connection the young person has with their own temporal being - and thus should be understood as suggestive to mature being in this very sense - can only be said to be an 'occurrence' in the space of its non-occurring: "The fundamental character of the being of Dasein is therefore first adequately grasped in the determination, *an entity which is in the to-be-it-at-its-time.*" (Heidegger 1992:153 [1925], italics the text's). The temporal particularity of Dasein is one of its most self-evident features, but this being so, such a feature is not immediately subjectively available to it. It is something rather that is observed, so to speak, only from the distance that each diverse and specific moment has toward its nearest and its farthest. In this understanding of punctuated time, what is near 'objectively' – the flux, the closeness of Nothing, the authentic – can be farthest subjectively – due to the loss of being in its modes of fallenness. The 'being of Dasein' is something that is in its own time, or better in a time which is its ownmost being. Like 'manufacturing a run' in baseball, the ownmost moment of play or even of playing along of the unstretched now is cobbled together, extended, stretched out, directed toward itself and into the consciousness of Dasein in that its source is the already always of the world's worlding. This even has personal overtones that take it yet further: "...the self is duration and the nonself extent: 'the unextended that endures is the self'. By intersecting with duration, a reminiscence joins together the subject and the world and unites duration and extent – 'the self becomes being'." (Kristeva 1996:263 [1994]). This is an ontological 'development' that, after constructing being in the face of Nothing, temporality in the face of the atemporal now, and acknowledging the closeness of that which closes upon us in a value-neutral manner, it then can construct the subjectivity of selfhood and its interaction with the 'object' of the world, both in its objectivity which is intersubjective and in its objection to our presence, which is objectifiable, 'hard' and something that we run up 'against' in our running-on-toward.

Just as Ricoeur declares that a trace or relic from the past is not a part of history until the historian appears to interrogate it (cf. 1965:23 [1955]), Dasein is not itself until the world objects to its being-there. Ricoeur cites Georges Canguilhem, Foucault's major mentor, for another exemplar of this dynamic: "...the scientific fact is what science makes in making itself." (ibid). Such an explanation, which Dasein renders unto itself, is kindred with an analysis, and not a synthesis (cf. ibid). And to close such an analytic circle, for the moment, Heidegger reminds us that 'significance' is something found in the 'structure of the now'. Succession does not permit these two structures, that is, significance and datability, to 'come to the fore' (cf. 1962:474 [1927]). Ek-static horizontality gets 'leveled' off by pure succession. Nothing can stand out, or perhaps, to pursue this potential extra meaning, Nothing gets stood outside of its authentic time. 'Being stood up' is, of course, a risk anytime one commits to an appointment. Here, redemption is made impossible from the beginning. The 'original sin' of whatever action does not so much occur, but is nevertheless there, already. But all is not necessarily lost. Missing a date might in fact save one from a variety of travails. Since the future is as yet unknown, and the stretching of the now brings only a probabilistic understatement of futurity into the purview of being the farther afield we venture, it may well be that the rejection exhibited in being stood up in various ways is in fact a good thing. Dasein comes home to itself through the casual expressions that are the equivalent of 'its their loss, after all', and the like. It is on the way to its ownmost being, even though rejection is part of the very ownness of Dasein as well as an element of the intersubjectivity of mundane time, though it is not, by this analysis, therefore quotidian.

But total rejection is rare. Usually, someone is simply late, 'after their time'. But since the appointment is co-decided, neither person, or no person, is 'in' their own time. This is one of the reasons the appointment, committed to and seen through, has its redemptive aspect. No one is favored, at least in principle. Certainly if we value the time spent with the other so much we may well acquiesce to meeting them solely on their terms at first, but this cannot last. Indeed, in the most intimate of desired circumstances, both persons begin to be unduly generous regarding what they imagine to be the other's 'valuable' time. 'Being late', behind, or tardy, after the moment or even 'losing the moment', speaking of intimacies and desired opportunities, we find ourselves kindred with the Nothing that is stood outside of its authentic horizontality. We empathize with that which is the very source of our Anxiety, and Anxiety in general. In fact, such Anxiety is transformed into a simple ontic version of itself, the suite of anxieties associated with impatience. Yet this too has its 'moments': "...the impatience which presupposes a punctual attitude is a socially patterned sentiment which promotes efficiency in modern society." (Schwartz 1975:153). But these 'sentiments' range far beyond mere efficiency, as Schwartz reminds us in his introduction, including a 'precise system of time accounting' and also the respect we show it which is necessary for it to take hold over us (ibid:8). Such respect is almost like a kind of filial duty. It replaces the demands made by parents, for instance, with those of the clock. Children are notoriously time-insensitive when time is considered only from this objectifying viewpoint. This is also true to varying extents of non-protestant Western cultures, pre-agrarians, and the sub-continent. These fellow humans, including children, exist in different time zones from the 'well-adjusted' modern. It is not that they are more authentic in their being, in their relationship with the interiority of time, let alone that they have somehow 'internalized' the imperative of ontologically reading Dasein only toward its ownmost being. But it might be said that the stretching of the now occurs more gradually in some cultures and regions than in others. This phenomenon is no doubt of historical interest, but let us not pursue that thread here.

Instead, let us conclude this chapter by suggesting that datability and significance, in whatever manner they are lived or extemporized, are almost one and the same thing when understood as part of what is closest for Dasein: "Death acquires a *date*; it is the first date, from the phenomenological point of view, that is inscribed on becoming." (Minkowski, op. cit:144, italics the text's). It is in the very nature of Dasein to stand up it own demise, to disregard its own completion. Yet death too is of our ownmost being. It is not part of the very ownness of the nearest because we cannot date it. We have decided to be the one who 'stands up' the ultimate other, until its own impatience with us proves to be our downfall. But that can wait.

It is a commonplace mystery novel idiom to have an 'appointment with death'. But "...if we knew the date of our death in advance, we probably would not be able to live at all. Like those obsessed, we would pass our time checking our watches, calculating the time that yet remained for us to live. The date of death ought to be ignored in life." (ibid:145). This Promethean gift has taken us far. Death is allowed to remain in the fullness of its authenticity. There is, in other words, no ontical death. Like Anxiety and the Nothing, or perhaps also the 'Never', recently purchased into a mythopoetic melodrama by the popular music group Metallica, Death 'occurs' in the temporality of its non-occurrence. It is part of an arbitrary, but still enlightening, parsing out of that which is closest to us. An end of all moments in the momentary with which we had made appointment simply by being born.

Chapter Three

The Restive: Schedules

> Lost in the making present of the 'today', it understands the 'past' in terms of the 'present'. (Heidegger 1962:443 [1927]).

The manner in which time is marked gets larger. If the appointment is the *punktus* of marked time, and one can make equally pointed remarks about it and upon it, then a series of appointments collaged into a schedule is the ontical intersubjectivity equivalent to succession proper. We have just seen how being gets 'appointed' to kept time, or preserved time. Onticality, by way of the factical apparatus of modernity, stretching out the now by extending the appointment backward in time – its preparatory work, as in reading the previous meeting's official notes, for instance – and forward from its own actual conclusion – by assigning 'homework', perhaps for the next meeting or other encounter. The facticality of the appointment is lent cantor by its appearance on a schedule. Most of these are formally kept official records of what is to come. What has past, also duly recorded, is no longer of the same interest. A schedule, by its very purposive venture and order of catalogue, is forward-looking. It seeks to control the future.

Given that this ideal of control is at best a probability, at worst, a tired metaphor, a phenomenological analysis might reveal more accurately what the schedule actually accomplishes, just as we have seen it do for the more syllabic content of the schedule. If appointments are words, the schedule is at least a sentence, sometimes a paragraph. Below, we might extend the sentimental analogy, that calendars are books, and deadlines are perhaps epitaphs. However this may be, it is clear that the schedule rests not upon the specific content of any or even all of its noted appointments and meeting times. Rather, *any* meeting or project will do to 'set' a schedule. The amount of sartorial humor we have invested against those who, through the bureaucratic bent, hold meetings simply for the sake of holding them, is too well known to discuss here. But such idiomachy does speak to our suspicion that, while we are committed to this or that appointment, more or less necessary given the degrees of direness we find ourselves in, we are much less committed to ranging along our existential horizons a slough of them, ordered and phalanxed, advancing upon us, we with only the small arms of our own dossier to protect us.

Let us discuss in turn then the manner in which schedules are first planned. A map of the future is no mean task. Indeed, we will find that we must immediately turn to something more serious, an attitude towards what is to come that breathes of the clandestine and the all too profound, that not of planning, but plotting. The course of events, like a navigational journey, must be plotted on top of being planned. Plotting is the sentential equivalent of the planned paragraph of time that most schedules hope to populate. Finally, with all of this planning and plotting behind us, we might think we have generated some 'free' time for ourselves. Thus the outcome of having a schedule is ironically to 'get round it,' just as Nietzsche said of the point of culture regarding its greatest persons.

3.1 Planning:

Primordial time contained no appointments, let alone schedules. Even time's cycle, drawn into itself along its selfsame torus and inundating the present with its own past, does not readily admit to any kind of chronology of events that might be ordered and preserved, looked forward to or hoped to complete. No, only with the advent of an eschatological outlook, the idea that, even if only a God could experience both the beginning and the end, that both of these *did* exist in any case, do we have the existential-temporal horizon necessary for setting up both the archive of the past and the cartography of the future: "Thus the discovery of linear time that makes possible a directed consciousness of limits and plunges everything into the light of the unique and unrepeatable raises man's conceptions to a new plane. World and man become worthy of being remembered in tradition, monuments, and documents." (Plessner 1973:237 [1951]). A schedule, seen in this way, is merely a future-directed archive, a mediocre monument, to be sure, as monuments might go, but even so, what it attempts to monumentalize has yet more scope than anything that has already happened. The casual phrases 'that's old hat', 'yesterday's news', or even 'you're ancient history, man', as in 'dead white European males' kind of history, speak to our awareness of this. Although lacking in relevance and ethic with regard to the history of consciousness and thought, there is a grain of validity to the criticism that reminds us that we cannot live in the past, no matter how grand or aggrandized. Our entertainment fictions ignore this warning to our collective peril, but in our personal lives, we are forced, reluctantly in many cases, to abandon or 'let go' as the self-help standard has it, whatever it may be, and more poignantly, whomever they have been, has 'occurred' to us in their very ownness of their being-occurred.

In doing so, our attention is turned toward making plans. And one only makes plans for something to come, for something that has not yet been done, even if by doing this in turn we are reminded of something that has already occurred, through cleaning up a child's mess on the kitchen floor to arrangements for the funeral and estate of a just passed loved one. The first is mindful of Heraclitus, the second, perhaps Plotinus, but either way, such events must be 'undertaken' with all due haste and seriousness, whatever their object. And since "All Objectification takes place in time-consciousness, and without a clarification of the identity of temporal position no clarification of the identity of an Object in time can be given." (Husserl 1964:88 [1905]), then we are immediately - one might aspire to say, immanently, but this is too much ontology too soon in the story here – placed into our own plans. But planning isn't just what it seems to be. It itself constitutes, if not a structure of temporality, then at least a mode of being-in time, the time-that-is-seen-to-come – without forgetting that this is a narrow interpretation of time because that which is unseen will also still come upon us – and a way in which to record one's faithfulness to the idea of a future. Depressive persons tend not to plan. On the other hand, over-anxious and neurotic persons will over-plan. The first have lost their faith in living on, the second in lived time. But most of us will plan accordingly. If each segment of a life project, like writing another book, requires a requisite leap of faith, then so too do the more syllabically oriented aspects of the 'to-be-lived': "Dailiness constitutes a frame of reference by which possibilities are determined in advance, and in which the boredom and dullness this generates sees constant diversion. The concept of everydayness therefore already embodies an interpretation of time." (Wood 1989:222). Both disclosedness and care are exhibited in the day to day. Not in their quotidian settings, which tend to be monopolized by publicness and the 'Das Man', but certainly in their mundaneity, wherein we are arrested by boredom, even ennui, and must do something about it. In this confrontation, even with what erodes our ownmost from one day to the next, we are called upon to pay the closest attention, through concernful being, to that which might enclose us. At the same time, this 'dailiness' exacts a price that estranges Dasein from what its ownmost being is capable of. Every plan that is made means as well one that is unmade: "Everydayness takes Dasein as something ready-to-hand to be concerned with – that is, something that gets managed and reckoned up. 'Life' is a 'business', whether or not it covers its costs." (Heidegger 1962:336 [1927]). Heidegger goes so far to suggest that conscience is itself in question because there is no guarantee, flowing from the ever-onwardness of the day to day, as to its right ontological interpretation. That's a shame, we might reply. But even so, shame on us, shame on me. For it is I as the virtual embodiment of the Dasein which is my very own that can take its business elsewhere. The stock ingratiation of 'this is yours to take and keep', when receiving some paltry piece of gratis in the course of an introductory meeting, for instance, with one's fund manager or accountant, real estate agent or even counselor, is an attempt at connecting the disparate dots of a being that has been made dissolute by 'management' and 'reckoning'. We are literally subject to a *dihairesis*, a 'taking together and laying apart' (cf. Heidegger 1992:64 [1925]), but within the scheduled meeting, the 'taken together' is no match for what is splayed out and distanciated from itself.

The phenomenology of the future could be considered both propaedeutic and analytic at once. It is but an introduction, as all future-looking can only be. Yet submerged problems come to the surface and are themselves laid apart for examination (cf.

ibid:79). Like the now that is stretched out, the schedule permits the stretching out of clusters of moments, meetings, encounters, and even 'off the record' conversations which 'clear up' things that might have had to have an officially scheduled meeting to come to grips with. 'Shop talk' of all kinds, in corridors, in offices, at mid-day meals and perhaps even in the proximity of pillows, has this social but also chronological function. It temporizes temporality, evens tempers out, and prevents the temper of the tempest from suddenly appearing as does a squall over the mountain range. Indeed, a schedule possesses the onticality of a phenomenological reduction. It is the obverse of the reductive coin, insofar as one is no longer immersed in the world, but one's stream of consciousness is directed along the lines of sight specific to this or that set of meetings and times (cf. ibid:100). If this is too pat and we have to pull up short of the eidetic reduction in which the structure of experience of this or that type comes into view, we can say that according to the principles of scheduling, once an encounter is formalized, it's position in the consciousness of chronology and the marking of the times which is to come is 'absolutely given' in the sense of the eidetic perception, while obviously not being its equivalent. Even so, it does share much of the attitudinal complex associated with the 'first' reduction; it has a 'binding force', it is something set out 'apriori', it is 'grounded' and contains within it its ownmost possibility (cf. ibid:162). It also sets forth a 'temporally particular scope of discoverability' in that whatever is to transpire within its scheduled time, the being of Dasein will adopt a new self-understanding because of it, even if this becomes, or is in the process of becoming, a mode of concealment. Here, especially, what goes on 'behind closed doors', or in some proverbial 'smoke filled room', conceals itself in its own beinghood, but not, contrary to ourselves, from its own being. In a way, its eidos is fully present in the act of keeping to a schedule, even down to the minute of observation. In general, adherence to schedules produces in unconcealed beings a mode of concealment and a manner in which to lose oneself in the world at large all the while pretending to be sharply focused, 'reduced' to those matters at hand and thus 'getting at' the truth of things through their transactions: "Here is the occasion for illusion; a single historical rhythm, in collusion with the time of mechanics, furnishes the canvas of dates, that is coincidences and rendezvous, like the measures on a symphonic score." (Ricoeur 1965:187 [1955]). Though a symphony performed could not be more different than a meeting undertaken – to be fair, improvisation often occurs during the most staid of meetings, and could not occur during a symphony unless it itself were scored ahead of time – the point regarding the ontic 'datability' of this kind of lived experience is taken. There are things that are to be held as necessary, essential, and hence the eidetic analogy which may indeed be more than that: "...temporal determinations of every kind are joined in a certain way as necessary consequences to every instance of coming to be and passing away that takes place in the present." (Husserl, op. cit:36). Husserl intones with a kind of surprise, that every real 'becomes ever and again non-real'. But what is this 'certain way' in which all things are joined in the present? We have already seen how the present stretches out the now, mostly in passing but also reaching forward and reeling it into itself. Surely our intents have something to do with temporality at this point. It may be, in principle, that 'every' thing is so joined in the consequence of coming to be, but this is an abstraction. One must construct time through an active agency. But is, for instance, Badiou really that far from Husserl here? "Time is not an illusion, but is a consequence of decision procedures." (Lampert 2012:193). The only form of known consciousness that *decides* is our own. We adjudicate the temporal through the now unlived experience of what has occurred to us, even in the sense of 'I just had an idea'. In this self-recognition, which happens both while we are immersed in the specificity of the hyletic realm or when we have practiced the 'first' reduction and have entered the realm of what is tantamount to form, it is a reflection and a realization that occurs, in its own time, after the fact. The thought has been succeeded by its appendix, including the insertion of the one who intended it. The thought might be unintended, as may be some of its consequences either in thought or action or both, but the self-recognition and the becoming conscious of the facticity of this thought and thus others is surely part of intentional lived experience. We realize this through recollection, no matter how little time has objectively passed, and we thus accrue to it certain expectations. Thought, like the now, becomes stretched out: "This knowledge asymmetry, by virtue of the difference between memory and expectation, yields our conception of succession. Time order is built into the notion of explanation in such a way as to imply that earlier facts may be taken to explain later ones." (Horwich 1988:13). So far, so good. We also know, up front, as it were, and as an expectation of any possible future explanation of itself, that only certain connections will in fact be made. A set of previous facts will be understood as being relevant to a corresponding set of future facts, which themselves are now just passed and thus also take on the burden of the most recent past. But the schedule of decision-making is more complex than it appears. We imagine the worlding-being-of-world to be in accordance with human intentionality. Not in the sense that what occurs in the world always does so according to our desire or follows our bidding. No one is that naïve. But less evident is the manner that we assume that what has occurred in the world as part of its actionable worlding follows the same kind of structure as does not only intent but also explanation. In fact, human consciousness stands utterly apart from the world into which it is thrown, and it strains the existential sense of the term 'being' to utter in the same sentence as 'world'.

This puzzles us because it is we who have to puzzle out the world, and not the reverse. The conceptualization of a mascot God solves the puzzle without resolving it. Here is a superior being who nonetheless has a human interest. However irascible or forgiving, what matters is not God's personality but His abiding *and* historical interest in humanity. But how can one be both superior and yet retain something of humanity, something that is shared with *being* human, as part of one's interiority, made manifest in one's intentions? These contradictory clauses of being may only be set apart by using some version of the schedule. Everything in its place. 'Every' thing made certain through the somewhat arbitrary temporization of temporality held within every schedule extant, from seven days of planned activities to the long day of judgement, where superiority demonstrates itself by working overtime. And all of this requires a series of decisions that cannot, on the face of it, be equal to its portentous moment. This is so because the act of decision cannot catch up to itself: "Decision arrives one moment too late to have been actual and too early to be actual yet." (Lampert 2012:188). The lack of simultaneity points up an absence of similitude. If the one is ontic and the second ontological, and we also expect that a God Himself is the second and His human interest the first, then our recognition of the presence of God comes too late for Him to have made effective His interests. Hence neither His wrath nor His forgiveness are, in the end, relevant.

Furthermore, since "…my decision did not bring about any past event, [ ] there is no conflict with the principle that events never precede their causes." (Horwich, op. cit:30). But it is just here that God is revealed in His nonhuman superiority. Time for the divine is non-linear, non-cyclical. It remains as it was 'in the beginning'. An 'entire chain of determination' occurs simultaneously (cf. ibid:136), as whatever occurs in a meeting does from the perspective not of the meeting in action, but of the schedule into which it has been placed. In coming to recognize the hand of God, if we are still so inclined, then we ourselves depart from our humanity. For 'symptoms' of causation in the human world, in the natural world drawn out to its maximum, and of course throughout history, need "...be neither essential, universal, or permanent." (ibid:141). Yet just here we at least aspire to that 'certain' sensibility that Husserl states must occur to 'every' thing that undergoes becoming. Even if we admit that in fact our access to the constitutional structures of Being are limited, and what they might indeed construct is very far from our imagination of what might have emanated from their source in the past, we are still left with the problem that decision-making is, in its own essence, a speculative endeavor to which laws may be applied only with reservation. We may think 'laws' in science and even within the legal apparatus of a state are 'special' because they enable not so much predictions to be made at all (cf. ibid:163) – anyone in an ill-lit circus sideshow can do this – but an order or predictive logic to be constructed that neither stands or falls according to its success rate. In this, we are finally approaching our version of godhead, for the logic of creation was assumed beforehand to be certain of not so much its outcome, but rather of itself.

Going about our lesser business, we humans construct things on the go. Our days fill up, sometimes within their own environs, but Heidegger cautions us about using such spatial metaphors that reify themselves all too readily. Scheduling aids in this illusion, because in fact "...all 'where's' are discovered and circumspectively interpreted as we go our ways in everyday dealings; they are not ascertained and catalogued by the observational measurements of space." (1962:137 [1927]). A schedule is a like a ruler applied to the future. Events are 'spaced' out, either as evenly as possible when they are related – a series of meetings or other kinds of transactional encounters from psychotherapy to drug counseling to early-on courtship ritual – and when too close a conjunction of events leaves us ironically bewildered and perhaps suspicious of its 'causes' – is there an ulteriority in my date's eagerness, aside from the obvious sexual one to which everyone has to at some point admit, even if not necessarily submit? Or such events are scheduled in a telescoped manner when they are, also perhaps ironically, unrelated, and when nothing in principle from the previous meeting can cloud the proceedings of the one to come so rapidly. The 'dialectic' of the schedule is thus exposed: the thesis should state the chronological order of one's expectations, the antithesis is the actuation of the events, and the synthesis the outcome of what is met and what remains unmet, producing further meetings on some points which are 'conserved' from the x-y axis of a dialectical triangle, and closing off or bracketing others. In characterizing scheduling in this way, we have a pragmatic metaphor that is at once well-practiced and too clear cut. It is part of a theory of the nearest, whereas a phenomenology of the marking of mundane time through scheduling etc. must reveal the closest to us, that which is an aspect of our ownmost being rather than that of the very own. Speaking of the purpose of the dialectic in history, Wood declares: "Essential to such an account of Time is the ability to identify and relate discrete underlying processes and forces whose interaction can be made intelligible in rational and teleological terms." (1989:322). If 'consciousness itself is a social product', the great epigram of *The German Ideology*, an existential *Erlebnisse*-oriented ontology is already present, predating much phenomenological understanding and specifically the Heideggerean version thereof. The very idea that today we can understand *telos* as rational at all seems to me to be entirely questionable, almost out of court. Hegel has fallen on hard times in many circles, but this is not of course the point. The purposive goal-oriented movement, whether instigated or further directed by a mascot god or no, has its home in the onticity of the schedule. It is no surprise that *setting* the time, aside from resetting it when the power goes out or one's batteries fail, should be the telos of much of today's technology, from the paper day planners of the 1980s to the portable multiplex digital knives of our own decade. The moniker of such devices is included in their messages, reminders of what is planned and what *has* been planned and exhortations to attend, lest quorum be lost. 'Sent from my so-and-so device' is a commonplace postscript to any such message, or others. Courtship ritual is both magnified and glamorized, made more serious, perhaps astonishingly, by the inclusion of such addenda. No longer would The Beatles' early hit 'P.S. I Love You' carry the same weight as a 'P.S. Sent from my device'. Perhaps a musical rewrite is of the moment?

All of this insidious hoopla also provides free advertising to manufacturers, and is in that sense no more interesting than what one sees following the car in front of you. Indeed, automobiles routinely give us much more information than we really need, if we need any at all, than does the shill of portable electronics. But the more important function of marking time so closely and then remarking about that every act by telling everyone involved *how* it was accomplished and communicated, is that we are attempting to reify what is really duration into a fixed measure. Rather, due to the vicissitudes of intersubjectivity on the one hand, and the worlding of the world-as-it-is on the other, "Such a duration is always interpreted in terms of well-accustomed everyday ways in which we 'make provision'." (Heidegger 1962:140 [1927]). Here what remains ready-to-hand does so through its being 'specifically within-the-world.' (ibid). It is not as if we simply slough off any attempt at precision. We do not disdain such estimations but use them as a tool, perhaps even as a benchmark, if we are practicing for a sporting event that is timed, for instance, or a more private 'personal best'. Even larger-scale projects, while not timed as intimately, take on their august character in part by marking 'how long' it took us to complete them. So, while precision time-keeping is of the essence in very few human endeavors, the *idea* of being precise, kindred with the faith and loyalty to punctuality we saw above, does animate us in almost everything we do.

How we square how long things 'actually' took, as when a meeting goes over its allotted time – more pointedly, its *scheduled* time, that is, what *should* have occurred in all of its teleological abstraction but also in reference, and deference, to the rest of the events so scheduled 'around' it – with the predictive estimate involves us fully in the experience of duration, something which is closest to us after all: "It is always the next perception, the delayed perception, that is the test of simultaneity. The result of the test refers back through time between first and last perceptions." (Lampert 2012:76). Here, what is simultaneous should not only be taken in the chronological sense. More importantly is the simultaneity of our expectations as laid down in the horizontal 'Mosaic' of the schedule when compared with the measured time of the actual event as experienced in the world. It seems that we are dealing with two *forms* of experience, and not merely two different kinds. Our first perception is that of a 'should' as well as a 'will'. But taking place, starting at this point, going for however long, and ending at another point, are presented as facts when in fact they are but the constituents of a theory. The last perception is that of 'having been', of 'happened', and of endedness rather than 'the end'. People straggling out by themselves, in twosomes or small groups, perhaps rushing off to their next scheduled appointment, heading to the restroom or back to the refuge of the office if the organization affords to its employees or the club to its members individuated spaces of that sort, all of this as well as the cleaning up of the tables, the erasing of whiteboards, the logging out of computer terminals and even the turning off of overhead lighting systems, is part of the experience of 'endings' and is not *the* end. So, "if we think of time as something *in which*, then the dimensionless time of the 'limit' can have no meaning of the sort that requires the scope for an event to occur." (Wood 1989:247, italics the text's). 'Shorn' of its inner meaning, what 'comes to an end' is experienced more on the order of 'what pushes us along', either to what is next up according to the schedule or towards the 'free' time, the phenomenological character of which to be discussed below. The difference between the 'should-will' and the 'having-happened-what', is the difference between chronology and duration.

Perhaps an historical example will help clarify this reductive and seemingly non-dialectical analytic: "We find a notion of psychological time among the ancient Egyptians, who divided the nights into twelve hours each of which increased or decreased in duration with the seasons. In this astropsychological time, the experience 'night' was considered to be a constant unit, independent of the duration in terms of (water-) clock time." (Knoll 1973:286 [1951]). Our 'night-time' is related to this notion in the manner of an experience form. We still abstract the happening of 'night', referring to it as 'at night', 'tomorrow night', or 'nightly at…' and so on. It is not even a reification in the usual sense. It is more like a trace of the closest inscribed upon the nearest. But like latex paint struggles to cover over that of oil-base, the nearest can only measure time, not mark it. Night is a *mark*, the number of hours on a clock a mere measure.

Another example: "…the Japanese used to measure time in hours of variable length." (Cipolla 1967:98). Cipolla reminds us that in China and even in Europe the system of 'unequal hours' had been in use but had been put to rest long before the advent of mechanical clocks and watches in any great number (ibid98ff). The sign of what is closest to Dasein has become the signage of what is only nearest to 'it'. Indeed, when we are accompanied by the nearest, we are no longer 'it' in that ontological sense wherein we recognize our companions as duration and the Nothing among others. We are not the one who is searched against nor are we expected to search for others in order to 'tag them up'. Instead, we can always consult the time and order our affairs thusly. The clock is 'it' when it comes to such decision-making. But has our very intentionality been submerged in the stretched out chronology of the schedule and its time-keeping devices? "Our clocks, it is true, have cast off this symbolism. For what we are concerned with measuring is unmeasured or abstract time. In the seventeenth-century clocks ornamented with moving figures, the twelve hours – represented as the apostles or as the figures of a dance of death – enter into a relation to that which is *above* time…" (Plessner 1973:247 [1951], italics mine). What overtakes all schedules is the passage through death to eternity. One cannot get there from here without dying. This is why such a limen is often represented as a tunnel or some other dark passage through which one must maneuver. Perhaps there is a bright light at its end, or perhaps it has no foreseeable terminus. Either way, it arrests our attention as a way 'out' of what we know, of what has been, and as an egress from time itself.

But the 'history of time' is not quite left behind as easily. For "Time is not number. Time is not things in movement. Time is the 'number of'. Time is number intentionality." (Lampert 2012:64). These Aristotelian notions are mindful of none other than settings in Sesame Street and other learning media wherein there are often portrayed personifications of abstract concepts, such as Time. The antiquated 'Father Time' or yet closer to Aristotle himself, Saturn, might appear alongside the number eight, which, or perhaps we should say 'who', is also real. The late nineteenth century idea that numbers were in fact real is also suggestive of this. But what then would be the character of this or that integer? Is 'Seven', due to how it is usually written down, angular, hard-nosed and pawkish, or is it - he? – a mystic simply due to the cabbalistic reference? Is the number eight not a he but rather a she, for curvaceous reasons? We immediately ridicule these kinds of analogies but when we read that time is the 'number of things counted', given that it takes some amount of time to perform this or that action, it suggests to us that as with Lampert, the idea of differentiality is already present, co-extensive with any definition regarding the being of time and its 'presence'.

If this differentiality is the source of all problems associated with schedules gone awry, it's tacit acknowledgement is surely also a motivator for the effort of scheduling, the reason why schedules are set at all. On the one hand, time is simply what is counted and what is to be counted, and how much of this or that there is or will be. But time is also that which takes its own time, uncounted and perhaps uncountable. For certain things are unique, like the hours spent with the beloved, that can only be remarked upon in the hindsight of coming back into a reality that is indeed shared by others outside this intimacy. Indeed, Van Der Leeuw reminds us that "Only when I take part in a race or when I am overtired is it different. Then I count the miles and move from milestone to milestone. But that is a subhuman process – as though I were to do nothing all day but look at the clock." (op. cit:327). So Aristotle cannot mean that we take counting so literally that we are made conscious of time as merely a measured passing. Scheduling does have this effect, of course. The milestones are simply transmuted into meetings, and we can remark to our fellows about 'last month's' get-together, poker night, Bible study or what-have-you. More ominously, the yearly employee evaluation or annual physical might also spring to mind. But what we are doing in these contexts is not merely counting, but recounting, just as schedules do not only mark the time but remark upon it. For something of note, however mundane, is to occur there. Something is going to happen. Not in any mystical or eldritch sense that such a phrase might conjure in myth or literature, but rather more strictly, 'some thing' rather than nothing, and certainly something other than the Nothing of which Anxiety is sibling. No, meetings populating a tightly packed schedule are the source only of *anxieties*, and these are never related to the idea of having a meeting rather than not having one, but always directed towards the specific content, or presumed content, of the encounter in question. The flip-side of this occurs when we are delighted to see someone or do something. Here again, however, it is the particular event that has been placed on our imminent horizon that we will to immanency with all the desire of the lover.

What is *shared*, then, is what makes time 'public'. It is not how it is measured after all. And scheduling encounters has the force of making time public in this more 'primitive' manner (cf. Wood 1989:239). "The difference between day and night, and the height of the sun in the sky, supply us all in a publicly available way with a grid for the assigning of times..." (ibid). Such temporality is the reason that clocks exist, and not the other way round. Heidegger himself puts it this way: "...the publicness of 'time' is all the more compelling, the more *explicitly* factical Dasein *concerns* itself with time in specifically taking it into its reckoning." (1962:464 [1927], italics the text's). How does Dasein accomplish this? Since the being of Dasein is care, it is oriented to the world which, in its facticality and in its already-thereness, persists in reminding us that we must be concerned with it, in a concerned-withness that does not lose itself wholly in its own temporality. "'Public time' turns out to be the kind of time 'in which' the ready-to-hand and the present-at-hand within-the-world are encountered." (ibid:465). Counting and marking are only a minor means of this encounter. But it is fair to say at this point that the schedule has become the 'grid' upon which we arrange who and what is going to be 'ready' or 'present' in the manner of factical handedness. But *Offentlichkeit*, wherein such a time as is its own transpires, rather than simply occurring, is not itself *Vorhanden*. It is what falls into the grid of the schedule that can take on this kind of language to itself, for its fallenness is arranged and calculated and not at all 'thrown' into the world. It has the meaning of a project only because we have seen fit to confer upon it such a potential. It is a secondary effort on our parts, and a wholly conscious one at that, to make such time public "...by the institution of measurement, and things can have times 'attached' to them as soon as they are seen to be 'in' this public time." (Wood 1989:244). Heidegger immediately reminds us that though the clock is the key element of this part of what is to be considered 'in the public', but even so, this is not its publicness: "The public dating, in which everyone assigns himself his time, is one which everyone can 'reckon' on simultaneously; it uses a publicly available *measure*." (1962:466 [1927], italics the text's). Importantly, constructing a schedule is not all about objectification in the quantifiable sense. We assign ourselves 'our time' in this way as well. But the fact that 'everyone' does so and in the same way smacks of Das Man. How then is this 'our' time? "When concern makes present by awaiting and retaining, time is understood in relation to a 'for-which'." (ibid:467). Heidegger is careful to also note that we have always a sense that this is the 'right time' or the 'wrong time' for something or other. This sense is not separate, not an entity standing aloof and apart from the 'thing' in question, but a constitutional structure of our experience of both time and the being of anything that could occur 'within' it, however public. Indeed, all the more so, publicness known in this way pushes our concern to the fore. This is eminently the reason why meetings are called in the first place, and the concern by which schedules are constructed refracts the concernfulness associated with thinking the right and the wrong in this manner.

We may of course be mistaken, pending the future outcomes of what we have constructed. This may not be 'our time' after all. But the assignation must take place even so. One cannot 'play the game' unless and until one 'plays up', so to speak. It may well be said that "...the time schedule – which may be the highest form of interactional rationality – states in an identical way how the time required for the performance of numerous activities can be covered by its anticipated availability." (Schwartz 1975:46). Schwartz's analogy, or yet homology, comes from Weber, whom he cites as stating that the budget is the highest form of 'economic rationality'. This being so, both could also be seen as the lowest forms of their respective Being. Everything is reduced and quantified. But this is only an appearance. What gives budgets and schedules their status is that they have, in a flattery and oblation that one might regard as both fanatical and yet also loving, transferred all of the existential sensibility being brings to itself into the 'within which' of public time. The being of the public, its 'open space', is the expression of what *can* be planned in finitude by those finite and those who face down what cannot be.

3.2 Plotting:

If planning carries itself into our ethical consciousness because it appears benign – it is 'only' a plan in this sense, open-ended, a chart of the route and not the route itself, a suggestion and not a demand – then there at once must be an underside to all schedules, something that has the force and will to undertake what needs to be done. This 'undertaker' is called plotting. It differs from planning in precisely the way private prayer differs from official genuflection, fees differ from fines, and requests differ from commands. The distinction between care and concernfulness is also relevant: "... care means being out for something; Dasein's concern includes a concern for its own being. As being out for something, it is out for *what it still is not.*" (Heidegger 1992:308 [1925], italics the text's). Our casual expression to this regard reflects this lack. 'He is out for something' always means that the person in question has at least a keen motive, even if the precise goal cannot immediately be identified, and hence the circumlocution. The plot is always keener edged than the plan. For a plot clearly has the expectation that the 'something' one is out for, out to get, or yet more shadily, the someone who one is 'out to get' in some other manner, will indeed occur in some form. A plan remains only a plan in this sense as well. We do not have the same expectations of it. The plan partakes in 'ordinary time' and the plot intentional time. The plan is more of a where and the plot a how, even a how-to. If "The ordinary interpretation of world-time as now-time never avails itself of the horizon by which such things as world, significance, and datability can be made accessible." (Heidegger 1962:475 [1927]), then the extraordinary concernful circumstance of the plot directs itself towards just this horizon. Things are much more exact. Planning a trip and plotting a course also reflect this difference. Errors in the execution of a plot are more 'significant' than those that may occur within the planning stage of any possible future. One hears this sensibility in managerial language when we are told that it is always better to encounter errors of judgement, timing, or even character 'in the planning stage', or 'before things get off the ground' and such-like. But within the plot that has been already plotted, such things are that much more serious. This is so at the existential level as well, for "In its preoccupation with the world the temporally particular being-in-the-world which the Dasein is temporalizes itself." (Heidegger 1992:168 [1925]). Our very being is at stake in the plot, because we are putting so much of ourselves on the line. If we are out for something, then we also 'put ourselves out' for something or someone and thence demonstrate, through the action of the plot, our willingness to do so at a moment's notice.

So we make ourselves temporal beings in the world by bringing world-time into the being-of-its-self-care. The world cannot know itself. It's worlding does not include a self-consciousness of any kind. This does not mean that we can presume to know it simply because we must confront the problem of self-knowledge and thus commit to the development of a self-understanding and the sense that one must make meaningful one's existence. Rather, the dialogue that takes place between Dasein and the facticality of the world exteriorizes both its objection to our presence and our subjection to its gravity. Like the confrontation with the tradition, the world 'itself' holds no specific hold over us in the way this or that cultural background does. But though the world is not our own, this distance is not quite the same thing as the manner in which the tradition stands apart from us. We live 'in' the world, but more in the manner of living *on* it. But we live *within* and with a tradition, in the manner that we live with one another. The world is the mediator between what is ready-to-hand and what is present-at-hand. It is the open space wherein these categories can be juxtaposed with Dasein, can be called into play by us, and can impinge on our ability to apprehend ourselves. We have seen that they can be a source of the loss of being, its forgetfulness, an aspect of its fallenness, and the surrounds of its inauthenticity. We need the power of the plot to negotiate all of this. The plan is far too airy a thing upon which to hang one's ontological hat. In this way we can be said to 'build' a future rather than live it (cf. Minkowski 1970:343 [1933]), and these 'previsions' by which we do not attempt to 'live the future' nevertheless are part of our being able to 'be ahead of ourselves': "The innermost structure of Dasein's caring about its being can be conceived formally as *Dasein's being-ahead-of-itself*." (Heidegger, op. cit:294). This is a unique feature of human consciousness. From this the concept of the future, as well as 'having' a future arise. Hence the themes of many Promethean myths around the cultural globe, wherein the moment of our death is hidden from us. From this all things suddenly become possible. Before this, we lived in the clamshell of animal-being, aware of only what was in the moment, schooled by the tension between instinct and habituation. Experience, in the sense of Erlebnis, did not exist. But once liberated from this truncated horizontality, newly *human* being took on the ability to be-toward. This being-toward included within its penumbra that of being-untoward as well, hence the ability to plot. Plotting is a way in which to live the future without having to admit to the future as it may be. One arrests it, rather than merely encounters it, as with a plan. So the content and content of a schedule that is plotted takes on a very different integer of meaning than one that is only planned. The sense of the 'right' and 'wrong' time for everything is heightened and transmuted into a weapon. Crises are plotted around. No plan is ever 'timely' enough to contend with them: "Even less promising situations can be influenced through their time element and by a correct timely attitude..." (Wilhelm 1973:228 [1951]). Being 'on time' in this sense is very much the same thing as being 'on task'. From the exhortations of kindergarten teachers to those of human resource professionals or physicians, it is made clear to us that we not only have a stake in our future - specifically and perhaps the more so, as individuals, with all of the problematic implications this contains for the future of the species as a whole – but that we can exert control over it if we try. Thus plotting is something built into the future in the manner Minkowski suggests that we 'build' it in general. Our being is 'out for' its own being, as Heidegger says. How it accomplishes this outward expression of the interiority of intentional concern is through this human uniqueness: "This being-ahead-of-itself signifies precisely that care or Dasein in care has *thrust* its own being *ahead as an existential facticity.*" (1992:295 [1925], italics the text's). We are always already involved in this, 'even' authentic being, which Heidegger seems to be surprised by, or at least wishes to make it perfectly clear, as he adds an exclamation mark to this addenda. The 'being in want' which is the interior implication of being out for something is itself a hybrid feature of consciousness in a world, a world that is not its own and was also not the source of its being. Wanting in this way includes both desire and need. The keener this is experienced, the more the plot comes into play. It offers relief from the awaiting-want in its wanton wont. It places into high-relief the 'wantedness' of what one does not yet have. We are overcome by such a thing. What we are does not match what we might think to be, or even what we will be, though this last includes the lesser as a possibility within its horizon. The gap between being-here and being-there is a constitutional article of *Fragwurdigheit*.

To assuage this alienating experience, the Nothing nosing its way into the interstitial vents of what is breathed into being by our being-ahead, schedules afford us the chart upon which our course may then be plotted. We line up, as it were, both ourselves into this or that queue to pursue a specific goal of the want, as well as lining up options and the wants themselves. For no want is in principal *the* want, or can circumscribe all wantedness. We must allocate what part of that which is to come within which the that-which-is-to-come, which includes something for us, coming to us and *for* us. Just as "...queue discipline may not be understood as an invariant allocational mode but, rather, as a strategy by which organizations accommodate themselves to varying levels and kinds of inundation." (Schwartz 1975:125), so too do we 'get in line' or make sure that the line between us and our want is as short and straight as could be. Now, the 'correct' and 'timely' attitude regarding subjecting oneself to the internal discipline of the queue as feigned facticity may have great bearing on its outcome. If we are light-hearted versus sullen, for example, then the waiting takes on a very different kind of atmosphere (cf. ibid:156). Even if we are in the minority regarding the kinds of wants we plot for, or yet the kinds of crises we plot against, we must take into consideration that we have not only not originated the contexts within which want itself is experienced as a part of the thrownness of human consciousness and the fallenness of Dasein's self-consciousness, we cannot in fact control them overtly and in every instance (cf. ibid:166 for a religious example of this 'martinet' quality exhibited by minorities at a larger scale public temporality). This is because the time factor is not negated by any kind of plot, no matter how involved and venerated: "In the two structural moments of being-ahead-of-itself and already-being-involved-in, there is a puzzling character which is peculiar to care and, as we shall see, is nothing other than *time*." (Heidegger 1992:295 [1925], italics the text's). On the one side, the presence of time as an 'independent' variable gives us the time we need to plot the most careful course we can imagine. This occurs always in principal, and just as always we experience a greater or lesser degree of this 'peculiar' quality in our doings. We may feel like we do not 'have the time' for this or that detail. On the other side, if there is too much time between plot and anticipated climax, the best laid things can also come unraveled. It is not as if care *makes* time by itself. But it does mark time. It cares to know the time. Its cares take place in time and because of this, make us feel like we are 'out' of time. It can dull our senses, in part by making us complacent – 'we have lots of time' – and also by presenting within its own ambit the unexpected, the other: "Time, the instrument of servitude, thus becomes a product of ignorance, resulting from a wicked imitation (evil in its intention and execution) of a sort of prototype that is infinitely superior, of something wholly other." (Puech 1973:71-2 [1951]). In this time of waiting and plotting, we are ourselves cast as the Gnostic Demiurge, holding to ourselves only a vague notion of what is to occur and how it will transpire, kindred to the partial understanding that we have and thus do not have of cosmic time. In a word the reality of that which is to come has been only imitated in our plotting regarding how it is to come about.

So we wait. Both on the outcomes of our plot and the chance of history, since both come together to make the peculiar character of the time 'between' intention and destiny. Even so, most plots do confer some small advantage upon those who construct them. They enable us to prepare ourselves for at least some of the likely outcomes. The trick is to not become to emplotted oneself. When things do not go as expected or planned, we might feel like giving up entirely. It is always better to wait it out, we might say, knowing that the 'less advantaged' we are, the longer we might have to wait. Of these persons, which is most of us over the life course, Schwartz drily reminds us: "While they might have something else to do besides sitting and waiting, they might not have anything better to do." (op. cit:22). The 'sub-human' quality of clock-watching is, as we saw above, tantamount to making oneself into a vehicle for measured objective time. In our age of the scientific testament, we may feel an odd superiority accruing to this kind of activity, simply because it appears to take us closer to the truth of the cosmos. But, like the wickedness of the calculated mimesis that pretends to know the truth and thereby uses this pretense to mask its own ignorance, this 'cosmosis' is a pale imitation of reality. At most, we are engaged in a flight from reality which includes ourselves: "You get absorbed in the observation of the clock and lose the thread that leads you to yourself – I am a clock myself, everywhere in me things always go pell-mell. I am all that myself – I lose it when I look at the clock on the wall." (Minkowski, op. cit:288). Here, a schizophrenic patient is cited explaining their fixation. But we cannot 'repeal' the past, just as tomorrow cannot be in the same stroke revealed before us (cf. Wood 1989:80). Watching the clock, though relevant in certain very specific contexts such as the players and coaches involved in a tightly contested sporting event, levels out experienced time into neither a subject nor an object. Time no longer objects to our presence in it, our being-in-time and the temporality of our being, which is lost to us like the 'thread' which leads to our lives, nor do we feel subjected to it. It is under our control. We are, after all, the clock.

This pale imitation of a being that is temporal through and through is yet a function of its concernfulness, which has 'the sense of a restoration of order' (cf. Heidegger 1992:188 [1925]), and a 'repairing'. We repair to the clock, and repair our senses thereby. Taking control in this way – 'you have five minutes remaining' – reminds us of two simultaneous things: that all things must pass in the brute sense of the momentary, and this may help get us through a crisis, such as all those who were interned in conflicts, and as well, that "…the very determining of the time should claim as little time as possible…" (Heidegger 1962:471 [1927]). The clock as a device used in a plot – how much time each incrementality of the how-to-be-ahead-of-oneself is of the utmost; one can only call to mind the satires of heists or assassinations, wherein the villain is marking the time by the minute to his or her compatriots – puts itself forward as the source of a banal intelligence, which, like the conspiracy, never quite divulges enough to vanquish itself. It rests on "…the *complicity* of references to the future…" (Wood, op. cit:367, italics the text's), just as logocentrism is said to. But surely this conspiratorial tone is more of an intonation. It does not merely project itself forward, as does a seer, prophet, or fortune-teller, using the already murky waters of what has not yet occurred to promote its own resourcefulness. The sheer nerve involved in prediction is something that not all of us are willing to exhibit. That alone places the plot inside the enchanted circle of Gnosis, or so it claims. It *is* true that we can know something of otherness in a variety of like circles, and "It is because understanding is drawn from the world that there is the possibility of understanding an alien world or a world mediated by sources, monuments, and ruins." (Heidegger 1992:243 [1925]). But this kind of knowing does not lay claim to the projection involved in prognostication. 'Prognosis' in its very attempt to be-ahead in the way Dasein is already, makes itself into the pale, and perhaps even evil, imitation of what is ontologically present. It tries to conjure the immanent from the imminent, and that at its best. Usually, events are non-present in this way. We do not know how close they are and, because we often mistake the nearest for the closest, as we have seen above, we conflate what the clock can tell us about our plotting and what the vital spirit of being-ahead-of-oneself says to Dasein. The first is a measured desire and the second an ability "..to see the future open in the élan vital wide before one…" (Minkowski, op. cit:39). What keeps the future open in this authentic sense concerns also what Heidegger refers to as 'reticence', which includes the 'genuine ability to hear', as well as *Mitsein* (cf. 1992:268 [1925]). Plotting is, because of its need to heed only itself and not the coming reality of a future beyond its complete control, could easily be categorized within idle talk. This is so simply due to the focus of the plot and how it must be communicated given the lack of experience with its actual outcomes. It is discoursed about as if anyone could speak of it and understand it. The plot is, in this way, anonymous: "What *one* says has taken the lead in all interpretation and thus taken over the temporalization of understanding. This means that what *one* says is really what controls the various possibilities of the being of Dasein." (ibid:270, italics the text's). Like other elements of the schedule in general, the plot relies on its apparent anonymization to engender group loyalty to it and to its aims. The actual process of plotting requires almost as much of this patriotism as do the contents of any specific plot device. One does not have to commit to the desired outcomes as such, at least, not yet. But one does have to throw one's hat into the ring within which there might be as much fire as that in the outside world one is trying to circumvent, just like the ill person who watches the clock all day and thus becomes it himself. As with plots of all kinds, if we are beholden to this or that course of action, we also instill in ourselves the sense that other activities can fail not only due to their apparent irrelevance but as well, if they had succeeded, they would have thwarted the main thrust of the plot: "The very condition that determines that act *A* will not be done *also* stimulates the futile attempt to do it…" (Horwich 1988:125, italics the text's). If we are determined *not* to do something, if we fail to do so, this is precisely part of the plot. Addictions may give us pause here, because we can plot a way of overcoming them and feel a keen sense of determination about doing so and yet still fail multiple times. Generally, however, the conflict between a projected desire and its surrogate – addiction may be seen as the evil imitation of an authenticity, a form of idle talk talking itself into idolatry – do not occur in the plots that show up in schedules or other kinds of long term plans. Indeed, institutional mission statements, annual reports and their projections, 'five-year plans' and the like notoriously ignore individual markers of time such as those of the addict, the ill, or the otherwise incapacitated. Not only this, the plot narrows the scope of action so significantly, that its enemies are also forced to watch the clock. Most entertainment fiction designed to push its audience to experience the tension of time 'running out' employs this dual feature. Can the heroes save the world before the villains destroy it? More sophisticated is the plot wherein the world is changed regardless. But the key point here is that in plotting, even more so than planning, time is given a direction and a *telos*: "If time here has a direction, it also has a meaning for the salvation of all mankind and of each man in particular. History is *Heilsgeschichte*" (Puech, op. cit:52). History also takes on a pedagogic function. The plot teaches us the 'how to' of its proposed future. In doing so, it transforms the studied dispassionate observer of the plan into the committed revolutionary of what is both staked out and now at stake. *I* may not have become death, but nevertheless, the old world must die.

3.3 'Free' Time:

Despite the sense of both urgency and propriety we might bring to the plot, its most likely goal is not to radically change the world entire, but adjust our own world so that we may liberate ourselves from a few of its burdens. Scheduling, including both its plans and its plots, has the unannounced but often assumed goal of giving us more time than we had before. This 'more' is then itself allocated into that which allows us 'free' time. Thus 'more free time' shows up as a major constituent in studies of motivation across workplaces and in the home life. Not to mention, young persons and children, when asked about their schedules, constructed for them by institutions and families alike, also tell us the same thing. Much vaunted then, is an outcome that seems to at first have little to do with anything other than self-absorption. We feel we need this, however, to balance the publicness of both idle talk and labor, everyday being-with-one-another and even the authentic and authenticating self-understanding of being-ahead-of-oneself. It is this last mode of Dasein that places closest to us the need for freedom. 'Free' time allows us to experiment along the edge of pale imitation, or better, rehearse for the completion of Dasein in its own demise: "…free time allows us to calm the mind and to contemplate our environment, to mingle with it, and, by plunging our attention to the depths of our being, permits us to come into intimate contact with our own selves…" (Minkowski 1970:3-4 [1933]). To reflect without object is the object of a time that is free in this sense. In this, it is the polar opposite of the schedule. The schedule's aim then is to get beyond itself, to overcome the need for itself, just as Dasein strives to overcome the need to be-ahead and reside only in the present, imagining that presence is thus contained there. My existence cannot be placed on a schedule. It is not based on a measured time, nor does it find its home within the objective time of the world already present-at-hand. Existence for human beings is never at hand in this manner. At-handedness is a feature of anything that can be marked in a schedule. Being remarks only upon itself: "Dasein does not exist as the sum of the momentary actualities of Experience which come along successively and disappear. Nor is there a sort of framework which this succession gradually fills up." (Heidegger 1962:426 [1927]). The apriori condition of Dasein is such that it takes care into itself, which is part of the 'experience' of a time that is free of objects and objectifications. And one does not object to free time unless one is enthralled with the idle talk of the object-life, unless one desires to place oneself at hand, or take oneself in hand. More darkly, to do so with an other to self marks us as wicked in the way in which the imitator of cosmic truth was. The beforehandedness of Dasein has to do with the 'ontological structure of being' (cf. Heidegger 1992:74 [1925]). Thus the 'earlier' is not a sequential concept. It is an element of how "...concern structures the world and is rooted in temporality, and the temporal way it structures the world appears as time." (Wood 1989:240). That we are so concerned about having free time is demonstrated by the lengths we go to enslave ourselves to that unfree. Aside from wage labor, the drive to imagine and then invent new technologies that 'save' time has been perhaps the most important marketing feature of commodities for the past century and a half. Improvements in this or that product invariably include at least the appearance of a time-saving mechanism. Of course, time itself may not be saved, especially in a finite lifespan. But all the more so, we are perhaps made aware of our mortality, though in an ironic fashion, by the shameless shill urging us to disregard it, or lending to us the pretense of overcoming it. With God's passing, the advertiser become the prophet. True, there is an homonymous motivation present, but nonetheless, the shorter term aside, consumer products of our own age exude the soteriology of distant and alien worlds. They are in this sense also, time machines., with the ability to transport us both backwards and forwards at once; backwards to the time when our ancestors might have actually believed in the afterlife – though there is a distinct paucity of data regarding how the great masses of historical illiterates thought on *any* topic, let alone those metaphysical or elite - , and forwards to that very afterlife which has been called into radical question by those very consumers.

So technology as applied to the commodity serves the desire to preserve time for oneself, the user of that technology. To use the more of it? Perhaps. But also to use it in a fashion that appears to promote the freedom occasioned by dwelling within that kind of time that is bereft of objects of all kinds. Does this merely imitate in-dwelling? "This is the pure state of hierarchy, a pure time with no concern other than to be at one with one's own code." (Kristeva 1996:312). But the imagination that can conjure its own purification through the focused use of objects that are at hand, is one that could be greeted with certain suspicions. If such an image is indeed a vision and not a mere mimicry, such time that is lost in making sure one has free time dispenses with the sense that all time is of equal value, and that some of it, at least, can afford to *be* lost (cf. ibid). In the context of a story, surely this might be plausible. The foreshortening that all narratives betray – no one would read every second of her life into a book and see it moment by moment reflected there as in a mirror image – itself betrays the sense of time that would be able to take time for itself. This is tantamount to "...the suggestion that narrativity might appear at the level of existence itself." (Wood 1989:353, and for a list of levels of time in narrative, see ibid:354). Art may mimic life, and then, in some refracted and usually degraded sense, some of us think to make our lives into a work of art, but the relationship between the two of them is not a form of similitude. Art exists in a different time than does life. It interposes itself, obtruding into the time of our lives in an uncanny fashion, or as a mnemonic, but never as an identity. In part this is due to the historical sequence of events that saw the sciences substitute themselves for their parent religions. With this, eschatological time lost its overarching meaning as an autoteleological antidote to any aporetic consciousness. 'Fragmented' time, one shard of which is 'free', is all we can now know (cf. Plessner, op. cit:259). But the 'imagery' of the *vision* still has resonance for us, especially if we desire to free ourselves from the time of objects and learn the object lesson of self-understanding shorn of all that we object to, in ourselves as well as others. To not present ourselves to the world in this way is to have *lost* all sense of time: "The person who says he has no time for this or that has (inauthentically) lost himself in objects of immediate concern, and is someone for whom the moment of vision is no longer operative." (Wood 1989:238). Contrary to this, the one who 'goes in for something' slows time down (cf. Heidegger 1962:218ff [1927]). Idle talk proceeds at a rapid clip, always moving on to what is of the moment and the latest thing, but the more relaxed, if not necessarily pedestrian, tempo of the specific something which is drawn from the present-at-hand and ready-to-hand out of their contrived *Offentlichkeit* and into the clearing, attains a space of indwelling and what is 'lighted'. What is lit up, as in, what is in the limelight, can never be also within the closest. Like the commodity which soteriologically *saves* time – to what end? – both idle talk and curiosity alike construct a kind of instant planned obsolescence that often looks like, from the outside in, another kind of plot. But the 'going in' produces a time that the public observes as passing more slowly. It is not a mere material coincidence that hobbies, however dreaded by the culture critic, focus on the archived objects of 'times gone by', such as philately or numismatics, the restoration of vintage vehicles or the acts of the bibliophile. These activities, 'gone in for', do not exhaust the manner in which temporality is experienced at a slower pace – the focus and discipline of the dancer or the athlete are other ways of bringing the nearest into the closest and indwelling with it, though none of these is 'authenticity' in any existential sense, contrary to some current interpretations of Heidegger – but they do underscore the idea that 'the soul is located in space' in the broadest sense (cf. 1992:122 [1925]). Recovering this sensibility from the world of objects in which 'the soul' or yet simply 'soul', as in soulfulness, is both a commodity and an object of desire, makes "...new demands on an inelastic supply of time [and thus] can only raise its value; hence the phobia of time waste and preoccupation with efficient scheduling..." (Schwartz 1975:2). Yet this very inelasticity which is at once promoted by the everyday sensibility that 'time's a wasting', has the latent function of being a benchmark against which Dasein can understand how and why it slows time or accelerates it. The focus of the gone-in-for accomplishes the first, the acts of love and friendship the second.

Not that such intensity is the sole guarantor of elastic time, the freedom of which we seek to be enfolded within. Pursuits that border on the fanatical, the fan of athletics or the workaholic, for example, exhibit as much or perhaps even more focused energy than do those acts which are on the way to being. Being a 'fan' of this or that raises the stakes of the future simply because no object of the fan can always perform to the 'live and die' exactitude of such standards. Placing Dasein in this kind of unfreedom, "...we now desire that our own future selfish desires will be satisfied, but we do not presently desire, to the same degree, that our past selfish desires were satisfied." (Horwich 1988:197). The hope of the sports fan, for instance, springs eternal, and in five years past where the Chicago Cubs won the World Series, Bob Dylan won a Nobel Prize and Donald Trump won the US presidency, it is clear that even the longest shots when considered historically or biographically will have their day, like the old saying has it. In the desire for the freedom of having made the right prediction and of having one's long-term loyalty fulfilled in the most public sense, we would certainly acceded to the idea "…that the values of certain future events are magnified compared to the values of similar past events." (ibid:196). That these 'certain' events are not at all certain, and indeed are much less certain the more extreme the fandom associated with them is – from the point of view of objective objection to their probability – does not deter their supporters. In fact, it tends to make them all the more vocal in their patriotic tones. They are as aware as everyone else is that they are fighting an unlikely, even a rearguard battle. This too explicates why neo-conservative religious communities can be so brash in their defense of 'values'. You might as well die with your boots on. Beyond even this, and perhaps also part of the nearest in a way that at least the vision of the religious fanatic could never be, is the simple facticality of dullness: "Brief life is here their portion, only because we are busy people or because we are bored with monotony." (Mabbot 1951, in Gave 1968:307). What gives them life at all, whatever its brevity, is the sheer fatal anomie of those who find themselves with either nothing, or alternatively, too much to believe in.

But since Dasein is time, its freedom is intimately imbricated with how it 'passes' or even how it 'spends' this time. For it is now easy enough to understand how "…temporality is not merely a subjective condition, but is constitutive of the world itself." (Wood 1989:234). At the same time, "…temporality is essentially falling, and it loses itself in making present…" (Heidegger 1962:421 [1927]). This is an insight that comes in part out of the ability to cast a parallax upon the everyday. Everydayness can be constituted as a problem, not in the social anxiety sense of course, but in the phenomenological and ethical senses. It is almost as if, in coming to grips with our own temporal 'natures', we must cast ourselves loose from Being and thus perhaps also cast ourselves *down* from it. Heidegger's ethical terms, though we are reminded more than once to take them as value neutral, do not only possess a descriptive flair. In much the same way, when one utters 'freedom', one is not meaning only to describe a state of affairs, however hypothetical. It is sage to note at once that the more hypothetical this or that theory of freedom posits its object to be, the more futural its temporality becomes *and* the more hyperbolic the means to attain it. But what if freedom and also free time are imbedded in the everyday, and it is the parallax of phenomenology that uncovers them there, in their thereness?

Like a protagonist struggling to find himself in his own story, the person dedicated to scheduling for himself enough 'free' time to be who he is, if only for a 'brief portion' of each day, such a person "...had to come integrated with it in order to disintegrate it more easily – for eternity. Was he at its periphery or at its center? It is a matter of mobility, of perspective, of the moment, of time regained and lost again so that 'pure time' can finally come about." (Kristeva 1996:158). The serpentine meanderings of the underground man, for instance, the guerrilla of a war on a drugged dullness and the enthralled ennui of a subsistence society, might move in such a manner as Proust's hero. Everything is made into a desire based in what may come, what might come, and not what *is* to come in principal, that is, that something or other *will* come to us and yet for us no matter our desires. "A conviction of potential richness of our existence *in time* is also characteristic of the imagination that is distinctively novelistic." (Sontag 2007:215, italics the text's). This distinction may be the mark of a great novelist, but its remarks on freedom within the temporal neither begin nor end there. Even if the 'narrative activity provides a privileged access' to the way we experience time, as Wood cites Ricoeur in affirming (op. cit:325), Wood is quite correct when he 'limits' the detailed extent of such a theory of temporal experience to having a common ancestor with existential time as well as time-consciousness, with its more phenomenological analytic in hand. In company with all of this future-directed desire for freeing up the time in one's life and days, and marking it as the absence of something in a formal way, as on a schedule – but, like the space on the road in urban settings, a length of asphalt may soon be filled up by other drivers – comes the sensibility that "It is not the pasts that actually took place, but the pasts that are still delayed and their forgotten futures that open up new lines." (Lampert 2012:165). A staple of speculative fiction, the idea of the 'time line' portraying events as they might have been had certain other things followed along from what didn't happen instead of what did, these 'forgotten futures', ones that could not be recalled as no mortal consciousness ever experienced them or even the thought of them, dramatize our desire that time itself be freed from the chains of history. The notoriously uncritical 'end of history', and its vehement if somewhat guttural denial as the 'absolute lie', might also be seen to have a more aspiring side. That is, one wishes to end its tyranny, let the dead bury the dead, and, as the heroine in one such fictional saga declared, 'The future cannot be guarded by those who hail from the past, it can only be guarded against.'.

Even so, as noble as these sentiments and desires may be and however suggestive they are of this or that ideal of freedom, authentically free time still seems both as elusive as it remains visionary. We are still faced with a key experiential objection to our subjectivity, and thus are subjected to it: "Experience once made is as complete as its occasions are past; that which is to be done in the future, which is anticipated in terms of an expectation, is scattered among an infinity of temporal extensions." (Koselleck 1985:272 [1969]). The dare is then made; *find that future in which your freedom be contained.* Not only this, do it before your own most certain future 'catches up' with you. The idiom is perhaps deliberately ironic. It suggests that we are running away from something rather than 'running on towards' it, which is the well known phenomenological ethic regarding human destiny. Idleness is not in fact, idle. It's 'talk' covers over Dasein's loss of the closest to it, its ownmost being. The idle found in what is public and everyday is hard at work, to the point of appearing to reverse what is ontologically the case, that we do in all of our existential facticity run towards something or other, and not away from it. But all that is unfree tells us that we are running away and thus we must run ever faster, lest 'it' catch up with us, or even catch us unawares, if we 'tarry' for too long and ourselves appear either as idle or as self-made idols. Heidegger then rephrases his question somewhat, to expose this problem: "Or is the Being of Dasein constituted first of all by historizing, so that anything like circumstances, events, and vicissitudes is ontologically possible *only because Dasein is historical in its Being*?" (1962:431 [1927], italics the text's). Two years prior, Heidegger had already stated unequivocally that a phenomenological interpretation of the 'phenomenon of death' is the only way in which Dasein's genuine being can be articulated to itself 'in its wholeness'. (cf. 1992:312 [1925]). That is, not only is Dasein completed, made whole, by and through its ownmost death - which is also its 'very own' in ontic life and the facticality of this not quite additional status is at first what we are urged to avoid by the 'running away' of distracted freedoms-to-be – it is the *ethic* of phenomenology, and not so much its ontological program, that discovers this. All 'discoveredness' in Heidegger's texts is both a function of the reduction and the critique that phenomenological analysis brings about. Indeed, the being-critical of psychologism was a catalyst that lingered in subsequent analyses, from Husserl onward. It cannot be summarily denied that culture critique, of the Weimar Republic in particular, gave wings to *Being and Time*, and exacerbated its authorial drive to place itself perilously close to the larger political reaction to it. These horrors at that time still to come and even desired by not a few, were also 'ambient events'. Our running on towards them is partly explained by the sense that "Time will not be empty for us; it will retain its *complete value*." (Minkowski 1970:338 [1933], italics the text's). Participation in events has nothing in common with 'presence', he immediately adds. Specific acts, whose being is neglected, serve only as a hint that the 'sense of being itself' has also suffered this same fate (cf. Heidegger 1992:115 [1925]). Because anything that remains unscheduled has the character of absence, it reminds us, however *sotto voce*, by whatever thread of the dreaming life, of the Nothing from which we hide ourselves, we must at least give the name 'free time' to the unmarked space within the temporal grid. We look 'forward' to these times, as they are imagined to be both beyond time – they have overcome the past in order to get to themselves, and get us 'into' them – and before the rest of the time – that is, the remainder of our days that also must then be 'gotten through'. The fetishization of free time is the ontic equivalent of our ethical desire for human freedom. But there is a disconnect; one that even those with the 'novelistic' imagination must pay heed to: "These nights beset with worry show a consciousness of responsibility, an awareness that in all such situations even a creative genius can act only in accord with the time." (Wilhelm 1973:229 [1951]).

Sleepless somnambulism aside, it is at least plausible that the imagination requires its possessor yet more of her time than even ascertaining when the time is 'right' or when one might be 'in accord' with it. No lasting eventuality can deny its presence, for it is one of the closest 'things' to us, in its ongoingness, and within its conscience, a self-consciousness that drives the future-oriented self-understanding not quite discretely from our desires. It is not mere *Orexis*, the desire born in and borne on a questionable ethic, but rather an attempt at *Phronesis*, practical wisdom given birth by the ethics of practice. And these ethics *do* occur in the present of the everyday. They do not attempt to conjure the future out of what is the case, but only insofar as they do not negate the future in the same way that the past has negated itself: "With poignant acuity a new element penetrates the past: the past not only has been but *is no longer*. Remembrance is born. Negation has penetrated time. From this moment, time rationalizes itself." (Minkowski, op. cit:167, italics the text's).

The schedule represents the most intimate portrait of that rationalization. Previous events are committed to its archive, to be recalled only if formally called upon. That which is to come, planned and plotted, with the desire that not all of it *will* come, or that something will remain even when *nothing* comes, including Nothing, is constructed out of desireful fetish. In between, we strive to avoid the full presence of that which cannot be either marked on a schedule or remarked upon by it; the restive renderings of a being so marked by time it has become indistinguishable from it.

Chapter Four

The Festive: Calendars

If both appointments and schedules discussed and even deadlines to come smack of modernity and nothing else, the remaining member of the substantive quartet has a more traditional ring to it. The calendar, found in ancient societies the world over, made all the more formal and sophisticated by agrarianism and writing, resonates in its residence into our own time and temporal consciousness. It's main theme is the celebration of cyclical time and life within it circumference and the ways of life found along its torus. The calendar, hung up on walls everywhere, accessed digitally on phones and computers, displayed in museums and archives and still given occasion for worship and oblation, is nevertheless an ironic anachronism: there are no 'special days'.

To imagine that there are is to deny the facticity of one's existence. But is that all one can say about calendrical events? Is there nothing else besides their inauthentic entanglement, the outcome of which is the loss of being in the being-with of the public and the everyday that includes its own fetish as days 'until' everyday can proclaims itself its opposite? Such a question can be investigated, but it cannot be asked at all from within the ambit of the calendrical circle. The would-be enchantedness of a bygone system of marks and signs, of late supplanted by the schedule as we have seen, clouds our judgement. I'd rather celebrate my birthday by not thinking along such lines, for instance, or 'take a vacation' where I am not writing or reading at all, about any topic. But within this desire, future-held and always desireful of itself as celebrated as 'special' and as part of the festive, cannot be entirely unthinking. Its schemes are not dissimilar from those of the schedule, but in the end, at the time in question, one is forced to confront the 'running on', the thrownness of our project. Each birthday and new year are, even if marked down as a part of an endless cycle, can be no less linear because of that. Calendars in their months and days look almost the same year to year, but the numeric of the year has duly changed before our aging eyes. It is a new year, but not in the old sense.

In turn, we will pursue the act of marking the date, of dating something, or even someone, and marking her with remarks to be made later, to either unmake our new friendship or to make it something more than it was, or perhaps ever could have been. Such a marking system differs extensively from that used by a schedule. Calendars are, as part of *their* constitutive essence, religious documents, not bureaucratic ones. Today this is used as a form of charlatanry that takes its place as 'idol talk' in the false durations of *Offentlichkeit*. Second, the mnemonic function of calendars will be discussed. The cycle never forgets anything, repeating it endlessly. But a linear cycle must remember things, and the sentiment 'forget me not' rises on its crest. Finally, our resolutions, so common a manner to ring in the new, or what can be the new in cyclic linearity, are examined. In the festive, we are resolved to both recall and yet not repeat everything that has occurred to us. This feat is to be accomplished by the sleight of handedness the object of the calendar presents to us.

4.1 'Mark the Date':

The calendar is not utterly bereft of contemporary relevance: "Every day is oriented to the position of the sun according to the official astronomical ordering of time. Every time we look at a clock, we are simply making use of the copresence of the world-system." (Heidegger 1992:193 [1925]). These days are marked on calendars. They come thus pre-marked, with usually square spaces within which we can detail the events, desired or feared, that are to come. What is allotted for each day becomes more clear the 'closer' we approach that time. Of course, events are rescheduled, as we have seen, across days and weeks and even longer, and when a certain threshold of time-length is encountered, the calendar comes back into play, and for a while, supersedes the schedule, which tends to mark itself in smaller increments. All of this is somewhat feigned: "Passage of time can never be represented by a straight line limited at its beginning and end by an initial and final event. [ ] ...time has a rhythm, it can never have an absolutely defined direction." (Puech 1973:42 [1951]). This is so due to its 'successive cycles', which are paid tribute to in the odd interweaving of a repetitive grid upon which are marked both cyclical and linear events. The annual physical is one such exemplar of this mixed metaphor. It comes 'around' each year or so, but its purpose is derived solely from linearity, that is, the aging process and its successive life phases. *This* succession is a line and a direction. Birthdays are another obvious example, perhaps the archetypical one, of the interstitiality of line and circle. The idea of 'tube' time, spoken of earlier, attempts to address this 'topological' conundrum, where the figure of time as lived does not adhere to this or that one-dimensional Euclidean vehicle.

Just so, as the dates marked on a calendar begin to recede from our viewpoint, all the more so when we turn the page on the months going forward, the manner in which these past events, somehow due to reappear once again next year or even the very next month or week, cannot be thought of in the same way as those to come, even if they are the 'same' event: "The passage of the past into the present does not have a linear character." (Minkowski 1970:165 [1933]). The markings on a calendar must be read more like a text: "*Unlike* linear time, the sentence reproduces a giant breath through explanatory detours or backward leaps that develop traces that had already been constructed, erased, and not absorbed." (Kristeva 1996:304 [1994], italics the text's). The content of the physical is again a case in point. We may well find something is amiss with us, or something that thus has to be monitored or medicated or even operated upon. These 'traces' of the future are now in the past, but they still have an unutterable power over us. They shape what is to come through the sophisticated evolution process that supersedes cause and effect as well as simple linearity. It is not at all clear that "…it takes as much time for the event to occur as it takes for the time to pass…" (Lampert 2012:110). But this is more of an extended metaphor, the very kind a sentence or a paragraph arrests us with and holds us within. From symptom to diagnosis to prescription and proscription, to intervention or prevention to prognosis is a kind of time that might be added up to a certain point objectively – we *could* time each instance where we are occupied specifically with our medical condition and nothing else – but this sum would not in fact exhaust the experienced time working within or 'dealing' with the phenomenon in question. It is no single thing that works upon us and within our interiors. It is only myself as Dasein that works in this way, and even then, such workings are generally obscured, as we have seen. No, it is more correct to state, as does Heidegger, that "The 'time' which is experienced in such reckoning is that phenomenal aspect of temporality which is closest to us." (1962:278 [1927]). From which comes both ordinary understandings and then traditional conceptions of time, including that which is both represented on, and revealed by, the calendar. So, first and foremost is my experience that while time has passed, the eventuality of the event in question may have experienced no passage of time whatsoever, as when one is on a waiting list for a medical procedure. Such 'wait times' as they have become known as, vary considerably country to country and procedure to procedure, of course, but nevertheless they all betray this disconnect between the 'time of an event' and the passage of time more generally. Even so, we cannot say that time has 'stopped'. Waiting has taken over from proceeding. It is the time passing within the wait that is now being experienced, and this still bears an indirect, and perhaps increasingly indistinct - the longer it 'goes on' for, relation to the 'main event' or the object of the variety of phases of the passage of time, or indeed, the different kinds of temporality experienced throughout a calendrically marked process – tempo and temporality. However much the monotony of certain aspects of mundane time are experienced as, their *Erlebnisse* cannot be considered to be the 'same' thing. The obverse also applies: "It is to be understood here that the *reliving* of an event, however vivid it may be, is not tp be misleadingly called an 'experience' of the event." (Grünbaum, in Gale 1968:336, italics the text's). Nation states notoriously contrive such events as if they can be both relived and experienced once again as they had been. The purpose of such contraptions is transparent, but more generally, the social control of large scale and diverse populations, from the standpoint of any centralized authority or attempt thereof, 'needs' to be summoned and rallied round some kind of incident that is supposed to have affected the collective imagination and thus may appeal directly to the collective conscience: "Such an anniversary serves a number of purposes. It is a day of mourning. It is an affirmation of national solidarity. But of one thing we can be sure. It is not a day of national reflection." (Sontag 2007:120-1). Indeed, I was working in the United States during the attacks of September 11, 2001, and even within the days immediately afterward in the region I lived in there was much diversity of opinion upon them, to the point that some American citizens stated quite unequivocally that 'it couldn't have happened to a nicer bunch,' or some such similar sentiment. I was not surprised by these reactions. In fact, the more patriotic the sentiment, the more suspicious of it one could generally be. For these persons, even such a shocking event as the '9/11' attacks was *not* experienced as a single thing or the same kind of thing. Over time, the nation state's attempts to create collective sentiment surrounding these events diminished and by now of course has entirely faded from view. This is a good thing.

Hence the ongoing presence of a calendar. The calendars constructed by institutions last far longer than those of individuals, just as with most other aspects of institutional life and the mortal and serial experience of it. The state has substituted its calendar for that of the church, but the 'holy days' of both remain marked together upon the what purports to ostensibly be the same grid. But like the disconnect between linearity and circularity, our modern calendar is actually two different and quite distinct documents passed off as one, not unlike the Judeo-Christian scriptures. State holy days, like those celebrated for past politicians or other leaders, present in every modern country, or those representing political entities - in Canada, there is 'BC day', for example, amongst many others –compete with our attention with the more ancient markings of the church or churches. A truly politically 'correct' calendar will list the important days of numerous world religions – though it is important to note that Western calendars to this day rarely note the holy days of Eastern religions – as well as days which are not holidays at all, such as those earmarked for the noting of social movements, like gay pride or black history or even those dedicated to medical conditions - national cancer day - or huge categories of personhood, like women's day. So by the time we have placed a new calendar on the wall or adjusted our electronic devices accordingly, we have passed through a myriad of dated days hailing from a chaos of cultures and representing a mélange of movements. No one could be expected to observe them all, and no one in fact does so.

Since that is invariably and inevitably the case, what then is the ultimate purpose of this aggrandized marking machine? It may be that "…while dating systems in principle allow any event to be uniquely located in a single temporal series [ ] there remains the possibility of establishing a number of more limited special series restricted by content and in which the actual order is not always of overriding importance." (Wood 1989:337-8). This is in fact what is done with calendars by their respective owners and observers. Hence the proliferation of versions calendars can be purchased in, once again, much like the versions of the holy scriptures of various religions and their associated, and perhaps all the more tellingly, disassociated, denominations. One can procure a calendar where almost none of the marked dates is familiar, and where almost all of them would be deemed archaic at best by 'mainstream' persons living 'today'. But do any of us really live in the present all of the time? The very presence of a device like a calendar argues forcefully to the contrary: "Whether this dating is factically done with respect to a 'date' on the calendar, must still be completely disregarded. Even without 'dates' of this sort, the 'now' and the 'then', and the 'on that former occasion' have been dated more or less definitively." (Heidegger

1962:459 [1927]). Wood characterizes the calendrical device as utilizing 'nesting orders' of temporal unit (cf. 1989:321ff). The basic unit of this order is the day, but this may be both divided and multiplied up and down an imbricated scale, like a set of Russian dolls. Calendars are thus able to play both multiple roles as a symbolic mnemonic as we have just seen, but also interdiscursive roles, such as being a device used in the sciences as well as more traditionally for the religious life. All of this figuring both up and down the scale of temporal chronologies is also a 'facticity' in the facticality of Dasein's existence: "And is it not also a Fact of existing Dasein that in spending its time it takes 'time' into its reckoning from the day to day and regulates this 'reckoning' astronomically and calendrically?" (Heidegger, op. cit:423). Taking time while spending it once again points up the dual feature of the calendar. It must mark two kinds of time at once. Before this, however, the ability to mark time must first be reckoned with, as Heidegger states a little ways later. This precedent, the kind of being-reckoned that precedes other forms of marking, also allows for their advent (ibid:456). The question, 'where does Dasein *take* time from?', and how does it both save and lose it at once, points us in the direction of a precedent, a manner of reckoning that does not appear on the calendar or other such grids. We will look much more closely at the character of this 'primordial' sense of ontological temporality in the final chapter, but suffice to say for the moment that marking systems announce its presence surreptitiously, as if to nudge us into wondering what exactly the space in each of the day-boxes which construct this or that month actually is itself made from.

If it is true that "...without ritual, time does not pass." (Plessner, op. cit:238), we must also agree that in myth there is no such time to pass or be marked as passing. But the calendar, no matter what its cultural origin and the numeric or mathematical system it itself relies upon, is our way of joining myth and ritual together. Its duet of being and becoming has a certain, imprecise rhythm to it; imprecise and ambiguous precisely because it is the join, the hinge, and neither side of what is joined, neither face of the door or the window that opens itself onto both us and to the beyond that awaits us. This has a larger implication for lived time and that which may occur within it or that which we may have imagined as potentially occurring before time existed and thus outside of it: "A real possibility cannot by definition be actual, but it also cannot merely be the product of imagination withdrawing from reality. It is the point of differing…" (Lampert 2012:130). Wood suggests that desire, flux, and even duration may be kindred with this limen of obverse and yet joined temporalities, but at once also says that they might not be fundamental for all that (cf. 1989:336). Dasein is said to possess both a 'temporal kind of Being' as well as being able to, more intuitively, find its 'meaning in temporality' (Heidegger, op. cit:41). Historicality is prior to history in the same way as being proceeds meaning. This does not shunt us away from the lived experience of an existential sensibility, but merely draws us into a circle of interpretation that calls forth to Dasein as time's interlocutor at an experiential level, rather than what, much later and much more formally, the historian does for time and meaning at that discursive. The blank spaces of calendar days restore to the objective world of the present-at-hand a ready-to-handedness that has yet to be experienced or even understood. At some point though, perhaps 'during' that very day in question, we have done it, or done some of it: "Not only have we done it individually, we have done it as a society, with shared calendars." (Lampert op. cit:130). When *we* 'do' this or that, when 'things' get 'done', and so on, it is not only the publicness of being-with-others that transpires or is lubricated with idle talk and suchlike. Before all of this, and in a sense, behind it in the way that something else lies behind what can be usually accessed or observed, is the temporal character of Dasein's 'existicity'. We might well mark down a measured point in time, as in an appointment, but we remark upon it in an experiential sense because we are temporal beings who exist because of time but also certain kinds of time exist because of our being present to them or as them. Being present as time presents to us our existicity, the facticity of existence set apart from factical life structures or histories. This alter being which only seems other to us because we are so adept at losing ourselves in the being of others, however inauthentic this may be for they as well, through the correspondence between acts that all people 'do', and have done: "And just as our calendars are thick with appointments with unpunctual people who will keep us waiting, so they contain the names of those whose fate is to be delayed by our own tardiness." (Schwartz 1975:3). This kind of realization, not quite trivially true because not in an identity relation with itself – one might not ever be late for something, or ever be delayed by someone else; inevitability is not identity nor even quite necessity – is the experiential version of the philosophical recognition that in any single philosophy, history and being are telescoped in a way that arcs toward their own completion: "Previous history becomes constructed in it, concentrated in its sources and its origins. All future developments, moreover, are adumbrated within it. It has its past and its future which are implied in a kind of absolute present which truly makes of it an eternal essence." (Ricoeur 1965:65 [1955]). This may sound grandiose, but the act of marking a date on a calendar carries with it much more than either the appointment as mark in a schedule or the once empty space unmarked and virginal. The gravity of the dated date, the remarked mark, or the overprinted print cannot be simply estimated as a possibility. It is both a probability excerpted from the regression of other odds-making points by our existential commitment to it, and it is the doorway or window which opens onto the beyond of a temporal being which has its own arc splayed outwards, beckoning a horizon not to recede, but to approach.

4.2 'Forget me not':

Part of the astonishing commitment we bring to the date, whether borne begrudgingly and resentfully or filled up with an anticipatory joy that would like to be boundless and yet bound to the beloved other at once, is that we simply do not wish to forget it. There is too much of our vanity at stake, subjectively, our reputation, objectively. Durkheim famously imagined mourning as the birthstone of all human memory, and it is interesting that paleoarchaeologically we find graves and nominal burial works at the dawn of the species we know to be our very own. But recalling something from mortal memory is of another order of experience: "Recollection, even though is not itself an original, self-given kind of experience, makes a particular positive contribution to the constitution of time." (Wood 1989:97). For recollection is specifically attuned to an object which is no longer an object, or no longer simply objective. Like the aesthetic work which comes to be used by us as a touchstone, talisman, mnemonic, or *memento mori*, what we can recall of this or that experience 'sticks around' as is said, because we need it to. Though much of our analytic therapy rests on investigating the negative consequences of these 'needs', this is not the whole story. Husserl states that we can relive the present without it ever being given as present again (op. cit:66). What then are we reliving, and why is this form of living a 're' and not simply another lived experience like any other? It is because we not only 'will' this kind of represencing but we also 'can' (ibid:67). This sounds almost like a form of self-projection, as if I am the only sentient being in the universe, a solipsistic sophronia of solo stunts. But what Husserl is presumably getting at is the manner in which I recall the living-present to itself, not how I imagine I can recollect into being-present that which can no longer be this way. Like any lost love anyone has ever had, there is at least one moment of recollection which wills the return of the one who was lost. But just so, it *only* wills it, and cannot accomplish it, unlike recollection proper. A recollection 'happens' again because it itself takes some present time to accomplish its return. Its is co-present with the living present as a form of lived presence. Memory is the ground of relived presence but not the source of the present as lived. Of course, one might note that our experience as recalled *does* help us live in the present, as in knowing how to do this or that task, or to be with this or that person, etc. Yes, this is certainly correct. But this is not a recollection *per se*. One cannot pin down to a point of recall called for by reliving a moment now past an entire suite of the stock of knowledge at hand. If one could, we would be forever trapped in an extended surreality of déjà vu.

If "...we tend to think that the past has 'more reality' than the future [ ] And this leads to the idea that the past is causally prior to the present." (Horwich 1988:143), it is because of the dual sources of recollection that this 'reality' the past is said to have and these continue to exert a force over our apprehension of both objects, others, and the lived time in its ongoingness. For 'will' and 'can' are also two crucial components of the present. They help us understand the character of possibility within the current human ambit, and just as importantly, they help us transcend whatever parochial limitations we as a species or as denizens of more specific cultures have and have had over time. They also aid in discovering a perspective that can be shared by both others within our own community and those beyond. This is not the kind of objectivity much vaunted by science or the legal system, necessarily. It is more a sense of how this or that time is lived and what can be said about the presence of the present: "Temporal objectivity can be established in subjective time-consciousness by virtue of the reidentification that recollection makes possible." (Wood 1989:101). Those in love notoriously tend to lack such a perspective, because nothing the beloved does should ever be lost to the past, should ever become 'only' a memory. Hence our familiarity with the common-place sentiments regarding time that lovers report. The 'food-tastes-better-colors-are-brighter' way of this new world does open up a lighted space of being-with for us, but it also narrows our sensibilities concerning what else is important. That it does so in a manner which does not excerpt oneself from empathy is no doubt a serious thing, for the use of hallucinogens and narcotics also promotes a perspective tangential to the everyday, but without the general succor of humane feeling. Such human feeling that not only remains but is heightened through the acts of love in the present bears a close kindred with acts by which the historian in each of us recalls the self to itself: "Since meaning appears through a specific act of 'recovery', the difference between *event* and *advent* therefore remains." (Ricoeur 1965:36 [1955], italics the text's). The event is something that cannot be relived as it was. But it reappears as adventitial through the act of recollection. This 'second coming' of all that has preceded what is now present no doubt betrays its eschatological sources, but at least as importantly for us in our own time is the sense that recollection 'saves' something in the memorial archive that can be accessed when necessary. There is a soteriological privilege conferred upon all that we do recollect, especially that which remains for us as something cherished. This is different than mere practical skills that are recalled through their practice alone. If we are not using this or that ability, it languishes, gets 'rusty', as we say. But the cherished recollection retains its vigor no matter if we have not thought of it in some time. Of course, even the most intimate and forceful memories fade over time. We no longer automatically feel the inspiration, the tingles up and down our spine, or to the contrary, the anger, even fury that the event itself once proposed to us. But the key difference between such a recollection and that which reconstructs part of the stock of knowledge at hand, that is, returns to us its at-handedness, is the difference between a gift and something one had purchased for oneself. Just as clocks were originally only gifts, and only later came to be used as timekeeping devices for, say, commercial transactions and scientific work, (cf. Cipolla 1967:92), the giftedness of something that can be recalled as a complex of experience and emotion is muted within the purview of the learned skill. Certainly we may think of those teachers who have given to us the great gifts of our own abilities, taught us not only these skills for the first time but also taught us how to hone and thus not forget them. But it is we ourselves who have had to continue the work involved in polishing and perhaps even bringing such skills closer to the perfection they both embody and idealize. What is gifted to us by another who is not a teacher, mentor, or some other kind of authority figure is something that is their own, and cannot ever become ours in the same way. We do not practice being in love with the lover who is now forever lost.

So not all of what is past can once again be present in the same way. Stocks of knowledge at hand can generally be so, as well as the more base compendium of idle talk and fashion, so practiced and yet so unskilled at once. The gift of the other, as well as more radically, the gift of otherness, most of which cannot be accepted through misrecognition of what it authentically represents to us, is never represenced in its original acuity and uncanniness. Even so, it is reasonable to claim, as does Heidegger, that "...'the past' has a remarkable double meaning; the past belongs irretrievably to an earlier time; it belonged to the events of that time; and in spite of that, it can still be present-at-hand 'now'..." (1962:430 [1927]). But his immediate example of an ancient ruin betrays the fact that whatever the past may be presently, it is not what it was, or what we might imagine it to have been. Whatever sentiment the obtrusive uncanniness of the past, no less in its present state, brings to us, we cannot help but accept that its 'original' state cannot be, in spite of the impressive simulacra of the museum or the consumer and entertainment landscapes of a Las Vegas. Not that there is nothing to be gained from such places. The 'Forum' at Caesar's Palace in Las Vegas is, for instance, quite beautiful in the way we imagine ancient Rome to have been, at least architecturally. The real thing would have smelled like its time. There is little danger in being accosted by a criminal in Vegas' assumed mimesis of Rome, nor are their present the variety of political and even, closer to our own time, metaphysical conflicts that animated the 'eternal' city. No, The Rome of Las Vegas has narrowed itself considerably, for the Saturnalia to which it pays homage brings to the present only what the present wishes it to. And why not? In doing so, we have authentically recognized the past for what it was in terms *of* the present of what *we* are, or what we aspire to become. Slavery, religious conflict, the subjection of women, children as chattel, animals as tools, caste like social structure, the *patria potestes*, and the infamous - if over-rated in its influence - lead plumbing; who needs any of those?

Thus modern Vegas is superior to ancient Rome in almost every way imaginable. Similarly, the wider society that constructed both respectively is the home to all of the differences exemplified and embodied in its creations. It is an over-used metaphor, but the city of the mind works the same way: even equipped with memory, nothing in it or about it is eternal. People have to live somewhere, but it is not so much where they live but how that is of the utmost, though the two are not unrelated. Since a simulacrum desires to present itself as stateless, we in turn desire to be within the state of grace that dissimulates itself. It is not real and yet it can be experienced as a present-day reality. It is a Heideggerean hollow of holy hoax. But it works: "…I realize I enjoy the anticipation and recollection of the ideal more than I enjoy any state, therefore I will live in the recollection." (Lampert 2012:61). No one who strolls the simulacratic boulevards of the 'Forum' in Vegas today can remember the 'glories' of ancient Rome. And we are thankful for that.

Yet the temporality of represencing that which cannot be of and in itself is an act of the memorialization of love. Unlike the skill set, the at-handedness of human feeling, when attached to a *specific* memory, falters. This is because we desire to stop time, to in-dwell within the lighted space that was once lit in a manner that was *only* of its time. In not accepting this, we *do* accomplish the end of history. But the world continues around us even so: "If time is not 'joined', if the calendar is not proclaimed, both cease to be; everything simply stops, as for the schizophrenic whose time stands still, or for Sleeping Beauty in the castle." (Van Der Leeuw 1973:328 [1949]). As Minkowski cites what Courbon says of a mentally ill person, "She moves about in a present which recommences endlessly." (op. cit:370). This is the function of contemporary entertainment. Time passes in narrative only, not in reality. We live, if we live only at the level of popular culture, in a recirculated atmosphere of the refashioning of fashion, the represencing of the retro, and more darkly, the understated intonation of the insidious self-represencing of the retrogressive, as when Branson, Missouri can be understood as the holier or more righteous version of Vegas, or that Vegas is itself a 'Disneyland for adults.' The danger of living within a simulacrum is well known, and it is not the purpose of a study on time to recapitulate such critiques as have been made about the topic. But it is perhaps important to note that the temporality of such spaces which are not actual *places* lends itself to the stoppage of time, just as specific recollections tend to excerpt themselves form their parent archive of memory. We place them 'above' other forms of memory or even memorialization. They are about anticipation, desire, and sometimes even joy. Yet it is not the recognition of historical horror that makes persons horrible, but rather the covering over it, the lying about it, and the pretense that the world as a whole is, or would be better off *as*, a simulacrum 'entire of itself': "...it could be mentioned that monstrosity stems from time implanted in men, that the hideous fable is the fable of memory." (Kristeva 1996:303).

Nonetheless, a culture memory is often considered to be something on the order of the sacred. Why would it have remained if this were not so, we might ask. But this is not even a rhetorical question. It does not require a response because it has been answered by the imagined presence, continuous and even infinite, of the memory in question. Memories are called into question, but memory is not. Plato is one of the major sources of this sensibility, and in the *Philebus*, as Lampert discusses it, "Memory is the preservation of sensation; it keeps us in the present of experience, where we can retain all our unfulfilled desires." (op. cit:61). Recollections that concern specific acts, events, feelings or indeed, sensations, are 'delayed' in their return. This delay occurs because a recollection is about something that has 'left' our consciousness or our bodies and thus is returned by recollection, hence the 're' in front of the usual term for everyday gathering or hoarding. Memory 'preserves' these things inside ourselves, and thus its version of delay passes through the same phases of temporality as did the original event. Recollection 'bypasses' this form of chronologically oriented 'delay', though it might be more accurate to simply say that the chronology of a memory recapitulates itself as the full memory, and has nothing to do with the passage of time *per se* either then or now. What is retained that can be so labeled is the sense that 'cause' precedes 'effect' (cf. Horwich 1988:109). Yet more telling, or more fundamental, is the preserved sense that in this idea of memory, judging the time can only be accomplished by reference to that which has altered, hence the passage of time as a facticity and not at first as an ordering mechanism is something characteristic of recall and recollection both (cf. Lampert op. cit:107).

Even more to the point regarding calendrical systems and their markings, is the sense we retain in memory of 'temporal distanciation'. We have already seen how noting a date or marking an event onto a static temporal grid like a calendar or other similar digital device gives to it an air of authority. It is no longer just something that could be done, and certainly far more that something that 'can' be done in the general sense of human ability. Whether or not it must be done or will be done, it has matriculated to the level of'should'. Once again, the 'will' and the 'can' of cherished memory comes to the surface, though this time we are trying to project those elements into the future. Marking the calendar is in effect the attempt at sacralizing that which may come. It is lending the future a degree of the present, and giving it a gift from the past. To a certain extent, we also do this to aggrandize ourselves: "...just as authority is affirmed by the placement of social distance between super and subordinate, so temporal distance subserves the ascendancy of the person who imposes it." (Schwartz 1975:35). Willing what is to come is of course one thing, but having the ability to accomplish this or that in a future time does give credence to the claim that a marked calendar is wont to make. This claim is not made on its own behalf; it is rather a trace of our desire to exert authority over that which is as yet nameless and placeless. Just so, we have named and placed it. For almost everything that we so mark in this way contains three things: a place, a time, and the core nature of the event in question. Sometimes this 'essence' can itself be named, as when we are to meet our spouse. So much might we trust this other, so significant is she, that we will be willing to meet her on a moment's notice with only time and place marked. The matter itself is of little or even no import whatsoever. Indeed, if we utter some caveat in our response to our most significant other, as in 'how important is this?', 'can it wait?', or even 'what is this about?' we are risking rather recklessly the inviolate nature of the trust between us. In this kind of situatedness of being, Dasein's authenticity comes to the fore. This *Mitsein* is not authenticated by our love for another or any feeling or sentiment relevant to such love. Rather, love places us in the foreground of our own finitude. One really *must* meet the other on their terms and thus the reality of our thrown subjection is brought home to us. That we desire this is secondary, for "...when historicality is authentic , it understands history as the 'recurrence' of the possible, and knows that a possibility will recur only if existence is open to it fatefully, in a moment of vision, in resolute repetition." (Heidegger 1962:444 [1927]). We *have* been here before. This kind of 'before' has both the ontic and ontological about it. The first tends toward a probability relation associated with a specifically known, or at least, knowable, antecedent that brings about "... one of the specially frequent states." (Horwich 1988:88). This is more or less pat, and constitutes the 'can' of previous experience. But the second is what actually gets us as beings to where we have marked, and what we have marked down. It is the 'will' of such a relation. We are aware of Schutz's borrowed indictment that we can 'never swim in the same river twice'. Equally so, however, is Husserl's 'I can do it again.' Once again, this time the second demonstrates the 'can' of recollection, and thus the first the will of memory. This Hegelian circle 'dissolves its own center' (cf. Lampert, op. cit:91). We return by not being able to get to the same place as before. Not exactly. For such a return when given its ipsissimous authenticity which is mine and mine alone, convinces us that we have come to the same place in the sense that it is our own. Once again, like the sentiments which we bring to the rendezvous, the 'sameness' of the place in any ontic sense is secondary, though not entirely beside the point. Romance aside, the call has been responded to and we are once again *present*. The future is no longer what is to come, and the past is no longer what is willed into the future in order that it *become* the present. This is why, at a more fundamental level, the markings on all of the dates of a calendar that precede today are naught. They 'exist' wholly differently than both those slated to come 'if I can' and those within which I now find myself and my will. This 'asymmetry' seems to have more to do with "… *justification* and with the reliability of mechanisms that link our beliefs to the world." (Horwich, op. cit:81, italics the text's). If the past is considered more reliable than the future – and given the character of human memory and recall alike, this is saying a fair bit – then we must all the more place our will on the horizon line between ourselves and the unknown. The reliability of the future as a possible present does not rest of course on our will alone. The stock of knowledge at hand, both personal, associated with a vocation or a means of labor, and present, though sometimes obscurely and cliquishly, in the culture around us, lend cantor to the idea of the 'reliable'. The domesticated dog is a metaphoric antidote for the well known human failings to these regards. Its obverse, the housecat, represents the reality of history and of others to self, who tend to go their own way in spite of our best efforts to control them. Of those who are pet owners of this kind, dog owners tend to be more controlling and desireful that their authority be accepted in the world around them, cat owners are more *laissez-faire*. Either way, neither of their predilections corresponds to the world in exact terms. Perhaps the allegorical snake is a better metaphor for the calculating interest we bring to the world, as well as all of our ulteriorities, and the bird might represent the flighty nature of all of those who obliviously wend their way round our desires and thus deny them. However this may be, it is at least clear that the future we imagine is not entirely shared, or hardly shared at all. It is this puzzle, and not chronology proper, that makes the future ambiguous, an 'open book'. Such an expression, kindred with others of its ilk, tends to contradict itself if taken too literally. If a book is open, we may of course read it. But the pages of the future are blank. That is, with the exception of our hopeful marks on the calendar to come. Through them we wish to make what is to come in general come *to us* in particular, and in a particular way. In doing so, however, we lose ourselves in the 'totality of public events', rather than maintain the question of being through understanding history as 'the mode of happening of the Dasein'. (cf. Heidegger 1992:129 [1925]). This act represents the desirefulness of desire, the *orexis* and the '*temptatio*' at once. Like the 'evil of evil' which Ricoeur has famously defined as 'fraudulence in the work of totalization', we imagine that we can bring about *all* of our desired outcomes by first planning, plotting, and then, marking. If this does occur, we can be assured someone else has suffered for it, or at the very least, has been persuaded by the snake to cage one of their birds as against its being eaten.

Yet these kinds of items have a way of themselves representing their order of relations and means: "A taste of the past, lurking deep within a memory and mistakenly believed to be effaced, returns to clothe the troubling resurgence with an image and a body." (Kristeva, op. cit:19). What speaks to us, what utters the proverbial injunction 'forget me not', is not the specific content of an experience recalled, but rather how we felt at the time. Only through this transliteration of what we had undergone, endured, or yet loved, would the contemporary experience of smelling an aroma, hearing a snippet of music, or feeling the sea breeze at a certain time of year be able to conjure to itself and by itself the entirety of a past experience, including persons, events, activities, and emotions. This suggests that recollection is not independent of imagination: "In going over into phantasy, the sensation preserves its constantly varying temporal character; from moment to moment the content thus seems to be shoved back more and more." (Husserl 1964:32 [1905]). Husserl then states that the sensation has itself become productive. Is this because it occludes a desire thought to have been 'effaced'? Minkowski suggests that the past 'turns back upon itself' but without losing its force (op. cit:157). Yet this is a necessary condition, and one that pushes our spirit toward the future. Indeed, he goes so far as to say that this is the one vital role of the past in our lives, and that 'perspective memory' surpasses its own pastness as mere biography or even historical experience (ibid). Thus we do not let go of this kind of past easily. No doubt. And yet the call to surpass what one has accomplished can even become 'violent', as he suggests in a footnote. The 'forget me not' of our own experienced sensations is, then, more powerful than any specific memory wherein it may have had, if not its genesis, then at least some forceful repetition of itself, as well as more vital than any specific future goal. To surpass ourselves by walking into the future is rather its sole mission. In doing so, however, there is no guarantee of effacing what has been for us. Perhaps it would be yet more accurate to suggest that we do not so much overcome ourselves as the content that has tied us to our pasts.

The 'history of the world' which incorporates what is both present-at-hand and ready-to hand also has this self-overcoming quality (cf. Heidegger 1962:440 [1927[). But pitched at a more macrocosmic level, 'world history' overcomes individual and even cultural suasion and worlds in its own way and as its own world. Dasein as individual being cannot accomplish this. The difference lies partially in the fact that the world and its objects contain no desire. The culturally modified aspects of nature insofar as they have become part of 'history', we are reminded by Heidegger, are thus called 'world-historical' (ibid), and in being so, we are to understand the nature of our apprehension of nature. The factical discoveredness of what the world is as well as what is in the world as it is, must make a severe and generally limiting impression on Dasein. So much so, that we ourselves do not wish to forget what we are. 'Who' we are is to bound up in the publicness of the everyday, as when one is inevitably asked 'what one *does*', as in what one does for a living. But what we actually *are* as a being with a history is quite different, and 'occurs' to us and within the world in an ontological facticity: "The being of having-been is the past, such that in such a being I am nothing but the *future* of Dasein and *with it its past.* The being, in which Dasein can be its wholeness authentically as being-ahead-of-itself, is *time.*" (Heidegger 1992:319 [1925], italics the text's). Here we have a precise statement of the implications of Minkowski's definition of perspective-memory. I am *nothing* but my own future originating in what I have been but am *still.* I have not forgotten myself, as the slogan on the Quebec license plate reminds its provincial residents, but specifically, those

Francophone, not to do. But what I have forgotten is that I have lived only in the past thus far, and cannot but continue to do so. I can live *for* the future but not within it. I can live *from* the past but also not in it. I dwell in both, however. Even so, the matriculation from dwelling to indwelling occurs for Dasein through the very rapprochement between what has been and what may be. Nietzsche was in fact correct about the ability to forget. It is precisely this human proclivity to surpass specific lived experience and yet retain the sensational palettes of both brighter colors and sparkling tastes that allows us a future at all.

4.3 New Year's Resolutions:

But there is also a history of forgetting. If all revolutions bring new calendars (cf. Lampert, op. cit:190), then we, who are to live within the chronologically marked territory of this new thing, must ourselves become new. Clocks are reset, the previous year is consigned to the dustbin of personal history, and explosions of various kinds are heard, from fireworks to the cannons of political revolution, fired perhaps from the clock towers themselves (ibid). But in becoming new, with all of the insideity that this implies, from the 'born again' of religious suasions to the rehabilitation of treatment programs, we must engage in some kind of effort to put the specifics of any lived past 'behind' us. "Lived succession is not a relation between what is and what is not; it only becomes so as any relation of a temporal order does when we attempt to rationalize it." (Minkowski, op. cit:28). Resolutions proper, wherein one is resolved to do something other than what one has been doing, feeling, even being, are revolutions writ small. They are the biographical mimesis of the apocalypse, for something of ourselves, tantamount to what we are, must be vanquished for all time. Recapitulating this same logic, 'worldly occurrences remain relativized' (cf. Koselleck 1985:179), because whatever we have been, done, or felt before is just that now, something about the way I was. Others may not be entirely convinced that we can exert such changes to our lives, but no matter. The nakedness of our own self-made weapon is visionary in that it has proclaimed not only the ability to change at all, but even what the specifics of such changes shall be henceforth. All of these kinds of calendrically marked and sometimes initiated claims are bold indeed. Akin to our personalized, and rationalized, version of Proust and others, we are likened to "…the narrator [who] constructs time regained while he is in search of lost time." (Kristeva, op. cit:128). What is recalled alters memory into perception anew. What is perceived confers upon memory the ability to recall. Everyone has 'fallen' into the publicness of the New Year's resolution, perhaps at varying points in the annual round. Notoriously, most of these declarations come to little or nothing. We lack the sociological data concerning what kind or even category of resolution *does* have a modicum of success, in that it is carried through with discipline and even a certain panache. We only know of our own failures. But their miserable character is enlarged, aggrandized, befitting the way in which they were announced. Something grand must itself have a grand demise. And we seek an audience for just this sort of display: "In thus accommodating Dasein with this unburdening of its being, the public maintains a stubborn dominion. Everyone is the other and none is himself." (Heidegger 1992:247 [1925]). One of the chief reasons why it is easy to proclaim a change and difficult to execute it, is that the character of temporality in the realm of public pronouncement is qualitatively different from that required by the focused and very much *private* discipline needed to do the work set out for oneself. Heidegger, later on, recognizes just this: "But when Dasein places itself in the reticence of carrying things through, its time is different. Publicly regarded, its time is essentially slower than the time of idle talk, which 'lives faster'." (ibid:279). The penchant for both major genres of so-called 'reality' entertainment places the onus on the doer of the deed in a very public way, so that Dasein is absent or wholly entangled in the skein of *Offentlichkeit*, which is not necessarily 'open' in any way resembling the 'lighted space'. It is lit rather by the limelight of being entertained. One the one hand, we observe the miseries of those who have tried but failed, and on the other, those who have succeeded, at least on screen, and are thus celebrated for their avowal of self-sacrifice. For it is literally the prior self that must be killed. It is a suicide of media proportion.

But if there really is an 'intrinsic' similarity between earlier and later (cf. Horwich 1988:47), then no amount of resolving on our parts would turn the trick of historical alteration. We count the hours based on our ability to access other kinds of archives, as when 'computational time' bases itself on that historical: "Such series-beginnings are always invested with meaning and value. Calendars are obvious examples." (Wood 1989:142). Heidegger refers to these 'stretched-out' temporalities as 'spans', in which "The making-present which awaits and retains..." only does so because it is 'ecstatically' stretched in this manner. (op. cit:264). Yet this too is an 'assigned' time, wherein every moment has its datability and spanned character. To live within the span of a calendrically markable temporality is to remain unknowing of the ecstatic nature of what occurs 'all day long' in a concernful manner. We are, as much as the event we propose or resolve is to be, transfixed by the datedness of the mark. It may well become a trace of failure when it itself has past, but for the moment, and even in the moment, it is a mark very much in the way one is marked for something; sometimes something grotesque.

Even so, we can also turn away from the proposed outcomes of resolution. We can rest and yet be aware that this too is a means to an end. The end is muted in rest, but the concern remains: "Taking a rest and relaxing is a mode of concern. For care does not vanish in rest, only now in relaxing the world is no longer appresented for the achievement of concern." (Heidegger 1992:276 [1925]). Circumspection frees itself from any specific task which has lain ahead of it. This is a 'projection' of the ability to be-ahead-of-itself that human consciousness uniquely, but also unquietly, possesses. Resting carries on the task, albeit more passively and perhaps with a liberated sense of reflection. In rest, one is resolved to redouble one's efforts 'later on'. We recover ourselves in this way, and this is why rest is different from the 'free time' discussed above. Rest is paid for by unrest. It is not at all free in any sense other than that it frees up our imaginations and our logic to cast their power towards the open futurity of our existence. Rest also confers the perspective that what has been changed is not so continuous and homogenous in its own character as to thwart any effort on our parts to apply our imagination. The world is not so cut and dried that only by burning it will we achieve the desired result.

At the same time, "...it is evident that emphasis on the uniform and the regular in the process of change in time represents a danger." (Wilhelm 1973:213 [1951]). Rest does allay our sense of vicissitude and diversity because it always comes to us in the same manner. Aside from purely physical fatigue, we find ourselves in the mode of being concernful about us alone. We turn inward and this is a sign of the necessity to step back from the task as it has been presented. Such an 'appresentation' differs profoundly from the pronouncement of resolution. Its very pronunciation is that of the annunciative, as if we were to ascend into another realm by way of rest; the realm of the imagination and the world as it is not, and not even not yet. Rest never announces itself to the world. 'I'm taking a break' communicates not rest itself but the reason why one is heading in that direction, or if not a reason per se, simply a declaration of intent.

And rest functions primarily as a kind of delay. Yet at the same time, time passes. In rest, we are aware of its passing but not its passage. Rest appresents an objective similitude that we will explore further below, but it does not allow itself to be presented to us in the full presence of its being-restful. To acknowledge this within the temporality of rest is to annul it efficacy. 'I am rested' is one thing, but 'I am being rested' or yet 'I am being-rested' are odd things to think to oneself. In rest, we have resolved not to carry on this or that project, but to carry *through* with it. What is delayed is the full recognition of what has occurred and what must occur: "If we live our lives at different temporal levels at the same time in different ways, each moment of life has its lived time at many times later than the time it is formed. The very structure of simultaneity *is* delay." (Lampert 2012:166, italics the text's). Aside from the famed 'delayed reaction' in Freud, the meaning of simultaneity must needs be historical and relatively conscious. It is rather similitude that holds within itself the full identity of difference in a trice. We know that the very character of recollection, so marked not on calendars but as the calendar itself, entails that the 'origin' of this or that tempo marking comes to be recognized in its fullness but also in its difference only over time. That which thwarts this effort smacks of fraudulence, and thus gives us the sense that it has learned at least part of the language of evil. We vainly attempt to mimic this with resolution, as if such things really were not only new but total as well: "The surprise is that Power has, as it were, no history, that the history of power repeats itself, marks time. The surprise is that there is no real political surprise." (Ricoeur 1965:248 [1955]). And after but a moment of reflection, we are no longer even surprised by this fact. But jadedness and even cynicism are not the necessary results of such a realization. If this is made into a self-recognition, almost in an Augustinian manner, are we not resolved to better ourselves in spite of it? In thise case, to wrest Power out of itself and reduce its nomenclature to what has power, who is empowered, when power acts and when it falls into rationalized reticence. For 'Power' never fails to act; it has its own claims on Being. Beings are hardly good enough for it, but may easily become means to the end which encompasses Being in its fraudulent envelope. The closet character of the resolution, so marked as to not require remarking upon, so unremarkable in fact that it also contains the surprise of no surprise, mimics Power and the means-end utility of beings; this time, ourselves.

Another aspect of the mistakenness of resolution, its too-well-made existential error, making itself without necessarily crossing the edgy threshold into ethical fraud, is simply the idea that what is to be changed is changeable by us, or the more so, that what has been can be made to have only nominal or residual bearing on what is to be. 'That is past' we tell ourselves. But "...the past is a field over which the searchlights of our vision continually play in order to extract different possibilities for our future; and consequently, the past is not external but internal to the present and also to the future, in the light of whose possibilities we are continuously restructuring the past." (Barrett 1968:365). This is a more general way of describing any state of affairs that includes within its category the resolution but is not thereby limited to it. It is true that it is rare to flip the calendar pages over backwards and rewrite what occurred in the basic terms of the appointment, event, or festive ritual. The detailed contents of any of these kinds of marked times never appears in the first place on such a prosaic document. There is no need to re-mark on such a device. Our concern is always future-directed. Whatever we may now say of what occurred, however we might engage in a politically motivated rewriting of how power appeared, was applied, discontinued itself at the 'appropriate' time, or other such sense and nonsense – particularly abused when attempting to convince children that *their* abuse was both necessary and ethical – it is the future which is at stake, and not the past: "...the primary item in care is the 'ahead-of-itself', and this means that in every case Dasein exists for the sake of itself. 'As long as it is', right to its end, it comports itself towards it potentiality-for-Being." (Heidegger 1962:279 [1927]). Resignation, often seen as the opposite of resolution, is still an attitude directed towards the future of being-present, 'here', and then 'there'. Of course, to solve something or other and to resolve it are two different things. Solutions are generally much easier to comprehend than are resolutions to apprehend. We know what must be done most of the time, including concerning world issues of poverty and geo-political conflict. Doing them, within the dynamic of politics, is often delayed unto the implausible. But reality is not beholden only to carelessness. One indeed takes care to show a lack of concern, since concernful being is a 'constitutive structure' of Dasein, of what we are. We always exist in care, even if that means we are careless toward others. We are so, when the stakes are high, with all due concern and seriousness. So it is not an ontology that resolves the world and its absence of being-concernful, but an ethics. We are reminded that for Dasein, there is always something still 'outstanding', something 'still to be settled' (ibid). That this experience that can hardly be called an experience without blushing, bleeding crimson across the world of absence and the world of the being absent from itself, is also no real surprise.

Chapter Five

The Suggestive: Deadlines

> Our contemporary history is a repetition of the actions and events of thousands of years, all in the briefest of possible periods. (Koselleck 1985:56 [1969]).

> ...in addition to the possibility of death and the possibility of alienation, there is the possibility of nonsense. (Ricoeur 1965:296 [1955]).

Making an appointment, drafting a schedule, marking the calendar, all are effects of something other than their own volition. A suggestion has been made, either graciously or no, but always with some centrifugal force, wherein we are brought toward the center of things. The central experience of Dasein is running onwards toward a moving horizon. But finitude runs along with us, whereas finiteness halts our progress on that 'one last perfect day'. The center of our being is, however, the sense that we are alive in the face of death, that we exist in spite of the possibility of non-existence, since before our births, and almost equally after we have ceased to be. The metaphysics of the social contract is so far behind us historically, that we no longer consider birth and death to be the same thing. Nor have they equal weight in our imagination. The finite and egalitarian pool of souls that must be recycled immediately and endlessly has long since fallen out of interdimensional favor, replaced at first by a hierarchical reincarnation, then a non-recycled judgement of various kinds, then our own somewhat ashen extension of ashes to ashes. Every conception of the afterlife reflects the social organization from which it has sprung forth.

But we are the only culture which has brought the judgement once reserved for the agrarian afterlife into our daily lives *while* we are still alive. This facticality itself merits some discussion, but beyond this, how such an idea is marked down and marked out in lived time, in the mundanity of all other tasks and desires, will at first be of chief interest here. Therefore we will take a brief look at three aspects of our ability to both have deadlines and thence rise to their occasion. What does it mean to be 'finished' with something? How can one tell this or that task with which we have been burdened, from those personal and intersubjective to those that are of the interior, to those, more rarely, of cultural note and those which emanate from a vocation versus a career, that generate works instead of labor, is finally complete? Secondly, what kind of vision do we bring to the sense of having a deadline? Why are some deadlines 'soft' and others 'hard'? What happens after the deadline, and how do we respond to a question that descends from a more perennial query regarding the human condition to which we as yet have no sure answer? Finally, who or what is it that enacts the deadline? Is there a judgement brought to us simply by the passage of time, and if so, what is its nature? The character of the visitation is also made more earthly in this mundane time in which I myself am marked.

5.1 Expectations:

Because we are by existential character future-oriented, based upon the constitutive structure of Dasein to be-ahead in various ways, we hold out a palpably poignant understanding that we can expect things to occur that have not yet existed. They may have existed before in some like form, or they may be some kind of mutation of forms thought long past. History has realized both and more. But for us, living only when we are living in this time and no other, expectation carries with it hope, desire, faith as well as lesser items such as propriety, vanity, egotism and the authoritarian version of projected authority. We *do* have expectations of ourselves, to be sure, but just so, our expectations of others tend to trump those we docket against ourselves. An expression of vanity alone would not have constructed such a vast edifice of unspoken and sometimes unutterable senses and suggestions of what 'should' occur in the day to day, as well as of course, what should not happen. No, expectation is clearly socially constructed in the usual manner of intersubjectivity and the social reality that such a world of humans brings about. But is this all there is to it?

Questions that arise from a basic social reality tend to reflect only those kinds of things that are present in order to keep things going as they are. This is a classic sociological formulation of the 'question' itself and needs no further development here. What is of interest, however, is the sense that not only questions may still be asked that are not of the mere technical variety and have their source in others than mere children - who are only incompletely socialized in any case, hence their excuse – and that our cultural imagination is still such that the quotidian subsistence of living on has not dulled our imaginations to the point where serious questions cannot be thought of in the first place. Most succinctly, in the realm of expectation, there is this kind of question: "What future has the future?" (Wood 1989:378). If we are to assume a future at all, and since the end of the Second World War this has become very much an open question, then of what nature will it, or could it, be? We humans are rarely content with pat responses outside of the realm of everyday life. Curiosity may be a way that Dasein loses itself in its own would-be future, but it is also a catalyst for imagining a future at all. 'What would it be like if I were...' or 'this was', or 'she had' etc. are all most familiar to us. And we do not grope blindly about with regard to such utterances, alit only through the vanity of our desires or aflame by virtue of our resentments: "...the future of every event contains many independent definite traces of its occurrence, although beforehand there need have been little or no conclusive indication that it would happen." (Horwich 1988:168). Another way of saying much the same thing is found somewhat later on, fittingly, in the 'future' of Horwich's volume that, from the reader's perspective back on the page whereon the previous citation was discovered, hadn't been written yet: "...there is always a characteristic antecedent event, but there need be no characteristic subsequent event." (ibid:199). There is more to this than the cliché about hindsight's precision pair of eyes. Of course we cannot conclude with certitude any statement concerning something that has not yet occurred, from our perspective. But we do, in our daily dealings, take others' words for a great deal. Something may well have happened, but almost everything that in fact *does* happen does *not* happen to us.

So we are bystanders for the vast majority of events. This is one of the major factors underpinning expectation. We act in orientation to moving toward a future, but it is otherwise with expectation: "In activity we tend toward the future. In expectation, on the contrary, we live time in an inverse sense; we see the future come toward us and wait for that (expected) future to become present." (Minkowski 1970:87 [1933]). Because we cannot possibly experience the actuality of almost everything that has or does or will occur, expectation presents itself to us as a kind of deadline to our imagination. Expectation is the end of speculation and the beginning of the facticality of the future itself. This is reflected in the history of personal development, from studies of character to ethics, to the cognitive reasoning of the various life phases, peaking at certain times and then falling off again, often tragically. 'Just so' stories, homiletics, morality plays and the like have as their lynchpin theme the contrasting and conflicting aspects of expectation over the life course. In and out of love, coming together and growing apart, growing up from childhood and perhaps becoming parents oneself, what is changed in us can be very often pinned down to the alteration of expectations within us about the world and others who live with us in it. We are listless in front of imagination's deadline only by virtue of our inexperience with life: "The spontaneous, unreflecting attitude of the young fool enables him to maintain himself in the heart (center) of time." (Wilhelm 1973:222 [1951]). The trite commentaries concerning the 'timelessness' of childhood or youth are well known. The tempo of living on appears, from the outside, to be much slower. Our memories of being young, non-responsible, and with, other things being equal, our entire lives ahead of us – 'entire' being taken not in the literal sense – may well be sentimental, but there is some truth to them nonetheless. One important mark of mature being in the hermeneutic sense is that we have become aware, very often radically so, of the Nothing that obtrudes its uncanny non-being into our lives, or can do so: "Nearness, which belongs to the structure of the encounter of the threatening thing, is here the acute form of encounter of what is not yet present, more precisely, of the 'not yet' which however can strike at any moment." (Heidegger 1992:287 [1925]). This is more than the also well known sensibility regarding the fact that 'I can die' transforming itself into 'I will die', with the lesser gradations of 'at some point, but not now' and 'at some point that could be any point' and hopefully much later, 'at some point soon' etc. The fullest maturity is never afforded to Dasein in the same way that completion ends its existence. The recognition of the ultimate existential deadline occurring at some point which could be any point is the general standard for social adulthood as well as hermeneutically authentic beinghood. This might be one of the few crucial points upon which these two 'traces' of that which is to come are in full agreement.

Given that birth and death happen to us in the radical manner of there being no other way around them, at least for the time being as well as for the time-being which is us, their necessity lends cantor and credence to the idea that deadlines can and should exist for us during the time of life we can call our very own and which *has* no authentic necessity to it. If it is correct to suggest "…that time is apprehended and suffered as a fatality…" (Puech 1973:66 [1951]), then we mitigate any rancor we may have regarding this fundamentally subjective reaction to thrownness by throwing ourselves in front of deadlines of our own construction. Even the most staunch and strictly enforced completion date or evaluation may be avoided if we are willing to accept whatever consequences it may entail. From the 'defiance' of a child to the unwillingness of an employee to the forced forgetfulness of an aged person, we are actually as familiar with missing deadlines as we are with meeting them. Everyone of us has done plenty of both. This can only suggest that the deadline 'itself' is mutable, that it mutates and that it can even be made mute. Expectation serves in the main to take horror away from fear (cf. Heidegger, op. cit:288). A specific deadline may be unexpected but the deadline itself is something very familiar. We fear it, perhaps, pending its content and ambit of concern, but we do not regard it with horror. This is reserved only for the utterly alien and uncannily radical to human life as we have known it. Death provokes this in us, but more as the idea of it than the moment when it comes. Generally, however, the one who sets the deadline likely has as much fear about it *not* being met as we have in being able to meet it. Everyone serves somebody, and if we fail this one person then they in turn risk failing the next, and so on. So what we actually experience with regard to expectation and deadline is that we work together to make sure we keep this or that project on track, whether it be the raising of children to productivity in the work-place to looking after our health and finances. Utterly inconsequential as all of these activities, and many others, are with regard to the Anxiety of Nothing and the *horror vacui* that accompanies it, nevertheless they serve as mundane surrogates for more existential puzzles. We ourselves may not know how to raise a mature being from total animal dependence, but it has been done in the past, and perhaps even by some of those we ourselves know in this life. We may not know how to secure our financial futures or adjust our expectations to the current conditions of our pocketbooks, but others apparently do and have done so. There is no real mystery, in other words, to living on in the social world. Everything may be made more or less pat. No, the true puzzle resides in the space *between* what is already known and what has yet to be accomplished in general, wherein no one who has *ever* lived has completed such an endeavor, and ironically, where *no* deadlines have yet come into being.

To wit, we collect a set of circumstances that have not yet been apprehended in this or that way and assign them a hypothetical time. We have not yet lived this time *as* temporality, so our experience is itself speculative. But the question, 'what will happen?" animates both our idle curiosity in the sense of the public, as well as our concernful being-ahead-of-itself:

"The concern which awaits, retains, and makes present, is one which 'allows itself' so much time; and it assigns itself this time concernfully, even without determining the time by any specific reckoning, and before any such reckoning has been done." (Heidegger 1962:462 [1927]). We are quite literally assigning ourselves when we agree to meet a deadline. Not so much in the sense of servitude or penury, nor yet in the sense that we are existentially enthralled to this and only this – though many job conditions attempt to theatricalize this state of affairs as a motivational tactic; this only adheres with a degree of success and for inexperienced workers, however – but rather in the sense of an ethic of commitment. We are ourselves beholden to the idea that we can, as individual beings, rise to the occasion of any evaluation. It is more than the bluff integrity of those with 'nothing to hide', as the saying has it. This kind of expectation rallies itself around both our vanity – they think that *I* will not be able to do it? – and our self-respect which is certainly still egotistical but not necessarily vain, in the same way that magnanimity is not arrogance. What greets us when we bring ourselves to the fore in this manner is, however, different from the deadline itself. This last is set up on a known horizon, which advances upon us. If *we* rise up and walk toward it, it itself appears much less threatening. In order to do so, though, we must pass over a kind of mundane abyss of meaning: "...the divide between previous experience and coming expectation opened up, and the difference between past and present increased, so that lived time was experienced as a rupture, as a period of transition in which the new and the unexpected continually happened." (Koselleck 1985:257 [1969]). The mundanity of such a passage should not understate its historical gravity. Such periods as these when experienced as a cultural whole are generally quite profound, but when lived through by persons, they may be merely pathetic or more simply a moment where we must steel ourselves and remind ourselves of who we are, and that we can 'do this', whatever it may be. Indeed, the only time we find ourselves mentioning these kinds of hortatory hallelujahs in the public sphere of everydayness is when we are helping our children or other adults who have fallen on difficult times, either emotionally or perhaps even cognitively. In a word, expectation betrays its continuous presence only in settings where one has lost the ability to expect anything from oneself, or considers oneself incompetent in the face of living on. In addition to this, and yet more squarely in line with our discussion, the sense that time moves ever 'onward' has also been lost or at least forgotten. For Husserl, memory includes expectation within itself, and if such 'intentionalities' are fulfilled in some manner, the present comes about (cf. Wood 1989:88). In Heidegger, disclosedness as the most authenticating aspect of talk reveals in itself expectations, both of itself and of the ability that all discourse is said to possess (cf. 1962:205 [1927]). This is more than the 'talking cure'. It is well-known how people are moved simply by the knowledge that others 'feel' like them, have 'gone through' similar things, know 'what it's like' and so on. All these items of discourse are euphemistic in the extreme, seemingly avoiding the deadline of disclosure more than meeting it. At the same time, however, if too much detail is granted them we may find that the other does *not* in fact know what it means to be myself in this very way, that my Dasein is only what it is and remains only so, and so does their own. This is correct, but it is not immediately helpful.

Beneath all of this discourse is, as it were, a structure of expectation that reveals itself as a mode of disclosed being. For we are to be made 'resolute' in the face of the deadline and the tasks which propel us toward it. This is so since "...temporality emerges as an articulation of modes of Dasein's Being, itself thought in terms of the structure of care, and of the 'authentic' care he calls anticipatory resoluteness." (Wood 1989:215). The chief factor in making oneself this 'way', is the sense that time is of the essence. Yes, this happens to be so, but not only in the sense that history is occurring while we speak. The shop-worn device of fiddling while one's surroundings are laid waste is the lesser part of the impulsion to resoluteness. Time is of the essence precisely because time is of *our* essence. In action directed to avoid missing a deadline, we experience this kind of authenticity refracted by the ontic herald, the pronouncement of what is actually an unpronounceable limen over which Nothing might suddenly appear. The anxieties we feel regarding meeting this or that deadline are the shadows of the Anxiety that is part our ownmost beings. In them we retain the alertness of Anxiety but without understanding it to be horrifying or Other to us. This is why fear is still a motivator, for one who is gripped by horror can do nothing in the face of Nothing. Speaking of the encyclopedists, Koselleck suggests that "The two men saw themselves as pressed for time; preparation of all technical potentialities and all knowledge had to be made in time for future action, even in the event of a catastrophe." (op. cit:248). The Encyclopedia was the Domesday book of its era. Just as the Norman Conquest had ushered in a new kind of local time and had accomplished the hitherto unimaginable – in the short lifetimes of the day, the previous and more or less regular conquests of Britain were already out of mortal memory – the French Revolution was the announcement that a new age had begun. New calendars with new nomenclatures, a new system of measurement, all of this proclaimed a new kind of time. But it was also unimaginable. More than the old time being replaced by that new, it had seemed like time itself had ended and for all time. The Interregnum in England has seen a similar kind of

Anxiety arise, also heralded by the monstrous forms at which human beings could only gape in horror. Nothing could follow the end of feudalistic monarchy, for naught could be imagined that could replace it unless of course the long awaited apocalypse had in fact finally occurred.

But since "The meeting of deadlines is after all not accomplished without cost, without diverting time from other potential uses…" (Schwartz 1975:79), we are cast in the role of manipulating time, altering its application, sequestering it or even placing it in a kind of quarantine, with its specifically dedicated activity area. The setting up of a deadline has in its own core the expectation that those who 'must' meet it will go to great lengths to do so, even at personal risk and sacrifice. In this, the deadline *is* the apocalypse writ small. Even the word itself, at least in English, betrays the character of its pedigree. Cross this line and die:" …then came a feeling of horrible expectation that I could be sucked up into the past or that the past would overcome me and flow over me. It was disquieting that someone could play with time like that." (Minkowski 1970:285 [1933]). Minkowski cites a schizophrenic patient to this regard, but who of us has *not* had the same feeling regarding one's own biography or yet even of the history of the species, given our ongoing geopolitical delicacies and sensitivities? Being overtaken by one's own past is in fact a regular occurrence for anyone who has lived outside of a monastic condition. Indeed, such data are clear evidence that those of us who fall victim to mental illness have indeed lived at some earlier time as 'normal' persons, within community, loving and losing, besting deadlines but also experiencing setbacks and outright failure. The feeling that one has neglected something or other in the past allows the past to overcome our present sensibilities, and since "There is neglect only because Dasein is defined as *care…*" (Heidegger 1992:136 [1925], italics the text's), there is yet more evidence that certain forms of mental alteration do not entirely excerpt us from our own shared humanity. It is well known that the 'delusions' of schizophrenics are borrowed from the popular culture of the day and are shared within the community of patients. From CIA experiments to the patient being a former intelligence agent, giving way in 1970s to extraterrestrial contact, or for those more rural and less consumptive of entertainment fiction, of being 'touched by an angel' or perhaps yet being one oneself, unrecognizable to the mere mortal doctors and nurses, as well as one's perhaps newly unrighteous family members, it is clear that certain diseases of the 'mind' are more importantly refractions of the publicness of consciousness, of the average in Dasein that has overtaken one's ownmost possibility. Time has stopped, the deadline of Domesday has arrived and the Encyclopedia of one's past action and thought has been compiled into stasis.

Therefore the presence of expectation is annulled in its forward-looking capability. One expects nothing other than to remain as one is, and the most absurd rationalizations are then given to make sure that this remains the case. If anything, the illness that assails us is committed to making sure its host cannot move away from it. Many are complicit at this juncture. And since we, as Heidegger maintains, 'exist finitely' (1962:378 [1927]), mental illness may be defined phenomenologically as the inability to put a stop to the stoppage of the finite. It is to turn finitude into finiteness, to lose one's anticipation but to *remain* resolute.

Thus expectation is itself value-neutral, kindred with the charisma that it helps engender. We look forward to something, to its advent perhaps or yet to its conclusion. We enter into a new milieu and at once exit that previous. We are not, usually and in the day to day 'overcome' by our past. Addiction and mental illness aside, we *do* move on, even if it is due to the unbridled publicness of a private curiosity in which we lose ourselves, or due to the entanglement which belies the public scrutiny of what we have been to ourselves and others – its very public reflection allows us to avoid any confrontation with it that might 'suck us in' – and this moving on is as much about endings as it is the future: "A concluded experience is both complete and past, while those to be had in the future dissolve into an infinity of different temporal perspectives." (Koselleck 1985:34). It is correct to surmise that in being overtaken by what one supposedly was suggests that this or that state or experience is not in fact complete, and that we still are, at least in part, something of our own past. But this is mere dwelling-in. It is a half-way house between tarrying along and indwelling. It is the private rationalization of public expectations that we indeed move on to the next existential address, but it is also the equally private vanity that promotes an unwillingness to do that very thing, in other words, to commit to not laying in state, but to live as Dasein is thrown. The combination of an *Offentlichkeit* of expectation coupled with a lack of will on our parts to overcome our own past without being overtaken by it, can only aid the rituals and ruins of everydayness in which we willingly become entangled. Losing ourselves in this almost patent manner is ultimately a way of avoiding expectations of any kind; it is a socially sanctioned mental illness: "At this extreme point, the triumph of consumer culture, universally identical and wholly anonymous, would represent the lowest degree of creative culture." (Ricoeur 1965:278 [1955]). Perhaps the first post-war statement of the 'comfortable numbness' which assails us from all sides in contemporary consumer society, Ricoeur is also simply a description of existential entanglement and loss of the authentic being of Dasein in not the unexpected, but the non-expected of a general deadline that has ironically become our collective lifeline.

5.2 Envisioning:

Just as the plot was more serious than the plan, the structure of the deadline also has a second moat, an inner circle of magical defense against the realism of lived time and ontological gravity. If expectation looks toward a certain horizon which approaches us, envisioning carries us beyond all such horizons and into a time wherein the horizon we can see must be approached *by* us. This deeper sense of deadline has at length a religious genealogy, and also reflects our native doubt regarding the ability to project ourselves into an amenable future within which we will find an enhanced viability and even vitality: "Anticipation is not as trustworthy as recollection, and this difference is reflected in the phenomenological difference between them, which in turn plays an essential role in our experience of the passage of time." (Horwich 1988:202). Given selective memory, we may question the first part of this statement. But to do so is not to invalidate that principal that time experienced is now of a different quality than that speculated. In part, what gives the past its unique quality is that we imagine we can have no further expectations of it. But this is in fact not so. As we have just seen, we must expect that the past not overtake us, and correspondingly, that we ourselves maintain a living pace that will always outdistance what we have already experienced. We cannot indwell the past, but rather must always outpace it. So not only do we have an expectation that the past stay 'where' it is, so to speak, in relation to our own motion and 'passage' through objective time, we also experience the ongoingness of meeting the temporal relativity of a deadline to this regard; that we meet the expectations the past has set out for us, then to overcome them and move beyond while letting go entirely select aspects of the past.

This is the point at which the projected vision appears. In this context, it is a tool we use to overcome the past, or at least, stay ahead of it. If we are to be true to our authentic nature of being-ahead, this must not only apply to the present, as Heidegger has discussed in depth, but also to the past. And this is not the mean feat that some aspects of phenomenological analysis have perhaps presumed it to be. If anticipatory resoluteness is a 'distinctive mode of temporality' which 'makes itself known primordially', as well as being experienced as 'authentic Being-a-whole', (cf. Heidegger 1962:351 [1927]), then we may also suggest that this distinctiveness is 'applied' equally backwards. Indeed, if we are 'coming towards ourselves' in our authentic Dasein by way of anticipation – that is, we recognize or at least approach our ownmost being as being-ahead and as *futural*, which is saying more fundamentally that we are also both future-oriented in relation to objective time and to that of the world as it is appresented to us – this also means that anticipation is only possible because we are futural (cf. ibid:373). That this is at least related to the past if not specifically and equally directed towards it Heidegger then recognizes: "Anticipation of one's uttermost and ownmost possibility is coming back understandingly to one's ownmost 'been'." (ibid). Like Ricoeur after him, Heidegger states most strongly that what is futural in Dasein must 'win' for itself what is to come not from what has been, either historically or personally, but from that which is to come into which Dasein would lose itself otherwise; the 'inauthentic future' (ibid:386). The inauthenticity of all human futures is the ever-present possibility of not only nonsense, as Ricoeur succinctly states, but also all that which entangles my Dasein and pushes it to lose itself in its ownmost possibility of inauthenticity, the sham existentiality of the public or of rationalized presence. Perhaps these are one and the same, but accrue to themselves different temporal signatures. On the one side, nonsense is the means of loss, on the other, inauthenticity the outcome of this loss. The 'passage of time' is here as well experienced differently, but to the same general end. The actual end of Dasein is as left behind, as if death were something that emanated only from beyond the grave, not only of others, but of history itself. Hence the fantasy regarding not my ownmost end, the death which is mine and mine alone, but the end of history, Against all of this, Heidegger restates his case later on. Ultimately, "Anticipatory resoluteness brings this Being-towards-death into authentic existence." (ibid:442). I want to highlight equally so that in doing this, the past is brought back into the relief of what has fullest presence for us, because it is only through the perspective of having lived, of the 'been', that anticipation gains the temporality of its own momentum.

Two ontic features lend themselves to this disclosedness, desire and activity. Yes, they are often responsible for the loss of Dasein's authentic Being-at-home-in-itself, but I also wish to highlight that equally so, they are phenomenologically rich with the authentic possibility of mine ownmost being-ahead: "In desire I am carried forward toward the future, as in activity: I live time in the same direction, but in so doing I look 'further' into the future. I feel myself related to a more distant future." (Minkowski, op. cit:95). Perhaps the deonticity of desire is its ability to retain the perspective not only of the undesired but also of desires fulfilled. Something once experienced and 'completed' is resurrected only in form. It is commonplace to critique desire as being in principal unfulfillable, but this stops short of giving it due credit for being a not unimportant aspect of the mode of being-ahead-of-oneself. Activity perhaps less so, as we have not time to reflect on what we are about, indeed, upon what we *are*, in the space of action. Even so, desire supplements will, as being-ahead-of-oneself specifies what 'being-ahead' itself means for Dasein: "The idea of the supplement can be said to capture the thought that the value of origin may be an effect of desire, generated perhaps from the sense that temporal representations cannot be all there are..." (Wood 1989:132). However 'metaphysical' this desire is, in kind or in the unkindness of reaching around behind itself and pretending to throw us into the future alone and aloof to our own histories, it is at least clear that our vision of the future is partially bent round the shape of recalling how the past had also once been but a vision for us. What has been envisioned then is an amalgam of the 'future of the past' and the present. They are not quite the same thing, though they exist in the similitude of a desiring being-present. This is so because all signification we apprehend as arriving from them to us by way of a modification of what desire impelled us toward before it could be said to be fulfilled: "These protentions were not only present as intercepting, they have also intercepted. They have been fulfilled, and we are aware of them in recollection. Fulfillment in recollective consciousness is re-fulfillment..." (Husserl 1964:76 [1905]). Though he immediately reminds us that 'recollection is not expectation', its horizon is still 'oriented on the future' (ibid). Our 'indifference' to this or that moment wherein our anticipated desire and thus our vision of it are awaited or delayed, might make us feel that time is a 'threat' (cf. Lampert 2012:42). That is, this point in time, this now-moment, does not fulfill me. What I desire is not present nor can it be anticipated to be fully present even in my vision, because there is nothing, once again, right now, that can be *envisioned* as being related to my desire. It is possible, at least, that the confluential force of desire and anticipation may actually construct a state of being that will correspond to a wider reality not yet experienced, as in one of Jung's characterizations of synchronicity: "The coincidence of a psychic state with a corresponding, not yet existent future event that is distant in time and can likewise only be verified afterward." (1973:206 [1951]). Such 'verification' may well be a form of self-fulfilling prophecy in the classic sociological sense. I feel the desperation and anxieties associated with a run on the banks, which is not happening yet. But in so experiencing this 'psychic state', I in fact actualize the very thing that I anticipated and feared (or desired). Before Robert Merton's formulation, based as it was upon Thomas' equally famous 'theorem', that 'if one believes something to be real it is real in its consequences', we have a sense that what is to come is in principal out of our ken and control. We experience this as a kind of attack upon our Dasein and its ability to be-ahead. If we are as ownmost beings being-ahead then why is it that we face down a futural disconnect that more often than not mocks what is our ownmost? Our best laid plans have again come to naught. Human consciousness, devised and reconstructed in evolutionary genius and perhaps gifted also from what is beyond its own knowing balks at this juncture, this 'turn' of events. The obverse of desire appears to be delay - which we also use in combatting the objection the future throws in our direction; Schwartz cites Meerloo on just this point, cf. op. cit:40 – which from the perspective of my desire can only *urge* us on: "*Urge is care which has not yet become free, while propensity is care which is already bound in what it is involved in in its very being.*" (Heidegger 1992:297 [1925], italics the text's). Though care 'itself' is not composed of urge and propensity (ibid), it is colored by them, given specific forms of temporality, and also for that matter, tempo. Urge is cut-time, time cut up and experienced in a staccato signal stultifyingly saturating us with its own kind of 'anti-being'. Propensity slows the pace considerably, to a more considered sense. If urge carries itself along on sensitivity, then propensity balances itself on the raft of sensibility. Urge desires us to reject all delay, propensity uses the newly found time as something discovered about itself – the wholly entangled version of this would be the advent of portable digital technologies that can be accessed during delay-times in waiting rooms or queues (cf. Schwartz's own situation in 1976 to this regard (op. cit:5) for contrast – and hence something that might be turned to a form of disclosedness. We may have reached a temporary limit, but urge alone cannot overcome it. It must change its name by way of propensity, as the color of care is so altered. This process has a wider relevance and historical pedigree: "Now creationism often belongs to the logical structure of a good many apophatic discourses. In this way, creationism would also be their historic limit, in the double sense of this word: the limit *in* history and the limit *as* history." (Derrida 1995:73 [1993]). Part Diltheyan, part Heideggerean, the character of our 'place' in history is such that we will likely never have such a place – that is, nothing will be written about us and our name will not have to be changed, trading the old name and taking on the new in an apophasis proportional to our historical place – and that this is the more authentic as Dasein does come to an end after all. At once, we are at home in our place in history and only in this specific place. This second feature provides the framework for all deadlines surrounding historical thought and how we interpret 'the past'; historization and historicism separated at birth and brought together in death. If we have objections to the first of these we risk an unnatural aggrandizement of our place as a culture in the historical tapestry of human consciousness: "...the fear of death is absorbed into the idea of a Time placed into the bodies of men, not to annihilate them, but to make them into giants." (Kristeva 1996:301). If we take too seriously our objections to the second we simply look like the fools we are.

Either way, we become 'monstrous', as we saw Kristeva note earlier, quoting Proust regarding a human being's length being measured in their years (ibid:302). This length, determined not even by time served or the species tenure on earth with all of its ambiguously 'placed' beginnings – we will never be able to pin down a moment that humanity was 'in place', nor exactly where this place was let alone 'who' can claim any present credit for it when the facts of the matter state unequivocally that no one can – is also imagined to be of human import relative to cosmic time. We may legitimately ask, in the context of astrological astronomy, so practiced for many thousands of years by almost all cultures known to us historically, the question of why, after the Age of Pisces, is there an effort to put an end to the Great Year, the procession of the zodiac? In 2150 the Age of Aquarius ascends, but far from ushering in a new self-conscious projection of finitude in this or that Western religion – the age of the bull, the ancient Egyptian beliefs, the age of the ram, ancient Judaism, the age of the fish, Christianity (cf. Plessner 1973:240 [1951]) – we expect rather to put an end to finitude itself. By this time, in our technological imaginations as well as in our technical souls, indefinite life of a *new* species should have been perfected. If there is still a need for religion or concepts of the afterlife associated with it for this hybrid organo-digital being, then we would not care to guess at the extravagance of such beliefs or their implications.

The urge for a vehicle that does not fall apart, either suddenly in a moment of ill-timed fate or gradually, in the agony of dying a slow but commonplace death, is marked overtop the propensity that rationalizes it. Why *not* live forever? What *is* forever, anyway, and how long could it be, after all? And if you don't like it, or get bored, just switch yourself off. Stop whining about the sacredness of life. What is life that it is seen *as* sacred? Without death, life would just be life, and isn't that better in the end? Indeed, there is something to these objections, even though they are made by us about our time and our place in history, and do not emanate from the objective pool of once-worlded objections to our presence as thrown beings-into-the-world which is not our own. This 'something' is given more precise symbolic form when compared to the perception of those with diagnoses, who claim to literally feel things 'coming apart' and that this makes a 'strange impression' on the one who witnesses it (cf. Minkowski, op. cit:322). Science fiction aside – and is there not a penchant for indefinite life expressed in much of our entertainment fiction to this regard; as Sontag suggests, another round of a perennial quarrel (2007:195), this time with the present cast as 'ancient' – we could list all of the achievements of technique that point to the advent of a new species. I, for one, aim to last just long enough to have my consciousness uploaded and thence downloaded into a new vehicle. Such vehicles might at some point be consumed as automobiles are today. Should I attend this function as the same *being* I was last week? Forget wardrobes or a new outfit, get yourself a new body, head, and perhaps even alter your personality, that is, more than we humans can already quite impressively do pending social context. There might never be a second date again.

The deadline that we approach more and more rapidly is projected into the world of objects and others. We envision a world of free market democracies, just give it enough time, we say to ourselves. We envision a species with at the very least easily replaceable parts, in the same way that 'thoughts' are traded in and out at will, partially by the idle talk of the public and yet also by more formal discourses. We envision the end for the reliance on recollection and the end of the need to be-ahead. 'Living in the moment' is the more pure bliss. This is why narrative can still entertain us even after so much time has passed: "By tracing beings and things situated in time, the novel becomes a journey to the end of memory." (Kristeva 1996:167). The 'flood of sensations' we are presented with mimics that of life-perception, lived time, and the plenitude of the world, but just so, it *only* mimics it. Art isn't life, and vice-versa. Even if Goethe is held out as an exception to this rule it is correct to say with Weber that a being such as Goethe comes round only once every thousand years – we may admire, though at a distance, the same sentiment directed at Weber himself by Leo Strauss, a regular opponent of Weberian discourse – and that none of us should be tempted to set our own standards by such a visitation.

Yet whether the topic turns itself toward the procession of constellations, indefinite life or a new human species, or the daily struggle to meet the deadline placed upon us as historical beings and as children of our own time and no other by these self-same others, we must adjust to the lens of a future not yet experienced but still able to uncannily observe our movements and even read our minds. But any and all of these exact a price: "The further we direct our gaze from the present, the more time seems to shrink, the more events are bound together, the more they become ordered into distinct periods of life." (Minkowski, op. cit:162). Realizing that we have impinged upon the world-being through our presence and truculently absorbing this worlding into ourselves by losing Dasein in the entanglement of its own diverse device, we nevertheless attempt to 'set things right' by ordering our temporality in a way that accedes to self-imposed deadlines along the way to Being. For us, this Being can only be discovered in the world, its very clearing to be bound to our discoveredness, that of the world's being which is already always, and that of others, some of whom *are* 'already' but none of whom will be 'always'.

And so with ourselves. What has been said about the 'non-violent' – and who among us is, like Goethe, present in, but also aloof to, one's time in this way? – can be said of any child, at least, and perhaps also the vast majority of nameless beings who live and die according to the deadlines of others: "...he is not on the fringe of time, he is rather 'untimely', unpresent, like an anticipated presence, possible and offered, of another epoch which a long and painful political 'mediation' should render historical." (Ricoeur 1965:229 [1955]).

5.3 Visitations:

It is our main objective, in the face of the world's objection to us, its objectivity about us, and its objectitude, its ability to remain aloof to our human concerns, to admit to the certainty of our own deaths without conceding that dying is the harbinger of death (cf. Heidegger 1962:300 [1927]). For Heidegger and others, this is the chief function of everydayness, and this may be revealed by our penchant for deadlines, which at once reminds us of the connection between world and being and also obscures it, makes it ambiguous or even promotes the entirely unfounded supposition that life is 'just a game' after all, and one should not take it all that seriously. Living on, perhaps. But life?

Without going too far back down the same road, back into sacredness and sanctity and, from our perspective, yet other rationalizations containing the secret of running-on within their disingenuous embrace, it is another thing to claim that life has no serious meaning and betrays no authenticity of Dasein in any way. In Heidegger, we are told that death is an event, historically locatable given time, but that this is also its most important attribute. "Opposed to it is the idea of death as 'possibility'. This may seem odd. Surely the ideas of 'possibility' and 'event' can be conjoined. Do not insurance companies deal precisely with 'possible events'?" (Wood 1989:182). But of course what Heidegger is driving at is the immanence of the presence of non-being, and not only the idea that one could 'die at any time', the fact of which most mature adults are quite aware. No, meaning for Dasein is only fullest, is only in its ownmost possibility, in the immediacy of the possibility of its not being present. We may complain of a Pauline tinge to this indictment of our perception of death and also our own deaths, but it is still a reasonable existential ethic: "Death, as possibility, gives Dasein nothing to be 'actualized', nothing which Dasein, as actual, could itself *be*. It is the possibility of the impossibility of every way of comporting oneself toward anything, of every way of existing." (Heidegger, op. cit:307, italics the text's). This 'possibility of my non-Being' is not only immanent (cf. Wood op. cit:182), but is itself immanence. Even so regarded, we are still at a distance from it. We cannot wholly apprehend this sensibility because it must first apprehend us. Comprehension is not an option. Once 'understood', Dasein has come to an end. Part of the attempt to remain aloof to this existential deadline that does not lose itself through entangled everydayness nonetheless preserves the desire for death to be only itself, and not include me in its self-definition. After all, time is apparently able to do this: "Flight from itself does not flee somewhere else, but is one of its own possibilities, which is the present. In the flight from itself, time remains time." (Heidegger 1992:227 [1925]). The totality of Dasein's being able to be is not so much rendered or yet rended in death, but is opened up to itself. My own death is as much a part of me as my own being-ahead, or my concernfulness in care, or as time. These are not metaphors. Care, time, death, and the futural *are* Dasein. Much later, Heidegger affirms that only a phenomenological analysis uncovers this facticity (ibid:312).

Gogol has the primogenitor to the 'music man' trade in dead souls. This is satire, but it is also history. Perhaps this is as well a Russian thing, given Prokofief's later Lieutenant Kije. Kristeva in turn muses on the abstraction that can be drawn from this: "Some believe that the souls of the dead are held captive in inferior beings [ ] transformed into something else, where they endure without our knowledge. Does this notion also apply to our past?" (op. cit:5). Conceptions of the afterlife differ in structure, as we have seen above. But is not any conception of afterlife a flight from itself as well? It is too well known a thing to speak of assuaging one's own mortality. Perhaps there is more: an afterlife annuls the pressing-in of any deadline. It gives itself up to the eternity of non-time and indeed, non-being, for what *is* can also not be. If the negation of being is taken away, then so is being. The afterlife is thus at least a contradiction in terms. One cannot simply be. This paradox is contained, as it so often is, within the term itself; 'life after life'. No, it must rather be framed as another life, and not 'after' anything, if it is to be conceived at all. It is also not thereby and through this strange plot device emplotted, put into a plot and then exhumed to be examined in aid of a sequel to itself, 'after-death'. Once again, we must reply in the negative. What may come is neither after death nor after life. It is different, or at least, we in industrial and technical civilization expect it to be – we have had occasion to note more than once that social contract societies did not see it this way at all – but it is also saying too much to impute that it is *difference*. We the living *can* experience the afterlife while we are still alive. Perhaps this is to be our only true experience of it: "She feels time passing, but at the same time she has to think in an obsessive manner of death, which closes in on her simultaneously with the passing of time, as if there were absolutely nothing between the present moment and death except the fruitless unfolding of time; this fills her with terror." (Minkowski, op. cit:304). The obsessiveness associated with manic depression, the one ecstatically unified with the desireful being of eternity and the other plunged into the abyss of both the absence of meaning and probably more saliently, of *meaningful absence*, is a clear exemplification of the afterlife within the emplotment of this our very own lives. It is a shadow image of what is ownmost for Dasein and for our being-ahead more specifically. We feel that we have met the deadline and it has felled us, but nevertheless a pyrrhic victory is better than no victory at all. We do a violence upon ourselves even so, because it is the other within whom we seek to annihilate ourselves besides: "...the intention of violence, the end of which it pursues implicitly or explicitly, directly or indirectly, is the death of the other..." (Ricoeur op. cit:227). This other does not have to be 'at large', as it were. He is almost never worldly either in his objectivity or most certainly in his objection to myself, my own presence in the world that was to be shared but has since fallen with the rest of it. But he is mostly other to my interior, refusing to become part of the existential envelope of general interiority, and opting instead for balking at it, sitting somewhere in a shadowed corner of an ill-lit indwelling. The violence involved in the death of the other ultimately seeks to vanquish otherness, and thus it thrusts itself into the breach only as a vanguard in service of the main force that desires destruction of non-being itself. If the Nothing, which is the source of Anxiety and also a staple of concernful being-ahead-of-itself, can be destroyed, then nothing, quite literally, can stop us: "Time can only be truly regained if it recuperates this sort of violence – a violence that is essentially one of archaic loss and vengeance. What gives me pleasure and abandons me also kills me, yet I am capable of putting to death that which gives me pleasure." (Kristeva, op. cit:181). The temporality of this 'regained time' is eternity. It "… appears as the temporal rhythm of men, as a structure of the plurality of consciousness." (Ricoeur, op. cit:228). Post-Babel, humankind are and remain conflicted, fractious, fragmented, and distanciated. But we are not necessarily alienated, anomized, annihilatory, and contrary. The one set does not inevitably define the other. For though the human condition may be blank, even bleak, we are not ourselves either of those things. What *we* bring to time is not only history, but temporality. Time 'itself' has nothing to be gained from it, let alone regained. The visitation of humanity upon time is, then, a re-creation of the non-being of primordiality in the face of the deadline. This is accomplished through a division of temporal experience, and is made manifest by the observation, once again, distanced, perhaps dispassionate, but still concernful and 'careful' in both the sense of being pronouncing part of its ownmost possibility but also in the more straightforward sense of being cautious, of ironically, the 'death of the other': "It is not my own death but simply my mortality that I witness in the presence of the death of someone else. It is as if a split in time were produced here; the present death is reflected as an inevitable event in the future." (Minkowski, op. cit:144). Is 'someone else' the 'other'? In a sense, yes, she is an other to myself, about whom I may know little or nothing. But she is also very much like me. The details of her biography appear, in the end, trivial when placed up against our shared fate. Minkowski puts it this way: "I would almost like to say, 'I know this person well, but in the end I know nothing about him.' And this is what constitutes the value of life." (ibid:177). This 'nothing' is not Nothing, of course, just as any one other is not herself Otherness in all its alien, and thus as well, alienating, horror. But what is meant here is rather that in our shared fate, the nothing which is to be known about an other - as opposed to our intimacy with *the* other, especially the other that inhabits our all too self-conscious self-consciousness – is also the something which is about to *be* known that overcomes the specific deadline of difference. We are in the end kindred. Birth and death have already accomplished this verdict. Overcoming both *en masse* would not change anything to this regard. We, all of us, would still be the same thing. There are multiple ways to lose oneself before this facticity, and it is *the* scandal of our shared existence that we attempt to *avoid* sharing it.

The desire for the death of the other is nothing other than the will to difference. In turn, this difference is to be used as against the sameness that we today loathe and fear and deny that we can understand what is ownmost about our being by pretending the very opposite; that we lose ourselves in the other or by acknowledging her in any way. The other is always our loss. But since the other doesn't authentically exist, there can be no ontological loss of this sort. 'Other' is the dubious word we consider to annul our own responsibility for being. In this, it is a word that must also be listed as preeminent (cf. Ricoeur op. cit:209). And not only this, the deadline the other presents to us is also a sham, even a 'fraudulence in the work of totalization' though it is we who are the source of this version of the 'evil of evil', for to equate the dull difference of the day with the Nothing of Otherness is to engage in what is at least assuredly an evil 'thing'. It announces itself, to no one in particular, that here has come a time to kill: "Yet it is also a time that 'prolongs' the dead by placing them in the gigantic space where they lived [ ] hence they resemble monsters..." (Kristeva 1996:82). This aggrandizement of merely what has been into that 'which should not be' is a patent danger in every world humanity has yet known. Its is casually referred to as our 'animal nature', but in fact no animal treats its species comrades in the way we do. 'Man's inhumanity to man' is a more accurate description, but it begs the question as to its source. Our desire to control the timing of our own deaths provokes these behaviors, and our resentment that we cannot in the end, set that most personal deadline, the one that seems to matter to us the most. We cannot set it, and we cannot meet it. It is not so much set for us, but rather meets us outside of any schedule, no matter how clinically calculated or precisely prognosticated. The extremity of this resentment tends toward helplessness and hopelessness. It is, writ large, what we have felt throughout the life course whenever we have faced a challenge where we are being judged on something we do not know how to accomplish – 'I don't know what the teacher, my spouse, my child *et al*, wants of me' – and thus we are made conscious of the unfairness of the condition of ambiguity in which we find ourselves. Life is *not* necessarily 'unfair', as we irresponsibly tell our children, but it *is* ambiguous. It is part of the will to life to attempt to ameliorate this ambiguity, but it is also partly our will to death. The deadline, set for ourselves or for others, who in this setting become surrogate selves, casts into high relief the intersection between our beings *being* time and the time of our beings to live within 'objective' time. At the extremity of the lost hope and the inability to aid ourselves or the other in any way, we telescope time into the temporality of the deadline: 'The future is found to be barred by the anticipation of torture or imminent death. The past is immobilized in the form of delusive ideas of guilt. As for the present, enclosed between the faults of the past and the expiation of the future, it is reduced to nothing." (Minkowski, op. cit:219). In doing so, we may be said to have 'devoured' ourselves.

The deadline that is visited upon us, without warning and leaving us without recourse to meet it even though it has already met us, does suggest that it is we who have been eaten. It reminds us, perhaps in the murky depths of a collective unconscious, of our primordiality as the species that had just become self-conscious and risen beyond instinct. In this time out of time in which no time had before existed, only the temporality of the moment, endlessly repeated until our first ancestors opened their eyes to themselves and beheld *nature* for the first time as something ranged against them, the deadline came in the form of that self-same nature. The leopard in the night, leaping upon us and burying its fangs into our skull. The flash flood carrying off our offspring. The endless hooves of the great herds of savannah ungulates trampling us down. This is what it meant to have become human.

Today, the only reminder of our true origins is the deadline that *is* visitation. It seems to end all things, but this too is a sham projection for the politics of our own time: "Indeed, the death of values that has recently been decried may have reached a point of no return. We risk the death of the psyche. Yet what would be a better antidote to this laziness, this eclipse of a civilization, than allowing ourselves to be devoured by time embodied." (Kristeva, op. cit:198). This more literal Saturnalia, wherein time stops its movement only to eat its annual meal of human desire and fraudulent immortality, betrays time itself in the guise of Saturn. But we willingly have leapt into his maw. We have recognized not so much the death of values, but rather the value of death.

Now, the so-called 'end of history', also recently decried, is part of this fraud. The deadline absorbs what we have been into it and into what it appears to us to be, almost like one who is devoured, but not quite. For in meeting any deadline we are also overcoming its fullest presence, which occurs, somewhat paradoxically, only *before* the time that has been arranged or marked for it. A deadline met is no longer a deadline at all. It vanishes with only the trace of its occurrence on a calendar or some other such grid that had the function now only of an archive. And an archive has no teeth. History does not end as long as humanity is extant, but the history of this deadline is complete. A deadline mimics the thrownness of Dasein in that it can only be complete after it ceases to exist. No animal has deadlines. It is the most human expression of lived time that a mortal consciousness can conceive. No wonder it looks like history has come to an end, and indeed, it can do so by way of an imagination that thinks the singular: "Perhaps this is the only meaning that can be given to the notion of an end to history. In a sense, every philosophy is the end of history. The system is the end of history because history becomes nullified in Logic…" (Ricoeur, op. cit:75). Like any stasis, the deadline appears to us a way to end something. Something or other will have ended by this time, something or other disappears, including the fangs deadlines possess. Any system presents to us the deadline of its self-regard. No more changes will be permitted 'after' the deadline. The deadline is a judgment – it might be the 'time's up' of the exam invigilator, the boss or indeed the physician or even the professional assassin – beyond which there can be no recourse. Extension of deadlines, so common on today's university campuses, for instance, are part of the fraudulence in which Dasein loses itself, imagining that it itself has an unlimited time in which to accomplish its being, and that there is always a being-ahead into which one can be bodily thrown. But something is in fact revealed by this inauthentic rendering of the deadline: "*Authentic Being-towards-death – that is to say, the finitude of temporality – is the hidden basis of Dasein's historicality.*" (Heidegger 1962:438 [1927], italics the text's).

Life is currently extended greatly from the longevity indices of previous eras. The fact that the average life expectancy in Botswana is thirty-six and that of Indigenous males in urban Toronto is thirty-five does not seem to make an impression upon us. These kinds of numbers are medieval in more ways than one. It is clear in a society that bears little resemblance to how we humans got our start, that even the concept of the deadline is something that can be both ambiguated for ourselves and yet visited upon others with a ruthlessness equaled only by certain *systems* of genocide. The 'logic' of this escapes us only because we live long enough to escape its lesser verdicts. Even if we cannot end history without losing the entirety of the species and likely the planet as well; even if we cannot put an end to the otherness that haunts us with its uncanny obtrusiveness, we can still end the history of the other. The genuine power of the deadline is to put an end to doubt. But to lose the ability to question is to lose what made us originally human, and thus to devour the deadline and make it outlast all further efforts to become humane.

Chapter Six

Conclusion: Temporal Ipseity?

> History is never identical with the source that provides evidence for this history. (Koselleck 1985:153).

What is the selfhood of time? 'We are our time', as Corbin states. But what does it mean, other than to be from our own time, in the sense that historicism both gains leverage from but also encounters it limits? The disconnect between what we can know of both human history and that of ourselves, individuality within a larger historical flux, identity with what is ours and ours alone, and not the stuff of history and whatever 'source' may be afforded to us, can quickly become a fetish. The *horror vacui* pursues us, and the sense that within any space unaccounted for the Nothing of radical otherness might spring forth assails us. Like the urban driver who knows that if he does not fill up the car length space in front of him it will be filled by another, there is a constant and consistent percolation of anxiety drawing upon our existential reserves. It also makes demands upon our reserve. We have reservations about it precisely because we did not make a reservation 'ahead of time'. We were caught *not* being who we are, without due nod to Dasein's being-ahead-of-itself. In a word, we were shown up for being the very Nothing which we so fear.

It is clear that Dasein is not only time, given that Heidegger also says it is care, being-ahead, and running-on-towards-death. Of these 'constitutive structures' of the being of Dasein, that which makes us our ownmost and provides for us the ipseity of Being, it is temporal selfhood that is, however, the chief ontological concern. Not to say that the study of Being necessarily trumps ethics or even knowledge, but it does, in certain instances, take precedence. Even so, its analysis, phenomenological or otherwise, is also a gloss for these others. What is self-knowledge for human beings if not self-understanding? What is being being-for in its concernfulness, in its care? And why is the 'nature' of a being who is nothing of nature at all but is of its own nature and nothing else, such an intricate subject that it invariably flows out beyond the boundaries of subjectivity and must needs approximate an identity with what is objective? Is this in principle an objection to Being? In particular, to our beings?

These questions and those related will be pursued in this concluding chapter. We will begin with the individualized version of what we took to be 'free' time above. This is commonly called 'personal time', and may be something that is said to be a formal benefit, as with a job or career from which one takes 'personal' days, often for medical reasons or other health-related questions, or perhaps time away from family, when one desires one's 'own company' the utmost. A related, but even more casual manner in which the mundanity of temporal ipseity is marked is commonly referred to as 'down time'. This is such a vague attribution that it is well worth to pause in our phenomenological investigations and query both its form and content. Finally, well embodied in a sentimental slogan yet also seemingly profound and singularly ipsissimous, an unfolding discussion of the 'time of our lives' ends the chapter. Who has it? How does one have it? Why do we need it? And perhaps most tellingly, the sense that this time, above all others, will never come again, animate the concluding pages of our brief study.

6.1 'Personal' Time:

We live in our own time but we do so with 'contemporaries'. One's temporal peers may be grouped in a great variety of ways, of course, and in so doing, we are also marking the kind of time we favor for ourselves. We are making personal, perhaps paradoxically, the time in which we happen to live by noting all of those other persons who, in their actual presence, would impinge on our 'personal time'. They nevertheless also contribute to it by their refracted presentation of themselves within such groupings. Much such comparison is motivated by our sense of vanity, but also by our almost equal sense that we need to know how others have fared, or are 'doing', or if they care to know about our own versions of these conditions. If one's vocation is thinking and writing, one might construct a list of one's generational peers who have the same mission in life. Pushing this, one might also construct, in picayune detail and involving some rather painstaking and obscure archival research, such a list that crosses many generations, but adjudicated by the exact number of years all of these writer-thinkers have lived and what they had accomplished when they were the same age as oneself. 'To what end?', is a reasonable question at this point. But such a compendium is more than a series of benchmarks or 'gold standards', if such can be judged. It presents to oneself a form of temporal ipseity. I am not merely like these others, I am *one with* them. I can take encouragement from their work, inspiration from their labors. If they can do it, so can I.

This is the first step in understanding the authenticity of temporal selfhood. It appears to be a contrary move, a step in the opposite direction, but it is in fact the way home to oneself. No one has accomplished anything in a vacuum. The vacuum, so horrifying to us at a deeper level is, at its surface, only devoid of that by which one can be compared and evaluated. History is our judge, we may feel, but we must also be its judge: "To accomplish this, there must be no more escaping into abstract time, the time of anonymous collectivities; there must be a rediscovery of concrete time, the time of persons." (Corbin 1973:xix [1949]). 'Unconditioned sympathy' is Corbin's wellspring of this kind of time, which lends itself to, once again in an apparently contrary fashion, personal time. The 'time of persons', of the flesh and blood of those who live and live on can indeed become over-personalized, as if one inverts the usual projection of presumed but mostly feigned individuality we observe in the day to day or the open publicness of our quotidia. We can be caused petty affront by the latter - as in the sudden recognition that someone else has 'taken' our self-advertisement and used it for their own purposes; they have the same bumper sticker as I do, perhaps, or the same recordings – as if it were a kind of 'identity theft', itself a way to lose Dasein in the entanglement of the idea that one's official archive of *identification* is the same as one's selfhood. Certainly, the everyday event of such a theft causes us endless bureaucratic turmoil. 'How can I prove I am me?' is a question that could only arise in our modern society, that of precisely the 'anonymous collectivities' of which Corbin warns us against. It is most telling then, that from such a society the idea of 'personal time' has arisen.

As such, it is inextricably linked with life phases and the expectations we and others serially have of them: "...the concept of time is developed by the human personality in life. As the human personality develops and expands, the experience of time is naturally expanded and developed." (Metzel 1970:xxv).

Children do not have the need to make such distinctions as 'personal' or collective, private or public, anonymous or intimate, for their time is one thing; a kind of dreamtime that is only broken away from during adolescence when relationships, nascent employment, serious study and independence all become both possible and necessary. Time does not become less 'structured' in the ontic sense, but is very much framed differently in each general life phase. The beginning of this partitioning of time into that personal versus other forms occurs in the encounter with the world as it is and not how it appears in the time of dreams: "The elemental worldly kind of encountering, which belongs to Dasein and is closest to it, goes so far that even one's *own* Dasein becomes something that it can itself proximally 'come across'..." (Heidegger 1962:155 [1927], italics the text's). Dasein 'finds itself' as such in the 'what' of this new time. The everyday gloss of this ontological condition concerns the efforts we make at remaking ourselves in our own image. Here the hobby once again may prevail, or some form of self-expression such as the amateur arts and crafts, the writings of the one who journals or commits musings to the diary. It may be encountering the wilderness, making assay 'back' into the very nature away from which we ran headlong into the culture we now try to escape from, if only for a moment and only in a very controlled manner. The whatness of the what eludes us, but this is also part of the goal and outcome of personal time. It is not meant specifically and solely for self-reflection, though such may come 'out' of its what and remind us of its whatness. 'Doing' always places us in the sphere of fallenness. Idle talk and even discourse alike perform a sleight of logocentric hand and we find ourselves necessarily entangled in them. Stepping back from this, taking it personally instead of making it personal, we find time to have not lost its ontological implication: "The ontological is always the *within-which*. It is also a non-thing. The ontological is the non-thing within which the ontic thing finds its place." (Barrett, in Gale 1968:361, italics the text's). The time of persons, even if it is but a historical figment, presents itself as a mode of the world-being of the species. But only in modern times can we say this of ourselves. Only now do we have the discourse *in which* to state its case for itself. We overlook the ontological, Barrett continues, because we are always seeing through it. We take a mistaken pride that we have 'seen through something' as in a plot or other device, but this is indeed *something* that can be seen through in this way. As well, we 'see through' a plan to 'do' this or that. We complete a task, or yet a mission. Wood adds that the idea which "...for Heidegger existential time is concerned only with the humanly meaningful organization of time is quite mistaken. This may be our loss. What he *is* committed to, it seems, is a sense of time or temporality in which the guiding thread is the transformation into a temporal framework of the problem of selfhood..." (1989:218-9, italics the text's). Clearly the phenomenology of the present analysis differs substantially from that of a fundamental ontology of Dasein. But not entirely: selfhood is the mediating space that Dasein brings to itself in order to understand the presentation of one's being ontologically, if not the full presence of Being. It is also clear that we cannot explain this being 'as an entity', nor yet only 'present for consciousness' as in immanentiality (cf. Heidegger 1992:217 [1925]). If the 'problem' of selfhood, originally cast as both a subjectivity and a subjection by Augustine, recast by Marx and others into a subjectitude, by Freud and Husserl into a subjectitudinal complex and so on, is to be temporalized, cast into Time as being is thrown into the World, then just as the world worlds *without* loss when encountering the various forms of the subject, so Time *times* its way along without regard to beings temporal or no. Why should it not be this way? If immanence is at least in part a subjective predicate, a projection into the world of the encounter with beings or with 'entities', this should not in any manner *necessarily* impinge upon the worlding or timing of what is the already-always. Beings come and go.

The temporal ontology of selfhood seems to take the time to make things all too personal: "The fact that experienced time obviously depends on lived time is a strong argument for the illusory character of time as a whole." (Plessner, op. cit:262). Life is not wholly a dream, and in addition, humans have the dream-life of both the unconscious and of the more idiomatic sense of desire and fantasy while participating more or less fully in conscious life. There is an 'extension' of time both in ourselves and in the encounter with others, things, and world, and like the concept of the aesthetic object, the 'temporal object' both challenges us and ameliorates its presence through an invitation to subjectivity that is also part of its *res extensa*: "By *temporal Objects*, in this *particular sense*, we mean Objects which not only are unities in time but also include temporal extension in themselves." (Husserl, op. cit:43, italics the text's). A tone can become an object, but not its duration, Husserl continues. There is a continual difference in the way a tone appears to us, but the simplicity of this series of appearances belies an act on our parts which could be referred to as a 'feature of intentionality' (cf. Heidegger 1992:61 [1925]). Husserl describes for us various conscious acts that have time as their focus or at least as part of their intentionality. This is not, in principle, lived time. It is the structure of how time is perceived by consciousness, and not even as an 'ego', which appears to be absent in the 1905 work. So Metzel is quite correct to suggests that the 'problem of selfhood' in this context "…is seen to be the problem of how consciousness constitutes an immanent object." (op. cit:xxxiv).

Now Heidegger seems to mock this tack, referring disparagingly to how epistemologies occupy themselves with the 'pros and cons' of such a question. Speaking of entities once again, that which is nearest to us, the Dasein 'which we ourselves are', we lack an 'originary apprehension of such' (cf. op. cit:149). Hence the novel sensibility that we must quite literally make time more 'personal', include it as part of our constitutive structure. Temporality in relation to Dasein becomes in its subjectivity almost a kind of personality. We do speak of atmosphere in relation to space, especially the social spaces of intersubjectivity. But of subjectivity 'alone', of what is my ownmost in that I am subject to it and to no other's subjectivity, the 'personality of time' takes on a different hue. Just as "A history is absorbed by its effect." (Koselleck 1985:216), Dasein is 'taken in' by its interaction with the world and with others, even with things, 'themselves' or no. Dasein is 'taken aside' by its own desire to understand its 'place'. It is counseled, perhaps even taken in hand, upbraided, worked over, not in any criminal sense, but in the atmospheric and personal facticality of changing times. We have already discussed how the schedule is subject to change. This has become in our society a commonplace expression, used as a throw-away line at the end of many missals, official or otherwise. It is a counterpoint to another problem of selfhood, that of a being which is at one place and at one time from the standpoint of others, so much so that we must needs construct an entire discourse alter to the subject - and perhaps also counter to it - to account for this problem: "…so unobserved time gained a function creative of knowledge that comprehended the whole of history." (ibid). At this level, the personhood of temporality drops radically off. It is the obverse of inner time consciousness, and might be referred to as a kind of 'outer time unconsciousness', if that were not too awkward and vague. Perhaps more accurately, discursive history is the *unlived* time of which we become conscious only through patient study. It is in part the 'confrontation with tradition' to which Gadamer exhorts us. Either way, the personhood of this kind of analytic of time has upshifted the notion of selfhood into a discourse foreign to its own experience of its ownmost. It is not even my very own, or that which is farthest from me, for it is not what occupies idle talk or the publicness of the everyday. We do not spend our small talk time speaking about the problem of human history in its relation to subjective perception of events. Perhaps ,'This is our loss', to echo Wood.

To travel to the other end of this spectrum, as with Husserl himself, we find that personal time is also effaced, this time not by history but rather by phenomenology. Even so, there remain some points of egress: "The formal description of inner-time consciousness must articulate with some persons' experiences of the beautiful, with others' experiences of the ineffable within themselves or of the peculiar but seemingly ever-present ambiguities of human existence, as much as with human experiences of the mathematical." (Larrabee 1989:388). That our perception of cosmos is undergirded by the mathematical does not, of course, make it any the less beautiful. Indeed, such a beauty is only enhanced by our knowledge of its formal properties. The aesthetic object, in losing its temporality for the ability to 'time' itself with our perception of it, glimpses on our behalf what Dasein authentically can apprehend about the world's being. Yes, we are at once apprehended by art - its radical wondrous beauty disallowing any patent summary, its scandal, even 'evil' to borrow from Ricoeur, disallowing any mindless complacency regarding the way things are with both us and the world around us – just as we are apprehensive about it for exactly these reasons. This is what 'apprehension' means to a phenomenological ethics, the 'hermeneutics of facticity' dovetailed with inner-time consciousness and such-like. It is the mother experiencing the desire for her daughter's well-being, the *Wesenschau* of subjecting oneself as Dasein to the objectivity of the world. The beloved other, herself a work of art in our perception, makes us not the artist so much as the one who, through the arts of concernful being, *cares* for the person and not only as Dasein.

And all of this, taking place in living time, is personal perception that occurs to us not merely *as* our very own but *within* our ownmost being: "An identical *flux* of existence lays the ground for all attitudes. It is because the same man *lives* in all attitudes that he 'suffers' the division of his life, he 'suffers' the plurality of his objects, the methods and his attitudes." (Ricoeur, op. cit:194, italics the text's). Though this flux is constitutive and ontological, the sameness it produces makes time personal and our experience of it as ethical. Such experiences do not retain their 'original' tone of value-neutrality as does the flux itself. 'Taking things personally' has this deeper meaning. 'Things' is not an odd-job term, personally not a reference to one's bruised or aggrandized ego. To 'take' in this way is to apprehend. Our experiences can differ radically across the life-course. We are not at all the same persons throughout our life, but we are made to shoulder the same burden, which is why Ricoeur uses the word suffering here. It does not necessarily entail emotional sorrow, but it is more like something which is carried along with us. It may not even stay 'within' us, and much of therapeutic discourse has this mandate: to expel the burden carried in this way. But what it cannot, and should not, do, is to convince the person that his burden is not very much his own. It may be carried in a number of ways, and it may not at all be transported only within the ambit of subjectivity and inner-time, but it nevertheless must be moved. It must be moved because it in turn moves us.

As with care, burdening is also part of the structure of Dasein, and may be better known somehow outside the definition of Heideggerean care, for it also contains within its presence carefulness and carefreeness alike. Unburdening can only occur if there as a burden in the first place. The *sans souci* is not knowable bereft of 'suffering' and 'division'. Even so, patient personhood, crafted by the art of time, negotiates this division and joins them inasmuch as it is joined with them: "Because the subjective meaning of the wait itself tempers and is in some respects affected by the kind of social relationship that immediately follows, these two parts, though temporally separate, are in fact aspects of the same whole." (Schwartz 1975:176). Just as the events of happenstance await their joining through a history compiled of them but within the crucible of discursive perception, so personal experiences must be attended to and attuned by the 'flux' made subjective. To reach this point is, of course, only to return. Not from whence one came, but by way of a reasoned and seasoned subjectivity that does not evade itself in the manner Dasein loses itself in the public or becomes entangled in inauthenticating discourse. The 'tube time' spoken of above has this subjectivity to it as well, for it is not merely an abstraction of the subtracted attraction we feel toward personal history as it 'should' have been. This is perhaps the most profound reason why "There is no history [ ] without an epoché of everyday subjectivity, without the establishment of the investigative ego from which history draws its excellent name. For historia is precisely the 'availability' and 'submission to the unexpected', that 'openness to others' whereby bad subjectivity is overcome." (Ricoeur, op. cit:31).

If we feel badly that our history is never entirely our own, we must understand that the source of this division lies not so much in the suffering of the 'same' person over time but the facticality, which is also a rare instance of facticity if it is apprehended as and through the 'historia' of the social world: "The experiential space of contemporaries is the epistemological kernel of all histories." (Koselleck, op. cit:137). Such a space has already undergone an epoché; that of what is worlded apart from the selfhood of disclosedness. What constitutes the disclosure of World is made manifest by the division of experience uttered not by one's own desires, but by the 'doings' and timing of others. This presents itself as a challenge, something to be apprehended. Once again, we ourselves undergo each of the aspects of self-conscious doubt as we did when faced by the aesthetic object, something out of time that is now 'back' in time, though not yet 'in time' with ourselves. This 'experiential space' is, then, something that has a rhythm of its own. It also partakes in its own ontic version of aesthetic experience that we cannot ignore: "Social life is always a spectacle. We must not close our eyes to this but go beyond it toward an extreme alternative to recapture time from our inner lives, a time that is all the more subtly reconstructed because it may *also* be the only conceivable and real exteriority available to us." (Kristeva, op. cit:170, italics the text's). This is its spectacular quality; sociality is only a means to further the ends of temporality and to allay our apprehension concerning the end of time. Once wholly divorced from primordial time and the nature which enveloped it, human consciousness has this and only this as its home. Temporal selfhood, the time of persons diluted into personal time, comes to terms with this 'reality' insofar as it comes to grips with the subjectivity of lived time experienced together and not alone.

The imagery we bring to a time which is our own but which does not discover my ownmost being as time within its experiential reality suffers then not from a lack of that reality *per se*, but an unwillingness on our parts to automatically share it. To do so might seem to be tantamount to making a spectacle of ourselves. Perhaps inevitably, we are more comfortable with doing this as a species, or as a form of consciousness unique and perhaps quite distanced from any other similar sentience if extant. At first, our local version of the dispassionate and the distanciated rests content with discursive descriptions and analyses simply because the responsibility for them is shared amongst more or less innumerable others. But there is more to it than selfish selfhood, a personality that declares 'this is *my* time', or even 'I've paid for this time, and it is thus mine and mine alone', ironically echoing the more ontological ethic of apprehending the completion of Dasein in its annihilation: "For the image of man is not just the portrait of man, but also the sum total of the ways in which man projects his vision on things. In this sense, a still-life is an image of man." (Ricoeur, op. cit:119). What is stilled is such an image is the multitude of living beings. What is distilled is the sense that our experience is our own and must be borne along with us, 'suffered' perhaps, but certainly 'burdened' in the sense of onto-ethical care. But what is still there, what remains and what has remained as careless as we may have been with our life or that of others, is the fact that any still-life is *still* life, still an image of what is. Once again, as history extracts from its own historia the historical endeavor, the narrative of a species-laden project, the project of self-understanding occupies any being who exists as its ownmost as time and not merely 'in' time with the world etc.. This rhythm is not lockstep, nor even something that swings along. It rather is agogic, perhaps aleatory, and certainly incomplete: "One might admit that something like systematic self-intelligibility is something people seek, without accepting either that they necessarily or actually achieve it, or that it is the only or supreme value. And yet existential temporality does make such a claim." (Wood 1989:328). 'Such' a claim does betray its grandiose side. It is *such* a claim to have made such a claim, if you will. Especially so when we so often fall *so* short of it in the modern anonymity of Das Man and everything it implies. But it is clear that even if it represents one of our more tacit and obscure ideals, in our time given over to the experts from which Weber famously warns us to steer clear of at all costs, it nevertheless points phenomenology along the way to being. Human consciousness is for us, first, an abstraction of self-consciousness. Time, the projected perception of the temporal self, and Being, the aspiration to become something more than oneself. What unites this modern trinity of human longing, to belong and to be along the way to, is the will not to know 'thyself' so much as to apprehend a time in which one comes home to oneself, when one can step beyond the stilled image of either the adventitial or providential Man: "Future history whose outcome is foreseen serves in this way as a relief – one's will becomes the executor of transpersonal events – and as a legitimation which enables one to act in good conscience." (Koselleck, op. cit:205). One must be careful here, however, not to presume that 'how things turned out' was a direct confirmation of one's desire. All the more so, the success of our actions do not make them in principle the manifestations of good conscience. Nor can we say, as we often do, 'well, it worked', without implying that things also were 'worked out'. Solution and resolution are, as we have seen, not the same. The outcome of that which has not yet occurred and yet is known, is a function of how closely we trust our will to execute in the space of action. This is one of the chief ways in which human consciousness makes Time into temporality: "Time, then, is not only *constitutive* of identity, rather than a mere medium in which things unfold, but is *itself* constituted by its role in supporting identities and differences." (Wood, op. cit:31, italics the text's). This second clause actuates temporality, which is always only incipient in the human perception of events. Objective Time, the time of the world and which times itself as the world worlds, at the same time though not necessarily *in* 'the same' time, could have been said to be that of nature. This is too pat a division for phenomenology as we have also seen above, but it does have the merit of reminding us that will has a limit. It is part of human finitude, and thus cannot overreach itself into the sphere of inexistence. Just so, a willed future does not entirely represent the image of man unto itself, just as it cannot be with certitude my own future into which I am throwing myself consciously and bodily. It is an expression of human freedom to imagine that we can even incompletely accomplish this or that act that we set before us, and it also reflects the will to life. But it is to time that we must grant the arbitration that in fact any of this *can* occur, and in so doing, we are not returning to the idea that time is but a 'medium', however objective and abstract. Rather, it is no different in metaphysical stature and status than a God must once have been. Our planning, plotting, and even praying have replaced the genuflections of antiquity but their object is still to free us from temporal finiteness: "To reflect on the radical evil of freedom is to forge beyond successive intentions, beyond the discontinuous choices which time scatters in every which direction up to this totality of self; at the same time, I discover this origin of the action whence regeneration may surge forth." (Ricoeur 1965:300 [1955]).

6.2 "Down' Time:

Unlike personal time, the other major kind of temporal space that we accrue to ourselves in our own day does not have to be spent alone, or at least, there is not the same kind of immediate expectation that I might have some other task to perform that only I can accomplish. The so-called 'down' time is also seen in itself as more task-less, so that whatever one *is* going to do with it, the sense that it must be done or that there is after all, a schedule in force through part of its duration is also lessened. Down time also never shows up in any official record. One cannot find in any employment or other contract the phrase that connotes a general sensibility that nothing may be done within its occurrence. It certainly can be planned, scheduled, and experienced, but it cannot hold appointments with others who are themselves working. This last is reserved, as we just saw, for personal time or 'personal days', which of course do occur in the official record of temporal transactions. Therefore down time betrays a slight affinity with the directional meaning held within the casual idiom. One is to 'go down', or one is already 'down', as in blue or slightly depressed. The 'up-down' signature is suggestive of things *not* happening rather than much of what we discussed above. But traditionally, going down has the connotations that other forms of idleness, at least since the Reformation, has had. That is, one might have another kind of appointment, one that cannot be foreseen, with a kind of devil: "It is the imminent possibility of degrading myself as a possibility of being free. Herein we meet once again [ ] with the ambiguity of history." (ibid:298-9). If 'evil never is, but always strives to be', as Ricoeur cites Jean Wahl as suggesting, this also fits within the ambit of the 'downward' motion associated with this kind of time. Falling itself does not stop. Just so, fallenness ends only when we have reached the terminus, the terminal point in which and at which Dasein itself is completed unknowingly. But this time any evil associated with our fall is not fraudulent. We encounter our fullest being-able-to-be in our death. We are as 'total' as a human being can be only at this point. Otherwise we are notoriously incomplete. So down time is not so much a rehearsal for death itself, its moment and advent, as we have framed deadlines to be in the above, but rather a practice run at nothingness, at what 'experience' might be like, if such a term has any purchase at all, *after* one dies.

If we are imminently capable of degradation in down time, its temporality belies its immanence precisely through its being imminent, especially if immanence suggests a kind of *Mitsein*, as Heidegger states (1992:103 [1925]). Being with another assumes that this other also has some 'time to spare', or perhaps is also engaged, as we are, in the experiencing of some 'down' time of her own. Immanence is a 'relation between two entities' and is characterized as being 'real-in-one-another'. It almost sounds romantic. Certainly our memories of down time, once 'taken', are more vague at the outset, before anything specific can or has occurred within its space, than in any other designated time. We keep the most casual of records of down time, perhaps these days a few photographs, because even a vacation or other major event involves far more planning 'ahead of itself' than can take place in the casual atmosphere of what is 'the down'. If it is generally the case that "The before and after of an event contains its own temporal quality which cannot be reduced to a whole within its longer term conditions.", then down time looks more like Koselleck's very next sentence: "Every event produces more and at the same time less than is contained in its pregiven elements." (1985:110). Since we do not have plans for such a time ahead of itself, as it were, it is plausible that something or other *will* occur that presents itself not so much as a plenitude or surfeit but as an addition to our expectations, which are set low or even near nil. This is the 'more' of such an 'event' or series of events. The 'less' is simply the sense that afterward, whatever has occurred, since it did also occur by definition within the ambit of designated down time, can't after all be all that important. The event occurring is the more, our interpretation of it's value is the less. Since this as well may be generalized outside of specifically designated down time, this kind of tandem suggests that *any* time may take on some of the character of down time. In a sense, down time has a kind of magnetic freedom, an ability to present itself in its relative non-presence at any point during the hours of the day, etc. This may seem oddly acausal, but "Problems only arise when we consider these causal chains to be located along closed timelike curves." (Horwich 1988:118). Akin to keeping a strict discretion between heaven and earth, or between sacred events and those mundane, even profane, temporal causality in this case is more of a model than anything 'real' or something that could be part of the human experience. Down time blends these differences in kind, giving it an acausal arc and flavor. The difference between discrete kinds of time is 'diminished' (cf. Koselleck 1985:172 for the archetypical case). But does not the temporal character of event and experience do this in principle? Since our sense of what has occurred or even more so, what is occurring just as it has done so without the possible benefit of additional reflection and the inevitable transformation underwent by the 'has been' in historical refraction, has the character of a flow on top of a phenomenological flux, 'kinds' of time are at best a kind of mental rubric. Down time presents itself as a kind of symbol of what happens to occurrences in general. It is the discretely partitioned sign of the *happenstance of occurrence.*

It is also plausible to suggest that what does occur in down time is the very diminishing of discretion. We might well participate in the spontaneity of private acts, since there is, for the time being, nothing else 'at stake' or at least nothing else to do. Happenstance then may be seen as being built into the structure of the occurrence but then experienced in an improvisatory manner. In a sense, no true 'event' can happen in down time. The downwardness of this symbol of the actuation of experienced time brings to the fore the process of being-time, brings into an impassioned but not altogether focused intensity of that which Dasein understands as its temporal being. Care, on the other hand, distances itself, as well as the feeling of being-ahead or 'running-on'. Phenomenologically speaking, down time is an experience of temporality without so much of the other constitutive structures of Dasein being 'consciously' present: "Temporalization does indeed in some sense involve a relation between an existent and a non-existent, an inside and an outside, but it can be best said to symbolize the inside/outside relation involved in phenomenological reduction." (Wood 1989:130). On the face of it, the simplest response to such a claim would be to understand what has been as the no longer existing. But we have seen that from Husserl onward this is not truly the case. Existence in this more narrow sense would clearly reference only the world and its eventualities. That is, a past event is no longer occurring in the same manner as it 'originally' occurred. In this, down time functions more like a memory or a trace of Memory proper. A time in which I am to do nothing in particular might well give rise to recollection. A temporality where being-time is experienced but no objective time passes insofar as there is 'nothing' which I *must* accomplish and only that which I might desire to do gives me the impression that at the same time, and in the mean time, nothing has been lost. Ironically, "This is the supreme example of time regained, the point where no memory ventures, the point where time leaves no memory trace, and is split from the mind." (Kristeva 1996:237 [1994]). The downwardness of this kind of solitary time which is given over to the solicitude of solitude cannot but bear its own memory in its descent. It is the *undertaking* of time, and we carry the casket of memory above us, since we are already beneath its weight, lower than it, and pressed ever downward by it. Yet my perception of this timescape, wherein the idleness bred evil as well as the nostalgia breeding more of itself can take place, continues both apace and consistently. The burdensome aspect to which Dasein is enthralled and under which it may falter from time to time, is lifted by our very downwardness. Perhaps what down time confers upon us is a way in which to experience the fallenness of Dasein's thrown project. Down time is thus aptly, if unwittingly, named as an ontico-ontological space of clearing. True, it is not yet cleared, and like evil, cannot be so in its striving to be. Our downwardness is the ontic conceptualization of our fallenness. We lose ourselves in down time like no other kind of time simply because time is, finally, ours to lose.

That we experience this motion as continuous even though what we 'do' with or in the time experienced is diverse, suggests that perception is itself a 'selfsameness' (cf. Heidegger 1992:43 [1925]), and thus it does not define itself by another kind of perception, and that "Temporality *is* only in its temporalizing." (Wood, op. cit:217, italics the text's). Down time recapitulates primordiality. In doing so it brings us as close as we can be to our ownmost being-in-time. We are struck by the absence of the event rather than by any specific kind of experience thereof or therein. Since it can also be the relatively undressed rehearsal for nothingness 'itself', down time presents itself to us as the 'from which' (ibid). Nothing else emanates from it, it is rather the wherefrom all events come to us. The happenstance of occurrence clearing itself before our eyes also implies a traditional sense of 'commensurability' that Heidegger comments upon as part of what it means to 'bring-into-coincidence' and retains, even in our own time, a distinctive mark of the truth about it (cf. op. cit:51). On the other had, however, any apodicticity is lacking. We do not have a clear and certain truth within the embrace of the downwardness, the down tempo of this time. But we also do not need it. We do not seek it. It is the opposite of the spontaneity that is born for downwardness. Do we wish to throw ourselves off a cliff? Is everyone else doing so? Why yes. Then, let us find our own existential overhang and drop therefrom. This too has a romance about it. But its metaphoric quality breeds not so much evil in time but an equality across diverse temporalities, as we have just seen with perception itself. It is, after all, a commonplace 'event' to have a Gestalt-like experience, to embody or find oneself embodied in a moment of clarity, wherein the ownmost of our beings has been cleared for us and we then are compelled to fill it up, to drop ourselves into its void: "A poet has a mental picture all at once, and then gives it Temporal expression. The timeless day of friendship could take a lifetime or a few minutes to act on. We have a thought, and the urge to make something in time out of it; action temporalizes ideas." (Lampert 2012:55). In this telescoping of what is imminent and what is immanence, there is no 'temporal succession' (cf. ibid:88). Sontag here speaks of a 'simultaneity' that is gained from travelling, and the difference this simultaneously different world has presented to one's home to which one cannot exactly now 'return' (2007:228). And what is simultaneity other than the bringing together of what could be differently experienced in the same experience? In the context of down time, just as it has announced the from-which, the 'bringing–together' is itself brought into similitude: "A full moment of time exists only when there are many time-lines. It takes two times to make one time, and one to make two." (Lampert 2012:227). Succession then is the experience of the similitude of simultaneity and delay. And so at the very beginning of Wood's actual analysis we find that "…the instant is a nonrecuperative opening out [onto what is other and yet] it is also an embodiment of all those identical moments it repeats."

(op. cit:11) while at the same time at the very end of Lampert's we read that "...we should not speak of 'one time' at all." due to the impossibility of clock synchronization across different space-time 'frames' (op. cit:230). At one level, time is here suggested almost in the sense science fiction uses as a time-worn plot device, while Nietzsche's understanding of eternal recurrence has more of the fantasy flavor to it. Lampert is finishing with the first and Wood beginning with the second. But more profoundly, the much-discussed 'moment', sometimes fully present and sometimes doubted to non-existence, has become the stretched-out nowness that characterizes down time. We even disregard the sacred device of the clock, since we are not 'due' anywhere at any specific moment. In this, the moment also both disappears in any adventitial sense, and completely takes over, for that is all there is remaining for us in a time where succession no longer matters.

If it is true that "A machine has a practical meaning only as an expression of man's response to the problems set by his environment and by his fellow men." (Cipolla 1967:89), then the presence of the clock fades to insignificance because the only 'problem' we face in the midst of down time is what to do with ourselves. Neither the world as an 'environs' or others as problem-posers exist. This setting is also the space wherein evil might begin to strive to become itself, but it is not necessary that we should heed its banal breath. We would rather make it come to us. We can patiently await its advent, which is never of the moment but always momentous even so, but we can also prevent our down time from becoming simply a limbo, waiting for it to end so that we can return to the regular everydayness of the schedule and the appointment. Not that waiting *per se* is all bad. Because down time does not require the 'articulation' of social relationships, waiting itself is downplayed: "Waiting periods thus represent part of the connective tissue by which interactions are held together and ordered, according to the principle that temporal separation of engagements constitutes the very condition of their inner coherence." (Schwartz 1975:192-3). So in fact what phenomenology has revealed about the moment and its similitudinal abilities is that its 'inner cohesion' rests upon the discretion accorded to temporalization. Such temporalization separates so that the experience of the moment may in fact be discerned in the first place. Sociology has come to this point rather more straight-forwardly simply by noting that what occurs in the stretched-out nowness that exists *between* moments is, also in fact, what makes them both cohere and coherent.

So down time has a 'cosmopolite' character to it, wherein the usual dualism of this time and that, or this action and that action, such is no longer extant (cf. Koselleck, op. cit:170). This is the bright-sidedness of down time. One need not be any one thing, as we are always supposed to be in any specific role context and its associated temporality, or for that matter, vice-versa. But in not being any 'one' thing, we are also not necessarily and immediately all things, the fullest expression of Dasein's ownmost being-able-to-be. Rather, and along with the sense that down time is a rehearsal for nothingness, we tend toward being no-thing at all, prematurely absconding with ourselves in the theater of anticipated but still played-with non-existence: "The compulsion to de-realize oneself in order to become paralyzed at the final stage of existence led also to an inversion of temporal experience. Past, present, and future ceased to be a framework for orienting behavior." (ibid:224). Oddly ahistorical contexts such as the Third Reich were 'addictive' in this sense. Their fraud was to permit time to become totality all at once, as it were, as if the messianic apocalypse of fascism could answer to all comers and, in a trice of duplicitous truth, become blinded by its own internal light. A light, however, that never illuminated itself.

Avoiding this and yet still being able to enjoy the non-entities and the nothing of down time requires, as do all ethical projects, more alertness on our parts, and more discrimination. Minkowski aptly sums it this way, also at the very beginning of his landmark study: "…it appears that this is the price we must pay if we are to free ourselves from the slavery to which modern culture subjects us through the idea of time that it imposes upon us. It is not a question of having free time but of learning how to live and to breathe freely and spontaneously in time." (op. cit:5). Indeed, this is what ultimately makes time personal. Once again, it is the potential for radical nothingness appresenting itself in down time that brings home to us the necessity for humans to apprehend the personhood of ourselves in time, and thus also the selfhood of time. Doing so makes us not more *than* human, but rather simply *more* human. This is not only the 'function' of down time, it is also that of history in general, as history extant cannot exist in the usual everyday sense of something that 'is' in its isness, for it is passed. The past exists, certainly, but what has passed does not. Therefore, since history *is* writ large what we are within down time, it is crucial to note that the downward nature of that which has passed but has also become the past has a similar humanizing quality about it: "For if history did not withdraw us from our customary surroundings, how could it enable us to find a subjectivity that is less egoistic, more mediate and, in a word, more human?" (Ricoeur, op. cit:32).

6.3 The Time of our Lives:

We ourselves are time. Presence 'arises' not for us but with us. Since nothing has been said ontologically when the expression 'in-itself' is used 'without further ado', as it were, then Heidegger begins the most serious of his analyses with these bold claims (cf. 1992:197 [1925]). The time of our lives is thus given a third sense by this kind of phenomenology. The casual idiom refers to subjectively experiencing the best time we have ever known. The objective sense of the phrase is quite literal and simply refers to the historical period in which we are alive. But the subject/object distinction is not of interest to a fundamental ontology of Dasein. It is a cleaved image, a misrepresentation of our relationship with the world and with others. Rather both 'presence' and 'the present' describe our encounter with the world (ibid:223). Thus 'the time *of* our lives' now also denotes that time which comes *from* us, it is *of* us, and of no other. But what, exactly, does the encounter of the world give to us and take from us? Does it withhold something from us? Do we in turn engage in some ulteriority in the face of its immanentiality? It is finally time to find out: "To understand any present, one has to grasp the contradictions at work within it, by which its capacity for (self-) transformation is marked. Understanding a state of affairs is to grasp its possibilities of change." (Wood 1989:364). Wood agrees that the future *is* possibility in the 'strong' sense. Hence the more full import of the present. The present's presence is, as the proverb runs, 'big with' the future. The presence of the future in tadpole form questions not only the present – it will be different in some way; change will be enacted at some point, etc. – but also ourselves within it. We are the agents of the change from present to future. The earth changes, yes, but far too slowly and gradually to be significant in this sense. Other forms of life also change by gradual evolution, once again, across time periods that may be geologic in length. No, it is we alone who alter existence and are thus altered by it. That is why phenomenology is not earth science. For it is 'World' that is of the moment, and 'World' worlds its way along because we are present in our presence and the world presents itself as the space within which time unfolds.

If it is also true that Dasein is "...the entity whose way of being is questioning itself." (Heidegger, op. cit:150), then this as well, like that which occurs in the time of our lives, has multiple meanings. We question ourselves. We *are* questioning. The residuum of faith lies in the continued ability to question. For to question is to enact the arc of a leap of faith. There may not be an answer in the form of a solution or resolution to my query, but I have faith that there will 'at least' be a response. Perhaps that is all there can ever be. In questioning ourselves we are enacting the imminence of the future in the present, just as the future does to the present 'itself'. In being the essence of the ability to question – we are the only known form of consciousness that does this – we are participating in the *immanence* of the present's presence, which also contains, as we have just noted, the seed of the future within it. Being-with the present means to question it. But it is also questioning itself, for to question something is to call it into being as it is *and* as it might be at the same time: "The peculiar meaning of history, such as that it is at the same time knowledge of itself, can be understood as a general formulation of an anthropologically given arc linking and relating historical experience with knowledge of such experience." (Koselleck 1985:92). Making history by living, thinking, and acting in the present occurs also because of necessity we are doing these 'things' in the presence of history 'itself' as well. The 'peculiarity' of this dynamic rests more in the sense that we can still effect change in spite of the weight of history proper, whose sometimes 'dead hand' rests so heavily upon us. This is what is more extraordinary than some laudation directed at reflecting and reasoning sentience. That is a mere contraption of a specific form of evolution, and not something to consistently 'write home' about as the history of philosophy has done perhaps once too often. Doubtless the idea that post-Babel we need something to hang our fragile ego up on drives part of that chain letter. But just here we also have the weakest point in our selfhood, the very point into which one can drive a pointed question: "It is not that we do not know what to think about time, it is that the solution to what time is may contain contradictory properties. Both sides of the aporia have to be right." (Lampert 2012:150). Since this is the case, 'solution' is too strong a term. More accurately, this kind of desire can be equated with the temporizing of the present that any future emanating therefrom brings. It is not a solution in the mathematical sense of the term. What the future holds for us is not exactly the same thing that it brings to us, nor, ultimately, gives to us. *Holding* is experienced by us in the present as one thing according to, and adjudicated by, who we are at that moment, and not who we will become in the future. *Bringing* to us undergoes and undertakes the same transformational processes. *Giving* finally gives up its presence in the fullest and ownmost sense. It is what will occur, without any more adjustments. But then by definition this 'gift of' the future is no longer the future at all. Just now we can ascertain what it is that *has* come, and not what it is that is still coming: "Duration becomes visible and death becomes visible. Just as the duration of the one time now relativizes the modes of temporality into aspects of a finite being, so death limits and transcends finite being, and confronts man." (Plessner 1973:252 [1951]). We apprehend the time of our lives as more than the 'one time' we thought we had the best time 'ever'. But *we* are apprehended by the facticity of finiteness in all of its obloquy, according to us, and even maleficence, another manner of bolstering our 'better' selfhood in its imminence. What is finite has become its ownmost aspect of finitude. Death is a finitudinal mode of being, and represents Dasein's ability to be-its-completion. When everything is said and done, the most authentic time of our lives is the moment at which all time stops.

Just as Koselleck reminds us that time is no longer a mere 'medium' but is a dynamic in its own right, (cf. op. cit:246), we are now aware that we ourselves must be our own time and not just 'have' it, as in the common expression: "What, on the contrary, it will perhaps have succeeded in doing is to *be its time*, its own time. And it is by being its own time that it will have realized its own *meaning*, willingly accepted the appearance of being untimely." (Corbin 1973:xiv [1949]). The presence of the future in the present is part of this untimeliness, like Nietzsche's 'underground' man, or yet his earlier meditations in essay form. Later, Russell too gives voice to this important critical movement, a movement that at once and in one motion makes its argument both untimely and 'unpopular', as Russell chose to designate his version of such meditations. In being our own time, like the casual idiom, 'doing our own thing, man', time is no longer that which is ranged entirely against us. We move closer to Heidegger's sensibility that we *are* time as well as being the question that occurs in time but also brings about time. Questioning, like humor, has a timing about it whose importance cannot be denied. And humor, like questioning, does question the presumed and assumed, which is where it gains the leverage for a laugh or two. In both, "Persistence, change, and novelty are thus conceived diachronically along the dimension of meanings and through the spoken form of one and the same word." (Koselleck 1985:83). The pun, the homonymal sleight of hand, the double or triple intent, all have both a smile involved in them but also a smirk. What is clever gives us a turn, for death has this same cleverness about it. It has an ability to fool even the most alert being. There are a myriad of examples even in the realm of popular culture, where we would not normally expect such audacity and slyness. The Canadian rock band *Rush* entitled their second live album 'Exit... Stage Left.' The face meaning is the most obvious, that one exeunts the stage to its left, the audience's right. But when one does so, the stage is left twice, as it were. It is left by itself, as the empty stage, and it is left by the people leaving it. So a triple intent emerges, which in turn mimics the number of personnel in the band itself, and hence the number leaving the stage itself, to then rusticate by itself. And so on. Puns of this sort can provide some mirth, but they also can become tiresome after a time. The 'past meanings of words' are brought together in such ways, and we are made aware that several things are happening at once that can be spoken of in apparently exactly the same way. It is diachrony applied to synchrony (cf. ibid:80). But this awareness is not automatic. One must be, or become, alert to it in the same way that the present may well be big with the future but unless one is oneself carrying this pregnancy and to term, it might escape unnoticed. It remains a contradiction even so, for how can what is present *be* what is to come, or even becoming what is to come as we remain *in* the present? "We do not recognize in our awareness of the times, the form of the reconciliation of historical contradictions. The spirit of our time is not even the sign that the negative mediatizes an actual subsiding of the sundering of consciousness." (Ricoeur 1965:294 [1955]). We do not feel ourselves back together; we have not yet been rejoined or reconnected. We are not reunited. But we were never apart after all. This *is* what human history is, and its 'ruse of reason' need not reconcile its oppositions. Indeed, it cannot, for it is the conflict that drives history ever onward, future-looking and over time, declining much of what it had been so fervently and loyally. Are we to castigate ourselves for having the time of our lives and then the very next time, at whatever future time this would have been *at* the time, having it 'again' and more so? How many times of our lives have we had, *can* one have?

As many as possible, would be the obvious response. And rightly so, given both the confluence of finiteness and finitude and the serial trust that we must bring to bear on any present's presence that announces itself as the bearer of that which it is not, or not yet. It was regarded as part of the divine mystery of godhead that time could hold itself aloof to its fullness by providing evidence that presence contained both itself and not itself. Surely only a divinity could apprehend such a contradiction: "This was the age when in the West the universe was regarded as a great piece of clockwork and God as an outstanding clockmaker; perhaps this is the reason Providence chose clocks to change the course of the event." (Cipolla 1967:83). The new age, our own, apparently does away with the accidental in history, but is this saying something radically different than attributing cause to providentiality? If 'chance loses its weight' as an 'accidental cause', how is this so different than uttering the divine reason of God embodied in the suasion of long-term human history? (cf. Koselleck, op. cit:127). In one sense, the subjectivity of history made our own in our own time, the 'having' of history as 'our' time and in 'our lives', deontologizes both chance and reason. There is neither accident nor ruse here. Instead, "…each moment of existence of our life represents a certain duration or, better, the *condensation* of a duration." (Minkowski 1970:364 [1933], italics the text's). What kind of duration? Why, any kind. Such a question is akin to asking after the difference between say, Peano Numbers and piano numbers. Once established, one can then ask whether or not one can play tunes on a keyboard that are themselves based on a series of related integers. The answer would be in principle, certainly, but whether or not any composer has used the former to construct the latter is something of which I for one am not aware.

That multiple events can occur 'at once', making themselves into another kind of event that is both perceived and also thence apperceived as something of the essence that has, accidentally or no, united this once multiplicity into a unity, is an experience with which we are, perhaps surprisingly, quite familiar. Indeed, we might well imagine that the time of our lives was built rather particularly and serendipitously on the confluence of a certain number of kindred events, events that 'loved' one another, so to speak. From this we might further speculate that we are loved by this time or by the world in this way and not necessarily others, or that a god loves us and has conferred upon us a beautiful moment, a moment of bliss, transpersonal union, or epiphany. But the construction of a unity out of disparate elements involves a constriction of the temporality which had to exist so that multiple events 'come together' in this or that way. Time is itself telescoped into something that it is not, and simultaneity therefore becomes both a problem, as Lampert notes early on in his analysis, as well as the framework by which we rebuild this kind of time (op. cit:9). But the desire to understand this same kind of time, driven in part, we suggest, by the very passion and/or compassion we experience when such a time arrives 'for' us - the holding, bringing and bringing forth as giving already accomplished by a once future, ambiguity fashioned into the surfeit of certainty, the plenitude of precision - retains its force, even if the aporia of accuracy also remains present: "In the immanent flowing-off of appearances, in the continual succession of apprehensions in phenomenological time which we call perception, there is constituted now a temporal unity." (Husserl 1964:119 [1905]). This is the 'lived synchronism' of Minkowski writ into the ontological 'vitality' of contact with 'dynamic nature'. If we are time and time occurs because of our presence, then this dynamic is, in oblique contradistinction to

Husserlian formulations, a kind of intuition of essence that we are: "Simultaneity, in short, is not an identity of what is present in a moment, but the experience of a staggered differential between two or more time-sequences." (Lampert 2012:28). Both intuiting that which we are and that we *are* in fact, present as we are, simultaneity as momentary and momentous at once *brings forth* the staggered experience. The multiple time-sequences noted are not then merely vehicles for events to have occurred or to yet occur, just as history is no longer a mere medium for such, but is more profoundly our presence as the being-ahead-of-itself through our very apprehensiveness regarding that which may come to us and that nonetheless we remain rooted to the temporal spot. However stoic the confrontation with the future may be or become, it is part of the 'scandal' of our existence - that part of our being to which the world utters an objection, to which objectivity submits us to an internal subjectitude and nevertheless, that also to which we utter our own nay-saying and in doing so make cowardice into a sensibility – to not *bring forth* future out of what was merely held and brought. But to in fact *do* so, to confront the future with our futural being, is the closest life can come to art: "As all great artistic creations always begin with some scandal, we can all the less forecast them: first of all, the false images which a nation or a regime form of themselves need to be shattered. The law of scandal answers the law of the 'false consciousness'." (Ricoeur, op. cit:281). This art, in its scandal, even evil, and in its critique of inauthenticity as well as more formally, ideology and just plain 'nonsense', to again borrow from Ricoeur, is "...the path of pure time embodied." (Kristeva 1996;159). If temporal ipseity can be said to have an ongoingness about it, that it does not only capture in its intuition of essence the moment which is history shattered and rebuilt in simultaneity, diachrony telescoped into synchrony and then embodying itself within it, pushing it ever along, then it is this 'path', on the way to Being, that announces itself through the art of life as scandal. Life as an objection to the objectitudinal aspect of World. Life as a declaration of liberty in the face of the clock, or the ruse that adjusts the hands on the clock face to reflect the time which we will take as our own and thus 'have'. Life as the disclosedness of our ownmost being-able-to-be, combining in the moment our being-ahead, our care, our resoluteness, and our running on, and mostly, our being-time.

Finally, we are made aware of this essential complex of constitutive structures by encountering, incipiently at first, the time of our life which is neither time nor life: "Under the eyes of death (which we do not see but which we know sees us) man's being is disclosed to him as temporality." (Plessner, op. cit:258). In this awareness, as well as with it, we give ourselves the ability to live on. We do not go forward in spite of death, living being cast as an unremitting stoicism in the face of a death which is mine ownmost possibility, but rather we step into the light of that which may come and by which we bring forth once again that which *will* come to us and for us alone because we can do no other thing. If we are time, and time is thus reliant upon us in this immanential manner, the selfhood of time has been given, and gives itself, a living temporality that no death can in principal vanquish. That death is at least individuated, even for collectivist or yet mechanical social contract societies, that those who live on feel that death and yet live still, testifies to this essentially temporal nature of Being. But death does appresent itself to us as something that is Nothing even so because, like a God, it knows itself as non-time and non-Being at once, and its purpose is thus drawn along a path that we never ourselves tread: "Beginning and end are thus bound up with one another and cannot be separated. From where something shows itself to be a beginning and what direction it will take both depend upon the goal." (Gadamer 2000:15 [1998]). Here, the telos of finitude is not to end time, but only to extract from all temporality the being which has brought it into existence in the first place. Seen this way, death becomes the *recompense* for life, not its price.

If this is so, temporal ipseity becomes a goal in its own right. Expressed more fully than we might have thought capable by the commonplace, including the idiomatic, 'having' this time as opposed to any other, experiencing it and knowing it to be the fullness of what is our ownmost being without being entangled by its reasonable ruse or yet losing ourselves in the sirens of its unreason, means to understand it as it is 'in itself', fully qualified and ontologically present: "What counts, in a word, is not the content of the unity that we envisage but the fact that there is a unity in lived time." (Minkowski, op,. cit:25).

It is true that we shun all forms of disunity at our peril, for they confer upon us the privilege of understanding what being-able-to-*Be* can mean within the envelope of finitude. That which we have and hold begins and ends in time. Calling forth its own temporality, it becomes the very being that we have questioned, cared for, ran from, and thus as well to which we have resolutely returned.

References:

Augustine of Hippo

1968 'Some Questions about Time', in Richard M. Gale, ed. *The Philosophy of Time: a collection of essays.* Macmillan, London. [400] Pages 38-54.

Barrett, William

1968 'The Flow of Time', in Richard M. Gale, ed. *The Philosophy of Time: a collection of essays.* Macmillan, London. Pages 355-377.

Cipolla, Carlo M.

1967 *Clocks and Culture:1300-1700.* Norton, London.

De Certeau, Michel

1988 *The Writing of History,* Columbia University Press, New York. [1975].

Derrida, Jacques

1995 *On the Name.* Stanford University Press, Stanford. [1993].

Gadamer, Hans-Georg

2003 *The Beginning of Knowledge.* Continuum. New York (2001).

2000 *The Beginning of Philosophy.* Continuum, New York (1998).

Grünbaum, Adolf

1968 'The Status of Temporal Becoming', in Richard M. Gale, ed. *The Philosophy of Time: a collection of essays.* Macmillan, London. Pages 322-354.

Heidegger, Martin

1999 *Ontology – The Hermeneutics of Facticity.* Indiana University Press, Bloomington. [1988].

1992 *History of the Concept of Time: Prolegomena.* Indiana University Press, Bloomington. [1925].

1962 *Being and Time.* Harper and Row, New York.

Horwich, Paul

1988 *Asymmetries in Time: Problems in the Philosophy of Science.* MIT Press, Cambridge, Mass.

Husserl, Edmund

1964 *The Phenomenology of Internal Time-Consciousness.* Indiana University Press, Bloomington. [1905 and 1910].

Jung, Carl G.

1973 'On Synchronicity', in *Man and Time: Papers from the Eranos Yearbooks, Volume Three.* Bollingen Press, Princeton, NJ. [1951]. Pages 201-211.

Knoll, Max

1973 'Transformations of Science in Our Age', in *Man and Time: Papers from the Eranos Yearbooks, Volume Three.* Bollingen Press, Princeton, NJ. [1951]. Pages 264-307.

Koselleck, Reinhart

1985 *Futures Past: On the Semantics of Historical Time.* MIT Press, Cambridge Mass. [1969].

Kristeva, Julia

1996 *Time and Sense: Proust and the Experience of Literature.* Columbia University Press, New York. [1993].

Lampert, Jay

2012 *Simultaneity and Delay: A Dialectical Theory of Staggered Time.* Continuum, New York.

Larrabee, Mary Jane

1989 'Time and Spatial Models: Temporality in Husserl', in *Philosophy and Phenomenological Research,* Volume XLIX, March, 1989. Pages 373-392.

Lingis, Alphonso

1989 *Deathbound Subjectivity.* Indiana University Press, Bloomington.

Mabbott, J.D.

1968 'Our Direct Experience of Time', in Richard M. Gale, ed. *The Philosophy of Time: a collection of essays.* Macmillan, London. [1951] Pages 304-321.

Minkowski, Eugene

1970 *Lived Time: Phenomenological and Psychopathological Studies.* Northwestern University Press, Evanston, Illinois. [1933].

Natanson, Maurice
1970 *The Journeying Self: a study in philosophy and social role.* Addison-Wesley Publishing Company, Reading, MA.

Neumann, Erich
1973 'Art and Time', in *Man and Time: Papers from the Eranos Yearbooks, Volume Three.* Bollingen Press, Princeton, NJ. [1951]. Pages 3-37.

Plessner, Helmuth
1973 'On the Relation of Time to Death', in *Man and Time: Papers from the Eranos Yearbooks, Volume Three.* Bollingen Press, Princeton, NJ. [1951]. Pages 233-263.

Puech, Henri-Charles
1973 'Gnosis and Time, in *Man and Time: Papers from the Eranos Yearbooks, Volume Three.* Bollingen Press, Princeton, NJ. [1951]. Pages 38-84.

Ricoeur, Paul
1965 *History and Truth.* Northwestern University Press, Evanston, Illinois. [1955].

Sontag, Susan
2007 *At the Same Time: Essays and Speeches.* Picador, New York.

Schwartz, Barry
1975 *Queuing and Waiting: Studies in the Social Organization of Access and Delay.* The University of Chicago Press, Chicago.

Toulmin, Stephen, and June Goodfield
1965 *The Discovery of Time.* Pelican Books, London.

Van Der Leeuw, G.
1973 'Primordial Time and Final Time, in *Man and Time: Papers from the Eranos Yearbooks, Volume Three.* Bollingen Press, Princeton, NJ. [1949]. Pages 324-351.

Wilhelm, Hellmut
1973 'The Concept of Time in the Book of Changes', in *Man and Time: Papers from the Eranos Yearbooks, Volume Three.* Bollingen Press, Princeton, NJ. [1951]. Pages 212-232.

Wood, David
1989 *The Deconstruction of Time.* Humanities Press, Atlantic Highlands, NJ.

Review Requested:

We'd like to know if you enjoyed the book.
Please consider leaving a review on the platform
from which you purchased the book.

CPSIA information can be obtained
at www.ICGtesting.com
Printed in the USA
LVHW091157201121
703452LV00026B/580/J

9 781682 355329

Contents

-flashback-How it all started...

I unlocked my door and walk inside after my tiring day of working at the cafe. "Aaron are you home?" I shout whilst placing down my bag on the sofa and hang the keys up. No reply. 'That's weird he said he was staying home today' I thought to myself. I kicked off my shoes and went upstairs so I could get in the shower since I smelt of coffee. I was about to turn the doorknob of our room when I heard noises. Moaning. I stepped back from the door and covered my mouth in shock.

No. No. No. This isn't happening. I opened the door only to see Aaron and a random girl fucking. "A-Aaron?". I was devastated, how could he!. He snapped his head round and made eye contact with me.

"Fucking hell. Baby? Wait, It's not what it looks like". I stood there frozen unable to move. So many thoughts were running through my mind but one kept coming 'she's so much more prettier than me, no wonder he's doing this'. I've always had insecurities about stuff like this. I hated everything about myself and seeing this scene happening in front of me has made it so much worse. 'Is everyone better than me?'

"W-why Aaron?. I haven't done a-anything to you". Tears start running down my face.

Aaron then starts laughing "Oh my god Aria, I needed to fuck someone! You always reject me when I want to do it with you!" I look down at my feet. He's right. I'm not brave enough to do it. I'm scared. "Your just fucking useless Aria!". I look back up at him with my mouth wide open. How could he say that? I suddenly had a boost of confidence and shouted at him back.

"I want to do it when I'm ready Aaron! Doesn't mean you just do this. Honestly I'm leaving, we are over."

I turn around about to walk off when he shouts back "you are not fucking leaving Aria, your mine and mine only". I scoff and started to carry on walking off until I felt a tight grip on my wrist that turned me around.

"Ow Aaron your hurting me!" He slapped me so hard that I fell on the cold floor.

Tears started to fall from my eyes. "YOUR STAYING HERE AND NEVER LEAVING. GOT IT?" I flinched from his loud voice. He then grabbed my wrist again and started dragging me out of the room.

"A-aaron stop, y-your hurting m-me. I manage to say through sobs but he doesn't listen. He then takes me downstairs and brought me to the cramped laundry room. The light inside never worked so it was always dark and we used a torch to see inside.

He chucked me into the room "this is your punishment little bitch until you realise your never leaving me". He slams the door shut and I start banging on it begging him to open it. After hours he finally opens the door and drags me out. "Now, your not going to leave me are you Aria?". I shake my head. "Good girl". He lets go of my wrist and I rub it trying to take the pain away. "Now go make me dinner and hurry up" I nod and walk to the kitchen to make his food.

Ever since then the same things happen. I need to tidy and clean the house, make him food, work so he can take the money. And if I do something wrong or even if I don't do anything at all and he wants to do it for fun he hurts me and locks me in that dark room. Being locked up in that dark room started having an effect on me. I suddenly got scared of the dark and whenever he locked me in there I start screaming and begging him to open the door, crying my eyes out until nothing left comes out. Whenever I'm in the dark for longer than 5 minutes I get dizzy, I sweat, I have trouble breathing, have panic attacks and sometimes even pass out. All because of him.

I just need to escape. If that's even possible...

□□:*°:✧□

"Wake up you stupid whore!"

I suddenly felt a stinging sensation prick my face which made me open my eyes as quick as I could, to see what was happening. I look up and see Aaron standing over me, his face red from all the anger he was building up inside of him.

"Make me fucking breakfast, you should of been up ages ago. You don't want to get punished again like yesterday, do you?" He smiles at me with a devilish side to it. I look down at my fingers and shake me head, to afraid to speak.

"Words you stupid woman" he grabs onto my hair and yanks it backwards so I was looking at him.

"N-no s-sir" I reply with a shaky voice. He lets go of my hair aggressively so I fall back onto my small mattress. Yes, if your wondering I sleep on a damaged, dirty mattress in a tiny room with a small window and a little light bulb on the ceiling and then small drawers for my clothes and makeup. Apparently "I don't deserve a good room to sleep in". He walks out of my bedroom and slams the door shut making the sound echo through my room. I rubbed my head since it was throbbing from his grip and patted my hair down now that it was messed up.

I stand up and a sharp pain shoots through my hip. I quietly yelp in pain and grab onto it with two hands.

________________________________-flashback from yesterday-

I sighed and held onto the kitchen counter with both of my hands. I had just finished making his dinner that he ordered me to make, since he can never get off his lazy ass and do it himself. I pick up the plate and start walking into the living room where I see Aaron sitting on the sofa, eyes glued to the tv and him gulping down his beers. I sigh and mentally roll my eyes and carry on walking. Everything was going good until I tripped up on the rug. Of course something like that would happen to me. I fall on my hands and knees and watch as I see the plate fly out of my hands, landing on the hard floor and breaking the plate.

"You stupid bitch, how fucking clumsy are you?" he yells at me whilst walking over to me with his fists clenched. I scoot backwards on my bum to try and get away. To be honest it was stupid of me to even think I would be able to get away with just doing that. Of course I didn't. He grabs onto my wrist and twists it whilst pulling me up from the floor. "You ruined my food, you ruined my floor and you ruined my fucking plate. So it's punishment time."

I felt tears run down my face as I begged him. "N-no please s-sir I'm so-sorry" he then pushes me down onto the floor and I land on my back. I arch it from the pain of the speed he pushed me down, he starts slapping my face multiple times and I tried to block my face as much as I could. He decided he got bored of slapping and so he went to kicking my stomach and hip. I scream in pain trying to get him to stop.

"Next time don't drop my food and we won't have a problem." He walks off leaving me broken on the floor. I grab my knees and curl myself into a ball and sob silently. How I wish I could just escape this.

I tip-toe down the stairs, quietly trying not to land on the creaky bits and tip-toe quicker to the kitchen hoping I won't bump into him. I lean back onto the counter and tap my finger on my chin thinking what I could make for him.

Nothing.

I thought to myself and made myself smile a little. I wish I could. I decided I would make pancakes so I grabbed all the ingredients I needed and placed them on the counter. Before my mum died she gave me her recipe book which I read almost every night and so I know how to make the best meals off by heart because of her. How I miss you mumma. I flipped the last pancake and placed it on the plate which was stacked of them. I grabbed a glass from the cabinet and got some orange juice from the fridge and poured it in the glass. I used my hands to fan myself since I was feeling really hot and sweaty, and I picked up the plate and glass making sure not to make the mistake of dropping it again.

I placed everything on the dining table in front of him and I noticed he was tapping his fork impatiently waiting for his food.

"Here you go" I whispered. He looked down at the meal in front of him, seeing whether or not he approves of it.

"Where the fuck is the syrup" he said whilst glaring at me.

"Oh! U-um I'll get it n-now s-sorry." I started walking off but he clawed onto my wrist making me whimper in pain like a little puppy. He slapped me around the face before I could even stand properly.

"It's sir Aria. Now repeat your sentence." I held my face which was stinging painfully with my free hand and I repeated my sentence.

"I-i'll get it n-now sir." He let go of my wrist and I quickly ran over to the cupboard and got out the syrup. I ran back over to him and placed it down.

"Now go get ready for work, and don't be late back" he warned me. I nodded and ran upstairs to my room to get ready.

After I was done brushing my teeth and washing my face I put on some black jeans with a creme woolly jumper and some worn out black trainers. I got some concealer out of my little drawers to try and cover up my bruises and my now recent one which was appearing. I looked at my reflection. Disgusting is what I would call myself. I looked a mess with bruises on my face that were pathetically tried to be covered up, my hair was tied up in a knot on my head, I had dark circles under my eyes from the lack of sleep and the tiring days. My nightmares of him didn't help either. I sighed wondering how much worse my life could get.

If only you knew..

I walked back downstairs to see him laying down on the sofa again watching his usual programmes on the telly. I'm actually surprised he hasn't started drinking yet. I grab my bag from the floor and put it over one shoulder.

"I'm leaving sir" I whisper. He doesn't hear me so I repeat it again just a bit louder. "I'm leaving sir."

He turns his head around and looked at me up and down before saying "bye baby" and looked back at the telly. I cringed at the words he still calls me. I'm not his baby. Not anymore anyways. I walked out of the front door and locked it, then I made my way to the cafe. I don't have a car yet so I have to walk mostly everywhere I need to go, but I don't mind I like taking in the scenery around me. I walk past a park and see little kids playing with their parents freely. Freedom. Something I don't have. Instead I'm stuck with a controlling, abusive, possessive ex of mine.

When I arrived at the 'Un Beau Café' I pushed the door open and the bell on top ringed. "Aria darling!" My boss Helen came towards me and pulled me into a tight hug, which I instantly returned it. I kept the pain from my hip to myself by biting my bottom lip. No one knows about Aaron abusing me mentally and physically, I just don't have the strength to tell anyone and also I'm scared of what he'll do to me or others. No one really cares about me and my life anyways apart from Helen but I don't want to bother her with my problems.

"Hey Helen" I finally reply after she pulls away from the hug.

"How are you dear? You look a bit exhausted" she said with a concerned look on her face. She always knows if something is up but

I always tell her I'm fine. Thats the thing with broken people. The people that are broken the most are the ones that fake their emotions better than anyone else. Ever since my parents died I had to live in an orphanage and I always used to get left out and was always lonely. But when I turned 18 I started working at the 'Un Beau Café' and Helen and I, instantly became close. She's like a second mother to me.

"I'm fine Helen, don't worry about me." I put on my most realistic smiles I could pull. She nodded and clapped her hands together.

"Let's get to work then." She winks before walking off and I couldn't help but smile.

□□:*°:✧□

After a couple hours of working I look at the time on the wall. ~Time: 5:50pm~I realised I only had 10 minutes left until we close, which also means 10 minutes until I have to go back to my nightmare. I have been thinking for a while now about escaping but I've never had the boost of confidence to do it. What would happen if I get caught? Will I ever make it out? All these little things are what's stopping me from doing it. But tonight I've decided to do it.

I'm going to try and escape.

I open the front door and see Aaron on the sofa still. No surprise there. Sometimes I wonder if he even moves at all. Once I close the door he whips his head around and see's me standing there playing with my fingernails. "Baby your finally home! Dinner needs to be made now." He smiles at me and looks back at the tv. Of course, I've just come home after a tiring day at work and now I've got to do more just for him.

I sigh and walk upstairs to get changed. I put on some light blue mom jeans and an oversized orange jumper to cover myself up. I never liked my body especially with all the bruises and scars on it. Whenever I see on Instagram i notice how beautiful everyone is and I always wish I could look and be like them, but instead I'm stuck with my disgusting self.

(A/N: hey angels I just wanted to say you are all beautiful and handsome just the way you are. Please don't change yourself to be like someone else, god created you to be unique and beautiful in your own way. NEVER believe what you see on social media because trust me, they do not look like that in reality. Be you and be the bad bitch you are!! Ily)

I then put my hair up in a messy ponytail and I walk back downstairs. I walk past the lazy ass Aaron and go to the kitchen to make dinner. He always tells me that I need to make his food and serve it before I do mine and eat it which I find annoying, but over time I've just gotten used to it. I felt tired already and I haven't even started, so I just decided to make cheesy pasta which was quick enough to do.

After I finished making it I got out a bowl from the cabinet and served up the food. I grabbed a fork and placed it in the bowl of pasta and filled his glasses of water. I grabbed his bowl and glass and walked over to the living room, placing it down on the coffee table. I managed to walk away before he could even say a word.

I started eating my stale bread. Yes my bread that's all I'm allowed to eat, I don't deserve a good meal either. I realised that this would hopefully be my last meal in this hell hole. I was praying that my plan would work and I'll finally be free. I finished up and gulped down my water and placed my glass in the sink quickly washing it up. I then crept past behind him making sure not to grab his attention and I walked up the stairs. When I was in my room I shut the door behind me as slow as possible. I looked around my room to find a bag to put my stuff in, in the corner I noticed a backpack and I quickly grabbed it. I then started shoving a few tops and joggers and jumpers, socks, underwear, bras, then I got my makeup to make sure I was able to cover up all my bruises and scars. Once I was done packing I went over to one of my drawers and pushed all my other old clothes out of the way and grabbed my spare money I was saving up for this day. I shoved it in the front pocket of the bag and I placed it under my pillow ready. Aaron never comes in to check on me anyways, he knows I won't escape. Until tonight.

I realised I had slept for a bit and looked out of the small window and saw it was dark. I noticed the time on my clock read 11:27pm. Aaron would be asleep by now so I quickly got off my mattress and grabbed my rucksack. I slowly opened my bedroom door and saw all the lights were off. I crept out of the room and closed the door quietly. I tiptoed down the stairs going from one side to the other making sure I didn't step on the creaky bits. I finally made it to the bottom of the stairs and I grabbed the keys. 'I feel like a spy' i thought to myself and smiled as I pretended to have a gun using my hands and started shooting around.

Enough of the messing around, get out!

My brain told me. I slowly unlocked the front door making sure it wasn't too loud and I opened it, the cool breeze entering and blowing on my face. I stepped out and closed the door behind me. I forgot how dark it actually was for a second, the dim street lights was the only thing helping me see but not much. Let's hope I get away safely. I start walking away from my nightmare but I realise I have to go down an ally way first. I sigh hoping I'll be fine and I start walking down it. Everything was fine until I see two men standing in front of an old man who was on his knees.

My conscience was telling me to run but I was a very curious person so I wanted to know what was going on. I hid behind a dumpster hoping they wouldn't see me and I started watching what was happening.

"Where the fuck is the money? Boss has given you extra time and you still don't have it?" one of the men started shouting at him in his face. I felt kinda bad for this person maybe I should help him?

"P-please I'll ge-get it s-soon!" the man on the floor begged. The other man then replied "Times up buddy." I then saw him bring out a gun from his back pocket and shot the man in the head. I watched in horror and my eyes were wide from shock. I now see the man laying lifeless on the floor, blood oozing out of his head. Who are these people and why did they shoot this man? I needed to get away and quickly.

□□:*°:✧□

I stand up as quietly as I could but then I accidentally knocked over some beer bottles. I look down at the bottles and back up to the men and found them both staring in my direction. "Who the fuck is there!" they shout. I waste no time and start sprinting as fast as my weak legs could go. I look behind and see they are close behind shouting at me to stop but of course I don't. I don't want to be killed thank you.

I look ahead again and it's pitch black so I didn't know where I was going. I look behind me again to see if they would of 'magically' disappeared or something I don't know but of course they were still there. I then suddenly knocked into something hard and thought it was a wall. I tried to move past it but then it went in-front of me and grabbed my arm. I was startled when I heard a low husky voice speak "going somewhere?." I look up and I'm greeted by a pair of twinkling hazel eyes staring at me. The street light above us helped me study this person's appearance and I saw he had dark curly hair, tanned skin, a faded beard, beautiful hazel eyes, lips which for some reason I really wanted to kiss and I noticed he had a hooped earring on his right ear which made him even sexier. Sexier? Aria snap out of it!

His hand was still holding onto my arm whilst I had my hand on his rock hard chest trying to separate us. Suddenly the men that were chasing me came up behind me panting trying to catch their breaths. "Sorry Boss we tried to get her, she saw it all." He didn't even look at the men that were speaking to him, instead he kept his gaze on me which made me fidget uncomfortably.

"P-please let me g-go" I whispered whilst looking down at my feet. He chuckled deeply and put his index finger at the bottom of my chin, lifting it up so I was looking at him.

"My apologies Hermosa but your going to come with us." I pushed his finger off my chin and tears started welling up in my eyes. I'm not going with a stranger, who knows he might be exactly like Aaron. I can't deal with that again.

"No, I'm not going with you!" I yell at him. I've only just left a nightmare and now I'm entering another one. I felt a sharp prick on my arm and I see a needle has been stuck inside of me. My legs suddenly go all wobbly and I feel dizzy. My legs then gave way and I was about to fall but strong arms caught me. "I d-don't feel s-so good" I whispered to him and he brushed a strand of hair out of my face. He then looked at the men and started shouting at the one that injected me but everything became faint so I didn't hear much.

"Did I tell you to fucking do that? No you stupid bastard!"

"Sorry Boss but she got annoying." One of the men said whilst laughing. Suddenly the mysterious man pulled out his gun pointing it to the laughing mans head and he instantly stopped laughing. "I give out the fucking orders and you do what I say, you don't do what you please got it?." I watched the man nod his head but I don't know what happened next since the darkness consumed me.

□□:*°:✧□

no song for this chapter-______________________________□••✎••□

~Matteo's POV~

When my men and I arrived back at my mansion I got out of the car and went round the other side. I opened her side of the door and picked up her tiny, fragile body bridal style and started walking inside my house.

I told my men to meet me in my office in 10 minutes so I could talk to them. I went up the stairs and walked down one of my long hallways and opened one of the guest rooms. I laid her down onto the bed and pulled the covers over her. I noticed some bruises on her face and I wondered if my men did that. I know I'm a ruthless killer but I never hurt women and won't allow it if one of my men hurt her either. But I also realise I'm only keeping her here because she knows too much. I'm not going to be nice to her because I don't have soft spots for anyone. And I have no time to have weaknesses in my job.

I roll my eyes and walk out of the room closing the door behind me not even looking back at her and started going towards my office. I open the big black door and shut it. I walked over to my desk and sat down on my chair tapping my finger on my chin waiting for my men.

After a couple of minutes I looked at my watch and wondered what's taking them so long. Before I could stand up from my chair I heard a knock on my door. "Come in" I yelled. Both of my men came in and shut the door. "What the fuck took you so long?" I yelled. I hate it when people waste my time and take forever, I'm a very impatient man.

"Sorry Boss we were just making sure the shipments where going smoothly." I nodded my head at them and put one of my ankles crossed on top of my thigh and leaned back.

"I want you to find all the information of the girl, I expect it to be in front of me in one hour, if not I'll shoot a bullet through your leg capeesh?" They both nodded nervously and quickly walked out of my office. I sighed hoping they would find something decent about her.

****-1 hour later-

I'm typing on my computer when I hear a knock on my door. "Come in" I yell not even looking up from my screen.

"Boss we have got information." I finally look up and watch as one of them place a file down onto my desk. I nod at them and they nod back understanding that I wanted them to leave. "Let's see then" I whisper to myself.

I move the file so it's in front of me and I open it to it's first page. _______________Name: Aria SkyGender: FemaleAge:

20Birthday: 4th September 2000Star sign: VirgoFamily: -Mother: dead -Father: none -Siblings: noneJob: Waitress at 'The Un Beau Café'Address: 83 Hanbury LaneIn a relationship with: Aaron Brown———Gender: MaleJob: noneAge: 21Birthday: 28th March 1999Star sign: Aries Family: mother and father who lives up in England. Extra info: has been in jail couple of times for bad drunken behaviour, speed driving, selling drugs, being in fights.__________

______

I read the file and realise that it says none next to her father. What does it mean that she has no father?. If he was dead it would say 'dead' but it doesn't. I'll have to look into that. I keep reading and see that her star sign is a Virgo. I'm a Capricorn and I read that those two are the best to be together. Not happening. I never do relationships, no point. My mother is always telling me to settle down and find someone but I'm a ruthless, emotionless killer I can't afford to have a weakness, I have too many enemies. And love doesn't exist to me.

I keep reading on and realise that she is with someone. Aaron Brown. Don't need to worry about that then. I see he has been in jail a couple of times and think what an innocent looking girl is doing with him? I mean I can't really talk, I've kidnapped her and I'm not exactly a saint but I'm still keeping her here anyways. I wonder how he'll be feeling right now realising that his girlfriend is gone. Oh well, I can't let her go even if she wanted to leave. She has seen too much. I flip the page and realise that's all the information. What the fuck? How is that it? She must have more information than that?

I grab my phone out of my pocket and dial one of my men's number. He picks up the call after one ring, knowing full well I don't like to wait."Yes Boss?" he asks through the phone.

"Where is the other information on Aria?" I hiss though the phone, slamming the file shut.

"I- uh Boss that's all that we could find on her." I was confused, how was there not more? I hang up the phone instantly and chuck it down onto the desk and run my hands down my face.

What do I do with you now Aria? I think to myself. A maid? Sure why not. It's better then doing nothing around this house anyways, since she's gonna be here a while.

I stand up from my desk and start walking out of my office to see if she's awake.

□□:*°:✧□________________________________

song-Name: EastsideArtist (s): Benny Blanco_________________________________□••✎••□

-Back to Aria's pov-

I slowly open my eyes adjusting them so I could see. A ray of sunlight was beaming down onto my face and I put my hand in front of my eyes blocking the light. I sat up and a massive headache shoots through my head. I groan in pain whilst rubbing my head. What happened? What time is it? I looked around and panic flooded through my body. Where am I? I look down and realise I'm on a bed. A very comfy one.

Now is not the time brain! I yell in my head. Suddenly the door opens and a man walks in. I realise it's one of the men that were in that ally way with that man that owed money to them, and it's the one that was laughing at me. I got up off the bed and backed myself up against a corner. "Don't come near me" I whisper. He laughs and starts walking towards me and grabs onto my wrist.

"You are coming with me." He tells me whilst trying to drag me out of the room.

I start screaming and hitting him to let go of my wrist. "Let go of me!" I keep shouting at him. He then pushes me onto the floor and points his finger in my face. Memories start filling my head. This is all so familiar.

"Shut up stupid woman and come with me!" He yells in my face. I bring my legs to my chest and look down at my knees, tears start building up in my eyes. He was about to grab onto my wrist again but then I heard a loud booming voice.

"What the fuck is going on here Edan?" He shouts. The men gulps before turning to face the man that just came in.

"I- well I was t-trying to bring her t-to you Boss" he stutters. Boss? So this is the powerful person that owns this place I'm guessing.

The deep voice speaks again. "Did I say drag her?." I look up and see the man shake his head. His voice yells again and I flinch. "Fuck off I'll deal with you later." The man instantly scurries off without even glancing back at me. I'm still looking at my knees when the deep voice speaks again. "We need to talk." I look up at him afraid. What does he want from me?

He sits on the bed. "Sit." His voice is so cold and dangerous but oozes with confidence and power. Who is he? I quickly do as I'm told like always and sit on the bed a look back down at my fingers, creating a distance between us. "Your probably wondering what I want you for is that right?" I don't give any reply but nod. "Words."

I hesitate before stuttering. "Y-yes sir." I can tell he is looking at me a bit confused.

"Matteo is just fine Aria." He reply's. How does he know my name? I can't call him by his first name. I just can't. I'm so used to calling Aaron sir and scared if he will hurt me like he does if I don't do as I'm told and call him sir that I don't trust calling someone by their first name apart from Helen. I look at him with wide eyes before shaking my head and looking back down at my fingers.

"I-I can't s-sir." I stutter again. I always get nervous around people, you can never know what they'll do to you. I can't help it now but feel paranoid about every little thing.

"Look at me when I'm talking to you Aria." He says coldly.

I quickly look up at him trying to look anywhere apart from those gorgeous hazel eyes. "Why can't you call me by my first name?" He asks. I just shake my head again. I can't tell him why. I can't tell him anything. No one can save me from my nightmare of a life. He will kill me otherwise. "Call me Matteo, Aria not sir. Only my men call me that or Boss."

"No." I say a bit louder this time. He looks a bit shocked about the way I said it and I realised I've messed up. I've just yelled at him and now he's going to hurt me. I watch as he gets up and I flinch. I notice he's staring at me with a puzzled look on his face and I quickly get myself back to normal and start rubbing my arm nervously.

I pray in my head that he doesn't ask questions and luckily he doesn't. He clears his throat and begins talking again. "So as you know you saw something.." he pauses for a second before continuing "saw something you weren't meant to see." I nod not daring to speak again just in case. "So that means your going to stay here for a while."

I snap my head up to look at him and my mouth opens wide. The panic floods my body again. This can't happen, I can't go back into another nightmare again.

I start shaking my head multiple times. "N-no I can't, p-please let me g-go." He chuckles darkly.

(hermosa: beautiful)"No can do Hermosa." He smirks at me.

"I'll just escape then." I say with a bit of confidence. I don't even know where it came from but I am going to escape. I don't care about the consequences. I'm not staying in another nightmare.

"Good luck with that angel I'll always find you again." He smirks so I glare at him hoping it would somehow intimidate him but I'm guessing it doesn't as he laughs again. "Anyways you will become a maid here and start working for me since you'll have nothing else to do. You can wear what you want but just make sure that breakfast is ready at 7am, lunch at 1pm and dinner at 8pm. I have another maid called Lindsey but she is the one that does the cleaning, she used to do cooking but now that's your job." I nod again taking everything in and making sure I remember all the times. I loved cooking so I guess that's a win for me at least.

"You don't have to work today but you'll be working tomorrow, I'll show you where the kitchen is so you know how to get to it, follow me." He starts walking off with his hands behind his back and I quickly follow him from behind.

□□:*°:✧□________________________________

song-Name:Be AroundArtist (s): Blooom________________________________□••✎••□

Once we reach down the bottom of the large staircase I look around in awe at the place. Gorgeous chandeliers are hanging from the ceilings, polished tiles on the floor, creme coloured walls, paintings hanging up. I could go on all day. I keep following him until we go round a corner and I'm greeted by a massive archway leading into a room (which I'm guessing is the kitchen).

He suddenly stops which makes me bump into his back. I quickly move backwards and look down at the floor. "S-sorry sir" I whisper just loud enough for him to hear.

He turns around and I feel a warm, large hand hold under my chin lifting it up. I look into his light hazel eyes which are staring deep into my dull blue ones. My eyes used to be a very light blue, but ever since I've become more miserable with my life they have just lost their colour. So that's why I always call them dull blue because that's all I see in my reflection. A broken, abused, tired and disgusting girl.

"Stop looking down all the time." He then roughly but gently at the same time, let's go of my chin. I nod quickly hoping I haven't made him mad. He turns back around so his back is facing me again. "This is the kitchen." I walk around him and start going into the kitchen looking around the place. The countertops have got white and gold marble on them, it has light cloudy grey walls with loads of bright built in lights on the ceilings, the floor are still white tiles, there are built in ovens and microwaves, there are built in stove top as well. There's just so much. Everything looks so fancy pancy, which makes me feel ashamed of where I was living, but I shake off that feeling.

Then an old women comes into the room with a bucket in her hand and she's wearing yellow gloves. She then notices Matteo and I standing in the same room and her face lights up. "Oh hello I didn't see you two here!" she giggles to herself. "You must be Aria." She places down the bucket and takes off her gloves and holds them in one hand, then starts walking over to me and embraces me into a warm hug trying not to get me dirty with her gloves in her hand. She releases me after a couple of seconds before saying "You've probably been told that my name is Lindsey so we don't have to go through that" she playfully rolls her eyes and I can't help but giggle quietly. She then looks behind me and notices Matteo standing there. She smiles at me once more before walking up to him saying "Matteo darling, how are you" then hugging him. To my surprise he hugs her back. "I'm good Lindsey thank you, how are you?." She releases his big body from her hug and smiles at him. "I'm good darling, should I start making dinner?."

Dinner? I think to myself. What time is it? I look around the kitchen and spot a clock. 6:48pmIt's still quite early why would he have dinner now? He said to me about how I had to have dinner ready by 8. Oh well his choice I guess. "No thank you Lindsey, you've done enough for today you can go home now we will be fine." A look of concern fills Lindsey's face.

"Are you sure? I don't mind making a quick something before I leave?" Matteo shakes his head with a smile.

"Honestly it's fine, thank you." She smiles at him back before nodding and leaving the room. He watches as she leaves before turning back to look at me. "I can order pizza if you want, I'll order it now because it takes about twenty minutes to arrive." I look at him confused. Yes I know what pizza is but I've never had it. I only made that type of food for Aaron. He only allowed me to eat stale bread but at least it was something.

I shake my head at his question. I can't have that type of food. "I- um I'll just have b-bread thank you" I say. He looks at me shocked like I'm a weird person for saying that. 'What it's what I'm used to eating?' I think to myself, of course I'm not going to say that to him though.

He starts walking over to me with his hands in his pockets. Then he stands right in front of me, towering over my small body with his tall one making me look up straining my neck. "Why the fuck would you only eat bread?" he asks with a confused face. Obviously I'm not going to tell him 'hey, yeah well basically my abusive ex boyfriend made me eat only stale bread everyday so that's what I'm used to eating you know my life was a living hell but it's okay!' If only I could.

I just shrug my shoulders looking away from his eyes that were staring at me. "I don't like to eat". And that is the truth, I've always hated my body so I guess I'm sort of glad I only eat a small amount of bread. I mean Aaron always tells me that i need to loose weight so might as well not eat a lot. I'm quite surprised I didn't stutter that time.

(A/N hey angels another message for you: I just want to tell you that all your body's are absolutely STUNNING and you don't need to loose weight just because someone told you to do it, or if they say you need too. FALSE INFO. 1: don't do it if someone tells you too, if they are helping you out that's okay but if they're saying it in a mean way then do it because you want to do it!! You don't need to loose weight unless you absolutely have to and if you want to do it for YOURSELF. Notice the key word 'yourself'. Make yourself feel good about that beautiful body of yours by hyping yourself up because ladies and gentlemen you look amazing And just know don't eat little or nothing at all because you think your gaining to much weight! Gurl no! If your eating that's good because your body needs that food for energy! Eat how much you freakin want! If need be have a workout routine to help with getting in shape! But please eat!! And if your starting to gradually eat again just know I'm so so proud of you and keep going! Never give up Do everything for you not anyone else and please show off that body of yours damn!! And remember never EVER compare yourself to ANYONE. OKAY!! good, you gorgeous bitch.) <3

"Aria, you need to eat other food not bread." He reply's with a concerned look on his face.

"I don't want to eat, I'm fine." I start getting a bit annoyed, he can't force me to eat. I'm not going to allow it.

"I'm ordering pizza and your eating some, final." He then walks out of the kitchen leaving me standing there. I huff and walk out as well going back the way to my room.

□□:*°:✧□

song-Name: Yes GirlArtist (s): Bea Miller________________________________□••✎••□

I walked into my room and shut the door behind me. He can't make me eat, I don't want to! I go over to my bed and sit down on it. I definitely don't deserve to sleep on this bed either, its to comfy and luxury. Something I'm not used to. It's fine I'll just sleep on the floor anyways. It'll be the same as when I was sleeping at the house.

I sigh deciding what to do. I found a book on a shelf called 'Cinderella'. I wonder why this type of book would be here, but I take it anyway and sit on the floor flipping the page to the first chapter.

I'm about halfway into the book when I hear a knock on my door which makes me jump. "Come in" I shout, inside walks in Matteo and he looks down at me on the floor and I smile shyly.

"Food is here come downstairs." Great I think to myself. I secretly hope that he didn't get me anything and hope that I just get bread. As I follow him we go into an unknown room to me, but noticing the massive flat screen TV and a large sofa I'm guessing it's the living room. Or a cinema, who knows I didn't even know you could have a living room this big to be honest.

I realised I was staring at the room for so long that i didn't even notice Matteo had already sat down on the sofa and turned on the tv. I awkwardly walk over to the sofa and sit down quite far away from him. On the coffee table in front I notice a box of pizza and see that Matteo has started taking one out of the box. Surprisingly he didn't eat it for himself he handed it over to me trying to get me to take it.

I shake my head and start playing with my fingers whilst looking at him. He places the pizza down back into the box and wipes his hands on the napkins and he grabs my legs and pulls me towards him which makes me gasp in shock. He picks up the pizza again and holds it in front of my face. I look at the pizza then back at him. "I can't eat it sir." I say to him. It's true I can't, I don't want to become even more fat.

"And why can't you Aria?" He reply's back. "It's pizza, and you need to eat it looks like you haven't eaten in months." That's not true! I think to myself. I hate this. I stand up off the sofa and his eyes follow my movements.

"I'm not eating, that's final goodnight sir." I begin to walk off but I feel an arm wrap around my waist pulling me back down onto the sofa. I huff and look back into his eyes and stare at him. "I said I'm not eating." I slightly raise my voice, but not to loud so that he won't get mad.

"Aria, you are going to eat even if it's just one pizza." I shake my head. No, I only eat bread. I don't deserve any other foods. Aaron says that I'm only allowed to eat bread. I'm not doing this. I don't want these type of foods! A tear starts to roll down my face from disappointment. Aaron changed me so much that I don't even want to eat anymore. Matteo places the pizza down and was about to wipe my tear that rolled down but I stop him. I push his hand lightly away and use my sleeve to wipe it away myself.

"I don't have fucking time for this Aria, just eat it" he raises his voice. I cover my ears and close my eyes tightly taking deep breaths. "Stop sir, I don't like it." I hear a low sigh and I open my eyes again to see him running his hands through his hair. He then looks back at me before saying "Aria, just one fucking bite." I sigh and hesitantly nod in agreement and he picks up the pizza again and holds it in front of my mouth. I look at the pizza, then at him, then back at the pizza and I take a shaky breath. Ok you can do this Aria. I close my eyes as I bite into the pizza.

Suddenly I get a explosion of flavour filling my mouth. Smooth tomatoey sauce, stringy cheese, pepperoni all the flavours just exploding in my mouth. It's been so long since I've had normal food that I forgot how good it tastes. I quickly open my eyes again whilst I'm chewing the pizza bite enjoying every second. My eyes are wide from the amazing taste of it and then I see Matteo smirking at me. "Is it good then?" I nod frantically at him and swallow my bite.

"Wow, I haven't had normal food in ages." I sigh in pleasure from the taste and close my eyes again. He chuckles deeply.

"What do you mean you haven't had normal food in ages Aria?" I snap open my eyes again and look at him, not even realising what I had said. Frick.

"I- uh" I stutter embarrassingly not knowing what to say. "N-nothing." I look back down at my fingers.

I look back up at him and then look at the pizza box. I watch as he grabs another slice and hands it over to me. I slowly grab it out of his hands and smile at him.

"Are you sure I'm allowed this sir?." He rolls his eyes and pushes the pizza closer to my mouth which makes me bite into it with a grin on my face. I see that Matteo is staring at me whilst I'm eating. Oh no did I do something wrong? I started panicking, was this all a test? "S-sorry sir was I al-allowed to eat t-this?." I watch as his hand comes closer to me and once it was near my face I flinch and put my hands up to cover my face.

After a couple of seconds I feel warm hands on my wrist pulling my hands away from my face. I open my eyes to see Matteo looking at me with an angry expression on his face. I quickly pull out of his grip and move away from him. My hands are starting to sweat and I'm feeling shaky. "S-sir I'm a-sorry, really s-sorry." I watch as his expression softens but I'm still panicking. He's going to be like Aaron. He's going to hurt me, I've made him mad. My breathing starts to go out of control and voices are coming into my head.

Your gonna get hit Aria You shouldn't of done thatGet away from himThis isn't going to end well

I start shaking my head frantically to get the voices away but they keep coming. I put my hand to my chest to sort my breathing out but it doesn't help. I hear another manly voice talking to me. "Aria, Aria calm down. You need to breath." I feel a warm hand grab onto my hands and another one holding my chin so I'm looking at a pair of hazel eyes. "Aria you need to calm down, breath at the same time as me."

I do as I'm told and watch his breathing so I try to match it with mine. After a while my breathing is back to normal and I've calmed down. I look back up to see his eyes and concern is written all over his face. But why is he so concerned about me? Then he covers it with his normal cold self. "Aria what the hell happened?"

"I-I just panicked that's a-all." I quickly said. I almost blew it. He can't know what happens with Aaron, I can't tell him. He finally lets go of my hands and chin and nods. "I'm going to sleep now sir,thank you for the food." I see he nods again and I walk off to go back to my room.

□□:*°:✧□

song-Name: My oh MyArtist (s): Camilla Cambel-lo________________________________□••✎••□

I closed my bedroom door as soon as I got in. You almost blew it Aria. Stupid, stupid girl.I sighed as I walked over to my bed and sat on the edge of it massaging my head. I got up and walked over to the bathroom which as soon as I walked in I was mind-blown by how beautiful it was. It looked expensive, so expensive that if I touched anything it would break. I was to tired to have a shower so I brushed my teeth with a new toothbrush that was on the side, and washed my face with a clean cloth.

I walked back out into the bedroom and look around to find any clothes. I look the draws and there empty. I sigh realising I have no clothes to wear for bed. Guess I've got to face him again. I walk out of the room and look down the hallways wondering which way to go. I shrug my shoulders and go right. Right is always right, right? I start my journey down the hallway looking around trying to find Matteo. After many turns and walking down long hallways I come across a room which has a big black door and a gold door knob. Looks like an important room.

I knock on the door and wait. After about a minute or so I was about to knock again but the door opened. I stood there awkwardly with my right fist up indicating I was about to knock again and my eyes wide with shock. I quickly put my fist down and cleared my throat.

"Sorry sir, I was just wondering what am I supposed to wear for bed?"

"Oh, yeah I forgot about that come in." He opened the door wider and walked back into the room and I reluctantly followed after him. As soon as I walked inside I looked around the room, it was very dark much to my disliking, the walls were a dark grey, same with most of the furniture and there was also a black king sized bed with a black duvet and pillows. Geez that's a lot of dark coloured things.

I jumped a little when I felt his presence in front of me again, I looked down at his hands and noticed he was holding some sweatpants and a white t-shirt. "These are the smallest things I could find" he said as he handed me the clothes. I took the clothes into my hands and nodded at him.

"Thank you sir" I whispered just loud enough for him to hear. I kept looking down and turned away from him and walked out of the room, closing the door softly behind me.

———

I was now back in my room with the long t-shirt on that reached just higher than my knees and currently wearing underwear underneath and also trying to hold up the sweatpants but failed because every time they decided to fall down. I groaned quietly and took them off instead. I folded them back up and started walking back to his room.

I knocked on his door again and the door instantly opened greeting me with a pair of gorgeous hazel eyes. "What now" I heard his low voice say with a hint of irritation in it. I looked back down at my hands holding the sweatpants.

"T-these don't f-fit me I'm s-sorry s-sir." I lifted my arms up with the sweatpants in my hands showing him. Suddenly warm hands grabbed me by the waist and pulled into the room with him closing the door afterwards. I gasped as I looked up and gazed into his hazel eyes that swirled around with emotions like anger.

"Why the fuck did you walk around with only my t-shirt on and nothing underneath! My fucking guards are around here and you're basically naked!" He whisper-shouted.

I flinched in his arms. How could I of been so careless! Only just realising what I'm wearing I looked down and gasped. "Oh fudge-sticks!" I murmured to myself.

I looked back up into his eyes and saw amusement dancing around in his eyes and he had a slight smirk on his face. I frowned and tilted my head to the side a bit. What's so funny? I stepped backwards but his hands tightened around my waist. "I'll just go back to my room now then sir" I said trying to get out of his arms but he didn't budge.

Damn what is he made of, stone? A small deep chuckle left his mouth and I blushed. Did I say that out loud? "Yes you did Aria." I quickly covered my mouth with my hand. Oops.

"Your not going back out there, tonight you'll stay here." He said as his hands tightened around my waist again pulling me a bit closer to him.

□□:*°:✧□

song-Name: 2 OnArtist (s): Tinashe ft. Schoolboy Q________________________________□••✎••□

"Your not going back out there, tonight you'll stay here." He said as his hands tightened around my waist again pulling me a bit closer to him.———

"W-what?" I looked at him in shock. "N-no sir it's f-fine I-I'll just quickly rush b-back" I said whilst trying to get out of his grip. Suddenly I'm being lifted up and over a very muscular shoulder. "S-sir!" I yell at him. "Put me down!" I start pounding my fists onto his back and kick my legs.

I scream when I'm suddenly dropped on a very very comfy bed. I quickly sit up and look around me. I'm on his bed! Oh shoot. I look back at Matteo and see him with a smirk on his face and I scowl at him. "I'm not sleeping here" I say whilst crossing my arms over my chest.

"I don't give a fuck what you say, but you're going to do what I say" he says whilst frowning at me. "Now I'm going to take a shower so don't move and go to sleep." I roll my eyes and get under the covers making sure my back is facing him. I'll just wait until he gets in the shower and I'll move to sleep on the floor. People like me are only allowed to sleep on the floor.

As soon as I hear a door close, I turn my head a little over my shoulder and check around the room and see that he's gone. I quickly get out from under the covers and step off of the bed. I grab a pillow and put it on the floor and I lie down putting my head on the pillow. I feel bad that I might make the pillow dirty but oh well. I deserve to sleep on the floor, not a bed. And with that, darkness surrounded me.

-: ✧ :-

~Matteo's POV~

As soon as I got out of the shower I wrap a towel loosely around my waist and grab another one for my hair. I go out of the bathroom whilst drying my hair so I can go and check on Aria. She better not of gone back to her room.

I look at the bed and see she's not there which makes me clench my jaw. Why didn't she listen to me. I go over to the bed and stop when I hear soft snoring sounds coming from the side of the bed. I look over and see Aria laying on the floor with her head resting on a pillow. You could tell she was cold by the shivering so I went around to her side and picked her up bridal style, careful not to wake her up. I place her on the bed gently and cover her shaking body with the duvet.

I go inside my walk-in closet and grab sweatpants and put them on. I walk back out and dry my hair more and chuck it in my laundry basket. I ruffle my hair whilst going round to the other side of the bed and get under the covers as well laying on my back and looking up to the ceiling.

I've never even let a women inside my bed, so why did I let Aria?

Stop Matteo, can't afford a weakness remember?

□□:*°:✧□

song-Name: Let's Go Home Together Artist (s): Ella Henderson and Tom Grennan________________________________□••✎••□

-Back to Aria's pov-

I groaned as I woke up and felt a weight around my waist which confused me. I opened my eyes and blinked a couple of times to get rid of the blur that covered my eyes. After I looked down at my waist I noticed a tanned arm wrapped tightly around it which made me gasp loudly.

I felt someone stir beside me which made me look at who it was, Matteo. He groaned as he started opening his eyes which made me panic even more so I quickly pushed his arm away from my waist and stood up from the bed. Wait bed? I looked at the place where I just stood up from. When did I get back into the bed..

"What's going on?" I heard a deep husky voice speak up making butterflies go around in my stomach. Then I realised we were in the same bed. Oh no he's going to get angry at me!

I closed my eyes and started rambling "I'm sorry sir! I didn't mean to sleep on your bed, I thought I put myself on the floor but then I woke up on your bed I don't know how it happened please forgive me! I didn't mea-" a large hand covered my mouth making the rest of my sentence muffled. My eyes shot open instantly making me see beautiful hazel staring right back at me.

"I put you on the bed Aria because you shouldn't of been sleeping on the floor." He slowly removed his hand from my mouth allowing me to speak.

I looked at him confused "But I deserve to sleep on the floor" I said quietly making Matteo look at me odd.

"Wha-" before he could say anything I started walking away.

"Sorry I'll go make breakfast sir." As soon as I reached the door his voice stopped me.

"We are going to the mall today to get you some things." I nodded my head and walked out.

———

So now here we are walking around the mall with many scary men behind us carrying bags of clothes, girl stuff, makeup you name it. I had a frown on my face with my arms crossed over my chest whilst we were walking to McDonalds.

"Stop looking so grumpy Aria, it's only a few things." Matteo said whilst texting someone on his phone.

I stopped walking and glared at his back that was moving further away from me since he was still walking. Noticing that I've stopped he turned around with his eyebrows raised. "That," I pointed at the many bags the men where holding "is not a few things, you spent way to much on me."

"I didn't spend that much" He argued.

"Yes you did."

"Did not"

"Yes"

"No"

"Yes"

"Yes"

"No- excuse me don't do that on me!" I raised my voice a little which made him smirk at me. Ugly hot smirk of his. "I don't need this much stuff."

"Oh my god Aria," he groaned "just let's go get some food and leave already!"

I huffed "I need a wee first be right ba-"

"How do I know you won't try to escape?" He had his eyebrows raised.

"I won't I promise, j-just don't hurt me!" He looked at me oddly but nodded slowly.

"Go then and hurry up about it." I nodded and quickly sprinted to the girls restrooms.

———

After I finished I washed my hands and checked myself in the mirror. I had slightly dark eyes bags underneath my eyes and my hair was a mess. I sighed before splashing cold water onto my face and trying to fix my hair.

I walked out of the toilets and started walking back. Suddenly I crashed into someone making me apologise and try to walk around them. "Now wait a minute doll" the person said whilst blocking me from walking away. That voice. No. No. Please no. I looked up and saw his dull dark brown eyes staring at me and he had a creepy grin on his face. Aarons brother. Also known as Gino.

"Nice to see you again doll, tell me why run from Aaron you know he's gonna get ya and trust me when I say he isn't happy with you" his creepy grin widened making me step back to get away. "He will find you, he's coming for you."

"N-no s-st-stop" I shook my head blinking hard and pinching my arm hoping this is a dream, a hallucination, anything apart from his being real. But no. It's real. I could hear him laugh manically making tears fall out of my eyes. Run Aria, go! My mind told me. So I did. I ran around him trying to get back to the only person that makes me feel safe.

Matteo.

I sprint looking around frantically trying to look for him but it was hard since it was so crowded. Luckily I spotted him standing looking at his phone with his men around him. I sprinted towards him whilst yelling "Matteo!" His head turned around and he made eye contact with me. As if he realised what I was about to do, he opened his arms wide whilst bending a little.

And I jumped.

I jumped into his arms wrapping my legs around his waist and my hands clutching onto his top, tears running down my face and soft sobs coming out my mouth. He's going to take me away. He's going to find me.

A warm hand started rubbing my back and Matteo's head went into my neck whispering near my ear telling me it's okay. God please make Matteo not like Aaron. He's the only good thing I've got at the moment. Make someone be nice to me for once.

Please...

□□:*°:✧□

song-Name: Baby I'm Jealous Artist (s): Bebe Rexha & Doja Cat________________________________□••✎••□

As soon as I was in his arms, I was suddenly grabbed by the arm harshly and was pulled backwards so I landed on my butt on the ground. "Ow" I whispered closing my eyes tight to get rid of the pain.

I looked up and saw a huge man towering over me with a gun in his hand. Wait a gun? My eyes widened and I sucked in a breath seeing the black pistol right near my face. "Don't touch the boss!" He yelled near my face. I pushed myself backwards trying to get away from the scary man.

"I-I'm sorry!" I said whilst coving my face with my hands, "I d-didn't mean t-to!".

A voice suddenly yelled louder "how fucking dare you!". I know that voice..Matteo. The scary man was suddenly pushed to one side and Matteo came towards me. Oh no he's angry at me! Why did I run into his arms!

"I-I'm sorry s-sir p-please don't hurt m-me!" I cried, tears coming down my face. I was suddenly picked up from under my armpits and one arm was underneath my butt keeping my up as I circled my legs around his waist and another arm was wrapped around my back securing me in this persons warm body. Matteo. "Shhh princess it's okay" his soothing voice calmed my whilst he used his hand to move my head into the crook of his neck.

I closed my eyes hearing Matteo shout at the man. "Don't fucking do that to her!" "You hurt her!" We started moving but I couldn't see where considering my head and face was still in his neck. He smells good. Shut up Aria. "Fucking twat" I heard him mutter under his breath.

~~~~

We where now back at Matteo's place and he told me to go to his room so we can talk which I'm quite nervous about. I hope he doesn't ask too many questions.

I was walking down the hallway to get to Matteo's room when suddenly a woman wearing a maids uniform and a lot of makeup on came up to me with disgust on her face. "Hello can I help you?" I asked politely.

"Listen here girl but Matteo doesn't like his sluts wondering around his place especially near his room so you need to leave." Sluts? I wondered.

"What do you mean? I'm not a slut" I said with a frown on my face which made the woman roll her eyes and look at me up and down.

"When Matteo has sex with women he kicks them straight out so I don't get why your still here wondering around so just fucking leave already" she gritted through her teeth. My eyes widened. He just kicks
~~~~

them out after have sex with them? How many girls has he done that too? Is he going to use me? Will he force me?

All these questions bought tears to my eyes and there was a slight pain in my heart. "O-oh" was all I could say. I then heard loud footsteps echo down the hallway making me freeze.

"Who are you calling Aria a slut Selena and how dare you be rude to her and why aren't you doing your job properly." His voice said eerily calm but he sounded angry.

I looked at Selena and saw her face full of fear. "I-I'm sorry s-sir" she bowed a little and scurried off somewhere. I released the breath I didn't realise I was holding in until Matteo started speaking again. "What did she tell you."

I stayed looking away from him and repeated the words Selena said to me. "She said 'When Matteo has sex with women he kicks them straight out so I don't get why your still here wondering around so just fricken leave already' and she called me a slut" I felt tears coming to my eyes and I don't even know why. Why was she so mean to me? It just reminds me of Aaron.

"A-anyways i'll leave n-now" I sniffed wiping my eyes a bit. I started walking away when suddenly a large hand gently grabbed onto my wrist and pulled my back into a hard chest making me shriek a little.

"Don't listen to what she said, it isn't true" his voice was low and angry. I looked into his eyes and shook my head.

"Listen sir I don't want to be used and kicked out like what you do to all the women you sleep with, b-but you carry o-on" I whispered hoping he won't get mad at me. He chuckled and whispered something under his breath but I didn't hear it.

~Matteo's POV~

"I won't do that now that I have you my Angel" I whispered under my breath. Thank you God for bringing me someone good into my life.

□□:*°:✧□________________________________

song-Name: What the Hell Artist (s): Avril Lavigne________________________________□••✎••□

It was now the next day and here I am lying on my comfortable bed doing nothing. Absolutely nothing. I turned at looked at the alarm clock at saw it was 3 in the afternoon. I literally have nothing to do.

I groaned as I sat up and crossed my legs. I sighed and got off the bed and walked over to the door. I opened it and looked down the hallway which was empty. I could literally imagine the bush things that roll around in the desert in this hallway. That's how empty it is.

"What am I even meant to do.." I groaned as I started walking down the hallway. I walked down the large staircase and started looking around the whole place not looking where I was even going. I heard voices but just ignored them but I then stopped looking when I realised that the room I'm in has now gone extremely quiet. I look ahead of me and see a group of men around the large counter - one of those men include Matteo.

"Uh-I-I'm sorry sir I'll leave." I said scared that I did something wrong so I started walking backwards.

"Wait!" One of the men said. I moved my head to the voice and saw it was a man that was quite tanned, had brown hair, had a beard and had a soft smile on his face. "Are you Aria?" My eyes widened. How did he know my name?

"Uh-um y-yes I am." Does he know Aaron?

"No! Don't be scared Princess!" He said clearly noticing my scared expression. He came over to me making me step backwards a bit but then I was pulled into a chest belonging to the man that was just talking to me. I stiffened but then heard him speak again. "My name is Micheal, nice to meet you Aria." I was about to hug him back but then another warm hand grabbed onto my arm harshly but gently at the same time making sure not to hurt me, and yet again I was pulled into another chest but this one was a lot warmer and I was much more familiar with it. You guessed it, Matteo.

"Don't fucking touch her Micheal!" He gritted out.

"Damn sorry, she's all yours babe." Micheal replied. Just hearing Michael so far, his personality is definitely an energetic one.

"Hey introduce us to her then!" Another voice spoke up.

"Fuck sake." I heard Matteo whisper under his breath clearly annoyed.

Matteo gently pushed me away from his chest and grabbed onto my face looking at me. "You ok?" He whispered and I just nodded.

"Stop being all lovey dovey and introduce us jeez!" Literally another voice spoke up. I saw Matteo roll his eyes and I slowly turned around to look at all the men in the room.

"Aria this is-" Matteo started speaking but was interrupted by Micheal.

"I'm Micheal!" He shouted whilst putting his hand up. I smiled a little making sure I don't laugh just in case I get told off.

"We fucking know that dipshit!" Another voice spoke up.

Matteo pointed to another man that had lighter brown hair, had no beard unlike Micheal and was much paler. "That's Noah." He said and the man named Noah turned to look at me and waved.

"Hey sweetheart I'm the funny one here." He said putting his nose high acting like he just won something.

"No you are not I am you butt!" Micheal spoke up whilst glaring at Noah and slapping around his head.

"Did you just- hell to the fucking no!" Noah started going towards Micheal and slapped his face.

"My precious face!" Micheal screeched.

"That's what you get you dick!" Noah screeched back.

"Fuck sake shut the fuck up you two I'm trying to introduce Aria here and you are fighting like children. Grow up!" Matteo yelled making me step away from him a bit but he just pulled me back to him.

"Sorry mom" they both said sarcastically.

Matteo took a deep breath and pointed to another man that had brown hair with some blonde bits, dark coloured eyes, shaved face and was a tan but light skin colour. "That's Jonah."

"Hey babe I'm Matteo's bestest bestest bestest buddy and he loves me the most." He said whilst winking at Matteo. I waved at him making him smile gently at me.

And lastly Matteo pointed to the last man that had almost black hair, had ear piercings, dark eyes and a slight beard growing. He didn't look as happy as the other boys which kind of intimidated me. "That's Sam." Matteo said and I hesitantly waved. Sam tilted his head a little like he was inspecting me.

He got off the stool he was sitting on and walked over to me making me move back a bit just in case. He was now stood in front of me looking down at me considering he was much taller than me. He then slowly opened his arms out making me look at him surprised. Does he want a hug?

I lifted an eyebrow and waved his hands a bit trying to tell me to get closer. Can I trust him? I slowly walked over to him and opened my arms a little hesitantly. Sam gently pulled me towards him and hugged me, sort of lifting me up at the same time. "Hello Aria." He said.

"Woah the big scary man just hugged someone!" I heard Micheal say.

Sam's head turned towards Micheal and glared a scary glare making Micheal be quiet. "Sorry." He muttered.

"Okay that's enough." I heard Matteo say behind me with his cold tone he usually has and I get taken out of Sam's hold and I turn to see Matteo had a frown on his face. "Well now I have introduced you all to Aria let's go back to what we are doing and Aria what are you gonna do?" I looked at him and shrugged my shoulders.

"Let's get food!" Noah shouted making me cover my ears slightly at the loud sound.

"I dibs going to McDonald's!" Micheal says.

"No I want KFC!" Noah says.

"No McDonald's!"

"No KFC!"

"How about we don't go at all!" Matteo shouts at the two making them pout.

"Can we go to this restaurant I know?" I quietly speak up making everyone look at me. "U-uh never mind sorry sir!" I say bowing my head so I was looking down.

"Excuse me but why does Princess call you sir Matteo!" Micheal says glaring at him.

"Don't fucking glare at me when I tell her not to you dumb ass!" He says angrily.

"If you two stop I wanna hear what sweetheart wants to say!" Noah speaks up.

"Um it's called Sunny Smiles, I've never been inside and tried it but it looks good but it's up to you guys!" I quickly say not wanting to make them mad.

"Yes let's go there!" Micheal says clapping his hands.

"Let's go then." Matteo says grabbing my hand and pulling me to the front door.

"Awe look at my boy growing up." I hear a fake sniffle behind me and recognise it was Noah that said that.

"I'm a proud parent." Micheal joined in both of them fake crying making Matteo shake his head and whisper curse words under his breath.

——————————————————(Inside of the restaurant)

We were walking through the doors of Sunny Smiles and looking around the place it looked cute but modern at the same time. There were small circle tables with chairs around them but there were also little rooms with booths in for larger groups of people. There wasn't a lot of people here which was good but overall it was a nice place.

□□:*°:✧□

song-Name: No money Artist (s): Galantis________________________________□••✎••□

"Can I help you guys?" A woman spoke up. I turned my head and saw she looked like a cliché bitchy model. Slim figure, blonde hair, blue eyes and of course the outfit that literally covers nothing.

"Yeah we need a table for-wait how many of us are there?" Noah said and I giggled quietly looking at his confused face and him looking around trying to count how many of us are here.

"There are six of us dumbass" Micheal said whilst slapping Noah's head making Noah hold his head whilst glaring at him. I looked at Noah worriedly thinking if he's ok or not.

"Oh my god, are you ok Noah!" I say using one hand to hold onto his head and one on his face inspecting his head. I suddenly get grabbed by the arm and pulled into a warm chest.

"He's fine Aria. Don't touch him." Matteo says in my ear and I look up noticing him glaring at Noah.

"No I think you need to kiss it better sweetheart" Noah says with a smirk on his face but when he sees me looking at him he pouts.

I hear Matteo growl behind me. "Shut up before I punch you in your throat." He says with a scowl on his face. He then turns back to the woman and speaks in a cold tone. "Table for six."

"Anything for you pumpkin" she winks at him and turns and walks away whilst swinging her hips and bending over a bit trying to give everyone a view of her bum. All the boys roll their eyes and start walking behind the woman and Matteo and I do the same.

===

We are finally sat in one of those booth things.Micheal, Noah and Jonah were all sat together whilst Sam, Matteo and I were sat together. Sam near the wall, me in the middle and then Matteo at the end of the seat.

"So my children what do we want for food." Jonah says whilst picking up the menus and giving us all one.

"Bread." I accidentally say out loud which makes everyone look at me with confused faces.

"Bread, why the frick would you want bread?" Noah says. I look around the table and notice everyone looking at me like the I'm the weirdest person ever. My gaze then moves onto Matteo and I see him glaring at me.

"S-sorry sir, I'm not ha-having anything am I" I say ashamed dropping my head downwards and putting the menu down.

I hear a gasp but don't put my head up. "Oh Princess of course your having something don't be silly!" I hear Micheal say.

"Why is she calling you sir Matt?" I hear Sam speak up.

"I don't fucking know ok! I've told her she can call me Matteo and she isn't listening! And you are not eating fucking stale bread Aria" he says whilst lifting my chin up so we are face to face. He then picks up my menu and gives it to me. "Now choose something or I'll choose for you, understood?" He says raising one of his eyebrows.

I nod and look at the menu but my chin is turned again and I'm facing Matteo's face again. "Words Hermosa."

"Yes sir" I say but he just shakes his head.

"That's not my name now is it Aria." I widen my eyes. It's disrespectful I can't call him by his real name in front of him. I shake my head slightly. "Aria I don't think you understand that I'll be more angrier if you don't say my real name but you keep thinking that I'll be mad if you don't call me Sir. Call me by my real name right now." He says with a deep scowl on his face, like usual.

I think for a moment. Should I risk it? Might as well. "Y-yes-" i take a deep breath. "Yes Matteo."

He lets go of my chin and a his lips tug upwards at the ends a little and he nods at me.

"Sorry to interrupt but are you ready to order?" A boy says. He had dark blue hair, he's pale, quite slim and around 5'7 ish. I realise he's looking at me and licks his lips making me feel a bit uncomfortable.

"Yes! I want a 10 piece pepperoni pizza and large fries and a large Fanta." Micheal speaks up bouncing up and down on his seat excitedly.

"Micheal you say you would like a 10 piece pepperoni pizza, fries and Fanta and after you say please." I say frowning a little at his lack of manners.

"Sorry Princess, I would like what I just said please." Micheal says whilst rolling his eyes.

===

Everyone gives their orders and then it's just me left. "What would you like sugar?" The boy says whilst winking at me. "We can meet up after my shift is done if you know what I mean" he says whilst looking at me up and down.

"That's it!" Matteo suddenly yells and pushes the boy making him fall on the floor looking at Matteo with scared eyes.

"Don't fucking speak to my girl you stupid piece of shit!" He yells whilst punching the boy.

"Oh my god!" I say coving my mouth and looking at the fight with wide eyes.

"Rip to that boy." Jonah says whilst rolling his eyes.

"We have to stop Matteo! He's gonna kill the boy!" I say yelling at them all which makes them all shrug their shoulders. I gasp at their carelessness and look back at the fight and see the boy almost unconscious.

"Matt-Matteo please stop!" I yell tears falling down my face. This is reminding me too much of Aaron. "Matteo stop!" I yell even louder covering my eyes whilst sobbing.

"It's ok Tiny I've got you." I hear Sam say hugging me and putting my head on his chest.

"Ok Matteo that's enough!" I hear Jonah yell at him.

"You're fucking fired. This is my restaurant you bastard and you thought you could get away with talking to her like that? Don't ever look or flirt with my girl ever fucking again!" Matteo booms, his voice echoing around the whole restaurant.

"Damn he's a jealous child" I hear Noah whisper under his breath.

I feel myself being pulled into someone else's arms making me cry harder having memories of Aaron touching and hitting me. "It's Matty Aria it's ok, I'm sorry" I hear a soft voice repeat in my ear. I wrap my arms around his neck and cry on his shoulder whilst he puts his head in my neck and I feel his harsh breath hit my skin.

"No one can take you from me. My precious girl." I hear him whisper in my ear softly and kiss my cheek.

□□:*°:✧□_____________________________

song-Name: Space SongArtist (s): Beach House________________________________□••✎••□

We were now in the car driving back to the house and an awkward silence filled the Tesla model X that we are currently driving in. I was sitting between Matteo and Sam, Jonah was driving and Micheal was at the front as well. And-

"Why do I have to be at the back by myselfff" Noah whined like a child.

"Because your annoying" Matteo said rolling his eyes. I heard Noah gasp.

"Sweetheart do you think I'm annoying?" I turned my head and saw Noah putting his chin on the top of my seat pouting his lips making me giggle. I shook my head whilst smiling at him. "Awe thank you sweetheart, you will always be my favourite." He smiled at me and ruffled my hair making me slap his hands away.

I turned back around and faced the front and started biting my nails. Why did Matteo do that in that restaurant? He almost killed

that poor boy. In the corner of my eye I saw Matteo looking at me with a frown on his face.

"Aria-" he started and raised his hand which made me flinch and lean into Sam. I couldn't help it, seeing him beat that boy with no emotion on his face made me realise that he can do that to me at any time. Sam turned to look at me and he put his arm over my shoulder bringing me closer to him. I watched as Matteo's jaw clenched and he narrowed his eyes at Sam. "Aria I won't hurt you, I promise" he said looking back at me.

I slowly put my pinky up and held it up waiting for him. "P-pinky promise?" I said hesitantly. He smiled a little and wrapped his larger pinky around mine. I nodded and slightly smiled whilst getting off from leaning on Sam.

"Are you ok now tiny?" I heard Sam say from beside me. I turned towards him and nodded whilst smiling. He ruffled my hair which made me frown having my hair messed up for the second time.

———

We were all getting out of the car and I closed my door behind me and watched as Sam was ahead of everyone. "Wait Sammy!" I call after him which made him turn around with a confused expression on his face. I run towards him and stop right in front of him. I slowly wrap my arms around him which makes him stiffen up and I almost pull away but he then wraps his arms around me too. "Thank you for being there for me" I whisper. I pull away from him and see he's got a small smile on his face whilst looking at me. "No problem tiny."

I feel large hands grab onto mine and start pulling me towards the house. I realise it's Matteo and he has a scowl on his face, like usual.

Once we get inside I looked at the clock on the wall and it read 6:43pm. I sighed not knowing what to do now.

Noah and Micheal ran through the door singing a random song and they then suddenly stopped and looked at us all. "Can we watch a movie?" Micheal said. "Oh yes! yes' movie time!" Noah said clapping his hands.

"Yeah whatever." Matteo said rolling his eyes. I looked down noticing that we are still holding hands making me blush. I tried taking my hand out of his grip but he only held on tighter.

"I want to watch Incredibles 2" Micheal said.

"No I wanna watch Moana!" Noah argued and then started singing. "And no one knowsss how far it goessss!-"

"Noah if you don't shut the fuck up right now I'm going to punch you in your throat with no regrets. You know maybe it will sort your voice out as well." Matteo said glaring hard at him.

"Why are people so mean to me." Noah sniffs dramatically whilst pouting.

"Why don't we watch a horror?" Matteo says which makes me stiffen. I hate horror films.

"Noooo!" Micheal and Noah whine.

"Excuse me Matteo but I don't want to not have any sleep tonight because of a film you wanted to watch" Micheal said putting his hands on his hips.

"Well tough shit we will watch it anyways, let's go" he says whilst dragging me to another destination.

———

Here we are now in Matteo's massive living room that had a massive TV on the wall and very very comfy sofas. Noah, Micheal and Sam are sat on a large sofa together and Sam didn't look happy at all whereas Micheal and Noah where happily eating their food. Me and Matteo where sat on a smaller sofa with a blanket covering us and Matteo was eating some popcorn.

I don't even know what film we are watching but it's one about a psycho man who kidnaps women and tortures them which is brilliant for me and my memories. I hope you know I was being sarcastic.

"Give me some of the m&m's you fat bastard" I hear Sam whisper yell to Noah.

"You're the one that's been eating them all!" Noah whisper yelled back. I look at them two and see Sam trying to snatch the packet from Noah but Micheal was just happily eating his sweets and looks engaged in the film. I see Sam finally managed to grab the packet and started eating them which made Noah huff and cross his arms turning to watch the film again with a scowl on his face.

A couple minutes later I see a bowl of popcorn go in front of my face making me turn to look at Matteo confused. "Have some" he whispered to me. I shook my head and whispered back "it's fine." He sighed and put the popcorn bowl in my hands. "Eat please" he replied making me sigh and look at the film again whilst slowly putting some popcorn in my mouth.

TW:describing abusive scenesHalfway in the film it comes to scene where a girl is laying down on this table and she's been tied down. The psycho man is circling her holding a whip. He starts humming the tune "run rabbit" and starts whipping the girl whilst laughing. I tense up whilst watching it and it carries on with my torture scenes. He grabs a knife and starts stabbing it mercilessly in her leg and carves out his name on her thigh. The girl is screaming but her scream is muffled from the tape that's covering her mouth. He shoves a flannel over her face and starts pouring water over her face making her scream more and choke.

It instantly made me remember what happened with what Aaron did to me. I zone out and all my focus on the film disappears and instead the flashbacks fill my head.

{FLASHBACK OF HERS} TW:abuse

I'm strapped in a chair tied up and tape is covering my mouth making my screams muffled and Aaron starts making lots of little cuts on my thighs. He chucks the knife onto the floor and slaps me hard across the face. "I told you not to try and leave me you slut!" He screams in my face. I shake my head wanting him to stop. "Thirsty babe?" he says walking over to the sink filling up a jug with water, tears leak from my eyes wanting this nightmare to be over. He walks over to me slowly with an evil grin on his face with a jug of water in his hand. I shake my head and more tears come out of my eyes. I try screaming for him to stop but my scream is more of a muffled cry. He rips my tape off my mouth and tips my chair backwards how I'm now on the floor looking up and see him looking over me. I scream but soon get cut off by him pinching my nose and pouring the water in my mouth making me choke on the water but since it keeps going down my throat it feels like drowning. I can't breathe he's holding my nose so I can't do anything. When will this stop...

{FLASHBACK OVER}

"Stop!" I scream closing my eyes. I suddenly can't breathe and I put a hand on my chest and bend over trying to breathe. I'm trying to suck in any air but it feels as if my airways are closing up.

"Aria open your eyes!" I hear people yelling but all the voices are muffled so I can't hear much. Someone grabs onto my shoulders and lifts my body upright making me snap open my eyes in fear. I'm still panicking about no air coming inside my lungs so tears start coming out of my eyes. I see Matteo in front of me and his lips are moving but I can't hear him. I feel someone rubbing my back and I notice Micheal and Noah behind Matteo looking at me concerned.

Matteo wraps his arms around me and brings me to his chest and instantly his strong comforting cologne fills my nose making me greedily trying to feel my lungs with his scent. I then hear him whispering in my ear "Angel I need you to breathe in and out for me. You can do it slow breathe in, yes good now slow breathe out." He rubs my back gently and tightens his hold on me. "Keep going darling you can do it." I copy what he's saying and my breathing after a couple minutes of him speaking to me and rubbing my back, finally goes back to normal.

"Are you ok now?" He whispers in my ear which makes me nod but I suddenly feel exhaustion hit me making me eyes droop. I think he noticed my tiredness from me cuddling more into his chest which made him pick me up bridal style.

And that's when darkness surrounded me pulling me into sleep.

□□:*°:✧□________________________

song-Name: Love AgainArtist (s): Dua Lipa________________________________□••✎••□

My eyes slowly flutter open from the sounds of people whispering. When my eyes are fully open but partly squinted from just waking up I groan and stretch my body out across the bed. I lay there just staring blankly at the wall beside me not even realising there's people in my room until someone yells "Sweetheart! Oh my god I've missed you!-" I scream in fright and turn my head to the person who just spoke.

Suddenly I'm engulfed into a massive hug by the one and only Noah. He's literally squeezing me so tight and saying how Matteo's been in a pissy mood since I've been asleep and how Matteo's been "hurting my feelings" as Noah's been telling me and how he's "breaking my heart." I don't even know I'm too busy trying to get out of Noah's tight hold on me that's literally gonna suffocate me

I tap his arm and try to speak. "No-Noah can't-can't breathe!" I croak out now slapping his arm.

"Oh right sorry!" He says letting go of me with an apologetic smile on his face. "I just missed you!" He says for 1000th time.

"Yes, I know Noah you've told me many times already. I've missed you too even though I've been sleeping" I chuckle.

I hear a throat being cleared and I snap my head round and see Matteo sitting on a chair with one leg over his knee and his arms crossed with a scowl on his face. "Sorry to interrupt your moment-"

"Oh that's quite alright Matteo we all make mistakes." Noah cuts him off looking at him with a cheeky smile. I hold in my giggle.

Matteo glares at him and starts speaking again. "As I was saying, I'm not sorry to interrupt your precious fucking reunion but Noah respectfully get the fuck out."

"But-" Noah tries speaking but this time it's Matteo cutting him off.

"No buts get the fuck out before I knock you unconscious and drop you out the window." He replies with anger written on his face.

Noah pouts and drags his feet across the floor as he walks out of the room, not before blowing a kiss at me and winks but when he noticed Matteo coming at him with his fists clenched he sprinted off shouting down the corridor "good luck sweetheart!".

Matteo turns to me with a soft look in his eyes and starts walking over to me. He takes off his shoes and sits criss-crossed on my bed. Once he's done he looks at my face and suddenly I'm being lifted on top of his lap making me squeal in surprise. "Matteo!" He hums but only puts my head on his chest and wraps his arms around my waist.

"You okay now Angel?" he says and I just nod.

We are sat there in silence not speaking until I suddenly remember something. "Hey you know what I've realised, you said for me to be a maid and I don't think I've been a very good one, I've done nothing really." I mutter under my breath but when I hear him chuckle I know he's heard me.

"I don't get why I told you to do anything if I'm honest Angel, you don't have to be a maid anymore" he says whilst stroking my hair.

"No that's unfair, you told me to be a maid so I need to I can't just stop, I haven't even started" I said whilst taking my head off his chest but he just puts my head back.

"I don't care love, your not a maid anymore" he says.

I huff annoyed. "What am I then" I question confused.

"Mine" he instantly says.

I gasp and move my head back looking him straight in the face and notice he's smirking amused. "W-w..excuse me!" I say shocked.

"You're mine." He says with a slight warning in his tone and he kisses my cheek.

"You don't own me, I'm my own person!" I say still shocked.

He scoffs and rolls his eyes. "Yeah I know you are your own person but your still all mine."He kisses my nose. "Mine." He kisses my forehead. "All mine." And lastly he kisses my neck.

Butterflies.

That's all I feel.

"Use protection!" I hear Noah yell as he sprints past my room.

"Fucking prick." Matteo mutters whereas I'm red as a tomato which Matteo notices making him chuckle and kiss my cheeks again.

□□:*°:✧□

song-Name: Not around Artist (s): Nova__________________________________□••✎••□

"What time is it?" I ask confused as Matteo gets off of me. How long have I even been asleep? Matteo turns his head to the side.

"10:38pm." He replies making my eyes widen.

"I've been asleep for ages!" I say to which Matteo shrugs.

I yawn and lean backwards making my back land on the bed but my legs still stay wrapped around Matteo's waist. "Tired again Angel?" he chuckles making me glare up at him.

"Maybe I am." I huff looking away from him.

"I was just joking my pretty girl, c'mon let's get you ready for bed." He says as he chuckles picking my up so I'm still attached to him making me squeal in embarrassment.

"Matteo put me down I can walk, that is why I have been blessed with legs! So I can walk!" I glare at him.

"And that is very nice gorgeous but I would prefer me carrying you" he smiles at me and kisses my nose. "You're too cute."

I look around and notice he's taken me to the bathroom, he places me down on the counter and pushes a strand of hair behind my ear. He bends down and grabs a new toothbrush, then grabbing the toothpaste he puts it on the toothbrush. He puts the toothpaste down and puts the toothbrush in front of my mouth. "Open up angel" he says which makes me pout.

"I can do it-"

"You can do it yourself, yes I know that" he says interrupting me. "Now open."

I huff and open my mouth making him put the toothbrush in my mouth and then he steps back and allows me to brush my teeth.

———

After Matteo help sort me out with my nighttime routine I'm sat on the bed waiting for him to get me clothes to sleep in. He finally comes out with some boxers and a long shirt and puts it on the bed. "Right these are some of the smallest clothes I can find" which makes me look at him oddly.

"You know you could of just got me my pjs from my room" I say, one of my eyebrows rising up.

"Yeah I know but I found these instead." He says rolling his eyes.

"Bu-"

"Just go to the bathroom and change angel" he interrupts me again.

"Stop interrupting me all the time!" I scowl at him and grab the clothes walking to the bathroom and closing the door behind me. I look at the clothes he got me and hold up the shirt and put it up against me. "Damn this is massive on me!" I say as I notice even when it's not on me it looks massive. I sigh and undress my dirty clothes and putting the clean clothes on.

As I look in the mirror I notice how ridiculous I look. "It's too big on me!" I say frustrated. "Ugh whatever" I roll my eyes and put my dirty clothes in the dirty clothes basket. I open the bathroom door and walk out noticing Matteo sat on the bed looking at his phone. I also notice he's changed into sweatpants and has no top on.

"Uh-i-um." I stutter. Sort it out Aria! "I-I'm gonna go to my room now" I mumble walking towards the door.

"I don't think so." I hear Matteo say and hear his footsteps walk fast towards me making me walk quicker to the door, and just as I'm about to open the door his arms wrap around my waist and pull me away from the door making me groan in annoyance. He kicks the door closed and carries me over to the bed and gently puts me down on it and he stands In front of me. "You're sleeping here" he says looking at me with a small glare.

I look at him slightly frightened. "W-w ho's room even is this?" I ask confused.

"Ours" he says with a smirk. I think what he meant was his. Wait. His!

My eyes widen. "No! I'm not sleeping here I have my own room remember!" I can't sleep here!

"I don't care this is our room now, you'll sleep with me here" he smiles at me making my cheeks tint slightly pink. Sleep here with him! I can't do that!

"Wha-no!" I attempt to stand up but he gently pushes me back down and leans down so we are face to face. "I-I'm sleeping on the f-floor then!" I say surprised with the close proximity.

He frowns at me. "No." I huff getting annoyed. He doesn't give up does he.

"Ughhh" I groan. "Ok fine you win!" I say which makes him smirk. "But you stay on one side I stay on the other."

"Yeah sure" he replies rolling his eyes.

"No funny business!" I glare at him pointing my finger at his face making him chuckle.

I climb under the duvet and he does the same slightly lying down. I grab one of my pillows and put it between us so it can be a wall so that he doesn't touch me. I feel his body moving and I can literally feel his glare burning through the pillow. "What the fuck is this bullshit" he says poking his head over the top looking at me.

"A barrier so you can't touch me." I say turning my body around so my back is facing him and I close my eyes taking in the coziness of the bed.

I hear him huff angrily and he moves around as well.

———

It's been a few minutes I'm presuming and it's dead silent. I'm pretty sure he's asleep now so that's good. My barrier worked! I silently laugh in my head. My laughing in my head is interrupted by Matteo, yes Matteo speaking.

"Fuck this stupid barrier shit!" he growls and suddenly the pillow is thrown off the bed and muscular arms grab my waist and tugs me into a warm chest. "Thought that would work didn't you my pretty girl, well you thought wrong" he whispers in my ear huskily making me gasp.

I try to get out of his grip but he just holds on tighter and softly kisses my neck making me stop moving around. "Go to sleep my angel" he whispers. I huff and pout angrily but just let it off since I'm tired and he's really warm and comfy. "Goodnight angel." I hear him whisper softy and feel him kiss my head.

And then I fall asleep.

□□:*°:✧□

{ THANK YOU FOR 18k READS WTF}

I slowly opened my eyes, don't even know why. The universe clearly just wanted me to open them. I stretched my body by literally spreading myself across the whole bed and clenched my butt. Weird but feels amazing.

It took me a few seconds to realise that the other side of the bed was cold which made me turn my head to see that Matteo wasn't in bed. I look on the nightstand and read the time on the clock that reads 8:12am. Ew why did I get woken up at this time why not like 5pm instead so I can sleep more. But no.

I groan and slide myself off of the bed and land on the floor on my stomach and my face buried into the carpet. "Hey tin- what in the fuck are you doing?"

I turn my head and notice Sam standing at the doorway face scrunched up in confusion. I huff and put my face back into the carpet. "Too early." I'm not sure he would understand what I said considering it was muffled from my mouth being covered by carpet.

"Uh..okay then?- well let's go get breakfast" he replied concern laced in his tone. I don't blame him if I'm being honest, I still have my face buried in the carpet and I'm just lying down not moving. You might mistake me for being dead. I'm alive but I'm dead.

I groan from how tired I am and roll myself over so I'm facing up towards the ceiling. "Can't you just carry me Sammy I broke my toes and legs so I can't walk." I hear Sam chuckle then hear his footsteps come closer towards me. Suddenly his face comes into vision from where he's standing over me with a slight grin on his face.

"Come on lazy bones" he says before scooping me up and placing my feet on the floor. Instead of me just standing like a normal person, I instantly just flop and fall into Sammy's arms not caring if he caught me or not. He obviously did though. "My god Tiny you really are lazy aren't you" he chuckles softly.

"Hop on then" he says before turning around so his back is facing me and he squats down a bit.

"Piggy back?" I question him.

"Yes, now hurry and jump on, I'm hungry everyone's waiting for you downstairs so we can eat."

Waiting for me? Why didn't they just eat. I would of anyway. I quickly jump onto his back and wrap my legs around the front of his waist and leave my arms dangling over his shoulders. "Take me peasant" I mumble making him turn his head around to face me and I notice he has a small smile on his face.

"You really are something Aria" he mumbles.

———

We reach the bottom of the stairs and Sammy makes a few turns and then opens some doors and...

...everyone's staring at me. On Sammy's back.

I shyly wave a bit embarrassed of how I'm on Sammy's back like what a child does to their parents or something. I really regret going on his back now.

Sammy just ignores everyone's stares and walks further in the dining room and gently places me in a chair. I smile a full teethed smile showing my appreciation of how he just carried me with no complaints even though I was probably heavy. "Was I heavy?" I blurt at him making him turn his head back around to me.

"Of course not tiny, if you jumped on my back at anytime I probably wouldn't even notice you jumped on me. It would feel like when a fly crashes into you, you don't even feel it. That's how light you a-"

"Okay I get it thank you Sammy. You just did a whole essay on explaining how light I am. Thank you very much I appreciate it" I cut him off with a slight pout. He's probably just saying that. I'm probably so heavy but he didn't wanna say anything so he's trying to be nice and say how light I a-

"What are you thinking about now miss moody pants" a voice from beside me says. I turn my head around and notice I'm sat right next to Matteo.

"I-oh uh..hey?" I say awkwardly not realising he was there. "W-where did you go this morning?" I blurt out before I could even realise what I said. Wait I didn't mean to say that!

"I-um I mean..." I scratch my head embarrassed, my cheeks turning red.

The corners of his lips twitch up into a small smirk. "Why did you miss me Princess?"

"Woah, that's my nickname for her you nickname stealer!" Micheal says making me turn to see his face and I see him glaring at Matteo.

"Ugh whatever shut the fuck up Micheal" Matteo rolls his eyes.

"Anyways where is my food I'm hungry!" Micheal says leaning back into his chair patting his belly.

□□:*°:✧□

•

THANK YOU FOR 32k AHHH!!

After we had finished our food we where all still sat around the table while the maids take our dishes out of the room.

"So anything we're doing today boss?" Jonah speaks up with a playful grin on his face, however Matteo's face is now in a scowl.

"Yes we are Jonah." Matteo says through gritted teeth.

"Aria I think you should come with us." Jonah replies looking at me with a smile on his face.

"She isn't coming Jonah so shut the fuck up." Matteo says glaring at him.

"But what would she do here all alone?" Jonah looks back at Matteo and puts on a fake sad face and pouts and Matteo just glares at him and doesn't say anything. "Yay you can come Aria!" Jonah looks back at me and puts his hands up in the air.

Matteo bangs his fist on the table and gets out of his seat. "Fine Aria get ready we leave in 5." He says angrily before walking off.

"You made him mad Jonah!" I say looking at him worriedly.

"No it's fine Honey Bun come on we need to get ready" he says playfully winking at me making me smile.

———

Now here we are getting out of the jeep. I looked up and read the neon sign saying "drinkers dreams." I turned my head and saw the whole crew; Jonah, Micheal, Sam, Noah and of course Matteo.

"Let's hurry this up." Matteo says still with that annoyed expression on his face. I didn't mean to make him mad. I watch Matteo's back as he walks into the club with a frown on my face.

"Come on Tiny" Sam says grabbing my arm softly and we both walk into the club. As I step inside I feel the heat from all the bodies and the smell of alcohol fills my nostrils. Why are people clubbing at this time anyways? Sam keeps on dragging me keeping me close to him and pushing any boy that comes near me. We were trailing behind everyone else but I couldn't help but keep my attention on Matteo.

He looks so angry and annoyed. Is it because I'm here? We arrive at a booth with black and red leather sofas and a black table in the middle. We all sat down and I ended up sitting next to Matteo and Sam. I looked down at my hands as soon as I sat down trying to distract myself. I started picking at my nails and started cracking my knuckles. I wonder who we are meeting?

A big tanned hand suddenly came into view and put it on my hands stopping me from cracking my knuckles and picking at my nails. "Stop that" Matteo whispered in my ear making me look up at him a bit fearfully.

"I-I'm sorry s-sir" I whisper looking into his eyes which have just turned darker. He suddenly moved his face closer to mine and looked straight into my eyes and his face was full of annoyance.

"What have I told you about calling me that 'sir' bullshit" he said with a scowl on his face. Before I could reply, another voice interrupted.

"Mr Bianchi! Ah it's a pleasure meeting you" the voice says and brings a chair at our table sitting down. Matteo still hasn't taken his dark eyes away from my face making me squirm in my seat and move backwards quickly and clear my throat. Matteo then turns to the man and nods stiffly at him.

Suddenly the other man notices me and smirks looking at me up and down. "Ah who's this lovely looking lady then." He brings his hand forward in front of me. "Name is Gino" he says looking at me still giving me the creepy smirk.

After a few seconds my eyes go wide with shock. Gino. Gino. Gino. You may be wondering who is Gino. Well let me tell you.

Aarons brother.

His smirk goes wider noticing that I've finally recognised him. I just nod at him and put my head down not even bothering shaking his hand. "Oh come on my precious why don't you shake my hand? That would be rude." He says with a warning in his tone making my hands start shaking with nervousness.

"Excuse me Gino but can we begin this meeting." Matteo speaks up looking at Gino with anger in his eyes and his jaw was clenched.

Gino finally turned his stare away from me and looked at Matteo. "Of course, my apologies."

They continue on with their meeting, Gino sometimes gave me the occasional smirk and I noticed Matteo clenched his fists tighter. I also noticed Sammy was coming closer to me and he looked angry as well. Jonah, Noah and Micheal were all glaring at him as well. Seems like no one likes him.

"So what do you think ay?" Gino says looking at Matteo and puffing his chest out to look manlier.

"No." Matteo says with no emotion on his face.

"No?" Gino says slouching again. "And why not?"

"Because it's a shit deal that's why" Matteo replies making Gino look shocked for a moment before clearing his throat.

"Okay, instead of $500,000 can I have something else?" Gino asks with a smirk on his face.

"Like what?" Matteo looks at him with suspicion.

"The girl." He replies simply making everyone tense up including me. I scooch closer to Matteo and grab his arm with shaky hands.

"Matteo." I whisper looking at him fearfully. I cannot go with Gino. "P-please don't make me." Tears start forming in my eyes. "Don't make me go w-with him. P-please" a tear falls and lands on his arm. He looks at me confused and with concern.

"Why don't you wanna come with me my precious darling." Gino speaks up making me snap my head to the side and see him smirking evilly at me. "Come back to where you belong" he says through clenched teeth.

I start shaking my head rapidly putting my hands on my chest trying to calm myself down but nothing was working. I was panicking I don't want to go back to him. I climb over Sams lap and get out of the booth. I look at Gino and notice him now glaring at me. I walk backwards clutching my chest and I try to breathe in and out and stop my panic attack but nothing is working.

Matteo gets up from the sofa and suddenly punched Gino straight in the nose making Gino 's head fall back and he starts groaning in pain. "Your scaring her you prick, no I'm not going on with the deal." Everyone else stands up and starts walking up to me.

"What's wrong Sweetheart." Noah asks me concern in his voice.

"Aria are you okay?" They all ask me apart from Matteo.

Matteo just comes up to me and lifts me up forcefully putting my head in his chest. He strokes my hair and whispers in my ear "calm down Ari your safe."

"I-I don't like h-him very much." I whisper as I feel myself moving since Matteo has started walking.

"Neither do I." Matteo whispers back holding me tighter.

3

Matteo opened the car door for me and held my hand helping me out the car making me reply with a quiet thank you and follow behind him as he walks to the house. All the others are behind us chatting away to each other whilst I'm in my thoughts thinking about Gino.

Why is he still here? Why can't he leave me alone? I look up when I notice Matteo has opened the front door and walked inside making me follow behind him. Suddenly I hear a woman's voice yell.

"Matteo my child, how have you been!" I look past Matteo's body and see a woman who looks to be in her 40s and looks almost the same as Matteo running up to him with her arms open. She wraps him into a hug and ruffles his hair.

"Momma Mel you're back!!" Noah yells pushing Matteo out the way and hugs the woman.

"Mel!!" Micheal yells hugging the woman as well.

"Hello you trouble makers." The woman smiles and hugs them back.

"I'm not even joking mom Matteo's been so mean lately, personally I think you should spank him." Micheal says crossing his arms childishly pouting.

"Awe you poor thing! Don't you worry hun I will" she smirks pinching Michael's cheek.

"Shut up Micheal I haven't done anything you prick" Matteo says rolling his eyes.

"Language young man!" She says glaring at him. Her eyes then connect with mine and a warm smile takes over her face. "And who's this cutie!" She says coming over to me making me feel a bit nervous.

"This is my honeybun Aria" Jonah says coming up behind me wrapping an arm around my shoulder then going in to hug the woman. She hugs back and says hello to Jonah then she looks back at me.

"Well hello Aria dear it's nice to meet you, you are a very pretty woman aren't you" she gushes making me blush and avoid her gaze.

"Thank you ma'am" I say smiling politely.

"Oh no dear call me Mel" she says pulling me in for a small hug. "I'm so glad there is another girl in this house that I can talk to that's actually a sweetheart!" She says stroking my cheek in a motherly way.

"Is dad here?" Matteo says looking towards us.

"Yeah he should be com-" Before she could finish her sentence a muscular man wearing a cold expression and looked like Matteo as well walked in the room. "Ah there you are honey!" Mel says going up to the man and be wraps his arm around her waist and kisses her on the cheek.

"It's my favourite dad!" Noah says running up to the man and wrapping his arms around his waist making the man roll his eyes but pat Noahs back anyway.

"You weird child" his deep voice says pushing his away.

"I'm not weird I'm unique" Noah replies flipping his non-existent long hair.

"Matteo son, how is it going?" The man says as Matteo walks over to him and gives him a small hug.

"Not too bad Dad, not too bad. How have you been?" He replies.

"Alright, I mean I'm stuck with this one" -he says looking at Mel- "which has been good"

"Just good! And what do you mean stuck you should be honoured to be in my presence." Mel says smacking the man on the chest making the man chuckle and kiss her on the lips.

"Of course I'm honoured sweetie." His eyes look at me then look away but he quickly looks back at me. "Who's this?" He says his cold expression taking over again as he looks at me.

"Honey calm down this is Aria" Mel says smiling at me.

"Why is she here?" He says looking at me coldly with a bit of confusion in his gaze.

"It's a long story dad" Jonah says rolling his eyes and putting his arm on one of my shoulders. "She is a cutie though isn't she, Dad honestly she is genuinely such a nice person so don't worry" Jonah says looking at me smiling and ruffling my hair.

I giggle and push his hand away quietly thanking him. Jonah goes over to Sam who's just standing next to Mel having a small conversation with her. Noah and Micheal are talking to Matteo about something which I have no clue what it's about, which means the man is stood there looking at me.

I gulp and look down at my feet. Suddenly I see a shadow in front of me and I slowly look up and the man is in front of me. "Carlos Bianchi" he says whilst sticking his hand out. I shake it nervously. "N-nice to meet y-you s-sir" I smile at him slightly.

"Carlos is just fine" he says turning around and starting to walk away.

He then stops and turns to look back at me with a softer look in his eyes making me push my hair behind my ears nervously. He walks back over to me and stands there. Then he opens his arms out. "Hug" he says. I tilt my head a little. He wants me to hug him? Really?

I slowly walk up to him and when I'm right in front of him I stand there. Should I hug him? He then wraps his arms around me first instead and puts my head on his chest. "Hello Aria" he says softly surprising me.

"He hasn't spoke soft like this in a long time to people he doesn't know, strange." Micheal whispers to someone but I heard it.

We pull away from the hug and he has a small smile on his lips making me return it.

3rd person:Carlos walked off to hug Mel and he whispers "I don't know why but she already feels like a daughter to me. She's giving me those good vibes."

Mel laughs and replies with "I was thinking the same thing honey, she seems like a good one for our Matteo." Which makes him nod his head at her.

□□:*°:✧□

•

|130k reads!! What the frickkk thank you! I love you all||

"Ok c'mon I'm hungry" Micheal says grabbing my hand and taking me somewhere.

"It's literally 10:36am and we had breakfast not that long ago and you're already hungry?" Matteo says scowling at Michaels back as all the others follow behind us.

"Yeah and we ate breakfast at like 8:40am something so I'm starving thank you" Micheal says turning his head around to look at Matteo for a second before turning back around as we walk into a room which looks like the kitchen.

"No wonder our food goes so quickly, it's because you're always eating it" Carlo says chuckling.

We arrive in the kitchen and we all sit on the stools around a counter. A very big and long counter that is. Whilst we sit down Micheal goes to the fridge and starts looking for food. "Excuse me it's not just me that eats all the food here! Noah does as well so boosh" he says sticking his middle finger up at Noah.

"Woah we are talking about you here not me, stop ratting me out you rat" Noah says folding his arms.

"Boys how about both of you be quiet, Micheal just get your snack" Mel says rolling her eyes. "Damn you boys and your food honestly."

I notice the boys are all talking to each other making me feel a bit left out so I just awkwardly put my hands in my lap and look around. The kitchen looks very..rich. Marble tiles, marble counters, white everywhere and even some gold. There's even a small chandelier hanging on the ceiling. It's very pretty, I wish I could have a kitchen like this one day but ya know #poor am I right.

Suddenly I'm pulled out of my thoughts by Mel starting a conversation. "So Aria how old are you my love?" she says whilst smiling at me.

"I'm 20" I say smiling back at her.

"You look very pretty and young, lucky girl I wish I was young and pretty again" she says sighing and putting her chin on her hands. I widen my eyes at that. What is she talking about she literally looks like a goddess!

"I don't mean to be rude or make you feel uncomfortable or anything but how old are you Mel?" I say asking her cautiously.

"I'm 43 years old dear, already ancient I know" she says smiling sadly at me.

"Oh my god no Mel! You are literally stunning! You don't even look 43, when I first saw you I genuinely thought you where in your early thirty's or something. You look so young! What do you use on your skin by the way, your skin is so clear which I'm so jealous about because although my skin is alright now it gets really bad sometimes and your-" I rambled on but when I notice she has tears in her eyes I instantly panicked. Oh no does she hate me? Did I do something wrong. She might hurt me.

"I-im so sorry! Did I say something wrong? Oh no I made you upset!! I'm sorry! I didn't mean to I promise, don't hurt-" I get cut off when I'm pulled into a chest and the faint smell of flowers fills my nostrils and I realise Mel has just pulled me into a hug.

"Oh my god you sweet sweet girl! I haven't heard someone else apart from my husband say those kind of things to me in so so long. You are such a lovely girl. Thank you so so m-much" when she finishes I feel some wet droplets land on me.

"O-oh it's quite alright M-mel" I say relieved she wasn't mad at me.

"Momma Mel why are you crying?" Micheal says coming back over with a pack of Oreo's in his hand looking at us confused. Micheal saying that made all the boys heads turn to look at us with confused looks on their faces as well.

"My sweet girl Aria just s-said the n-nicest things to me e-ever" she said sniffling. She finally releases me from the hug and holds my shoulders and making me look at her. "You my sweet child deserve the world, I can see in your eyes how much of a genuine nice girl you are. I will always be here for you my love, I know this is quick but I already consider you as my daughter" she finishes with a warm smile on her face.

I tear up a little thinking that someone actually thinks of me as their daughter. My real mom died so Mel saying that really does make me happy. "Thank you Mel" I say smiling back.

"Oh my gosh this is so beautiful" I hear Micheal say from beside us. I look at him and notice that he's pretending to wipe tears from his eyes. "But I'm still your favourite aren't I momma Mel?" he says rapidly batting his eyelashes trying to look cute.

"You're all my favourite silly" Mel says laughing and then she looks at me and whispers "but I like you just that little more then all them annoying lot" she says winking at me making me giggle, and making Micheal look at me confused to why I'm giggling.

"You better not be talking bad about me behind my back" he says jokingly glaring at us.

"Course not son" she says laughing.

———————————————————————

I look at the clock in the living room after the show I was watching on the TV had finished and notice the time says 8:52pm. I found out that Matteo's parents don't live too far away from him but they are getting their house re-done so they are staying here for..well I don't actually know how long. Until their house is finished I guess? My stomach makes a small sound showing that I'm hungry. I don't really feel like eating though. Lately I've noticed that I look a bit fatter so I need to try and loose some of it.

When I'm about to turn the TV off I hear noises and footsteps and everyone came into the living room. So basically the boys all had work to do and Mel was meeting one of her friends she I was left at the house by myself. She invited me if I wanted to come but I politely declined because I didn't want to intrude. And yes you must be thinking why haven't I ran away when I had that chance but I couldn't. Matteo hired a lot, and I mean a lot of bodyguards to surround this place to make sure I don't escape.

I was gonna try but when I realised how many guards there are I gave up and decided to watch TV. Anyways back to present time, I noticed that Noah was holding a white plastic bag and he started walking over to me and sat down on the place right beside me. "We went to a burger place after we were done with our work and we have burgersss" he said grinning at me whilst taking the wrapped burgers out of the bag and placing them on the big coffee table in front of us.

I smiled back at him but then frowned thinking of how much weight I will gain from eating the burger. Maybe it's not such a good idea to eat it. "T-thank you b-but I'm not really hungry" I say forcing a smile. "T-thank you t-though, I might just go to bed." I stood up and walked out of the living room hearing Matteo call my name behind me but I just carried on walking pretending I didn't hear him. I know he will make me eat if I stayed.

I looked down at the floor whilst walking to my room thinking. I am really hungry but I really need to lose that weight. It's fine, I'll be fine. It doesn't matter, i don't really need the burger I can survi-" I'm brought out of my thoughts when I crash into a hard wall. Or should I say chest. I gasp and quickly look up thinking I walked into a guard or something. I was going to apologise but realised who I bumped into.

Carlos.

"I- oh golly! I'm re-really sorry S-sir!" I say lowing my head again. "I was just lost in my thoughts I didn't realise an-" I was cut off when he chuckled lightly.

"It's okay Aria, don't worry about it" he says smiling a little bit. "Where are you off too anyways?" he says furrowing his eyebrows.

"Oh! I was g-gonna go to sleep" I say fiddling with my fingers.

"Have you eaten already then? That was quick" he said tilting his head looking more confused.

"Oh n-no I didn't eat the burgers" I said laughing nervously. "I'm not really that hungry."

"Have y-" as he was going to finish his sentence my tummy just had to make a grumbling sound. Thanks a bunch stomach.

"Have you eaten anything apart from breakfast today Aria?" He said looking concerned and a little angry. Oh no what have I done! He's gonna hurt me. Just lie. It's fine. He'll believe me.

"Y-yeah I have" I said looking away. Great lying Aria.

It goes silent for a couple of seconds before he picks me up and puts me over his shoulder. Woah it's high up here!

"Carlos it's really high up here, please may you put me down! I've eaten I promise!!" I say gripping onto the back of his shirt.

"Bullshit, you haven't eaten and I'm not going to allow you to go to bed when you haven't eaten since breakfast you silly girl" he says with a bit of anger to his tone whilst still walking back to the living room.

But I don't wanna eat... I think sadly. All those extra calories! I don't wanna do this...

□□:*°:✧□

song-Name: DNAArtist (s): - BTS______________________________□••✎••□

As soon as we walk back in the room, all the chattering instantly stopped and it went so quiet you could hear a pin drop.

"Sweetheart why is Carlos carrying you on his shoulder?" Noah says confusion laced in his tone. I sigh when Carlos finally places me down on the ground. Thank freak for that. I turn around and see everyone looking at me and see Noah and everyone else looking at me with confusion on their faces. The one who looks most confused is Matteo though.

I fidget with my fingers anxiously and tuck my hair behind my ear. "U-uh I'm not really sure" I say looking down at the lovely floor.

"Bullshit, she hasn't eaten anything since breakfast and I could hear her belly rumbling from ages away that's how loud it was" Carlos says butting in making me blush in embarrassment.

"I thought you did eat?" Matteo says making me look up at him and see he has an angry expression on his face making me even more nervous. "Mom told me that you told her you ate lunch and snacks whilst watching telly, why lie."

I open my mouth to speak but nothing comes out so it just makes me look like a fish. "Get over here and eat right now" Matteo says patting the space beside him. I lower my head and slowly walk towards him and sit down beside him. He puts a plain cheeseburger on a plate and some chips and puts it on my lap. "Eat."

I look at the food disgusted. How many calories does all this have? I can't eat this. It's too much for me. I'm trying to loose weight not gain weight. I slowly shake my head. "I-I don't want to" I say placing the plate back on the coffee table. I feel long fingers hook under my chin and move my face to be faced with Matteo's and he looks impatient.

"You are not leaving without eating most of this food on your plate" he says wiping a tear from my cheek that I didn't even realise has fallen. I turn my head around and look at everyone watching the telly and eating their food peacefully. Why can't I be like that. No worries about what I'm eating or how many calories it has. Why?

I look back at the food and pick up a fry with trembling hands and slowly bring it to my lips. I take a small bite into the chip and chew it. I feel disgusted with myself. How can I eat this stuff? I'm absolutely disgusting.

——————————————————————30 mins later

I put the plate on the coffee table and lean back into the chair holding my stomach. I look at the plate and see I've eaten half the burger and most of my fries. I look down at my stomach and see how much fatter I've gotten. I knew I shouldn't of eaten it. Now I'm even fatter than I was. Suddenly I feel warm lips touch my head and I look up surprised to see Matteo looking at me with a content look on his face. "Good girl" he says looking back at the telly. A small smile pulls at my lips. I've made Matteo proud? Just from eating food?

But that still doesn't help the fact I feel disgusted with myself.

——————————————————————9:40pm

I'm in my bathroom in my pj's, brushing my teeth getting ready for bed. I spit the toothpaste in the sink and rinse off my toothbrush and then I clean my mouth and wipe it dry. As I start to brush my hair I look in the mirror and lift my top up slightly and pinch my stomach feeling the fat. I wince in disgust "I shouldn't of eaten that meal."

I sigh and lower my top and carrying on brushing my hair. Once I was done I walk back into my room but squeal in surprise when I see Matteo sitting on the edge of my bed looking spaced out. I slowly walk in front of him and start waving my hand in front of his face which seems to get him out of his trance and look at me straight in the eyes. "Are you okay Matteo?" I say concerned, he looked really deep in thought about something.

"Yeah I am, what about you though?" he says making me confused. "Yeah? Why do you ask" I say confused.

"Then why did you look so disgusted when you lifted up your top in the mirror and looked at your stomach." he says making me look down at my feet in shame.

song-Name: You're never fully dressed without a smile Artist (s): Sia ______________________________□••✎••□

'Well shoot what do I say now?' I think to myself. Just try and change subject Aria. I look back up at Matteo. "Um so how did you find dinner?" I say chuckling nervously whilst avoiding eye contact. After about a minute I haven't heard any reply so I finally look Matteo in the eyes and see he's looking at me with a confused expression. Great changing of the subject Aria, I mentally slap myself on the forehead. Luckily Matteo didn't push further and just stood up off my bed and brushed imaginary dust off him.

"Ok well tomorrow I'll be late coming back from work" he says. "What kind of work?" I ask him.

"I'm not just the leader of a gang Aria, I own hotels and clubs and restaurants and then I have my bigger company 'The Bianchi' where I just plan and organise all my small businesses ideas etc and help other businesses" he says shrugging his shoulders.

Wait I've heard of the company before! "Wait that's the most successful company in the world!" which makes him nod. But then my brain processes what he just said. "Wait. Did you just say gang?" He sighs and ruffles his hair. "Yes Aria I'm the leader of the gang 'Black Vipers'" hearing him say that makes my eyes widen and my jaw drops to the floor. After a couple minutes I try to speak but nothing comes out until I manage to just say "u-um ok.." which makes him furrow his brows in confusion.

"Ok?" which I just stupidly nod my head to. He nods slowly in confusion and walks out out of the room closing the door behind him. I slowly walk to the bed and get under the covers and look at the ceiling. "What the frick" I whisper to myself. I'm in a house with a gang leader...Brilliant.

———————————————————————

Next day

I wake up to the sound of people shouting. "You ate all the pop tarts you fat bitch!" Noah shouts. I rub my eyes and groan at the fact I've been woken up. I look to the side and notice that the time is 8:36am which makes me groan even more because of how early it is. I put my pillow over my head and cover my ears hoping to get rid of the people shouting downstairs. "He what!" I hear Micheal join in. "No! My pop tarts!" he fake cries.

"They're just pop tarts" I hear Jonah say. I hear a two loud smacks followed by two "ow what the fuck!"and hear Matteo tell Noah and Micheal to shut up. I push the covers off my body and stretch my muscles. I get out of bed and walk to the door of my bedroom whilst running my fingers through my hair trying to make it look more presentable because let's be real it probably looks like a birds nest.

I arrive at the kitchen and see Noah and Micheal sat on stools at the kitchen island eating what I'm guessing cereal from their bowls and they both are frowning, and Sam eating a pop tart whilst looking at his phone. "What's going on?" I ask whilst walking to where the boys are. "That mean dickhead ate the last of our pop tarts!" Micheal said glaring at Sam. I look at Sam and see him look away from his phone to look at Micheal and then he shrugs his shoulders and goes back to looking at his phone. "There where only 2 left anyways" he says.

"There where 5 left dumbass!" Noah says angrily crossing his arms. "Oops" was Sam's unbothered reply. Before the boys could argue anymore Matteo walks in wearing a suit and looking very professional, and hot. Shut up Aria. "Have you guys stopped arguing over a fucking pop tart now?" he says annoyed whilst putting on his watch which two grumbles where heard as a reply. Matteo looks up and we make eye contact straight away. "Good morning Aria" he says whilst fixing his hair.

"Good morning" I reply. "So all of us are going to work now but you still have all the maids here if you need anything" he says. "Don't do anything stupid, I have guards everywhere don't forget" he adds raising his eyebrows in warning which makes nod.

"Let's go then guys" he says walking out of the kitchen with the guys following him. But before Noah and Micheal leave they both hug me and give me a kiss on the head and tell me to have fun then they leave.

Right. What do I do now then...

□□:*°:✧□

CPSIA information can be obtained
at www.ICGtesting.com
Printed in the USA
LVHW052028090123
736787LV00009B/342

9 781837 617357